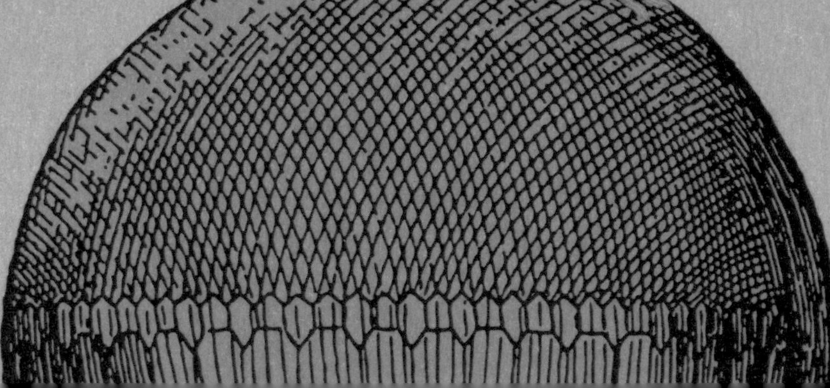

monkey

Also by Agnes Bushell

After Mistra
Asian Vespers
Days of the Dead
Death by Crystal
Death in Arcadia
The Enumerator
Fabrice in Flight
The House on Perry Street
In the Garden of Nicholas Treeson
Local Deities
Mothers and Sons
The Oracle Pool
Shadowdance

MONKEY

Agnes Bushell

A Russian Novel

Littoral Books
Portland, Maine

The author gratefully acknowledges the kind permission of Larissa Volokhonsky and Richard Pevear to quote passages from their translation of *The Master and Margarita* by Mikhail Bulgakov published by Penguin Books, 1997.

Drawings by Judith Allen-Efstathiou
Monkeys from Georges Louis Leclerc's hand-colored engravings in Comte de Buffon's Planches pour L'Abrégé d'Histoire Naturelle, *1790 (on pages 79, 137, 417, 563, and 609)*
Cover design and book design by Lori Harley

ISBN: 978-1-7357397-6-2

Littoral Books
Portland, Maine
www.littoralbooks.com

In memory of Nick

...there was something
gorgeous about him,
some heightened sensitivity
to the promises of life,
a romantic readiness
such as I have never found
in any other person
and which it is unlikely
I shall ever find again.

–F. Scott Fitzgerald

contents

BOOK ONE

The Barakovs of Oak Hills

BOOK TWO

Autumn in St Petersburg

BOOK THREE

The Amazing Adventures of Blavatskaya and Fyodorov

BOOK FOUR

Romance in the *Demi-monde*

BOOK FIVE

An Episode in Odessa

BOOK SIX

The Final Dispensations of Fyodor Fyodorov

BOOK SEVEN

Death and the Poet

BOOK EIGHT

Passage to Panama

ILLUSTRATIONS: JUDITH ALLEN-EFSTATHIOU

PRINCIPAL CHARACTERS

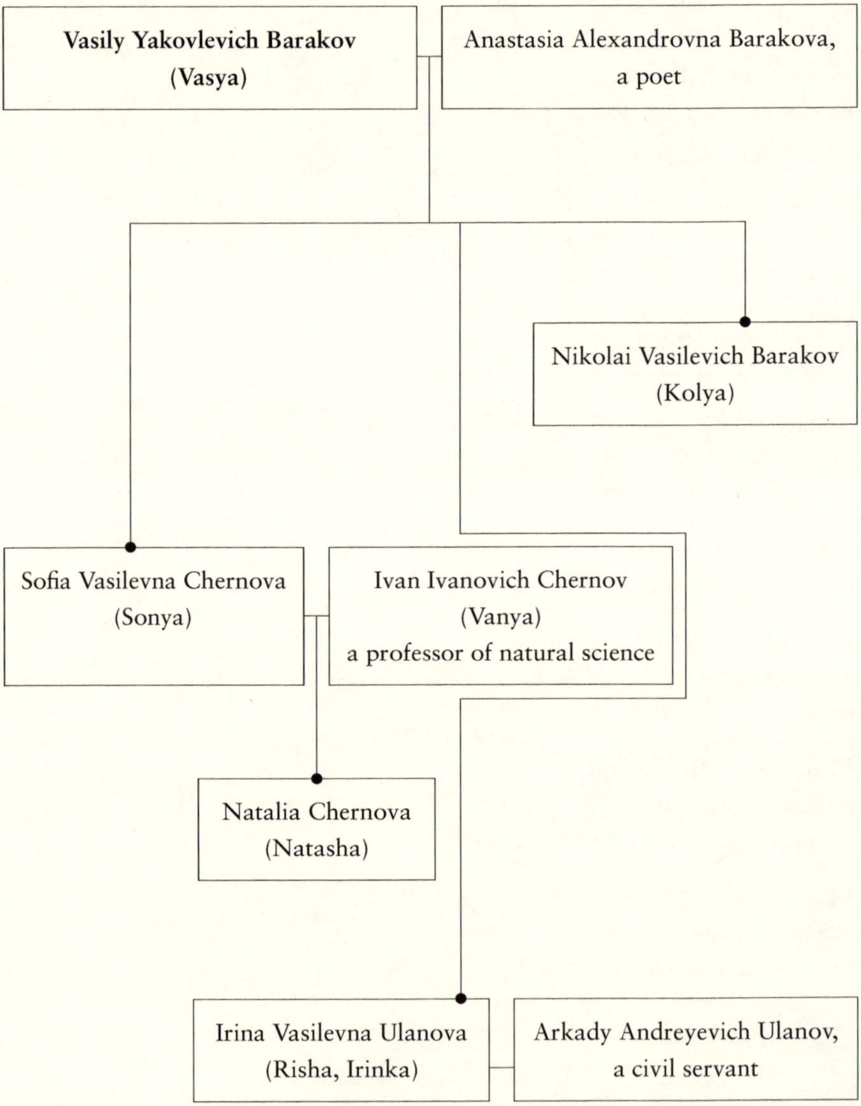

Princess Tatyana Andreyevna Volkonskaya, Anastasia's oldest friend;
Margarita Mikhailevna, her adopted daughter

Yevgenia Dmitriyevna (Zenya) and Mariya Sergeyevna (Maryshka),
friends of Anastasia

Aleksey Konstantinovich, "Uncle Alyosha," friend of the Barakovs

Marko Volchek / Valentina Grigorevna Markova, writer;
Pavel Damianovich (Pasha Damianich), Marko's valet

Pyotr Illych Panov, a traveling actor

Marina Fyodorovna Vilinskaya, an editor

Sofya Fyodorovna, her sister, a painter

Elena Petrovna Blavatskaya, a medium

Fyodor Fyodorovich Fyodorov, a cosmist philosopher

Serafima Vadimovna, a madame

Katerina Ivanovna Gutieva (Katya), mistress of Nikolai Barakov;
Ilya Ivanovich Gutiev (Ilyusha), her brother, a friend of Nikolai Barakov

Pavel Pavlovich Beriosov, deputy director
of the Third Division, State Security

Alejandro Azara (Sasha), an Argentine scientist

Odysseus Dimitrakos, a taverna owner and ship's captain

Alexandra Kirillovna Kantrovskaya (Sasha), a friend of Nikolai Barakov;
Countess Mora Khayimyevna Sabanska, her cousin

BOOK
ONE

THE BARAKOVS OF OAK HILLS

CHAPTER ONE

The Missing Son

Early one summer morning, just as the sun was rising over the hills, Vasily Yakovlevich Barakov, dressed in his gardening clothes, straw hat on his head, cane in his hand, was strolling through his flower garden. The air was cool and fragrant, drops of dew lay scattered on the grass like tiny diamonds, birds greeted the dawn from the treetops: nothing was amiss in the world. But Vasily Yakovlevich had been unable to sleep, he had been haunted all night by his usual worries, and so he had risen and dressed and gone to visit his roses in the hope that beauty might dispel care. So far, it had not.

He paused in front of *Rosa paestana,* a perfect flower, now in full bloom. One could become fanatical about flowers, as one could about anything, acquisitive, competitive, greedy. Still, he thought, gardening itself, the actual work of gardening, was a humbling enterprise, got you onto your knees in the dirt. And, then, once you lifted your eyes from the ground and looked around—and he did lift his eyes and look—there was work to be done everywhere. The bathhouse needed a new roof; the pond was being encroached upon by willows; the path to the hill was becoming overgrown; the wood was steadily creeping up to the old labyrinth whose hedges needed cutting; the fountain was dry and clogged with dead leaves; and just beyond the cultivated flower garden, wilderness reigned amidst the lilacs and rhododendrons, the hazel, elder, and honeysuckle. His heart yearned for the wilderness to take over everything. Yes, take everything! The fields, the village, the entire estate, for what men imposed on nature was unnatural, barbarous, rooted in human misery, a blight on the face of the earth.

If his son did not return, if he maintained his silence, if he refused the land, as it seemed he would, in fact, as he already had... A memory came back to him then, as memories so often did now. It had happened one summer morning, thirty-odd years ago, his father was still alive, they were visiting his estate, and Nikolai, little Kolya, four or five years old at the time, by an unfortunate lapse of attention on someone's part, had been playing near the stables on a day designated for punishment, and had run into the stables at the very moment a serf was being flogged, probably for good reason, Vasily always believed, since his father had not been a cruel or unjust man. Still, there was the poor soul, tied prostrate on the ground, there was the bailiff leaning over him with a whip, and just then Kolya came running in. They had found it funny, what the child did, even the bailiff himself had laughed at it, and the story was told for years: how the master's grandson, little Kolya, had run right up to the bailiff and, to stop his blow from falling on the miscreant's back, had grabbed the bailiff by the beard and pulled at it. Yes, everyone had thought it amusing. But Kolya had not found it funny at all. He pulled the bailiff's beard and then burst into tears and they had to comfort him and carry him back to the house.

But why tears? Vasily Yakovlevich had always wondered about it; now, for some reason, it was a question that haunted him. Why tears? For whom was his son crying? For the man being flogged? For the bailiff, whose beard he had pulled? Or were the tears for the loss of his own innocence, for the grief that had come to his soul, seeing what he had just seen, the obscenity of one man beating another? Vasily wished with all his heart that he had asked his son that question.

So then, he thought, stopping in front of his *Rosa damascena,* using his cane to dig out a small weed growing near its roots, if Nikolai did not want the land, he would give it to his serfs. That's what he would do. He would give them the land. Isn't that what they wanted? Isn't that what he wanted for them? Land and freedom. Isn't that what the young advocated? So he would do it. He would give them the land. The house along with it. The roses. Everything. Yes. If Nikolai did not come home, did not ever come home, and if Anastasia approved, which he knew she would, he would free his serfs and give them the land. Before he died, he would do it, finally. They could move to Odessa and spend their last years by the sea.

Having dug out one small weed, he noticed others.

What else could he do? If his son returned, that was a different matter. But he'd had that nightmarish dream again; it was the dream that had awakened him and after that there was no sleeping for the rest of the night.

He was looking out across a vast plain of sand at a line of blue, which he knew was the sea, but a sea that had ebbed away leaving a desert behind. He began to run toward it, over the sand, over shells and stones, running toward the still ebbing sea...until he realized that if the tide turned and the sea rushed back, he was so far from the shore that the sea would drown him. Then he heard a roar, the roar of surf, and he looked out and saw, coming toward him at great speed, an enormous wall of water.

The dream was simple and obvious; yet, while he was dreaming it, each time, it held the same power, it filled him with the same terror. Probably all over Russia men were dreaming the same dream. The sea could only ebb for so long. Eventually the tide would turn. And those who were standing there, gaping, would be drowned in the flood.

Perhaps his son was smart to stay away, to find another life. There were many ways of living, as many ways of living as there were people alive. The trick was to find a way to live that didn't murder your soul. If his son had managed to do that, then he could be proud of him, once he stopped being angry at him. He had stayed away too long, and for what? Why this long absence, this silence? He didn't have to visit them, but how hard was it to write a letter?

Having paused in his thinking at that point, the point to which he always came whenever he thought of his son, he heard the glorious sunrise symphony of bird song, and then other sounds, from the stables, the barns, the house. As though he stood in the center of the world and everything was awakening around him. He glanced up at his wife's windows. Was she awake as well? Perhaps today she would come down, for Irina and her children were arriving that afternoon. She was being foolish, staying up in her rooms. But the children reminded her of Kolya when he was small, and made her miss him more. She had told him that. How the children, the little boys especially, only made her miss him more.

He slapped the dirt with his cane and thought it was about time he got to work. Coffee first. Then the accounts.

Natasha, peering through the leaves from her perch in the great lime tree, watched the caravan appear at the crest of the hill and begin its descent into the village. It slipped down the green hill like a snake, twisting its way first to the left, then to the right, slowly filling the whole road from top to bottom. How many carts Aunt Irina had brought along with her! Were they moving to Oak Hills forever? How nice that would be, if her own family could stay, too, if they could all live together in the big house and be happy. Or, better, if the parents lived in the big house and the children lived in the trees! Oh, that would be glorious! They could hang lanterns from the boughs and light them at night. They could build little houses amidst the greater tree limbs—oh, how lovely it would be!—and when Masha brought their meals, they could hoist them up on the same sort of machine that the old monks used who sat on pillars in the desert. They would carve stairs into the trunks to help the little ones climb up, and they would all slide down on ropes.

But she had no ropes now. She thrust her book into the pocket of her smock, turned to face the gnarled old trunk, found her first handholds and lowered her legs, letting her feet search around on their own until they found some purchase on the lower branch. Yes, a rope would be much nicer, and faster… or a ladder made of rope, perhaps… or a different invention entirely, a winged chariot like the one in the little theatre on the neighbor's estate in which Saint Ilya had descended onto the stage from heaven.

Thinking about ladders and wings and ropes and hoists, she made her way down. She had to take care not to catch her skirt on the tree's rough bark or entangle her hair in its branches or, worse, disturb the bees that were drawn to the piquant sweetness of the linden flowers. To return home in a torn dress covered in pollen trailing behind her a retinue of buzzing bees might not go unnoticed even with the arrival of Aunt Irina. Though if they were not very loud bees… And then there were the crows to think about. Her crow poem was very much on her mind. She did like how it began, the rhythm of it; she liked it very much:

Summertime is rolling by
The crows are in the wood.
Their black wings are against the sky.
Are they doing what they should?

But would Anastasia like it, too? She would certainly like the rhymes. Anastasia's poems all had wonderful rhymes. Or used to have. Now she wasn't writing poems anymore and visiting her meant sneaking up the stairs and not letting Mama know, otherwise she would be asked all kinds of questions, which made her feel like she was spying. Grandmama knew about this, of course. No one could trick her, and Natasha would never try. They knew each other perfectly, Natasha having spent most of her childhood on the estate while her parents were living abroad. When they returned and set up their own household, she had been forced to leave Oak Hills to live with them, and she had suffered quite a bit from it. To suffer a bit was necessary for a poet, but suffering too much made one ill. It was making her grandmother ill. If only they could discover what was causing her suffering! Then Grandfather would give Grandmother whatever she wanted (because he always did, according to her mother, who often complained about it) and everything would go back to the way it was, Grandmother would write her poems again, and everyone would be happy.

So she descended slowly, thinking as she went.

Back on solid ground, she straightened her clothes, and looked about her to make sure she had not been seen. No one was in sight. Everyone must be gathering along the drive to welcome Aunt Irina and help with the carts. And having decided that, Natasha began running toward the house until she saw Yuri, one of the gardeners, and remembered she should not be running in front of the servants. It was one of Grandfather's rules: do not place the servants in the awkward position of having to choose between their affection and their duty. It had been drummed into her long enough that she now stopped running and pretended that she had never run ever in her life. Yuri greeted her and she greeted him back. A successful navigation. Grandpapa would be proud.

Of course, she could run with her brothers, or with her cousins, if they were playing tag or ball. It was just running from place to place that was against the rules. Going into the woods alone, also against the rules. Speaking, usually, unless spoken to. Repeating family conversations. Then there were the Bigger Rules. She still had only glimmerings of those. They were the ones the breaking of which resulted in serious harm. Uncle Nikolai, she knew, had broken them more than once. She had learned this through listening to those family conversations which she was forbidden to repeat to anyone.

She walked sedately along the path through the flower garden toward the house, but already she could hear the sounds of the wagon wheels, the horses' hooves, the shouting of the drivers, and other voices, deep adult voices, and higher voices, squeals and shouts, and those were clearly her brothers, squealing and shouting, and other children's voices returning the squeals and shouts. The cousins had arrived. There were no servants around now so she ran.

Within an hour, the carts had been unloaded, the guests had been settled in their rooms, and the children, adamantly refusing to nap, had been sent outside to play. Irina, on the other hand, was exhausted and fell asleep the moment she lay down on her bed. Sofia arranged with the kitchen for an early supper, and with the nannies for an early bedtime.

She had just returned to the drawing room when all five children, screaming with laughter, burst into the room, chased by their grandfather who was making horrid grunting sounds, pretending to be an ogre.

"Papa! Please! You're getting them overexcited."

Laughing and out of breath, Vasily Yakovlevich sat down heavily on a chair. "Go along, children. The ogre has to rest. Run outside now. Go!"

And off they went, out the door and into the hall, running and laughing.

"What a wild mob," he said, catching his breath. "A bunch of hooligans and Jacobins. Gives you some idea of what emancipation will be like, eh, Sonya? Except they'll be carrying torches and pitchforks. Not that it's undeserved, mind you. I've been saying it all my life. When it comes, it will be like the apocalypse itself, the logical end of a ruinous reign."

"Shshsh!"

"Nonsense, Sonya. We are at home."

"Even at home, Papa."

"No, my dear. It is a rule of mine. At home, we act as though we were free. I insist on it."

"I agree. But when Arkady Andreyevich comes—"

"Bah. I will not be silenced in my own home. Anyway, he's not going to denounce us for sheltering a pack of baby Jacobins, is he? Not when they are members of his own family."

Sofia sat down beside her father on the sofa and, in an entirely uncharacteristic gesture, took his hand.

They were so alike, Sofia Vasilevna and her father, sitting there, side by side, both small but sturdy in build with light blue eyes and thick curly hair, hers rich auburn, his now white. They were even dressed similarly, in simple, serviceable clothing, since they both preferred physical activity to socializing in drawing rooms. Vasily, in fact, always credited his good health and strong constitution to a lifetime of work, the physical labor needed to keep up his estate and the emotional labor needed to keep up his marriage, for it was a well-known fact that his wife, our beloved poetess Anastasia Alexandrovna Barakova, led him quite a merry chase through all the years of their long and happy marriage. Having answered the so-called "woman question" for herself long before it became the subject of intellectual debate, she had lived an emancipated life from the first days of her marriage, and wrote about it in many of her poems. One would be hard-pressed to find a woman of our class unfamiliar with Anastasia Barakova's most famous poem which begins: "If you truly wish to love us, first let us breathe..."

Sofia, the eldest child of this marriage, not only took after her father physically, but also temperamentally, although it might be more accurate to say that he took after her since she had been born even-tempered, calm and patient while he had had to acquire these virtuous traits over time in order to continue living happily with his wife. It was only because Sofia was so easy-going by nature that when something was seriously bothering her, as it was now, the contrast to her normal tranquility made it appear to her father that she was utterly distraught. The fact that she had taken his hand was even more troubling.

"What's happened, Sonya?" he cried, seizing her hand in both of his, and rubbing it between his palms. "Tell me, sweetheart! I must know."

"Oh, Papa, if only we could all stay here forever."

"You can, my dear. Why not? The house is big enough. The land—"

"I don't think Vanya would be happy, living in the country. He has his position, you know."

"He's an important man, your husband. I have always said it."

"He's doing important work. That's quite different. How long he'll be able to continue..."

"Why shouldn't he continue?"

Sofia released her hand from his, and stood up. More and more these days she found she could not sit still.

"These troubles can't last, my dear," Vasily said.

"Can't last? They've already lasted my entire life. And the children..."

"All is flux. It will change."

"So you always say."

Sofia walked across the room, and stopped at the window. The children were chasing each other around the fountain in the garden.

"I am worried, Papa. I am so afraid. I feel like something terrible is about to happen to us. And the more people you love, the more danger you are in."

"In danger of...?"

"Suffering."

"Sonya, darling," he said gently. "What is it?"

She turned from the window and returned to sit beside him on the sofa. As she spoke, she dropped her voice to almost a whisper, which in itself convinced her father of her fear. Why whisper in her own home? It was outrageous, intolerable. Thinking this, he wanted to hold her in his arms, but instead he merely took her hand again and listened carefully (for his hearing was not as keen as it once was) so he could catch every word she was saying.

"Every day something ghastly happens, Papa. You hear about it, but you can't do a thing about it. For years it has been like this. Vanya's students disappear, they are arrested for talking, for reading a book, for writing an article... He makes an inquiry, he is warned. Some goon from the Third Section comes, threatening him, silencing him. And so he feels powerless and he becomes like a wild man. He becomes careless and drinks. He carries on... One of his best students threw his life away just this spring, shouted something in public... against the Tsar. Can you imagine? And it was like a lightning bolt that went through everyone who heard it. The shock of it. The terror and the... glory of it. That one moment of freedom."

"Yes."

"We don't need a tsar, he said. We don't need a king. We need liberty... Just words. And he will die for them."

"Foolishness."

"Is it?"

"Of course it is. To die for words."

"What did your friends die for?"

"More than words."

"Still they failed."

"They tried to force a change before the time was ripe for change to come."

"Oh, Papa, change doesn't just come. It isn't a force of history. That is a lie. Change has to be created by men. But it seems men don't have a clue how to create it. All they can do is talk. Talk, talk, talk, day and night. And nothing comes of it. Nothing whatever."

Vasily Yakovlevich tried to think of an answer to his daughter's charge, but he was an honest man, and so he could not. It was a problem he had been thinking about his entire life. He might have used the excuses he often did when talking to himself, that thirty years of repression had made it impossible for them to think as free men, that they could not even imagine what change might look like. But he knew that was a lie. They could imagine all they wanted, each man in his own mind, but they could not speak together and they could not act.

How right Herzen was when he wrote that the only free men in Russia were philosophers and beggars, and often they were the same. Everyone else was a slave—the serfs, slaves of the landowners; the landowners, slaves of the Tsar. Oh, he had a way of turning a phrase, Herzen. Yet it was the truth. Vasily Yakovlevich was himself a slave and he would remain a slave so long as he owned the land and the serfs who were bound to it. Unless he took his own philosophy seriously and did what he should have done twenty-five years ago. But he couldn't do anything until he talked to Nikolai. Nikolai was his heir.

There are some who always say that it is better to know nothing, to think nothing, to retreat to the country and live as happily as one can. Vasily Yakovlevich had listened to those voices. After university, he had used a small inheritance to purchase a farm in a provincial district, and there, with his wife and a group of friends, following the philosophy of Fourier, he had established a kind of phalanstery. When this experiment in utopianism failed, he took a position in the civil service, working for the provincial Court of Justice. So he thought he had saved himself from complicity with the evil of our times. But it was no good. First he inherited his father's estate, then his uncle's. Once a landowner, he gave up the reforms he had once championed, he hesitated to emancipate his serfs. He was learning the hardest lesson a man can learn: that he could not at the same time be an honest man and feed and protect his family. Instead, to raise them, to keep them safe, he had to become complicit in a system he detested.

No, he had not escaped. Nor had he resolved the questions he had wrestled with in his youth. As hard as he had tried to shake himself free, his daughter was right, he had failed.

Natasha spied Masha climbing the stairs with a supper tray. Stealthily she followed her up, and slipped into her grandmother's apartment behind her, and hid behind a high-backed chair, squatting down behind it like a cat, and like a cat made herself invisible. Peeking out, she scanned the rooms in which her grandmother spent her days: the study itself, with its wonderful library, and beyond it, the cool and comfortable bedroom. All around her were the things she had loved to play with when she was smaller—and loved even now though now she felt too old to play with them. There were the dear little altars, the dear little stone gardens, the painted boxes, the little figurines, the pictures in golden frames, and all the books, the gorgeous books, ones with pictures and gilded pages, ones in boxes, ones with little red ribbons, and the great desk always covered with pages of writing, and the drawers of the desk she loved to open and explore, so many dear little things in the drawers that she loved to touch or hold in her hand.

Then there was the sound of voices and Masha waddled out of the room, still holding the tray, and the wind took the door from her and slammed it shut, and Masha opened it again and said she was sorry, Madame, very sorry, and closed it very gently behind her.

Natasha sighed and crept around the side of the armchair and stood up and walked into her grandmother's bedroom.

Anastasia, wearing an indigo dressing gown, her head wrapped in a light blue turban, was sitting up in the bed with her back resting against a mass of pillows. Her face was pale and lined, her cheeks were hollow, her eyes were dim and seemed almost to have lost all their color. Natasha did not notice these things. What she noticed was that Anastasia wasn't wearing any rings on her fingers. She always wore so many rings. Natasha could not remember ever seeing her grandmother's hand so bare.

"Good evening, Anastasia Alexandrovna, dear little Grandmama," she said. "I am here to help."

"Then come here and kiss me, *mon petit chou*, and tell me all about your day."

Natasha scrambled onto the great bed, bouncing just a little (how she had bounced on this bed when she was little!) and gave her grandmother a kiss.

"I climbed into my tree and read a book. I saw Aunt Irina's carts come down the hill like a giant snake. I played with Sasha and Andrushka and Katya and Misha and then we were called in for supper. How are you feeling? Why didn't you eat supper with us?"

"I don't feel like eating," Anastasia said. "I just had Masha take the food away. If I'd known you were coming up, I'd have had her leave it for you."

They smiled at each other. It was true Natasha was always hungry and the meals Cook made for Anastasia were much more delicious than what the children were given to eat.

"Will you come down later? Aunt Irina is here. I'm sure she would love to see you."

"I don't feel like talking either."

"You could be quiet."

"I don't feel like seeing anyone."

"Except me."

"Except you. Did you write a poem today?"

"I finished my crow poem."

"Recite it for me."

And so she did.

Summertime is rolling by
The crows are in the wood.
Their black wings are against the sky.
Are they doing what they should?

They're monstrously big and very loud,
They come in family groups
And always travel in a crowd
Like actors in a troupe.

They caw and clack and rattle so
They yell from tree to tree.
The squirrel ducks his head down low
So does the chickadee.

I think they're reconnoitering
To keep the bears away.
It looks like simple loitering
But tomorrow's picnic day.

Then they'll come a hundred strong,
And fall on us like thieves.
They'll caw until we run along,
Then steal our bread and cheese.

Anastasia smiled at her granddaughter. "Reconnoitering and loitering... a very nice rhyme, little cabbage."

"You helped me with that one."

"Not at all."

"You did, Grandmama. Don't you remember?" But then she noticed Anastasia's smile, and realized her grandmother was only teasing her and not "going soft in the head," an event her mother greatly feared, which, as far as Natasha could understand it, meant Anastasia would forget who everyone was and begin walking around the house without any clothes on.

"I love rhymes," she said.

"Well, thank you for reciting the poem. You must always memorize them so they will never be lost."

"I will. Now, Anastasia," she said gruffly, since this was her job, to get her grandmother to write, "it's your turn."

"I did not write a poem today."

"Why not?"

"I did not feel like it."

"Not even one little line?"

"No."

Natasha said, "I think you are too sad to write a poem."

"Yes, Natasha darling. I think I am."

"I don't see what she has to be sad about," Sofia said. "We're all here. She should be happy."

"We're not all here," Irina said. "Kolya isn't here."

They were walking along the garden path. The evening was a soft blue-grey, the air was soft, too, and fragrant with the many scents wafting all around them from the beds of herbs and flowers their father had planted over the years.

"Oh—Kolya! But he's never here. He hasn't been home for a summer visit since Sasha was born. And that was five years ago."

"Has it been that long? Five years?" Irina turned away from her sister and looked across the garden to the house. "Hasn't she come down at all?"

"Not since I've been here."

"Well, Sonya, it's absurd. Unless she's ill. Is she?"

"Natasha doesn't think so."

"Natasha is a child. Perhaps a doctor would be a better person to send up to her."

Sofia didn't reply. Irina was probably right. In theory, at least. In practice? It seemed hardly likely to happen. Anastasia Alexandrovna hated the sight of doctors almost as much as she did the sight of priests.

"So, tell me, why is Mother so sad? You've been here all month. What do you think?"

"She isn't writing."

"Ah. But is that a symptom or a cause? Is she sad because she is not writing, or is she not writing because she is sad?"

They had reached the fountain and by silent agreement turned back toward the house. The lower floors were all alight, but in their mother's apartment, only a single candle seemed to be burning, a single light, like a beacon, shining into the night.

"Or is she sad because of Kolya?"

Sofia hesitated to answer, hoping her sister would add something more. When she didn't, Sofia said, "What about Kolya?"

"He has stopped writing to her."

"Did he ever write to her? I mean, except to ask for money?"

"Evidently, yes."

As they approached the house, they heard the rather piercing sound of children's voices raised in laughter or in tears, it was difficult to tell.

"Still awake," Irina sighed. "Papa's keeping them up."

"Not for long," Sofia said, and went striding into the house.

But Irina sat down on the terrace and tried to remember her brother. Every memory she had of him was by now nearly twenty years old, it had been that long since she had spent enough time with him to create any memory of him at all. What she did remember: how, when he was very small, she and Sofia used to dress him up in their party dresses, how they used to torment him, hide from him in the garden, the two of them, until he cried, poor little boy. Then they would jump out of their hiding places and tickle him and make him laugh. He had the best laugh, rich and musical, and how they had loved him, their blue-eyed baby brother. Later they all three played games together, learned music and magic tricks, ran wild in the woods. Then suddenly everything changed. Great Uncle Andrey died, their father inherited his land and serfs, there was terrible consternation in the family which at the time she could not understand. Sofia was sent abroad to school, and she herself soon followed. Kolya moved away from home, too, to the capital, where he made dangerous friends and picked up dangerous ideas. Then there were years of worry. He was arrested and released, arrested again and held for months. Yet his crimes were minor, more like pranks than serious crimes, and so he had not been sent into exile, or into the army, or to the mines. He might still have gone to university and made something of himself, but he had refused to go. Refused to go to university, refused to enter the Guards, refused to help manage the estate. Refused everything society offered him. Nothing satisfied him, nothing was good enough, pure enough. You offered him bread and he asked you whose labor produced the grain. You asked him a simple question—had he read this or that, had he gone here or there—and next thing you knew he was condemning thick journals, George Sand, the Moscow-Petersburg Express.

And yet, she thought, smiling to herself there on the terrace, bathed in the warmth of the gentle evening, there was something admirable in that stance. If the world was corrupt—and she had no doubt it was, through and through—then perhaps he was right in rejecting it. Though how one lived then, how one survived from day to day, what one did… this she did not know.

These thoughts all passed through her mind rather quickly, as thoughts do, in quick-moving images, and feelings, ending finally in an upsurge of affection which instantly gave way to the darkest sense of fatality and fear. Now at last she understood her mother, locked upstairs in her room, waiting for word, hearing nothing, expecting a catastrophe which was bound to come. The image of her own dear son Andrushka came to her, and suddenly terror rose up inside her and a feeling of deadly cold. Shivering, she rose from her seat and went into the house.

As far as Natasha was concerned, the summer holiday had only now really begun, now that the cousins had arrived. Finally there were enough of them to make playing tag or hide-and-seek worthwhile. They swam in the little pond while the adults went riding, played tennis, or drank on the terrace. When it rained (and we had great thunder and lightning storms that summer), there were games in the game room, and puzzles to put together, and chests in the attic with dress-up clothes they could try on and play in. Natasha took charge of the attic and distributed its treasures with the economy of a thrifty housewife. "They're really too little for the attic," she complained (and in fact they were), but the rocking horses came downstairs and some of the ancient toys, bald dolls and broken soldiers and carved animals on tiny wheels that the littlest children loved pulling around behind them by a string, and miniature doll furniture and tea sets and all these gave the children endless hours of pleasure on rainy days so Sofia could read in peace and Irina could play chess with her father and occasionally even win.

Anastasia stayed stubbornly in her study. Natasha visited her every day.

"Anastasia Alexandrovna, I have written another poem!"

"Let's hear it."

Natasha recited:

Oh how the stones shine prettily,
Oh they are so glittery.
But I fear they are slippery.
It makes me feel quite jittery.

"That is a lovely poem! Come here to me, little cabbage, and let me kiss you."

Grandmother hugged her and kissed her all over her face, her eyes, her nose, her cheeks, her mouth.

"You have the gift, Natalia. You have the gift of loving words."

"Is it a gift?"

"Oh, yes. For a while, at least. Yes, at least for a while."

"Do they take it back—after awhile?"

"No. It just turns into something else. A curse. Yes, the gift turns into a curse. Like when someone gives you a pretty little bear cub. Then one day—"

"It grows up and eats you."

"Yes. It chews you right up."

Hugging her grandmother again, she asked, "Will the bear cub eat me, too?"

"If you keep it too long. Bears belong in the woods."

"And where do words belong?"

"That's a good question, Tasha. Where do words belong? Or how can we get away from them? They're everywhere. Unlike bears. Maybe to escape words you have to go into the woods with the bears."

Natasha laughed and so did Anastasia Alexandrovna, the poetess who had tired of words.

It was some days later, in the evening, that Natasha, dancing in front of the staircase while Irina played a mazurka on the piano, glanced up to the second floor and saw, ever so briefly, her grandmother dancing "a dear little mazurka" (as Natasha put it) down the hallway.

"Well," Sofia said, "she can still dance at least."

Something about this particular event—if it could even be considered an event—so alarmed Irina that the next morning she sent for me.

CHAPTER TWO

Marina Vilinskaya Comes for a Manuscript

"Fortunate is the man who inherits a task," wrote my mentor in one of his books. "He can accustom himself to it early, without wasting half his life on the choice. He can concentrate, and he gets things done. But we really don't want to do anything, or if we do, we venture onto the boundless steppe where no matter what you do or where you go, you get nowhere."

Fortunate is the man who inherits a task. Perhaps. But then it depends on what kind of task. If the task is maintaining Autocracy, Orthodoxy and Serfdom, as our Minister of Interior believes it to be, then one might be better off on the boundless steppe, doing nothing and getting nowhere.

I had given my mentor's book to Nikolai when it was first published, the year before the great revolutions swept Europe and our lives here changed so dramatically for the worse, and so I feel I must bear some responsibility for him. After all, despite what some young people say, books can change the world, and some actually do.

But Irina Vasilevna had not summoned me to talk about Nikolai. It was her mother she was worried about.

♣

It was evening when I arrived at Oak Hills. I had the coachman stop a short distance from the house so I could approach it on foot along the lime-bordered avenue that led up to the wide and welcoming front door. It was a house I had loved ever since I first set eyes on it long ago when I was young. This was not so much because of its architectural grace or beauty; from the outside it looked like any other three-storey, wooden house, its shingles as brightly painted as an icon, its window shutters and balustrades fancifully carved, the sort of house that is so common in our district. But inside, its rooms were open and airy, not crowded with heavy furniture, bric-à-brac, or ostentatious decoration. Around it were Vasily Yakovlevich's beautiful gardens, behind it, the stables and barn, the bathhouse and little pond, and down the road, the village and the church, everywhere a sense of peace and order. Granted, the house had become a bit ramshackle over time, was in need of some repair, had a sense about it of slight neglect as though waiting for the true owner to appear, waiting for Nikolai Vasilevich, the son and heir, to return. Still it was here within these plain and simple walls that Anastasia Alexandrovna had spent most of her life, and written almost all of her poems. It made Oak Hills a sacred place.

So I arrived at the house, and Masha answered the door, welcomed me warmly and directed me to the terrace where Irina was waiting for me.

I had not seen her for several years, but she looked the same as always, her hair still golden, her strong features so like her mother's, and she greeted me with the nonchalance of a friend whom one sees every other day. This was a characteristic of the entire family, this easy amiability, and one I always found greatly appealing. She suggested we take a turn in the garden together before joining the rest of the family for supper when the children returned from their outing. I told her I had supper plans. That settled, we started strolling along the pathways, heading toward the fountain.

We had known each other a long time and didn't stand on ceremony. Irina explained the situation quickly, and asked for my help. I said I would be glad to help but I had no idea what she expected me to do.

"You know her temperament. You know ... the difficulties. She's becoming childlike, I'm afraid. And her editor has written. They are coming here. I don't know what to do."

"And she's not writing?"

"I don't think so. But I don't know."

"What does your father say?"

"He doesn't think she's writing either."

I consulted my pocket diary. Yes, Marina Vilinskaya had written to me as well. In three days, she and Sergei Kataev were due to visit and retrieve, by force of arms if necessary, the latest collection of poems by Anastasia Barakova, a book long-promised, long-delayed, and now long-overdue. If Irina was right, they were about to be gravely disappointed.

"Is she ill?"

"I don't know. I haven't seen her since we arrived. It seems only Natasha is granted daily audiences with her. And Masha, of course."

"What is it you want me to do, Irina?"

"Go and see her. Talk to her. Find out what's happening to her. This is so unlike her, so … disturbing."

"There's no one in the family who can do this?"

"I could ask Natasha, but she is not entirely trustworthy."

"Her loyalty is with Anastasia. As is Masha's."

"She gives them both sweets."

"We have no sweets to offer them?"

"Perhaps you might try bringing *her* sweets."

We had been walking and now stopped at a particularly lovely and fragrant rose bush. How bright their colors, how thick their thorns! They are made to be seen and not touched. They are like your mother, I thought. At the same moment, Irina said, "Sweets, but never flowers. She hates them to be cut."

Of course, I agreed to see Anastasia. After all, it was what I wanted to do in any case. We spoke for a few more minutes, but our business was finished, and soon Irina embraced me, wished me a good night, and returned to the house.

But I sat on a wooden bench in the garden, overcome by the opposing forces working their power within me, on the one hand, the warm, earthy sweetness in the air, on the other, a cold and bitter sorrow that rose along with it, and a sense of outrage at God for creating such a world and putting us in it, sensitive creatures, yoked to time, driven to desperation by the horrors that surround us, thrown here so carelessly (yes, God! carelessly!) like stars thrown into the heavens, like handfuls of sand thrown by children at the seashore. Oh, how careless He had been with us, and yet, ironically, how precise and perfectly ordered the rest of creation was, these roses, for example, and the bees who attended them, and the rain that watered them.

And I went on in that vein for some time because it is an ongoing argument between me and God, and we have yet to settle it. I doubt we ever shall.

Then I laid the argument aside—it would keep—and let my mind be flooded with memories of Anastasia Alexandrovna as she was when I first met her. How lovely she was then, how brilliant, how willful, how self-assured. In those days for a woman to show such spirit was unusual. In those days for a woman to publish under her own name was more than unusual, it was unheard of, and had been ever since Anna Burina had been subjected to mean, vicious, scornful attacks by male poets, even by Pushkin himself, who was so threatened by her voice that he stooped to laughing and jeering at her. Well, Anastasia Alexandrovna did not disguise herself by taking on a pseudonym as other poetesses did, and if a male critic spoke harshly about her, she only laughed and wrote her own review of his review—this indeed under a male pseudonym—and made a fool of him. In those days she was indomitable. Her figure was slim, her step was brisk, her eyes flashed and her fair hair floated around her face like a cloud of gold. Of course, she had the voice of an angel.

A difficult woman, everyone said, but well worth the trouble.

Then time, that devil, stole up on her.

We keep the images of those we love burnished and candle-lit, keep them on the altars of memory, and there they are beyond time, beyond change, perfect like the resplendent bodies of the saved which the holy saints assure us will be our own perfected state. In just such a form I kept the image of Anastasia Alexandrovna on all my travels and through all the years so that when I returned home at last and saw an old woman sitting at Anastasia's desk, I did not know who she was. And Vasily Yakovlevich had come to resemble an old peasant gardener in a straw hat, the man who had once been a fiery orator, a forceful official in our district, a man capable of furious rages and fateful decisions—now overseeing the composting of leaves, the planting of vegetable plots.

All of us indeed will sink into the earth. Bodies broken. Voices silenced. Thoughts ended. And the argument with God settled at last, of course in his favor, who will have the last word.

Finally, having followed the familiar track through my mind to reach at last a place of quietness and surrender (how can one not surrender to such overwhelming force?), I rose from the bench and made my way along the garden path, now in a deep purple shadow, to the terrace steps, and through the terrace doors into the house I had once lived in and knew so well. Again it was filled with children and the excitement and noise and joy of life that only the young can bring to a household. The piano was open, someone had been playing, and there were toys scattered on the rug in the game room. Clearly the children had returned, swept through in a great wave of energy and movement, leaving their traces behind, and were now being washed and dressed for supper. Someone had lit all the lamps, and the floors and woodwork shone in the soft light. Even the wooden rafters seemed polished and bright. It was the house as I had known it so intimately when I, too, was young.

I did not take the main staircase but went up the back stairs. Supper was being prepared in the kitchen so Cook was not about, nor were any of the other house serfs. Still I crept up as quietly as I could, past the bedroom corridor, and up to the top floor and the door I knew led into Anastasia's library. It would not be locked, and I would enter and surprise her, though if she were sitting at her desk and not resting in her bedroom, she would see me directly as I came through.

And she was sitting at her desk, staring at the doorway in which I must have appeared like a specter, but before I could speak, she said, "Oh, here you are. I've been expecting you. Sit!"

She waved her arm at me, and I sat down in an armchair facing her desk.

"Forgive me for frightening you, Anastasia Alexandrovna."

She lifted her eyebrows. No, indeed, I had not frightened her. She looked like a woman not even death would frighten. Her hair was completely white, her face thin and lined, the skin puckered in places where the flesh had once been firm and smooth. She was dressed entirely in black, as though in deep mourning, with no jewels or rings, she who had once worn great emeralds and amethysts, and there was a sense about her of vacuity, as though she herself were not present, that her imagination had not died but had deserted her, that it existed still but was dwelling in a place beyond her reach.

And then, after I had come to such grim conclusions on the basis of a mere look, she erased it all by smiling at me and saying my name. The warmth of her voice had not changed.

"So Irina called for you, did she? It had to be Risha. Sonya would never ask such a favor, but Risha, yes. Nothing is beyond her. Still, it's good to see you. You are looking quite well. You have had adventures!"

I thanked her for the compliment, and we smiled at each other. Was her smile different now, did it mean something or nothing, did it hold deep significance or was it merely a habit, a courtesy? She was a hard woman to read.

It was never clear to me whether Anastasia had known my feelings for her when I first met her, when I was not yet twenty, and she in her forties and at the apex of her career. Oh, how extraordinary she was then! I had come to Oak Hills as a French tutor for Nikolai, and I gave him books by George Sand to read, and talked with him about socialism and the ideas of Saint-Simon and Fourier. I was still naive, and did not realize how dangerous these ideas were considered to be, and living in the country, I did not know how people suffered merely for thinking about them. I loved Nikolai dearly and wanted to share everything I knew with him; as for his mother, she was the greatest star in the firmament and I adored her. So when Nikolai left home to live in Petersburg, I stayed on as Anastasia's copyist, secretary, courier, and tea-maker. But now something had ground her down, and her light—what had become of her light?

"Those two dragons, Vilinskaya and Kataev, are coming here soon," I said. "And Irina wonders..."

"Does she? So she has sent you to see whether there will be war or peace when the dragons arrive at the door? Will I have gold for them or must we sacrifice a virgin? Does she worry it will be little Natasha? Would the dragons be satisfied with Natasha on a plate?"

"Anastasia," I said. "What has happened?"

Then I saw something I never dreamt I would ever see: tears! Tears filled her eyes and flowed freely, unchecked, down her cheeks. I wanted to spring up and take her in my arms, but the desk, a wooden barrier, its clear surface shining like a glacier, stood mountainously in the way. Still, crying, "My God! What is it?" I started to rise, but she held up her hand imperiously (she could be imperious in this way) and so I sat down again and waited and feared the worst.

"He is lost," she said. "I feel it in my heart."

"Who? Who is lost?"

"Kolya. My Kolya. No word from him for months, and I cannot go to him. But the silence, the silence, the emptiness... the darkness..."

"Anastasia! What do you mean?"

"I mean, I must find him, or I will die."

So it was about Kolya after all. I should have known.

He had not written. He had been writing to her once or twice a month, sometimes every week, then abruptly the letters stopped. She kept writing to his address in the capital where he had taken rooms. The letters were not returned, but neither were they ever answered. Where had he gone?

"And he didn't mention moving from his rooms in any of his letters?"

"Not a word. Nothing."

He was always unreliable, Kolya, not that his mother would admit it. He had strange ideas. Of course, in our time the whole world has strange ideas. Even in our district there was political turmoil and agitation, a new governor had been appointed, there was what we called "disorder" among the peasants, and groups of students had come from Moscow with the idea of "educating" them. Wherever students and peasants gather to talk about the land there will be religious fanatics of one sort or another to proclaim the holiness of the Tsar, or, alternatively, his wickedness. These things go together like political pamphlets and the secret police. In fact, representatives of the Third Section were always present at such gatherings. There had been arrests.

Arrest was certainly a possibility. And the arrested often disappeared without a trace, without a by-your-leave, and wrote no letters home to their mothers with the news.

"What was he doing with himself? Surely he wrote about that."

"He wrote to me about little things. People he saw on the street, boats on the river, what was sold at the markets, the weather, the changing colors of the sky."

Anastasia got up and went to her bookshelf. I assumed she was going to get a book, but instead she reached behind the books and retrieved a bottle of vodka and two glasses. The sight of the bottle was—sobering.

"You see, I am trying to become my son," she said, filling the two glasses. "The better to know him, the better to find him."

"I think this search might best be left in my hands," I said.

We emptied our glasses and the agreement was sealed. I do not drink vodka on an empty stomach as a rule but there are occasions when one must throw rules out the window.

Before I left, she gave me a few of Kolya's most recent letters, in case there was something in them she had missed, some reference to a place or a person I might have knowledge of or recognize, and she asked me to intercept the dragons at the coach station and keep them away.

"You must discourage them from eating little Tasha."

"But is there gold for them? Is the manuscript ready? It's what they want and I doubt they will leave without it."

"There is no manuscript. Tell them that and make them go away. Poetry is dead. Words are dead. Life is all that matters, and life is not made of words."

What is it made of then, I wanted to ask her. But I did not.

♣

For some of us, life is made of words.

Perhaps that is the problem.

As for Nikolai Vasilevich, if we were to find him, words were all we had to use, and there were not many of them and they were not very useful. That was my conclusion after reading a dozen pages of his letters. They contained no personal information at all, and for "recent" letters they were quite old. It appeared that Kolya had not written to his mother in well over a year.

A year is a very long time.

♣

I knew Marina Vilinskaya and Sergei Kataev quite well. They were not unreasonable people. They had been Anastasia's publishers for many years and, in fact, it was due to Marina's connections in Europe that Anastasia Barakova had become as well known there as she was, her work having been translated into both French and German and having been well received by critics in both countries. In short, Anastasia Alexandrovna had much to be grateful to Vilinskaya and Kataev for, if Anastasia Alexandrovna were the sort of woman who felt grateful to anyone. A sense of gratitude was not one of her virtues, however, particularly not in this realm where she felt, probably rightly, that what mattered were her poems and not Vilinskaya and Kataev's skill at publishing them.

I met them at the coach station and informed them that Anastasia was too ill to see them and that they would have to return the way they had come, sadly, without even a short interview...

"Ill?" Kataev cried, loudly, as though one of our wasps had just stung him. (In fact, there were a number of wasps buzzing about.) "We had not heard she was ill! Has she seen a doctor? Who is her doctor? Good God, we should have ours sent immediately. There are nothing but quacks out here, probably still prescribing hot baths and valerian drops!"

He continued in this manner while Vilinskaya called a porter.

"Why, she is a national treasure! A living saint! An inspiration! It is her destiny—her destiny!—to be known, to be loved..." (This is how Sergei Kataev spoke when he was himself inspired. Enthusiasm sometimes took him in its claws and flew away with him.) "Her life is precious. Precious!"

Meanwhile Marina Vilinskaya had engaged a carriage to take us to Oak Hills. So, porter trailing behind with their bags, we three left the coach station, somberly, in military file, as though en route to a war we could never hope to win.

So much for my attempt to shield Anastasia Alexandrovna from her destiny.

I expected that the publishers' interview with Irina Vasilevna would be short, no matter which way it went, so I waited for them on the terrace. If Kataev could only calm down and focus his mind on the actual problem, we might possibly save Russian poetry after all.

Or it might rest on my own shoulders. Finding Nikolai, saving poetry. An absurd, far-fetched, romantic idea, worthy of Anastasia Alexandrovna, whose poems had moved the hearts and souls of Russian women for decades, yes, but had done little else, if truth be told. But what does poetry do, in any case? It can move a heart, perhaps, but when it comes to moving a piece of furniture or an emperor's national policy, one needs more than beautiful rhymes.

I knew, or could guess, some of the temptations Nikolai encountered in the city. Not the simple temptations (he had already encountered them right here in our own district), but the more complicated ones, the temptation to imagine yourself God, to change the world, save the oppressed, free the imprisoned, raise the dead. There in the city you see—if you dare to look—more misery than can be excused by the rational arguments of philosophers, and so one reaches for blunter instruments, for guns, for bombs. I knew Kolya. He was above all else, above, that is, all the irresponsible traits he displayed so proudly, a sensitive and compassionate man. Injustice outraged him though he disguised his outrage under a veil of irony, the clever man's shield against his own sensitivity and vulnerability. But righteousness can lead a man to desperate acts, to take into his own hands things that belong by right in the hands of others. Yes, he might say, but what others? And what if those others neglect their duty to see that justice is done? What then?

This is the argument our Nihilists make. Who is responsible? Where is the leader who will take on the work of reform? There is no such leader, you say? Well, then, if no one else will act, we must. It cannot be reformed, you say? Then the entire structure must be torn down and built again.

And this was why, thinking of Kolya, I found myself becoming more and more fearful. I had no important contacts in the capital, but Marina Vilinskaya did, and when she put her mind to it, Marina Vilinskaya could move a great deal more than hearts and souls.

I was just imagining her doing it when the woman herself swept onto the terrace and sat down beside me. She was immaculately dressed as always, immaculately groomed, but I could tell she was deeply upset. Her lovely cheeks were slightly flushed and she had put her left hand glove on her right hand and was pulling on the fingers to get it off.

"Irina Vasilevna has forbidden us access to her mother."

"I expect it's more the case that Anastasia Alexandrovna has forbidden you access."

"And she says there is no book."

"Yes," I said, taking her hand and pulling the glove off for her. "I believe that is the case."

"Why not, for the love of God? The woman is a poet. She must be writing."

"She is in despair."

"Despair? Aren't we all in despair? Why isn't she writing about despair?"

"She is afraid for Nikolai."

"In trouble again, is he? But he's been in trouble all his life."

"This time he has disappeared. She has had no word from him in more than a year."

Marina sat very still. Her hands, ungloved, were clasped in her lap, her face, a perfect oval framed by sleek plaits of golden hair, betrayed no emotion at all. She barely breathed. When she spoke, it was as though a very small ripple was for a mere second whispering above the deep stillness of a pond.

"So. What is to be done?"

"You will have to find him."

"I? I am an editor, not a finder."

"Of course you are a finder! You find writers, you find poets. Think of him as a writer whose manuscript you must capture for Kataev. You have tracked down and trapped many poets in your day."

"In my day! How funny you are, Marko Volchek."

She turned her brilliant smile on me, and as usual, when faced with the full force of her charm, my heart pounded a bit harder. Oh, Marina Fyodorovna! How many poets have fallen into your sweet trap! That thought led to another but I stopped myself from thinking it and carried on.

"Listen, Marina, Anastasia will not write another word until she knows her son is safe, so we must assure her of that. If you want your book—and all Europe seems to be waiting for it—"

"So we are off on an adventure, you and I! Of course nothing can be done in August. The city is deserted in August. I am going on holiday myself now. You will have to come see me in the fall. We shall lay our traps then."

"Good. In the meantime I will stay here and watch for mail. Perhaps he will write."

"Or arrive."

"That would be best."

"You think it unlikely?"

"The best things usually are."

Sometime later Vilinskaya and Kataev, having refused Vasily Yakovlevich's offer to spend the night, left Oak Hills to begin the long journey back to the city. They left empty-handed except for a basket of garden vegetables that Vasily Yakovlevich presented to them on the steps of the house as their carriage approached along the drive.

"The poetry of the earth," he said with all the seriousness of the gentleman farmer. "Beautiful—and edible."

He was always a bit of a joker, was Vasily Yakovlevich. His children would laugh at him and say he was the only person in the world who was made happy by bad news. Bad news confirmed his belief that the world was in the hands of an evil archon and there was no use struggling against that cosmic fact. Be grateful for small favors. If the sun shines, the plants grow, the birds sing—thank your lucky stars. If you happen to marry the woman you love and are able to live with her without killing her—aha! he'd smile—thank God for that too.

Anastasia Alexandrovna once wrote a poem about passing by a lover on the stairs. "The shadow that lies between us is the shadow of the truest love..." The truest love—was that Vasily Yakovlevich? I think it always was.

CHAPTER THREE

More Guests Arrive

Oak Hills settled comfortably into summer like a child snuggling with a favorite doll. The sun shone, the plants thrived, the birds sang, and the children played in the garden (much to the distress of the gardeners), swam in the pond (much to the distress of their nannies), and rode ponies over the meadows and along the woodland paths (much to the distress of just about everyone). It was idyllic; no catastrophes occurred, no bones were broken, there were no fevers or attacks by wild beasts, though the children would have enjoyed seeing a wild beast or two, a bear lunging out of the woods, a golden-eyed wolf, tongue lolling from a tooth-filled mouth, leering at them from behind the trees, even a vixen screeching in the night would have delighted them. But Oak Hills was not in a wilderness, not in the deep forests or the high steppes, more's the pity, as Vasily Yakovlevich would say, bemoaning the advance of so-called civilization, the ruination of the country, but it was to be expected, he would say, since everything good was being destroyed, there was only bad news and more bad news, while upstairs in her study, Anastasia Alexandrovna sat and stared and stubbornly refused to write a single word.

Even in the country our summers can be stifling and humid, and that summer was exceptionally so. The forests surrounding the estate gave no relief; it was as though instead of absorbing the heat in their shade, they concentrated it, and then there was fear of fire breaking out, especially during some of the powerful thunderstorms that struck that summer with unusual regularity and ferocity. Yes, the air in the woods was suffocating, the water in the pond was like a bath, the earth itself, the very stones of the earth, exuded heat.

The house guests sat all day on the terrace, drinking tea or something cooler. The animals lay panting in the shade. Only the children seemed immune to the weather and continued to run and play, to get overheated, to have their faces washed in cold water, and to be confined in the

NIKOLAI BARAKOV

There were pictures of him as a child, and as a student,
and as a handsome grown-up man,
bearded and wearing a lovely fur hat and a dashing coat.

afternoons and forced to rest in darkened rooms. All the children except Natasha, who spent her afternoons in Anastasia Alexandrovna's study, writing poems in her journal or drawing pictures or reading from her grandmother's collection of books. When she came downstairs for supper, Irina always asked, How is your grandmother? and Natasha always answered, She is well.

"Is she writing?"

"No."

"What does she do up there all day then?"

"She is listening."

"Listening? To what?"

"She is listening for a sound. She is listening to the trees."

"Does she sleep?"

"No. She sits at her desk or in her chair."

"Doesn't she speak to you?"

Natasha laughed. "Of course she speaks to me. We talk about everything."

Irina was quite unable to get more information from Natasha than that.

Still, Anastasia Alexandrovna would not come down and she let no one else up. Tasha and Masha, just those two, and Vasily Yakovlevich for a goodnight kiss.

In the afternoons, hot though they were, her room was always cool, shaded by one of the great oaks, and the fragrance from the flowering hedge and the climbing roses filled the air with sweet perfume. There were the cool stones of the stone gardens to touch, and Natasha loved to handle them and water them as though they were plants—for stones only showed their true beauty when they were wet and shining—and there were the little altars her grandmother had set up all through her rooms where pictures of Uncle Kolya stood in place of the icons other grandmothers might have placed around their rooms and high up in the corners. There were pictures of him as a child, and as a student, and as a handsome grown-up man, bearded and wearing a lovely fur hat and a dashing coat. Natasha loved looking at the pictures and placing her own found treasures on Uncle Kolya's altars—bird feathers, rose petals, a perfectly round white stone.

"Will he ever come to see us?"

"Yes, he will. Of course he will," Anastasia Alexandrovna said. "We shall write notes to him telling him to come, and burn them. Then he'll dream of what we've written. We shall write: Kolya, please come home to see us. Do that for me, Tasha, dear."

Natasha carefully wrote the words on a piece of paper, Anastasia lit a candle, and they held the paper over it, Natasha on one side, Anastasia on the other, until it burnt to ash.

"Now the words are in the air and can travel to Kolya wherever he is."

"How do they know where to go?"

"They are words. They know."

"Are they like spirits?"

"Yes, like angels. They are messengers. Which is what angels are."

"Did I ever meet Uncle Kolya?"

"Of course. You don't remember?"

"No," she said, and stared hard at the picture of Nikolai as a young man. It was an ink drawing and made Nikolai look stern and somber like a cavalry officer about to ride off to war and a heroic death in battle.

"You were a little child. Let me think. It was Christmas, you were almost three. Sasha was an infant and Kolya was afraid to hold him. But he played with you. I remember. He sat on the floor and rolled a ball to you and you rolled it back. He taught you a song."

"What color was the ball?"

"Red and blue."

"Ah. I remember the red and blue ball. And what was the song?"

"The Little Fir Tree."

Natasha closed her eyes tight and tried to remember the ball, the song, tried to remember her uncle, but she couldn't remember anything at all. She tried to remember back as far as she could go…

"I remember a pony, someone holding me so I could sit on it, being very high up…"

Anastasia shook her head. "That was not Kolya. That was someone else."

♣

When she was not with her grandmother, Natasha liked to take walks around the estate. She had special routes she would follow, secret paths she took, and visits to make along the way. There were certain trees she visited, a certain little clearing amidst the trees of the wood, and a certain little fountain at the very back of the garden around which there was a circular maze, a darling little pathway she loved to walk along, one circle within another circle, and certain little ways blocked, the entire path encircled with hedges higher than her head covered with little white flowers that smelt divine. The bushes were filled with chattering sparrows and sometimes little golden finches or yellow or green warblers. The fountain never had water in it but it had a lovely statue of a water sprite which Natasha loved to draw pictures of in her book.

No one ever came to this part of the garden, it was really left quite wild, and there were places to hide under bushes, wide and clear spaces completely hidden, secret places under the boughs of rhododendrons, that she loved more than any other places on earth. No one else knew about those secret places and no one could ever find her when she was there. But she was always careful to return when she heard the bell ring out, calling the children home for meals. Better not to alert anyone to her secret places, her secret life.

Here under the great bushes near the dry fountain and its labyrinth she wrote the story of Prince Nikolai and the Magician whose red and blue ball was really a magic globe through which one could see into the future, a globe Prince Nikolai had to find in order to free Princess Zinaida from the evil powers of Pasha Khan.

And she wrote poems there to bring the next afternoon to her grandmother, to please her, because she loved to listen to poems and especially loved to hear Natasha recite her own.

Misha likes to wash the stones
In Grandmama's stone garden
He likes to sit there all alone
And asks nobody's pardon.

Anastasia Alexandrovna liked this poem very much.

Natasha said, "I wish you would read one of your poems to me."

"I will, someday. I will have to think of one that you would like."

"I would like any one. If you wrote it, I would like it."

Anastasia only shook her head and smiled.

As the summer progressed, the feeling in the house changed. A more severe attitude began to prevail. Schedules were created and enforced. Children were admonished. Their movements around the estate were restrained.

The husbands had arrived.

Natasha, being the oldest, suffered the most from the restrictions placed on the children by her father and her uncle. Her dignity was offended by such rules especially since she thought of Oak Hills as her true home, as her own possession. She was mistress of all she surveyed… so to be forbidden to climb trees, fish in the pond, or hide in the woods felt like imprisonment, felt like usurpation, felt like ... a coup d'etat.

And then, with men in the house, there was less laughter, and the adults began playing cards in the evening, and stopped letting the children dress up in fancy clothes from the attic and put on funny plays after supper or dance around to Aunt Irina's piano-playing or be read stories in the drawing room, but instead they had to go straight to bed.

The husbands also had quite different ideas about Nikolai Vasilevich. They did not think of him as a prince. The more their wives worried about him, the less good they had to say about him.

"A disappointment all the way around," Ivan Ivanovich sighed sympathetically one evening when Nikolai's name came up, which it often did when they were all sitting around the card table.

"A wastrel," Arkady Andreyevich grumbled, tossing his hand of cards onto the table in disgust.

"One man's wastefulness is another man's generosity."

"Easy to be generous with someone else's money. He's never succeeded at anything."

"But smart. Talented. Charming…"

"A fabricator."

"Granted he can spin a tall tale—"

"One would not call him a liar—"

"Not to his face. He'd call you out on the spot. I expect he'd enjoy a good duel."

"Full of opinions, nothing to back them up."

"Always likes a good argument."

"A contrarian with anarchist tendencies."

"Well, he's a typical nihilist."

"And an atheist."

"But with no rational arguments. No belief."

Ivan Ivanovich grimaced at his cards, and then gazed with some of the same disdain, just the slightest scornfulness, across the table at his brother-in-law, the up-and-coming official, Arkady Andreyevich.

"No belief in his unbelief, you mean?" Ivan Ivanovich said.

"Yes. He doesn't even believe that he doesn't believe."

"Ha! He believes in nothing, not even that he doesn't believe."

Sofia Vasilevna, who along with her sister had remained silent through this entire exchange, said quietly, "I would ask you both not to speak of our brother like that." She laid her cards on the table. "I believe I have the winning hand, whether you happen to believe it or not."

The husbands scowled.

"Well, what are we going to do? We can't entertain guests, not if your mother is as ill as it seems—"

"No one said she was ill."

"That's because no one has bothered calling the doctor."

"She won't see a doctor. She never would."

"Everyone sees doctors!" Arkady exclaimed in annoyance. "Who does she think she is? Why she's—"

"Arkasha!" Irina cried out, stopping him from expressing in public what he said often enough in private, that Anastasia Alexandrovna was acting like a spoiled tsarina when she was only a third-rate versifier.

She is a female Nekrasov! Irina would say, and Arkady Andreyevich, who had never read a word of Nekrasov, nor, for that matter, a word of Anastasia Barakova, would only laugh and mock her by reciting the only line of poetry he actually knew, thinking himself clever by changing the gender of the pronoun: *Beside the desolate waves SHE stood and thronged with mighty thoughts stared out...*

That evening, however, with both sisters staring at him so sternly, he did not say any more. But Ivan Ivanovich, who by then had drunk quite a bit of Vasily Yakovlevich's French brandy, was less restrained.

"She's behind the times, let's admit it. She's old-fashioned. She has lived long, God bless her, but now she is out-of-date."

For some reason, he found this expression charming, and repeated it several times.

"But why are we discussing Anastasia Alexandrovna's poetry when it's her health that is at issue?" Arkady asked gruffly, pleased with himself at grasping the bull by the horns. "What is to be done with her? That is the question."

At that point, Vasily Yakovlevich entered the drawing room and all conversation regarding the art and health of Anastasia Alexandrovna immediately ceased.

"Have you been up to see Mama?" Irina asked.

"Yes, I wished her a good night."

"And did you ask her to come down?"

"Of course," he said, and poured himself a brandy from the nearly empty bottle on the sideboard. "She did not feel like it tonight."

At that Irina sprang up from the table. "Why won't she come down? Why, Papa? Isn't she part of this family? Doesn't she care about us anymore? What is wrong with her?"

Clutching her hands together, she began striding around the room, her skirt swishing around her, all of her intent on movement. She had been sitting too long, listening too long to insipid conversation and disdainful insults to her entire family. She was suddenly in a mood to break something, and was actually looking around for some innocent object to smash onto the floor.

Sofia also rose from the table and went to her father. "Come, Papa, sit down."

"Poor Irinka, she is upset."

"She's always upset about something. Come and sit."

Irina glowered at her sister from the other side of the room.

"Very well. I'll say nothing more. Let's all sit down here and grumble about her and complain about her and do nothing. And it will be just like what we do about Kolya, grumble and complain and do nothing. And, now, see what's happened!"

"What? What's happened?" Vasily asked in alarm. "Have you news—?"

"No. No news. Like with Mama. No news." And Irina, to everyone's surprise, even shock, sat down on the nearest chair and began to cry.

Then everyone gathered around her and tried to comfort her, and Arkady Andreyevich, not the most sympathetic of men, got on his knees and put his arms around her while everyone else called for Masha to bring water or tea or more brandy and when Masha did not instantly appear, Ivan Ivanovich went himself to fetch these things while Sofia settled her father on another chair and brought him his brandy.

Then as suddenly as this squall began, it ended, and everyone settled down with the feeling that Irina's outburst had been far and away enough drama for one night, and they simply forgot what she had said, what they had said to spark her temper, the entire incident simply ceased to exist for them for they were a group of people who, unlike most of their fellow countrymen, lived lives without passion, not because they had emptied themselves of feeling through overindulgence but because they valued tranquility and order and habit and calmness. Those were the virtues Vasily Yakovlevich had acquired from living his long life with Anastasia Alexandrovna, he had trained himself in such virtues, and passed them down through his example to his daughters and they in turn had demanded them from all their suitors and potential husbands. They were by no means the virtues of Anastasia Alexandrovna herself, nor, needless to say, had they been acquired by her son.

One afternoon I stopped by Oak Hills to ask after Anastasia's health, and ran into little Natasha on the doorstep, rushing to fill a jug with water for Anastasia's stone gardens.

"Is she writing?" I asked, since this was the only question worth asking and I knew I had very little time in which to ask it.

"Yes. She writes," Natasha said. "May I give you a kiss?"

I accepted the kiss gratefully, and pressed on.

"Poems?"

"No. She writes letters. But she doesn't send them. She writes to Uncle Kolya and puts the letters in her desk drawer. She says when he comes home he'll have hundreds of letters to read and he'll know everything—and how sad he'll be."

"Why will he be sad?"

"To know how much she suffered. But she will burn them when he comes so he won't read them and be sad. She'll throw them all in the fire."

"Have you seen these letters?"

"No. She locks them in her desk."

So, there's hope, I thought. Anastasia is writing, and how could she be writing anything but poems? The idea of it—perhaps hundreds of poems locked in her desk drawer—so delighted me that I almost sang for joy.

"How is your grandmother feeling today?" I asked Natasha, feeling some small pang of guilt at interrogating a child. But little Natasha was no fool and simply smiled at me and sped off to fetch water for the stone gardens.

Seeing her with her jug, however, had given me the strangest feeling, for I, too, had once been charged with watering the stone gardens in those days—blissful beyond compare—when I was Anastasia's secretary, samovar-minder, and willing slave. I remembered how absurd it seemed to pour water on bowls and trays of stones, and yet how miraculous the transformation was when they were glistening with water and sparking in the sunlight.

There were such stone gardens scattered all around the house when I first met the Barakovs and they were quite lovely when the sun shone on them. Still there was something childish about them, and the way Anastasia attended to them, like a child would. Later, in addition to the stone gardens, there were little stone altars at which she left offerings of petals, dried flowers and herbs, bird feathers and bits of bark she found on her walks, that is to say, before she stopped taking walks. These were altars to the Muse, or attempts to lure the Muse, depending... and when she walked (or used to walk) she would stop at certain places, her "stations," she called them, like the rituals of someone following a pilgrimage route... and all this was quite childish, too, but she was an artist and so no one ever suggested her actions were signs of imbecility. Now, however, it struck me that, added to Anastasia's refusal to leave her rooms... and especially should she stop eating (and I was not sure whether she had or not)... the stone gardens and the altars might be seen, by someone, as a sign of decline, and some intervention might be determined necessary. Though necessary to whom?

Irina and Sofia were children who could not help their mother.

Anastasia was a mother who could not help her child.

It was a damnable situation all the way around.

As the blistering days continued in the country, the cities were sizzling in the heat and so more and more refugees arrived at Oak Hills, some on long-planned visits but others merely fleeing unbearable conditions with no notice of their arrival but a message delivered while they themselves were already en route. So within days of each other there arrived on the estate Anastasia's oldest and dearest friends Yevgenia Dmitrievna, Mariya Sergeyevna, and Tatyana Andreyevna, known to all and sundry as the "aunts" or "great aunts" or simply "the ladies." Soon afterwards Vasily Yakovlevich's oldest friend Aleksey Konstantinovich, known to all as Uncle Alyosha, also pulled up somewhat unannounced in his britzka, to the great excitement of the children who loved to ride in it (and of course with its facing seats, it was big enough for all six of them to squeeze in). Then a group of young people arrived, friends of Irina's, with several new children in tow, along with governesses and nursemaids, and more husbands, city men, brash, loud, impatient, demanding, all titular councilors, in other words law clerks working for the Department of so-called Justice, on their way up the ladder toward titles of nobility, currently on the lowest rung but feeling terribly important, and in their presence Arkady Andreyevich and Ivan Ivanovich themselves became puffed up and important and very busy and impatient and demanding. Fortunately there was a summer house on the estate for the overflow of guests and so the younger visitors were shuttled off to the other side of the pond while the older people remained in the comfort of the big house where conversations were calmer, quieter, and a good deal slower.

Still with four aunts, an uncle, two daughters, two sons-in-law, five grandchildren, and half a dozen random guests with their own collection of nannies and servants, all forever coming and going, having meals, drinking on the terrace, swimming in the pond, running through the garden, throwing balls on the lawn, swinging from trees (as the children did), playing cards (and gambling on them, as the men did), and forever trying to find each other and forever losing each other, the Barakov household was in a state of constant turmoil and upheaval, every part of it except for the rooms where Anastasia Alexandrovna stayed and perhaps looked down on the mad chaos below as a bird perched on a high branch might gaze down at movements on the ground with no interest in their patterns or intents.

Of course everyone asked for her, was constantly asking for her. Was she ill? Obviously she was ill or she would come down to welcome her guests, eat with them, talk to them, play cards with them (though in my recollection, Anastasia never played a hand of cards in her life). Had a doctor been called? Or a priest?

♣

"Yak, yak, yak," Anastasia Alexandrovna said, dismissing it all with a wave of her hand when Natasha repeated some of these conversations to her. "A doctor, a priest, a burial—all in due time. Meanwhile I hope they are enjoying themselves. Yevgenia, Mariya, Tatyana—are they getting along?"

Natasha thought they were.

"They only sit and talk."

"Of course. They're too old to do anything else."

"They also drink and laugh and play cards."

"Good for them!"

"They really want to see you, Grandmama."

"Are you their advocate?"

Natasha shrugged and kept drawing. She was making a picture of rooks to go with her new poem.

The Rooks

The rooks are black and very loud.
They caw and cackle in a crowd.
They sit on branches all the day,
And there they sleep the night away.
I do not know what else they do.
I do not like them much. Do you?

Her rooks looked more like ducks.

"Aunt Zhenya says you are writing your epic."

"Zhenya has always expected a great deal from me."

"Aunt Maryshka says you are being historic."

"Historic?"

"Something like that."

"Histrionic, perhaps. Or hysteric. Yes, she would. And Tatyana?"

"She says you are like someone in an opera."

"A diva?"

"No. She said—she was talking to Aunt Maryshka—that people

who live in operas have to sing. They sing about how they feel."

"Yes? Go on."

"So you, Aunt Tatyana says, have to sing but you are not singing."

"Perhaps I don't like the opera I'm in."

"Don't you?"

"No."

"What opera is it?"

"A very sad one."

Natasha put down her pencil and looked at her rook. It had turned into a great beaked creature. She couldn't tell at all what it was.

The men loved to talk about land and wealth. How much land Prince So-and-so had, how many serfs Count What's-his-name owned. They talked about disorders among the peasants as though they were personal insults aimed specifically at them. "We only killed five hundred of the filthy scum. Should have killed five thousand," they would say, while at the same time they denied up and down that there were any organized peasant disturbances to begin with. And why would serfs rebel against such a benevolent system and way of life? Of a population of sixty million, fifty million were serfs; a hundred thousand landowners owned two-fifths of them, while the state owned the others. How could anyone possibly complain about a system so fair and mathematical and just? Naturally these numbers were open to debate, some claiming the number of landowners was altogether too low, others that it was too high, some insisting that the imperial family owned twenty million, others that the number was half that. No matter. The arithmetic spoke volumes no matter how many pieces the pie was sliced into. The fact was the "land problem" consumed all our energy, all our creativity, all our lives, and there was no solution to it except the unacceptable one. We all knew what it was, but we also knew that to mention it in public meant torture, exile or death. It was a strange, surreal world in which one could not name, think about, or discuss the one thing that in the end might save the world, or destroy it.

One afternoon when I was visiting the house I happened to overhear a conversation between several of the husbands, including Arkady Andreyevich. (Interestingly, Ivan Ivanovich was not party to this conversations. I would soon learn why.) I did not mean to eavesdrop on them, but they came onto the terrace to smoke their pipes while I was sitting in a shady corner and they did not see me.

I was thinking about Anastasia, and so paid little attention at first. It was, in fact, the low tone of their voices which first drew my attention since they had always before spoken quite loudly. So, a group of men whispering? It meant either a surprise name day party in the planning stages, or some revolutionary activity. Given the men in question, the latter seemed highly unlikely. Out of sheer curiosity, I pricked up my ears and listened.

"... all over Petersburg. Like a thunderbolt from the blue."

"What do you mean, all over?"

"Plastered up on walls, left on café tables, floating in the gutters."

"I heard that a horseman even rode up Nevsky Prospect flinging them all around."

"Absurd. Well, the miscreants will be dealt with soon enough."

"But what if it's true? What if there are hundreds of them?"

"Hundreds of what? No, I can assure you, the great revolution consists of five students with a printing press."

"Don't forget what else they want." This was Arkady Andreyevich's voice, louder now, full of derision and scorn. "Besides freeing the serfs and the Poles. The emancipation of women, the abolition of marriage and inheritance, the closing of monasteries!"

There was general laughter at these absurd and childish notions.

"And the drunkenness and debauchery among them! This is what comes of trying to educate peasants. They can't be educated. Chernov doesn't seem to understand this."

"No. And don't bring it up around him."

"Is he involved in any of this?"

"Ivan Ivanovich is my brother-in-law. Of course he's not involved."

"But, Arkady Andreyevich, think! If he were—"

"He's not!"

Many voices shushed and soothed a somewhat irate and annoyed Arkady Andreyevich.

"The liberal press, of course, is almost sympathetic."

"To revolution? I doubt it."

"To freedom with land."

"Nonsense! That *is* the revolution. Give them freedom, yes, all right. I agree. But the land? Never."

"Well, the journals will be shut down soon, believe me, and any presses not under our direct control."

"The Third Section is being kept busy these days."

"Yes. We're working hard. Some changes are coming. Forbidding public lectures, for one thing, and unauthorized meetings—that will silence the ruffians. And we'll be far more vigorous about investigating anyone who complains about it. Everything will simmer down, you'll see."

"What about Herzen? You can't silence him."

At the mention of my mentor's name I felt a blow to my body sharp as the thrust of a knife into my heart.

"Because he's in London? Don't be so sure."

Who was this man from the Third Section? Who was this devil in disguise, here in the home of Anastasia Alexandrovna? I was about to leap up in rage, but caught myself in time because the devil was still speaking and I wanted to hear everything he had to say.

"Our Imperial Highness can do many things. His reach is long. And a man who writes the sorts of things Herzen does, well, it is intolerable. 'Only the oppressed can overthrow the order that oppresses them…' What nonsense! Thanks to our Tsar there are no oppressed people in Russia. The peasants should be grateful to the Tsar who protects them like a father."

Someone gently chuckled and there were other mirthful sounds that suggested that even this group of patriots was finding some humor in their friend's paean to the benevolence of the Tsar.

"Ivan Ivanovich teaches natural science, you know. He is not a member of the philology faculty."

"It's coming from the school of medicine, in fact. Science and technology. All of them are atheists, materialists, nihilists and anarchists. The women are worse than the men. We'll get them out soon enough."

"But Ivan Ivanovich—" Arkady began again, in a whisper, but at that point I heard Ivan Ivanovich's voice greeting his brother-in-law as he came up the stairs from the garden, and the conversation turned abruptly from political repression to vodka and cards.

The countryside of our district in summertime is covered with endless cornfields spread out like golden lakes ruffled by the breeze, dotted with islands of houses and villages, white churches visible here and there like the sails of ships, while forests of various shades of green frame the picture, and rivers flow across it like bright ribbons of sparking light.

That evening around sunset I walked up to the hilltop just beyond the bathhouse and stood under the great oak trees, listening to the soft whispering of their leaves. From below came the lowing and bleating of sheep, the barking of dogs, the sound of bells ringing in the distance. I smelt the scent of smoke from the corn kilns and felt the light breeze moving over the land, arising from some secret source where before there had been no movement in the air at all. Herzen, my mentor, had written about just such a scene. "The soaking dew begins to spread like smoke over the earth, the wind seems to walk audibly over the trees, the sunset glow sends a last faint light over the world."

I sat down on the hillock, my back against a sturdy trunk, and thought about the world in which we lived, its beauty, none of our doing, its horrors, entirely of our own. How we could enslave other men so that their labor was the necessary condition of our lives, and how we could live with this situation, how we could eat and drink while other men labored, play while they suffered, demand that they wash us, massage us, dry us and dress us in our bathhouses, all the while complaining or gossiping or, worst of all, philosophizing… how we could continue living under such conditions, these were the great questions of our time. We had to act but we didn't know how, we didn't have the patience to learn, we felt time was running away with us, we had to do something now, but what could we do? So Kolya must be thinking. Surely he must be in the thick of things, somewhere, writing pamphlets, writing manifestos. Drinking with the peasant students so derided by Irina's friends' husbands… Does Irina know what kind of men they are? Should she be warned?

I sat on the hill until darkness fell upon me like a cloak, and pondered and wondered, and still did not know what to do.

CHAPTER FOUR

The Aunts Become Concerned

Already a sultry morning, birds singing and chirping and calling in the oaks, the lindens, and the birches, children singing and crying and calling in the summer house. It was Saturday so there was great fun in store that evening when all the children would fill the bathhouse with laughter and make Masha and the other servants go crazy trying to keep them from splashing each other, which was the whole point of bathing so far as Natasha could tell. It also meant that today she could get as dirty as she wanted because no one would know after her bath except for the fact that her clothes would be dirty also, and that was a problem but one she was not interested in solving at the moment. At the moment she was interested in sitting as still as she could under the orange berry bush, as still as a stone, and listen to the birds eating berries just over her head, and not disturb them, but only listen and watch and imagine being a bird, having wings and feeding babies by thrusting chewed berries into their open mouths.

Suddenly there was a warning call and all the birds flew out of the bush in a great cloud of beating wings.

They came along the path without speaking, though there was no mistaking the sound of heavy boots crunching loose pebbles, but instead of passing by, they stopped just in front of the bush, not three feet away. One of them was speaking; the other grunted now and then. Two men with low, growly voices, muttering together like bears. She heard them, but could not make out what they were saying. Who were they, and what were they doing in her garden? As silently as she could, she stretched out on the ground and peered up from beneath the boughs of the bush. She could not see their faces, only their legs and feet. One wore a pair of shoes, clean and polished; the other, a pair of high riding boots, dusty and scratched. After a few minutes, Boots clicked his heels, turned neatly, and strode away. Shoes stayed a bit longer, pacing back and forth, and then followed him down the path.

Natasha stuck her head out and watched the man's back as he walked away. One of Aunt Irina's friends, the father of little Boris and red-haired Klara who always tattled on everyone. Natasha didn't like Klara and didn't think she liked Klara's father either. She would have to find out who Boots was, and where he had come from, and what he was doing in her house.

⁂

Later that morning, the air humid and heavy, rain clouds thickening on the horizon, Tatyana Andreyevna and Vasily Yakovlevich were also walking in the garden, and stopped in front of the same bush to sit for a few minutes on the stone bench beside it, disturbing the birds and interrupting their lunch. Tatyana had a deep, melodious voice in which she expressed her opinions with confidence, whether she was discussing art or music, the foibles of Muscovite society, or the personalities of her friends. She was a brilliant woman, and an insightful one, and she had known Anastasia Barakova longer than any other person still living for they had been childhood friends. Such a long friendship gave Tatyana Andreyevna certain rights, candor being one of them. She was being quite candid now.

"Fathers and sons have a much more fraught relationship than mothers and sons. And, remember, Kolya saw you fail."

"How could he? I failed before he was born."

"Vasily—he *saw* you. He knew you. Your anger—"

"I am not angry."

"Vasily, my dear... May I continue?"

"Yes, go on. Skewer me as you always do."

"I only tell you the truth. You may not be angry now, but you were for thirty years or more. I must say, you have taken to retirement well, however. You seem quite calm these days. A pleasant change."

Vasily grunted and kicked at some pebbles at his feet.

"You can't help sounding patronizing, can you, Tatyana? It must come from living with princes."

She laughed. It was a full-throated, hooting laugh, a solid, undisguised laugh, and one he loved to hear, though not necessarily at his own expense.

"Jealous?" she said, and laughed again.

They were silent for a few minutes, while she recovered herself and wiped her eyes.

"You are a funny man, Vasya. Now listen. I love you and you know I do. But this situation with Kolya—"

"What situation?"

"The one no one discusses. The one that is keeping Anastasia in her cave."

"She has said nothing to me."

"Hasn't she? She sends messages through Natasha. Does no one listen?"

"What messages? I don't know what you mean."

Tatyana sighed. "Are all men so oblivious or only old ones? She is not writing. Why not?"

"Perhaps she has nothing more to say."

"Yes. And perhaps the earth will stop turning and the sun stop rising… or however it goes."

Now it was Vasily's turn to smile. "Clearly you think there is something I should do and you are about to tell me exactly what it is. Well, go on. Issue your *ukas*. 'The Tsar commands!' Go ahead, my imperial one. Speak."

"Tell me this. Are you still so angry at Nikolai that you don't care what might have become of him?"

"Who says I am angry? You just said I wasn't. And who says something has happened to him? No one says that."

"So you know where he is?"

"In Petersburg."

"Really? You know that?"

"That's where he lives. Why should he be somewhere else?"

"And has he written to you?"

"He never writes to me."

"Nor you to him. You are still angry at him, Vasya. Admit it."

"All right. I am. He had every opportunity—education, position, wealth, connections—and what has he done with it all? Nothing. Nothing except waste everything, ruin himself, disappoint everyone, cause misery. I have a right to be angry, and I am."

"And what if he is organizing peasants or—"

"Nikolai? Organizing peasants? Come now, Tatyana. More likely he's getting drunk with them."

"You used to get drunk with them yourself."

"Yes, I did. When I was seventeen. I soon grew out of it."

"You must have been lovely when you were seventeen."

Vasily Yakovlevich shook his head. "Not as lovely as you were, when you were seventeen."

"Was I seventeen when we met? Really? I thought I was eighteen."

"Call me a liar for a year."

"I will not call you a liar for anything, dear Vasily. Our lives have been entwined for too long, and our lies also."

"What lies are they?"

"The ones we have told ourselves since we were—what? Surely not eighteen. Twenty-four perhaps."

"You were twenty-four. You both were, you and Anastasia."

"Well, then. You remember."

"I am hardly likely to forget... So you think we've been lying all these years?"

"Haven't you?"

"No. I told the truth then and I'll tell it now. I loved her. I loved you. I loved you both, but it was not permitted. It caused the skies to fall and the earth to open! You do remember, don't you? Anastasia did not take it well. She was outraged."

"She was wounded. That is different. The outrage was yours, dear Vasya—that you could not have everything you wanted. You wanted a revolution, the world changed top to bottom, not only no more autocracy, no more serfdom, no more repression, but also no more possessiveness, no more jealousy, no more strife, everyone living together in harmony and peace. And you convinced us it was possible. You persuaded us, you and Fourier. You were always excellent at argument and rhetoric. Passionate about what you believed. A passionate man is hard to resist."

"Go on," he said, sulkily. "I'm sure you're not finished yet."

"Only to add what you know: that what sounds like a good idea in theory can sometimes not work out so well in practice. I am quite finished now."

"No, go on! Tell me that as a result of that failure, I turned bitter and retreated to the country, Tell me that I, too, have wasted my life. That like my son, I have done nothing of value with the gifts I was given. That I, too, was educated, I, too, had wealth and position, and did nothing with them. Say it! I know you think it."

Tatyana sighed deeply but said nothing.

"I did some good here, you know," Vasily said. "I advocated for the peasants. I spoke for them and protected them. I never used corporal punishment. I educated them—"

"I grant you all that, Vasily. I never said you were not a good man. You are a good man, and an admirable man. I am merely suggesting that we all had ideas when we were young, and ideals, and desires… that we learned, bitterly at times, that we could not achieve what we wanted, even though what we wanted seemed so simple and so right… And then we kept living and told ourselves—what? That we didn't really want those things, or that it was better not to want them, or that we had been foolish, or had acted like children… Be that as it may, it is all in the past. But now there is your son, Vasily. Can't you see that he may be more like you than you wish to believe? That he may have some ideas of his own? That you might want to listen to him?"

"You say it's all in the past, but I lost both of you then. It was never the same."

Tatyana smoothed her skirt and sat up a little straighter. The bench was terribly uncomfortable.

"Of course not. How could it be? Anastasia was a romantic, and you betrayed her idea of romantic love… Well, you both were romantics then, weren't you, and you were so handsome, Vasily, with your sword and spurs and that wonderful Arabian you rode… Bedouin, was he called? I remember that horse! How very young we were!"

"She punished me for it, you know. Oh, I had to pay, believe me. What a creature she could be!"

"Let's walk a bit," Tatyana said.

Standing, she was several inches taller than he. Her hair, gathered at the nape of her neck, retained hints of its former auburn color through the grey, her figure retained hints of its graceful lines, her mind and her tongue were as sharp as ever. She was aging, yes, but gradually and carefully, taking her time, still wearing fine clothes and expensive perfume. Her current male companion was an Italian prince.

"Yes, we were all wounded," she said as they strolled along the path toward the rose garden. "And once so wounded in love one never dares love with such abandon again."

"Did you feel the same, my dear?"

Tatyana smiled at him and tucked her arm into his.

"It was a dream, Vasily. You know that, don't you? Now let's not get sentimental. Come back to the present and the problem at hand. Something is very wrong here. What is it? Why is Anastasia confining herself in her rooms? Why does she refuse to see me?"

"She refused to see you? That is troubling."

"Tell me why, Vasily. You must know."

"She is worried about Kolya."

"What does she think has happened to him?"

"How do I know? But he has stopped writing to her. Perhaps she thinks he has stopped caring about her."

"That's the most ridiculous thing I have ever heard. Kolya adores her. If he's stopped writing to her it's because he cannot write to her. So what might have happened to him that would make it impossible for him to write to his mother?"

As though the truth had finally struck him, Vasily stopped short in front of his beloved Rose d'Ispahan whose scent, filling the air they breathed, could not be ignored no matter what emotional turmoil he was in.

"No, Tatyana," he said. "It is not true. Kolya is not political. He finds politics boring. He might comment, ironically, yes, but he would never involve himself."

"In this world, commenting *is* involving yourself. Men disappear every day for commenting. Vasily, you know this."

"That's what we hear, but is it true? Arkady Andreyevich assures me it is exaggeration and lies promulgated by the liberal press."

"Does he? Well I can assure you it isn't exaggeration or lies, but perfectly true. Do you think the Third Section is a myth? Vasily, you've been hiding here in the country too long. You with your roses, Anastasia with her poems, both of you, hiding. And now she is enacting a full-on military retreat. How much farther into retirement can she go? Can she crawl under the eaves, fade into the very walls? Your son had disappeared, Vasily. Think. He may be in Peter-Paul Fortress, suffering.

He may be in Siberia, dying. Are you going to hide on this estate and do nothing?"

They saw a flash in the darkening sky and heard a not too distant clap of thunder. As though God, listening all the while, had decided to add some emphasis to Tatyana's exhortation, as though God had decided to speak at last.

Vasily and Tatyana walked briskly up the path and climbed the steps to the terrace, reaching it just before the first drops of rain began to fall. The husbands were standing there, watching the approaching storm and smoking their pipes, Ivan Ivanovich and Arkady Andreyevich, whom Tatyana knew well, and two others whose acquaintance she had just made during this visit. There was another man, standing with them, a man to whom she had not yet been introduced. She recognized him at once; she knew his mother.

It was utterly impossible that Vasily had invited a high-placed official of the Third Section to be a guest in his house. But someone had. Vasily needed to be informed. Over a brandy, she thought, in his study. The walls had ears in most houses in the capital, but she felt here in the country it might be safe to speak in private, even with a member of the secret police in residence, though he would not be in residence for long. They would find some way to get rid of him. An outbreak of disease on the estate, perhaps. The rumor of typhus was always a fool-proof instrument, in her experience, for shooing away unwanted guests.

On the way to the study, they encountered Yevgenia and Mariya. Vasily offered his brandy, and they accepted.

Uncle Alyosha was already settled in the study, in Vasily's chair, with a snifter of brandy in one hand and a pipe in the other.

"Vasily Yakovlevich, we shall need another chair," Mariya said.

"No, dear lady, you may sit on my lap," Alyosha said, chuckling.

Then everyone was calling for chairs, moving chairs, getting up from chairs, and old, arthritic, white-haired Dusha brought in several straight-backed chairs that looked like instruments of torture, although all that needed to be done was to move a pile of books from the settee, which Mariya did, and she and Yevgenia made themselves quite comfortable while Tatyana took the second deep armchair and Vasily, once he had distributed the glasses of brandy, the voltaire.

"You don't make terribly good use of Dusha," Mariya said. "He should be your butler not your furniture mover."

"Dusha is a renaissance man. He does everything."

"Have you freed him?" Yevgenia asked, somewhat brutally.

"I offered. He declined."

"They all do," Mariya said. "The house serfs, I mean. They fear the world."

"That is why we must educate them," Vasily said.

"To do what?"

"Well, whatever they show interest in. Art. Music. Medicine. I have a doctor on the estate who was born a serf. And several musicians."

"But they're still on the estate. Did you offer to free them?"

"No. We need a doctor here. We need a cellist."

Alyosha sighed deeply and stretched his back.

"And I need a few hours in your bathhouse. It is Saturday, isn't it? I must have steam and heat. All my joints are stiff."

A great clap of thunder sounded directly over the house, startling all of them.

"The weather this summer seems quite extraordinary," Alyosha said. "It reminds me of the summer of 1810... "

"—and the gypsy encampment down by the river," Vasily said, smiling.

"Oh, what fun we had, remember, Vasya? It was your first—"

"Now, now, Alyosha, ladies present."

"I was going to say your first river bass."

"Oh, yes! Fishing!"

"And the storms we had!"

The room had fallen into a darkness like night. The door opened and little Galya came in to light the lamps. Suddenly the rain began to pound ferociously on the terrace outside and against the windows.

"Oh, such storms!" Alyosha went on. "Lightning like you've never seen."

"Night lights, too. Great colored lights in the sky. We thought it was the end of the world, and they played with us, remember? And made us think they'd never seen such things before, but it happens every year."

"Oh, and the dancing! You learned them all, didn't you, Vasya, and I stumbled through. Oh, we were young blades then. Not yet even twenty..."

Tatyana stirred in her chair. She had no patience with this sort of sentimentality. She waited until Galya had left the room, and Alyosha had run out of breath before she said,

"Forgive me for interrupting, but you do know, don't you, Vasily, that there's a man from the Third Division staying in your house."

The silence afterwards was profound for the moments before another great thunderclap shattered it.

"It's right over our heads," Yevgenia said in a whisper.

A moment later, thunder rumbled again, loudly, threateningly.

"Oh, God," Mariya said. "One of the guests? Tatyana, are you sure?"

"I am. The question is, what's to be done about it?"

The lamps flickered as a draft of air came through the room, and Masha appeared with a tray of nuts, grapes, bread and cheese, sausages and dried meats.

"Sofia Vasilevna says if you are going to drink before dinner, you have to eat something."

Another horrific crash of thunder overhead made them all jump, and Masha almost overturned her tray.

"What about Anastasia Alexandrovna?" Vasily asked. "Have you been up to see her?"

"Yes. She is well," Masha said.

"It's what she always says," Vasily muttered as Masha left the room. "She is well. How can she be well?"

"It's frightening," Mariya said. "The secret police here? How could that happen?"

"He is married to one of Irina's friends."

"Irina should choose her friends more carefully."

"Irina's friends should choose their husbands more carefully."

Yevgenia held up her hand to silence everyone, and everyone stopped speaking at once. The thunder rumbled on, now at a slight distance. The rain still pounded down. The darkness did not lift.

"I talked to one of the young women earlier today and she told me they are all planning to return home tomorrow, so there is really no need to do anything but wait until they're gone. After all, they've been here for weeks. If he was hoping to find any of us engaged in subversive activity, he would surely have done so by now."

"My God!" Vasily cried out, and jumped to his feet, "The bastard's been looking for evidence against Nikolai! Where are my pistols? I'll kill him!"

Then the room broke into an uproar. All three women rose at once, meaning to grab hold of Vasily, Uncle Alyosha, attempting to rise as well, managed to tip himself, with a great thud and cry of pain, onto the floor. Yevgenia ran into the hall to call for Dusha while Vasily and Mariya tried to get Alyosha onto his feet. But Tatyana turned directly to Vasily's desk, unlocked the drawer with the key he always hid in the same place under his humidor, and took out the box in which he kept his pistols. She looked around, made a quick decision, and slipped the box under the cushion of the settee. It would not take him long to find it, but long enough, perhaps, for his temper to cool and his reason to assert itself. She had the feeling that dear old Alyosha's fall had been staged to do precisely the same thing. In the hubbub that followed, Vasily would come to his senses. One cannot call out a member of the Third Division no matter what sort of devil he may be. There is honor, yes, and then there is power. We admire the former, of course, but we bow to the latter. In this we are no better than slaves, no better than the men we call slaves, who must do what we command. We are all slaves of the emperor. Not one of us is truly free.

"One wore riding boots. The other was Boris and Klara's father."

"Little Pavel Beriosov. Who grew up to be a big bad wolf."

"Do you know everybody, Grandmama?"

"Of a certain class, I know a great number. Of other classes, I know no one at all."

"Why is he a big bad wolf?"

"He dresses up like a sheep..."

"So he can get into the sheepfold and eat them."

"Precisely... I remember him as a boy. I knew his father, long ago, and slightly, as one knows very many people. He made a good marriage." She laughed, a bitter little laugh. "Yes, a good marriage, meaning he acquired land and serfs and a wife who was presentable in society. What more could a man want? Pavel was a beautiful little boy, as I recall. It is extraordinary what happens to children. They are so lovely and full of life. Then they grow up and turn into cruel, nasty, selfish brutes. Not all of them, of course. Not you, cabbage."

Natasha said, "I wish I knew who Boots was. I looked at everyone's feet—everyone was wearing their boots this afternoon because it was raining—but I did not see the boots he wore. They went all the way up his leg, and they weren't polished, you know, the way our boots always are."

"I imagine whoever it was came only to see Pavel Pavlovich, and left directly after delivering his message. We've had no other visitors today."

"And tomorrow they are all leaving, all of Aunt Irina's friends."

"Are they? That is coincidental. Well, he came and left and no harm was done. Now, tell me, do you know what today is? Your favorite day of the week."

"Saturday! Oh, the bathhouse is so lovely! Will you come to the bathhouse, too, Grandmama?"

"Of course I shall. I am not a barbarian."

"I never see you. What if I stayed up very late?"

"No matter how late you stayed up..."

"Because you are magic and make yourself invisible."

"Precisely."

They smiled at each other.

"I want a poem," Natasha said.

"Then you will just have to write one yourself," said the poet Anastasia Barakova.

So she did.

Prince Nikolai is very brave
He's also strong and good and grave.
When he whistles the birds all sing
And when he claps the church bells ring.
He loves to ride his horse so gay
But always gives his gold away
And cares for people rich and poor
And animals that growl and roar.

"Animals that purr, too, and howl and squeak and bleat. Maybe I should include all the animals. What do you think, Grandmama?"

"I think you should just keep writing your poem and see what happens."

"That's a good idea. Is that what you do?"

"What I used to do. Oh, I don't know what I used to do! Let's have some tea," Anastasia said, and rang the bell for Masha.

"Aunt Tatyana would really like to see you."

"I would like to see her, too."

"You can! She's just downstairs. I can run down now and get her."

"I will think about it. Perhaps."

"Animals that purr and squeak, and ... hoot and honk and bark and bleat." Natasha wrote the poem down in her notebook so she wouldn't forget it. She liked the rhyme of squeak and bleat. What about birds that chirp? Her poem could become a huge inventory of all the sounds animals make.

She glanced up at Anastasia who was sitting in her chair looking out at the sodden garden, watching rain drip from the leaves of the oak trees, and she wondered what it might be like to live for so many years. For the first time in her life, Natasha felt very, very young.

Tatyana Andreyevna, Mariya Sergeyevna and Yevgenia Dmitrievna had also lived many years, as many as Anastasia herself. They were, in their own ways, remarkable women, women ahead of their time, as women so often are, "our time," no matter when it is, usually being somewhat backward in relation to women. Like all of their generation of educated, liberal-minded, Western-looking young people born at the end of the century, they were deeply affected by the Guards Revolt of December 1825. For Mariya and Yevgenia, the affect of the rebellion was also deeply personal since both of them had relatives involved: Mariya's father; Yevgenia's cousin.

When the rebellion was crushed, when hundreds of the conspirators were arrested, when the long, dark repression that followed it first began, the heavy whip of punishment fell not only on the conspirators themselves but on their wives and children. The wives of the heroes and martyrs were deprived of all civil rights, lost all their property and their place in society. Many of them followed their husbands into exile in Siberia; many of them died there. While so many male relatives of the rebels denied them like Peter denied Christ, or worse, became zealots for tyranny (as Herzen put it), the women stayed true to their husbands and brothers and fathers, and joined them in their suffering. Mariya's mother was able to send her daughter to relatives abroad before joining her unfortunate husband in the east where once the Dukhobortsy had fled to establish their radical "ideal communities" but which our emperor had turned into a hell of penal colonies. Mariya never saw her parents again.

Rather than make them fearful, the sufferings of their families acted as an inspiration to Mariya and Yevgenia, making them strong financial supporters of liberal causes and especially the liberal press, and firm believers in all those fine ideals so dear to the hearts of the generation born at the end of the last century, beliefs whose gravestones bore the year "1848." As for Tatyana, though not personally affected by the Guards Revolt, she adopted the daughter of a distant relative imprisoned for life as a result of the Petrashevsky conspiracy, and raised her as her own.

Anastasia, Vasily, Tatyana, Yevgenia, Mariya... upstanding members of the older generation... a generation we can't condemn for their failures though their failures led to the absurdity of our own dire times whose entire nature can be encapsulated in the charming words of our Minister of Public Instruction: "The only thing wrong with political repression is that there is not enough of it."

And what of us, of our generation? What have we accomplished? We came of age in the heyday of Hegelian philosophy which told us everything except what was to be done, not by History but by men. The "accursed questions"—how to live, what to do—could not be answered by studying philosophy, though study it we did. Eighteen-forty-eight marked the death of all that, and left us with nothing but despair. Or as Herzen put it in a letter dated June, 1848, "Universal grief is the supreme characteristic of our times."

But the Aunts did not indulge in grief. I had never known them to stumble, to waver, to weep. They were fighters, warriors, but, as women in a patriarchal society, what they did was barely noticed, and the older they got, the more invisible they became. Ironically, it was their invisibility that made them so powerful; they could get away with anything because no one really paid any attention to them at all. They were all in robust good health, too... except now, Anastasia. She had appeared so frail to me when I last saw her, and somehow diminished as though she were fading away. How to stop her from leaving us, for leaving us was what it seemed she was set on doing—this was the question I had to pose to the Aunts, now that they had assembled, and now that I had some sense of the dangers facing Anastasia, both near and far. There was a man from the Third Division in her house. That news alone should alarm the Aunts if nothing else did.

I arrived at Oak Hills on Sunday afternoon, just as carriages were being loaded and visitors were being kissed goodbye on the porch. Irina's friends were leaving, en masse. Perhaps the Aunts had already taken steps to deal with the situation; I would not have put it past them. I strolled around the house to the garden to wait until the guests departed, and found the Three Graces themselves, sitting on benches in the rose garden. They greeted me warmly.

They had always thought of me as Anastasia's protégé, and they treated me accordingly, that is to say, they loved me and spoiled me and ordered me around. I opened their champagne bottles and admired their hats, bridled their horses, posted their letters, laughed at their jokes, and basked in their light. When I was young and just beginning to find my way in the world, they made sure I had warm clothes in the winter and new boots, and in the summer they dressed me in the best of taste and always indulged me and called me Marko Volchek and flattered me with their loving care. They were curious about my life but never inquisitive. Being women, they understood the desire to be free, the lure of entering other worlds, of walking the streets unmolested and unnoticed. The freedom free men own and waste... no, not waste, but simply take for granted, unthinkingly, the way fish take for granted the sea, that freedom is unimaginable to those who don't have it by right of birth.

This was why I could never agree with Herzen about liberty. "Do not quarrel with the world," he wrote, "but begin an independent, self-reliant life." He believed men could choose to live free lives, as though the world had no power to prevent them. Of course it is possible to choose freedom, one glorious moment of freedom... but such acts of radical freedom must sometimes be paid for with your life. I chose a free life. I put on trousers, cloak and hat, and went out into the world, but what world did I enter? A world of pretense and disguise, betrayal and faithlessness, corruption and deceit—the world inhabited by men. What price had I paid? "We could hardly believe," Herzen wrote to me after the failure of 1848, "that after so many ordeals, after all the trials of modern skepticism, there was still so much left in our souls to destroy."

I kissed each of the Graces, and took a seat among them. They were drinking some cool concoction made mostly of vodka and encouraged me to pour myself a glass from the bright red pitcher on the garden table.

"You all look like cats that have swallowed canaries," I said, and they laughed quite merrily. "Well, tell all! What's going on? Or is it that you've been sipping vodka all morning?"

"We are just pleased the youngsters have left us in peace," Aunt Mariya said. She had acquired a pince-nez since I'd seen her last and looked quite shockingly modern in it, like a member of the intelligentsia. Her hair was now completely white, snow white, and she was wearing a dark blue dress with a wide collar which suited her full figure perfectly.

"I doubt that peace is what you wanted. More likely you wanted that imperial spy out of your hair."

The Three Graces shot me looks of various intensities and meanings. I always enjoyed shocking them, as much as they enjoyed being shocked, but this time I had perhaps gone a bit too far even for them.

"You know there are no secrets in Russia," I said, and when Tatyana lifted her eyebrows at me, I added, "I overheard them talking on the terrace. And you?"

"I recognized him," she said. "He was not wearing a disguise. His name is Pavel Beriosov. I don't know his rank. I knew his mother. That was bad enough."

I let the name linger in my mind a few seconds while I searched my memory for a picture of the man. I had heard his voice, but did I remember his face? If I thought very hard, I could remember Irina introducing us, but only vaguely. Rather short. Pale skin, pale eyes, faded red hair. The sort of man who left no impression.

Then I was asked a question, and forgot all about him again. The question was whether I had any news of Anastasia. The answer was no.

"Now that we've dealt with the problem of Pavel Beriosov—or it dealt with itself," Aunt Yevgenia said, "we have another problem to solve. It is called Anastasia."

"A harder nut to crack," Tatyana said.

"To lure her down or to invade, that's the question."

Tatyana, who was facing the house, said, "There are her windows. I have been watching in the hope that seeing us here in the garden drinking from this bright red jug might be lure enough. But she hasn't looked down. You've seen her recently, Marko. What's to be done with her?"

"Yes, is there any good reason why we shouldn't just troop up the stairs and see her?"

Mariya was a brave woman and believed in the all-out assault on the castle fortifications. I tended to agree with her. I too thought trooping up the stairs was the simplest solution.

I began telling them what I knew, what I thought, how I felt. I told them about my visit to Anastasia's aerie, about the non-existent poetry manuscript, about the letters Anastasia stopped receiving from Kolya, about her worry and sorrow and about the tears on her cheeks. By the time I was finished, all four of us were like Anastasia, worried and frightened and wiping away our tears.

"Oh, Kolya, Kolya!" Yevgenia sighed. "I remember him as a child. I've never known a sweeter little boy."

"He was sweet and he was smart," Tatyana said, "and that is a terrible combination for a young man living in this country. I think that once he saw the world for what it is, he decided he wanted no part of it."

"None of us do," Mariya said.

"None of us do. But we continue to live in it. He does not. He has escaped. He has slipped through."

"So you know where he is?" I asked, suddenly filled with foolish hope.

"No. Of course I don't. I only know where he is not. You will not find him in drawing rooms, discussing the latest opera, I can assure you of that. The last we spoke, many years ago now, he told me stories about his life that astonished me, stories about people he knew and things he had done. At first I thought that if even half of it were true, he must surely have decided there was no future for him and so it didn't matter what he did. But I was wrong, as I discovered after talking to him at length. He believed in the future. It was just a very different future from what everyone else expected. And yet it turns out that he was ahead of his time. The young radicals of today, from what I understand, have abandoned liberalism for anarchy, and now believe in 'going to the people,' as they say, but Kolya has always been an anarchist, and has been drinking and arguing and enjoying himself with 'the people' all his life.

He watched his father wrestle with his conscience and lose. He spent no time wrestling. He just walked away."

"Retreat from the world. Don't we all live like this?" Yevgenia said, sadly, staring into the distance as though hoping to see there some vision of happiness.

"But the problem remains," Mariya said. "We must find him. So what are you doing about it, young Marko Volchek, sitting here with us old ladies in the rose garden? Why aren't you out looking for him?"

I had no good answer, really, Why wasn't I out looking for Nikolai? Because it was August? That was Marina Vilinskaya's excuse; it should not have been mine.

"We need to make a plan," Mariya continued, pressing on, seemingly oblivious to the sentimental feelings Tatyana's recollections had aroused in all of us, myself included. "We all have contacts in the government. Let us send out our inquiries. Let us marshal our forces. For God's sake, we ought to be able to locate the son of Anastasia Barakova, if he's not in the east. Even if he is. He's not exactly unknown."

"If he was sentenced at a secret trial, he may have been sent east without anyone we know learning about it," I said.

"I have a friend in Justice. I will inquire," Yevgenia said.

"Isn't Arkady Andreyevich a ranking official in Justice as well?"

"My friend is a better source."

"And if he has gone into hiding?"

"Then it is no use trying to find him, and we may even endanger him if we try."

They continued talking in this vein, deciding whom among their friends in the government it was best to speak to, who would make the overture, when it would happen. As for me, I knew what I should do, and what I should have done from the very beginning. I had access to places none of Anastasia's relatives, friends, acquaintances, servants, lovers, or devotees could enter. Other people could inquire about Nikolai through official channels, but only I could go into the underworld to look for him, and it was there, if anywhere, that he was most likely to be found.

CHAPTER FIVE

Natasha Takes a Walk in the Woods

Once the other children left the estate, along with their parents and servants and nannies, Natasha felt gloriously free again and happy. She could wander wherever she wanted without being followed by a trail of squawking little children, she could run with her brothers and cousins without being reprimanded by some nanny she didn't even know and told to act like a little lady, which she wasn't and never even wanted to be, she could sing and dance in the evenings again when Aunt Irina played the piano instead of having to be quiet so the stern and gloomy fathers could concentrate on cards, and she could climb her tree and hide in her secret places without being afraid some nosy boy would find her. In short, she was like a queen who had reclaimed her kingdom after the barbarians had been driven away.

Not that everything returned to normal. There were still many people sitting down every afternoon for dinner and every evening for supper: her grandfather, her mother and father, Aunt Irina and Uncle Arkady, Uncle Alyosha and the three Aunts, and, of course, the empty place at the table where her grandmother should be sitting but wasn't. She sat at the children's table with her brothers and cousins, but she ate quickly so she could go upstairs behind Masha and slip into her grandmother's room. All the servants knew she did it, and all of them approved.

"Please, dear Grandmama, taste a little of this darling fritter, take just a spoonful of this lovely pudding, try this sweet little mushroom pie Cook made especially for you…" And she got her grandmother to laugh at her and eat some of the food Masha brought up for her on the tray.

Then they would sit together and write. Natasha would write a poem. Anastasia would write a letter. Natasha kept the poems in her notebook. Anastasia put the letters in her desk drawer. When they were finished, Natasha watered the stones, Anastasia listened to the trees.

Then Natasha would go outside and play. Our summer days are so long, it was like you could live an entire life in one of them, the way mayflies do or day lilies. Natasha loved every day, and every evening when the fireflies came out and danced about like fairies over the lawn, she was so supremely happy she thought she might simply explode with joy.

♣

It was on one of those soft, quite ethereal summer nights not long after the departure of Irina's friends that Natasha dressed herself in her most suitable- for- tree-climbing clothes which she had set aside for herself earlier, tip-toed out of her enclosed corner of the nursery, and crept as silently as she could along the corridor and down the back stairs. Everyone in the house was asleep, her parents and aunt and uncle in rooms at one end of the corridor, the three Aunts in rooms at the other, Uncle Alyosha in the study downstairs, where they had set up a little bed for him (he liked to sit up smoking his pipe and reading thick books about the fall of Rome), Grandpapa in the big bedroom right across from the nursery, where Grandmama should be sleeping, too, but wasn't. She could hear him snoring even through the closed bedroom door.

Once downstairs, she slipped out the little door from the kitchen to the kitchen garden, glided along beside the herbs and through the darling little wooden gate, and into the flower garden. The air was sweet here, and moonlight, falling on the trees and plants and flowers, gave them dancing shadows and made them shimmer.

Everything in the world was fluttering with joy, plants fluttering their leaves, night birds fluttering their wings, insects fluttering their little legs to make their music, and frogs making music too, and, oh!, the fireflies, like diamond-covered fairies dancing at a ball, lighting up the space between earth and sky, how beautiful they were! Natasha's heart was fluttering too with sheer delight. How free she was! How magical the world! She stopped beside the flowering hedge and breathed in pure sweetness, the scent of the earth and of zephyr breezes and of cool water. Yes, she could smell the cool water, and hear quite clearly the frog and insect symphony coming from the banks of the pond. There was another sound, too. She listened.

It was music.

Faint, yes; she had to listen hard to hear. But there it was again! It sounded like a shepherd's flute, the kind they made of birch bark and played to comfort the lambs. She could not make out a tune, just a note here and there wafting to her on the wave of a breeze—oh, how lovely! She might follow the sound if only the player continued to play, and who knew where it might lead?

She passed the entrance to the maze; the music was not coming from there. She walked past the maze and into the woods. Now the ground under her feet was soft and buoyant and although it was darker in the woods, darker under the shadows of the trees, she knew the path and knew every tree, and the sound of the flute was clearer here, the player closer. She walked carefully on the carpet of moss under great swaying limbs, under the canopy of green, into the small clearing with its low laurel bushes and its dear little meadow of wild flowers. The moon had blanched the sky, she could see everything quite well, and now she heard the mysterious music clearly. It was not a tune at all but only sound, a series of long notes, like sighs or the sound of wind blowing across the steppes, a foreign and mesmerizing sound, and she thought how nice it would be to listen to this music as she was falling asleep, for it conjured up pictures in her mind of a small boat floating on a gentle sea under full sail... She stood under a tree at the edge of the clearing and watched, hoping the flutist would appear.

For a long time nothing moved. Then a figure did. It rose from the ground in the center of the clearing, a human figure, wearing a long cloak. At the same time another figure stepped out from the shadows on the other side of the clearing. This figure was also human, not a bear or an elf. But who was it?

She wasn't at all afraid, though she should have been. All she wanted was to learn who these people were. It was as though she had walked into a story, and these were the characters in the story. Perhaps the figure from the woods was Prince Nikolai. Perhaps the cloaked figure was Princess Zinaida. If so, the prince was dressed rather badly, as she could see as she crept closer, for it seemed he was wearing a peasant blouse and baggy trousers and had a long shaggy beard. As for the princess, Natasha could not see her face at all, or hear her words, but she could see that the princess had a package of some kind and passed this package to the ragged peasant prince who took it, bowed politely, and disappeared back into the woods. When the cloaked figure turned around to make its way back across the meadow, Natasha saw her clearly. The princess, hooded and cloaked, was none other than Anastasia Alexandrovna, her own grandmother!

If Natalia Ivanovna had been a wiser child she would have followed her grandmother back to the house, tiptoed silently up the stairs to the nursery, climbed into her bed, and gone to sleep. She knew—for she was adept at listening to adult conversations while pretending she was not listening at all—that there were brigands in the countryside, and gypsies, and crazy holy fools, and communities of wanderers, harmless people, but odd, that there were also criminals at large, and idealistic though possibly revolutionary-minded students trying to educate the peasants, and religious fanatics who preached the end of the world, and Old Believers who wanted everyone to live like Jesus, and escaped prisoners and fugitive serfs. There seemed to be an entire world of people hiding in the woods, traipsing around the countryside by night, stealing food and scaring people on the roads. But she was intrigued by the peasant prince, and she felt she simply had to know where he was going, whether it was to a gypsy encampment or a brigands' cave or his magic castle hidden deep in the forest, and so she waited until Anastasia had crossed the clearing and entered the woods again on her way back to the house, and then she ran in the opposite direction into the dark shadows of the trees.

She followed her peasant prince at some distance, keeping him in sight, or at least the movement of shadow that indicated where he was. He moved quickly and silently, but once, coming around a large tree-trunk, she nearly ran right into him. He had stopped and was standing perfectly still, looking in front of him through the trees, as though he had seen something there, a bear perhaps or a deer. He hadn't heard her, though, and she immediately darted behind a tree so if he turned he wouldn't see her either. Then she held her breath until he began to move again.

She wondered why she didn't want him to discover her even though she was following him for the very purpose of learning who he was. Still, something kept her wary. He was a strange man, they were in a dark wood, it was night. And even though he clearly knew her grandmother, he did not know her, and seeing her without warning, he might startle, like horses sometimes do, and attack her out of fear.

There was another reason, too. She was sure he was returning to his home, and there would be something marvelous about it, it would be a secret cave or a castle or a great pavilion like the ones pictured in books about Prince Igor. She was afraid that if he discovered her before he arrived there, he would insist on escorting her back to Oak Hills and she would never see the wonderful place where he lived.

So she followed. The trees thickened all around her and so did their shadows. It was becoming harder and harder to see the man moving ahead of her. Then she lost sight of him entirely. She stopped and listened. She could not see very far ahead of her, but she could hear. It seemed she was hearing voices, and it seemed they were nearby, but it could have been the rustling of the trees or the tinkling of little bells or water bubbling in a stream, if there was still water flowing in streams, the summer had been so hot and dry. She tried to stretch her ears to catch any sound, every sound. And, yes, she was hearing something now. Voices certainly. And now there was a light shining in the gloom, and then several more. Moving lights, lanterns, no doubt, and moving toward her. Suddenly she was afraid, and turned to run back the way she had come. But the lights were behind her now, they were all around her. She was encircled by them. Out of the shadows figures appeared, figures of men. They had encircled her, they were closing in on her. She had been caught in a trap.

Vasily Yakovlevich was not a sound sleeper. Sometimes the wind rattling the windows disturbed his sleep, sometimes it was a stomachache, and sometimes his own snoring woke him up. That night it was something else, a banging door, a barking dog. Whatever it was, it was enough to rouse him from sleep, from a dream, and then try as he might he could not get back to sleep. This was usual, or not unusual, and his remedy for such insomnia was a brandy in the library and a few pages of a boring book.

He was down the stairs before it occurred to him that his library was currently in use. Though knowing Aleksey Konstantinovich as he did, he suspected it was quite possible that the old man was awake, too, and drinking brandy over a volume of Gibbon. And in this suspicion, he was absolutely right.

"A lot goes on in this house after dark," Aleksey Konstantinovich muttered, kindly pouring Vasily a glass of his own cognac. "People coming and going at all hours. You'd think it was—"

"Who was coming and going?"

"Why... I don't know who. Down the stairs, out the door... Trying to be quiet, you know, but the ears pick up sound like nobody's business in an old house like this."

"Hmm. Maybe I should take a little walk around. I don't like the idea of people sneaking in and out of the house in the middle of the night."

"Well, I'll join you, Vasya. Be happy to. A little night air."

They went out onto the terrace and down the steps. Vasily had brought a lantern but it wasn't necessary; the twilight lasted long this time of year, and the full moon added its own illumination. First they walked around the house, then they walked to the pond, and then through the garden to the edge of the woods. They saw no one. Of course, talking as they were, even in low voices, they would have alerted anyone who was about and wanted to remain unseen.

They had been discussing the ever-vexing question of whether it was more economical to buy tobacco or grow it, when Uncle Alyosha said, "I have been thinking about that swine Beriosov, Vasya. It's been disturbing me, that he was here in your house. It's been keeping me awake."

Vasily grunted in agreement.

"What have you done about it?"

"I asked Irina how he happened to be invited. It seems she hadn't heard from the Beriosovs in years. Then out of the blue she received a letter from her old friend Anna Beriosova saying that they would be so happy to come for a visit. Quite extraordinary. Well, what could Irinka do but invite them? They had already invited themselves."

"That makes sense, then. That's better news."

"Than what?"

"Than that he's a friend of Arkady's."

"Good Lord, that would be terrible. Terrible. No, the girls knew each other at school."

"So it had an intention, this visit. And you think he was looking for evidence against Kolya?"

"Damned spies! Devils, the lot of them."

"What's Kolya up to, Vasya? What trouble is he in now?"

"Don't know. Have no idea."

"What do you mean, you have no idea? You're his father."

"And he's my son. But we don't see eye to eye and he doesn't inform me of what he does. Or Anastasia any more, for that matter. Which is why she's in the state she's in."

They had reached the edge of the wood, peered in, and turned back toward the house. In the moonlight, it looked grand, Vasily thought, like a country palace, spread out as it was under the moon, shaded by ancient trees, encircled by fragrant gardens, a paradise of peace and love, a safe haven, and yet it had been invaded, it had been assaulted. And what if they really were after Nikolai, what if he really was in serious trouble... then having a safe haven meant nothing, having a little paradise in the woods meant nothing, and there was no safety anywhere.

"No, we don't know. We know nothing. Not even where he's living now."

"No address? But, Vasya! What's happened to him?"

"I don't know. I don't even know where to look."

"Well, I know one place we could start to look," Alyosha said. "Actually, I know a few, and so do you."

"Tatyana Andreyevna?"

"She, certainly. For the kind of information she can gather. But I was thinking more of looking for him in places he might actually be."

Vasily laughed, and laughing made him feel quite relieved, suddenly quite free of care. "You old—! But, God bless us, Alyosha! Do you mean what I think you mean?"

"I think I do," he said, and took out his pipe.

"Our old haunts. Not where Kolya would go. No, not at all."

"Our old haunts will have new faces. Our old companions will have sons. Kolya loved those old wagons, those encampments, same as we did. And they move around, they see the whole country, those families. They are a great source of information, though untapped by our so-called intelligence service. But don't think other services don't use them! Don't think other governments are as foolhardy as ours. We kill their children, arrest their sons, rape their daughters—we do that! Of course they won't talk to us."

"Who will they talk to?"

"The Turks. The Greeks. The Austrians and Moldavians. The Poles. The Serbs and Montenegrins. The Slovenes and Ukrainians. The Finns."

"Everybody but us."

"Yes. But they will talk to *us*, to you and me."

"Will they?"

"Yes, Vasya. We'll bring those travelers the best bottles of cognac they've ever tasted. Wherever do you get it from? And they'll point us in the right direction."

Vasily grunted again. "To hell, no doubt."

Uncle Alyosha chuckled to himself. "Oh, I can taste that roasted lamb now! But what about Anastasia? Will she let you go?"

"Let me go? Don't be absurd. I come and go as I want."

Now Alyosha laughed out loud. "Come now, Vasya!"

"Anyway, this will not be a Bacchanal, or a... fishing expedition. It will be serious work."

"Indeed it will. And if we're looking for Kolya, she'll be happy to see us go."

"Wait!" Vasily said in a low voice, grabbing Alyosha by the arm. "Listen!"

They had been walking slowly and had only now reached the steps to the terrace. Someone was sitting there, someone who was humming softly... and then a voice, a lovely voice, Vasily thought, recognizing it as his wife's, called out, "Did I hear something about a fishing expedition, my dear? Or was it a Bacchanal? Are you running off with the gypsies again? Come up here right now, and explain yourselves, old men! What devilment are you two planning?"

"I'm glad to see that at least you come out at night for some fresh air, Anastasia," Vasily said gruffly.

"Don't change the subject, my dear."

Alyosha laughed again. He was feeling quite merry. Everything would work out, everything would be fine. They climbed the steps and sat down on the terrace and, watching the moon sink slowly behind the hill, they told her their plan, or at least Alyosha did, who was the one who knew it.

When he was finished, Anastasia said, "Do you know that Pyotr Panov and his troupe are nearby, Vasily? I believe they have an encampment in the woods."

"In our woods? Well, well."

"Panov," Uncle Alyosha muttered. "Name sounds familiar."

"All names sound familiar," Vasily said, and yawned. "This one is a conjurer of sorts. A magician."

"A magician? Really?"

"Well, he worked his magic on us, at one time," Vasily said.

"He travels with a troupe of actors—"

"Devotees, more like it."

"So he puts on shows, does he, this magician?"

"Shows, yes. Music. Dancing. Singing. Costumes. There's a good deal of spiritualist nonsense involved in it, too. Mumbo-jumbo. He's a—what would call him, my dear? A holy fool would be putting it mildly."

"He comes from a family of Dukhobory. Come now, Vasya, don't disparage the Spirit Wrestlers. They are good, peaceful people, and terribly persecuted. When Pyotr was young, the decrees against dissenters were promulgated. His father and uncles were conscripted, the family was forcibly resettled in the Caucasus. Thousands of families were broken up, whole communities were destroyed. Terrible things."

"Our government is a clever one indeed," Alyosha said, "to manage in one generation to turn peaceful, hard-working religious people into rebels and revolutionaries."

"Pyotr is not a rebel or a revolutionary," Anastasia said. "He's an actor."

"Well, what do you say, Vasya? A place to start, eh?"

"With actors?"

"He's right here in your woods. He travels around. Did Kolya ever meet this Panov?"

"Kolya? Did he, Anastasia? I think he must have."

"Yes, my dear. I'm sure he did."

"Well," Vasily said, standing, "I am going to get that bottle of cognac, shall I? My dear, you would like a small glass, wouldn't you?"

"That would be very nice." Just then a small breath of cold air brushed by her. "The night seems to be getting a bit cool."

"Perhaps we should go in then," Vasily said, who had also felt a slight chill in the air. "Better to have that drink inside."

"Easier to see each other," Alyosha said brightly."Easier for making plans."

❦

"Well, well, what have we got here?" one of the men encircling Natasha said. "Not a wild beast at all."

"A wild child, though," another said, holding his lantern high and peering down at her. "What's it doing out in the woods at night?"

"Must be lost, poor lamb," said a third.

"Poor lamb, you say?" said the peasant prince with a laugh. In the lantern light he looked much older than she had imagined. "Why, she has tracked me all this way like a perfect bloodhound. How do you do, child? I am pleased to meet you, Natalia Ivanovna."

"And who are you, sir? If you don't mind."

"I am called Pyotr. I am your friend. But if I don't take you home right now, your dear grandmother, Anastasia Alexandrovna, will have my head."

"Can't I please see where you live first?" Natasha said. "Please, dear Pyotr."

"We live nowhere, dear girl. We only travel from place to place."

"But you must sleep somewhere!"

"Indeed. In the forest, in the trees. In the meadows. Under the stars."

"Look at the poor lamb!" another voice said. "She's bone weary, Pyotr Illych. She needs to rest."

"I'll run quick as anything, Pyotr Illych, and tell Madame Barakova that the child is safe," a boy piped up, not much older than Natasha herself.

"No, she must go home tonight. Listen, child, there will be great upset in your house if you're found to be missing, so back you go now. I will carry you if you are too tired to walk."

"I am not at all too tired to walk," she said, proudly.

"Good. Because I am too tired to carry you," and he laughed again, quite a merry laugh.

"But can I come back tomorrow? And see your camp?"

"If we are still here. As we go back now, I'll show you the way to find us again."

She glanced around at the lantern-lit faces around her. She loved all these dear men, outlaws they must be, or gypsies, and she didn't want to go back home at all. But Pyotr was already leading the way into the forest, and so she followed after him, as meekly as a granddaughter of Anastasia Barakova possibly could.

They moved quickly through the woods; it seemed to take half the time returning than it did arriving. Soon they were crossing the clearing, and then they were within sight of the house.

"No one's raised the alarm yet," Pyotr said, "or the house would be all alight and they'd have roused every poor soul in house and village to go out looking for you. And that would have caused quite a lot of trouble, dear child, which I am sure you would not have meant."

"No," she said. "I only meant—"

"Yes, to have a little adventure. And you did. So now let's try to get you back inside without a mis-adventure." And this struck him as funny, too, and he chuckled under his breath. "How did you get out?"

"The kitchen door."

"Shall we try that, then?"

"First, Pyotr Illych, please tell me why my grandmother gave you a present."

"Why does anyone give someone a present, dear child?"

"Is it your name day?"

"A fine guess, but no. There are some people, like Anastasia Alexandrovna, who give presents only because they like to make other people happy."

"Did what my grandmother give you make you happy, Pyotr Illych?"

"You are very curious."

"No. I just want to know."

"That is what being curious means, wanting to know. Let us go now."

They left the shadows of the trees, and crept up through the garden.

"But will you tell me please what was in the package she gave you?"

"I have not opened the package, so how can I tell you? But if I had to guess, I would say she has given me a book or two, perhaps a bag of gold coins, a honey cake, several bottles of vodka, a cart and horse, a little puppy, an elephant and a mouse, a goose, of course, and a small writing desk, and—"

"A stone garden," Natasha said, laughing at the game, "and a fur coat and an almond tree, and—"

"Sshh," he said, but she had heard, too. Voices from the terrace.

"Anastasia," he whispered. "We're in for it now. Come, let's just confess and take our punishment like Christians."

"But we are Christians," she whispered back.

"Then we are used to suffering."

"But I don't want to suffer," Natasha said, whispering still. "Please can't we wait until they go in?"

"And if they do go in, will you promise not to sneak out at night again?"

"Not ever in my whole life?"

"No. Just not again this summer. Will you promise?"

"Yes. I promise."

"Let's wait a moment then," he said.

They had stopped beside a flower bed, but it was night so of course the flowers were sleeping. To her surprise, he bent down, and started brushing the tops of the sleeping flowers with the palm of his hand, and then he picked one. It was a weed, a dandelion that had gone to seed, and he held it up and blew the seeds into the air, as children do.

On the terrace, Anastasia shivered as a breath of cool air passed by her, and Vasily suggested that they go inside.

Natasha was about to look for a dandelion too when she saw that the people sitting on the terrace were finally going back into the house.

"Well, I see you are a very lucky girl," Pyotr said. "Now let's see you slip back through the kitchen door, and no one's the wiser."

"Thank you, Pyotr Illych. I will see you tomorrow," Natasha said, giving him a little curtsy, and then she did slip away, across the kitchen garden and into the house.

He watched until she was safely inside. Then he watched a little longer. No new lamps were lit; the house remained mostly dark, and very still. He waited longer still, until even the lamps in the upper rooms were extinguished and the dawn brightened the eastern sky.

♣

It was not a sensible thing to do, he knew, but Vasily Yakovlevich had been sensible for too long, he had made sensible decisions, he had lived a sensible life. And what did he have to show for it? A lost son, a desperately unhappy wife… and two lovely daughters, let's not forget that, he told himself. Two lovely daughters, who had blessed him with five grandchildren. Let's not forget. It wasn't all wasted, he had done a few things right. But now he had to do something else right. He had to fix this problem, he had to find Nikolai, he had to restore joy to his home. And if that meant dressing like a peasant and traveling around the district with a band of spirit-conjuring magicians, well, then, so be it.

Anastasia had listened seriously. She had not dismissed it as a mad idea. On the contrary, she had welcomed it, she was thankful, she thought it was a wonderful plan, a clever way to get information... And yet, something in her voice, in her face, told him she held out very little hope.

They let it be known they were going on a fishing trip, they packed up what they needed, and set off one morning on horseback, taking the path through the woods. Only Anastasia knew the truth, and Natasha, who was not supposed to know, but did, because she had overheard her grandfather and Uncle Alyosha talking about it. She so much wanted to go with them, to travel with the actors and their dear horses and their magical wagons and search the whole country for Uncle Nikolai. It sounded like the best adventure ever in the world.

The day before the expedition was to begin, Natasha slipped away into the woods and ran to the encampment. She had visited it several times; she would have liked to live in it. There were several children her age, and lovely young women who were probably their sisters, and older women who were probably their mothers. And then the wonderful costumes, the puppets, the musical instruments, the wagon that turned into a stage, the gentle horses. But they were not staying, they were only stopping a few days, they would be traveling south, they had many places to visit, performances to give. Eventually, they would go all the way to Tiflis in the Caucasus.

"And on the way you will see many marvelous places," Natasha sighed, longing to see those places.

"Yes. And many sad places, too."

"But you will cheer up the sad places," Natasha said.

Pyotr smiled at her and kissed her head.

Then the day came, and the fishermen set off. It was only to be for a few days, and no one but Natasha and Cook, who had prepared bundles of food for them to take on their journey, paid much attention to their departure.

"They'll have eats for some days anyway," Cook said. "Even if they don't catch a single big fish."

NATASHA

She so much wanted to go with them, to travel
with the actors and their dear horses and their magical wagons
and search the whole country for Uncle Nikolai.

And that was good, Natasha thought, waving goodbye to them, because it was unlikely, highly unlikely, that they would catch any fish at all.

But they would not go all the way to Tiflis, they would not be away for months. There were many bandits in the Caucasus, as well as hot springs and spas. Rich people went there and so the bandits did, too. Where the rich go, robbers follow, her father always said. No, they would not go beyond the borders of their own district, not unless they had a good reason to, Uncle Alyosha had promised her grandfather. "Of course, a good reason would be a good thing, too," he had said. "We want a good reason, don't we?"

They were talking secretly and so not saying what they really meant, but Natasha knew. A good reason would be news about Uncle Nikolai, and if they discovered that good reason, they wouldn't stop at the borders of their district. They would go to Odessa, if need be. They would go to Tiflis. They would probably go all the way to the ends of the earth.

BOOK TWO

Autumn in St Petersburg

CHAPTER SIX

Marina Vilinskaya Hears about a Dangerous Book

Two women were sitting side by side on a rough-hewn stone bench overlooking the gardens surrounding the famous mineral spa in Pyatigorsk high in the mountains of the Caucasus. They had only recently been introduced, though they were known to each other by name and reputation. One was a painter, the other, a medium. The painter was thin, lithe and of a nervous disposition; the medium was short and stout with large, bulging eyes. Both were holding glasses of mineral water, and wearing straw hats.

"I am glad to see you again, Sofya Fyodorovna," the medium said. "I have a message for your sister, the countess."

"My sister? Really?"

The medium closed her eyes and sat very still. Moments passed. Sofya Fyodorovna wondered if her companion was quite all right. It was warm on the bench, the air was heavy and still. It was possible to become ill even at a health spa. She herself was not feeling particularly healthy. The mountains did seem to close in on one so...

"Are you unwell, Elena Petrovna?" she asked softly.

"No. I am looking into my mind."

Sofya Fyodorovna felt it was best to sit silently and wait for this operation to be completed. What an interesting face, she thought. She was sorely tempted to reach for her pad and pencil.

"The message for your sister is this," Elena Petrovna said solemnly. "Find Nikolai Barakov's book. You must deliver this message to her in person. It is important that you do."

"Oh. Very well. I shall tell her when I see her. Though a letter would get to her much faster."

But Elena Petrovna was already standing, already waddling away on her short, sturdy legs.

"Wait! Elena Petrovna! Who is Nikolai Barakov?"

"She will know," Elena Petrovna answered over her shoulder. "He is Anastasia's son."

"My goodness," Sofya Fyodorovna said to herself as the figure of the medium slowly disappeared down the hill. "A most interesting face."

Marina Fyodorovna Vilinskaya smiled sweetly at the old villain with whom she was having tea and agreed with him entirely. Yes, it is certainly true that Russian literature since Pushkin... Of course, Prince, a genius... No, no, there never will be another Alexander Sergeyevich... (Thank God, the man was a monster.)... And she sipped her tea demurely and smiled.

The old villain, Prince Kirill Pavlovich, was, in truth, neither terribly old nor much of a villain, but rather a minor poet, an aesthete, a devotee of the theatre, of opera, of all things French and some things English (hunting dogs, whiskey, English tea), a man who, in his youth, was reputed to have kept several mistresses and survived several duels (with minor injuries to himself, more fatal ones to his opponents), but who now spent his time in drawing rooms, in idleness, in good clothes and French cologne, and in uselessness, like so many of his class.

"Take this novel, Marina Fyodorovna, which you were so kind to bring me," Prince Kirill said, nodding to the slim, attractive volume he had placed on the small table beside him, a scandalous tale by an English writer, difficult to obtain in Russia, but one Marina felt sure Prince Kirill would find to his taste since it was written by a member of the British Parliament. "No Russian would have the imagination to write such a book."

"No Russian publisher would have the courage to publish such a book, dear Prince. Our censorship laws—"

"Exactly. No, it is not something you'd be likely to publish here, not with our good censors at work."

Marina Vilinskaya smiled again.

"Tout comprendre c'est tout pardonner."

"Indeed. But, censorship aside, our contemporary literature seems to me so dull. Of course, I place Anastasia Alexandrovna in a different category altogether," added the Prince, gallantly.

"Yes? What category is that, Prince?"

"Why, she is a woman, my dear! And among women, she is without peer. Without peer."

"She speaks of women's experiences with complete faithfulness, it is true."

"Does she? Does she indeed? You would say so, would you? Because to me, well, sometimes I wonder if women actually think the sorts of things Anastasia Alexandrovna thinks they do. I mean... herself being an exception, of course. Do women think at all? This is the question."

Prince Kirill blinked at her over his pince-nez (the pince-nez was another affectation, Marina thought cruelly) and smiled. She noticed that his eyes had become smaller since she'd seen him last, and his jowls fatter. His entire body had thickened remarkably. She wondered if he suffered from that very English affliction, gout. She rather hoped he did.

"I assure you, Prince, women do think."

"Yes, yes, but about womanly things, don't you know? Parties, ball gowns, feelings. Isn't that true? They think about love, so to speak. Yes, feelings are the province of our women poets, and Anastasia Alexandrovna expresses feelings beautifully, beautifully. It's when she starts to think... that's when I lose interest, I suppose. Because really do we care what women think? I ask you, a woman... perhaps it's an unfair question. Of course you, Marina Fyodorovna, you must think about your journal, your readership, of course you must. Business. Yes, a woman who understands how to run a household understands business. It is completely reasonable. But when a woman starts to think about the social questions, the accursed social questions, and to think about politics... good Lord! Really, is this why we read poetry? To think about such things?"

"Nekrasov is not adverse to writing about social questions or political questions. Nor was Pushkin himself, of course."

"Different times, my dear. And as for Nekrasov, he does walk a very thin line at times, very thin indeed. Still, when he takes risks they are purposeful."

"Ah, Prince, I take your point. Men think about such things to a purpose."

"Exactly! Exactly right! Nekrasov thinks about these things to a purpose. Very well put. As for Anastasia Alexandrovna, I have not seen her latest work. Of course, I don't read the journals as thoroughly as I should. I wonder what she's written lately. But I expect you are preparing a manuscript even now, aren't you, my dear?"

"Yes. And you will enjoy it, Prince. It is full of feeling. Full of emotion."

"I am glad to hear it."

"Indeed. Her new work is elegiac. She writes about grief and sorrow. Women know these emotions very well."

"Is Anastasia Alexandrovna in mourning? Poor soul. Tell me, is it Vasily Yakovlevich, at long last? Is it he who has died?"

Marina Fyodorovna, who prided herself on her ability to read character, to see through artifice, to alight on the vulnerabilities and the particular vanities of men, and in this way to achieve her goals, could also appeal to the last vestiges of chivalry in them, when forced to such extremes by sheer necessity. The image of Anastasia Alexandrovna's book, propped up in a bookstore window, in front of which stood an eager crowd of people, the title of the book now appearing in her mind in Russian, now in French, and again in German (and why not in English as well?), stiffened her backbone and strengthened her resolve. Tears welled up in her eyes, she searched in her sleeve for her handkerchief, and from her breast she released a half-stifled sob.

"Not her husband, dear Prince. It is her darling, her most beloved, her son. He has disappeared, and poor Anastasia is out of her mind with worry. Oh, can you help her, Prince? You know everyone. If only she had news, any news at all..."

So that wheel was put in motion. Prince Kirill would gladly make inquiries. He knew everyone in the government, but in particular he knew Mikhail Nikolayevich Muravev, known as The Hangman for his preferred method of dealing with the Poles. The aristocracy were all related in any case; they were probably cousins. Not that being family would necessarily help. This was Russian politics in a nutshell: one half of the family worked for the autocracy, the other half tried to overthrow it. The Decembrists themselves were all members of the ruling aristocracy, even the ones who were hanged. So were most of the political prisoners currently in Peter-Paul Fortress or exiled in the east. How that had happened was anyone's guess, but it wasn't necessary to wonder about things that were incomprehensible. Marina Fyodorovna could report back that she had done her duty, unpleasant as it was.

"You're becoming a veritable Charlotte Corday," Kataev laughed after she recounted her conversation with Prince Kirill to him. "Next you'll be stabbing men in their baths."

Marina Fyodorovna did not find this image particularly appealing but she only shrugged and smiled. They were sitting in Kataev's study where they met regularly to review correspondence and discuss issues concerning the press, issues that often concerned finances, especially now that Anastasia's manuscript was so delayed. Marina had been leafing through an album of critical notices which Kataev kept on his desk. They were dispiriting, as most critical notices were, critics being far more interested in hearing their own voices than listening to the voices of the writers whose work they were meant to discuss.

"Next I will have to visit Nekrasov and that menagerie of his at *The Contemporary*."

"Whatever for?"

"Just to visit. Just to catch up on news."

"Be careful. Prince Kirill is right about Nekrasov. The noose is tightening around some necks over there."

Marina Fyodorovna shrugged again. Nooses were always tightening. Everywhere.

"We'll see," she said.

"Don't be a fool, Marina Fyodorovna. You know as well as I do that men have been exiled and imprisoned for writing poems, for publishing poems, and for reciting poems over a dinner table. It happened to Herzen in '34, and is still happening today, as it did just recently to Mikhailov. It was only under the disguise of literature that we were ever able to think and speak freely, but now that disguise is wearing uncomfortably thin on all of us, Nekrasov and his editors especially. They can't help it, things being what they are, but soon they will be exposed. There is no hope for them unless what cannot be said aloud actually occurs. And God help us if it does."

"Listening to you, Kataev, one would think the very ground was seething beneath our feet, and fires were burning down the dachas in Pargolovo. With whom have you been talking lately that has made you so dramatic?"

"Never mind with whom, the point is I would stay away from *The Contemporary*. If you must speak to any of them, do it in a drawing room or over a dinner table, not in their offices, and for God's sake be discreet. They're unlikely to know anything about Barakov in any case. He isn't a writer, never published so much as a letter to the editor. Why would that bunch know anything about him?"

Marina Fyodorovna did not reply. She didn't want to tell Kataev that she just had a feeling... an intuition... She knew Kataev. He would only laugh at her.

She turned another page of the album on her lap. Some of the notices were full of lavish praise, except those aimed at women writers which were invariably either scornful or patronizing. Even when the critics tried, they could not help but be insulting, as in the one to which her eyes now were drawn, which Kataev had marked as a rave: "The best poetry that ever flitted onto paper from a lady's sweet little fingers."

Marina Fyodorovna found her right hand had closed into a fist.

Sweet little fingers indeed.

Marina Vilinskaya was a woman of great determination. Warnings for her were more like invitations. And yet she did not go to the offices of *The Contemporary* that afternoon, nor indeed the next day nor the next. She had preparations to make for her Thursday night salon... that was one reason. But not the real reason. The real reason came from a different source altogether. Her sister Sofya had stopped by for a visit.

Marina Vilinskaya came from a literary family. Her mother had hosted a salon that included many of Moscow's leading intellectuals and writers, and the children of the family had received excellent educations, having as tutors not only professors of literature and botany, law, archeology and languages, but poets and writers as well. Her brother, Alexander, was a playwright and philosopher; her sister, Sofya, was a painter.

Like her siblings, Marina also pursued a career in the arts. She began as a translator of French novels, moved on to editorial work at various journals, and finally became an editor at Kataev's publishing house. Her salon in Petersburg, like her mother's a generation earlier in Moscow, was a meeting place for intellectuals, poets, philosophers, and artists. It wasn't often that her sister attended it, but she did pay calls now and again, and this afternoon she happened to be in town and stopped by.

"Hello, Countess!" Sofya Fyodorovna said, embracing and kissing her sister. "You're looking well, as ever. How was your summer? It was dreadful here. I didn't stay at all. I went south to the sea, and then to visit the Tatars. I did some excellent work, mostly terrible work… Let's sit in the garden. Oh, I have so much to tell you!"

When she was young and foolish, Marina Fyodorovna had married a French count who was soon after expelled from the country for dueling. She did not join him in his French exile, however; she even stopped using his name, taking instead her mother's maiden name as her *nom de plume,* and, in fact, she soon forgot him entirely. Sofya was the only person in the country who called Marina by her title; she knew how much it annoyed her sister, and she enjoyed annoying her sister immensely.

Tea was requested, and the sisters went into the garden and sat at the table under the trees. The sun was still warm but the air was cool; late summer had almost imperceptibly slipped into autumn. The leaves were so crisp they crackled at the slightest hint of breeze; the flowers in the garden were poised at the very edge of the abyss; their final, fleeting hours were upon them, golden as they still were. Marina tightened her shawl around her shoulders. Autumn was her least favorite season, it was so obviously a season of death.

"You had an interesting summer, Sonya," Marina said. "Tell me all."

"All? Impossible! I met a lovely young exile, a poet, of course, adorable. I painted him. It was lovely. What else? I saw a great deal of horsemanship. They ride like madmen in the Caucasus, I must say. I got quite ill from something I ate, and there were flies everywhere. I went to several spas. You'll never guess who I met, though."

"I never will. Who?"

"Elena Gan's daughter, Elena Blavatskaya."

"The medium? Did you go to a seance, Sonya? Oh, tell me! You did, didn't you?"

"Certainly not, Marysha. I barely spoke to her. But…"

"But what?"

"Well, it's rather odd… I don't suppose you believe in apparitions? Because… well, it's all very strange."

Marina settled more comfortably in her chair. It appeared she was about to be subject to another of her sister's endless and pointless stories.

"You saw an apparition? Tell me."

"I think that's what it was. Or it was a dream. It had to be. How could it not be? I was sitting on a bench and Elena Petrovna appeared to me... She was not there, then she was... and, Marysha, we were four hundred versts away from Tiflis. Did she just drive over the mountains for a morning at the spa? Because when I asked no one else had seen her. She wasn't there... I mean, in Pyatigorsk. But if I was dreaming, it was the most life-like dream I have ever had in my life... Tell me, are you and Kataev still publishing Anastasia Barakova?"

"Yes. If she'll only give us the manuscript."

"She has a son, doesn't she?"

"Yes. Nikolai Vasilevich."

"Yes. I thought so."

"Well? What of it? Was he there?"

"No. Not that I know of. But he was spoken about."

Marina took a breath, kept her temper, did not jump up and shake her sister. The tea arrived, was duly poured into cups, the sugar was passed...

"In what context was he spoken about?" Marina asked, as calmly as she could.

"It was so odd. It seemed after my dream... if it was a dream... many people were talking about him, but the first was Elena Petrovna... I was at the hot springs, like a character out of Lermontov... The whole thing was very much like one of Pechorin's tales, in fact. The spa, the ladies taking the waters, the gigolos hanging about. I had met Elena Petrovna in Tiflis in June, then there she was again, in August, four hundred versts away in Pyatigorsk."

There were little cakes with the tea. Sofya chose one and began to nibble it.

"She can be very ... portentous. I suppose it comes with being a medium. Anyway, if it was really Elena Petrovna and not a dream. We sat on a bench together and spoke for a few minutes. She said she had a message for you."

"For me? I don't even know the woman. What was the message? What did she say exactly?"

"She said, 'I have a message for your sister, the countess.' Which is strange in itself. No one calls you countess. Do they?"

"Only you."

"So I thought. Anyway, I said all right. I would see you when I returned home, though a letter would get to you much faster... These cakes are quite good."

"Sonya!"

"Does this matter so much?"

"How will I know if it matters or not until you tell me what it is?"

"Then I will continue. She was sitting right next to me on the bench. She is younger than we are, you know, but she speaks and acts and dresses like someone much older. I suppose it is part of her ... mystique. I would not say she's a particularly attractive woman, but there is something—"

"Sonya, if you don't give me the message this instant I will hurt you."

Sofya Fyodorovna laughed, merrily, a laugh that Marina found particularly annoying at that particular moment. "You are so impatient, Marysha. The message is nothing. I mean, it seems to me to be nothing. Let me think now. She said she had a message for you, and I told her I would give you the message. She closed her eyes, and for a moment I thought she'd fallen asleep, but, no, she was looking into her mind... or so she said when I asked her if she was all right. How odd this all is! Then she said, 'Tell the countess to find Nikolai Barakov's book.' I said I would do that and then I asked her who Nikolai Barakov was and she told me he was Anastasia's son, and then she got up, rather abruptly, and stalked off without even saying goodbye. Later, I mentioned this to my poet, and he seemed to know all about Nikolai Barakov and his book except what you'd expect someone to know about a book, like its title and subject matter. But he knew someone who knew someone who had read it, or part of it, or had heard about it from someone else... To make a very long story short, it appeared that everyone in the Caucasus had heard something about this mysterious book but no one had actually read it. But evidently the spirits want you to find it, Countess, so you'd better start looking."

"Did you ever discover the title?"

"Someone said it was called *Monkey*. A strange title for a book, I thought. But I don't know how reliable that information is. And I'm not sure if it's the title of the book or if it's the subject. Though more likely the subject is nihilism, which is all the rage in the provinces. You think Petersburg is bad. All I heard all summer was the most dismal philosophizing. Life is meaningless. There is nothing but death and annihilation. What is the point of living? Only live so long as you can remain intoxicated. As soon as you're sober, you see it's all a delusion."

"That's just old-fashioned romanticism. Our real nihilists are much more optimistic. They think if they burn everything down, they will be doing something useful and sublime."

"My poet, the exile, is very much of that school. He is a firebrand, I must say. You might actually be interested in his work. Though he's too political for Kataev, I'm sure."

"Kataev dislikes taking risks."

"Well, who enjoys taking risks anymore? Only crazy wild poets..."

The conversation continued in this desultory manner, though Marina Fyodorovna soon stopped paying much attention to it and began, instead, to wonder how Elena Petrovna Blavatskaya had learned of her interest in Nikolai Barakov, and when she had. Her own trip to visit Anastasia had occurred in early August, at just about the same time Sofya would have made her visit to Pyatigorsk.

Suddenly Marina felt a chill go through her. The leaves crackled overhead. The sky was clouding over.

"Let's go inside," she said.

So Nikolai Barakov had written a subversive book. It had to be subversive. Why else circulate it in secret? Writers in her experience wanted to be published, wanted space in one of the thick journals, wanted to be read. Why write a book and keep it in your desk drawer unless publishing it was impossible, unless it would bring nothing but grief, unless it was a dangerous book?

And if Nikolai Barakov was going to write a book it would have to be a dangerous book. Of course it would. The boy was nothing but trouble, had never been anything but trouble, had done nothing but vex his parents since he was old enough to be vexing... And this—if it got out—this would be worse than anything he had ever done. It would destroy Anastasia's reputation.

Or perhaps not. Perhaps it would enhance it. One could never tell.

Later that afternoon, while Sofya Fyodorovna lounged on a divan and paged through a French novel, Marina Fyodorovna sent notes to her acquaintances informing them that she was hosting her salon again this season, and inviting them to join her Thursday evening. Among those she sent a special invitation to was not Nekrasov himself, but the two young editors he had recently brought onto the staff of *The Contemporary*. Under other circumstances she would not have any reason to think they would attend, but it was always possible that they, too, had heard rumors of this mysterious book and so would have their own reasons to want to talk with someone as close to Nikolai Barakov as the publisher of Anastasia Barakova.

"You'll come Thursday evening, of course, won't you, my dear?" Marina said to her sister as she was leaving.

"Oh, Marysha, you know how I feel about—"

"And mention the rumor you heard. To certain people."

"Oh. But why?"

"To watch their faces, especially if they say they have no idea what you're talking about."

"Oh, Marysha! This is so exciting. You are going to try to find the book! But why? What's it all about?"

"It's a mystery, isn't it?" Marina said. "I'm intrigued. Aren't you?"

"So you want me to help you ... investigate?"

"Yes, darling. I want you to gather information. See if anyone else has heard about this book. But don't tell the story of your meeting with Elena Petrovna or all we'll hear all night will be stories of ghosts and seances."

"I like stories of ghosts and seances... But, all right, I won't mention it. Anyway, I'm still not entirely sure it even happened."

Marina thought it was as likely that it didn't happen as that it did. Perhaps it was a case of telekinesis. Telekinesis was a fascinating idea, and people were getting interested in it. Perhaps she might find some writer willing to explore it. In capable hands an investigation into the subject might be extremely entertaining. It might even become a best-selling book.

As it happened, the young editors of *The Contemporary* did not come to Marina Fyodorovna's salon that Thursday evening, but many other editors and writers did. Sofya Fyodorovna chatted them up with her usual exuberance. Prince Kirill was also in attendance and lingered afterwards to speak privately with Marina Fyodorovna. He had information, and it turned out to be rather important news.

CHAPTER SEVEN

MARKO VOLCHEK VISITS TWO FRIENDS

My last interview with Anastasia Alexandrovna took place on one of the first autumnal days of the year. The birches had already begun to change from green to gold; the sky was high and clear; the air was becoming crisp and light. It was the sort of day that stimulated the wanderlust, and made the clicking of spurs and the whinnying of a horse fill the heart with desire for adventure and the winding road. Anastasia sat in her high-backed chair. She was wearing a silk dressing gown of Oriental design with little slippers to match; her head was once again wrapped in her green turban; she had put kohl around her eyes, perhaps to disguise the dark rings of sleeplessness and strain. The total effect was unnerving and theatrical. Then who was I to speak of theatrics? I came to her in a disguise of my own, having raided Nikolai's old wardrobe for traveling clothes.

"Marko Volchek," she said, looking me up and down as though I were a newly captured Circassian brigand and she another Queen Tamar. "I see you have dressed for your journey. What's that you're wearing?"

She reached out to me, I took a step closer, and she laid her hand on my sleeve. Her touch was so light I barely felt it through the layers of wool and linen; yet, from the expression of pain on her face, I did feel something, a stab of guilt and shame, and it struck me to the heart, as sharp as a blade.

"His jacket," she said.

She stroked the sleeve, once, then lifted her hand. I wondered what hurt her more, touching it, or letting it go.

"Forgive me. I will take it off."

"No. No, it fits you well, my dear. Perhaps wearing it will bring you luck."

A jay flew by her window, squawking loudly.

"So then," she said. "You are taking someone with you?"

"Pavel Damianovich. On your recommendation."

"Ah, the young Frenchman! As a valet?" She smiled, slightly. "Can he fight?"

"If need be."

"Look on my desk." A thick wallet lay there. "Take it."

"Anastasia..."

"For Kolya. When you find him."

"All right."

"And here." She handed me a small journal covered in soft Moroccan leather. "There are names inside. Friends of his. Ones I can recall. And his most recent address. I am of no help. I have such little information."

"It will be enough."

"Marko, don't do anything foolish."

I wanted to say the entire venture was foolish. I held my tongue.

"What else can I give you for the journey? What do you need?"

"Only your blessing."

She smiled and recited a few lines of a poem she knew I loved. Then she stood and embraced me and kissed my cheeks.

So dressed in Nikolai's clothes, with his money in my pocket, his friends' names in my vest, his mother's kisses on my cheeks, and the sound of her poem still singing in my heart, I set out. It was fine day for the sort of quixotic adventure I was embarking upon, myself and my Sancho Panza, young Pavel Damianovich. What dangers we might face were of little concern to us then, and so it should be when going adventuring, for if we knew what awaited us in the course of time, there would be few of us indeed who would ever leave the safety of our houses, the warmth and comfort of our homes.

❦

I kept an apartment in the capital and it was there that I decided to spend the first few nights. I had various people to see, some in high places, some in low ones, and these visits had to be done in the right order so that information concerning my presence in the city did not pass too quickly from one group to the other, and so that the authorities did not find me out before I made more secure living arrangements.

I hoped to have two or three days grace before someone reported that I was in town. They like to keep an eye on writers in this country. They do more than keep an eye on us. They falsely accuse us, try us in secret, lock us up in prisons, destroy our presses, harass our families, burn our manuscripts, destroy our reputations, starve us, persecute us, drive us to suicide.

The first person I wanted to see, my mentor, was already living in exile.

The second person, I discovered, had that very summer drowned himself in the Baltic.

The third was Marina Fyodorovna Vilinskaya, and she, at least, would be at home since she was holding her usual Thursday night salon that very evening. In a different mood or on a different errand, I might have attended her soiree, if only to hear the latest literary gossip, but under the circumstances I decided to pay a more clandestine call on Marina Fyodorovna.

I dressed in black and, arriving on her street, crept unseen into her courtyard, climbed up the thick trunk of the old wisteria vine that covered the wall below her bedroom window, unlatched the window lock, and slipped in. Like a thief in the night. *Who comes like a thief in the night?* Kolya would ask. *Jesus. Jesus comes like a thief in the night.* He used to laugh at the idea of it, being, at times, a thief in the night himself.

I had made this ascent before—and the descent as well. Still I might have frightened Marina Fyodorovna had she been sitting at her dressing table, but she was not. It was already late, her guests would have assembled hours before, there was nothing for me to do but wait. I stretched out on her divan and picked up the book that lay on the table beside it. It always interested me to see what other people were reading. Marina Fyodorovna appeared to be midway through yet another novel by that most prolific of writers, George Sand.

"She must not see me suffer," he told himself. "She must not miss this chance for happiness. I must not stand in the way of her marriage. It is the only way I can make up for my shameful behavior toward her. She must not see my pain..."

I closed my eyes for only a moment...

A loud masculine voice brought my nap to an abrupt end. Instinct instructed me to make myself invisible. I rolled off the divan and slipped under it, where I would be hidden by its tasseled skirt. From there I could not hear what he was saying, lingering there in Marina's doorway. Perhaps his intention was to linger in the bedroom itself. Marina might not be adverse to his lingering but it would certainly be quite a bother for me, cramped up as I was under the divan. There was nothing for it but to create a diversion. I remembered the delicate little liqueur glass standing on the table beside the George Sand novel (how steadfastly French Marina's tastes still were!), and felt briefly sorry for sacrificing it before tipping the table gently with my foot. The tinkling sound of breakage was discreet, but loud enough to alert Marina that something was amiss in her bedroom. A few moments later, she came in alone.

"Whoever you are... before I scream for help..."

"It's only I, Marko," I said, and pushed myself out from under the divan. "Didn't you get my letter? I wrote I was coming."

"I expected you days ago. Well, get up, dust yourself off. I will have to speak to Lenka about cleaning under the furniture. Goodness, Marko. Look at you!"

I looked in her mirror. My hair was disheveled, and probably too long to be fashionable in the city. I have noticed that in the world of male fashion, it is the length and style of hair that is the most mercurial. Other than that, and some dirt on my nose, I seemed to be in good order.

"Was that dear Prince Kirill Pavlovich, with whom you were chatting just now?"

"It was. What can I do for you tonight, Marko? It is very late."

She was understandably grumpy after a long evening entertaining the literati and denizens of high society. Who wouldn't be?

"It's not late at all. You're only bored. Talking to the likes of Prince Kirill."

By then I had stretched out on her bed.

"Do make yourself comfortable," she said, and, taking out two more delicate glasses from a cabinet, poured us each a dose of vodka. What I always loved about Marina was her ability to anticipate other people's desires. She handed me a glass and took her own to the divan, where she lay like an overdressed odalisque.

"So, Marko, do you have Anastasia's book with you?"

"I do not. Do you know where Nikolai Barakov is?"

"I do not."

"In that case, we both have some work ahead of us, since the one follows from the other. Will the prince be of any help?"

"I believe so. He can make inquiries. He is very close to Muravev."

"The Master of Spies himself? I hope Muravev has never have heard of Nikolai Barakov."

"I hope so as well. But tell me, Marko, what are you doing here? I mean, here in the capital? What do you intend to do?"

"I've come to help you lay traps, of course. Dear Marina, have you forgotten already?"

"Things here are complicated. You have been away."

"Only a year."

"A lot can happen in a year."

"Like what? You fall in love. You fall out of love. You go abroad. You come back. You change your hair style—"

"You are the one who has changed your hair style. Not in a terribly attractive way either, if you don't mind my saying—"

"You decide to read French philosophy—"

"Never!"

"Or start chanting with an Indian swami and become a vegetarian."

"I said complicated, not ridiculous. Complicated... and more difficult. The political climate has changed noticeably. The Third Section of His Majesty's Secret Chancellery is more active and more virulent than ever, there are more spies in Petersburg than rats, and they breed like rats, too, there have been more arrests, more disappearances. People are more frightened than usual, and it is far harder to worm the least bit of information out of anybody. It has literally taken me weeks."

She smiled at me craftily over her glass.

"Marina Fyodorovna, you vixen! You know something! You have news! Out with it!"

Marina laughed. "All right. It's true I haven't found Nikolai himself, but I haven't been entirely useless since I saw you last. There is a rumor about a rather provocative novel that is circulating *sub rosa,* and causing quite a stir among our intelligentsia. It is highly subversive. If what I hear is true."

I smiled at her delicacy. Marina would never use the proper word for underground publications, *samizdat*, as though merely by naming them she was somehow colluding with their existence. Publishers want to publish, editors want to edit, just like soldiers want to fight, and the existence of an alternative, underground literature, unpublished, unedited, beyond the reach of critics and censors alike, simply offended Marina's sense of order the way the existence of a guerilla army offended the Hussars and the Guards. Nevertheless a guerilla army proved to be quite useful for stirring up trouble in the mountains of Chechnya, and *samizdat* proves to be quite useful in stirring up trouble in the salons of Petersburg. Such is life—unruly, unscripted, unmanageable, irascible... I was pouring more vodka into my glass and thinking of adjectives when Marina added, "Rumor is that the author is Nikolai Barakov."

"Hah! That's a lot of nonsense. For one thing no one in their right mind would write a subversive novel using his own name."

"I said it was rumor. Please pay attention, Marko. The Petersburg literary circles comprise a very small world. Everyone knows everyone else. Everyone has even slept with everyone else. They argue, they make up, they make love, they cut each other, they hate each other, all with equal passion, changing positions from one day to the next."

"This is your world. Not Kolya's."

"No. But once a manuscript is let loose among these people—and this one seems to have broken out of its cage—then everyone wants to know about it, and must discover who wrote it. The Big Whigs are interested. You know who I mean."

"No, I don't know. The Big Whigs in Interior, or the Big Whigs at *The Contemporary*? Or the Big Whigs in London?"

"All of the above."

"Well, I don't think it's an issue. Nikolai isn't a writer."

"Isn't he? Are you sure?"

"Anastasia would have been so pleased and proud. She would certainly have told me."

"She might not know. Listen, if this novel is what it sounds like it is... well, he wouldn't tell his mother about it."

"What does it sound like it is?"

"Let us just say that a censored version of it wouldn't fit on a note card."

"So you have read it?"

"No. I am reporting the rumor."

"Ah. It sounds like what they always say about a book before they read it. Then it turns out to be another off-color peasant tale by a Gogol *manqué* or a poor imitation of a tale of the heart *à la* Elena Gan."

"What if it's true, though?"

"What if it is? It seems to me it makes everything a good deal harder."

"Because he'll be in hiding?"

"Because he'll have left the country. If he can."

"If he had left the country, the exile community would know about it."

"True. He would go to Herzen."

"Of course he would. So, he's still here. And if he has written this book—"

"Marina, I promise you he has not."

"But if he has, or even if they only think he has—"

"Ah. Yes. If they think he has—"

"We won't be the only ones looking for him."

I got up and refilled our glasses, drank mine down in one gulp, and poured myself another.

"Dear God," I said, feeling the vodka burn, seeing the image of a parade of fools marching around the city, searching for Nikolai Vasilevich Barakov. "It will be a fox hunt. He'll go to ground, then. He'll bury himself somewhere. If he hasn't already."

"By the way, have you heard the latest about Elena Gan's daughter?"

"The mad one who travels with a troupe of *esprits frappeurs?* What about her?"

"You've heard about the escapades in Pskov? She caused quite a sensation. Now she's gone to ground herself. In Tiflis."

"She's hardly gone to ground if everyone knows where she is."

"I'm hardly *everyone*. She's a writer, you know. Her travel stories are quite good. Now she's writing a book."

"Of course she is. *Conversations with Ghosts*. Or perhaps *The Secrets of the Dead.*"

"Mock all you want. It will sell. The point is—"

"Don't even suggest I go to a medium."

"She is a very clever woman and she knows everybody."

"Living and dead. I am surprised at you, Marina Fyodorovna. To traffic in such nonsense."

"Is it nonsense?"

MARINA VILINSKAYA

"Now, come, give me a kiss, Marko!
You haven't kissed me in so long."

"What else can it be?"

"In this world, anything is possible. But let's not dwell on Elena Petrovna. I will see what I can find out from Prince Kirill. The most pressing question is where Nikolai is. They are our secret police, after all; they should know where we all are at any particular moment."

I smiled, and agreed this was the best first step. Meanwhile, I said, I would look up Nikolai's friends.

"You must be very careful," Marina Fyodorovna said softly. "Now, come give me a kiss, Marko. You haven't kissed me in so long."

She had drunk a good deal of vodka and champagne. Her cheeks were flushed, her eyes were sparkling on the verge of becoming a bit glazed. Marina Fyodorovna, my beloved editor, lying on your divan, surely you do not mean to seduce me tonight? Or do you?

I went to her, knelt beside her, and kissed her cheek, and very gently, her lips. Her perfume went to my head more quickly than the vodka had.

"Good night, dear Marko," she said.

"*À demain, cherie*," I answered, kissing her again.

"Go, you rogue!" she said. "Or I'll make you stay."

Laughing to myself at such charming coquetry, I rose and bowed and left the way I had come, through the window and down the wisteria vine. Pavel Damianich was waiting patiently for me at the gate. He took my arm, and together we strolled back along the river, under the stars.

The following night I set out again, this time alone, and made my way to quite a different part of the city. The narrow passages and alleyways I traversed were shadowy except for the firefly twinkling of smokers' pipes and cigarettes and the occasional light that flooded the street when a tavern door opened or an upper window was uncovered. The smell of tobacco smoke did not successfully camouflage the other more unpleasant smells of these squalid passages, of beer and urine and garbage and bodies in various states of sickness, debauchery and decay. Stolyarny Alley, the goal of my journey, was notorious for its concentration of drinking places and bawdy houses. Often one had to step over bodies in Stolyarny Alley, most of them only drunk, though once in while a corpse would turn up. The murder rate in the capital was low, but what murders there were usually occurred in the district around Haymarket Square, a place not unused to the flow of blood since it was the site of executions and public floggings. So I was not overly shocked to have to step over a few bodies en route to the Stardust, whose rooms would be more fragrant than this wretched alley, and whose denizens would be far better dressed.

I walked briskly, not wishing to be accosted by panhandlers or drunks or the more desperate ladies of the night or the more aggressive officers of our Tsar who liked to flash their epaulets in the alleys of the capital. In fact, I was forced to push an older gent aside just at the entrance to the little courtyard of the Stardust. The old drunk was unlikely to follow me in; Little Abrasha, the bouncer, was unlikely to let him.

"Evening, Your Excellency," Little Abrasha said, bowing deeply, after I pressed a coin into his hand and started up the steps. Your Excellency, indeed! He must have confused me with someone else.

But Serafima Vadimovna would not confuse me with anyone else. She noticed me the moment I entered her drawing room, and came to me straightaway like a goddess flying in a chariot drawn by a flock of birds. Statuesque, with raven hair, pale skin, and sapphire eyes, and dressed in a dark silk gown of Parisian design, she was a lovely creature, and well she knew it.

"My darling Marko Volchek," she said in a voice that was resonant and deep. She smiled down at me, for she was several inches taller than I.

"My angelic Serafima Vadimovna," I answered, bowing.

"You have been away so long. I hope you have missed us."

"To distraction, dear lady. You received my note?"

"Of course. Though you were as cryptic as ever. Have a drink?"

"With pleasure."

These formalities completed, we sat down together at a small table, huddling around a bottle of brandy like the conspirators we were. At other tables, couples were chatting, smoking, sipping flavored vodka from tiny glasses or popping open bottles of champagne. Every so often a couple would come to some decision, rise and leave the drawing room for one of the smaller, more private rooms upstairs or farther in the back. The ambience was as always refined, luxurious and calm, with none of the raucousness and belligerence one usually finds in houses catering to a different clientele.

Though located on one of the roughest alleyways in the capital, Serafima Vadimovna's house might have been tucked away in a casbah for all one saw or heard of the city outside its doors. Little Abrasha was only the first guardian of the Stardust's heavenly gates. There were other musclemen in the corridors and on the stairs, and then, too, its inner rooms, besides being guarded, were also fairly unknown. Secrets are rarely kept in our fair country, riddled as it is with networks of spies, but for some reason, perhaps because even to admit to a knowledge of the existence of such a house was compromising in itself, this particular secret was well kept. So Serafima Vadimovna, most mysterious of women, was mistress of a rich and secret world, entrusted with knowledge she could easily use to make herself one of the wealthiest women in the city. She did use it, but for more admirable ends. More dangerous, too, I thought, because it is one thing to part with money, quite another to part with information. Money can always be recouped, but information, once shared, can never be recovered.

Serafima was smiling at me, that secret, wicked smile I knew so well, and I felt myself responding to her in a way I had hoped I would not.

"You are looking quite dashing, Marko," she said. "Though I may have to take you to Weichmann's. Your jacket is just a bit out of date. And I am not sure about the tie. The devil is in the details, you know. Assuming you are planning to continue with this… adventure."

"Style is not going to be important where I'm going."

"My dear Marko, don't be foolish. Style is always important. Especially where you're going. The young are far more critical than the old. If you are not meticulously careful they will see right through you."

"The young are more forgiving."

"Not this generation, I assure you. They have no feeling for art. They think we are merely degenerates."

"Then they have no feeling for liberty either. But I assume you mean young men. I am sure young women—"

"A different species, yes. Young women have better things to do than gather in secret and plot. And better places to be than en route to Siberia."

"Our youth sacrifice everything."

"They are children. They throw away their lives."

Serafima's voice was cold, her eyes were hard. It was because she loved those boys, those heroic and foolish boys who threw their lives away, who stood up for one moment and spoke the truth, futilely, yes, but they did stand, they did speak. We could, if we wished, recite their names, and there would be so many, and even then we would not know them all.

"Of course you are right. You have more pressing concerns than wardrobe. A lost boy. Very well. What can I do to help you?"

I must have glanced around furtively, as though looking for spies, for she put her head back and laughed with delight. "Come upstairs," she said. "You must take off that jacket, loosen your tie, put your feet up, fill your pipe... and tell all!"

She paused to give her vicar a few instructions before leading me out of the reception room and up a short flight of stairs to her private suite. I knew these rooms, candle-lit, spacious, high-ceilinged, done in red and gold. Champagne was cushioned in a silver bucket of ice, a servant was poised to open it at a word. The word was given, the cork was popped, the champagne poured, the servant dismissed. If only all human actions could be so precisely ordered, so deftly performed, so gratefully received.

Settled with my tie loosened, my jacket off, a champagne glass in my hand, I felt foolishly like the master of my fate. This was Serafima Vadimovna's art, to indulge all our fantasies, to permit us to live these other lives and imagine ourselves free. She herself was an actress of great talent; she had been on the stage in her youth and might have had a successful career had she pursued that life. She chose another. Or perhaps it chose her.

Briefly I expanded on my errand, and what I hoped she might provide.

"Going to ground in a brothel! Oh, Marko, how clever of you to think of such a thing! Perhaps you are putting it into a novel? *A Romance in the Demi-monde!* Oh, dear, I believe Avdotia Panaeva has already written that novel. But surely there is room in our literature for another. And I doubt hers takes place in a brothel, especially not one like this."

"Are you insulted?"

"Insulted? Why should I be? It is a clever idea. Assuredly no one will look for you here."

"If I'm careful enough, no one will look for me anywhere."

She glanced at the clock on the mantel. "Indeed. Well, just to be sure no one is looking for you tonight, you will stay here. There's a light supper in that cabinet. Eat, and when I return you must tell me everything." She rang a small hand bell and rose magnificently from her chair. It was the theatre, no doubt, that had trained her to make such grand entrances and exits.

I found I was starving and ate with relish. I was just finishing a plate of dumplings when the bedroom door opened and a man emerged, tall, blue-eyed, flaxen-haired, wearing a silk caftan tied with a Turkish sash. He poured himself a glass of champagne (the servant had brought in another bottle while I was eating), and took a seat across the table from me.

"How was your meal?"

"Delicious. I did manage to save you a few cheese tarts." I smiled at Serafima with admiration. "It is miraculous, really, how wonderfully adept you are at turning yourself into a woman."

"Thank the theatre. They have been perfecting the art for centuries. I brought one of my dressers over from the Aleksandrinsky, and the other from the Mikhailovsky. He was so tired of opera singers. We cannot begin to guess the sorts of torture the likes of Bosio and Tedesco can put a dresser through."

"Still it is amazing how paint and powder, gown and wig can create such a transformation. It is a kind of magic. The only thing that remains the same is the color of your eyes."

She—he—smiled at me. "I am merely creating an illusion, my dear Marko. And illusionists—well, as you know, one does not create such magic simply by changing one's clothes. It is a matter of faith, always a matter of faith. You must believe you are who you pretend to be. If you don't believe it, no one else will. If you do, everyone will believe along with you."

"A matter of faith?" I said, laughing. "How religious you have become, my dear."

He laughed. "Yet I always keep in mind that bit of old Arab wisdom: Trust in God but tie your camel. It is one thing to play my games here in my own fortress, but I would not try it on the streets of Moscow or

Petersburg. Paris, yes. Not Petersburg. Now, tell me, dear Marko, who is this lost boy, Nikolai Barakov, and why are you risking life and limb to find him?"

"Not a boy. A man. He is well into his thirties by now. Son of Anastasia Barakova."

Serafima—though now it might be better to refer to him as Serafim—had placed a cigarette in his cigarette holder and lit it. Smoke rose up into the air like incense smoke from a censer. Some of the candles were smoking, too; in fact, the boy was even now replacing them. Smoke-filled semi-darkness always reminded me of being in church. Odd how the mind works, weaving memories together, connecting us to the past in every moment of the present.

"He was only twelve when I met him," I began, now summoning from my store of memories the image of Kolya as a boy. "The sweetest boy, and smart, polite, with a keen sense of humor, filled with ideas and energy. But even then, even then… well, he was very clever, and, as they say, too clever for his own good. He could see through the little deceits, the little compromises, he could see the abyss between what we say and what we do. It didn't take long for him to understand that as much as his father talked about liberalization and emancipation, he had not, in fact, done anything about it. This was around the time Barakov inherited his uncle's estate with its thousand serfs. Before then, Vasily had attempted to live a pure life, the sort of life we should be able to live, a life without guilt, without causing others to suffer… Then Andrey Barakov died and left Vasily a rich man. But that was only one of the problems for Nikolai, and I think by the time the inheritance was finalized he had already turned his back on his family and taken up with people as unlike his family as he could find. That, at least, is what I imagine he did. I don't know his motivation, only the events and the results. Several times his father had to use his wealth and position to extricate Nikolai from situations that might have led to prison sentences. Not for subversion, mind you. For brawling in public, for dueling, and once, I believe, for stealing a coach and four. He lived with outlaws; he became coarse; he drank too much. Why? The last time I saw him—many years ago now—we shared a meal and talked for hours and finally I said, You are so intelligent, so clever, you can do anything. Choose something and do it! Then you will be happy. And he smiled at me, such a cynical smile,

I will never forget it, and he said, Surely, Marko, you know as well as I that it is impossible in this world for a man to be both intelligent and happy."

"So he is a lost boy," Serafim said sadly. "There are so many of them! I have heard stories like this before. Some drink themselves to death, some take laudanum or smoke opium, some sink so low... and they all began as sweet, smart little boys with no future before them but to become monsters like their fathers. No wonder so many choose death instead."

"Vasily Barakov is not a monster."

"He takes part in a monstrous system. Come, tell me, has he freed his serfs?"

"I see freed serfs everywhere in the cities, homeless, starving, without work, without hope. Freeing serfs willy-nilly and forcing them into destitution is not the answer."

"You are right, it is not, and I don't know what the answer is. But I am merely the madame of a brothel and can't be expected to have an answer. And this, I imagine, is the excuse everyone uses: it is not my job to have an answer. So no one answers and the evil goes on and on."

"Perhaps given the chance serfs themselves might come up with a solution. It is their lives after all."

Serafim laughed. "How radical of you, Marko! Yes, let's give serfs the vote and see what they would like. And being the son of a serf myself I can tell you immediately what they would like. Land. Land. Land. Very good. Then once you know that, try giving it to them. No, you would have to give them arms first, give them weapons, give them the army, in which so many of them already are forced to serve, and then see if they can take from the aristocrats what they want and deserve. Good luck to you in that particular enterprise."

"Is there no solution?"

"There is. I just told it to you. Or as much of it as I dare say even to you, my dear Marko. You can surely work out the rest. But enough politics. Do please carry on with your narrative. I have an image in my mind of young Barakov. He sounds quite the young corsair. But you haven't told me yet why you are in search of him."

"He stopped writing to his mother."

"Ah."

"You are laughing."

"I am not. So during all this ribaldry and rough living... he wrote to his mother."

"Regularly. Until, without warning, he stopped."

Serafim rose from his chair and stretched his neck and back in a most graceful, swan-like manner. He walked across the room, slowly, and back again to his chair.

"She fears he is dead," he said at last. "And has sent you to determine it. Poor woman!"

"Yes. That is her fear. But I am hopeful that I can find him. I want to talk to his friends. And I will need to seek out the radicals. He may be known in those quarters, among students and their secret societies."

"Poke around in that hornets' nest at your peril, Marko."

"I know. But it is a likely place. And there is some rumor about his having written a novel... I will have to speak to the journalists and critics, much as I dislike the idea. "

"I can't help you with the nihilists. Needless to say, they don't come here. We are far too bohemian for them. They really are quite moralistic and prudish. I sometimes think with all their talk of martyrdom and self-sacrifice they are against all art and beauty and all human feeling entirely. Not that I've met any of them, mind you, but I read their articles and their journals. On the other hand, in respect to journalists, I can arrange a meeting with Avdotia Panaeva, of *The Contemporary*, if that would be of help. Of course, you could always go to her."

"I could, but I want to keep this as quiet as possible."

"Yes. And you don't trust the writers at *The Contemporary* to keep it under their hats. Well, I think you're right. They are a noisy bunch, most of them are drunk half the time, and they have too many nosy hangers-on around them. But Avdotia Yakovna knows everything that's going on among the literati and the intelligentsia, and she's trustworthy. If Nikolai Barakov is known to that circle, Avdotia Yakovna will have heard about him."

"A meeting with her would be very helpful."

"What else can I do? If you are going to explore the underground you had better take a bodyguard with you. I can provide someone."

"I brought someone with me. He acts as my valet."

"An armed valet, I trust. If you are really going into those districts.

It's hard for me to imagine a son of Anastasia Barakova sinking to such a level. Grigoriev, yes, that terrible drunkard, yes, someone like that might live with gypsies and runaway serfs and opium smokers and thieves, but the son of Anastasia Alexandrovna? It breaks my heart."

"Apollon Grigoriev, the poet?"

"The same. It's a tragedy. He once could write, but he's always drunk and has embraced the lowest elements and most absurd notions. He's in debtor's prison now, poor soul. Oh, Marko, it's such a terrible story you've told me! I am amazed that you still have hope."

"I must. And, if the worst has happened, it's better that Anastasia knows. She has a right to know."

"A right? Who in this foul country has rights? No one, as you well know. If he's been arrested, for example, one would have to have a friend, a well-placed friend, to get any information. Do you have such a person?"

"Yes."

"Good. So you have a solid three-pronged approach, like a general going into battle." He smiled at me with some pride and lifted his glass. "To victory," he said. Then, refilling my glass, he added, "And to love."

By the time I left the Stardust it was nearly dawn, a grey and somber one, the sky overcast, rain clouds gathering in the east, the air chill, the wind raw. Petersburg is always a cold city, even when the temperature is warm and the sun hot. The architecture is heavy and imperial, nothing human about it. The only street in the city dedicated to human needs and desires, Nevsky Prospect, appeals to the lowest of them, to consumerism and commerce at one end, and the most sordid of vices at the other. It is at its worst in the early morning when the accumulated dirt of the night clutters the sidewalks and the detritus of wasted lives washes up against the curbs. And overseeing it all is the monstrous fortress of Peter and Paul, our Bastille, which some day, like its Parisian counterpart, will surely fall. How many poor souls were even at that very moment locked within its dreaded cells? The thought that one of them might be Nikolai Barakov spurred me on. *Arise from your sleep!* Yet I needed a little sleep, or, in the alternative, several glasses of very strong tea, then a change of clothes, and a bit of good luck. The rain began to fall, a strong and steady shower. It was not promising to be a very lucky day.

CHAPTER EIGHT

The House across the River

The poorest, meanest districts of our cities often lie cheek by jowl beside the most exclusive ones. So across the river from the most fashionable section of Petersburg was the most squalid; only the river separated them, and a pontoon bridge. Across that bridge I went a few days later, dressed in the oldest clothes I had, or rather the oldest clothes Pavel Damianich could find for me and would allow me to wear: a shabby grey overcoat, a worker's peaked cap, scuffed boots with worn down heels—clothing typical of impoverished students and unemployed clerks, those poor young men of Petersburg, "down at heels and out at elbows," as the English so poetically put it.

It was a cold, damp morning, the wind coming in off the gulf, the river choppy, gulls crying and swooping in the grey air. A cold-hearted city, this, built by a cold-hearted tsar on the scourged backs of millions of slaves. It was an enterprise typical of my country; it was its signature piece. As for the men who lived here, and the work that was done here... it was enough to crush the heart to think of it, enough to crush the soul. And overlooking all the despair, the brutality, the suffering—no matter where one was in the city, one had only to lift one's eyes to see it—rose the tower and spire of Peter-Paul Cathedral, set in the heart of Peter-Paul Fortress, a constant reminder of the power that oppressed us, ever-vigilant, ever-watchful, forever gazing down on us like the very eye of the Tsar himself, which is to say, the eye of the Third Section of the Secret Chancellery, whose headquarters lay in the cathedral's shadow, in the Zotov Bastion, near the dark stone torture chamber of the Trubetskoy, where so many of our bold and young had lost their lives. The thought of Kolya imprisoned in that hateful place tormented me day and night.

Just as I reached the bridge a squall came rushing down with a burst of cold, punishing rain that nearly drove me into the river. I struggled on against the traffic coming at me, jostled by a mass of men on foot, and splashed by water and mud churned up by the wheels of carriages and carts and the hooves of beasts. Here on the street a poor man becomes anonymous and inhuman, simply an impediment to other men's wills. This was another truth I had discovered early on, and I often felt—as the educated argued and debated what was to be done—that all they needed to do to achieve understanding was to dress themselves as poor men and take a walk on the city's streets.

Once I attained the farther shore, I still had to find the proper street, and by the time I did so the rain had already caused my poor coat to become shapeless and soggy. The street itself was narrow and strewn with garbage. On one side it was lined with apartment flats, on the other with large houses, most of them in obvious disrepair with broken windows and collapsing roofs. The air, even after the sudden cleansing shower, smelt of rubbish, spoilt food, and other filth. Some raggedly dressed men, talking loudly, seemingly already drunk, had assembled on the crumbling steps of one of the houses. There was a steady flow of wagons and carts, for a market was nearby.

Suddenly a voice was raised, there was a good deal of shouting, the group of drunken men dispersed, down the steps, down the street, and I saw an old man at the doorway, holding what appeared to be a sword in his hand and shaking it at the loiterers… or perhaps it was a cane or a broom handle. I had only a glimpse of him before he re-entered the house and slammed the door.

It was, coincidentally, the very house I was seeking.

Having seen his swordsmanship, I waited a few minutes for the doorkeeper to calm himself before approaching the house and knocking on the door. This time it was opened by a younger man, not in answer to my pounding but because he was on his way out on some errand of his own. Without even asking my name, he called me friend, gestured me in, and directed me to the back of the house where he said I could warm myself and get dry.

The house was gloomy and rambling with crepuscular rooms opening up on either side of a long, squalid hallway littered with pieces of broken furniture, sacks of rotting vegetables, and piles of torn and faded newspapers, yellowed by feline urine, an overwhelming stench. Hanging on hooks along the corridor were buckets and baskets and odd tools and coats, but other things were thrown carelessly on the floor, and the walls themselves were covered with odd symbols and designs scrawled in red and black paint.

I followed this corridor deeper and deeper into the bowels of the building, past alcoves and stairways, following the sound of voices, until I came to the kitchen. Here the air was warm and steamy, pots were bubbling on the stove, a battered old samovar squatted on the sideboard, and five men in shirt sleeves were sitting around the table with glasses of tea in front of them. There were two other people in the room: the old swordsman I had seen earlier was chopping cabbage at the cutting board, and in the corner a strikingly beautiful young woman with long, dark hair hanging down her back was paging through a thick book whose pages, I could see, were filled with numbers and equations. Six of the seven faces turned to me as I entered—the old man did not stop chopping his cabbage—and on all six faces I saw a similar expression. Not surprise, but indifference, and, in one case at least, slight disappointment.

"Downstairs," one of them said gruffly. "Kitchen's only for official residents. That means people who live here."

"But I am looking for someone who lives here."

"Is that so? Because you look like you're looking for one of the heroes printing seditious nonsense in the cellar. Doesn't he? What do you say, Ilyusha? Eh? Doesn't he look like one of those milk-drinkers down there?"

"He does, Gavriil Mikhailovich. One of those children, those little boys, playing with ink too black and ideas too grand—"

"Who is it you're looking for, friend?" the girl in the corner asked me, interrupting Ilyusha, who, if he was Ilya Ivanovich Gutiev, was precisely the someone I was looking for.

"Friends of a friend," I said. "Friends of Nikolai Barakov."

At that, a sudden and absolute silence fell on the room. The swordsman stopped chopping his cabbage, the mathematician stopped flipping her pages, the tea-drinkers put down their glasses and their pipes. Their looks of surprise changed quickly to expressions of fear and suspicion.

"Is he here?" I asked as off-handedly as I could though I knew very well he wasn't.

Gavriil Mikhailovich—another of Nikolai's comrades whose names appeared in Anastasia's notebook—was the first to speak. "Who the devil are you anyway? Who sent you?"

"My name will mean nothing to you. It is Valentin Grigorovich Markov. But as to who sent me, her name will mean everything: Anastasia Alexandrovna Barakova. And the reason I am here? To discover the whereabouts of her son."

This caused the men at the table to sit up and take notice, at least.

"She has been writing to him at this address," I continued, sternly, "but has received no reply for over a year. What has happened to her letters?"

"I have them," the mathematician said quietly from her corner. "And I am pleased to meet you, Valentin Grigorovich. I am Katerina Gutieva. I have been saving Nikolai's letters for him. For when he returns."

I bowed to Katerina, but before I could say anything more, a dark young man thumped his fist on the table and cried out, "When he returns? He's not returning. Never!"

"Where has he gone?" I asked, but my voice was drowned out by loud exclamations from others at the table, calling the speaker—Mikha was his name—a rat, an idiot, and a fool, all in the most vulgar terms imaginable. They attacked him on all sides, four against one. Katerina Ivanovna said nothing, nor did the swordsman. When they were done yelling abuse at him, Mikha started shouting back. He stood to shout; he was not a tall man by any means so standing did little to make an impression. Still he stood, he raised his voice, in equally violent and vile language he accused them of craven self-deception, contemptible selfishness and cowardly refusal to see things as they were. Then, just as abruptly as he had stood, he sat down.

It occurred to me that he and possibly everyone else in the room (Katerina excepted) had been drinking all night and were only now sobering up. This thought was confirmed when the old swordsman strode to the table with a bottle of vodka in his hand and plunked it down with curses and a warning that if they awakened Taras Maximovich there'd be hell to pay. Then addressing me, he said, "He's not here, understand? Nothing here for you. Be on your way."

"You can't throw him out like that!" Gavriil Mikhailovich cried out. "Who gives you the right?"

"Shut up, Mikhailovich," Gutiev said. Then turning to me, "Go on up, if you want. There's nothing up there. Not one damned thing."

"Now you're giving strangers the run of the place!" the old man said fiercely. "Who gives *you* the right?"

"Thank you, Ilya Ivanovich," I said, ignoring the old man. "I will go and take a look at his room."

Gutiev gave me a furious look. "Do I know you?" he asked sharply, taken aback by my use of his patronymic.

"No. But you are known to me. You are Nikolai's friend and—" But before I could say more, our conversation was drowned out by the continuing altercation at the table between Gavriil Mikhailovich and the old man. Suddenly, all the others jumped up again and there was a kicking of chair legs and the table rocked a bit. I sensed someone moving behind me; a gentle hand tapped me on the shoulder. I turned away from the fracas and as discreetly as I could followed Katerina out the door and into the hall.

"They are like children sometimes," she said. "I'll take you up to his room."

We climbed two flights of stairs to the top floor of the house and entered a room with sloping ceilings and a tiny window overlooking the street. There was a bed against the wall, with a mattress of sorts but no blankets; a cabinet; a table and chair. The stove was unlit; the room was cold and had been thoroughly stripped. If it had once held books, papers, clothing, lamps, blankets or boots, there was no trace of them now.

"If you want the letters to bring back to his mother..."

"Yes. I will take them back to her."

"Then I will go and get them for you," she said.

As soon as she was gone, I searched the room. I searched for floor boards that were loose, for cleverly made holes in the walls or the ceiling, for crevices around the windows. I searched the empty cabinet thoroughly for hiding places. I felt sure, sure, that Nikolai would have left something behind, some clue, some token, but I found nothing at all.

When I felt I could search no more, I sat on his chair at his table and looked out the window. If he had written a book, he would have written it sitting here. He had written letters to Anastasia, sitting at this desk. I had read a few of those letters. There was nothing in them at all. One wouldn't know, from the letters, that he was living in a communal house on the Vyborg side of the river, in the worst neighborhood of Petersburg, with student drop-outs, thieves, drunks and subversives (for I had no reason to think his friends downstairs were anything but that). From the letters, he might have been anywhere, doing anything. I had never read such vague prose before; it was an art in itself.

I remembered some clever thing Nikolai had said to me once, clever but cruel, as truth for us so often is. "Our grandfathers did nothing but dress up and pretend to be French. Our fathers did nothing but dress down and pretend to be poets. What do we do? We do nothing but undress and pretend to be peasants." It was not entirely true. Our grandfathers had fought the Great Patriotic War against Napoleon before they decided to spend the rest of their days dressing up and pretending to be French, and our fathers had fought, but lost, the great fight for a republic before they realized they could do nothing and took to dressing down and pretending to be poets. Only we, having grown up under a repression, had done nothing at all but wallow in drunkenness and despair. Twenty thousand of us, the so-called educated elite, among a population of sixty million. Was it any wonder Nikolai had sat at this window writing pages of empty pleasantries to his mother? Was it any wonder he lived as he did?

Katerina Gutieva found me there, staring out at the drizzling rain and the windows of the apartments across the street, imagining myself being Nikolai Barakov, sitting in this chair, looking out this window, writing to his mother, saying absolutely nothing.

I stood; she smiled. "We are not so formal in this house, Valentin Grigorovich," she said, sitting down on the old mattress and patting the space next to her. Instead of joining her there, I pulled the chair over so I could sit and face her.

"Here are the letters," she said. She was holding a thick stack of them, probably two dozen or more, tied together with a blue ribbon. She held them, but she seemed disinclined to hand them to me.

"Tell me, Katerina, how did you come to live in this house?"

"Ilyusha is my brother."

"Ah. So that explains it."

"Explains why I am living here? Is this house so strange to you? Many people today live in similar houses."

"Similar, perhaps, but not ones with illegal presses in the cellar."

She smiled at me, quite an endearing smile. "You are worried about me! How kind of you! Now may I ask you a question? Did you find anything when you searched the room?"

"How do you know I searched the room?"

"I know you did," she said. "I know you didn't find anything. I have searched the room too, and found nothing." She gazed around at the barren space. "I used to live in this room. It was a cheerful room once. We were happy here."

"You and Nikolai?"

"Yes."

"So that's why you kept his mother's letters?"

"Yes." She put the packet of letters beside her on the bed. "I never opened them."

"Katerina Ivanovna—"

"Call me Katya, please."

"Don't you have any idea where he is?"

"No."

"He didn't tell you where he was going?"

"No."

"He wasn't arrested? You are quite sure no one come for him during the night?"

"Don't you think if that had happened I would have done everything, everything, to get him back? I would have written to his mother. I would have done whatever was necessary. But no one came in the night or in the day. No, he just packed a bag one morning and left and didn't say where he was going. Over a year now, he's been gone. Almost two."

She stood up and began pacing the room, from the bed to the window, from the window to the bed, ringing her hands as she walked. I had never seen such signs of obvious anguish in real life though romance writers describe it often and in just such a way. I hardly believed it, to tell the truth. I waited to see what else she would say or do.

"Sometimes I come into this room," she said, "and I wait to feel him… and sometimes I do. Sometimes it's like he's here, but he's a ghost."

"A ghost?"

"Not that he's dead! But he's sending a projection… an image. It has to do with magnetism. Fyodor Fyodorov understands the principle involved. We have talked about it often."

"Fyodorov the philosopher?" The quack, I wanted to say, but I restrained myself.

"Yes. He rents a room in the house, though he does not stay here as often as he used to."

She had stopped pacing and was standing by the window. A bit of light was shining on her; the drizzling rain must have stopped. In that pale light she looked quite extraordinary with her ebony hair, dark complexion, high cheekbones and slightly slanted eyes. Tatar blood, I thought. She is exotic like a woman from a story by Lermontov. She is just the sort of woman Nikolai would be attracted to, who rejected what other people prized, and prized what other people rejected.

Suddenly she came up to my chair, knelt before it, and gripped my hands.

"Listen!" she whispered. "I know who you are."

"What do you mean?"

"He told me everything. Everything about his father, his mother, her friends. He told me about his bedroom when he was a child, about the toys he had, about his sisters, how they teased him when he was little. He told me about you. I know who you are. You are the writer, Marko Volchek."

She looked into my eyes. She knew more than that, I was sure. She knew the whole truth, but she was keeping her knowledge secret, either from delicacy or wariness, I could not tell which.

"Nick told me everything."

"Nick?"

"He hated being called Kolya. You didn't know? He hated it. He wanted to be called Nick."

"Like Herzen's friend, the poet Nikolai Ogarev. He is also called Nick."

"He probably knows who those people are. He knows everything, my Nick. I don't know them. I am a mathematician. I know about numbers, not about poets."

"Did you know about his book?"

"Nick's book? Of course. He was always working on it. He had so many notebooks filled with ideas. He must have taken them all with him, because they weren't here."

"What was here?"

"Nothing of his. All that was left were things that belonged to me. All the pretty things, all the luxuries, the comfortable things. He was always bringing me presents but he never owned anything himself. Just some clothes. His notebooks. His knife. He always bragged that he could carry everything he owned in a sack on his back. Or that he didn't own anything he couldn't leave behind. He gave his books away, he would read them and give them away. He even gave away his clothes. He wanted to be free. He wanted to be able to pack up and go whenever he wanted."

"And you have no idea where he might be now, Katya? No idea at all?"

"No. I already told you. At first I thought he might have gone home, but his mother kept writing to him so I eliminated that. Then I thought he might have gone to see Little Mikha, who was serving in the Crimea, until Little Mikha showed up here looking for him. But Nick has friends everywhere. Friends in the Caucasus, in the Crimea, in the Ukraine, in the east. In Europe. In England. He could be any place. Until he writes to me, how will I know? Unless you find him. You'll keep looking, won't you? I know you will. Not for me, but for his mother. You are looking for him on her behalf, and you love her, so you'll do what she asks."

She was still on her knees gazing into my eyes; hers were so brown they were almost black. Nikolai's were dark, too, but blue, the darkest blue. The memory of his eyes, coming so unexpectedly, sent a cold shiver through me. I suddenly felt a sense of loss. Was it possible Nikolai was dead? The thought had not really found purchase in my mind before; it was an idea that had no resonance. Why then in his empty room did I feel this emptiness in my soul, this profound emptiness? Fortunately I was able to disguise my feelings, and smiled at her as I rose and helped her to her feet.

"I will," I said. "I give you my word."

"Marko Volchek," she said softly. "He read all your books, you know. He always spoke so highly of you. I can see why."

I kissed her hand, took the package of Anastasia's letters, and left the room.

Downstairs they were still sitting around the kitchen table drinking, though some had left and others had arrived. One of the new arrivals was Taras Maximovich, recently awakened by the look of him, and starting his day with vodka and tea. He was notorious among the Barakovs for being the friend who had led Nikolai into grievous trouble when they were young. It was Taras Maximovich who had introduced Nikolai to drinking and gambling and dueling. It was Taras Maximovich's idea, according to the family, to steal the coach and four and drive it to Moscow… to challenge a drunken titular counselor to a duel… to raid a princess's dinner party… to bring a bear cub to a ball. I had never met this evil genius before, and I was interested to see how he would stand up to his own legend. Of course, all those adventures had occurred long ago, in another time, in the golden age, the romantic era of our cultural life, when dueling and smoking opium and taking a bear to a ball were not so outrageous as they would be considered now in these more moralistic and somber days.

One look at him slouching at the table was enough to see the legend had far outstripped the man. Taras Maximovich was bloated from alcohol, scarred from fighting, worn out by prison and poverty and rough living. It was impossible now to see what charisma he had once had, to get a boy as smart and educated and well-loved as Nikolai to follow him on his criminal escapades. How close Kolya had come to disaster, even I didn't know fully. But Taras Maximovich had continued his career of crime to no good end, and had not escaped the full weight of the law. He had been sentenced to years of penal servitude; upon his release, he was arrested again, sentenced again, spending still more years in the east. How he came to live in this house, worming his way back into Nikolai's life and affection, I could not imagine.

He squinted up at me with red-rimmed eyes.

"They're all downstairs, your lot," he said. "In the *underground*. Up to their old monkey-business."

"Monkey-business?" I asked, too quickly, because now he sat up a bit and looked me over.

"Oh, go to the devil," he said. "Or go down and help your little friends get themselves hanged."

"It's you I want to talk to," I said, and pulled out a chair and sat down. Like one man, the other three drunks at the table got up and left us alone.

He poured another shot of vodka into his glass. "Never talk with strangers. That's my motto. Nothing good ever comes of it."

"I am not a stranger."

"No? Oh, that's right! Friend of Barakov's. Grigorovich, isn't it?"

"That's right," I said.

He smiled wickedly, wagging his finger and shaking his head. "Can't fool me, my lad. You're something else, you are. Who sent you? And don't tell me it was Anastasia Alexandrovna. That's a damned lie if I ever heard one."

"I'm not the police," I said. "If that's what you think."

He laughed, if you could give that name to so short and bitter a sound. "No. I don't think you're the police. Someone hired you, someone high up, someone who wants something, but take it from me, Grigorovich. You are not going to find him. He has done it, you see. He's a magician and he's done the perfect magic trick, the perfect vanishing act. Now you see him. Then... poof!" He snapped his fingers in my face. "He's gone."

I followed Taras Maximovich's advice and went down to the cellar to see what sort of monkey-business was going on down there. As I expected, they had set up a print shop with an old printing press, illegal, of course, since the government strictly controlled the ownership of printing presses in our fair country. And what would they be churning out on this little hand press, I wondered? Anti-tsarist manifestos, of course. The ink hadn't yet dried on some of the flyers. They were having tea and discussing their distribution strategy.

Monkey-business, indeed.

This time my entrance was not met with indifference. There was a general scrambling, and before I knew it, there was an arm around my neck and a knife at my throat.

"Password!" voices yelled at me.

Child's play. I disarmed the boy with ease and took his blade away so he would not hurt himself with it. I straightened my cap with a studied nonchalance and stared at them all sternly. They might have been schoolboys by the look of them.

"What are you?" I asked. "Are you all ten year-old children? What are you doing down here in an unlocked cellar in a house full of drunkards and ne're-do-wells and thieves? Are you all out of your minds? Password? God in heaven! That should be your password. A little prayer before you are taken out and hanged."

I picked up one of the broadsheets and scanned it quickly. *The Tsar is the enemy of the people… To your axes!… Land and freedom!… Long live the Russian Social and Democratic Republic!*

"Well, you have put your heads in the noose, haven't you? Good thing I'm not an agent of the Third Section."

"Who are you then?" a flaxen-haired child asked. He might have been sixteen, at a stretch.

"Kill him now!" one of them cried out, but without making a move. He was in charge of the press, no doubt, since his shirt sleeves were rolled up and there was ink on his hands.

"A good idea, that. All you need is a corpse to go with your land and freedom manifesto. Want to know how I got here? I just appeared at the front door and they let me in and directed me down here. You might be running a bordello in this cellar for all they know or care upstairs."

They looked at me stupidly and that only made me angrier. A sip of vodka in the morning is bad for my digestion, especially since I'd eaten nothing solid for a very long time.

"Well, I'm not your guardian. Do what you want. Die young."

"We are patriots," one of the boys said. They were all philology students by the look of them, pale, bespectacled, ardent. They'd be sent to the front or the east in a heartbeat and die of starvation or typhus before the year was out.

"You are idiots," I said. "Do you think we need more exhortations, and from the likes of you? We light our pipes with your manifestos."

I turned back to the stairs.

"Are you just going to let him go?" someone with a high voice said to no one in particular.

They would debate the question for few hours, I imagined. By the time they decided on an answer, I would be on the other side of the city.

♣

"How did it go at the communal house?" Pavel Damianich was bound to ask when I returned, and so as I walked back the way I had come, over the river and through the crowds on the Nevsky Prospect, past the arrogant, sauntering rich, the officers in their gold-braid, the over-indulged ladies in their perfumes and pearls, past Gostiny Dvor, the shopping arcade, the Court of Merchants, past the exclusive Ruzonov's, past Weichmann's, I tried to formulate a quick and yet truthful reply. How had it gone? Not very well, I would say. I had learned very little for my trouble. If I were to believe the denizens of his former household, Nikolai Vasilevich had vanished into thin air.

On the other hand, I had met Katerina Gutieva, I had retrieved Anastasia's letters, now nestled safely in an inside pocket, I had insulted some poor, idealistic students—not bad for a morning's work.

"What now?" Pasha would be sure to ask, being a young man of optimistic disposition. "What's your plan?"

My plan, Pasha darling, I would inform him, is to have a good dinner. And then, after a meal and a few glasses of liquid inspiration, we shall have to decide where to pursue our inquiries. I was confident by now that Nikolai was not in Petersburg. Therefore we would have to look elsewhere. But Russia is a fairly large country, and then there was Europe, Asia, Africa, the Americas...

If this were one of my novels, it would be at this very moment, while walking the streets of the city in despair, that the heroic investigator would encounter an old friend and invite him to dinner, in the course of which the friend, quite innocently and nonchalantly, would reveal the secret whereabouts of the man the hero seeks. But, alas, life does not imitate art. I walked all the way back to the apartment without meeting a single person I knew.

Pavel Damianich, aside from all his other virtues—punctuality and prudence, orderliness and forethought, civility and reasonableness (none of which, needless to say, are Russian virtues, rather the contrary)—also enjoyed good food and could even prepare it, given access to a well-provisioned kitchen and the appropriate culinary tools. In a pinch, he could also go to the markets, and that was what he had done that morning. As a result our dinner table was well-laden with pickled onions and herring, smoked sturgeon, a variety of meat and vegetable pasties, a walnut cake, a selection of wines from Denker's, and a bottle of Armanac for a *digestif*. By the end of the meal we were satisfied and relaxed and ready for a smoke and a bit of thinking.

We conversed in French, as we always did when we were alone, and since that language was his native tongue, our conversations offered him ample opportunities to practice the additional virtues of patience and fortitude—and good humor. All in all, we got along rather well.

I began by recounting the events of my morning visit to the communal house. Pavel Damianich listened with interest. When I finished, we sat for a few minutes in silence, sipping our brandy.

"You are a fiction writer, after all," Pasha reminded me, gently. "What would your hero do?"

"Just what I'm doing, I suppose."

"Wrong hero," he said, smiling. "The hero of the story isn't you."

"It isn't?" I laughed. "I am always the hero of my stories."

"Not this time."

"Who is then? Nikolai Vasilevich?"

"Why not? He is the perfect hero of our time."

"How do you mean?"

Pavel Damianich had rolled himself a cigarette, and now lit it, put his head back, and blew a plume of smoke up toward the ceiling. This meant he was thinking, or trying to put his thought into a precise and well-constructed sentence. He often spoke in aphorisms. I had even used a few of his cleverer sayings in my most recent story. Thankfully, he didn't object; perhaps he didn't know.

"I mean that he has done what all our pundits, intellectuals, philosophers, anarchists and agitators spend their time arguing about, but would never once consider actually doing: he has abandoned his class and joined the masses. He has become one of the invisible men. Which is why he cannot be found."

"I never thought of Nikolai as a political radical."

"And that is the sheer perfection of what he's done. He didn't do it for any political or moral reason. He's not a member of the holier-than-thou repentant nobility. Thank God. No, he lives the way he does simply because he enjoys it. Now imagine that a man like this is the hero of your novel. He's living in Petersburg in a communal house with his old friends and his beautiful mistress. What does he do with his time? He drinks and gambles, eats and argues, makes money here and there, makes love, lives his life just like anyone else, whether gentry or peasant or freed serf. When he can, he works on his novel. From what you say, he is living in a house with a cast of characters who could easily make their way into a book. Very well. He lives in this house for three or four years. Then one day he packs up a bag and leaves. Where does he go?"

"And why? If we knew why, we might guess where."

"Maybe he finished his book."

"Possibly. But then why leave one of the few places in the country where people actually read?"

"When you finish a book, what do you do?"

"Get drunk."

Pasha laughed. "Then what do you do?"

"Give it to my editor. But this book, if what I've heard about it is true, won't have an editor. It won't have a publisher. Not here in Russia anyway. He would have to smuggle it out of the country. And what's the point of doing that when no foreign publisher would care about such a book? Its audience is here, but it can't be published here. It has to be circulated secretly, it has to be printed up in cellars on illegal presses like the one in the cellar of his house. If only I could get my hands on it! Someone must have a copy."

We were still sitting around the table in the dining room of my apartment. Several paintings hung on the walls of this room, and I happened at that moment to lift my eyes and look at one of them. The afternoon light was already fading, and old Nadya, who lived upstairs and minded the apartment when I was gone, and kept it clean and warm for me when I was staying in it, had come down to clear the table and light the lamps. Just as my eyes rested on this particular painting, Nadya lit a lamp beneath it. The image of the painting, a two-masted ship gallantly sailing on the high seas, sprang to life before my eyes and with it a thought sprang to mind, like an inspiration from the Muse.

"What do you know about Fyodor Fyodorov?"

"The cosmist? The man who thinks we should live under the sea or travel to Mars? I've read some of the nonsense he's written. Why do you ask?"

"He is one of the cast of characters. He keeps a room in the house, according to Katerina Ivanovna."

"Interesting."

"I thought so. He's not there at the moment. I wonder if he knows anything."

"He knows a good deal of nonsense," Pavel Damianich said, kindly refilling our glasses. "Calls himself a scientist! The man is insane."

"Philosophers often are."

"Well Fyodorov certainly is. He thinks men can be sent into space, and live on other planets. He thinks that it will be possible in the future for science to make us immortal. No one will ever die. Our body parts will be replaced as they wear out. He even believes that one day science will be able to resurrect the dead."

"Yes. His association with Nikolai and that household is—intriguing."

"Colonies on other planets. Spaceships. Raising the dead. It's lunacy."

"Perhaps he's been inspired by Jules Verne. A Frenchman like yourself, though still rather unknown even in France, but his publisher in Paris is Anastasia's publisher as well so I've heard of him and even read a few of his fantastical stories. He sends his characters on adventures to other worlds, into space and even under the sea, in amazing vehicles that he describes in such a way that they almost seem real… I wonder if Nikolai and Fyodorov are friends."

"You think he may be with Fyodorov?"

"Who knows? He has to be somewhere. And I feel—I am almost certain—that he's not in Petersburg. But even if he isn't with Fyodorov, his book may be. If he was going to entrust it to anyone in that household, Fyodorov is the most likely person. For one thing, he might actually be interested in reading it. And he might have access to a printing press."

"You are thinking like a writer. You are thinking that all Nikolai wants to do is publish his book. But let me ask again: if he were the hero of one of your novels, where would he be now, and what would he be doing?"

"I will have to think about it. But first—"

I was cut short by a loud and insistent pounding on the front door.

My brave Pavel Damianich jumped to his feet, pulled a poker from the stand, and strode into the foyer.

"Pasha! Don't!" I cried.

"Get dressed!" he shouted at me. He can give orders when he needs to, and when he does I usually obey.

While I rushed into the bedroom, I could hear that Pavel Damianich was not discussing philosophy with our guests in the front hall. There were clear sounds of struggle, of raised voices and things being knocked about, or perhaps people. Pasha could knock heads together if need be. He was giving me time.

Nadya, bless her, was still in the apartment, and followed me into the bedroom to help me. God knows, one cannot dress oneself in this absurd world in which we live. Shirt and trousers off, so much was easy. For a moment I gazed around at a loss, but Nadya quickly fetched a dressing gown from the wardrobe, a turban to wrap around my head, and slippers for my feet. *Voila!* I was ready to march out to face my guests.

I stepped out into the hall, into the battleground of my foyer, now crammed with half a dozen security police in their ugly uniforms. I noticed that a vase had crashed onto the floor, the flowers it held were now crushed under the *gendarmes'* boots, and that angered me almost more than seeing Pavel Damianich, his mouth and nose bleeding, being held in a white strap's grip while another was about to drive a fist into his face again.

"Stop this instant!" I cried. "How dare you enter my house, destroy my property, and assault my servant! Who are you?"

The policemen stopped what they were doing—hitting, holding, milling about, crushing glassware under their feet, or holding their heads in spots where Pavel's poker must have landed—and stared at me. Then out of the mass of uniforms a civilian emerged.

"My apologies, Madame Markova," he said, sarcasm dripping off his tongue like venom. "The deputy director of the Third Division of His Imperial Highness's Chancellory would like a word."

CHAPTER NINE

IMPRISONMENT

They gave me time to dress since one could not have a word with His Imperial Highness's Deputy Director in a dressing gown. While I did, with Nadya's help—poor woman, how she despaired of my wardrobe, my gowns and dresses so dreadfully out of date, and my hair, barely long enough to put in a chignon—the white straps hit Pasha a few more times and then went through my desk. A preliminary search. They would certainly rip the entire apartment apart before they were done, and break more vases while they were at it.

It was quite dark when we arrived at the building where my interview was to take place, and passed through its rather elaborate gate. It was not, thank God, the Vasilievsky Gate of the Peter-Paul Fortress, over which might well be written "Abandon all hope, ye who enter here," but rather led to a wide, imperial courtyard. From the coach we were hustled up steps and along a corridor to a door. Nadya, who had accompanied me, was ordered to wait; I was invited to enter.

This was not an ordinary arrest. I knew a good deal about ordinary arrests from my correspondence with Herzen, who had been arrested several times, and from stories one hears. So many people get arrested in Russia, it is almost a rite of passage for the young. Of course it's quite a different story for peasants and serfs and poor people in general, who suffer greatly at the hands of the police, often without ever being charged with a crime.

The man who turned from the window to face me was short, pale, and ginger-haired. I recognized him immediately as Pavel Beriosov, the spy who had been a guest at Oak Hills. He was dressed in a formal black tailcoat as though he was on his way to the opera, and perhaps he was, but had decided to stop off en route and whet his appetite for tragedy by torturing a few subversive serfs and students. We stared at each other over the space of the room. His smile was lecherous.

"Madame Valentina Markova. We meet again."

"Pavel Pavlovich, what is the meaning of this? I demand to know why you have had me brought here in the middle of the night."

"Now, now, dear lady, there is no need to get dramatic so early in our discussions. Do please take a seat. It's a chilly night. Perhaps you would like some tea."

"I would not. Nor do I want a seat. I want to know what I am doing here."

He didn't reply, but went up to his desk, a grand affair the size of a sledge, and stood next to it and ruffled through some papers that were lying on top of it. All for show. He was a showman, and all this drama, as he put it, was part of the process of intimidation they were all so masterful at, when they weren't using truncheons and knouts and hot irons.

Finally, he looked up as though he had just remembered I was there, and in a voice so weighed down with sarcasm he could barely utter the words—one imagines the Third Section gives lessons in such vocal techniques to their interrogators—he said, "I am relieved to see that you have dressed appropriately for our interview tonight, Madame Markova. Transvestism, as you undoubtedly know, is a crime in this country."

Transvestism? Good Lord, I thought, feeling unduly optimistic, was that all they had against me?

"A crime? I wish I had known. I shall have to ask Nadezhda Durova how she managed in that case to receive a medal from the Tsar. I believe at the time she was dressed as a cavalryman."

"*Sed alia tempora*. Well, I shall have some tea." And he jangled his little bell and ordered tea from the old man who came in answer to it.

"Yes," he said, dreamily, drawing out his chair and taking a seat at his desk, "a crime, and a sin against God and his Church as well. Yet, you are correct in saying others have committed the same crime without being punished for it. There is Lady Hester Stanhope, for example. She was a well-known transvestite. She traveled the world dressed as a man..."

I sighed, and since I was tired I sat down in an armchair, and when the tea arrived and was offered, I took a cup. Meanwhile he talked on and on as though attempting to bore me to death and so relieve himself of the trouble of doing it more brutally.

"... and stopped once at the home of Elena Pavlovna Fadeyev, the mother of the writer Elena Gan, who was herself the mother of another

Elena, Elena Petrovna Blavatskaya, also a writer, and a fortune teller or medium.... So many Elenas in that family. The current one, Madame Blavatskaya, might well be a man herself. If you've ever seen her..."

"I have not," I said. "Is there a point to all this, Pavel Pavlovich?"

"There is, Valentina Grigorevna," he said, and then, in a different tone, jarringly different, he said, "I want you to tell me why you do it. Is dressing in men's clothing exciting for you?"

I put my cup down and stood up.

"I am leaving now. And if you don't allow me to go—"

"You'll do what?" The scorn in his voice was simply appalling.

Then he rang his little bell again.

"But, of course you may go. You may go from here to a cell, Madame Markova. Perhaps dressing as a man is not a serious crime, but conspiring with subversive elements certainly is. I have a report here that informs me that you visited a certain house today where manifestos threatening the life of our Imperial Highness were being printed, and printed on an illegal printing press, I might add. You will be given paper and pen in order to write your confession, and give us the names of your confederates, and when you have finished writing it, I will interview you again."

At that point two soldiers entered the room, and escorted me out. Nadya was no longer sitting on the bench.

"What have you done with her?" I cried out to the guard standing by the door, but he did not reply.

♣

The soldiers bundled me into a carriage, and drove me out of the city. It seemed we drove most of the night. The place where we finally stopped, at the end of a long tree-lined avenue, was a large house with a high, round, windowless tower, like the minaret of a mosque or a medieval *terem* where in ancient days noblewomen were confined to prevent them from running off with their lovers. They took me there, up the circular staircase, to a cold, cell-like room, gave me the promised paper and pen, and left me behind a locked door.

It is not easy to write a confession when one has committed no crime. To what is one to confess? To being alive? To being human? To thinking? I confess I am alive, I am human, I think. I also feel. Oh, horrible crime! Our Lord was silent before his accusers. We learn from him, we Russians: when there is nothing to say, it is best to remain silent. What choice is there? I had nothing to confess, no confederates to name, no secret plot to expose, so even under torture, what could I say?

One day passed, and then another.

It amused me to think about how perplexed they must have been, trying to decide what to do with me. While being examined prisoners are usually held in a police barracks, but since they could hardly keep me there, they had devised another plan and sent me to this house in Pargolovo, a small resort town about ten kilometers north of Petersburg, and put me under house arrest. According to the old woman who brought me food and who was not in the least adverse to answering my questions, I was now under the close supervision of no less a personage than Pavel Beriosov's own mother, Svetlana Beriosova.

They sent a man to collect my confession.

"You must write!" he said.

"If I don't write... what will you do?"

"You must write," he said. "If you want to eat."

"Ah. And what if I need tobacco in order to write?"

"Why didn't you say so, Madam?" he said, smiling, relieved.

"And some brandy," I added.

Soon I had cigarettes and brandy, paper and plenty of ink. Why not write? What better place to do it? How many great books have been written in prison cells? *The Consolation of Philosophy*, *Le Morte D'Arthur*, *Don Quixote... La Philosophie dans le boudoir* (a favorite of Serafima Vadimovna's) to name but a few. I kept asking for paper, and paper was brought. Of course, whatever I wrote they would read, and use against me if they could. But I would write tales of fantasy, and at least amuse myself.

Another day passed, and another. And another.

There was a single window in the tower room through which I could view the world below, and the great expanse of sky. I could see weather coming in, cloud barriers, storm fronts, flurries of snow. I could watch sea birds flying by, for the sea was near. I had time and peace and beauty. What more did I need? Only hope, but hope had abandoned me. For I was not a fool, not an innocent, I knew very well what became of people once they fell into the hands of the Third Division. It was no secret:

they disappeared. They were taken off the streets or out of their houses, and no one ever heard of them again. And this was how it felt, to be the person taken in the night, the person who vanishes without explanation. This was how it felt: being alone in the dark, isolated in a frigid tower room, utterly dependent on the whims of one's jailers.

Who, I wondered, was the snitch in Nikolai's household? Who among them was the rat, the informer? Someone in the house had reported me to the Third Section, that was certain, but who was it? Taras Maximovich? The old swordsman? Little Mikha? Had this person betrayed Nikolai as well? And how was it that, if there was an informer in the house, he had not also informed on the cell of subversive students churning out manifestos in the cellar?

And why was the Third Section interested in me at all? What had I done to attract the attention of the likes of Pavel Beriosov? Was it simply that by asking about Nikolai, I had become complicit in his crime? This was how Herzen had come to be arrested, merely by inquiring about the fate of his friend, Ogarev. "The Tsar commands" is how all our imperial decrees begin, and one of the things the Tsar commands is utter passivity. He would prefer it if we were all asleep. Perhaps, better yet, if we were all dead. So when a friend or relation disappears, it is best not to inquire. Inquiring only brings the questioner trouble, as my inquiring about Nikolai had brought trouble for me.

Thinking along these lines, in rage and despair, the truth came to me at last. They had made Nikolai vanish, they had sent him to the mines or to a penal colony in the east, or they had killed him in secret for the crime of mocking them or for the far more egregious crime of putting that mockery into a book. And they had arrested me because I was asking awkward questions about him, whom they had snatched away to murder without charge or trial.

It surprised me that I found all this shockingly cruel, for I believed myself to be inured to the injustices and cruelties of life, and hence to feelings of outrage and anger. That I could still feel rage and grief over what was the normal course of events in our pernicious times only told me how deep my love was for him whom I now, in my heart, had given up for lost.

I did not have paper enough to write all day, and so I had many hours left to think. I thought about the people I loved, and about all the places I had yet to see and the things I had yet to do. I could hear noises from the cellars far below, and I imagined the suffering of the poor souls Beriosov kept there, their cries and moans rising up through the walls. Some nights the sounds of weeping and groaning filled the tower room and seemed to issue forth not from living men held in chains below but from ghosts of the dead. I wondered what death was like. Such thoughts, I knew, were the beginning of madness. Prayer might have filled some empty hours, but I had long ago given up prayer. Poetry can be recited, and, indeed, it is for just such times that we memorize poems, for imprisonment or long journeys or for working in the mines. Yet I found little consolation in Pushkin or Nekrasov. Only Anastasia filled my heart with hope, even the saddest of her poems, for I could hear her voice in them, the clear rhythm of her voice.

I could not sleep and so I lay,
listening to no sound,
the street, snow-powdered,
the garden, frozen ground,
the spruce no longer sighing,
no wind to make it sway.
Yet clouds, thick and lowering,
kept light from dissipating,
kept the world illuminated
and the night seemed bright as day.

Here, then, the mystery of being:
the soul, the god within,
is sometimes sleeping,
cannot be awakened out of season;
when questioned,
does not answer;
when appealed to,
turns away.

You are on your own
in the night, bright and silent,
and alone
with your sorrow.
Keep it close then,

and guard it.
It is all that is given,
the key to some door
you have not yet had to open.

The poems I had loved without knowing why now were like chants, like prayers. But how, I wondered, how did she know how to pray, how to mourn? How did she know about being alone with grief, living as she did in such security, surrounded by so much faithfulness and love? How did she know what she knew? And I myself—how did I know what I knew? What I wrote always seemed to come to me from somewhere other than my own mind, seemed to be told to me, so that I was merely recording what was being whispered in my ear, or what I saw before me when I closed my eyes. It was ever so, even in that tower room.

Every night I tossed the pages into the fire and watched them burn.

And every few days, when the man came to collect my confession—a poor man, merely a servant, his orders quite beyond him—I would beg his pardon and hand him a single sheet of nonsense, a discourse on *The Republic*, a summary of the plot of *The Inspector General*.

And so the days passed, and the nights. The days passed quickly, steel-grey, cloud-filled, more dark than light; the nights seemed to last an eternity. Winter was coming.

All I could do, finally, was wait. One day they would come, either to release me or send me to some other prison or to exile in the east. Or perhaps they would not come at all, no one would come, and I would die in this tower of hunger, thirst, and cold. In the meantime, when all paper was gone, I huddled by the stove, my mind filled with words, and ideas, and images, with which I tried to fashion a different place, a different world.

Marko Volchek

What I wrote always seemed to come
to me from somewhere other than my own mind.

BOOK
THREE

The Amazing Adventures of Blavatskaya & Fyodorov

CHAPTER TEN

INSIDE THE GYPSY CARAVAN

At the hour of the cool autumn sunset two citizens appeared at the Patriarch's Ponds. One of them was a stout, untidy woman, approximately thirty-three years of age, wearing a shapeless black dress under an equally shapeless black cloak and hat. The other was a thin, fair, bespectacled man of around the same age, also dressed in black, holding a cane and a leather case. They sat side by side on a bench under the linden trees, and together gazed at the pool of water.

The first was Elena Petrovna Blavatskaya, journalist, world traveler, and spiritualist medium. The second was Fyodor Fyodorovich Fyodorov, scientist, inventor, and cosmist philosopher. They were waiting for a third. While they waited, Blavatskaya smoked a cigarette, Fyodorov fingered his pipe but did not light it.

"The only two questions of concern to us are these," Fyodorov said at last, as though continuing a conversation that had been in progress. "One: why is there suffering; two, is there life after death."

Blavatskaya blew smoke rings out of her mouth. They floated toward the Patriarch's Pond and then dissipated in the shadowy air. Dusk was rapidly falling.

"Does the Holy Orthodox Church answer these questions for us?" Fyodorov continued. "Yes. It gives us the words of God. Think of it! The words of God. Entrusted to the Church, and by the Church preserved."

Still Blavatskaya said nothing.

"Why then look to the East? To savages in the jungles? To pagans, heathens, foreigners? To imams and yogis and dervishes and—voodoo priests? Worshipping idols! Why one might as well become a Catholic!"

"If you believe the promises of the Orthodox Church, why then do you seek immortality in this world, Fyodor Fyodorovich, and the physical resurrection of the dead?"

"For the happiness of mankind."

"Why not leave that work in the hands of God?"

"God invites us to participate. Evolution is in our hands now. We must be co-creators. It is the destiny of man. Our God-given task."

"Ah," she said. Having finished one cigarette, she immediately put another into her amber cigarette holder and lit it. "Have you ever smoked hashish, Fyodor Fyodorovich?"

"No, Madame. I have not."

"You should," she said.

Minutes of silence ensued. It was Fyodorov who once again was the first to speak.

"How was your stay in Kislovodsk? The mineral springs there are said to be the finest in all the Caucasus."

"It is popular, that is true. Countess Kiselev enjoyed the baths. I myself was more interested in the visitors. I had many notable conversations."

"Speaking of visitors... isn't that Nikolai Vasilevich now?"

A man had emerged from the shadows of the trees, and was walking steadily toward them along the path. He was a broad-shouldered young man dressed in a top hat and overcoat, but as he came closer it was clear to both of them that he was not Barakov. The man tipped his hat to them as he walked by.

"I fear he is not coming," she said. "It is worrying."

"He said he would. This place, this day, this hour."

By then darkness had fallen.

"Do you have it with you?"

Fyodorov pressed the leather case he was holding closer to his chest, but he did not answer. He was squinting at another figure approaching through the smoke. But where had all this smoke come from?

"Is the city on fire?" he asked, too loudly

"No. It is only remembering fire. It is only remembering being burnt to the ground."

Fyodorov began coughing. Apparently they were now entirely surrounded by smoke. Then out of the smoke stepped the man he had been watching. He was dark like a gypsy, and dressed as a peasant with a belted smock over his shirt and pants. He had no hat to tip, but he bowed to the pair on the bench as he passed. He, too, was not Barakov.

"Who are these people?" Fyodorov asked, angrily. "They seem like spirits of the dead."

"The dead don't come to us. Why should they? They live in a state of bliss. No, these are just drifting spirits. Pay no attention to them."

"I am getting thirsty," Fyodorov said. "The air is becoming very warm. Are you sure there's no fire?"

"They are burning down the city," she said. "Not here in Moscow. In Petersburg. A great conflagration. I can feel the heat from it here and smell the smoke. See how it thickens?... Perhaps you are right, and it is not too soon to plan for the perfection of men. Perhaps sending them into space is the best solution. Or undersea. Underwater, under wave, with the fishies of the deep, and the silent swimming Leviathans, and the eight-armed octopuses, the ocean's monkey gods..."

At that very moment, the smoke parted, vertically, like the opening of a theatre curtain, and out sprang four black horses and a coach. As it reached the bench, the coach came to a halt, the coachman lifted his hat, while simultaneously the door of the coach swung open.

"What luck!" Fyodorov said, standing. "Come, Madame. Let us take this carriage and leave this dire place."

"You call it luck?" she said. "We'll see."

He helped her step into the coach, and called out a destination to the driver before taking the seat beside her.

"If he won't come to us, we'll have to go to him."

"And do you know where he is?"

"I know where his friends will be."

"Not quite the same thing," she said. "Nevertheless, doesn't the scripture tell us that where the body is, the birds of prey will gather? Isn't that the correct text, dear Fyodor Fyodorovich? So then we shall go in search of the birds of appetite. I believe it will be a long night."

Meanwhile the horses were trotting along, the coach swayed and bounced on its springs as though it was traveling on a country road, not on city streets, and when they looked out to see where they were, all they saw was darkness.

"It's a black night," Fyodorov said. "What's happened to the street lights?"

In the darkness inside the coach, all that could be seen was the red glow at the tip of Blavatskaya's cigarette; in the darkness outside, there was only darkness in differing degrees, only lighter and deeper shadows.

"Hecate," Blavatskaya said, "is the great goddess of the night, of thresholds, of crossroads, of the underworld. Do you know her?"

"Know her? How could I know her? Pagan gods are merely demonic fantasies, and demonic fantasies do not interest me."

"Oh, I would take care, Master Fyodorov! I would take care, insulting the host while you are riding in his carriage."

Fyodor laughed at the jest. At the same moment the coach hit a bump in the road, took to the air, hit the road again, bounced, turned sideways, spun back around, and at last came to an abrupt and bruising stop. It took them several moments to collect themselves. When they had, Blavatskaya flung open the carriage door and stepped out. Fyodorov, for no very good reason, followed her. He was about to address the coachman and inquire where they were when, without a word to his passengers, the man cracked his whip and the horses drove off, leaving them standing in the dusty road.

Where were they? Not on a busy street in Moscow but in a fairgrounds, by the look of it. There were several large round tents, lit from within so they seemed like golden globes shining in the night, and scattered around them other smaller tents and unhitched wagons. Campfire smoke filled the air, and the odor of roasting meats, and the sound of voices singing gypsy songs, so commonly heard on the streets of the city. Knots of men were squatting around the fires, playing games of chance in the dirt; women were gathered here and there in groups, or were walking singly or in pairs. It might have been the set for an Italian opera or a performance of commedia dell'arte; perhaps a play or opera was about to begin.

"Ah," Blavatskaya said, "here we'll find a reader of cards, or a seer with a crystal ball. If you want to find something that's lost, this is as good a place as any to start."

"Nonsense," Fyodorov said, but he followed along behind her as she strode toward the nearest tent, and went in.

Though a few candles burned inside, everything in the interior was grey, as though the air were filled with smoke or haze. Two old women and three younger ones were seated around a table playing cards. A boy in a tattered jacket was serving them tea; the scent of the tea floated in the hazy, smoky air. The tent was spacious but nearly empty except for a few odd objects, all of them broken and useless: a cracked mirror, a hand cart without a wheel, a large clock without hands, and in the very back, an old man lying on a divan, smoking a water pipe.

One of the card players was chanting as she dealt the cards. "Thirty rubles a month for three rooms in the city. Ten rubles a month for tea. Seven hundred rubles a year for eight rooms. Sixteen hundred a year for twenty-one."

"Arise from your sleep!" yelled the old man in the back.

"Shut up, Danielovich!" said the very old woman. "Or join the *pyaterki.*"

"He's too old for revolution," one of the younger players said with a sneer. "It's Apollon who should be joining Young Russia. Isn't that right, Apya? Spill one drop and I will beat you!"

The boy, who had finished pouring the tea, retreated quickly to the back of the tent.

"Land and Freedom!" the old man shouted.

"Don't listen to him," one of the women at the table said to her partner. "It's your turn. Play!"

But it was hard not to listen. The old man was chanting loudly in his hoarse, cracking voice, a song whose melody was familiar:

The poor man, the lost man, the bum on the street,
the one you step over, or kick with your feet,

"Make him shut up!"

... lives like a king, like a bird of the air,
with nothing to hold him, no nets to ensnare—

In fury, the very old woman picked up her cup and flung it in the old man's direction, but only doused herself, her companions and the cards on the table top with scalding hot tea. Everyone at the table jumped up, screaming and yelling in pain and anger.

"This is the wrong tent," Blavatskaya muttered under her breath, turned on her heel, and made for the tent flap, while from the back of the tent the old man's voice continued singing his plaintive song.

"A close call," Elena Petrovna said once they were back in the open air again. The smoke had cleared a bit; it was easier to breathe.

"Why do you say that?"

"Don't you know who they were, those horrid women? Cruelty,

Complacency, Arrogance, Covetousness, and Indifference. The scourges of our time. Come along. Let's try another."

Off she stomped, Fyodorov trailing along behind her. Meanwhile the opera had begun. All around him, men and women in festive costumes were strolling and singing. It was a *romansy* song, sung in the Roma tongue. But then a man stepped forward from the crowd of singers and when he sang, in a fine tenor, it was a song whose words Fyodorov understood.

Enjoy your life, have no regrets,
Never worry, don't sit and fret.
Leave nothing behind, and pass like a shadow.
We're here today, and gone tomorrow.

"Be careful!" Blavatskaya called to him over her shoulder. "Don't listen to the songs!"

"Why not?"

"Don't be a fool, Fyodorov. There are many kinds of sirens in this world."

Then she stopped in front of another tent, opened the tent flap, and strode inside. He followed sheepishly after.

Here the darkness was also filled with smoke, thick smoke that smelt of rosemary. In a corner, candles had been lit in front of a golden icon, and there a long-bearded priest was bowing and chanting and swinging a censer from which the smoke billowed while behind him stood a number of men dressed in rags and bare-footed women, all of them bowing toward the image.

"Wrong again," Blavatskaya said huskily and backed out of the tent.

"Wait! These are holy people!" Fyodorov cried.

"Then stay here with them," she said. "But you won't find Barakov in there."

With that she walked away, and into a crowd of young ruffians, smoking cheroots and passing around a bottle of yellow vodka. Fyodorov hesitated for a few minutes, drawn to the icons, the incense, the chanting, before turning away to follow his companion.

The boys had made way for Blavatskaya to pass, and, holding his cane up horizontally like a spear, Fyodorov trotted along in her wake, and emerged from the crowd just in time to catch sight of her climbing up a few steps to enter one of the covered wagons.

"Dear Lord!" he said to himself. "She must be mad." Still he followed along behind.

But then he found himself caught up in another crowd gathered around a single performer entertaining his audience by chanting a rhythmic, sing-song rhyme, all the while pointing to them and gesturing, moving his hands and arms and body like a marionette. The children in the crowd were particularly entranced by him since the chant was the sort of rhythmic rhyme children sing when they are bouncing a ball or jumping rope, but the words were nothing like the words of a children's song:

Think you can run, think you can hide,
Think that you're free to enjoy the ride?
Pray to the Lord and don't relax.
You got a monkey on your back.

You want a wife, you need a job,
You know it's a sin to steal and rob.
You want to live to get old and fat,
But you got that monkey on your back.

Can't shake him off, he's holding on tight
Makes you crazy, makes you want to fight.
Makes you drink 'til the world turns black.
You got a monkey on your back.

Now the crowd was stomping its feet to the rhythm and shouting out the words along with the singer. For a terrible moment Fyodorov was afraid he had been caught up in a mob of rowdy anarchists.

You think there's nothing to be done.
You want to keep going and enjoy the fun.
One day the earth will quake and crack,
Then you'll get that monkey off your back.

The singer moved on and, cheering, the crowd followed him. Fyodorov stood still and let them all wash past him like a receding wave, leaving only a single word behind. *Monkey!*

Oh, what had he done? His cane was in his hand… but where was his case? Then the full catastrophe was revealed to him, the full and complete disaster of this ill-conceived journey. He had left his little satchel in the coach, and the coach had driven away with it, and he would never find it again.

And what of Elena Petrovna? Had he lost her, too? He stared around, trembling with anxiety… He was surrounded by gypsy caravans, some dark, some lit from within. He chose the nearest, climbed up the steps, and entered through the door.

It was a small space, crowded with young men and several young women, some sitting at a table, some standing, all of them smoking cigarettes and shouting at each other. One man seemed to be in charge and he was attempting to speak above the cacophony, and pounding on the table as he did.

"Listen! Listen! Please, comrades! Please, stop shouting!" Finally, he picked up a handbell from the table, and rang it loudly. This seemed to do the trick. The yelling stopped, and faces turned to him, some angry, some expectant, some merely bored.

"The series of events that have transpired in the provinces have only proven the truth of the words of our collaborators and comrades, which is to say that, if circumstances are favorable, existing Socialist currents can develop towards a full, coherent and extensive program of federalist Socialism…"

"Socialism be damned!" a deep voice called out. "Death to the Tsar!"

"Political liberty will not come from liberal demands or petitions to the autocracy, it will not come out of the barrel of a gun or from the hands of a few agitators throwing bombs—"

"Though a bomb wouldn't hurt!" another voice shouted.

"—but from the mass movement of free, independent peasants themselves, peasants capable of standing upright—"

"Show me a peasant who can stand upright!"

"More like a peasant to fall down drunk!"

The speaker pounded again on the table for order.

"A revolutionary party by itself never has the strength to overthrow the state. Revolutions are made by the people."

A dark-haired boy pushed back his chair and stood up. "Why are you boring us with this nonsense?" he said angrily. "What we need to do is kill the murderer! Death to the Tsar!"

"Then what? Another murderer will just take his place."

The thick tobacco smoke that filled the small, enclosed space in which so many people were crammed had been irritating Fyodorov's throat. He tried manfully to suppress his cough but just as at the theatre when a tickle in the throat becomes impossible to suppress, and the more one tries, the more impossible it becomes, so too here, at this meeting of bomb-throwers and regicides, Fyodorov found himself choking back his cough until it burst forth in a torrent of hacking sound. In a single movement, the group of madmen turned as one and stared darkly at Blavatskaya and Fyodorov.

"Has Third Division of His Imperial Highness's Chancellory dropped in on us?" asked the young man with the handbell. "Is this a social call? Perhaps you've come for tea?"

"So sorry," Blavatskaya said in her deep, throaty voice. "I see this is a meeting of a secret society. We are looking for a fortune teller."

"You don't need a fortune teller," someone yelled out. "I can tell you your days are numbered."

There was some scattered tittering at this clever remark.

"And you don't need a weatherman to know which way the wind blows," Blavatskaya said, prophetically. "Still, is there a fortune teller?"

"Sophia Palaeologos," one of the young women said. "Two wagons down."

Blavatskaya turned back to the steps.

"Long live the Tsar!" Fyodor Fyodorovich Fyodorov shouted and shook his stick at them. "He is God on earth, you fools!"

Then he too left the wagon, a burst of angry catcalls and curses following him out.

"You are very young to hold such old-fashioned views," Blavatskaya said to him. "How come you by them?"

"How come I by them? Why, they were taught to me as a child. Elena Petrovna, I must speak to you. Urgently."

"Yes, yes. But as for your beliefs, it amazes me that you believe in them still. The Orthodox Church. The Tsar. I suppose you believe in the holy soil of Russian, too, and that in the heart of the average peasant resides the genius of the people."

"And you? Do you believe in nothing?"

"I believe in many things. Now let's see if I can believe in our card reader, Madam Sophia of the family Palaeologos. Were they not once

Emperors of Byzantium? Were they not once themselves gods on earth? Let us see how the gods have declined in our age."

They walked a few paces to the next wagon. A man was sitting there on the steps playing a small accordion, and singing:

There's nothing to do, the world can't be fixed,
You know your fate can't be different from this.
Just live in joy, have no regret,
Never worry, don't sit and fret.
Leave nothing behind, and pass like a shadow.
We're here today, and gone tomorrow.

"It all sounds quite promising to me," Blavatskaya said cheerfully as she put her foot on the first step, nudging the musician off as she did.

"But, Elena Petrovna," he said, following her up the steps. "It's my satchel, you see. I'm afraid I've lost it. It's a disaster. I left it in the coach, and—"

He stumbled into the wagon, another dim, enclosed space, not smoke filled, thank goodness (for he was still coughing and needed desperately to drink something to soothe his throat), but oddly lit, its several lamps giving off an eerie, ethereal light by which one could see that the walls were hung with tapestries, the table covered with a richly woven cloth and the floor with thick carpets of Turkish design, and that sitting at the table was a gypsy woman of indeterminate age, her head covered with a scarf, gold earrings dangling from her ears, her large, lustrous eyes darkened by kohl, her bodice and skirt glittering with golden coins. It was such a perfectly typical scene—as a painting it would be called "Inside the Gypsy Caravan"—that he almost did not believe his eyes.

"Now this is more like it!" Blavatskaya said, and without further ado, pulled out a chair at the table and sat down.

"You wish your fortune told?" Sofia Palaeologos asked in an oddly accented, and Fyodorov thought, highly ironic voice.

"Not at all. I know my own destiny very well."

Sofia Palaeologos took Blavatskaya's hand and glanced at the palm for a moment. "Do you indeed? Very well. Then why have you come?"

Fyodorov could not hold his tongue any longer. "You would think," he said gruffly, "a real fortune teller would know the answer to that question."

"Ah," Sofia Palaeologos said softly. "You travel with a skeptic, Madame Blavatskaya. How amusing!"

Blavatskaya shrugged. "My companion is thirsty. Have you something for him to drink?"

A few minutes later, Fyodorov, no longer so skeptical, was reclining comfortably on a low divan, sipping a glass of kvass, or something rather like it. It was cool and fruity, and, he had to admit, really quite delicious. It certainly soothed his throat, and seemed also to concentrate his mind. He lay back in delicious comfort, and stared up at the ceiling. It was draped with cloth hung in such a way as to give one the impression of being in a pavilion, or, he thought, even a vehicle of some kind, a kind of bubble or ship, a sort of spaceship, perhaps, in which one could fly, one could soar upwards into the sky... into the very heavens... and hear the music of the spheres.

His body was feeling heavy and lethargic, but his mind was alight with ideas, so many, in such swift order, he could not keep up with them. Why, for example, did Blavatskaya laugh at him for desiring a new world? Why not desire? The world as we know it is itself impossible, and irrational. Ergo, if the world as you find it disappoints, why not conceive of the existence of a better one? And what a man can conceive in his mind, he can build... He could see it even now... right in front of him... as though he had stepped into the other world, already there, created by perfect beings, perfect men, deathless and content, from whence they gazed down on Earth, a great circling wheel, and pitied her... And as he himself gazed, he saw more wheels, wheels within wheels within wheels, from the most enormous to the most minute, a great wheeling entity, the Cosmos, not unlike a great living machine, the most magnificent invention of the Great Inventor...

All at once, a wheel split off from the machine, and, in a swift descent, came flying down on him, a wheel with spokes, a carriage wheel. The wheel bounced onto the ground, rolled along the road, attached itself to a carriage; the carriage, racing ahead of him, struck a child playing on the side of the road. A crowd of angry men and women gathered around the coach, seized hold of the coachman, threw him onto the ground, began stomping on him, driving his face into the mud. Other men took clubs to the horses; the animals screamed in agony and terror. *Stop!* he cried, or tried to cry, but no sound came out of his mouth.

Now he was sitting at a table in a smoky room filled with men shouting and drinking. He glanced across the table. A man he recognized was sitting there, a woman on his lap, a pen in his hand, a notebook on the table in front of him. *What do you think of my story, Fyodorov? Every word of it is true. You've seen it all yourself—the dead child, the angry crowd, man and horses, beaten to death. Yes, it's good to pity the Earth, Fyodorov, but better to escape her. Such a shit hole of a planet, when you really think about it.*

I know you! he thought. *Nikolai!*

It was the last thought he had before he fell into a deep and comforting sleep.

♣

Madame Sofia of the family Palaeologos gazed across the table at Elena Petrovna Blavatskaya. On the table between them stood a large globe of crystal glass, precious and very old.

"Look into it and you will see your future. The journeys you will take. The mountains you will climb. You will see your fame spread across the earth. It will never die."

"Why look to see what I already know? I told you my destiny is written. I want to learn something new."

Madame Sofia covered the globe.

"A reading then?"

"I have a specific question."

"Very well. The Ruling Card?"

"The Fool."

Madame Sophia raised an eyebrow, plucked the Fool from the deck, and placed it in the center of the table.

"The vagabond with his bindle and stick, his little dog at his feet. Folly, extravagance, intoxication. Very well. Keep your question in the forefront of your mind, Elena Petrovna."

They shuffled the cards, three times each. As they shuffled, the lamplight shifted subtly in color, from golden, to amber, to green… until all color retreated entirely and only the table top was lit with a greenish glow. Blavatskaya cut the cards three times.

The first card to appear was the Eight of Swords. "Bad news. Crisis, conflict, chagrin. This is the energy that covers the enterprise, that stimulates all activity." Sophia glanced up from the table, realized no more needed to be said about this card, and continued. "What impedes you in your enterprise..." she turned over the second card, the Two of Pentacles, "... is a lighthearted young man. He has written something troublesome to you. He travels by sea."

The third card was Justice; the fourth was the Knight of Swords. "I see you expect to be vindicated and that you have at your disposal not only personal skill and bravery, but the power of great enmity, warlike energy, and wrath. This young man must take care against you."

"This is all known," Blavatskaya said. "Please answer the question!"

More cards were laid upon the table. Blavatskaya frowned at them as one by one they told her what she already knew. The last card, however, was intriguing: the Magician, reversed.

"Let us try the question once again," she said, picking up that final card. "With this."

"Reversed? He is the black magician, the shaman, the necromancer. A card of madness."

"Let us see."

Once again they shuffled the cards. Once again, Blavatskaya cut them three times.

"I request a specific answer," Blavatskaya said.

"The cards have a will of their own. Let us listen to what they say and welcome their advice."

The first card to appear was the King of Swords.

"Judgement. A force to be obeyed. Or a powerful male figure. An officer of the law. Someone in authority. A servant of the autocracy, perhaps." She turned over the second card. The Queen of Cups. "Ah! What opposes the male energy. The creative energy of dreams and visions. A woman, devoted and loving. An artist. These two opposing energies, they are a knot. Let us see if we can untangle them... "

"Not entangled," Blavatskaya said. "They are his parents, the parents of the mad magician. All is well. Go on."

Sophia turned over several more cards, cards of oppression, disguise, adversity, calamity, flight. "We are getting there," Blavatskaya muttered. "Go on!"

"The cards act in their own good time," Sofia said. "Let us be patient."

The next card was The High Priestess.

"Bah!" Blavatskaya cried out. "I don't need the cards to tell me I am involved or that there is a mystery behind this!" She was angry, and nearly broke the reading by getting to her feet.

"Stay!" ordered Madame Sofia. "The High Priestess signifies more than mystery or your own presence, Elena Petrovna. The feminine energy here is very strong. Can't you feel it?"

She turned over the sixth card. "Holy Isis!" she cried out.

It was the Queen of Pentacles.

"He is surrounded by women, this mad magician about whom you inquire. He is protected by women, and loved by them, sometimes for good, sometimes for ill. And see here where the energy is flowing, away from concealment and toward the Queen of Pentacles."

"Yes. That's all well and good. The energy is flowing away from concealment. Soon he will be discovered and the mystery will be unveiled. Let us get on with it then!"

"The cards sometimes answer not the question you asked, but the question you should have asked."

"I would prefer them to answer the question I did ask. I need a location."

"The cards are not always so specific."

"Perhaps this time they will be. Proceed."

The next few cards Sofia turned over quickly, and indeed a clear and specific message was there. Seeing them on the table, Elena Blavatskaya only laughed. Cards of trickery, loss, betrayal, deception, these images might as easily refer to the cards themselves as to the world in which Nikolai Barakov lived.

At last Madame Sofia revealed the final card, the card of divination.

"Ah," Sofia sighed. "Dame Fortuna! The great wheel. The wheel of life and death."

Blavatskaya stared down at the card, the Wheel of Fortune, and guffawed. It was not a pleasant sound. "Your deck has become whimsical, Madame Sofia."

Sofia Palaeologos took a pipe out of her bodice, filled it with leaves from a leather purse on her belt, and lit it. A sweet smoke soon drifted in the air. She passed the pipe across the table to Elena Petrovna.

"Whimsical? Not at all. Here," she nodded to the table, "is a great Power at work. Around this question you asked, look at the powers that have gathered, the High Priestess, even Dame Fortune herself, Lady of

Permutations, the card of change. Whoever it is you seek has a powerful destiny, many lives will be touched by his and many hopes will gather around him. The cards say all this. Why then do you say they are being whimsical, Elena Petrovna?"

"You don't see the humor? But see how very clever they are, how very amusing. My dear lady, I asked a question, and they answered me. I asked for a specific location, and they gave it to me. Evidently I will find the man I'm seeking at a gaming table. Come, Fyodorov. Wake up!"

She stood to go, but she found herself sinking instead. Gravity was pulling on her, the comfort of the divan was luring her, a dream was already taking her into its arms. The smoke had been so sweet... and before her she seemed to see already the cold, deserted wastes, the high, stone towers of the snowy Himalayas rising above her, the narrow track leading upward, the brightly painted stupas, the prayer flags flapping in the wind, the monks in red robes...

"Nonsense!" she said, shaking herself. She grabbed Fyodorov by the collar and pulled him to his feet. "Come along, Fyodorov! We have no time for these sirens! Take hold of yourself, man! The game's afoot!"

Out of the gypsy wagon they fled, Blavatskaya half-dragging Fyodorov, half-carrying him in her arms. This time it was a britzka, not a coach, that drove up beside them, a carriage long enough for a man to lie down in, which Fyodorov did directly, and went back to sleep.

"We're in a hurry," she told the driver.

"Isn't everyone," he replied. "And where are you in such a hurry to get to?"

The britzka was already moving, the driver already encouraging his horses with a light touch of his whip.

"I expect you already know," she said. "I need to find a game of roulette."

CHAPTER ELEVEN

In the Gambling Den and the Home of the Poets

They arrived in the city in the early dawn, only a red streak lighting up the eastern sky, and were deposited by their driver at the end of one of those malodorous and loathsome alleys where merely breathing the air puts you at risk of contagion, and if breathing doesn't kill you, a knife in the back will. Fyodor Fyodorovich was more than a little reluctant to enter, but Blavatskaya took his arm rather forcibly, and strode forward. She had a good sense of direction, and had taken control of his cane, which she was not adverse to using, and so between the cane and her own sturdy physique, she managed to steer them around bodies, some leaning, some staggering, some lying on the ground, and past clumps of men stooped over dice games or over women plying their ancient trade, and onward to the far end of the alley where a small sign over a stone gateway pointed in and down. They crossed a dirty courtyard cluttered with rubbish and broken furniture; they entered a ruined house and followed a pointer down a dark and crumbling staircase.

"This can't be the place," Fyodorov mumbled. "No gambling man with money in his pockets would dare come to such a hole."

"Down such devious paths," Blavatskaya said as though she were quoting something. "Perhaps danger is part of its charm."

"Charm! My dear lady..."

The staircase, such as it was, brought them to a dark passage lit only by ornate bronze candelabra set on gilded table-tops. They followed the passage to the end where they found a circular staircase, winding upwards like a snake. Sitting on the first step was a hall porter dressed in livery who looked them over, then rose in silence and let them pass. Up the steps they went, Fyodorov leading the way, higher and higher, until he began feeling quite dizzy. And just as he felt he could go no farther, he reached the top of the stairs and emerged into a dazzlingly bright room filled with people and noise, the rather inhuman sounds of men gambling away their lives and fortunes, that is to say, the sounds of laughter and tinkling glasses and the call of numbers and the occasional cry of pain or glee.

"What is this place?" he asked, turning to Blavatskaya, offering his hand to help her up the last few steps. They stood there at the edge of the staircase, looking around them, and Blavatskaya muttered a line of Pushkin's under her breath: "*No fancy could imagine it; around a table monsters sit.*"

And indeed some of the guests were wearing monstrous masks as though they had come directly from a carnival ball, or wished to conceal their identities, or had, indeed, taken on the physical form of their inner beings: a dog's head, a fox's, a cockerel's, a bearded goat, a donkey, a skull. Around the green baize gaming tables and the roulette wheels, they all sat or stood, fascinated, mesmerized, watching their destiny turning as the cards were dealt or the wheel turned, all of them drinking, laughing, shouting...

Fyodorov stared around in disbelief. "Are we in hell?"

"Not at all. Though we are in the underworld. If I'm not mistaken, this is the Dancing Serpent, Suvorov's gambling club. We came in the exit, you see. The escape route, in case the police should come. Let's see if there's anyone here we know."

"I assure you there's no one here I know."

"Place your bets!" a voice cried out above the cacophony.

"Let's visit the tables, and see," she said, and strode into the room.

"What game is that?" Fyodorov asked, peering at one of the tables.

"Faro, I imagine. A deadly game of chance. Want to play?"

"I might try. How does it work?"

They stood at the table, across from the banker, and watched for a little while as men lost hundreds of rubles at the turn of a card.

"Put your money down!" the banker cried, and the punters did, and as easily as they placed it down on a card, it disappeared.

"It's utterly simple, as most evil in this world is," Blavatskaya said. "They've laid out a suit of cards. Spades, not that the suit matters. You're betting on a number or one of picture cards, one of the thirteen. You place your bet on the card you want. Then the dealer draws two cards. The first is the bank's card, and if anyone has placed a bet on that card, it's forfeited to the bank. The second card is the player's card, and if the player's card comes up, he wins and the bank pays him the amount of his bet."

"Well, perhaps I'll try it. Let's see if I have a few kopecks in my pocket."

He did and moved to the table to lay them down on a card.

"Minimum bet at the table, one hundred, Your Excellency," the dealer said.

"One hundred—what?"

Blavatskaya, at his elbow, gently pulled him away.

"Did he mean roubles, Elena Petrovna?"

"Shocking, isn't it?"

"One hundred roubles! Are these people mad?"

"Look there!" she said. "It's Nekrasov!"

She gestured across the room to another table around which a crowd of excited people had gathered. A thin, well-dressed man with a high forehead and a small mustache was sitting at the table, playing vigorously.

"Our greatest living poet," Blavatskaya sighed. "It's a pity."

"It looks like he's winning."

"He won't win," she said. "He's a gambler. If he wins, he'll keep playing and so he will end up losing everything. Let's see if we can intervene before disaster strikes."

But it was already too late. The crowd was dispersing, disappointed, or perhaps secretly glad, for no one really likes a winner unless he's likely to treat the house to rounds of champagne. Nekrasov stood, as melancholic as a gambler can be when the Lady of Permutations changes her mind once again and looks away. He had been handsome in his youth, charismatic, brilliant, but even then he was subject to bouts of melancholy and misanthropy. Russia was no place for sensitive men. He was not in good health and tonight looked rather more sickly than usual. He was also, quite naturally, in a fiendishly bad humor.

"It might be best to leave him be for a few minutes," Fyodorov said, as Blavatskaya began striding toward the poor man. "He is not going to be—"

"Nikolai Alexeyevich," she said, extending her hand, "what a joy to see you!"

"Madame Blavatskaya," he replied, taking her hand and kissing it.

"The joy is all mine." But he did not seem in the least joyful, except perhaps when he caught sight of a servant carrying a tray of champagne glasses in his direction. "This seems an unlikely place for you to be."

"*The year doesn't matter, the land's not important, but seven good peasants once met on the high road...*"

Nekrasov bowed low. She had quoted the first lines of his poem *Who Can Be Happy and Free in Russia*?

"Unlikely as it is," she said, "here I am. And this is my companion Professor Fyodor Fyodorovich Fyodorov." The men bowed to each other. "Like your seven peasants, we are here on a quest, dear Nikolai Alexeyevich. We are looking for Nikolai Barakov."

"Anastasia's son? This is indeed an unlikely place, then."

The servant approached offering champagne; all three of them took a glass.

"Or, alternatively, anyone who might know where he is."

"Or might have some knowledge of his book," Fyodorov added, and immediately regretted it since both Nekrasov and Blavatskaya looked at him sternly and Elena Petrovna even mumbled some insults to his intelligence under her breath.

"This is hardly the place," Nekrasov said. "Come with me."

"First I wish to watch a game of roulette," Blavatskaya said. "Then we will come with you."

In a serpentine fashion, passing many crowded gaming tables, they wound their way to the far side of the room and the roulette wheel. Blavatskaya paused there and studied the faces of the players, all of them seemingly mesmerized by the spinning wheel, fascinated by the sound of the ball skipping across it, all of them intent on winning... what? Didn't they know what the wheel meant? Didn't they know—or perhaps on the deepest level of consciousness they did—that every life was tied to the wheel of birth, death, and transmigration, that the wheel was the Great Breath of karma, change, and return?

"Do you see him, Fyodorov?"

"No. He is not here."

"Look carefully at every face!"

"He is my friend, Madame. I would know him at once. He is not in this room."

"This way!" Nekrasov said, urging them on, and, disgruntled as they were—Fyodorov at Elena Petrovna's petulance and Elena Petrovna at Madame Sophia's cards—they followed him through the billiard room where more intense play was in progress, into a drawing room where ladies were sitting at small tables playing whist, and through that room into a smaller one, a kind of alcove, where a servant, who had been sitting half-asleep in one of the chairs, was soon rousted, and sent off to fetch a bottle of vodka. "And ask Madame Panaeva to join us, there's a good man," Nekrasov said, passing the servant a tip. Then the three of them sat down in the quiet room, so quiet after so much noise that it was uncanny somehow. No one of them seemed inclined to be the first to speak.

"Barakov," Nekrasov said at last.

"Yes," Blavatskaya said. "In short, he was supposed to meet us, he did not come, so we are in search of him. I was told he might be here. Clearly, he is not."

"That is very short indeed. What's this about his book?"

"You know about it?"

"Of course I know about it. Everyone *knows* about it. No one has *seen* it, however. And I would dearly love to get my hands on it."

"From what I hear, I doubt you could use it to fill your pages."

"Madame, I am not entirely a philistine."

"My dear Nikolai Alexeyevich, I hope I am not suggesting that. You are the greatest poet living in Russia today, and the most beloved."

Nekrasov rose to his feet, bowed deeply, and sat down again.

"But if not to print it," Blavatskaya continued, "why would you—"

"To read it, of course. One does read... And to save it from destruction. I can get it to London."

"Excuse me," Fyodorov said, breaking his silence, "but if you haven't read it, how do you know it is worth so much trouble on your part?"

"I know Barakov. Not well, but I've played billiards with him. I've heard him talk. I've heard his stories. If he wrote down even a fraction of them, his book would be a work of genius. He is better than Gogol, who only repeats what he hears. He is better than Turgenev, who is now utterly out of date, and better than Dostoevsky, who has become a religious maniac, and better than Goncharov, who is long-winded, and Tolstoy... Count Tolstoy, that is... who only cares about the psychic processes and the purity of moral feeling... Well, who knows? Who knows, damn it!" His exclamation, so angry and forceful, occurred at the same moment the servant entered the room with his tray, and so startled the poor man that he very nearly dropped it.

"Give it here," Fyodorov said, and took the tray with its trembling glasses and its careening bottle, and set the whole thing on a small table.

"Fyodor Fyodorovich knows Barakov quite well," Elena Petrovna said. "They lived together in the same house."

"Really? What is your sense, then, of his literary talent?"

"I... I must agree with you. But I was wondering... You see, I have read some of his work. An earlier work. I even had it in my possession... Oh, God! How could I have lost it?"

"What in God's name is he talking about?" Nekrasov cried, staring not at Fyodorov but at Blavatskaya. "Is the man mad?"

"Of course he is," she said. "This is Fyodorov, the cosmist, the man who wants to send us all to the moon. In the name of Isis, of course he's mad!"

"No madder than you, Madame," Fyodorov said, straightening his back. "For you believe that men can become gods."

"I believe men are already gods," she said, huffily. "Man is an animal plus a living God within his physical shell. What is human mind in its higher aspect if not a portion of the essence of a higher Being? You'd have to be mad not to see that!"

"You believe man has already evolved—"

"Your idea of evolution as linear progression is incorrect. The cosmos is a wheel, my friend! A circle not a line. We return again and again. I myself am an ancient soul. And as for the evolution of matter—"

She might have continued pontificating in this manner for many hours, much to the consternation of the poet, had not the door opened again and a woman entered. But what a woman! Avdotia Yakovna Panaeva, acknowledged as the most beautiful woman of her generation, was even now in middle age a dazzling beauty. Her beauty lay not only in the perfection of her features and figure, the perfection of shape and line, the curve of her neck, the gleaming black of her hair and eyes, her pale skin and red lips; it lay also in the spirit that animated those perfect features, that gave radiance to her smile and richness to her voice, nobility to her carriage and grace to her movements. No one who saw her could resist her charms; yet she wore her beauty lightly without vanity or pride for although she could not fail to be aware of the impression she made, her beauty meant little to her, she knew how worthless it was in the face of grief, that it had no power and brought no consolation. Suffering had made her sensitive to the feelings of others, and she was skilled at setting men at ease in her presence, for acting was in her blood. In fact, it was to escape from her theatrical family and a career on the stage that she had married Ivan Panaev at a young age. But all her children by Panaev had died in infancy, and their marriage was already merely a formal arrangement when Nekrasov met her and fell in love with her. For well over a decade now they had been lovers; their relationship was well-known and accepted by everyone, including Panaev. All three lived together in the same house, and jointly owned and edited their journal *The Contemporary*. Panaeva was herself a writer whose novels were extremely popular. Women especially admired her not only for her style of writing but for her style of living. Dressed now in a gown of midnight blue silk, she stood poised in the doorway, taking in the scene before her—the short, plump woman in black, gravely expostulating; the thin, heron-like man, seated across from her, seemingly in a state of mental distress; her lover, glass of vodka in hand, looking both angrily perplexed and faintly amused.

The men stood and bowed to her; Blavatskaya, in the very midst of her exposition, tried not to scowl.

"My dear," Nekrasov said, after making the introductions, and gesturing her into a chair. "We are having a most interesting conversation."

"So I gather. I heard only a fraction of a sentence, but it seemed of great interest."

She smiled, insincerely, Blavatskaya thought.

"Mostly we are discussing Nikolai Barakov," Nekrasov added quickly. "And Fyodorov here was saying—"

"What he was saying is not entirely to the point," Blavatskaya interrupted. "We are trying to find Barakov, that is the point. It is essential that we find him."

"Well, we don't know where he is, do we, Nekrasov?" she said, smiling at him. "We know nothing, like all Russians. We can be of no help at all."

"You think we are spies, don't you? Government snitches. Dirty tattle-tales. Madame, I assure you—"

"Please be calm, Elena Petrovna," Panaeva said gently. "I knew your dear mother, Elena Gan, who left us far too soon, may her soul rest in peace. I would never take you for anything but a noble woman of high moral character. But, in fact, we can be of no help. I have not seen Anastasia's son in—oh, three years? I think it was three years ago, or maybe four. It was in Odessa, after the war. Oh, don't you remember, Nikolai? We went for your health, for the spas and the beaches and the long avenues, the warm golden sunlight! And there was Kolya Barakov… of all people… running up the Primorsky Stairs."

"I have seen him since then," Nekrasov said. "But still it's been well over a year. Is Anastasia worried about him? I can see why she might be, in this political climate."

"And you haven't a copy of his book, I suppose," Fyodorov said, addressing Madame Panaeva.

"Of course she doesn't!" Nekrasov said angrily. "And neither do you, or if you did, you lost it."

"I told you. What I lost was not his novel. It was something quite different. A different manuscript."

"What sort of manuscript?"

"A play."

"A play! What is the title?"

"*Wide and Crooked.*"

"Ah," Nekrasov said, smiling after a moment's pause. "I see. Wide and crooked, as opposed to straight and narrow. You see, a clever man, Barakov! I would have been glad to have it. Whatever did you do with it?"

"I left it in a coach."

"It burnt in a fire," Blavatskaya said.

"No, it didn't."

"Yes, it did. Remember the smoke?"

"Manuscripts don't burn," Nekrasov said.

This gnomic statement left them all somewhat perplexed. To cover the awkward silence that followed it, Fyodorov poured them all another glass of vodka. Panaeva sipped from her glass of champagne.

Suddenly Fyodorov burst into tears. "Running up the stairs! I remember him, too, how he ran up and down the stairs! Two at a time! Such a noise he always made! Yes, I remember him!"

Everyone sought to comfort the poor man. Panaeva took him by the hand. Nekrasov patted his arm. Blavatskaya lumbered out into the salon, collared a servant, and ordered him to bring in a cool towel. None of this did any good. Fyodorov wept like a child. He sobbed, he cried out, his chest heaved, his nose ran, tears flooded his eyes and tumbled down his cheeks, and all the while he tried to speak but the words were suffocated by his sobs.

"What the devil is the man trying to say?" Blavatskaya asked, accepting another cigarette from Nekrasov and a light as well.

Panaeva, who was kneeling beside his chair, put her ear close to Fyodorov's mouth.

"I am afraid he's becoming apoplectic," she said. "He is saying words but not in any language I know."

"Call a doctor, idiot!" Nekrasov cried to the servant, who rushed off.

"The poor man," Panaeva said. "He is overcome with guilt. And for what? People leave manuscripts in coaches all the time. They usually find their way back."

"Not from this coach," Blavatskaya said.

♣

They called for a coach themselves and soon had Fyodorov settled in a bed in the Panaev-Nekrasov flat where he immediately fell into a deep sleep, aided, naturally, by a few drops of laudanum prescribed by the doctor, who was happy to leave the small bottle behind for the rest of the household to use as needed.

"Twice in one day. He'll soon become addicted," Blavatskaya said. "He will be able to write another *Les paradis artificiels. Confessions of a Russian Opium Eater.*"

The three writers were sitting in Panaev's study which doubled as the office of *The Contemporary* and so smelt of stale tobacco smoke and alcohol, and was crowded with wooden chairs and piles of books and disordered papers, while the floor and the desk were littered with half-read, half-edited manuscripts. They had gathered in a corner where there was a comfortable divan with pillows and an even more comfortable sofa, and were stretched out in various attitudes of repose, drinking brandy. Panaeva had changed into a silk dressing gown, and Nekrasov into a smoking jacket. Blavatskaya had removed her hat and cloak and shoes and was wearing borrowed Persian slippers and smoking her pipe.

It was altogether a peaceful domestic scene.

"Now that you have brought up the subject," Panaeva said with a sigh, "I wonder where Barakov has gone off to. You've looked in the obvious places, I'm sure."

"What would those be, my dear?" Nekrasov asked. "The pot houses? The beer halls? The wine cellars? The brothels? Ah, forgive me, Elena Petrovna, for mentioning—"

"I am aware of the existence of such places. Where else would you look, Nikolai Alexeyevich? Besides saloons and bordellos? I gather you think he is a true artist, and therefore a dissolute sensualist and debauched degenerate. Perhaps. But if he has in fact written this book, he is a courageous sensualist and degenerate, and so I admire him. I believe cowardice is the most terrible of vices, and courage, in and of itself, wipes away a multitude of sins."

"Well put, dear lady. Of course, Barakov is just that much younger than Avdotya and myself, ten years or so, I would say, and for that generation, who grew up under the present autocracy, who never knew in their entire lives a single day of freedom, who are always and forever tormented by the censors and the secret police, who are hounded day and night by spies, who are never at liberty to think what they want, to say what they want, who have to be suspicious of everyone, and doubt their closest friends, who are subject to the worst education, the most fearful militarism, the paralysis of economic growth, the lack of any imaginable future, forbidden to travel, to study abroad, then even to read foreign newspapers and books, all of this crowned by a full-scale war and total and complete defeat and international humiliation... for that generation—indeed, it is your generation as well, is it not?—truly, it is a miracle if any one of them accomplishes anything in this foul country other than drinking himself to death or drowning himself in the sea."

That tirade completed, Nekrasov rose and began pacing up and down the room.

"Of course they drink and gamble. Of course they have sex as often as they can with whomever they can. Of course they take absurd risks, join secret societies, publish subversive manifestos, practically dare the Third Section to come after them. Of course they do. They can do nothing else. Nothing. Wherever they turn, they find barriers and blockades.

Try being imaginative in this country, try being creative, inventive, try making something new, a new device, a new tool, try reorganizing your estate, try bringing in a new agricultural machine, try building up a business, even if it is only publishing a journal of poems and stories. Poems! By God, not even a poem can get printed in this country without a damned censor ripping the soul out of it... "

"Darling, please sit down," Panaeva said. "You will only make yourself sick."

"Make myself sick, Dunya? I am already sick!"

But he sat down.

"And, you know, my dear, you and I were also raised under Nicholas's dark cloud. It began with massacre. We knew even then, though we were children."

"Only the peasants know how to live," Nekrasov said, and quoting his own poem, he added: "*Shouting and singing, swearing and fighting, falling and kissing.*"

"*When things are in this state, a man who is sober feels nearly as awkward as one who is naked,*" Panaeva finished the line, and then laughed.

"*The quiet night is falling,*" Blavatskaya said softly. "*The moon is in heaven, and God is commencing to write his great letter of gold on blue velvet, mysterious message which neither the wise man nor the foolish can read.* You also are a man of courage, Nikolai Alexeyevich, for your poem exists, despite the censor, and unlike God's message in the heavens, we can read it and understand it. But I agree with you about Barakov's generation, which, as you say, is also my own. We are the same age, he and I, born only two years apart."

"I have great hopes for his novel, Elena Petrovna, and for that very reason, that it might speak for your generation, and tell the truth of what life really is in these times. And told in a new way, breaking the old mold. We need an altogether new narrative form, the old fashioned novel is dead, it can't speak to us in these times. No, I am looking for something innovative and personal, angry and ironic, and yet a comedy, a dark comedy, if you will, but it must make us laugh because laughter alone has the power to diminish a tyrant's power. I expect *Monkey* is such a book, from the little I've heard of it... and the little I know of Barakov's life. A life of adventure, from what I hear."

"Of desperate acts and narrow escapes," Panaeva said, a smile in her voice. "The life of the hero of a novel rather than the writer of one."

"The life of a fool, then," a voice said, and the study door swung open and Ivan Panaev stuck his head in. Like Nekrasov he was clean-shaven except for a small mustache and his hair hung in curls over his forehead. He was dressed in formal attire; he had been at a ball at the home of Countess Elizaveta Sailas de Tournemire.

"When she's giving a ball she's Countess de Tournemire," Panaev laughed, lighting a cigar. "When she's behind her desk editing her journal, she's Yevgenia Tur. I am not sure which of these ladies' company I enjoy less."

"Who was there whose company you did enjoy, my dear?" Avdotia Yakovna asked with a smile.

"No one at all, my dear, since you were not present."

It seemed to Blavatskaya that it was now time for her to leave the *menage á trois* to gossip about their literary friends, and so, after introductions were made, for she and Panaev had not met before, she made her apologies and retired for the night. There was no question of her leaving the house; it was already after four in the morning. A servant led her up the stairs to a bedroom.

♣

No sooner had a lamp had been lit, a glass of water poured, and the servant dismissed than she knew where she was. Someone had attempted to disguise the room by adding an armchair and hanging Chinese silk on the walls and placing porcelain shepherds and shepherdesses on the dressing table, but she knew the moment she entered that this had once been the nursery and that it was here that Avdotia Yakovna's infants had died.

It is the case, as she well knew, that the air around us is filled with spirits of various kinds and determinations: everything that exists is animated by Universal Soul. Some of these spirits, elemental spirits without immortal souls, inhabit certain places, drawn by strong emotion, and of these spirits some are vicious, some fractious, some merely curious and impish, tricksters who enjoy tormenting those who pay excessive attention to them. There are other spirits as well that dwell here, or are sent as messengers, but one kind of spirit never comes to our sphere, the spirits of the dead, beloved and longed for as they may be, for once they ascend we can only see them again in dreams.

Still there was some presence in this room. She felt it, like a texture in the air.

The lamp light did not illuminate the entire space; deep shadows formed in the corners like rain clouds over mountaintops. The air tingled, vibrated, as though somewhere in that enclosed space a violin string had been plucked. She stood quite still, and listened. Sound was gathering around her like an invisible mantle. She shook the sound away. *I am thirsty,* she said aloud. *I am going to drink some water. I am going to take off my dress and lie down on the bed and sleep. Do not disturb me!*

In reply, the room… blinked.

Nonsense, she thought, and picked up the glass of water the maid had poured for her from the pitcher. These sturdy objects were admirable: pitchers, glasses, lamps. They were anchors to this plane of reality. They rooted one in time and space. And as she thought this, at that very second, there was the sound of something cracking, and the glass she was holding broke in her hand.

And there she stood, holding a cracked glass. The part between her fingers was still solid, but all around her hand, which had not been cut, were sharp, pointed shards. Pieces of glass both large and small had fallen onto the table. Tiny, shimmering slivers clung to her fingers but had done her no harm. Cool water ran in tiny rills down her palm to her wrist and wet the sleeve of her dress.

Slowly she put the glass down again.

All right then. I am very tired, but I will listen. Do you have a message for me?

To this question there was an immediate response.

A great wave of grief came at her from a shadow in the room. It came, it roared, it overpowered her, it forced her into a chair, it held her down so she would hear it, the roaring of it, the rage of it, its uselessness, and impotence, and powerlessness… a child's impotence, a child's helplessness, a child's grief. She could almost see them, infant spirits, flittering in the shadows.

There is Bliss waiting for you. Why do you linger here?

It seemed then that the wave ebbed somewhat, the anger ebbed, there was a quietness in the air. A pause. The inhale of the Great Breath. Soon enough the exhale came, the Great Breath exhaling its elements: the lesser elemental spirits in the room dashed themselves helplessly against necessity and a higher wisdom while, with the rushing sound of raging water and lights flickering furiously on and off, the house itself rocked as though the very earth were shifting beneath it.

Spirits, speak! What do you want?

We want our mother!

Mothermothermothermothermother Their cries, echoing, spiraling, resonating, beat into her, beat within her with her own heartbeat. **Mothermothermother** The sound of it, the power of it, never had she experienced such fury, such fierce, senseless, raging, helpless grief, as though the world, the earth itself, were cracking open and all the sorrow of a million generations of lost, abandoned, heartbroken children were pouring out. She could not withstand it, she could not control it, it was a great wave, coming at her with a gale force behind it, stirred by unimaginable winds, fed by cataclysmic storms, against which no power of her own could contest...

But, Elena Petrovna, you are the storm.

The screeching, pounding, wailing spilled over her like water spilling over a fountain, yet she heard the voice.

You yourself are calling the spirits, Elena, you yourself are animating them, you are the abandoned child, Elena, my dear Elena, you, the seeker of what cannot be found on this earth.

The air was thickening before her, a shadow was coming closer, and inside the shadow, a figure, **not mother, mother cannot come, mother cannot appear**, but a figure nonetheless, floating closer... slowly materializing, slowly taking on form, slowing becoming a young man, dark-haired, tall, lanky, handsome, with the easy, loose-limbed stance suggestive of the *raznochintsy,* the bohemian, the déclassé, wearing the ragtag remnants of a military-style uniform of the kind students were made to wear at school, a staff in his hand and a pack on his back. His approach quieted the air, settled the spirits; she could breathe again.

And breathing again, she recognized the truth of what he had said: the angry spirits were her own creatures, their sorrow and fury were the sorrow and fury of her own grief, their desire was her own desire, their rage her own rage. Even as she thought these things, all the furious forces and energies in the room were dispersed and absorbed into the ether, and the figure who had spoken to her began to fade.

Wait, Messenger! Tell me who you are!

A foolish question, Elena Petrovna, and you are not a fool.

The Messenger laughed, and the ripple of the sound made all the glass in the room tinkle like tiny bells, like troika bells one hears coming from a distance on a winter's night. Then she did know him, of course she did, the archetype of life and freedom, the mad genius of the Cards, the Fool.

Oh, what a fool she had been, not to know him, not to ask him…

Where is he, Messenger? Where is Barakov?

It was impossible that she should not have the power to hold him.

Speak, Spirit! I must know where he can be found.

But too late! Oh, how infuriating it was to be too late! For the spirit vanished, the lamp light strengthened, the shadows in the room disappeared, and a sweetness permeated the air, like a garden of roses.

Fool! she cried. *Fool! I am a fool! And you leave me with roses!*

Yet the scent of these roses was intoxicating, and so, despite her vexation, she fell into a deep sleep in the chair where she was sitting, and did not wake until the morning.

CHAPTER TWELVE

Evil Doings in the House of Pavel Beriosov

The Panaev-Nekrasov household did not rise early. It must have been nearly noon—though who could tell the hour under such a grey sky?—before they and their guests sat down for their morning coffee, and even so they all looked half-asleep. Everyone had had dreams during the night, and wanted to bore everyone else with long descriptions of them. Panaev had dreamt about traveling to a river to go swimming, and all the difficulties of the journey. Inns had been full, roads had been flooded, his driver had gone missing, and he had brought too many things with him—satchels and parcels, a bottle of beer, several coats—which he was constantly mislaying. He never did arrive at the river, and never had his swim. Nekrasov had dreamt about a page of writing he was trying to read but couldn't decipher although he was sure it was about the Holy Ghost. Fyodorov had had a very long narrative dream the details of which he could not remember except that Nikolai Barakov was a character, there had been a fight with knives and fists, and there had been brigands and horses and a woman in a gypsy skirt…

"Goodness, Fyodorov Fyodorovich, what an exciting night you had! Even a gypsy girl! It makes my swimming adventure pale by comparison."

Panaeva at first claimed she could not remember her dreams, but with a little prodding recalled one small image from the night, that she was following a small child up a flight of stairs. All she could remember were his little red shoes.

Blavatskaya said she had not dreamt at all. She was a truthful woman and this was not a lie.

After breakfast, the three journalists went into their office to work while Blavatskaya and Fyodorov sat at their ease at the table, sipping coffee. Outside the window was a terrace and beyond the terrace, a garden, now, it being well into autumn, gone completely to seed. A few sparrows were flying in and out of the bushes and pecking about in the weeds. There was also a small pond, now covered in dead leaves. Altogether it was a mournful sight.

"Tell me more about your dream," she said. "You dreamt about Barakov?"

He did not reply at once. He was thinking and did not particularly want to share his thoughts with Elena Petrovna.

It had been a strange dream, if dream it was. A very long, strange dream, so detailed, so real... Yes, as real as real life, as real as sitting here at this table, he thought. What made it less real than this? He remembered it as well as he remembered anything. It was almost—and he did not know how to think this thought clearly—almost as though he had gone into another world in which these events had actually happened, and then returned to this one, the one in which he was sitting in a dining room drinking coffee with Elena Petrovna. And yet how was such a thing possible?

Perhaps it had happened.

And then, of course, he remembered that it had.

"I must tell you how I came to live in the phalanstery."

"Indeed, you should. I had no idea you lived in such a community."

"It was a rather odd one."

"I expect so."

"Smaller in scale, of course, than Fourier suggested, and not as organized as he might have wished. In fact, it was rather anarchistic. But the idea of living and working together, of sharing everything, of creating a community based on friendship and equality... well, this was Barakov's plan, you see, and that's how he came to rent the house on the Vyborg side of the river. But he wound up taking in all kinds of strays, and ne'er-do-wells, old friends who found him and asked for help, which he gave, of course, and soon the rooms were all filled with drunks and brawlers and the utopian elements of the house more or less fell by the wayside."

"And you, Fyodorov? How did you...?"

"I will tell you. One night some years ago I was coming into the city to give a lecture..."

Elena Petrovna, preparing for a long Fyodorovian tale, settled back comfortably in her chair.

It had been a moonless night in early spring. The roads were terrible and mud-clogged, the carriage he was traveling in barely exceeded a walking pace, and so it was very late, far too late, by the time he arrived in the city. Once there he discovered that the inn he had planned to stay in was completely filled so that he was obliged to go in search of another. But he was hungry and thirsty and decided to take some refreshment where he was. He paid little notice to what was going on around him, being tired and hungry and distracted by some new ideas for his lecture, which he wrote down in his notebook, and so after his meal and his glass of beer, or perhaps he had more than one, he quite carelessly wandered into the street in search of a cab to take him to another hostelry.

Before he knew it he was surrounded by a gang of thieves who seized hold of him, ran their hands all over him, took things from his pockets, grabbed his small case, struck him on the head, threw him to the ground—and did all these things at once so that he could not even tell what was happening to him at any given moment—and would have done God knows what else to him except that within seconds of the assault another group of attackers arrived, and poor Fyodorov thought now indeed he would be killed because these bandits must be even more evil than the first, coming at them with such ferocity, yelling at the top of their lungs and pounding them with their fists. Blows were exchanged, shouts and cries filled the air, men were falling onto the ground. One man in particular, a bearded, broad-shouldered villain, took on one of the first thieves and beat him mercilessly until not only he but all his comrades fled off into the night, but not before the new thieves robbed the old ones not only of all of Fyodorov's possessions but all of their own as well.

Then, breathing hard and rubbing blood from his face, the bearded fighter looked down at Fyodorov, who was crumpled in a heap on the muddy ground, holding his head and trembling in terror, and he laughed.

"Well, Your Excellency, what do you say? Can you stand?... Give him a hand up, Taras, and give me that bottle...The professor here could probably use a drink, too. "

And then, before he knew it, strong arms were hauling him to his feet, his hat was restored to him, and his valise, and a bottle of vodka was thrust into his hands.

"Did you get it all?" someone asked, and then he felt sure he was about to be robbed again, though this time by more gentlemanly thieves.

"Let's sort it out inside," the leader said, for the ferocious bearded fighter was clearly the head of this group of brigands, and so they all returned to the inn, from whence, it turned out, the group had come, and sat down at a large table, and one by one the good thieves dropped onto it in handfuls all the objects that had been in Fyodorov's pockets or on his person: his watch, his flask, his wallet, his passport, his precious notebook, some coins, a medal, a packet of papers, a handkerchief, a knife with a silver handle, keys, a pen… even a gold ring from his finger which the first thieves had slipped off his hand without his even noticing.

"Is that everything?" the leader asked, looking around the table. "Nobody's holding out?"

"That's everything," Fyodorov said, although he wasn't sure it was since he had no idea he carried so much around with him to begin with. Then he stood and bowed and introduced himself. "I am greatly in your debt," he said, hoping he wasn't too much in their debt as he had very little money to reward them with. And what was his life worth, really? He had heard of a man being rewarded with fifty roubles for pulling a drowning man out of the river. He did not have fifty roubles.

"No debts involved," said the leader. "We all love a good street fight."

"Or a bar fight," someone else said.

"Or any kind of goddam fight," said the one called Taras, a bear of a man with a head of curly hair and a scar on his cheek."

One by one the men introduced themselves. None of them, Fyodorov noted, was called Yuri the Corsair or Igor Knife-in-the Back, but the leader's name, Barakov, rang a bell.

Another bottle appeared on the table, its contents immediately poured into glasses, one of which was set before him, and he drank it down, and drank the next one, and the next. They were laughing at the escapade and talking about others of the same kind. Meanwhile Barakov had taken on a truly piratical appearance, having wrapped a rag around his head to staunch a wound—one of the thieves had cut him with a knife during the fight—which was now quite bloodstained. The brigands had been well-armed, though not strong enough to withstand the assault from these young ruffians. He was not sure how he was going to extricate himself from them, for by now they were all quite drunk and the night was passing by and he was tired, weary down to the bone, stiff and sore and still had no idea where he was going to spend the night.

"I have studied medicine," he said at last, "and I think you should let me look at your wound, Barakov. Then, gentlemen, I must try to get some sleep somewhere."

"Somewhere? We can offer you a bed for the night. And then you can sew me up. I'm sure you'll do a better job than Voloshin here." Barakov laughed, and punched his friend on the arm. "He's pretty wicked with a needle and thread. I can show you, if you have the stomach for it." Pulling up his sleeve he showed Fyodorov a long, ugly scar.

♣

"... So they took me to the house on the Vyborg side, I sewed up Nikolai's head, and then they gave me a bed in a room on the second floor, and there I stayed... for quite some time. The best years of my life I spent in that house, Elena Petrovna, and the joy I felt there, with those boys, so full of life, so much sheer fun... It was never the same after he left. It changed entirely."

"I have met with brigands in my travels," Blavatskaya said. "They have usually been dressed in brightly colored turbans, dolmans of thick cloth, loose, knee-length shirts tied with broad sashes around the waist through which they thrust evil-looking daggers and yataghans, and they wear high boots or beautiful slippers on their feet. Such ferocious men! I gather Barakov was not of such disposition."

"Indeed not. As I recall that night, he and his friends were dressed as workmen, and they had no daggers or yataghans. We were in the city, after all, not on the steppes."

"And a good man, from what you say?"

"Barakov? Yes, a good man, and a loyal one. He could be fierce and angry and I never saw him back away from a fight, and I saw lots of fights during those years, lots of drinking and brawling. I did quite a bit of bandaging and sewing up, I can tell you. It was a different sort of life than I was used to. But Nikolai himself—he has a noble heart, Elena Petrovna, and I would not say that about many men. We are the same age, you know, and even born in the same month. Born under the same star, he used to say. Star-brothers. And it pleased me so much, I can't tell you, Elena Petrovna, it pleased me so much that he would say that and he never let anyone insult me or disrespect me or my work. He always asked me what I was thinking about, and he'd sit and talk to me, and listen to me… with sincere interest."

"A writer must listen with interest."

"He told me once that everything he did in his life was research for his book."

"He was researching his fellow men?"

"Yes. Assembling characters and events. Though of course he was also taking part in those events. He is a character in his own book."

"Nekrasov seems to have high hopes for this novel. Justified, would you say?"

"I have not read it, you know. But the play—"

"Yes, what of the play?"

"It is startling, Elena Petrovna. Funny and sad, filled with characters one would never imagine existing, except that I have met some of them, living in that house."

"Is he another Griboyedov, then? And has he written another *Woe from Wit*?"

"Not at all. Griboyedov is a genius of the French classical school of dramatic farce. Nikolai's work is utterly different and unique, and quite unlike anything I have ever read before."

"And did you remember him clearly in your dream? Was it convincing? Was he brought back to you in a way that left no doubt it was he himself?"

"No doubt at all. It was as though I was reliving that event, it was so real."

"I suppose, all things considered, one might have expected that at least one of us would dream of Barakov last night since he is on everyone's mind. Indeed, it appears we all had significant dreams of one kind or another. Yours about Nikolai Barakov, Nekrasov's about a coded letter from the Holy Ghost, Panaev's about searching for the water of life, Panaeva's about following her dead child… "

"Dead child? How do you—"

"My dear Fyodorov, please do not attempt to tell me the meaning of dreams."

"But why a *dead* child?"

"Because all her children are dead, dear man. Yet the bond of love between mother and child is stronger than death. Alas, the spirits who loved us best will not approach us. They have no need to since they have us with them in Devachon, that state of bliss in which the monads are surrounded with all those and that which they have loved, objects of spiritual aspirations as well as human entities. Only in dreams can we see those we love who have departed this plane of existence, and so Panaeva was dreaming of the child... dreaming of following the child into bliss."

"So your Devachon is another word for heaven."

"It is a temporary heaven, before the soul is reborn."

"How very complicated your thinking is, Madame."

"It is not my thinking, Fyodorov. It is the thinking of the occult sciences, the thinking of the Tibetan lamas, it is the essence of all religious teaching, its doctrines are found even in the philosophy of Plato and Plotinus, it is the first and supreme wisdom. I am merely a messenger."

Fyodorov got up from his chair and, cup in hand, walked to the window and gazed out at the dead garden, the stifled pond, the bare, brown trees, the little brown birds. Never in his life had he felt so unmoored. Nothing was secure, steadfast; nothing could be relied on. He was adrift in a strange world with a strange woman. And how did he get here? What was he doing here? How had this happened?

"In any case, we need to leave this house today and continue on," Blavatskaya said.

"Where are we to go?"

"Let us see where our feet take us. As your story itself proved, dear Fyodorov, often our feet know where to go when we ourselves do not."

♣

It was rather later in the day that their feet took them away from the house, for they were persuaded to stay for dinner and very nearly for supper as well. Only Blavatskaya's iron will got them out of the house and onto the street by late afternoon, or rather early evening, since it was by then nearly five, the hour of sunset.

"There is only one place left in the city to search for him," Fyodorov said sadly, "and that is our Bastille."

"Nonsense," said Blavatskaya. "He is more likely to be in a bedroom than a prison cell."

"Whose bedroom?" asked Fyodorov who, for all his imaginative cosmology, was really quite a literal thinker.

Blavatskaya didn't answer, but merely lifted her arm and immediately a carriage pulled up to the curb, and once more the steps were let down, and they climbed in.

"Where to?" the driver asked.

"Pargolovo," Blavatskaya said. "We need some country air, I think."

"At this time of night?" Fyodorov asked, startled.

It had suddenly become quite dark.

"And whose house is this?" Fyodorov asked as they descended the steps of the carriage and found themselves in front of a set of much grander steps that led to a rather grand front door.

"We'll just have to see," she said.

It was becoming annoying, this habit she had of being unnecessarily secretive and mysterious. Fyodorov, thinking of his friend, tried to imagine how Nikolai would treat this mad woman. As a gentleman, no doubt, which is to say, with tolerance and humor but also with a good deal of skepticism. Fyodorov himself was probably not skeptical enough. Yet it was true that they were moving around the country quite rapidly, in vehicles that seemed to appear and disappear at Blavatskaya's command, while carrying on conversations he had to admit were of a good deal of interest to him, and meeting intriguing people like Madame Sofia, and also famous ones like Avdotia Panaeva and Nikolai Nekrasov, whose work he had long admired. But he had little time to consider the relative merits of his journey because they were already climbing the steps to this mansion whose windows let out streams of glorious golden light. A servant in livery opened the door before they even knocked... and yet he was almost reluctant to enter, the air of the park in which the house stood was so fragrant, the night sky so clear, the stars so voluptuous and bright, and the planets so near, the planets that called to him... but then they were in the hall and a tall, middle-aged man dressed in a long sheepskin coat with a thick belt, a red velvet cap on his head, was holding out his hands to them, welcoming them.

"Very good to see you both, very good indeed," he said. "My mother will be delighted. We are just sitting down to supper. Do please join us."

Servants took their coats and hats and Fyodorov's cane, which by some miracle he was still carrying, and their host, if that's what he was, led them into the dining room where a group of women, one quite elderly, the other three in middle-age, were sitting at a long, candlelit table.

"Guests," their guide announced.

"How nice," said the dowager. "Right in time for supper. Have you come far?"

"From the city, Madame," Blavatskaya said.

"Dmitri, dear, do introduce your guests," said one of the women.

An awkward silence was bound to follow this request so Fyodorov introduced Blavatskaya, and then, bowing low, himself.

"Not Fyodorov the cosmist!" the man in the sheepskin coat cried, seizing Fyodorov's hand and shaking it warmly. "I have heard you lecture, dear professor! I am a great admirer of your work!"

Then everyone at the table began talking rapidly, and servants brought plates and glasses, and chairs were moved around. Blavatskaya was seated across the table from the elderly woman, whose house this was, though her name was still unknown to her guests.

"Madame Elena Blavatskaya," the elderly woman said, as though searching her memory for some recollection of the name. "Ah, yes. You are a medium, I believe."

"I have that gift, yes."

"A great gift it is, too. Though I imagine it can be trying at times. Can you turn it on and off at will, or are you subject to the whims of the spirit world any time of day or night? Which I should think would be ... unpleasant."

"I have attained the power to control such apparitions."

"Very good. Because we certainly don't want any apparitions around here, especially not at suppertime."

Then the old woman laughed with a patronizing amusement that infuriated Blavatskaya, so much so that she almost did call a few elemental spirits, a few tricksters who would teach the old biddy not to make fun of the occult science. Fyodorov, meanwhile, had managed to be introduced to the ladies, to Dmitri's wife, Elizaveta Pavlovna, to

Anna Alekseyevna, wife of his brother Pavel, who was not at home at the moment, and to his mother, Madame Svetlana Beriosova. The other lady at the table, a faded beauty in a lavender gown, was introduced only as Cousin Margarita.

Supper consisted of buckwheat pancakes and butter, sourdough pies, and tea.

Fyodorov, seated beside Dmitri Beriosov, was immediately asked questions about the principles of cosmism and the mechanism necessary for inter-planetary travel. These he tried to answer as concisely as he could while continuing to eat his pancakes, for even earthly travel gave him an extraordinary appetite. On the other side of the table, Blavatskaya was also being interrogated. Svetlana Beriosova was a curious woman and was particularly interested in learning about seances, how successful they were in calling spirits, and whether they were, in fact, real or fanciful.

"I would so much like to experience one," she sighed. "Perhaps it can be arranged."

"Arranged?" Blavatskaya replied, archly. She did not take kindly to overbearing women.

"Yes. After supper. It would be so amusing."

Blavatskaya smiled in reply. So, she would have to sing for her supper. Very well. It might turn out to be very amusing indeed.

"I am somewhat fatigued from the journey. I shall have to rest a little while after supper."

"Of course. And you will have to tell Dmitri what sort of furnishings you will need. I leave it in your hands," Svetlana Beriosova said.

The expression on her face, Blavatskaya noticed, was not so much satisfied as grim.

"Come here a moment. I need to speak with you," Blavatskaya said to Fyodorov as they reached the door of her room. She grabbed him by the arm and pulled him through the doorway, shooing away the servant who was accompanying them, and shutting the door. "We must be very careful here."

"What are we even doing here?"

"I am not sure. But it is a dangerous place."

Fyodorov sighed. "I suppose you have a good reason for thinking that."

"For feeling it, rather," she said. "I feel… oppression. Who is that woman in lavender? That so-called cousin?"

"Margarita?"

"Yes. Margarita. With no patronymic, no surname, wearing thick make-up of the cheapest kind and a worn and faded dress, who trembles whenever anyone looks at her and does not say a word all through supper? She is a prisoner here."

"A prisoner? My dear lady!"

"Do not 'dear lady' me, Fyodorov! She is in terror of her life. And there is something very wrong about—"

They were interrupted by a knocking at the door and the servant entered. She was an old woman with a grey face and a bent back. Without saying a word, she made her way around the room, fussing with lamps.

It was a warning, Blavatskaya realized. The walls have ears, the house serfs are slaves, and the house is old enough to have secret doorways and passages. It was as dangerous to speak in the bedroom as it was in the drawing room. But how was she to alert him? And he would keep talking!

"I just don't understand your thinking, Elena Petrovna. We are being treated so well here, a good supper, beds for the night. And Beriosov is quite informed about my ideas. You would be surprised—"

At which point, the maid having momentarily turned her back to them, Blavatskaya seized Fyodorov's arm, pressed it hard, and put her finger to his lips.

"I am not at all surprised, Fyodor Fyodorovich. The Beriosovs are a noble family, and generous, and, of course, they would take in poor travelers like ourselves, and show us hospitality."

"Ah," Fyodorov said. "I take your point exactly."

"I think I might take a walk in the garden. A little fresh air is the best medicine for a weary mind. Would you care to join me?"

The night air was chilly, and since their outer garments had been taken by the servants, who were now nowhere to be seen, they were outside with no cloaks or coats. Once in the garden, Blavatskaya lit a cigarette; Fyodorov warmed his hand with his pipe and hummed.

"What's that you're mumbling?" Blavatskaya asked.

"I am not mumbling."

"You are humming something."

"Am I? Just a childish little rhythm. I heard it in the gypsy camp."

"Are there words to it?"

"Words? Why, yes. Let me think. How does it go?"

The rhythm was in his mind; the words came back to him quite easily.

Think you can run, think you can hide,
Think you are free to enjoy the ride?
Pray to the Lord and don't relax.
You got a monkey on your back.

"Sshh!" she said, fiercely. "Don't you realize where we are?"

"No. Where are we?"

"Beriosov! Doesn't that name mean anything to you?"

"No... Oh! My God! Yes! Not the head of the Third Division, but close enough to the top to lick Dolgorukov's boots. That's what Nikolai used to say. He knew all their names."

"I know their names, too. Some of them are relatives of mine. Well, my friend, we have ended up in Beriosov's house."

"How did this happen?"

"There is a reason for everything."

"Is there? Then what's the reason for this?"

"I have yet to learn that. But be careful here, Fyodorov! Don't mention Barakov, or his book."

"*Monkey*?"

"Yes. Don't say its name. And don't sing that song! Remember men are sent to their deaths for singing songs in this country."

"Nikolai had a friend sent into penal servitude for singing the *Marseillaise*. Though I expect singing wasn't all he did."

"No singing, Fyodorov. No mention of Barakov. No talking about his book. Clear?"

"We should leave at once, but I suppose we have to stay the night."

"I want to find out why that poor woman is being held here against her will."

"How do you know she is?"

In a small fury, Blavatskaya knocked the end of her cigarette out of her amber cigarette holder and immediately replaced it with another.

The utter denseness of men, their total lack of observational skills, their inability to sense the most obvious things... as though they were blind and deaf... as well as dumb! She herself was not a very feminine woman, and did not care about fashion or physical appearances, but even she knew that no woman who could choose otherwise would appear at supper in such a dress with such clumsily applied powder... perhaps necessary to cover a bruise? Perhaps the poor soul was being tortured in this house and then forced to eat supper with her tormenters? It was too horrible a thought to consider.

Yet she was considering it.

She was considering what a man in Beriosov's position of power might find to be a source of amusement. After all, they had nearly unlimited power, the high level operatives of the Third Division. They wove such webs, they kept such thick dossiers, they knew everything about everyone. No one but the Tsar himself could overrule them or rein them in, and why should he since everything they did was for the purpose of preserving his power? No, they had *carte blanche*, and could do whatever they wished.

"Tell me now, Elena Petrovna. Do you intend to rescue this woman?"

"We'll have to see what the spirits have to say."

"What spirits?"

"Have I not told you this before, Fyodor Fyodorovich? I am a medium. I call on spirits and they come."

"Do they really? How extraordinary!"

"You will see just how extraordinary it can be. I think there are many elemental spirits in this house. I imagine they will be quite delighted to have the chance to display themselves."

She sucked a good deal of smoke into her lungs and let it out slowly, in smoke rings. The smoke rings drifted into the air, floated over the dried stalks and grizzled bushes of the garden, and rose in ever-widening circles toward the heavens where a nearly full moon was slowly showing her smooth round face through the clouds. Gazing upwards, she found her eyes following the swooping flight of a small bird. No, not at this hour. It was a bat. She turned around and faced the house. The lower floor was lit; the upper floors were in complete darkness, all but one window, and that quite high up. So there was some sort of high tower room, for old servants, no doubt, and for bats.

"Go back inside, Fyodorov. I need to sit out here alone and meditate for a few minutes."

"Yes, of course," he said, and knocking out the last embers from his pipe, turned and walked away.

The night closed in.

All her senses were now alert. She felt the air moving beneath the swift wing-beats of the circling bats. She heard the deep hooting of an owl in the park, and, closer by, in a nearby tree, its mate, answering. She smelt the dried leaves and the damp soil and burning tobacco ash and some lingering scent, a cologne or perfume. Moonlight dappled the garden path; then the light disappeared as clouds covered the moon. Everything in motion, everything alive, spirits saturating space so that one breathes them in and out like the Great Breath breathes Being in and out, in and out, like the moonlight dancing in and out on the garden path. Oh, how mysterious and sacred! And, oh, how villainous those who attempt to command it or defile it. But Socrates was right. No evil can befall a good man, either in life or after death. He and his are not neglected by the gods.

Yet in this world, on this plane, there dwelt many spirits of ill-will. There were the mischievous elemental spirits, the fractious imps, the gnomes, undines, sylphs, and salamanders, quite able to wield the elemental forces they embodied; there were the not-yet-ensouled spirits of the unborn, playful spirits mostly, but not adverse to tormenting living beings with the lingering shells of the dead; and there were the vampire souls, the disembodied spirits of vicious, malicious, unredeemable men who had destroyed their own immortal souls and were now wandering the earth on the verge of their utter dissolution, seeking succor from those as evil as themselves. She felt the presence of all these spirits now, hovering around this house, waiting to be summoned.

She was a strong and powerful medium, but she was still young and so, at that moment, her will wavered, and she found that she was filled with fear. Fyodorov's little song came back to her, the cheery little song of despair. *Think you can run, think you can hide? Think you're free to enjoy the ride? Pray to the Lord and don't relax. You got a monkey on your back.*

Prayer was not in her nature. Her Master, who had first come to her in Saratov after her mother's death, had not come because she prayed—she would never have thought to pray for such a vision—but of his own desire, to help her gain her powers. He had revealed the secret of the subtle bodies, instructed her in astral travel and projection and telepathy. He was still her Master but she was now an adept. She could deal with this crowd of petty elementals and as for the vampirish spirits, even they could not touch her. No, it was not they, but the very human evil inside the house that she felt most strongly, the evil which, as Dante himself shows, can cause a man's soul to be cast into the Ninth Circle of Hell long before his physical body dies. She had a sense of that same evil now, and it chilled her to her very soul.

♣

Fyodorov was glad to go inside and feel the warmth of the stoves. In fact, the rooms were perhaps too warm, overheated, as though winter had already set in. There was activity in the hall, and as he passed through the drawing room to the stairs, he realized that more guests were arriving, and at such a late hour, too. Or was it late? He had really lost all sense of time with all the traveling they'd been doing. He was on his way to his room, he had just reached the staircase, when Madame Beriosova appeared at his elbow, and took hold of it.

"Come along, Fyodor Fyodorovich, and join us in the drawing room. My son Pavel Pavlovich has just arrived and will be most happy to meet you."

Pavel Pavlovich Beriosov was a rather short, middle-aged, fair-haired man—fair but thinning, to be sure—with a straight carriage, a small mustache, thin lips and a frowning brow. He did not seem in the least happy to see Fyodorov, but then he had just arrived and had barely had time to allow a servant to take off his coat. The rich, as Nikolai used to say bitterly, don't even undress themselves. And this one not only had servants to dress and undress him, he had squadrons of *gendarmes* at his beck and call. Fyodorov, poor son of a poorer priest, educated out of his class, but still very much aware of it, was sensitive to even the smallest displays of privilege and power, the way a man will expect someone to take his coat off for him or open a carriage door for him or pour his vodka into a glass.

"Fyodorov is traveling with Madame Blavatskaya," Svetlana Beriosova told her son almost as soon as they were all seated in the drawing room. "She is going to hold a seance for us later tonight. You arrived just in time for it."

"Mother, I do not think holding a seance here is at all appropriate."

"Of course, you wouldn't. But it will happen nevertheless. This is still my house."

Pavel Beriosov bristled noticeably at this rejoinder. Fyodorov, feeling he was about to witness a domestic spat which would be awkward and regrettable, made a move to excuse himself, but Beriosova restrained him with a gesture of her hand.

"You will enjoy it, Pasha. Believe me. It will relax you and take your mind off all the nasty things you think about all day. Madame Blavatskaya is a famous medium, very well-known, even abroad. You would not want to miss such an opportunity."

"And what is Madame Blavatskaya doing here in Pargolovo? It seems a rather out of the way place for a famous medium."

Both Beriosovs turned to Fyodorov for an answer, Pavel sternly, Svetlana with a saccharine smile. Fyodorov, feeling both sets of eyes on him, became flustered. What in heaven's name were they doing there? He hardly knew. How could he answer?

"Well, Fyodorov?" Beriosov of the Third Division asked, and Fyodorov's heart began pounding, sweat broke out on his brow, and his mouth went completely dry.

"Yes, Fyodorov," added Beriosova in a simpering voice, "Surely you are here on some mission, aren't you? A quest, perhaps?"

"Why yes," Fyodorov said. "A quest. That's it exactly."

"So you are a knight errant! How marvelous!"

She leaned toward him, offering him a glass bowl of chocolate sweets, one of which he chose, and then, not knowing exactly why, thrust not into his mouth but into his pocket, where it would later melt.

"But do tell us, dear Fyodor Fyodorovich, what are you questing for? Not the mysterious Firebird, surely. Perhaps the Holy Grail?"

"No, no. Neither Firebird nor Holy Grail," he said. And then, feeling her green eyes (how very green they were!) resting on him so encouragingly, or so it seemed, and with a smile of such expectation, he added, "Unless, of course, one thinks of Barakov's book as the Holy Grail."

The words were no sooner out of his mouth than he felt a shadow pass over him like death itself.

In the doorway Blavatskaya stood, *and thronged with mighty thoughts stared out*, like Tsar Peter in Pushkin's poem, and, glaring at him just as ferociously as that autocrat, bored into him with her bulging eyes, and damned him for the fool he was.

"Nikolai Barakov?" Pavel Beriosov said in a voice as low and menacing as a viper's hiss. "So you are looking for his book, are you? May I ask why?"

"I can answer that," Blavatskaya said, striding into the room.

"Madame Blavatskaya," Beriosov said, standing.

"Monsieur Beriosov," she said, coming toward him and holding out her hand, which he had no alternative but to kiss. Attuned as she was, she felt the frigidness of his soul slipping from his lips to her hand, and creeping from her hand to her arm, and reaching for her very heart.

You got a monkey on your back.

She heard that phrase in his mind, like an echo. Had it come from her? In that case, his power was surprising. Instantly she closed her mind to him, sealing it against him. He released her hand at the same moment; she dissipated the chill he had left in her by the force of her will.

Then there was the sitting and the smiling and the servant carrying in drinks and the sipping and the heat flowing from the glass into her veins... and all that happening while she prepared an answer to the question he would be sure to ask again, and then did ask.

"So you are looking for Barakov's book. What do you know about it?"

"What everyone else knows."

"And what is that?"

"My dear Pavel Pavlovich, surely I need not tell you what you of all people must certainly already know far better than anyone. Indeed, about the dangerousness of Barakov's book, I am quite sure you could instruct me. You could tell me—everything."

He fixed his viper's eyes on her. What a duel! Each was attempting to probe the other's mind, but to no avail. When he spoke again, it was in a tone of resignation. He would get nothing from her.

"May I ask another question then? *Why* are you looking for it?"

"To destroy it," she said.

"Destroy it?"

"Of course. Why else?"

"Many others are searching for it for that very reason."

"Indeed. And we have joined the search party."

"Well," Pavel Beriosov said, utterly nonplussed, "that's good of you. Very good of you."

"And now," Blavatskaya said, glancing at the clock on the mantel, "we ought to start the seance. If Madame Beriosova is still interested in communing with spirits."

"I am, very much so," that lady said. "Nothing would bring me more joy."

Blavatskaya tried not to snicker at the idea of anything bringing Svetlana Beriosova joy.

"Who will be joining us? Once we begin there should be no interruptions." She turned to Beriosov. "You will sit with us, won't you, Pavel Pavlovich? As a man of science—"

"My education in that area is sadly lacking."

"Nonsense," she said. "I don't believe it. Your brother shows such knowledge of science. He and Fyodorov talked incessantly at supper. I can't imagine you don't share his interest. Or surpass it."

After such a challenge he could not refuse.

"And the ladies, Madame Beriosova?" Blavatskaya said as they made their way to the study. "I see your daughters-in-law are here, but what of your cousin Margarita? The more people at the table, the better the results. You would not want to be disappointed."

"Margarita is feeling unwell tonight," Beriosova said. "I doubt she will be able to come down."

"Yet the spirits might advise her in regard to her health. One can never tell. I have often received messages from healers. It is not at all uncommon to hear from a healer when an ill person is sitting at the table. I recommend that she be present. We shall wait for her."

And so Cousin Margarita came down from her room.

The drawing room was prepared for them in so much as it needed preparation. There were eight chairs and a table; no other furnishings were needed. The drapes were already closed, the lamps already lit.

They took their places around the table: Madame Beriosova; her sons Pavel and Dmitri; their wives Anna and Elizaveta; Cousin Margarita in her faded dress, Fyodorov and Blavatskaya herself. Seven, and the medium.

The spirits were so eager they began rapping on the walls and the furniture almost before everyone's hands were resting on the table in a complete circle. Some candles were blown out while a previously unlit lamp began to blaze brightly; the table shook. Elementals acting up.

Blavatskaya gazed around the table. A formidable group. If they were cards on Madame Sophia's table, the three men would appear as cards of trickery, deception, and betrayal (though Fyodorov's betrayal was innocent enough, the poor man was more a fool than a traitor) while the three Beriosovas would be three queens, reversed, their feminine powers turned evil, to jealousy and deceit, to cruelty and malice, to sterility and corruption. And then there was Margarita, sitting at her right hand, the mysterious Margarita. And what was her ruling card? Was it Dame Fortuna, perhaps, the card of destiny?

While she took the measure of the table, the elementals bounced about the room. Very good. Let the guests be entertained for a little while, and let the spirits have some fun. So she allowed the impish and mischievous elementals to break a few glass bowls, throw chocolate candies into the air, knock over some porcelain statuettes, make roaring noises, like winds or pounding surf, and engage in the sort of banging and clanking they always seemed to enjoy so much.

The younger women grew pale, of course, and clutched the table; Fyodorov and Dmitri Beriosov took on that skeptical air men of science assume when they have no idea what is happening but want to insist they are still in control of everything and everyone. But Pavel Beriosov was smiling scornfully and Svetlana Beriosova had closed her eyes... Margarita, sitting beside Blavatskaya, was muttering something under her breath.

Pavel Beriosov growled at her to keep still.

The growl had not come entirely from him. No, a vampire spirit was standing just behind him, a ghastly soul, no longer immortal, which, having given itself over entirely to evil, was about to plummet into eternal darkness. It had been its voice, resonating in the air. *Woman, keep still!*

Thus the battle lines were drawn, the struggle commenced. For some could still be saved.

"Is there a specific spirit to whom you wish to speak?" she asked

Svetlana Beriosova.

"There is one," the woman replied, while another voice, a spectral voice, unheard by anyone but Blavatskaya herself, added, "*And you know very well who it is!*"

Clearly, the powers that resided in the house were strong, but insufficient to accomplish their will. They had need of her, for only an adept of the occult arts could summon a subtle body from the astral plane, especially if the spirit were unwilling. Nikolai Barakov would be unwilling, but many others were willing indeed. She sensed them now, angry, wounded souls, and she did summon them. They came rushing in, a river of souls, rushing in from all directions, and flooded the room, their subtle bodies bearing witness to horror, for they came in shackles and chains, beaten, starved, branded, broken. One flickering spirit, a young man, a student, thin, pale, consumptive... how he wanted to speak! But she could not hear him. He was far, far away, dying of cold, dying but still alive... had traveled here to say his few words. Why couldn't she hear him? The Other was exerting its will. What she produced from the astral plane, he thrust away as easily as a man might brush away a fly.

She concentrated her power; she pushed against what opposed her; she forced the door open and held the Other at bay.

I shouted once in the street, Pavel Pavlovich. That was my crime.

The boy stood firm before them. They all heard him now.

Svetlana Beriosova opened her eyes, green and luminous like a cat's eyes gleaming in the dark. "Remove these creatures!" she said in an oddly deep voice that did not sound in the least like her own.

Just as she spoke, a mischievous elemental swept by her and lifted the wig she was wearing right off her head leaving her head quite bare and bald.

"Devil!" she cried. "Demon!"

Dmitri Beriosov reached for the wig as it hovered just in front of his face, and reaching, over-reached, toppled forward, and fell face-first onto the table. He was helped a bit by an impudent, fun-loving sylph. The wig floated by Fyodorov, who made no attempt to touch it, and then came to rest on Anna Beriosova's head. She screamed and pushed her chair back from the table...

While this vaudeville was in progress, the astral bodies of the poor prisoners melted away, returning to the places from whence they had

ELENA BLAVATSKAYA

She sensed them now, angry, wounded souls, and she did summon them.

come; yet the room was still filled not only with irascible elementals but with empty shells left behind by the dead. Upon one of these shells Pavel Beriosov was attempting to project an image... was reaching into someone's mind, someone at the table... to retrieve an image... to attempt to materialize it onto the shell... She could feel him scrounging like an animal, a rodent, scrounging, searching for a mind open and innocent, a mind vulnerable to him and his vampire companion... and few minds are invulnerable when assaulted by such power.

And then the spirit appeared. He was a young man dressed in a worker's smock, tall and lean, with close-cropped hair, a trimmed beard and cherubic cheeks, and shining dark blue eyes under long lashes and thick brows. He stood quite at ease, and looked around at those seated with an expression of ironic amusement. He was holding a sheaf of papers in one hand and a pen in the other.

The sight startled Fyodorov, while Margarita, sitting beside Blavatskaya, began trembling violently and pulled herself to her feet.

"Nikolai!" she cried out in a hoarse and desperate voice.

Then, as quickly as she had stood, she sat again, as though all strength had left her body. Svetlana glowered at her across the table. Blavatskaya, however, addressed the apparition.

What is your name, Spirit?

My name? I no longer have a name. I renounced it, as I generally did everything in life.

"No, no!" Margarita cried out. "You have a name! Nikolai!"

The materialized spirit turned to her, smiled at her, a sweet, sad smile, and spoke: *Love leaped out in front of us like a murderer in an alley leaping out of nowhere, and struck us both at once."*

"Nikolai!" she cried again, and this time she began to sob and tears ran down her cheeks, and as they did, the chalk-white make-up on her face began to disappear, the thick powder streaked her cheeks, and her hair came loose from its combs and fell in curls down her back, and under the powder that had turned it almost white it shone raven black in the candlelight. "Oh, tell me you aren't dead, Nikolai! It can't be true!"

"It isn't," Blavatskaya said. "What you are seeing is a trick, a projection."

"Our medium renounces her own powers," Svetlana Beriosova said, sarcastically. "She calls the spirits of the dead and when they come—"

Fyodorov, now shaking fiercely and feeling his own life coming to an end, cried out, "Oh, Nikolai! Nikolai! My friend—"

"I do not call the dead," Blavatskaya said in her deep, husky voice. "I do not practice necromancy—"

But a louder, deeper and huskier voice interrupted her, the voice of Pavel Beriosov, or the vampire spirit at his shoulder. "Nikolai Barakov, I command you to speak! Your novel—where is it? Tell me now!"

Beriosov might have powerful abilities, but he was not as powerful at Elena Petrovna Blavatskaya. She closed her eyes and called on fire. The salamanders, the fire elementals, flamed up in delight, sparked little fires in all the corners, set alight the table cloths, the wall hangings, the rugs, the furniture. Spirals of smoke began ascending from all parts of the room.

The three Beriosovas jumped up, screaming in terror. The circle was broken; the apparition vanished. Then the brothers Beriosov, grabbing their mother and wives by the arms, pulled them away from the table toward the door, shouting for servants who could not hear them, all the doors and windows being securely closed. Black smoke, now billowing, filled the air, angering the sylphs, enraging the undines, irritating the gnomes... but the salamanders were filled with childish delight and ran around the room in crazy joy. Fire suddenly burst up out of the very walls...

But Blavatskaya had already turned to Margarita, and with the words *I have come to free you, Madame! Quickly, Fyodorov!* had seized the poor woman by one arm while Fyodorov, who had been seated on the other side of her, seized her by the other, and the three of them had run like a phalanx out through the French doors and into the garden just before that doorway was completely barred by flames.

They kept running, through the garden, onto the drive. Horses neighed gently at their approach; three of them were standing already saddled and waiting for them. No sooner had they mounted than the horses flew off down the drive and into the night while behind them the mansion of Svetlana Beriosova burned.

CHAPTER THIRTEEN

THE TIME PORTAL

"You must stop crying," Blavatskaya said, a bit more gruffly than she intended, and yet she was feeling testy and annoyed. She was tired, and being tired made her irritable. And Fyodorov would keep questioning her, and Margarita would keep sobbing, and the inn they had stopped at was quite primitive, there was no coffee, and they had not slept all night. She was in a vile mood.

"You must stop crying, Margarita," she said again, more forcefully, "and you must tell us who you are. We saved you. We rescued you. The very least you can do—"

Fyodorov, always the gallant, interrupted her, rushing to the defense. "Elena Petrovna, please! The poor child is distraught."

She looked the poor child over with a disdainful eye. Yes, it was true. Cousin Margarita was no faded beauty of a certain age. The deception created by a little conjuring and a little more powder could not withstand a flood of tears and a modicum of daylight. All was revealed: Margarita was a raven-haired young woman whose beauty was in full bloom. Even so she was not a child. Elena Petrovna had married Blavatsky at seventeen and almost immediately run off to Egypt without him; Margarita was at least twenty, and twenty was not all that young.

"Please try to get hold of yourself," she said. "And, Fyodorov, for the love of God, go and try to get that barkeep to give you some brandy or vodka, and something to eat. If we must spend the day here..."

For indeed it seemed they must. It had been barely dawn when the horses had stopped at the gate as though they had arrived at their own door, and refused to go any farther, and then to top it off it had started to snow.

"We must be in Finland," Fyodorov had said, and they probably were.

Now Fyodorov obediently left in search of nourishment, and Blavatskaya took hold of Margarita's hand, turned it over and studied her palm. She was not a palm-reader, but it did not take much intuition to discover information from looking at a person's hand. This hand had done very little of note in its life. There were no signs of physical labor, no scratches, callouses, or broken nails, no indications of its owner having indulged in bouts of sewing, embroidering or violin playing nor of having written letters with a leaky pen.

"Your full name, please, with patronymic."

"Are you interrogating me?"

"No. But I must know who you are."

"Why must you know that? Isn't it enough to know I am miserable, I am grieving? Isn't my suffering enough for you?"

"But we have rescued you, my dear."

"From what? From that house? That house is the least cause of my anguish. Their tortures are nothing compared to the agony of my heart. I do not know whether I love a living man or a dead one. And whether he is living or dead, I am separated from him now, and possibly forever. What suffering is worse than that?"

"Is it to Nikolai Vasilevich that you refer?"

Margarita turned her flushed and tear-streaked face to Blavatskaya, but before she could answer, Fyodorov came into the room, followed by the innkeeper carrying a tray. The stove was fed with more wood, vodka duly poured into glasses, little pies distributed on tiny not quite clean plates. There was also a variety of cheeses, for, indeed, if they were not in Finland, they were very close.

"Let us eat now before we say anything more or attempt to make any decisions," Blavatskaya said while Margarita wiped her face and blew her nose.

To this everyone agreed.

Soon enough then, warmed with food, drink and fire, and feeling far more comfortable, they settled down before the stove, and Blavatskaya lit a cigarette, and resumed her questioning.

"Margarita, my dear," she began, "we must leave this place soon, we must decide where to go, and for that, we need to know where to take you, and into whose care—"

"I understand. I will answer, if I can. First you will want to know how I came to be in that loathsome house. How I fell into the clutches of Pavel Beriosov, who is the worst sort of devil, liar, manipulator, torturer, kidnapper, defiler of women—"

"Oh, my dear girl!" Blavatskaya cried, knowing full-well about those horrible defilers of women, which was why she had run away from her husband on their wedding night.

"He did not touch me. Not in that way." A fierceness showed in Margarita's eyes. "That he did not dare to do. Nikolai would kill him if he had. Nikolai might kill him anyway, if the brute survived the fire. And if Nikolai is still alive."

"I have no reason to believe he is not."

"Thank you, Elena Petrovna. But then how was it that his ghost appeared? How was it I saw him so clearly?"

"It is a skill that some psychics have, my dear, that allows us to materialize images that otherwise only dwell in the mind. Beriosov is a powerful psychic. I believe he was able to extract this memory from your mind, and—"

"No! I would never let him do that! Never!"

Blavatskaya, who had some powers of her own, though she was always restrained in her use of them, now tried to gently probe Margarita's mind. She found, to her surprise, that the girl's mind was—unfathomable. Either Margarita was herself a powerful adept, able to protect herself against the psychic interference of others, or her mind was—empty. Not vacant, but new-born, unblemished, clear and cool and fresh as a crystal spring. It was like no mind Elena Petrovna had ever encountered before.

"Perhaps if you told us who you are..." Blavatskaya suggested, with some caution.

"And continued your story of how you came to be in that house," Fyodorov added, with no caution at all.

Margarita, who had been becoming more and more restless as the conversation progressed, got up from her chair and walked over to the stove. Standing there, with her back to them, she sighed deeply, and seemed to mutter to herself. Surely some sounds, some words, were coming from her, but neither Fyodorov nor Blavatskaya could understand what they were.

"Would you believe me if I told you I don't remember..." she began. "No, it isn't that!" Turning from the stove, she began pacing up and down the room, clutching her hands. "I don't know how I came to be in that house. I was in Moscow, sitting on a bench by the Kremlin wall, looking at the Manège. I closed my eyes against the sun… Someone sat beside me and said, Margarita Nikolaevna, I've been sent to you on a little business… I thought he was a criminal, or the police. I called him a scoundrel and got up to leave. Then he quoted a passage from Nikolai's book… a few sentences, but I recognized them. He told me he knew where Nikolai was, and if I went with him, he would take me to him. So I went with him, of course, and ended up in Beriosov's house. More than that, I cannot say. Except—"

"Except?"

"Except the passage was not from Nikolai's book at all, but from Bulgakov's. And my name is not Margarita Nikolaevna but Margarita Mikhailevna."

"Uncanny, indeed," Fyodorov mumbled to himself. "And who is this Bulgakov? I have not heard of him."

But his words were lost, drowned out by Blavatskaya who, at the same time, asked, "You did not recognize the man who sat beside you?"

"No, I did not recognize him. But Beriosov, I did." She sat down in her chair again, and ran her hands through her dark hair, pulling it back from her face. "And if he survived the fire, Nikolai will kill him, I know he will. He knows my mother, you see, Beriosov. Or rather, his mother knows my mother. They are not friends, of course. But known to each other. So Beriosov invited himself to the Barakov's house at a time when my mother, Tatyana Andreyevna Volkonskaya, was visiting—"

"Your mother!" Blavatskaya interrupted in surprise. "You are the daughter of Princess Volkonskaya? How very interesting!"

"He came there in order to spy on us. He spread his net wider, he began investigating my mother, and then me. Someone informed on us. So he had me snatched off the street. He is a monster."

"Informed on whom?" Fyodorov asked, having lost the thread of the conversation.

"Because you and Nikolai are lovers," Blavatskaya said, somewhat reluctantly since she hated to state the obvious. "Isn't that true?"

"No. Not because we are lovers," Margarita said. "I am Nikolai's wife."

"Well," Blavatskaya said. "That *is* news."

She filled three glasses with vodka, and, wishing Margarita happiness (a rather foolish hope under the circumstances), they toasted to the joyous news, for it is far better to drink to good news than to bad, though they are so often intertwined. The vodka went down smoothly, so smoothly Blavatskaya was quite convinced they really were in Finland. She smoked another cigarette and Fyodorov lit his pipe.

"So, now we have some answers. You are Margarita Mikhailevna, adopted daughter of Princess Tatyana Volkonskaya, and you have contracted a secret marriage with Nikolai Vasilevich Barakov. And you kept it quite secret indeed. I'd heard nothing of it. Had you, Fyodorov?"

"Not at all, Elena Petrovna. Not a whisper."

"But Beriosov learned of it. So he kidnapped you and kept you prisoner in his house in the hope that Nikolai would offer himself up as ransom... or offer his novel, which Beriosov considers dangerous and desires to destroy."

"Yes. But then, after all that, they couldn't find him to tell him they had captured me. And really there's no point holding someone for ransom if you can't locate the person you want to collect the ransom from. And they couldn't. Beriosov had the entire division looking for Nikolai, all their blue-coated *gendarmes*, all their overseas agents, all their local spies, all their snitches among the student societies, everyone. The entire Third Division looking for him, and they could not find him anywhere. It annoyed him a great deal, as you can imagine."

"But he couldn't very well release you," Blavatskaya said. "It would be a terrible scandal, and reflect badly on him. Failure of that kind might even threaten his position. So he kept you locked up in his mother's house, disguised as an old woman, and drugged on laudanum, too, I would imagine. How dreadful it must have been for you!"

"But then you two arrived," Margarita said, smiling at them. "My saviors. I wonder how you even discovered the truth. You are an amazing woman, Madame Blavatskaya. And you, Fyodor Fyodorovich, are a brave hero. You are like characters in a story!"

The vodka had been working its usual magic on Margarita's state of mind. Blavatskaya smoked and wondered, but Fyodorov had more questions, and asked them.

"So, my dear, what shall we call you? Madame Barakova?"

"No, please don't! Call me Margarita. We are such good friends now. And anyway Nikolai and I are Fourierists and believe in equality." Suddenly tears sprang into her eyes again and ran slowly down her cheeks. "Oh, what has become of him! I am so afraid that he is—"

"Don't even think it, my dear!" Fyodorov said kindly, quite moved himself by her tears. "But please continue. Tell us how you met Nikolai Vasilevich. Was it through Tatyana Andreyevna's friendship with the Barakov family?"

"Yes. Indeed I have known Nikolai all my life, or the greater part of it. I often saw him at his parents' house when I visited there with Tatyana Andreyevna. And later we met again in the city. We spent many lovely days together, lovely summer days..." And once again she sobbed and her whole body shook with grief. "But now he's dead and only a ghost!"

"I told you already," Blavatskaya said sternly, "that is not true. It is a trick, to project an image, to materialize a mental image."

"And Beriosov did that? He took the image from my mind? Oh, it's horrible!"

Margarita jumped to her feet again and resumed pacing the room, clutching herself and sobbing loudly.

"It was Nikolai, though, his sweet face, his eyes, his voice! But why didn't he speak to me?"

"He did address you, I believe," Blavatskaya said.

"But not in his own words. Everything he said came from Bulgakov's novel."

"And Bulgakov is...?"

"A thought in my mind," Margarita said, now pulling at her hair in her distress.

"Elena Petrovna," Fyodorov shouted, "you must stop this madness!"

"What madness? You saw the apparition yourself, didn't you? With your own eyes?"

"Extracted from the child's mind? Are you mad?"

"Beriosov did it, nevertheless. How else? Unless he himself knows Barakov. Does he?"

"No. He does not know Nikolai," Margarita said. She stopped pacing the room and threw herself into a chair. "He has never met him. Though he certainly wishes to. The horrible, cruel, evil man!"

"Well, then, unless Beriosov has power to summon the subtle bodies of men through the astral plane, and that I doubt very much, what we saw was the materialization of a memory."

"Oh, God!" Margarita cried. "I thought I had told him nothing at all, and yet it seems he was able to creep like some vile creature into my mind and—Oh, it is a horror!"

"It also seemed to me you were under some spell or in a trance state at supper last night. Did they mesmerize you often?"

"Yes. Svetlana did. She had acquired the skill in Paris. From the mesmerist Victor Michal. She was quite proud of it."

"Was she indeed?" Blavatskaya murmured. She herself had studied mesmerism in Paris. Most people thought of it as a kind of after-dinner entertainment, but it had a deep and dark side to it. Even French security agents were known to experiment with it, for in the right hands, or the wrong ones, it could become a powerful weapon.

"And they gave me laudanum," Margarita was saying. "I had taken a few drops before supper last night."

"Yes, laudanum would calm you and in large doses it would send your mind on its own voyages and make you quite impervious to questions from the likes of Beriosov." She paused for a moment to consider whether it really was the opium that was shielding Margarita's mind from her psychic probing. She had never encountered such a result before.

"I still cannot believe he could do that to me."

"But it appears he did since you recognized the apparition and the words he spoke. Fyodorov also has memories of Nikolai, of course, but you did not recognize the words, did you, Fyodorov?"

Fyodorov shook his head, and, having expected such an answer, she carried on, "No, I didn't think so. So therefore, it had to come from you, my dear. Beriosov is an accomplished psychic. Earlier in the evening he projected into my consciousness a bit of song we heard in the gypsy camp, a song about a monkey. He must have extracted that song from your mind, Fyodorov."

"My mind?" Fyodorov cried, feeling the same sort of horror that Margarita had given voice to. "The devil! How dare he—"

"A mistake on his part, to show himself to me so soon. It alerted me to the danger. But he is a proud, arrogant man, and assumed he was my superior in the occult sciences, a foolish assumption to make, and one that he paid a high price for in the end."

Elena Petrovna surely did not lack amour-propre, Fyodorov thought, which idea made him think instantly of his friend, and what admirable self-regard Nikolai had, especially in the presence of ladies, how confident he was with them, how charming he could be, yet he always spoke with complete sincerity, he always believed everything he said, no matter how absurd... *Love leaped out in front of us like a murderer in an alley...* Surely he had heard Nikolai say something much like that to some young lady, sitting with her at a small café table, laughing at himself as he did, and she, laughing along with him. And surely, when asked his name by someone to whom he did not wish to give it, Nikolai might well have answered, with modest pride, *I have renounced my name, as I have renounced everything else in life...* Perhaps Elena Petrovna was wrong, and the image of Nikolai and the words the apparition spoke had not been drawn from Margarita's mind after all, but from his own. But then who was Bulgakov?

"Pavel Pavlovich was always thinking about *Monkey,*" Margarita was saying. "He was obsessed with it."

"Nikolai's book?"

"Yes, his wonderful book!"

"You've read it?"

"Parts of it. Those lines the ghost... the apparition spoke... those are from his book."

"Are they?" Fyodorov cried. He felt he was becoming feverish, or perhaps going mad. "But I thought you said they were from Bulgakov's book."

For a moment, Margarita looked at them in confusion.

"Well... yes. They are. But Bulgakov's book is also Nikolai's."

"Ah! He is writing under a *nom de plume,*" Blavatskaya exclaimed. "Well, at last he's being sensible. He should have done it from the beginning."

"So," Fyodorov began, in a state of confusion of his own, "if I understand this... there are two books now? Both written by Nikolai? Or is there only the one?"

"There are two books," Margarita said. "But one of them has not yet been written."

Fyodorov and Blavatskaya looked at each other in surprise.

"What book has not yet been written?"

"It will be called *The Master and Margarita.*"

"Ah, and Nikolai is going to write this book, and you are going to be a character in it?"

"Yes. But he will write it under a different name."

"Bulgakov?"

"That's right. Under a different name, and in a different time."

"But you have already read parts of it," Blavatskaya said. "So he has written some of it, at least."

Again Margarita looked at them in confusion. "I am remembering the future," she said, and burying her head in her hands, she cried, "Oh, I don't know! I don't know! I shouldn't be here! I must go back!"

"You poor child," Fyodorov said, filling their glasses again. "We must take you home. To Princess Volkonskaya's? Is that where you wish to go?"

"I am lost!" she cried.

Fyodorov searched in his pocket for a handkerchief to offer her, but Blavatskaya sat back in her chair and closed her eyes. She concentrated her mind, exerted all her power, reached out with every particle of psychic energy she possessed... and met a solid wall.

Fyodorov had found his handkerchief but before he could offer it to the weeping Margarita, Blavatskaya seized it from him and wiped the perspiration from her brow.

"Tell us about the different time, Margarita," she said in her gentlest voice. "A different name, a different time. What different time are you talking about?"

"Oh, that," Margarita said with a small shrug. "I don't understand it at all. But you, Fyodorov, you do! He often talked to me about you and your experiments and your ideas about traveling into the future. Time portals and time travel. He finds these ideas so fascinating. And he knows so much, Kolya... He knows about the planets and the stars, and the atoms that make up matter, and about space..." She opened her hand and stared down at her palm. "We are made of pure energy, you know. Of tiny invisible particles of energy... just like the entire world... all of it, emptiness and energy and light... though Kolya says there is a kind of dark energy as well... out of which everything comes... and the totality filled with wonder and mystery... and the greatest mystery is Being itself, and the greatest question, why anything exists at all."

"Yes, yes! We used to talk about all that," Fyodorov said with enthusiasm. "We'd stay up all night talking about space and time."

"I was always jealous of you, Fyodor Fyodorovich, spending so much time with him when I could not."

"And why couldn't you?" Blavatskaya asked. "If you were married, why didn't you live together?"

Margarita smiled at her, a very beautiful, an almost beatific smile. "Live with Kolya? It would be like trying to live with… the Lampyridae."

Blavatskaya raised a questioning eyebrow at Fyodorov. "Fireflies," he said.

"Or with the Raskolniki," Margarita went on, "or far in the east with the Dukhobortsy, the Spirit Wrestlers. Or wandering with gypsies or the Sarakatsans of Roumeli, and being drunk all day long. Or flying to the stars in a rocket machine or floating over the ocean in a balloon. He lives in a different world from the rest of us. You understand, don't you, dear Fyodorov? You know what he's like. He is a free spirit. You can never rely on him for anything, even to be in a certain place at a certain time. Anyway, you're quite right, no one knew about our marriage. Kolya wanted to keep it secret. He thought it would be too dangerous for me if it were known. Of course, it is known now. The Third Division found out about it somehow. They can suborn anyone, I suppose. Though I can't imagine who told them."

"And you were married to him all this time?" Fyodorov asked.

"All this time!" she sighed. "A hundred years would not be long enough."

"Well, he never said a word about it to me."

"Perhaps he told one of his friends when they were drinking together. When he drank, well… It's hard to lie when you are drunk, isn't it? It seems drunken men are more likely to speak their minds and open their hearts. Perhaps he told one of his friends, and that friend told someone else. That's the only way they could have found out."

"What I would like to find out," Blavatskaya said, "is where exactly he is at this moment. He and his book."

"And this is the question I have been asked a hundred times, and I don't know the answer. The last time I saw him… we spent some weeks in the country… he returned to Petersburg. He said he would come back to High Meadows, but he didn't come back, and I don't know where he is."

"And the manuscript of *Monkey*, I expect, went with him."

Margarita stood and walked to the window and gazed out at the falling snow. Everything was white, the sky, the trees, the ground, and every object that had been left in the courtyard was now merely a white mound. The wind was blowing hard, and somewhere a bell was ringing. Behind her, Fyodorov began reciting:

Bells are ringing
and gongs sound, heavy,
as though in a Buddhist temple
or a monastery.
The bells are not a call to prayer,
but resound freely in the arctic air.
The shadow of a gull is passing,
skimming over snow-white ground,
and chimney smoke, like incense rising,
briskly floating, southward bound.
And all the trees are bowing down,
bending back and forth,
back and forth,
in the gale.

A silence followed. Then Fyodorov said, "You must recognize that poem, my dear Margarita."

When she did not reply, he added, "It's a favorite of Nikolai's. I believe his mother wrote it. He always recited it when it was snowing, didn't he? Part of his arsenal of snow poems, as you must know yourself, Margarita Mikhailevna."

Margarita turned from the window and faced them. And Blavatskaya, still reaching out psychically to find any crack in the mental carapace Margarita presented to her, suddenly heard her thoughts. *Who are they, these heroes, these saviors? A short, stern, squat woman in black, perhaps a witch. A skinny, nervous, bespectacled professor, perhaps a madman. What can they know about love, true, faithful, eternal love? Love—fierce, powerful, bright, infinite, unremitting, never quenched? What do they know about sacrifice? And about eternal loss, eternal grief—what do they know?*

"He did not take *Monkey* with him," she said. "He burnt it."

And look at them! Are they even surprised? Fyodorov only stuffs more tobacco into his pipe, in such a desultory and slovenly way he leaves a cascade of tobacco leaves on his shirt and jacket. And she, she merely stares at me with a completely vacant expression, as though she were about to fall asleep. How witches wait. Or how they cast spells.

And at that, Margarita's mind slammed shut against Blavatskaya.

"He did it one afternoon while I was out," Margarita continued. "He stuffed the pages into the stove. Written pages burn reluctantly… as Bulgakov says… My Nikolai was stubborn. He ripped the pages, he used a poker to ruffle them so they would catch fire more easily, so the wonderful words he had written would turn to black ashes and dust. He burnt the notebooks as well, tore them apart with his hands, fed them to the flames. By the time I returned, all but a few pages were destroyed. Oh, how I wept, how I beat his chest in rage… How could he have done it? The few pages that remained, blackened pages… I pulled them from the fire with my own hands, and preserved them, and smoothed them… maybe a dozen pages in all. And why did he do it? It was too dangerous for me, he said. He did it to protect me from those monsters… those beasts that want to destroy everything beautiful and free. They had condemned the novel before they even read it. Well, how could they not? If they read it, they would fall in love with it, it would change their hearts and their lives, and then they would no longer be the monsters they are paid to be."

"My goodness," Fyodorov said. "What a tale!"

Yes, a tale indeed, Blavatskaya thought. *And quite a fanciful one at that. It sounds like it came straight off the pages of a novel.*

What she said was, "If we are going to set forth later today, perhaps now we should all try to sleep."

The vodka, the food, the warmth of the stove, the wind rattling the shutters, the dimness of the light, all these things were conducive to sleep, and Margarita, lying on the sofa, was soon breathing deeply, and Fyodorov, in the armchair, was nodding and snoring softly. Only Blavatskaya was fully awake, awake to the dangers that surrounded them, and the danger that was in the room with them. The girl seemed so innocent, her story was so convincing…

But she is no more Nikolai Barakov's wife than I am.

Then what was she?

Her thoughts were utterly opaque. Her stories were literary and romantic, like the one about Nikolai burning his manuscript—for love!—that no one who had ever set pen to paper would ever believe. Even the story of the secret marriage seemed preposterous. A great secret no one knew, except Pavel Beriosov; a great secret she had kept from everyone and yet had told to them, easily, eagerly, for no good reason.

And she did not recognize Nikolai's favorite poem.

Was she a spy, then, an agent of the Third Division… a psychic adept, recruited by the Ministry, schooled in mesmerism, taking on the role of a fictional wife and sent out as a lure to entrap others, perhaps the Barakovs themselves? But for such a deception to be successful, she would have to be the real Margarita Mikhailevna, daughter of Tatyana Volkonskaya. Was she? Had they really been able to recruit the daughter of Princess Volkonskaya? Was this possible?

Well it's a pretty puzzle you've set us, Cousin Margarita. A pretty puzzle indeed. Blavatskaya lit a cigarette. While she smoked it, she thought.

Her own dear Master had sent her orders, and she had willingly obeyed. To rendezvous with Barakov, or, if that proved impossible, to find his book.

What had Nikolai Nekrasov said? *Manuscripts don't burn.*

An absurd statement, she had thought at the time. Now… she accepted it. She was convinced that Barakov's book still existed; therefore, her orders stood.

And what of that other book, *The Master and Margarita*? Was there such a book? And this Bulgakov—was there such an author? And what did it signify that Margarita insisted that this book was not yet written but would be written *in a different time*? There was some deep mystery at work here.

She herself was familiar with mysteries. She had travelled far and wide; she had met many remarkable men and witnessed extraordinary events. Many secret doctrines had been imparted to her. In Central Asia she had met shamans who could so easily project their astral bodies that they were often seen in two places at once. In Hungary she had met mesmerists who could hypnotize entire villages, and in Siberia, sorcerers who by the use of magical instruments and incantations could materialize the spirits of the dead. Necromancy was a powerful craft, a dark art; yet it was practiced, fell and benighted though it was.

Pray to the Lord, and don't relax.

Yes, there were times when it was fruitful to pray, times when it was not only fruitful but necessary. As the poet so truly said: the bells are not a call to prayer, yet the trees bow down.

By the time the sleepers awakened, she had come to a decision.

"We shall flee under cover of darkness," Blavatskaya announced.

"Flee? Where?" Fyodorov asked. He was busy searching about the room. "Blast it all! I have lost my cane!"

Margarita was stretching beautifully and tying back her long, curly, black hair. She had a fulsome figure, more apparent now that she had flung off her shawl. Her cheeks were rosy and her lips were pink. She looked like a portrait of a perfectly healthy young woman just awakening from sleep.

As though she were a character in a book.

Blavatskaya looked up and saw a little impish elemental balancing on the icon stand in the upper corner of the room. A moment later, the air was filled with bits of paper, shreds of the *Moscow News,* which had previously been stacked in a basket beside the stove. Laughter came from all corners of the room. The samovar was shaking noisily, the bottle and glasses on the table started to rattle.

"Yes, I think it's best we leave right now," Blavatskaya said. "Cane or no cane, Fyodorov."

"I will not leave," Margarita said.

"What do you mean, you won't leave?" Fyodorov asked crossly. It had just occurred to him that he must have left his cane behind at the Beriosov house.

"She means she won't go with us, isn't that right? You have to wait for them here, don't you? But they are not coming, Margarita. They are not coming for you."

"I don't know who this *they* might be that you speak of, Elena Petrovna."

Sleep had done wonders for Margarita. She looked young and fresh, she looked like a young goddess.

It was in that instant of pure vision that Blavatskaya finally understood. Had she really thought of Margarita as a spy? What an absurd idea! She was not a human being at all.

What an amazing opportunity she was being offered! Rarely, if ever, was one offered such a chance, and a kind of fierce joy rose up in her. Yes, it would be a test of her powers, to see if she could force her will on one of the Divine Ones. What a glorious moment it would be! So without any hesitation, she went up to Margarita where she was sitting on the sofa, and grabbed her roughly by the arm, and pulled her to her feet.

"Listen to me! I said I would save you, and I will save you. You are coming with us, and we are leaving now."

The girl started shaking in Blavatskaya's grip, but Blavatskaya had no intention of letting her go. "Who are you? Tell me your name! Speak!"

She did not speak. Instead, while the elementals tossed objects into the air, and rained down bits of paper and ash on their heads, Margarita began to grow tall, taller and taller, and her arm thickened and became muscular and furry.

Blavatskaya held on.

"Fyodorov! For the love of God! Open the window!"

He opened it, and a small mountain of snow fell into the room and a harsh wind followed it. The fire in the stove crackled, the ash in the air blew in circles.

"Come now. This won't do," Blavatskaya said. The huge figure looming over her had taken the shape of a ferocious black bear. The animal growled menacingly; she tightened her grip on its arm. "Turn into a dragon, if you must, but I am not letting you go."

Then she cried out loudly to Fyodorov, "Open the door!"

He flung the door open, a snow-laden gale blew in, and they heard the cheerful bells of an approaching troika.

"Well, that's a good sound to hear," Blavatskaya said, pulling at the arm she was still gripping. "Come now, Little Bear, come along nicely. No biting!"

But now the figure began shrinking again, the bear's arm became human once more, soft skin and smooth cloth replaced fur. Margarita—for she was Margarita once more—suddenly stopped growling, stopped fighting, stopped pulling and twisting this way and that, and now standing quite still and closing her eyes, began reciting words that even as she spoke them were moving her to tears so that she wept as she spoke.

"*Listen to the stillness, listen and enjoy what you were not given in life—peace. Look, there ahead is your eternal home which you have been given as a reward. You will fall asleep with a smile on your lips, sleep will strengthen you, and you will no longer be able to drive me away. I will watch over your sleep...* This is what I said to him, my beloved, these were my last words to him."

"To whom, Margarita? To Nikolai? Was it to Nikolai that you said them?"

"Yes! Yes! Don't you see? I must go back now!"

While they were speaking, Fyodorov had thrown their cloaks around them, and was gently pushing them toward the open door. Suddenly, Margarita thrust herself forward and strode out through the doorway, outside into the air, under the starlight and the moonlight, for the snow had stopped falling and the sky was bright and clear. The troika was waiting for them by the gate, the horses stomping the ground and whitening the air with their breath.

Blavatskaya and Fyodorov hurried out after her, but some force stopped them on the threshold. They could only watch from there while, standing alone in the moonlight, something remarkable happened to Margarita. It was as though all the light from the cold stars, all the light from the moon, was passing through her, making her first luminous, then diaphanous, and finally, right there before their eyes—invisible, as though light itself had carried her away.

"A time portal is merely a thought experiment," Fyodorov said. "It is entirely theoretical. But there are incidents which suggest that time and space are not entirely what we think they are. Weird things do happen."

"Indeed they do."

"As we have just witnessed."

"Yes, as we have."

The troika was carrying them through the still and snowy night to God only knew where, and yet, despite the rather bizarre events of the day, there were things they had to discuss, calmly and rationally, and so that was what they were doing, huddling under warm sheepskin blankets, perfectly comfortable and at ease.

"You think Nikolai Barakov might have discovered one of these time portals?" Blavatskaya asked. "Is that what you think?"

"If they exist, someone is bound to find them. Maybe many have. All those people who just disappear. How would we know?"

"But you conceive of it as a sort of tunnel... that people might use to go back and forth?"

"Why not? People from our time might go into the past or the future, people in the future might come here."

"And objects could be brought back and forth as well?"

"Again, why not? People. Objects. Ideas. Anything. It would explain why they are expending so much time and energy searching for Barakov. It seems excessive, wouldn't you say, for just another writer of subversive novels. Of course, Beriosov was no more serious in saying he was searching for the book in order to destroy it as you were. It was a clever ruse, to tell him that. But what are your intentions should we find it?"

"Don't concern yourself with my intentions, Fyodorov. But what you say is of interest to me. And so you think Barakov might have described this time portal in his novel and that's why our Third Division is so determined to find it?"

"It is certainly possible. When Margarita mentioned the book that doesn't yet exist, she said something about *remembering the future*. Not the sort of idea many people have."

"But one might have such an idea if one were traveling through time. Is that what you mean?"

"It is one explanation. And she did disappear. We witnessed it. Where did she go?"

"Yes, a time portal is one explanation. I have another."

"I suppose something from your occult world?"

"No. And not Beriosov's either. To conjure up such a creature would be quite an accomplishment for him. A necromancer might attempt it, but Margarita had a sweetness about her one does not find in the spirits of the reanimated dead. Though, granted, they are a very skillful family. Svetlana, a mesmerist. Pavel, a necromancer..."

"And Dmitri, a physicist of some talent and erudition. He knew my work and had ideas about it. If *Monkey* is about time travel, he's clever enough to have understood its scientific significance… Did they all die in the fire, do you think?"

"I doubt it. They are too evil to kill off so easily."

"Assuming this theory about *Monkey* is correct, and it does describe these portals or give instructions of some kind, then we really do need to find it, Elena Petrovna."

"I understand, Fyodor Fyodorov. And we shall. But I believe we shall find it in this time, in this world. And speaking of this world, do you happen to know which direction we are going in?"

"I would say now we are journeying south, toward Petersburg."

"I will not remain there. I believe to find Barakov's book we must go east."

"I will remain there, for a little while, anyway. I have some ideas I want to pursue in my laboratory."

"I hope you don't think you can find this time portal, Fyodorov. Don't waste your time on foolishness. The book exists. It can be found. What you seek is pure chimera."

"Perhaps you are right, Elena Petrovna. Tell me, you mentioned you had another explanation for what occurred that was neither a feat of necromancy nor an example of time travel. What is your explanation?"

Blavatskaya leaned back against the soft sheepskin rug and closed her eyes.

"It is not an explanation, Fyodorov. It is the truth. Margarita is a Muse. She is Nikolai Barakov's Muse. Perhaps also the Muse of this Bulgakov. But a Muse is what she is, a goddess. We were in the presence of a goddess, Fyodorov. How did it feel? I myself felt mostly annoyed with her. That is quite odd, isn't it? Anyway, it appears she allowed herself to become trapped by the Beriosovs, and she suffered a period of confusion before marshaling the strength to return to her own cosmic sphere. Poor goddess, she seemed utterly befuddled by love. However that may be, now I have told you the true explanation for the phenomenon we witnessed, you must abandon your experiments, Fyodor Fyodorovich, and come with me. We will find *Monkey* in the east."

Fyodor, utterly amazed by this explanation, could not reply. Meanwhile, Blavatskaya was thinking of high mountains and prayer flags and stupas and the gentle rhythm of the moving sleigh was lulling her, lulling her gently, and so, slowly and gently, she drifted into sleep.

Fyodorov did not sleep. Something in his world was not right. Not right at all.

A goddess? A Muse? What nonsense! Was it possible?

He tried to remember... How did it happen that he was now riding in a sledge in the night with the notorious Madame Blavatskaya? How had that happened?

They had been sitting on a bench, waiting for someone.

But how did I ever come to meet her in the first place? he asked himself. He could not remember. *And who told us to wait on the bench at the Patriarch Ponds? And who was supposed to meet us there? For whom were we waiting?*

It was much like the experience Margarita had described. You find yourself sitting on a bench, beneath the Kremlin walls, at the Patriarch Ponds, perhaps even at a spa in Pyatigorsk. You have no idea how you got there. It is like a dream in which things are happening that seem to have been happening for a long time, though you have only just become conscious of them and of having a role in them.

And before that, where had he been? Had he not been in his laboratory? Had he not been ... reading a book? But then something had happened, and it had thrown the entire rational universe out of whack. Muses were visiting, spirits were traveling in the astral plane, perhaps a time portal had opened.

He had to get back! He had to return to Petersburg as quickly as possible!

He shouted to the driver, but there was no answer.

BOOK FOUR

Romance in the Demi-monde

Chapter Fourteen

Stardust

I was a prisoner in the tower and the only person I saw was the old woman who came every day to bring me food, water, and wood for the stove. God bless her that she came, though as the days passed she spoke less and less. Perhaps she had been warned not to befriend me. I never learned her name.

One night, one of those very long winter nights that last eighteen hours and are reluctant to leave even when the day breaks, I heard different footsteps on the stairs, and knew they were coming for me at last. They were not the heavy, tired footfalls, accompanied by snorts and groans, of the poor old woman, but were light and difficult to hear, but I had been listening for them, listening all the time, and so I was able to hear them when they finally came.

I waited, listening... until I knew they were just outside the door. I had no weapon, nothing with which to defend myself. There was not even a decent stick of wood. Very little good that would do anyway. All I could do was stand in the dark and wait. Then, with a rush of cold air, the door flew open, and light from a torch illuminated the man who stood in the doorway.

My heart nearly stopped, I had to breathe hard to keep myself on my feet, when in a deep voice that seemed in that silence like a shout, he said, "I have come to free you, Madame! Come quickly!"

And Pavel Damianich, grinning—the crazy fool, I thought, my heart filling with pure joy—threw a cloak around me and literally pushed me out the door and down the steps. Down we went in a great rushing plunge, the staircase being one of those twisting, circular affairs, steep and dark. Down we flew, or fell; then, pushing me still, he guided me through dark passages and finally out a door into the night.

"Sshh!" he whispered, though I had hardly made a sound, only a sigh of joy and relief, and tugged me along after him, hugging the walls, trampling bushes and flower beds in the process, until my eyes made out a figure in the night... My heart leapt. Was it friend or foe? Neither, a mere statue... We kept creeping along, Pasha holding my hand so tightly I thought he might crush my fingers. And yet to breathe the air! To be under the great sky! To be free! It was worth it, broken fingers or even death—well worth it.

I breathed deeply, and smelt smoke. Then we were running over a lawn, and then into a darkness, under the limbs of trees. A boy and two horses were waiting there. I was lifted onto a saddle, Pavel and the boy mounted the other horse, and off we rode, off into freedom! Down the long drive, galloping now, and no one could catch us.

I glanced behind me and saw a red glow coming from the house as though a fire had been loosed there. Subversives are incendiaries, as we all know, and burning the houses of the rich delights us more than gambling or drink. So, laughing at the great joke that was our lives, I rode on into the wild and glorious night with Pasha, my savior, while behind us the mansion of Svetlana Beriosova burned.

We rode on like brigands in the night, Pavel Damianich and I, like wild Tatars, like Cossacks, like the very wind, from the place of my imprisonment to the outskirts of the city. There, at dawn, we left the well-rewarded boy and his horses at the stable from whence they had come, and hired a carriage to take us a bit farther into town, and then another to ride around in circles until Pavel was sure we were not being followed, and could safely walk through a few nasty alleys to the nastiest alley of all, and to the secret side door of that most disreputable of houses, the Stardust.

Serafima's fortress had never seemed so secure, her brandy had never tasted sweeter, though she herself, having spent many anxious hours waiting for us, was not in the most dulcet of moods. Still, once relieved of her fears for us, she wanted to hear the entire story in detail, and while listening, devoted herself to our comfort. So I found myself transported within hours from miserable imprisonment to the luxury of a sultan's tent where I was wrapped in warm blankets and fed delicacies while a handsome boy massaged my feet.

"Well, you've certainly had an adventure, both of you," she sighed when we finished our tale. "And I am sure burning down the house was the *coup de grace*."

"Oh, God! Were there prisoners in the cellar?" I had suddenly remembered the voices I'd heard. "I think there were, Pasha."

"There were not. No prisoners in the cellars. I know. I hid down there for a night and a day. Nobody in the cellars but rats. As for the fire, it provided a helpful diversion, wouldn't you say? I'm sure you were more than ready to relinquish your role as maiden in the tower... what was her name?"

"Rapunzel," Serafima and I both said at once.

"She doesn't have the hair for it," Serafima said.

"Nor am I a maiden. So, no, the *terem* was not a place for me... Where did you get the explosive?"

Pavel laughed. "What explosive? Listen to her! Not a maiden in the tower, but an interrogator. You have missed your calling, Valentina Grigorevna."

Since it was clear from his smile that I was going to get nothing more from him about the cause of the mysterious fire, I turned my thoughts from the past to the future. We were safe for the moment, but how long could we remain in a brothel no matter how delicate the sensibilities of its clientele? And if we were to leave, where would we go? And for what purpose, now that I had resigned myself to the bitter truth of Nikolai's death? It had gripped me so intensely, this notion that Nikolai was dead. I could think of no other reason why I should have been arrested.

I told them what I feared.

"Nonsense," Serafima said, dismissing the entire notion with a sweep of her hand. "If they had disposed of Nikolai secretly, why would they want to draw attention to it by arresting you? You do have some measure of fame, dear Marko." She smiled at me, endearingly. "Sooner or later you would be missed."

"But there must be a snitch in that house. Beriosov knew about the press in the cellar. And—if they knew about the press, why didn't they raid the house? Or did they?"

The thought of Katerina Ivanovna in the hands of those brutes almost roused me from my couch.

The tale that Pasha then related to us was almost unbelievable, as so much is in our country, so much so that we no longer know what normal human behavior is, or have a sense of the difference between the farcical and the real. We no longer understand satire because our lives have become satirical. We no longer fear the worst because we are living in it. And yet the worst can get even worse, and when it does, we laugh and say, This is absolutely unbelievable! The story Pasha told might have been a comedy, it might have been one of those farces French playwrights are so fond of, or the kind of slapstick found in British music halls, or it could have been what it was: an example of the workings of the Third Section of the Imperial Chancellory.

This, then, is the gist of the story Pasha told:

The same night Beriosov sent his bullies to my apartment, he also sent a squad of white straps to the communal house. They surrounded it in their usual subtle manner—all blue uniforms and prancing horses and sabre rattling—and banged on the door. When no one answered, or didn't answer quickly enough, they broke it down and rushed inside. One group took the cellar, another the kitchen, a third the upper rooms. As usual, the highest ranking officer waited in the hall, nearest the exit, in case there should be fireworks of some kind, these anarchists being notorious for their bomb-making apparatuses as well as for their highly explosive reading materials.

Down from the upper rooms they dragged two ancient, odoriferous men, and a skeletal woman, dressed in a decrepit grey night shirt. The woman was still asleep and could not be awakened. It soon appeared clear even to the clueless white straps that they were trying to awaken a corpse, and not a new one. They immediately arrested the old men, either for the crime of possessing a corpse or the crime of creating one. Meanwhile from the kitchen, another group retrieved a rather large pig, terrified, naturally, obstinately resisting arrest, and screeching in that high-pitched way pigs have of making their discomfort known, and this noise and struggle upset the chickens that were also living in the kitchen and woke the cock who started crowing angrily though it was hours before dawn. The glorious *gendarmes* were still attempting to control the livestock when from the cellar there emerged first the grossest of odors—a dank, swamp-like miasma—and then, straggling up from below, coughing and retching, several sterling members of the imperial secret police covered to their thighs in river mud and sewage.

The Third Division had raided the wrong house.

One must not laugh at power. This is one of Serafima's Laws. Never laugh at a man while he is performing a sexual act, no matter how absurd or grotesque it may look. Very well. Never laugh at the secret police either. But in both cases, we have to laugh. Power in the hands of men can be frightening, but it is also often very silly. What is one to do? Laughter is inevitable when men make fools of themselves. In any case, we could laugh safely in Serafima's rooms, and laugh we did.

"As for the right house, which I know you are keen to ask about," Pasha added, reading my mind, "they did finally send some minions there the next day, but by then the story had traveled throughout the neighborhood with the speed of an express train—the pig, the sewage, the corpse, and the poor old stinking men, let's not forget them—and so by the time the white straps arrived, of course everyone had left, and taken the press with them. And that was that."

I didn't believe it.

"How on earth did they manage to go to the wrong houses? I would think such errors would be—unacceptable."

"Your friends were just lucky," Pasha said.

I turned to Serafima. "Luck?"

"Perhaps. Or perhaps someone in the Ministry didn't want that press seized quite yet."

"You mean—those boys are *agents provocateur*?"

"My God! I think I have shocked you, Marko! My darling, have you really never considered this?"

"Well, of course, I know they have spies everywhere—"

"Yes, and more than spies. They have agents trained to provoke action, then they move in and punish it. It is what they do best, and some day they will do it so well that the Tsar will be assassinated at the hands of a man employed by the Tsar's own secret service. Mark my words."

"Then why bother raiding the place at all?"

"One hand doesn't always know what the other hand is up to. One group within the Ministry has this set of agents working for them; another group has another set. And their plans are jealously guarded, and there are plots within plots. Oh, it is a nest of vipers, and sometimes they bite each other. A most gratifying sight."

"Those stupid boys in the cellar. It's hard to believe."

"Not at all. A spy service wants stupid boys in cellars, arrogant and stupid boys. At least we know that Barakov's friends got safely away. One of them even found his way here."

"What do you mean? Who?"

"Fyodorov," Pasha said. "Remember? You mentioned him—"

"Fyodorov is here?" I found it—unbelievable.

"Oh Lord, I have shocked you again," Serafima said, laughing. "But, really, darling, you should rest. Bathe, eat something, sleep... We'll talk again later."

The tale of the odoriferous old men had reminded me of my own odoriferousness. A bath and a meal... yes. Then I would have to have a nice long talk with Fyodor Fyodorov, cosmist philosopher, author, quack, and former housemate of Nikolai Barakov, whose presence in the Stardust was so startling and miraculous I felt as though a bag of gold had just fallen into my lap. But before I could talk with Fyodorov, I had a few other pressing tasks which, since I could not do them myself—being once again under a kind of house arrest, though a voluntary one—I had to send someone to do for me. Pasha was willing, but I was afraid he was something of a marked man having blackened a few eyes and knocked out a few teeth during that fist fight with the *gendarmes* in my vestibule. Serafima had a boy to lend me, but he was too pretty by far to send out into the streets. No, I needed someone like Little Abrasha, the bouncer, a sturdy, compact, bruiser of a man, but still somewhat inconspicuous in a crowd. It was a sign of how much affection Serafima had for me that she agreed to lend Abrasha to me for an hour or two that afternoon.

That settled, I bathed in peace, wrapped myself in a borrowed kimono, and sat down to an excellent meal. Life was good again, for the moment. But moments are all we have. Relishing the good ones when they come may be the true art of living. Anastasia once wrote a little poem on this very theme, a poem I recalled with pleasure:

Under a shroud of grey, a lowering sky,
A flash of red against the somber trees.
He calls to her, and her quick reply
Tells him she is close. Then on the breeze,
And calling to each other still,
They fly upon their separate ways.
But, oh, how their ardent hearts must fill,
Knowing the freedom of uncounted days,
The quick uplift of flight, a daily bliss,

As thrilling to them as a lover's kiss.
And so, enraptured by the moment's song,
Its benediction, like a flow of grace,
I thank you, Life, for blessing me so long,
A willing captive in your sweet embrace.

"Tell me about Pavel Damianovich, your *soi-disant* valet."

"What do you mean, *soi-disant*? Pavel Damianovich is my valet."

Serafima rolled her beautiful eyes at me. Her dresser was just finishing her hair. She looked divine.

"Marko, my dear, please do not play the fool with me. Young Pavel Damianovich is as much a valet as you are the Queen of France. He is your lover. Why be coy about it? He is perfectly presentable. He is charming, and quite delicious in every way. I must say, it is heartening to see a man so in love. Of course, he is young, and young men do tend to become worshippers."

"I hardly know what to say," I said, for indeed I was quite nonplused.

"Say nothing, if you wish, but at least let us stop the charade. You are residing here for a time, where we celebrate love in all its myriad forms. There is no need to continue this pretense. We are all very discreet. Now, you wanted to ask me about Fyodorov. What he's doing here. All I know is that he is rehearsing a play."

I was still reeling from one revelation—that Serafima, seemingly so astute and pragmatic in matters of love, should harbor such romantic illusions about me. Now to hear that Fyodorov the Cosmist was an actor—

"Oh, I am so confused! Though I suppose you think confusion is my constant state of being."

"Not at all. You will just have to investigate what he's doing. You are the investigator, aren't you?"

"Am I? All I've investigated so far are brothels and prison cells. Perhaps you'll tell me that's all there is. Pleasure and punishment."

Serafima was dressed to administer both. She was wearing a tight-waisted gown of black silk which accentuated her regal stature, and was holding a short riding crop. She looked ravishing.

"He is rehearsing now, I believe. I allow it in the sitting room, before clients begin to arrive." She looked me up and down with some disapproval. "What are you going to wear?"

"Little Abrasha will be here soon with my trunk," I said, and indeed at that very moment a boy came in to announce that my trunk had been delivered, and that my neighbor, Nadya, about whom I'd been worried, was at home and well, news that greatly relieved my mind.

Fyodor Fyodorov was much younger than I expected him to be, perhaps in his mid-thirties, slight of build, fair haired and bespectacled, formal in his dress, fussy in his mannerisms, with a soft speaking voice which became somewhat high-pitched when he raised it, which he was doing at the moment I entered the sitting room. Rehearsal was in progress, and he was commenting on it, which annoyed everyone to a degree which made me suspect the entire project was doomed.

"It is not a French farce! You will not be wearing powdered wigs and French cloaks! Why are you playing it like it is a vaudeville?"

"How else are we to play it?" one of the actors cried. "It is a comedy, isn't it? The audience must laugh at it!"

"The audience will laugh because of the irony—the IRONY—not because you actors are tumbling around like circus clowns!"

"But, Fyodorov, it is *impossible*!" another actor said, literally wringing his hands."The language! It's not poetry. My character speaks like a peasant!"

"He speaks like a peasant because he is a peasant!"

"But not even peasants should speak like peasants on the stage!"

At this Fyodorov threw up his hands. Then he caught sight of me.

"Actor?" he asked.

"Bystander," I replied, and asked him what play they were rehearsing.

"One that cannot be performed, evidently. One that isn't *French* enough."

"Fyodorov, *really!* You are browbeating the poor boys, and that is my job!" This from a gaunt man, tall from the look of his outspread legs, with expressive eyebrows and a small mustache, sitting in state in a high-back voltaire with a small dog at his feet, holding a copy of the script.

"Why don't we let our bystander be the judge?" one of the actors asked, a dark young man, lean and good looking.

At that, one of the young men rushed over to me and took me by the arm.

"We'll run through the act for you. New eyes. New ears. Very valuable."

"What is the play?" I asked for the second time. "And who is the playwright?"

"The playwright is anonymous. The play is *Wide and Crooked.*"

The title was unknown to me, but an anonymous playwright meant either the work was subversive or so bad the author was ashamed to claim credit for it. But since I had no other plans for the afternoon, I agreed to act as critic and took a seat.

The drapes were closed as usual, so once the lamps were extinguished, the room was quite dim with only a single lamp in the front of the room to illuminate the actors. The set consisted of a table and a few chairs, a bottle of vodka and glasses. The scene began with several actors slumped over the table, one standing in the back, and another, a woman, sitting upright in a chair in the corner.

One actor, shaking his head as though trying to wake himself up, raised his hand and banged his glass onto the table and shouted a single word, a word one only hears in the gutter, a word everyone knows but no one says, a word never heard on a stage before. It shattered the silence. Then he shouted it again.

And so from the drawing room of a high-class brothel, I was transported to the steamy, dingy kitchen of that house across the river, eavesdropping on a conversation that I might easily have heard in person while I was in that same room. One by one, they all appeared—Taras, Ilya, Gavriil, Mikha, Katya, the old man, and even a mad philosopher. Was he not Fyodorov himself? They were all there, under different names. And there was another, too, Veniamin, called Venka, played by the lean, dark-haired actor, playing the naif, the innocent… the fool.

If I had not been in that house myself I would never have believed it, how they shouted obscenities at each other, kicked at their chairs, banged down their glasses, addressed each other only by their patronymics, swore and ranted, argued and joked, said outrageous things in the language of the gutter, invoked the highest and loftiest ideals only to turn them on their heads, and wove revolutionary slogans into their talk as though they were phrases you might yell out the window at the lamplighters. The actors were right: it was not the sort of drama we were used to. It wasn't like art at all, but more like life. It was literary realism, yes, but not the dark, bare, humorless, brutal kind so favored by our younger critics. No, it was an exposure of human life as it was really lived, with its sensuality and its crudity, its insults and its laughter, its politics and its pretenses, its sentimentality, its cruelty, its desperate hopes and its deepest fears. It was like looking in through a window at people living their uncensored lives.

I had never seen anything like it on a stage before.

The plot revolved around the Taras character, here called Arif, a typical violent, dishonest, and cowardly brute. Evidently, earlier in the play, he had been arrested and released on the condition that he collect evidence against his friends in the household, whom the security police believed to be part of a secret conspiracy against the regime. Drunk one night, Arif confesses everything to Venka, who offers him a means of escape, but this act of generosity only angers Arif and turns him against Venka, whom he must despise in order to betray. Only Venka's lover, Monika, sees what is happening and tries to open Venka's eyes to the truth.

Her last attempt to save him from his friend's betrayal takes place in their bedroom, the illusion provided by a settee, a pillow, and a blanket in disarray. Monika, played by a young actress of considerable talent, is trying to persuade Venka that his sense of morality is quite different from the amorality of his friends, that they are nihilists but he is not. He replies that he doesn't consider himself a nihilist any longer, though there was a time when he did.

I had reason later to memorize much of this play, and these last lines especially I soon knew by heart:

Monika *(sitting up in bed)*: You? A nihilist? Impossible, Venka! I can't believe it.

Venka *(stretched out beside her, his feet sticking out from beneath the blanket, holes in his shoes)*: You haven't known me very long. Before... for most of my life... I felt empty inside, like I was missing something. A soul, maybe.

M: A soul?

V: Call it what you will. Whatever it was, I didn't have it. Life had no meaning for me, and seemed absurd. Nihilism justified the way I felt, gave it a name, made it seem important and philosophical. And, of course, universal. Since I have no purpose, the world has no purpose. Since my life is absurd, the world is absurd.

M *(kissing him):* But your life is not absurd, Venka.

V *(sitting up, taking her hand)*: It was before I met you. It's like I was born blind, and so I thought the world was dark. Then suddenly one day I woke up and I could see… light, color, trees, flowers, people, everything! I always knew they were there, but now I could see them. That's how it feels. You have given me a soul, Monika, or maybe it's your soul I'm feeling. Maybe you're sharing your soul with me.

M: No, it is your own soul. I recognized it as soon as I saw you. A shining soul, just a little down at the heel… *(She indicates his shoes; he smiles at her, ruefully)* But now you must listen to me, my love! Listen, please. You are in terrible danger. You are not safe here. I know you don't want to face this, but you must now. You love Arif like a brother. But, Venka, he is no brother to you, and no friend, not to you or to anyone. He's a devil, a murderer, a betrayer. He's a snake, he slithers and simpers and sneaks. He's a drug addict, too, and, worse, he's a rat. You know this, Venka. You think he won't betray you, but he will. He would kill you to save himself. Not with his own hands, he is too cowardly and weak. He'd let others kill you for him. They'll take him back to the mines anyway. He's doomed, but you can still escape, Venka. You must!

V: But Arif? I can't believe it… How do you know this?

M: You just told me you've begun to see the world as it is, but I've been looking at the world for a long time and I can see what's right in front of my eyes. I know they are coming for you. I know it. I feel it. You offered Arif a way of escape. Now you need to take that way yourself. You must, Venka. If the ship is ready, you must go.

V: All right. I will, if you say I must. But only if you come with me. I can't go without you. You know I can't. I won't.

Suddenly there was a great pounding at the door, and I jumped out of my chair… but the actors went on since the pounding was part of the play. I felt quite ridiculous and sat down again.

(Pounding at the door. Instantly both Monika and Venka throw off the covers and get up from the bed.)

M *(taking him in her arms)*: You see? He's betrayed you, and now they are here. Hurry! You must leave, my love! Now! You must go!

(Venka does not move but stares out at the audience with a pained expression on his face. The pounding continues.)

M *(releasing him, pulling on his arm)*: Venka! You must leave. Now!

(He turns to Monika, and embraces her.)

V: All right. I will. But not without you. Come with me!

(Venka goes to the wall, pushes against it. A hidden door opens, revealing the machine.)

Here some imagination was required of the audience. This was a bordello, after all, not the Aleksandrinsky Theatre. Venka led Monika by the hand over to a curtain meant to be the wall of the bedroom. He pushed the curtain aside, and revealed *the machine.* A *deus ex machina* without the god in it: just the machine.

I took one look and started to laugh, as I am sure I was meant to, as I had to, the image was as absurd as the idea, for they had fixed up a chair with an open umbrella over it and some sort of wings made out of heaven only knew what—silk perhaps or bed sheets—and created some vision from a child's imagination, a child's dream of a flying machine, a child's idea of a means of escape.

V: Here it is. The professor's magic ship. Ready and waiting for us.

M: Where will it take us?

V: I was thinking of a city far, far away, a place where it's always summer and we can be together and be free.

(The pounding stops and a rush of people enter onto the stage. Leading them is not Arif, but the student, Semyon. He has a pistol in his hand. The group comes to a halt, waits.)

(No one moves. Lights go out.)

The stage went dark for a moment. Then the lights came up again, and everyone relaxed. The gaunt man in the director's chair turned toward me as though inviting me to share my reactions with him. I had only one reaction, though, and it was not for him.

I knew who the anonymous playwright was.

Of course, Anastasia Barakova's son would have enough talent to write like that. It was the sheer daring of it that surprised me. Now, of course, I understood what Fyodorov had meant when he talked about vaudeville and comedy and irony, for the play could be read in a number of ways, and the ending was especially dependent on the director's interpretation, for it could be played as romantic farce—the lovers escaping in a flying machine!—or as tragedy, a good man's fall into madness and self-deception, or as a political metaphor, the only escape from tyranny being some fantastic invention, a contrivance of imagination and hope.

What I had to do immediately was talk to Fyodorov. I looked around for him, but he was no longer in the room. He had slipped out before the end of the act, they told me, but no one could say where he had gone. Did he have his own flying machine so he could escape so easily? I went downstairs and upstairs, and yet could find him nowhere. The musclemen guarding the stairways hadn't seen him either. He seemed to have the power to make himself invisible.

"He's probably in his laboratory, miss," Serafima's dresser told me when I finally made my way back up to her rooms. The dresser was a theatre man himself and knew all about quick changes, trap doors, and flying machines. Stage craft. The art of the grand illusion.

"What laboratory is that?"

"He has a place he works in. Does all sorts of experiments, so I'm told. Makes queer machines. Never been up there myself."

"Is it here?"

"More or less. You can get there from here, though I'm not sure you can get back." He gave me a smile… but what sort of smile was it? A magician's smile. And I knew I'd get no more out of him, not that day. For the afternoon was already fading, evening was rapidly approaching, and Serafima needed his magic to create an illusion of her own.

"Just tell me one thing," I said to her as she swept into her room, "and I won't bother you for—I don't know. Hours."

"Darling, you never bother me. What can I tell you? How was the play?"

"Quite good. Where does Fyodorov take himself off to when he's not in your sitting room chastising actors?"

"He disappears into his laboratory."

"Yes, but where is it?"

"Ah. It's terribly secret. Perhaps you might ask him yourself. I invited him to have supper with you."

"You did?"

"I hope that fits in with your evening plans."

"I have no evening plans."

"I didn't think you would. I ordered some sturgeon and fruit and... what else?"

"Champagne, Madame. And pies."

"Thank you... Yes, champagne and pies."

"And where is this supper taking place?"

"Right here... Well, you can't entertain him in your room, can you? I've invited Pavel Damianovich. The three of you will get on famously. I will pop in for a bit around midnight."

"I doubt I'll still be awake at midnight."

Serafima smiled at me. "You never know. He may be more interesting than you think."

♣

I had hours to fill before my supper guests arrived, so I decided to see if the young actor who played Venka was somewhere in the house, or somewhere that I could find him, for aside from the common rooms—the reception hall, the drawing room, the gaming rooms, and the parlor—the Stardust was something of a labyrinth, with many stairways and passages, many little rooms tucked away, many winding corridors, a warren, in fact, cunningly designed. It was a house with many secrets exits as well, many ways of escape.

The young actor was not hard to find, however. He was sitting at a table in the parlor, laughing and drinking champagne with another one of the actors, the one who had played the evil Arif. When they saw me, they immediately stood and invited me to join them with the sort of fawning respect theatre people have for journalists and critics, the monsters who can make or break them with a finely turned sentence or two. Their obsequiousness was not completely serious, of course; after all, we were in the parlor of a brothel.

"We were honored to have you in the audience today," the dark-haired one said, bowing. "We are not supposed to know who you are, but I'm afraid we do."

"Yes," the other said gayly, "someone let the cat out of the bag. Not the staff, mind you. They're as close-mouthed as the grave. It was one of us. Young and overly excited. It will go no farther. Promise."

"Then we should be properly introduced," I said. "I am Marko Volchek."

They were Yuri Pashkov and Valerian Brianski. All the bowing completed, we sat down to have a drink.

They were both very young, and I must confess that being around admiring young men can be quite flattering. They had read my work in the thick journals; it had surprised them when they learned that Marko Volchek was a woman writing under a male pseudonym. It had intrigued them. They both loved the popular society tales of star-crossed lovers, and romantic adventure novels; they were familiar, in fact, with all types of romance novels, and even some erotic novels by English and German writers which circulated secretly only among very special friends.

I asked them to recount the plot of the play to me since I had only seen the final act.

"Simplicity itself, really," Pashkov said with a smile. "And yet has any playwright dared put it on the stage before? Things that happen every day. Our reality. And yet who dares speak about it? Only this genius, whoever he is, God bless him and keep him safe!"

We raised our glasses to the health of the author and wished him long life. Pashkov continued.

"Venka and Arif are childhood friends. In the first act, they do all sorts of wild things together, they break all the rules, they are free... or think they are. But Arif enslaves himself. He is a thief, yes, but worse, an opium addict, and so when, in Act Two, he is caught by the *gendarmes,* he has no inner strength to fight them with and he offers to betray his friend without a second thought. He agrees to bring an *agent provocateur* into the household, he agrees to entrap his friend by embroiling him in a revolutionary plot. Monika knows what's going on, but Venka cannot believe it, he refuses to believe it, until that pounding on the door. I have to work harder on that moment. It's all in his expression, you see. When he realizes he's been betrayed by the man he loved as a brother."

"But it isn't Arif at the door, is it?" I asked.

"No. That's the real twist. It isn't Arif. It's Semyon."

"And who is he? The *agent provocateur*?"

Pashkov smiled at me. "I guess you'll just have to come tomorrow and watch us rehearse the second act."

"Well, Yuri Pashkov," I said, "I thought your expression at that final moment was not only quite believable but rather marvelous."

Actors crave praise, as do we all, but I meant what I said and he knew it. He was a good actor but he could not conceal his pleasure at my words: he blushed quite adorably and gave me a smile of almost child-like delight.

"The last scene is a brilliant finale," I said. "It conveys at once a complex mix of romantic sentimentalism and bitter, realistic irony, of comedy and pathos. One simply does not know how to respond, at the end. It's utterly brilliant. I must say I am very interested in the playwright. What do you know about him?"

"Nothing at all," Brianski said. "Fyodorov knows but won't say."

"How did you come to get the play then?"

"Now that's a story! Shall I tell it, Yuri? You see, dear Marko, your words have affected him so much he is no longer capable of speech. Very well. I will begin. This is what happened..."

I listened to the story Brianski told, and it made me smile, it was so typical of our times, of the accidental quality of our lives, the element of chance, of luck, of randomness which embellished and enlivened our otherwise predictable days, for life under a tyranny is nothing if not predictable, enclosed, limited, and banal.

It appeared that the unknown playwright, genius that he was, gave the one and only manuscript of his play to Fyodorov for safekeeping. But Fyodorov, a rather absent-minded man, put the manuscript in his satchel and then left the satchel in a cab. Luckily, the next person in that same cab was the actor, Aleksey Bunin. He saw the satchel and opened it. There was the manuscript with no name on it and no address.

"It's all so remarkable, it's like something you'd put in a novel, isn' it? But who would ever believe it?"

Aleksey took one look at the play, and decided to bring the satchel home with him. There he read the entire play with rising excitement. He loved it. He was enraptured by it. But as it had no author's name on it, no address, nothing, he couldn't return it to the playwright. Aleksey was something of a denizen of the Stardust and he was sitting right in the parlor one night when Fyodorov himself came by, all upset, very nervous and stuttering, completely out of place, but determined to question all the actors he could find, no matter where he had to look. For as soon as he realized he'd left the manuscript in the cab—it had taken him some hours to make this discovery—he ran back to the cab stand to try to retrieve it, but of course the cabbie was out driving around and did not return for a very long time and by then had quite forgotten all about Fyodorov and had no memory of who might have entered his cab after him. Fyodorov had to badger the poor man, buy him vodka, buy him dinner, do everything in his power to get him to remember who his fares had been that morning, but finally together they pin-pointed the two or three possible suspects, that is, men who might have walked off with Fyodorov's manuscript.

At that point I had to interrupt the story to ask why Bunin had not returned the satchel and its contents to the cab stand immediately or given it to the cabbie, for surely the owner would have come back for it.

"He would never have parted with it. Imagine entrusting it to a cabbie who might think nothing of just tossing it away! Imagine it in a rubbish heap! The thought is unbearable! No, he opened it in the back of the cab and began reading it and after that, why he'd die before giving it to anyone but its real owner."

Fyodorov, then, having succeeded somewhat with the cabbie and having the descriptions of several gentlemen who may have taken his satchel, began his search, but the only one he could even begin to look for was Aleksey Bunin because the cabbie remembered where he had dropped him off—at a theatre—and said he had the *mannerisms* of an actor. ("Mannerisms, indeed!") Fyodorov, figuring an actor was likely to pick up a script in the back of a cab, went to that theatre, and he asked and inquired. He asked and inquired, again and again, and the word spread, of course, that some crazy professor was looking for a lost manuscript and there would be a reward for anyone who found it. He was not very subtle and people began to become alarmed, he was making such a fuss. Finally, someone took pity on him and directed him here. He was completely baffled by it all. But he wanted his manuscript back so he persevered.

"But I thought he lived here. Or that his laboratory is somewhere in this building."

"It is, yes. But Fyodorov lives in a another world, as philosophers do.

Cloud-Cuckoo-Land, as Aristophanes calls it. His laboratory is up in the clouds, under the eaves. And, believe it or not, he had absolutely no idea what went on below him."

"I think the first person he spoke with was Ivan the Terrible," Pashkov said, taking up the story while Brianski filled our glasses again. "Who is enough to baffle anyone. You saw him at the rehearsal. He's the chap pretending to be our director. He isn't, of course. Aleksey is directing the play. Ivan, though, is quite a character himself. Always wears tight black clothing and a short black cape and is usually enshrouded in a cloud of tobacco smoke. He has eyes like a fiend, and a smooth, lean little dog he calls Vlad the Impaler. An admirer of the work of the Marquis de Sade."

Despite Ivan the Terrible, however, Fyodorov persisted, and he and Aleksey met. Immediately they began plotting together. Aleksey wanted to produce the play, but in secret, of course, and Fyodorov wanted to see it produced. But he never told anyone where he had come by it or who the author was.

How I wanted to tell them! But, of course, I could not. Instead I said, "*Wide and Crooked* is so new, so bold. I find it extraordinary."

"Yes, it is rather," Brianski said. "It gives one a sense of freedom just saying the lines, if you know what I mean. My character, for example, Arif... he says such terrible things! It's difficult sometimes for me to say them, yet when I do, my God, the feeling!"

"Indeed, your role as Arif, the beloved traitor, is most difficult, Valerian Brianski, and to my mind you play it quite brilliantly." At this he stood and bowed to me, a rather lovely response, but I had more to say and continued. "You must have to think somewhat kindly of Judas, playing that role. For surely even to the very end Venka continues to love him. Yet it isn't Arif who betrays him, is it? Or is it, and Semyon is only the police agent who comes to arrest him? A Third Division man, no doubt. Well, I shall have to see the rest of the play. I long to see it. It is an important work, and Aleksey was right to keep it and produce it, even if he must do so clandestinely. But he must, for it is a dangerous play. God only knows what the censors would do to it. Destroy it, of course. And arrest the author, if they could find him. He would need more than a fantastical flying machine to save himself from them."

The fact that I knew who the author was now seemed to me to be the greatest secret I would ever know and be required to keep. Yet how I wanted Nikolai's name to be spoken, how I wanted him to be acknowledged, to be praised. What restraint he himself must have, what discipline, to keep his work hidden! My admiration for him now knew no bounds, but I had to have discipline, too, and prudence, and restraint.

"Aleksey played the professor exceptionally well, I thought," I said, for there was praise enough to go around. "I imagine he used Fyodorov as a model for the character."

"Aleksey has borrowed certain *mannerisms* from him," Brianski said, laughing.

"The way he fidgets with his pipe," Pashkov added. "The way he swings his cane."

"His voice, too," I said. "It's low, until he gets excited, when it rises…"

I mimicked it a bit, and they laughed, and we drank the champagne and talked about the Russian theatre and its discontents. Before I knew it, the parlor was filling up with guests, and it was time for my supper with Fyodorov.

I thought I knew the cunning passageways of the Stardust quite well. I was good at labyrinths, at finding my way through Moroccan kasbahs and the twisting streets of old medieval towns; I had even been able to walk around Venice without getting lost. The Stardust was only a house, after all, yet for some reason that evening I could not find Serafima's rooms.

I left the parlor, and took the flight of stairs that should have brought me directly to her floor. The stairs were steeper than I remembered; I attributed this steepness to the champagne I had drunk. The slight roll underfoot, as though I were on a sailing ship—this also I attributed to the last few glasses. But how many glasses had there been? Three of us drinking, and we had only polished off a few bottles… So I climbed the stairs, a bit bemused, but not yet… not yet disturbed.

At the top of the flight of stairs there was a landing, and a corridor. The corridor had an unfamiliar turn to it; I knew this was not Serafima's corridor, not her floor, and not her stairs. Nothing about it was right. The Stardust was tastefully decorated; its wall coverings were subdued; its artfulness was unobtrusive. Subtlety was its virtue. But this corridor—there was something sinister about it, something grotesque. I was reminded of *Yevgeny Onegin* and Tatyana's dream: the faces around the table, turning toward her, the horrible mixture of animal faces, of horns and tails and ears and teeth, the merging of the human and the non-human, something devilish and queer. Yet there was nothing in the hall at all; it was entirely a feeling, a sensation. And yet the floor was rocking gently under my feet as though I were on the sea. Perhaps I should have tried to return the way I had come, but the thought of descending those steep stairs while the floor rolled beneath my feet ... there was something so nauseating about it that I simply could not attempt it.

Still very little I had done in my life took more strength of will than walking down that empty corridor. I knew it was not empty, though there was nothing to be seen. I knew it was teeming with forms being made and unmade... with forces, with energies... and yet ... there was nothing there. Everything and nothing: that was its true horror.

I walked and the floor beneath my feet rose and fell, the air tingled, there was a sound like a buzzing, but lighter somehow, and such a sensation... not of falling but of being about to fall... and the lamps flickered constantly, on and off. Then something like a prayer came to me, one of Anastasia's, and I whispered the words to myself as I walked:

In the dusk of early evening,
in the dusky afterlight,
night approaches over the lawn like a dark wave,
birds sing their last notes before roosting,
bats, flitting and diving,
stream from their cave.
Oh, how strange
this hour of the gloaming,
neither fish nor fowl, night nor day;
it does not beckon, does not harken,
more a loss than a gain.
Then one by one,
the lamp-bearers,
those flickering fairies,
the Lampyridae, come.
The night is a ballroom,
dew flows like champagne...

I was not sure the words were quite right, I thought I had lost a few lines somewhere, the rhyme was not at all correct, but the sound and the flow and rhythm of the words kept me going, kept me on my feet, upright, despite the rolling swell... But there were other words in the ether through which I was traveling. Barely discernible words, strange words that made no sense to me, that came to me on dark waves, while lights flickered around me like fireflies.

I persevered down the corridor, I had reached the place where it turned, when the floor beneath me lurched as though the little vessel I was on had been struck by a massive wave or a leviathan... for I could not help feeling that I was at sea in some sort of ship... and I was transported—I can use no other word—around the corner. One moment I was facing a wall; the next moment a new corridor stretched ahead of me. I turned to look behind me; the wall was there. I took a few steps back and peered around the corner: there was the corridor I had been on, or one quite similar to it, at least. But some invisible force prevented me from going any farther in that direction, and I had no desire to enter that hallway again in any event. This new one seemed somehow—calmer.

Calmer and easier to walk down, certainly. The ship's roll had ceased, as had the flickering and tingling in the air. This corridor, in fact, seemed quite normal, except the light was different here. It seemed like daylight, though I saw no windows, and, anyway, it should have been night. Then I noticed that the material composition of the corridor was unusual, too, for when I touched the wall—it wasn't there. I was walking through a tunnel made of light and air, if light and air were solid enough to make anything like a tunnel.

Walking down that corridor into some mystery that could have been death, I felt a stirring deep inside me, an ancient recollection, like the intimation one has as a child that the world is magical, that anything can happen, and one can never predict what it will be. Suddenly and unexpectedly I understood that something mysterious and wonderful was hidden behind the empty banality of our lives; and I was approaching it, not to understand it, for that would have to be impossible, but only to be awed by it, by something so great and vast and sublime it could not be touched or made small and vile by the actions of men.

Yet even as I thought this, some part of me, the rational part that did not want to act the fool, refused to believe that it could be true. No, someone had conjured up this hallway; it was theatrical, it was fake, it was meant to make a fool of me. I would not be made a fool of.

At the end of the corridor was a door. I strode up to it, touched the latch, and the door swung open.

CHAPTER FIFTEEN

Fyodorov Philosophizes; Blavatskaya Holds a Seance

Pavel Damianich opened a second bottle of champagne, filled his glass, and set to work on the sturgeon. There was no point waiting any longer. Evidently both Marko and Fyodorov had forgotten about him. So be it. There was supper to be eaten, and he never turned down a free meal. It was a matter of principle, for when one was starving, as one would surely be some day, one did not want to regret not having eaten when one could. Regret was a terrible thing.

"Regret tears at the soul," Pavel Damianich said to the very pretty girl, dressed in a wood nymph's tunic covered with a cascade of leaves, who was standing by to wait on him. "And yet, every day that passes... there is something to regret. Something one didn't do or see, something that passed by unnoticed. Our time is so short. Absurdly so."

He raised his glass to the shortness, yet the richness, of time.

"But what is time?" he asked. It was a rhetorical question.

"A little past nine, sir," the wood nymph answered.

"Oh, do come and sit with me and have a glass," he said. "You don't need to wait on me while I am waiting... We are both people-in-waiting, aren't we? Come, sit, drink."

Making guests happy was her job. She was pleased to sit and drink and laugh at the gentleman's jokes about time.

Meanwhile, time passed.

"It is rather unlike her to forget about supper entirely," he said. "I hope nothing's happened."

"Anything can happen," the wood nymph said, philosophically. "And things do happen, all the time."

"Finish the bottle," Pavel said, and got to his feet.

♣

"Tell me, what did Volchek think of the play?"

Pavel, halfway to the stairs, swung around and found himself facing a short, stout woman dressed in black garb somewhat reminiscent of a nomad's tent.

"I beg your pardon, Madame," he said, bowing slightly. One never knew, in a place like this, whom one might be addressing. He had nearly collided the day before with a prince.

"No need to beg my pardon. Just answer my question. I hear she watched the last act this afternoon. I merely wondered what she thought."

"Ah. I fear I have not spoken with her since this afternoon."

"Indeed. I saw her chatting up the actors earlier. Must have gone off with them. Always wandering about and never studying their lines. Not all of them. That Yuri fellow is quite good, I think. Anyway, never mind. Is Fyodorov in there?" She nodded toward the door he had just come out of. "Well, is he or isn't he? You just came out, you ought to remember."

"No, he is not."

"How annoying the man is!" With that, she turned around and walked back down the hall the way she had come.

He barely had time to wonder when a tall, gaunt man appeared at the top of the staircase and strode toward him. He recognized him; he was the same Prince Ivan he had encountered just yesterday, a rather brusque man with harrowing eyes.

"Did she pass here?" he asked rudely.

"Who?"

"Blavatskaya. Short, ugly, wearing a black—" With a sweeping gesture, he indicated size and scope. "—thing."

"I have never met such a woman," Pavel said.

"I didn't ask if you met her. I asked if you saw her. Never mind. Thick-headed, aren't you. But—" He cocked his head, and scrutinized Pavel's body, his gaze settling intensely, and with great interest, on a certain part of his anatomy. "—charming."

"Please excuse me," Pavel said coldly, with a slight bow.

"By all means," Prince Ivan answered. "I will excuse anything. Eventually."

Then, raising an eyebrow and nodding, he stepped aside by perhaps an inch, giving Pavel just enough room to pass.

The parlor was filled at this time of night with all manner of people in all manner of dress. Costumes seemed to be *de rigueur,* the more fantastical, the better. There were figures dressed in feathers and figures dressed in furs sparkling with jewels; there were men wearing animal masks and men wearing gowns. At one table a group of women dressed in dinner jackets sat laughing loudly and smoking pipes, while at another a group of men dressed in Roman togas were doing the same. A very tall young man was walking around with an exotic bird perched on his shoulder. But Marko wasn't in the parlor or in any of the common rooms. He couldn't identify the actors the woman called Blavatskaya had referred to, and he knew it was useless to ask the staff, for they might as well have had their tongues cut out, the amount of talking they did. What you want in a private club for degenerates, he thought, yet annoying if you needed a bit of simple information. He went down to the courtyard to have a smoke with Little Abrasha, who was not bound by the rule of silence and would at least give him the time of day. Little Abrasha had not seen Madame Markova that evening either, but her absence at supper worried him.

"Sturgeon, you say? And meat pies? And champagne? Hardly likely she'd miss that, mate."

Pavel stamped his feet for warmth and fretted and smoked.

"She didn't leave the building, so she must still be inside."

"Maybe. There are other ways out. She could have left with no one seeing."

"How many other ways?"

"Oh, plenty, I'd say. Even I don't know 'em all."

"But she could still be inside."

"Sure she could. It's a big place."

Pavel gazed up at the building. Its height was deceptive; from the street level it looked like it had four stories, but he knew for a fact it had more.

"There's a tower up there, isn't there? That you can't see."

"Oh, yes... It sits back some, and it's a rambling affair, that whole floor. Connects somehow or other to someplace else. I got no need to go up there myself. I did once for Madame, and I did not like it. All attics and rafters and bats and such."

"What about cellars?"

"Of course there's cellars. Storage cellars. Wine cellars. Play rooms, too, they call them. Dungeons for those what likes that sort of thing."

"Not real dungeons?"

"Oh, they're real enough. Thing is, you only get put in 'em if you want to be put in 'em. Funny stuff goes on in this place, I'll tell you."

"How would I get down there?"

"Ah... well, Madame has the keys. You'd have to ask her."

Pavel looked up at the building again. From the outside, it looked deserted, with light coming from only a few small windows on the ground floor. Above that, the building was dark, all the windows being double-shuttered as well as covered on the inside with thick drapes. He loved Marko, but suddenly he wanted to be somewhere else. *What the hell is she doing in there?* The thought demanded an answer, but what his body demanded was fresh air, a walk along the river, or better, a fast gallop under a wide sky.

"Damn her," he said to himself, and threw down his smoke and went back inside, now forced by conscience to seek out the keys, to trundle down the stone steps into the cellars of the Stardust, to poke into store-rooms and playrooms, so-called, the pretend dungeons in which pretend tortures were administered to pretend slaves by pretend masters. Ivan the Terrible's domain.

He would search faithfully but he would not find me there. For I had opened the door to a different domain. I had entered Fyodorov's world.

He was standing at a table in his shirtsleeves, pen in hand, while in front of him some mechanical contraption, something like a wind-up toy, was emitting flashes of light. The toy was connected to a wire, the wire was connected to a gauge, the gauge moved, and Fyodorov was watching it and making notes. Or so it seemed to me in the moments before he noticed my presence, which startled him a good deal and caused him to switch off his instruments.

I introduced myself, and tried to excuse my rudeness, bursting in on him, interrupting his work. Terribly sorry. Just wandering about. Had no idea...

"Madame, please," he said, taking me solicitously by the arm and guiding me into a chair, "you seem quite distraught. Has something upset you? May I get you a brandy?"

"Yes," I said. "A brandy… very… kind…"

I could not seem to find words.

While he bustled off to find his brandy and his jacket, I gazed around, incredulously. I had never before been in a laboratory, and I could never have imagined one, certainly not a place like this. The room was long and narrow with a row of small windows along one wall and exposed rafters, a garret, surely; it even had the feel of an attic, being cluttered with objects of all sorts. But what odd objects they were! Work benches lined three of the walls. One bench held a veritable forest of flasks and beakers and burners and tubes; another was littered with metal-working tools, and half-built machines; webs of wires attached to instruments I could not name rested on the third. Suspended from one corner was a huge spherical machine, large enough for a man to sit in, while in another corner was a contraption with sails and wheels attached to it. The walls were plastered with star maps and graphs; precise anatomical drawings of bird and insect wings were set beside sketches of fantastical winged vehicles, some having rotary blades attached to the wings while others were propelled by steam engines and still others by balloons. Exotic lamps hung from the rafters, the floor was decorated with drawings of giraffes and constellations. Even the air had an oddness to it, a fragrance I could not define, like the freshness of tingling mountain air mixed with the sweetness of just baked bread. Altogether it felt like a place apart, a magical aerie, a fantasy, or a dream.

He returned, in jacket and tie, and carrying a bottle and two glasses.

"Forgive me for my importunate entrance," I said. "I mean, unfortunate." The words still sounded wrong. "Or maybe disordinate. Or discordinate?" Did I even know what I was saying?

"Don't apologize, please, my dear lady," he said with what seemed to me to be unwarranted enthusiasm. "I am gratified to see you here."

"You are?"

"Yes. Very much so… Why, we were to dine tonight, weren't we? Oh, dear! And I completely forgot! How kind of you to come get me. Yes, very kind indeed."

"But… I didn't plan to come here."

"No, no. One rarely does."

"I mean, it was not my intention to come here. I was going to Serafima's rooms to meet you for supper. But I seem to have gotten lost on the way. And I felt something strange out there in the corridor—something very strange."

"It sometimes happens," he said.

"What do you mean, it happens?"

"It occurs."

"But how?"

"Ah. How. I suspect it is a kind of magnetism."

"You mean, I was mesmerized?"

"No, indeed, though the word is often misused in that way. Magnetism in the scientific sense is not a psychic phenomenon but a physical one. We live and move and have our being, so to speak, within an electro-magnetic field. The English physicists have done remarkable research in this area. Just the other day, I read a paper by—"

While he explained to me, to no avail, I might add, the incredible work of someone named Maxwell, I sipped my brandy and gazed around like a child seeing something extraordinary for the first time. Something about the place was simply enchanting, like a nursery or a child's playhouse or a toy workshop, where the most fantastic toys were being imagined and made.

When he finally paused for a moment, I asked him what exactly it was he did here.

"You mean, am I like that infamous Doctor Frankenstein, creating monsters up here in my tower? An excellent play, by the way. A pity no one produces it these days. But I have read it. How does it go at the end? 'Life and death appeared to me bounds which I should first break through and pour a torrent of light into our dark world. I might renew life where death had apparently devoted the body to corruption. I have myself been blasted in these hopes, yet another may succeed.' To renew life where death had devoted the body to corruption, surely it is an honorable goal. But not mine, not at the moment. I have several other works in progress, to borrow an expression you writers use. One is to construct a reactive device that might ultimately be powerful enough to propel a ship into space. A propulsion engine, in a word. The others are... somewhat more difficult to describe."

"To go into space?"

"A voyage of exploration, yes."

"But why?"

"A good question. I must admit I am beginning to doubt the usefulness of establishing off-world colonies, an idea to which at one time I was deeply devoted. We change our minds. Or our minds change. It is extraordinary."

"You are seeking something."

"Indeed. Aren't you?"

"Yes. I am. I am seeking a person."

"I am seeking an answer. Harder to find, I think."

"What is the question?"

"Ah. *Touché.* But before we begin to philosophize, dear lady, perhaps we should have a bite to eat. Or should we go down to Serafima's? Since we are both here, perhaps it's best to stay."

I agreed that staying was preferable. I had no desire to return the way I had come. He seemed pleased with that choice, and went to a cabinet, returning with a platter of bread, pickled vegetables and cold meats, and a decanter of wine.

"Modest fare, I'm afraid," he said. "I am sure supper at Serafima's would have been far better."

Modest it might have been, but it was delicious, and we ate it with pleasure, as one always should.

"So," I said, after we had cleaned our plates, and were sitting back in our chairs, relaxed and well-satisfied, lighting respectively a cigarette and a pipe, "we were about to indulge in some philosophy. But from now on you must call me Marko. I detest being a dear lady."

"I shall be happy to oblige. And indulging in philosophy together makes us comrades, indeed. Shall we?"

"Why not? But, tell me this, will philosophy explain how I came here tonight without intending to, the strange sensations I felt in the corridor, why it seemed that daylight was flooding the hallway when undoubtedly it is night, and why you say this is all a result of some field of magnetism?"

He smiled, then he laughed. "Perhaps we should start with a more basic question."

"Very well," I said. "We have all the time in the world. Let us begin at the beginning."

"Well, then, the first question I ask myself is: must there not be more than this? It would be a disappointing universe if this were all there was."

"What do you mean by *this*?"

He gestured around the room. "This! And the rest of it, of course."

"You mean, the rest of the world?"

"Yes, the world."

"And it's not enough? But there is so much already! Stars, trees, oceans. The giraffe," I added, nodding to the drawing on the floor.

"Yes. But what is it all doing here? And what are *we* doing here? Or better: what *is* it? If we knew the answer to that, we'd know all the answers."

"I don't understand. What is what?"

"Very well. Look at it like this. We land here—or, as we say, we are born. We become aware of this place. We don't know how we got here. We don't know what sort of place it is. Extraordinary, that, don't you think? Yet, pretty soon, we stop being curious about it. We stop being strangers here. We adapt. Yet, think of it! We are on this planet, in this galaxy of stars, in a universe that is immense. Where did it come from? What is beyond it? *Is* there a *beyond it*? If not, are we the only sentient beings in existence? The only conscious minds? If I answer *yes*, we are alone, then I must conclude that the universe is absurd, that there is no order in it and no reason for its existence or for ours, that everything we love will ultimately perish, and the world will end in tragedy and dissolution. If I answer *no*—"

"Wait! If you answer no, it leads to only one conclusion. God must exist."

"Yes."

"But it's impossible!"

"Why do you say that?"

"You are a scientist."

"That does not make me a materialist. Materialism takes us down a path to utter despair and ruin. Reason refuses that path. You yourself must concede that."

"Not willingly."

"Of course not willingly. Yet I believe the existence of God is a concession that must be made. A concession to reason, which demands it. Otherwise what we have is an irrational universe, cold, immense, empty, accidental, purposeless, existing for no reason, yet obeying reasonable laws—"

"Perhaps that is the case."

He smiled at me, indulgently, I thought. "Perhaps it is, and we must embrace the absurd."

I studied him carefully, this small, bespectacled man in an old-fashioned suit, puffing on his pipe. Some years younger than I, and well-educated, over-educated, some might say, certainly educated above his class, and so, like many young men of our time, utterly superfluous in a society that had no need of either intelligence or enterprise—yet what a mind he had! Discussing philosophy with him was making my brain hurt, it had been so long since I had engaged in such a debate. Yet he seemed quite unfazed by it; in fact, he seemed quite cheerful. He perplexed me.

"Tell me, Fyodor Fyodorovich, how can you live with such thoughts?"

"I have never lived without them."

"But how can you?"

"How can you live, knowing you will die?"

"Everything dies."

"Tell me, then, what is the point? What is the point of all this energy, this endless production, and reproduction, this endless repetition—what is the point of it?"

"You sound like a nihilist."

"I am not a nihilist. I do not object to the world, I merely want to understand it. Its banalities and cruelties, which nihilists seem to find personally offensive and insulting, I acknowledge, as any sane man would. At the same time, I observe its inherent order and symmetry and predictability. The universe follows certain rules, and the rules are understandable to reason. We can detect them, and they make sense to us. It is not random chaos, is it? Yet, it seems to have no reason for being except that it happens to be."

His thinking in this regard was not entirely unlike my own. I, too, had noticed Nature's order and symmetry and good workmanship, and contrasted it with the senseless randomness of human life, its disorderliness and the proliferation in it of useless suffering. Perhaps I did find life's cruelties personally offensive, but this did not make me a nihilist, only an unbeliever in any divine providence, or even in any divine being.

"We tell stories," I said. "We create stories to explain where we came from and why, in order to make our lives bearable, even meaningful."

"Yes, we do. And think of the stories! Take Plotinus and his Emanations, for example. From the One to the Many. All very orderly. And yet fantastic."

"So you want to go out into space—to see if there are other sentient beings? To discover whether they have found better, less fantastic answers to your questions?"

"I once thought one might find some answers there, yes. Now I rather think the answers are better sought elsewhere. By different methods."

"What methods, exactly?"

"Ah, that is the question! We must find new methods for new problems. New methods of exploration when we find new worlds to explore. For you see, dear Marko, we are so used to thinking that there is only this one world, the world we experience, the sensuous present we live within. But what if this is not the case? What if there are many worlds, not just this one we live in? What if these worlds are connected to each other like rooms in a huge palace, separated from each other by locked doors? Imagine if we could find the key that unlocked those doors, so we could move from room to room, from one world to another world. Imagine if we could even travel back and forth in time." He smiled at me "You see, as the poet says, I do believe that there are more things in heaven and earth than are dreamt of in our philosophy. Though what poet said it, I can't quite recall."

I could not recall either, and I was too perplexed to try. Travel in time? I had never heard of such a thing. Could these ideas of his shed any light on what I had experienced on his stairs or in his hallway, the feelings I had had of terror and of joy? Could they explain the light that shone on me from no source I could see? I did not know how to frame such questions so I asked another.

"Did you talk about these things with Nikolai Barakov?"

All this time Fyodorov had been at his ease, or as much as a man can be at his ease who is talking about things of so bizarre a nature, but the mention of Nikolai's name startled him.

"Nikolai! Oh, my dear Marko! Yes we did, always. Nikolai loved to talk about these things. He'd been thinking about them all his life, so he found great pleasure in being able to discuss them with someone who had also been... haunted, shall we say, by the same questions. The idea of parallel worlds was one he especially enjoyed."

"What is that—parallel worlds?"

"It simply names the notion I tried to describe, that there are many different worlds existing at the same time. Though our notions of time are not helpful in talking about these ideas. They are difficult ideas to communicate in a satisfactory way using the language we have."

"Please, Fyodor Fyodorovich, using the language we have, can you tell me where Nikolai is? Do you know?"

"He is traveling."

"Where?"

"Traveling by its nature has no *where*. It is movement. By the time I learn where a traveler is, he is sure to be there no longer. He will be elsewhere."

"I am searching for him for his mother's sake. Can you tell me nothing more?"

"Elena Blavatskaya... have you met her? an extraordinary woman ... believes he has gone to Tibet. It is her own desire to go there, so I do not trust this idea of hers."

"Elena Blavatskaya? What does she have to do with Nikolai?"

He frowned, wrinkled his brow, rubbed his nose, pulled at his ear. He was clearly perplexed.

"Now that is a very good question," he said. "You know, I am trying to remember, but I simply can't recall having spoken to her about Nikolai, yet somehow I know that she is also interested in finding him."

"Is she? And she believes that Nikolai has gone to Tibet? And you, Fyodor Fyodorovich? Do you believe this also?"

"No. I believe he has gone—elsewhere. But it is my own desire to go there, so I do not trust this idea either."

"Where exactly is *elsewhere*?"

Fyodorov smiled at me. It was a warm, charming, innocent smile.

"The future, Marko," he said. "The future."

♣

However engaging Fyodorov's ideas, they were still cockeyed, and only the fact that I was a guest in his laboratory kept me from saying so. Worse than that disgruntlement, I was feeling deeply disappointed, for all this time I had nurtured the hope that if I found Fyodorov, he would be able to help me, or even tell me where Nikolai had gone. Now it seemed he knew as little as I did. Unless, of course, along with the play, he had in his possession a copy of Nikolai's book.

"By the way," I said, as casually as I could, "when did Nikolai give you the script of his play?"

That remark must have surprised him; he gave me a look of wonder as though I had just spoken in Chinese or told him the city had fallen to the Finns.

"Do you deny that he wrote it?"

"No, no. But how did you know?"

"Come, come, Fyodor Fyodorovich, I have been to his house. When did he give it to you?"

"Just before he left."

"Did he give you *Monkey* as well?"

Again, he looked at me with some astonishment. "You know about that too? What don't you know, Madame Volchek?"

"I am not Madame Volchek, dear Fyodorov, and what I don't know is where Nikolai is. That is the issue, the question, the goal, the mission, the quest—do you understand? I don't know where he is. I also don't know where his novel has disappeared to. Do you have it?"

"I do not have it."

"Do you know anyone who does have it?"

"No."

"Have you read it?"

"He read a few pages to me once... and before you ask, I don't remember them. I was too drunk to remember, I regret to say. At the time, I was happy listening, but afterwards I could not recall what the story was about or why it had made me so happy."

"Too much vodka, no doubt," I said with a sigh. He was a most infuriating man. "So, in short, you don't know where Nikolai is, you don't know where *Monkey* is, you have no idea what the novel is even about—"

And, I added to myself, bitterly, now all my hopes are dashed, every one of them. I had found him so easily, it had seemed a stroke of luck that he was right here, in the Stardust, and yet he was useless to me. I had reached another dead end in the maze; I had to go back to the last false turn, and pick up the trail again.

While I was letting myself feel the magnitude of my disappointment, Fyodorov got up, went to another cabinet, and started rummaging around in it. He returned holding a map. Maps always interest me even if I'm not intending to go anywhere, so the appearance of the map raised my spirits a bit.

"Now, let's see," Fyodorov said, spreading the map on the table and adjusting his spectacles. "Ah, look! Here is the world which we Russians are not permitted to see. Here is Europe, which is forbidden to us. Here, in the other direction, Siberia, which too many of us see who would rather not... but beyond it... ah, look! North America! Quite recently I learned that the navigator of the expedition to Alaska in 1732 was a Fyodorov, Ivan Fyodorov. It is a small fact which pleases me greatly. Now Nikolai never traveled far, but he often said that if he could go anywhere in the world, anywhere, mind you, it would be here."

Fyodorov moved his finger from the coast of Alaska, where it had been pointing, slowly downward. Down, down, his finger went, following the North American coast. "Here," he said. "The city of San Francisco." Then, still following the littoral, his finger swooped down, farther still, all the way to the Equator, where it stopped... and then moved slightly to the west, into the Pacific Ocean, to no place I could see on the map. "And also here. The Enchanted Isles. The islands that appear and disappear."

"San Francisco I have heard of. But enchanted islands? Are they real?"

"Voyagers have visited them, yes."

"But why would one go such distance, to such places?" I asked, horrified.

"For the adventure. For the joy. To discover the earthly paradise, Eden before the Fall. Perhaps just to be free, Marko, free and far from the reach of Autocracy. At least Nikolai saw it like that. He put that very image at the end of his play."

"It was a vague place, as I recall."

"Not in the original. No, indeed, it was quite specific. I changed the wording a bit, I must confess, for I felt our audience here at the Stardust might not understand the reference. What he actually wrote was, 'I was thinking of San Francisco, a city far, far away, a place where it's always summer and we can be together and be free.'"

"But surely you don't think he has actually embarked on such a journey?"

"I don't see why not. If one wants to see something that is at a distance, one must traverse that distance. That is the only method I know of for getting from one place to another. Unless there is some other way we do not yet know... or some way of being in two places at once."

"You amaze me," I said.

"Forgive me. Amazement was not my intention."

"But if you are right," I said, mostly to myself, "and he has begun this journey... if he began it over a year ago... how far might he have already gone? Merely to travel the breadth of this country might well take a year. Then to voyage down the North American coast... Oh, imagine the distance! It is unbelievable!"

"One could, of course, go the other way. That is, one could go west instead of east. Like this." I followed his finger again: from Petersburg to Odessa, Odessa to Constantinople, Constantinople to Cape Verde Islands, across the Atlantic to Panama, across the isthmus to the Pacific coast. "Then one could travel either north to California or south toward the Equator. Ships are so much quicker than other modes of transport. If you can bear them."

Together we leaned over the map, studying the possible routes. Would anyone attempt such an adventure? I could hardly believe it. It seemed as insane as anything else Fyodor Fyodorovich had said to me.

My head was swimming. I needed a bed. Yes, a bed. A delightful bed, a bed of my own, in a room of my own, in a high-class brothel, in Tsar Peter's city. Fyodorov, being something of a mind-reader himself, kindly offered to guide me down the stairs. So it was that when Pavel Damianich finally found me, hours later, I was in bed sound asleep, and he was just tired enough to crawl in beside me and either kind enough, or annoyed enough, not to wake me up in the process.

The next morning, I entertained Pasha with a description of my evening with Fyodorov and he entertained me with tales of the various sexual escapades he had inadvertently witnessed down in the dungeons. We talked about leaving Petersburg, but decided that first we needed to discover whether there was a hue and cry out for me. It certainly would not do to walk out of the Stardust into the arms of Pavel Beriosov or his minions.

That afternoon I found myself in the parlor again while a rehearsal was in progress. One of the actors had quit in a fit of chagrin, piqued by some slight, and since I was there, I was quickly recruited to read his lines.

"Keep the script," Aleksey, the real director, said. "You like this play. Now you're in it!"

"When is the actual performance?" I asked.

"Haven't set a date. Perhaps we'll stage it in December. Perhaps around the fourteenth."

The fourteenth of December, a grave date on our calendar, the date of the Officers Uprising of 1825. Had they only succeeded! If they had, our lives would so different. We would be living in a free country, with no autocrat, no secret police, no institution of slavery, no rule by knout and noose, no ignorance, no poverty, and all our doors would be open to the world. And with that thought, a memory came to me, and instantly from a gas-lit parlor in a Petersburg brothel I was transported through space and time to the morning room at Oak Hills, and sunlight was pouring in, and I was bending over a map with Nikolai Vasilevich. Oh, how young and slim and tall he was! His eyes were dark blue under long lashes, his beard was just coming in, his mind was sharp, his heart ardent... his anger, deep and cold and bitter. For the Tsar had issued a decree. By order of the Tsar, all our borders were to be closed and all foreign travel was to cease. All students studying abroad were recalled, and henceforth no young people would be permitted to attend foreign universities... and this a month before Nikolai was to go! Oh, he was enraged! So I had taken out the map, and now we were imagining... traveling down the great rivers, crossing the oceans, visiting exotic places. The names alone thrilled us. But they were forbidden. Even the cities of Europe, the centers of human endeavor, of creativity and thought—all forbidden to us. The Emperor had sealed us off from the world, turned the entire country into a prison. *But it can't last...* Later we learned about escape routes, about the art of slipping over borders, forging papers, making contacts, the art of bribery, the art of the wink and the nod. I had traveled in such a manner. Perhaps Nikolai—

"... assuming we are ready, of course. So, study your lines. I'll expect you to be off book in exactly two days."

"Off what book?" I had been pulled back into the present from the past, an eerie feeling, almost physical.

"It means you know your lines," Aleksey said with a grin.

"Yes, of course," I said. "I will certainly know them."

I had no idea what I was saying. What I was thinking was: the world is vast. Will I search all of it for him, will I search my whole life, what if he cannot be found? But it was far too soon to indulge in such dark thoughts. I had spent more time locked in a tower than I had looking for him. And now I was locked in again. I needed an escape route myself.

The actors adjourned to the drawing room, and I spent the remaining hours of the evening drinking and smoking with them until with a shock I remembered that Serafima had asked me to come to her room at a certain hour, and that that hour had now, unfortunately passed. I rushed up the stairs, and had just arrived at her door when it opened, an arm reached out, a hand seized me by the wrist, and I was pulled quite forcibly into the room.

Inside, it was all shadowy; there were only a few candles burning though an obscure light came from a lamp concealed behind a screen. A group of people were gathered around Serafima's table. I could not make out who they were. The short, stout person clutching my wrist had a man's grip, but was wearing some flowing garment that might, in some foreign land, be deemed a dress. I was about to object strongly to being manhandled in such a fashion when the bedroom door opened, a shaft of light entered the room, and Serafima herself appeared, like a goddess at the door of a temple.

"Ah! Here you are at last," she said. "Now we can begin."

"Begin what?" I said, shaking off the hand on my arm.

"Madame Blavatskaya has graciously offered to hold a seance for us tonight. But only if you attended. I see you've met."

So it was she who had hold of my arm, Elena Petrovna, the mad daughter of Elena Gan.

"I have not had the honor," I said.

"Yet we have many friends in common," Elena Petrovna replied. "I am pleased to finally make your acquaintance."

Nice enough, I thought. And so I was introduced at last to Madame Blavatskaya, Marina Fyodorovna's future best selling author, her potential cash cow. She did have a rather bovine figure, and a cow-like expression, with those big, wet, protruding eyes. I had never seen a woman quite so unattractive. But it was more than her appearance that repelled me; something about her seemed flawed and uncanny. Whatever it was, it made my skin crawl.

One by one the other guests rose and bowed: a fat man named Pavlov; a gaunt man in black, Prince Ivan Ivanovich, whom I recognized as the infamous Ivan the Terrible; a dark young man who spoke French like a Spaniard; and an old geezer named Orlov, who peered through his thick spectacles at everyone in a most disconcerting way. Fat Man, Skinny Man, Spaniard, Spy. The Spaniard had a rather dashing appearance, and Skinny Man, the Prince of Darkness, had a certain Gothic style, but the other two were sartorially indistinguishable from the average titular counselor or clerk. Why they were here at the Stardust, gathered around Serafima's table, guests in her private sitting room, was quite beyond me. But then, appearances *were* deceptive, especially here. All four were smoking, they all had drinks at their elbows, a servant hovered in the background ready to refill their glasses at the merest gesture… and they seemed, not agitated, exactly, but nervous, twitchy… expectant. Yes, they had been waiting in expectation of something, and now that something was about to occur.

Perhaps it was because I had so recently been acting a part in Nikolai's play, perhaps it was having his words so fresh in my mind, the sound of his caustic humor, his wicked sarcasm, his delightful sense of irony, but this whole seance affair was irritating me. Calling on spirits of the dead! It was laughable.

"Will you sit with us?" Blavatskaya asked.

"I am really not interested," I said. And then, so she would understand my meaning unambiguously, I added: "I think it's all a great deal of nonsense."

Someone at the table tittered, someone else discreetly coughed, some feet shuffled a bit. Were others at the table as skeptical as I? The thought made me smile—and at that very moment, something large flew right by my head, hit the door behind me, and fell with a thump onto the floor.

I nearly jumped out of my skin, while everyone at the table stood up or tried to. "Who threw that?" Serafima demanded. Only Blavatskaya remained perfectly still.

I bent down to see what it was. I thought perhaps a bird had flown in through a chimney, though birds rarely fly into rooms in the middle of the night. But no, it was no bird. It was a book. I picked it up to read the title, though the light was so dim it was hard to see. When I did see it, it made my head spin. I had to sit down. "Vodka!" I said, like I owned the place, and someone poured me a glass.

It wasn't possible, and yet there it was. The book was one I had written myself, years ago, and presented to Serafima. I doubt she had ever read it, but I was glad to see she had kept it on a shelf, from whence it had evidently hurled itself at me, most sentient of books. It was a collection of stories inspired by Ukrainian folk tales. Its title was *The Girl Who Did Not Believe*.

Blavatskaya was explaining to Serafima that no living person had thrown the book, but that it had been the action of one of the impish elemental spirits who do so enjoy creating havoc. She would have to assert control over them. Now if everyone would take their places... And she guided Serafima into the chair beside me. Since I was sitting at the table anyway, I submitted to the greater force and joined hands in the circle of fools and waited for a spirit to make an appearance.

Elena Petrovna was sitting across the table from me. I watched her carefully. I was sure this spirit nonsense was a form of theatre, that the flight of the book had been orchestrated, somehow, and that if I paid attention, I would see how it was done, despite the dimness of the light, and the smoke in the air, and the fact that Blavatskaya herself was in shadow, since the only light in the room was coming from behind her.

Now that we were all settled, Elena Petrovna informed us that she was hoping to contact her own spirit-guide who might answer our questions. However, she could not predict what spirits might materialize. She was aware of very strong powers present in the room, and strong psychic forces at our very table. At this remark, we all glanced at each other in alarm, surreptitiously for the most part, although Spy was more overt, peering at each of us in turn quite solemnly through his thick spectacles. These powers, Blavatskaya explained in her deep voice, might well impede the transmission of messages from her spirit-guardian, but might result in significant communications themselves. One could not know these things in advance. She then instructed us to relax and breathe, to empty our minds, to be receptive, and so on. In this way the seance began.

They all seemed so restless, though, my fellow seekers. Restless, nervous, twitchy. The room seemed restless, too; the house was settling, and making the sorts of noises old buildings make at night. Then closer to the table, something started rattling, and there was a sense of things shuffling around, shifting. At the same time, Elena Petrovna began speaking in a foreign language I could not identify. The charade was getting on my nerves. Suddenly she seemed to grow even larger, and as she spoke her voice became singsong, and very low.

I saw nothing, of course... until I did.

It was a figure, a bent old man with a long beard, quite visible, despite the dimness and the smoke. Everyone else saw it, too; the shock of the apparition jolted the table like a lightning strike. Spaniard, sitting beside me, squeezed my hand so tightly I thought he would break it while Fat Man, sitting on the other side of him, cried out, "Father!"

"Do you have a message, spirit?" Blavatskaya called out in her husky voice. "Can you speak?"

There was a groaning sound, like the sound one hears walking down an old staircase in the night... a groaning, suffering sound.

Fat Man began struggling out of his chair. "Father!" he cried again.

Then a bit of chaos ensued: another chair was pushed back, a glass was upset, the vision vanished. Fat Man sat mopping his face with a handkerchief; Prince Ivan called for vodka. It seemed the session was ending, and I felt a slight disappointment, as though I had paid for an entire opera and only heard the first aria. But Blavatskaya knocked on the tabletop and commanded us not to break the circle but to stay in our places. She extended her arms over the table, the black material of her long sleeves hanging over the space like a shroud, and closed her eyes. Several moments passed; then she cried out, ominously: "He is coming!" And then, more ominously still, "He is here!"

At the word *here*, every light in the room—blinked. How else to describe it? The few candles, the lamp behind the screen—all were extinguished, and relit... in a moment. It was quite a trick, that moment of blackness, of utter darkness, the length of a heartbeat; yet it had occurred. Again, we looked at each other in amazement and confusion. But we had no time at all to recover ourselves or to end the charade, which I still believed it was. More was to come, I was sure, and I braced myself for more shenanigans, feeling almost shamed and misused, embarrassed for Serafima, angry at being made to be part of such a farce.

Such was my state of mind when I looked across the table, past Blavatskaya's formidable girth, to the space just behind her, the only spot in the room clearly illuminated by the single lamp behind the screen, and in that almost radiant place, uncanny and impossible as it was, a man's figure appeared. He seemed as real as any of the men sitting in the room with me; he seemed, in fact, somehow more real than they. He had a look about him that was familiar, and as I kept my eyes fixed on him, he became more familiar still. But it was hard to fix my eyes; the vision shifted like everything else in the room, for at that moment everything in the world seemed to be in flux. And yet, even so, he became more and more clear until, unless I doubted the evidence of my own eyes, I was looking at Nikolai Barakov.

I tried to speak, but my mouth was so dry I could not move my tongue. I could not move my limbs. The only part of me that could still move was my heart, which was beating so hard I felt my chest was about to burst.

Stupidly, I tried to stand.

Everything in the world went black.

CHAPTER SIXTEEN

"THE WOMAN IS AN UTTER CHARLATAN!"

Blavatskaya and Fyodorov left the parlor, where they had been watching the rehearsal, gathered their cloaks, and took the stairs down to the courtyard. It was snowing and the air was tingly and glittery and very cold.

"Ah, fresh air!" Fyodorov said, breathing deeply before lighting his pipe. "What joy!"

"You are in a fine mood today, Fyodorov," she said. "I envy you."

"The seance is still upsetting you, dear lady? But all's well that ends well."

"I have no idea what you mean by that tired cliché. What has ended well?"

He did not answer, but rather attended to the lighting of his pipe.

"Or do you refer to the fact that Marko Volchek will be staying here for some time, resting. We shall have to rename this place the Stardust Sanatorium. If only there were a hot spring, other cases of nervous exhaustion might be treated here as well. As for the seance, the results were poor indeed, no matter what Serafima says. My Master did not even manifest. Instead I was blind-sided completely by Pavlov's father. A damned soul, at the verge of extinction, and still as evil as ever, follows the poor man around, hounds him..."

"Why does he put himself through it?"

"He is mad, of course. Why else? Souls of the damned cannot be appeased or reasoned with. They are beyond care or reason. As for the others, Serafima wanted to impress them. I believe she has endless plots. She is a spider."

"And they were impressed, certainly, by the appearance of—what do you call it? The astral body?"

"It is easy to impress the uninitiated. For me, it was a failure. I could not communicate with the spirit. There was too much interference."

"Those who saw it said it was a young man."

"The astral plane is filled with young men."

Blavatskaya placed a cigarette in her amber holder; Fyodorov offered her a match.

"You have an interest in Marko Volchek," she said. "I find it curious."

"Marko is acting in the play."

"Is that all it is?"

"What more could it be?"

"Volchek is a strange bird," she said. "I would be wary."

"I am a Russian," Fyodorov said. "I am always wary."

Little Abrasha approached them. "Your carriage is waiting at the end of the alley, Madame."

"Well, Fyodorov, I am off. Good luck, safe travels."

"The same to you, Madame."

He bowed, and she waddled off through the gate, leaving a wide path behind her in the snow.

It was a great relief to see her go. She was a psychic and a mind-reader, and yet he had managed to conceal something from her she might well wish to know. He had not told her about Marko Volchek's interest in finding Nikolai Barakov, and she had not sensed it or intuited it or whatever it was she did to elicit information from the depths of people's minds. He had outfoxed her. It made him rather proud.

He took a leather-covered journal from his pocket, and a bit of pencil, and wrote himself a short note. His mind was filled with ideas, and he had been lax about keeping notes about them. He had been lax about his work altogether these past days. How many days had it been? He had even lost count of the days! It seemed now that his life revolved entirely around this woman, and what a fool he was, and he knew it, and yet it made no difference. He would go to visit her now, in her bedroom, where she would be sitting up in bed, bolstered by pillows. She would welcome him easily and naturally, without any feminine fuss or bother, one human being to another. Everything about her was simple and natural: her oval face, her pale complexion, her dark eyes, her short-cropped hair, never curled or adorned with ribbons and bows, nor was her face ever dusted with powders or rouge, nor her eyes accented with kohl, nor did she ever act or speak flirtatiously, or disguise her feelings, but was always straightforward, and, indeed, in appearance, far less like a woman than a young man whose outward demeanor was stern, sober and sad. Yet if he could make her smile, and he sometimes could, her smile so sweetened her expression that the sight of her filled him with joy. The truth was, he could not keep away.

But what a baffling woman she was, Valentina Grigorevna! How to predict what she would do? Then, was it ever possible to predict what anyone would do? He himself, for example—what person, knowing him, would have predicted he would be spending his days in a place such as this, putting his mind to work on puzzles of this sort? He might as well be working for the intelligence service himself, the amount of information he was amassing! And how easy it was, how irresponsibly and wickedly talkative men were, how willing to reveal each other's secrets, to gossip about each other. Then there were the uncanny coincidences. He was unwilling to accept them. The extraordinary return of Alejandro Azara, for example. Fyodorov was not suspicious by nature, but he suspected Azara. But of what? Of being involved in intelligence work? Was it possible? Why not? He knew far too much about everyone concerned, he was far too helpful, far too... willing. Then again, he wasn't Russian. It wasn't fair to judge him by the standards of men who suspected their own brothers of spying on them, and whose brothers probably were.

With all this on his mind, he made his way up the stairs to his laboratory, but found himself instead taking a hallway to another flight of steps and stopping in front of Marko Volchek's door. He scratched on it softly, and went inside.

♣

"Finally!" I said, looking up from the notebook on my lap. "I got your message, and I've been waiting. So, it's true? He's a rat?"

Fyodorov sat down on a chair beside the bed, and took up the sheaf of papers lying on the table.

"Yes, I believe so," he said, glancing down at the top sheet.

"What are we going to do about it?"

"Stay away from him. Stay away from the whole thing. Lie low."

"No. We have to do something. We need to protect ourselves."

"From what? You've been listening to too many socialist agitators and drinking with too many petty conspirators. You think the white straps are interested in people like us? We're not worth the trouble. As long as we keep our distance from him, we'll be all right."

"Are you really willing to risk it? Anyway, there's a principle involved. Even if we're not the target this time, a stinker's a stinker, a rat's a rat. We should do something about it."

"*We* should? What are you talking about? You're a university student and a rich man's son, not a Chechen brigand, enforcing some tribal law of revenge. It's not up to you to do anything."

"I realize that. But, think! We can do this and get away with it. We're smarter than they are. We'll never get caught for it. And we'll be ridding the world of a snake."

"You know how we can make sure we don't get caught? By doing nothing. Trust me. Arif will destroy himself without any help from us."

"But just think how easy it will be! We'll agree to meet him, to give him copies of the pamphlets. That's what he's been asking for. That's the evidence he needs against us. We'll choose a place somewhere out in the woods, kill him there, dump his body into a pond, and no one will be the wiser."

"Now listen to me, Semyon Semyonovich. Do you know you're talking about killing my best friend? Do you think for one minute I'd allow you to do that?"

"Listen to yourself, Veniamin Yakovlevich! You are letting your emotions interfere with your judgement. The man is not your friend. He's out for himself. Look at what he's doing. He may not give you up, but he's giving up all his other so-called friends, all the men who once trusted him. He's doing it to save himself. If the situation were reversed, do you think he'd have any qualms at all about eliminating you? Look, Venka, life's a game and these silly little ideas like morality and loyalty are handicaps, handicaps your friend Arif obviously doesn't have. You realize this. I know you do."

"Silly little ideas, are they? Is that what they teach you at university? Or is it just the practical wisdom rich men pass on to their sons instead of a conscience?"

"I never took you for a fool, Venka."

"And I never took you for an assassin, Senya."

"Forget it, then. Just forget it. But remember I offered. You can always come back to me, boss, if you ever change your mind."

I spat out that final line the way Aleksey had told me to. Then, stepping out of character, I grinned at Fyodorov and said, "Lights!"

"Bravo!" Fyodorov cried in delight, putting down the script he had been reading from. "You have your lines down perfectly. Well done, Marko!"

I had to admit that his praise cheered me. I still considered him an odd man with unpredictable enthusiasms, *Wide and Crooked* being one of them, and yet indulging him made us both happy. At least taking on a part in the play relieved my boredom. I had little else to do.

"How are you feeling today, my dear? You look better."

"I must have looked really awful yesterday if you think I look better today."

"And you are beginning to sound like one of Nikolai's characters."

"*What are you talking about?* Yes, it is a problem, isn't it? You get the rhythm of the lines into your head and can't get them out. I often find myself saying *You do realize that, don't you?* It's not an expression I normally use."

"As long as you don't find yourself using some of his raunchier expressions."

"Semyon Semyonovich is too much an aristocrat to use some of the raunchier expressions, the stinker."

Fyodorov laughed. "What can I get you, Madame? Have you eaten?"

"Yes. But I can eat again. And drink, too. Perhaps there's a bottle of vodka somewhere in this miserable cat house."

"I imagine there is. Let me see what I can do. Anything else you'd like?"

"Information."

"Of course. But first things first."

He went to the door, collared a servant in the corridor, ordered fish and vodka, and returned. As soon as he was sitting again, I asked him what he'd found out for me.

"Shall we wait for the vodka?" he said.

"All right. What's new then? What am I missing?"

"It is snowing."

"Ah! Now that's news."

"Madame Blavatskaya has left the building."

"Indeed? Is she en route to Tibet?"

He gave me a look of some perplexity. "I believe she may well be.

How did you know?"

"You once told me it was her desire to go there."

"Did I? And you remembered?"

I laughed at him. "I am not senile yet, dear Fyodorov."

"No, no! It is only that so few people actually listen when I talk."

Dear man! I wanted to pat him on the head, but of course I did not.

"I'm sorry she left before I had a chance to talk to her," I said, though, in fact, I found I was quite relieved that now I did not have to.

There was a scratching at the door, and the servant came in with a tray, a young man I had not seen before.

"Who are you?" I asked him as he set the tray on the small table beside the bed.

"Madame?" he answered, taken aback by the question.

"I asked you who you are."

He was a young man, perhaps not even out of his teens, with fair hair and skin, which caused his cheeks to flush easily. They were flushing now. "I am Artemey Efimovich, Madame. I am at your service. If there is anything you would like from me... if you wished to request me..."

"No, no! No, thank you, Artemey Efimovich. But do you always work on this floor?"

"I am often on duty on this floor, Madame. In the daytime."

"I see. So were you here yesterday?"

"Yes, Madame."

"I am asking because I don't remember seeing you."

"Perhaps I came when you were asleep."

"Did you come when I was asleep?"

The poor boy was blushing so fiercely it looked like his face was on fire.

"Yes, Madame."

"For what reason?"

"Madame Serafima wanted to be sure you were comfortable."

"So you came in to see if I was comfortable. And was I?"

"You seemed to be, Madame."

"All right then. Thank you, Artemey Efimovich. You may go."

The boy left, his face still burning.

"Poor lad," Fyodorov said. "Put on the spot like that."

"Poor lad, indeed! Fyodorov, we are in a brothel, remember. And someone has been spying on me. I think it's your poor lad, there, Artemey Efimovich. Isn't it amazing the way serfs give their children such grand Greek names. I suppose if you have nothing else in life, you can at least take some pleasure in being called by the name of a god."

"Spying, in what way?"

"Spying in the good old-fashioned way. Opening closets and drawers, going through my papers, reading my journal. I can tell when someone has been looking through my things."

"On whose orders would he do it?"

"Anyone's. Anyone could pay him. I am sure many people do."

"You had better tell Serafima."

"I'll think about it. Meanwhile, pour me a glass of vodka, Fyodorov, for the love of God."

He poured me a glass, and one for himself.

"Happy days," he said, raising his glass to me. "Oh, she gets the best vodka, our Serafima. The best pickled herring, the best sturgeon, the best smoked salmon. She is a person of style and taste. I wonder how she manages."

"You have some thoughts on this subject, dear Fyodorov?" I said, smiling at him. I was becoming used to his manner of approaching his subjects, somewhat askance, like a sailor tacking obliquely against the wind.

"One thing Nikolai taught me—oh, he taught me many things, but one that applies here—always look for the money."

"And what did you take him to mean by such a statement?"

"I expect he meant that you learn a great deal about an enterprise by finding out where the money is coming from, or where it's going to. Your comrade offers you dynamite. The first question you ask is: where did it come from? The same logic applies here. Serafima gets excellent fish and vodka. Where does it come from?"

"Go on. And pass me the bottle, while you're at it."

"Here you are. Very good. Now a few days ago you mentioned being curious about the men who attended the seance in Serafima's rooms. I've made some inquiries for you, and I must say I was intrigued by the results."

"Were you? And do these results have something to do with Serafima's vodka?"

"Everything to do with it."

"What riddles, Fyodorov! I do wish you would speak more clearly."

"May I smoke? It will make my speaking clearly easier."

"Of course. And I will join you. And that will make my listening easier."

We prepared our tobacco, lit respectively pipe and cigarette, and once we were quite settled, Fyodorov began to speak.

"When he's acting as a businessman and not as a madame, our Serafima is a very clever person. His father was born a serf, you know, but served so bravely in the Patriotic War of 1812 that he was liberated, and he became a doorkeeper and clerk on one of the Stolypin estates not far from Moscow. Very good. Our Serafima grew up surrounded by neo-classical beauty, was well educated along with the sons of the family, and went to Moscow for university. So far, everything seems quite normal. Then his life took a rather radical turn. He discovered the underworld, and took to it, well, like a duck to water. Or rather like a swan. Yes, he became a diva of the demi-monde, he transformed himself... into Serafima. On the way, he made some startling discoveries, and the biggest was that his demi-monde was not solely the province of the abnormal and rejected but in great part it was filled with members of society, with the rich and the ennobled. These were men who appreciated the presence in that world of someone clever at business who also possessed taste and style and discretion. Discretion above all. And they were, and are, willing to pay for it. Hence the Stardust. To a great degree it is more like the English Club than a whorehouse. Wouldn't you say?"

"Now that you mention it... not that I have ever been in the English Club."

"Nor have I," he said. "However, you asked me to discover the identities of the guests at the seance...your Fat Man, Skinny Man, Spaniard and Spy... They are not unfamiliar faces around here, though you were quite right in thinking that the names they use here are false, all except for your Skinny Man, Prince Ivan Ivanovich, who really is who he claims to be. They are—investors, let's say. Three of them, in any case. And as such they were being treated to a private event, quite exclusive, of course, which gave it added value. Everyone enjoyed himself immensely. I regret to say, even your fainting fit added to the pleasure they took in the evening, being men of... abnormal sensibilities."

"If it was such an exclusive event, what was I doing there? I didn't even want to be there. I was strong-armed into it."

"I believe..." Fyodorov began, but then abruptly stopped, and seemed to sink into thought. I knew enough not to interrupt him. He was like Socrates who is said to have had the habit of stopping in the midst of a walk, and standing in one place, perfectly still for hours, just thinking. Fyodorov did not remain silent for hours but for a few minutes. Meanwhile I smoked my cigarette and thought my own thoughts.

"It was either Serafima who wanted you there," he said finally, "or Blavatskaya herself."

"It was Blavatskaya," I said, having just remembered. "Serafima said it. Elena Petrovna would hold the seance only if I attended... But why? She doesn't even know me."

At that, Fyodorov suddenly struck his forehead with his fist, and cried out, "Oh, what a fool I am! How could I be such a fool!"

I had never seen him in such a state of emotional distress. I tried to calm him. I refilled our glasses, and encouraged him to puff more energetically on his pipe. Finally, he smiled at me.

"I am a foolish man, Valentina Grigorevna," he said. "I thought I had tricked her. You cannot trick that woman... But she deceived me, pretending she didn't know anything about you. She must have known about you all along. And she uses people's minds and memories. Don't you see? The entire seance was held merely to use you t..."

Fyodorov stopped speaking so abruptly that he didn't finish the word he had just begun, "to" perhaps. *Used you to* was what he was about to say, before he caught himself.

"Used me to do what, Fyodor Fyodorovich? Finish what you were saying!"

"Excuse me. I cannot."

"You can. You must."

"Please, Marko. All right. But first tell me again what you saw at the table that night."

"I saw figures. First an old man, then a young one. Standing behind Elena Petrovna. Or hovering, I suppose. Smoky, unclear figures. Fabrications. Smoke and mirrors."

"The young one resembled no one you knew or could identify?"

"Of course not."

"Very well. Then I will tell you. I believe Elena Petrovna wanted you present so she could attempt to use your memories of Nikolai to summon his astral body."

"His *what?*"

"Astral body. It is a term of art in the spiritualist world. It refers to a body composed, I believe, of light or energy, which co-exists with the physical body of every living person, and can travel through the astral plane from place to—"

"Wait! You said *Nikolai's*? Is that what you think she did?"

"I believe that was her intention. You did not recognize the figure, though."

"Perhaps—there was a slight resemblance." I felt a chill go through me. "My God! Did you say a *living person*?"

"Yes. Elena Petrovna does not pretend to summon the dead. She insists that the dead cannot be summoned to our plane of existence, they are far too happy where they are."

"So what I saw was not a ghost? What a relief!"

"I detect a note of sarcasm in your voice, my dear Marko."

"No, indeed. It is a relief. Yet how very appropriate that an *astral* body should make an appearance in a house called the *Stardust*!... But why would Blavatskaya want to call Nikolai's... *astral body*... in the first place?"

"I imagine she wished to ask it where exactly Nikolai is. Evidently, one can question an astral body."

"Surely you can't believe such nonsense, Fyodor Fyodorovich! The woman is an utter charlatan!"

Poor Fyodorov! I was being unfair, forcing him to defend Blavatskaya's ideas when he was already so terribly annoyed with her.

"Well, I am very glad you told me this," I said in my most conciliatory tone of voice. "Now I don't have to worry that I saw a ghost. That idea was a bit disturbing, I must confess."

I had no sooner spoken than a memory came to me of another conversation about seeing ghosts, Kolya's ghost in particular. It was Katerina Ivanovna, in that cold, empty room in the house in which they had lived, who first mentioned sensing... not Kolya's ghost, she said, but an image... a projection, she called it... something Fyodor Fyodorovich might be able to explain. How odd, I thought, that I should be talking about ghosts again, this time with Fyodor Fyodorovich himself. Or, if not ghosts, astral bodies.

Bewildered and bemused by the whole subject, I turned the conversation back to the less fraught issue of Serafima's investors and what Fyodorov could tell me about them. He had discovered that one of them was of particular relevance, but before we got to him, Fyodorov felt obliged to tell me a great deal about the others.

Fat Man, Pavlov, as he called himself, was the son of a priest, now deceased. Sons of country priests tended to become extremists of one kind or another. Evidently Pavlov had become an extreme degenerate, and an extremely rich one. Having begun as a clerk in the Department of Crown Property, he had raised himself up to a position of authority in an eastern province, and made himself rich by collecting bribes and stealing Crown lands which he then deforested, selling the lumber, and making a fortune at it. When he had accumulated enough, he moved to Petersburg and obtained a position with the Ministry of Justice.

"He has attended several of Elena Petrovna's seances in the past, in an attempt to rid himself of his father's ghost. A futile effort, I would think. The man must be haunted by his conscience which takes his father's form. But his interest in ghosts has been a boon to Elena Petrovna, who cultivates men in ministerial positions who can obtain favors for her, and his interest in boys has been a boon to Serafima, who has a similar interest in cultivating officials in the Ministry of Justice, as you can well imagine."

Orlov, my Spy, was a German merchant, and, Fyodorov assured me, richer than Croesus. His interest in Serafima was economic as well as hedonistic. He saw the Stardust as a good investment, but his interest in spiritualism was quite sincere and mystical.

"He has been longing—ardently, I would guess—for the pleasure of attending one of Blavatskaya's seances. And so he obtained what he desired, which is the service Serafima renders to her clients and to her economic investors, no matter what form their desire takes."

Skinny Man, Prince Ivan, was an *habitué* of the house, a sexual connoisseur, with unusual tastes.

"The actors are well-informed about him. He pays well for services rendered, and is even sought after by those who desire to experience the kinds of punishments he is famous for exacting on his willing victims.

Forgive me speaking of these things to you, my dear—"

"Nonsense, Fyodorov!"

"He comes from an old, aristocratic family. He is sophisticated, educated, and has a mordant sense of humor much appreciated by his acquaintances. As to why he was present at the seance, he is evidently a student of necromancy, according to my sources, if they are to be believed. It is possible they were practicing their own mordant wit on me."

"How typical of his class each of these men is—the degenerate priest's son, the degenerate merchant, the degenerate aristocrat. We are a country of degenerates, Fyodorov! But what of the last man, what of the Spaniard? What sort of monster is he?"

"Ah, the Spaniard! Your ear for accents is quite sound, Marko. The Spaniard is not Russian, nor even European. He is Argentine. Real name, Alejandro Azara, born in Buenos Aires twenty-eight years ago. His father was a naturalist and cartographer who traveled with Humboldt during his journey through Spanish America back at the turn of the century. Young Alexander, named after Humboldt, of course, attended university in Freiberg, at the School of Mines, Humboldt's own college. As you might know, Humboldt visited Russia, in the year '29, advising the government on the organization of mines, so when young Alexander completed his studies, he came here with the idea of traveling to the east as Humboldt had, and looking at our mines. How naive men of the West are, thinking they can simply travel around the country freely, visiting our mines! He soon learned what Humboldt himself learned thirty years ago: one does not move about freely in the empire of the tsars. He ran into serious trouble, did young Alejandro Azara. And can you guess who got him out of it? Nikolai Barakov."

He was pleased to see how truly stunned I was by this bit of news.

"I recognized him the minute I saw him. As well I should. He stayed at the house for several months, and we spent many a night drinking and arguing with each other, the three of us... Yes, he stayed some months. Nikolai managed to get him papers, and a passport, and hid him until the whole affair died down. Which it did, naturally, with the aid of a little gold passing into the right hands."

"What is he doing here?"

"Here? In Petersburg? On holiday, he says. More than that I don't yet know. I spoke to him only briefly. He came to the seance, however,

Alejandro Azara

"But if he is a spy, in whose service is he working?"

at the special invitation of Serafima. He believes she's taken a liking to him."

"A liking to him? I don't believe it. I don't believe it can be mere coincidence that he was present that night. Can you?"

"No. Mere coincidence is not the way I would describe any of this. In fact, if Azara's presence in that room at that time happened to be the result of chance it would be quite alarming. I would have to revise my entire philosophy, which, as you know, is based on the belief that the world is a rational place."

I couldn't help smiling at him, sitting in his chair, smoking his pipe, so formally dressed, so professorial; yet he was no older than Nikolai, which is to say, still rather young.

"How do you explain it then, if it was not chance? Is he a spy? Is *Wide and Crooked* about to move from the realm of art to the realm of life? Must we assassinate the rat?"

"This thought has occurred to me. And, you know, the character of Semyon Semyonovich could easily have been based on Alejandro Azara. Something about his pride and arrogance, his sense of privilege, his easy dismissal of those very virtues Russians hold most dear—loyalty, self-sacrifice, passionate attachments—"

"But if he is a spy, in whose service is he working? Surely not ours. Although I suppose this would be an excellent place to plant an agent. Think of the information you could collect, the pressure you could then exert."

"Yes," he said. "And imagine getting permission for doing it from the likes of The Hangman."

The name sent a shiver of terror through me. It was the sobriquet of our Director of the Third Division. Well-earned. He had been in charge of putting down the Polish Revolt.

"No," Fyodorov continued thoughtfully, "I doubt that Azara is working for Russian intelligence. Perhaps he is playing a more dangerous game. But as for his presence at the seance, it is possible that it was arranged by Elena Petrovna for her own ends."

So we were back to Blavatskaya and her tricks.

"What ends? Ah, calling the spirit from whom she might obtain Nikolai's address! Utter foolishness, Fyodorov! Surely, you can't believe in it."

He gazed at me for a moment with an expression of such utter and painful seriousness that I reached out to him and took his arm.

"My friend! What is the matter? Have you been taken ill?" And I nearly called out for Pavel Damianich, but instantly Fyodorov shook his head.

"No, no, forgive me, I am fine. It is my memory. For some time now I have been trying to remember precisely how it is I know some of the things I know about Elena Petrovna. A thought occurs to me, but how did I come by it? It is puzzling, almost troubling. Perhaps I had a conversation with her once during which she explained some things to me about her art, and now I can recall the information without being able to remember the conversation itself."

"This often happens to me, dear Fyodorov, and it is nothing to be concerned about. I remember all sorts of information but forget who told it to me. I would make a very poor spy, I'm afraid."

He smiled at me and thanked me for reassuring him. "In any case, what I remember learning from her is that a psychic like herself can not only read minds but can extract images from them and give them form. When she does this it appears she is summoning spirits, but it is not the case. Of course, she can summon spirits, too, but it is a different process, or so I believe."

"I find this information astonishing."

"And you think me mad for giving it any credence. Yet there is the evidence of the seance."

"First you must tell me how you, a scientist, can possibly explain these so-called psychic phenomena."

"I am not prepared to make a rational, scientific defense of them, my dear. But it is the case that much of our physical reality is both intangible and invisible to us. Matter, after all, is composed of atoms we cannot see. No honest scientist would deny that the universe is much more mysterious, much more complicated, and much—denser—than we know. Psychic phenomena posits the existence of just such a layer of reality, invisible, ineffable, yet co-extensive with the one which we experience every day, and as a scientist I would not disagree that such a layer of reality exists. But the psychic—animates it, I would say, populating it with spirits, and claims to have access to it and to have the power to stimulate the forces or energies which inhabit it. One might say that when Blavatskaya enters her trance state and contacts what she calls the spirit realm, she is really stimulating the mental and spiritual energies around her in the same way we move the physical and material objects around us. Nevertheless, we can't deny that when she does this, something happens just as, according to your own description of it, something happened to you at her seance."

For an instant I recalled the two apparitions, so clearly, so distinctly... and in a kind of mental horror, immediately thrust them away.

"So you believe that she read my mind, and discovered a memory of him, and somehow extracted it and projected it into the room?"

"That would be the occult explanation, yes."

"But what of Azara? Why would she require his presence? For his memories? But why would he even be thinking about Nikolai?"

"Why wouldn't he be? He is in Petersburg on holiday. Surely he would want to visit his old friends here. Surely he would be looking for Nikolai, especially, given the debt he owes him."

"All right. So we both have memories of Nikolai in our minds. And she has brought us both to the table for that reason. She extracts the image of Nikolai from my mind or from his, and she *materializes* it. But stop there, and listen, Fyodorov. Even if I accept this possibility, even if she were able to do this, a projection of a memory could not possibly provide her with *news*. It could not provide her with Nikolai's whereabouts. Not unless one of us already knew it."

"You are quite right. Perhaps she hoped that one of you did know it. Or perhaps she needed your presence in order to summon Nikolai's astral body. She has never met him, you know. She might simply have wanted to see what he looks like. There was a manifestation of some kind, wasn't there? Unless your eyes deceived you."

"I would rather believe my eyes deceived me than that Nikolai's astral body made an appearance at a seance in this whorehouse. To be honest, I would rather believe I was mad."

"But I don't believe you are mad."

"Perhaps I saw Nikolai only because I wished to see him."

"It is true that our affective lives can often seem far stronger than our material ones."

"Indeed," I said. "To become enslaved by one's emotions is far more unpleasant than to suffer from hunger or cold. Is it possible that Azara does know where Nikolai is?"

"I think it unlikely, but I will inquire tonight. I have an appointment to meet with him."

"Do be careful. He may be a dangerous man."

"I will take care. But as Nikolai always says, fortune favors the bold. And I am now very curious about him. Indeed, I am."

He sat back in his chair and gazed at me with great pleasure, as though at a child to whom he was about to give an unexpected gift. At least, that is the way I interpreted his smile after the fact. Otherwise, I would not have known what to make of it, such a loving look from a man I barely knew.

"If I may change the subject entirely, I have one more piece of information for you which I believe will cheer you and set your mind at ease," he said. "Beriosov did not have an order to arrest you or even detain you. He acted without authority."

"Without authority?" I cried, almost jumping out of bed in my excitement. Joy was filling me with a kind of mad glee. "You saved the best news until last, Fyodorov, you wonderful devil, you monster! Is it true? I don't need to fear arrest?"

"Not at all."

"But what about the fire? Could we not be charged with the crime of burning down his mother's house?"

"Officially, you were never in his mother's house, so the fact that his mother's house caught fire has nothing whatever to do with you."

"Well, this is all exceptionally good news, Fyodor Fyodorovich, and I can't thank you enough for it. However did you find this out?"

He gave me that smile one gives a fool who asks an inappropriate question.

"Right," I said. "Never mind. You knew whom to ask."

"I know someone who knew whom to ask," he said, smiling at me. "It comes from a high source and a trustworthy one. But not being wanted by the secret police and being safe are two quite different things. You are not safe so long as Beriosov wants something from you. Therefore, staying out of harm's way for awhile seems to me to be a judicious choice."

He refilled our glasses, and I emptied mine in one gulp like a good Russian. "I must rest now, dear Fyodorov. Too much vodka in the afternoon."

"I understand completely," he said, and formally kissed my hand. "With your permission, I will visit again tomorrow, after I meet with Azara. Perhaps I will have more information for you then."

The door had no sooner closed behind him than another door opened, and Pavel Damianich stepped out. Immediately he filled and emptied Fyodorov's glass.

"Thirsty work," he said, "listening at keyholes."

"You could have come out."

"Yes. But eavesdropping can be quite interesting."

"What do you think?"

"I think our timing is just right. He brought good news, yes, but we are not out of danger yet, and I am a bit concerned about this fellow Azara. I must say, though, I've come to like Fyodorov. He isn't half the crackpot I once thought he was."

"Still I simply can't believe in that supernatural layer of existence he talked about."

"It may not be supernatural at all. There is a strangeness here that is so strange it can only be natural. Whenever I think something is too strange to be a product of Nature, all I do is ponder the existence on the same planet of the electric eel and the giraffe."

"I thought of the giraffe myself quite recently."

"It is an animal worth thinking about," he said. "But not now."

"Very well," I said, and with some force, pulled off the bedclothes and jumped out of bed. While Pavel gathered my things, I dressed quickly and wrote two short notes, one, scrawled onto the script of *Wide and Crooked*, for Fyodorov, another, sealed, for Serafima. It is always important to thank your host even though you might also wish to wring her neck.

"One always wants to warn people not to irritate writers," I said, "but such warnings always fall on deaf ears. It's true our revenge is slow in coming, but when it does… well, if you doubt me on this, just read a little Dante."

"I never doubt you on anything, Marko, my dear," he said. "Are you ready? Our coach awaits."

"Yes. Now all we have to do is leave the building without being seen."

"Just follow me, Madame. This place is like a sieve, there are so many ways out of it. Practically every wall is pockmarked with secret doors."

He glanced around the room, noticed the half-empty bottle, and stuffed it into his pocket. Then, assured that we were leaving nothing of value behind, he thrust my satchel under his arm, picked up a candle, opened the bedroom door, and led me cautiously down the empty hallway until we walked into a wall—which, at a touch, swung open for us and closed again behind us, leaving us at the top of a steep flight of steps circling down into darkness. Pasha lit his candle, and by its dancing light we made our way down until we reached the bottom and another door. He pushed on this door, and we stumbled out into cold, grey, snowy air, and a narrow, cluttered alley. We trotted down this alley as quickly as we could without slipping into snow drifts, rounded a corner, and there, like a miracle, was an enclosed sleigh, horses hitched, coachman waiting.

"You are a prince!" I said to Pavel Damianich. "*You do realize that, don't you?*"

He laughed like a boy, lifted me into the carriage, climbed in himself, and signaled the driver that we were ready to go.

"Have you mapped out our journey?" I asked. I was feeling quite delighted with this new adventure.

"To the ends of the earth," he said, and he sounded delighted too.

And so, with a small jolt and a rattle or two, we left the Stardust and its denizens and its deceits behind, and set off again in search of Nikolai Barakov.

CHAPTER SEVENTEEN

The Argentine Enters

Alejandro Azara's apartment was not in the student district near the university as Fyodorov had expected, but in a rather fashionable neighborhood close to the river, in a building that, in sheer size and quantity of stonework, aimed for a certain grandeur. It was an impressive place for a poor mine inspector. Or perhaps Azara had now become a man of importance. Perhaps young Azara had acquired a patron, or patroness. It struck Fyodorov as the sort of building a patron would put his protégé in, for safekeeping. The interior of the apartment itself was elegantly furnished, and decorated to suit masculine taste, that is, in dark colors, with solid furniture, Oriental rugs, and pictures of hunting scenes on the walls. It came equipped with a man-servant dressed in the sort of livery one might expect to see on an English butler.

Azara greeted him warmly, with what appeared to be genuine pleasure. He had always been an easy man to take a liking to. Even Nikolai Barakov, not especially impressed by displays of cheerful enthusiasm, had found Azara's sincere friendliness hard to resist. So they expressed joy at meeting each other again, happiness at observing each other's good health, and curiosity about their current respective scientific interests. That they had happened to renew their acquaintance at the Stardust went, for the moment at least, unremarked.

The liveried servant announced that supper was served.

"Nothing fancy," Azara assured his guest. "As Barakov would say, just a little something to absorb the vodka."

They went into the dining room and sat across from each other at a long table laden with enough food to feed an entire household: soup, dumplings, meat pies, smoked fish, pâtés, and several varieties of cheese. Azara shooed the servant away and poured the wine himself.

"So," he said, smiling across the table at Fyodorov and lifting his glass, "shall we drink to lucky circumstances, or to the lovely Serafima Vadimovna, who seems to have been the catalyst which brought us back together?"

"I don't believe in luck," Fyodorov said, "but I will be happy to raise my glass to Serafima."

"The goddess of Stolyarny Alley!" Azara said and laughed.

Fyodorov did not like the sound of that laugh.

He did not like the servant in livery.

He did not like the chandeliers or the crystal glassware. He did not like the silver cutlery.

He wasn't sure he liked the wine either. It was a little too sweet.

He glanced across the table at his host, and felt a sudden urge to get up and leave. To break something first. Yes, like Nikolai would! Indeed, he would! He'd drink half the bottle of vodka first, then stand up and break something, and then stride out the door... What would he break? Fyodorov looked around the room until his eyes fixed on the exact object practically begging to be smashed, an extremely ugly, elaborately decorated, brightly colored glass fruit bowl, probably of Murano make, sitting placidly on the side board.

"I must say I was surprised to see you at her establishment," Azara said. "I suppose you were as surprised to see me."

"That is true."

"Please, help yourself, Fyodorov! The soup is excellent, I think."

Fyodorov admitted that it was.

They ate for a while in silence. Fyodorov had not had a good meal in some time. It was only by eating that he realized how very hungry he was, and the more he ate, the clearer that understanding became. He put the wine aside and poured himself a glass of vodka instead. It went better with the fish and dumplings and pies. He was eating with the concentration of a glutton, and he knew it, and he didn't care. He didn't care about the seance either, or about Blavatskaya, or about astral bodies. He almost didn't care about Marko Volchek, as he spread liver paste thickly onto his bread, but when he drank Azara's vodka he remembered her all too clearly, and felt a pain in his heart, and banged the glass down on the table and stared almost viciously across the table at Azara's good-humored face. Was Azara laughing at him? Did he think he, Fyodor Fyodorovich Fyodorov, was one of those degenerates who frequented Serafima's brothel? Of course he did! He had to, since he himself was one.

And a foreigner, too. A foreign spy.

He picked up his napkin and wiped his mouth, feeling disgusted with himself, and yet at the same time quite pleasantly full.

"Smoke if you wish," Azara said. He was still picking at his fish. "I find that smoking after a meal is a real delight. You smoked a pipe, as I remember. I have some very fine Turkish tobacco you might like to try... Shall I get it for you?"

"I have my own, thank you," Fyodorov said, and took his pipe from his vest pocket, and his tobacco. He hardly knew what he was doing, but a pipe would certainly help to concentrate his mind.

"So," Azara said, still smiling his false, foreign smile, white teeth flashing, dark eyes shining in the candlelight, "there's so much to talk about. Your work. My work. Our friends. Are you still living in that house on the Vyborg side of the river? How is Nikolai Barakov? I think of him so often. He was such a help to me years ago. How is he keeping himself?"

"So many questions! Where shall I begin?"

"With Nikolai," Azara said. "I yearn to see him again."

"Ah. Well, unfortunately, I can be no help to you since I don't know where he is."

"What do you mean? He's left the city?"

"He has, yes. But as to where he's gone, I don't know."

"And lovely Katya went with him?"

"No. No, he went alone and told no one where he was going."

"What a shame! I was looking forward to seeing him so much."

"You didn't see him the other night at the seance?" This was a dangerous move, but Fyodorov was tired of fiddling with pawns. A knight's move was what the game needed. A leap.

"At the seance? No. Did you think he was one of the guests? No, indeed. He was not."

"I did not mean as one of the guests."

Azara had been playing daintily with the food on his plate, moving bits from one place to another with his fork. Suddenly he tapped the fork on his plate, and the servant appeared, seemingly from out of nowhere. He gave Fyodorov quite a start.

"More vodka, and take all this away," Azara said. In minutes the table was cleared, a new bottle was brought and a box of cigars, one of which Azara chose but did not light.

"You did want to talk about the seance, didn't you? And what I saw at it. But surely you have attended other seances. You know how they work. You are a friend of Madame Blavatskaya's, I believe."

Fyodorov stuffed tobacco into his pipe and made a great show of lighting it. He needed a few minutes to think of how to reply to this rather forceful and aggressive move. Azara was bringing out his queen.

"Each seance is different, and as you know, I was not present at this one. I understand that it was of great interest in that Madame Blavatskaya was able to materialize an astral body. This is quite extraordinary. I am sorry I missed it."

"It was quite extraordinary indeed."

"Did you actually see the spirit?"

"I did, yes. Two, in fact. One was an old man. I saw it quite clearly."

"And the other?"

"The other, not quite as clearly. But do you think that the apparition I saw was Nikolai? Did someone tell you that it was?"

"Yes, someone did. But you yourself did not recognize him?"

Azara looked up at that—he had been studying his cigar—and stared quite seriously into Fyodorov's face.

"Strangely," he said, "now that you ask, I think I did. Just for a moment. Well, it only lasted a moment, really. Then one of the other guests cried out, tried to stand, and fainted quite away. All very dramatic. I assume it was all part of the show."

"You took it as a show?"

"Of course. What else could it be? I don't believe in ghosts. And I certainly have no reason to think that Nikolai is dead, or that his spirit is susceptible to the summons of a psychic like Madame Blavatskaya. Not at all! No, it is all done by suggestion, and some kind of mesmerism. The idea is planted in the mind that you will see something, and then with the shadows, the spooky lighting, the expectation, the vodka... And he has been on my mind as well, you know. I do so want to see him again."

I wish I knew if he was sincere, Fyodorov thought, for at that moment he was tempted to open his heart to this man, to tell him about

Valentina Grigorevna, known to the world as the writer, Marko Volchek, and her own search for Nikolai Barakov, her loyalty, her bravery, the strength of her character. Oh, how tempting it was to speak about her, and yet he had to resist. Resist with all his might! He could not trust him. But why not? Was it the apartment? Was it the man in livery? Was it the totally impossible and inexplicable coincidence of Azara's presence at the same seance table as Marko herself? Was it because he felt a need to protect her? Was he in love with her? Was he now completely mad and utterly lost?

"So… is it work or study that brings you here?" An awkward question and one he had already asked several days before. But Azara answered without a second's pause, as though it followed quite reasonably from a discussion of the appearance of an astral body.

"Neither. I am here for pleasure. I am on a holiday."

"Ah. A holiday in Petersburg, in the winter. How delightful. Well, the social season should be in full swing soon. Do you have many friends here?"

"Some. And I am making more every day."

"How ever did you find your way to Serafima's? The Stardust is a well-kept secret in the city, I think. I am surprised you found it out."

"A friend introduced me. And you?"

"I came to find actors," he said. Then, realizing how that might sound to someone of Azara's tastes, felt himself go red with embarrassment, and quickly explained that he had been searching for an actor who had a play in his possession.

"Not the very play that was being rehearsed in the drawing room? I watched a bit of rehearsal the other day. Quite interesting."

"Nikolai wrote it," Fyodorov said. He immediately regretted his words.

"Did he? I was sure he had! Just hearing that little bit of it, I was sure! Well, that is excellent news. Does he know you are producing his play?"

"In a whorehouse? No, he doesn't. As I said, I don't know where he is."

Suddenly Azara laughed. "In a whorehouse! Oh, Nick would love it, wouldn't he? His play produced in a whorehouse!"

The sound of that unusual nickname, used only by Katerina Ivanovna until Azara came and began to use it as well, filled Fyodorov's heart with unexpected joy, as did the idea, which for some reason he had not considered before, of how very amused Nikolai would be to learn that *Wide and Crooked* was being premiered at the Stardust. Oh, yes, he would most definitely be amused.

"I shall have to come and see it when it is ready to be seen. Do you have an opening day?"

"December 14th," Fyodorov said, and waited to see if this date made an impression on Azara. It appeared it did not.

"I shall make a note of it," Azara said. "Now, please, tell me what you are working on. I am eager to hear how the plans for your spaceship are coming along."

♣

It was hours later before Azara, having wished his guest a safe journey home, finally closed the door on the by now tottering figure of Fyodor Fyodorovich. His face, which had all evening borne an expression of delighted curiosity, now relaxed into a more natural one, a look of sober concentration. He walked from the foyer into the study, took a seat at the desk, and resumed the letter he had been writing before Fyodorov arrived, and which he had suspended in order to include whatever information he may have gleaned from his guest. There was very little to report. And he had to take great care in deciding how much to reveal of what he knew. Any letter could be read, any desk could be searched, any paper could be seized. Russians knew how to read between the lines, Nick always said. Read between the lines, slip between the lines… And now where the hell had he slipped away to?

♣

Meanwhile Fyodorov made his way back to his rooms.

He did not know why he was feeling the way he was, why he was on the verge of panic. He walked slowly, but all his instincts were shouting at him to run, to flee. He felt eyes on him; he felt he was being watched. Yes, he was pretending to be drunk, but perhaps it was no pretense, and he really was quite inebriated, and all these feelings were merely hallucinations brought on by an overindulgence in alcohol. On the other hand, perhaps he was finally seeing everything clearly. He had told Marko his suspicions, but he had barely believed them himself. Now, however… What was Azara doing in such a palatial apartment? What was he even doing in Petersburg at such a time of year? If he was a foreign spy, he would be known and he would be watched, and so would everyone who came in contact with him.

But if a foreign spy, for whom was he working? And to what end?

In any case, she must be warned.

He quickened his pace. To run to her, to save her… that was the absurdity. Yet there was nothing he could do about it.

Love leaped out in front of you like a murderer in an alley, eh, Faya? It's what Love does. You do realize that, don't you?

He stopped running, and stupidly looked around. It was late, the street was in shadow. Was there someone there? Of course there were, many people, walking rapidly through the snow, and more snow was falling, light, delicate flakes of snow, falling on his upturned face.

Fortune favors the bold.

Better to live one year as a tiger than a hundred as a sheep.

Words Nikolai had written in bold letters on his walls of his house. His mark. His creed.

Cheered by these memories and feeling somewhat restored, Fyodorov took a deep breath, smiled to himself, straightened his hat, and walked on.

Alejandro Azara laid his pen down and reviewed the document. It would be as disappointing to read as it had been to write. Better to wait to send it until after he saw Marko Volchek, for surely he would get some information from her. Women were notoriously unable to keep secrets, especially from men who were exceptionally good at extracting them. If she knew where Barakov was, or even had a suspicion, he would soon learn all about it. Of this, he was quite certain.

He was a young man, full of himself, and this was how he thought.

So it was with some dismay that he learned the next evening, when he stopped at the Stardust to drink with his new actor friends, that Marko Volchek had secretly left the Stardust the day before, and that no one knew where she had gone.

The Stardust held no more interest for him. He had many invitations, an attractive young man, born in the exotic American jungles (though Buenas Aires was hardly a jungle), well-traveled, and visiting from one of the great European capitals, and so most nights he could choose where to spend his time. It was Thursday evening, and the Prince was dropping in at Marina Vilinskaya's literary soiree. He had not yet met this woman whom the Prince thought so highly of. It was time he did.

"You are most welcome, Monsieur Azara," Marina Fyodorovna said, offering her hand. "And you have arrived at an opportune moment indeed. We have just decided that German philosophy is dull, Italian painting is frivolous, and English poetry is sentimental. Having dismissed Europe out of hand, perhaps we can find something about Spanish America that displeases us too."

"Marina Fyodorovna is being too harsh," a young, long-haired man standing beside her said and laughed. "We also decided that French poetry is divine, and also that George Sand is the greatest genius of our time."

"She is indefatigable, at least," another man said.

"He is a poet," Marina Fyodorovna said, nodding at the long-haired man. "All he wants to talk about tonight is Baudelaire."

The young poet might have been one of Madame Vilinskaya's protégés, yet she seemed somewhat peeved at him. Perhaps she did not approve of this Baudelaire. She did seem to approve of his companion, a man in his late twenties whom she introduced as the new owner of a bookshop and circulating library on Nevsky Prospekt.

"He is also a great admirer of the poetry of Nikolai Ogarev," Marina Fyodorovna said, smiling at him. "He does not think Baudelaire can hold a candle to him."

"We cannot discuss Russian poetry at all," a young woman sitting alone on a sofa said. "There are too many critics in the room." She sounded peeved as well. It appeared he had interrupted some literary argument.

"Well, now that Monsieur Azara has joined us, perhaps we can turn the conversation to other topics," the bookshop owner said. "You have been traveling around the country, I gather. How did you find the state of the roads? I think it is still safe to criticize the roads in this country, isn't it?"

"The roads, but not the railroads."

"No. One must never criticize the railroads. They are imperial rails."

"I came here by train," Azara said. "The line from Warsaw is quite good."

"Yes. Built to crush the Polish revolt," the bookshop owner said with bitterness in his voice. "We are quite good at crushing revolts."

"We can be proud of our railroads," another man said, joining the conversation. "After all, we started with a mere seventeen kilometers of track twenty-five years ago, and now we have over six hundred kilometers. Think of it! Six hundred! Of course, the Americans, from what we hear, have over fifteen thousand kilometers of rail lines, and they'll have finished their transcontinental railroad soon. But we can go from Moscow to Petersburg in ten hours."

"Tea, anyone?" Marina Fyodorovna asked, sweetly.

"Our country roads, I find, are better in winter than in summer," the young woman on the sofa said. "In winter you can get to places quickly by sleigh. In summer, the roads are dusty or get boggy or bumpy, and in the spring they are entirely impassable."

"Are you planning to travel on our roads in winter?" Marina Fyodorovna asked Azara.

Before he could answer, a servant came by with glasses of tea on a tray, and glasses of vodka. He chose the vodka.

"I may," he said. "Traveling by sleigh would be quite a different experience for me."

"Yes. Prince Kirill has just been telling us about your thrilling adventures in the great American jungles. I was terrified just listening to him. I am delighted you are here now so we can get more details about your journeys."

"I undertook those journeys many years ago, Madame Vilinskaya. When I was young and foolish."

"Come sit with me, and tell me what you remember from so long ago. Just one story, and I'll let you go."

He sat down beside her on the sofa. Immediately a small group of eager listeners pulled chairs up closer around them, serious men in black jackets, and women in rustling gowns, ribbons and pearls. He had not planned on being the center of such attention, though he might have expected it, being the house guest of Prince Kirill. Very well. As a traveler he would be known, a lover of adventure, and so no one would inquire too closely about what he might be doing in Petersburg in the winter.

And so, encouraged by his own natural optimism, he launched into a tale which he had told so many times that he had almost come to believe it had really happened to him. In fact he had taken it directly from the pages of Humboldt's *Personal Narrative*, as he had taken virtually all his jungle stories, for he himself had never ventured farther into the equinoctial regions of Spanish America than a short visit to the city of Caracas while en route to Paris.

"We were sailing down the Apure River, a territory inhabited by tigers, crocodiles, tapirs and peccaries. It was like finding oneself in a new world, in wild, untamed nature. Sometimes we saw a jaguar on the banks, the beautiful American panther, sometimes birds, the black hocco, the *Crax alector*, strolling along. All kinds of animals, one after another. It is like paradise; yet when you observe the animals, you see they avoid and fear each other. The golden age has ended. For example, as we sailed, we would see crocodiles, ten or more in a group, their jaws wide open, stretched out on the sand, lying side by side without the least sign of sociability, unlike other animals that live in groups. During rutting season, the males fight and kill each other. There were so many of these great reptiles, we could always see at least five or six of them, and we were told that hundreds more remained buried in the mud. Not a year goes by without those great, carnivorous lizards tearing apart and eating two or three people, mostly women or girls fetching water from the river. The Indians told us a story of a girl from Uritici who saved herself from the jaws of one of these monsters, though she lost an arm doing so. It happened like this..." And so, with some minor embellishments, he told the story of the Indian girl from Uritici who lost an arm but saved herself from death by sticking her fingers into a crocodile's eyes.

"Extraordinary!" Madame Vilinskaya said when he had finished, and all around there were similar expressions of delight and murmurs of amazement. He accepted this praise humbly along with a well-earned glass of champagne, and was just about to swallow it down when a low voice quite close-by said, "It certainly is extraordinary. If I'm not mistaken, a very similar story is told by Humboldt in his diaries. Why, I read that volume not a month ago. Though I suppose those miserable lizards are still swimming in the Apure river, and still making meals of poor Indian girls. Not much changes in our world, does it, Marina Fyodorovna?"

Azara looked around, and discovered the speaker standing just behind him, leaning over the back of the sofa, a thin, sickly-looking man, with a high forehead and a small mustache, whom he recognized immediately as the poet Nikolai Nekrasov.

"The bad things don't change, no," Marina Fyodorovna replied, and introduced the men to each other.

"Were you oppressed by those clouds of biting insects Humboldt describes with such skill one almost feels them crawling under one's clothing and into one's nose? They alone would probably prevent me from such a journey."

"They are inescapable in those jungles, I am afraid."

"Well, after such a tale I for one need a breath of cold air. Join me, Monsieur Azara?"

"Gladly," he said, "If Madame Vilinskaya will excuse me?"

"Be gone, both of you!" she laughed. "I have a roomful of guests to amuse me."

"And we can have a smoke," Nekrasov added slyly. They crossed the room and Nekrasov opened a French door that led onto a snowy terrace. He pulled his muffler from an inside pocket, and wrapped it around his throat. "We can just pop out here for a few minutes."

Azara had been in the world long enough to know that this tête-à-tête was more than a pleasant opportunity to take an innocent breath of air on a cold terrace. He had been warned, most recently by the Prince, that many interests were at stake, and that he was to trust no one. But that was the Russian way, he had learned. Trust no one, they say, and then they tell you everything. Absurd people. Or maybe simply too childlike. They had not suffered through three centuries of the Inquisition; they had developed no skill in dissimulation.

Nekrasov offered his cigarette case; Azara accepted with thanks.

"How are you enjoying your stay in Petersburg so far?"

"I am enjoying it very much."

"I understand you are staying with Prince Kirill. An interesting fellow. I had a long talk with him this evening about books."

"Not a poet, is he?" Azara asked, knowing very well he was not.

"Not he, no. More in the diplomatic line, I would say. He must have quite a library, though."

"I believe he keeps most of his books in his country house."

"Ah, yes. Eclectic tastes in literature, I think. Not the sorts of things we publish."

"In your journal, you mean?"

"In Russia," Nekrasov said.

"I imagine many books easily obtained in Europe are difficult to find here."

"Indeed. And there are many books written here that are also difficult to find here."

They smoked in silence for some minutes. Then Nekrasov flung his cigarette into the snow and said, "Freezing out here. But you must visit us before you leave the city. Madame Panaeva, my partner, would be so delighted to make your acquaintance."

"I will certainly do that. Thank you."

"And then perhaps we can talk about your friend, Barakov. Don't be surprised, Monsieur Azara. Prince Kirill told me you and Barakov are old friends."

"We are, yes."

"And we might also talk about his book."

"What book is that?" Azara asked, quite amazed.

"Ah, you mean you are not looking for it?"

"Believe me, sir, I have no idea about any book."

"Well, then, my dear Azara, you are the only man in this room who doesn't."

With that, Nekrasov opened the door and they returned to the warmth of Marina Fyodorovna's drawing room.

Azara looked around at the people gathered in the drawing room with new curiosity, and wondered if he had understood correctly what Nekrasov meant. It was ambiguous, what he had said. Had he meant that everyone in the room had ideas about books, in general, or had he meant that everyone had an idea about Barakov's book? The latter seemed highly improbable, if the book in question was the one Nick had been writing years ago. Why would this elite group of literati be interested in a rather absurd little novel by his old friend Nick Barakov? No, that could not have been what he meant.

"Isn't it freezing outside?" Marina Fyodorovna asked, approaching him with a smile and a thin, dark-eyed, scarf-draped woman on her arm. "I am so glad you've come in. I did so want to introduce you to my sister before she leaves. Sofya, this is Monsieur Azara, of Vienna. My sister, Sofya Fyodorovna."

"A pleasure," he said, bowing.

"I am so happy to meet you, Monsieur Azara," Sofya said. "I have just been talking to Prince Kirill and learned that we have a mutual acquaintance in Elena Blavatskaya, and that you have seen her recently. It's been such an age since I've had the pleasure of speaking with her. I must ask you how she is."

"I barely know her, I'm afraid. I did attend one of her seances recently."

"How extraordinary! You must tell me all about it!" Marina Fyodorovna by this time had moved on to another circle of guests and Sofya had expertly guided him to a sofa and invited him to sit beside her. "I had occasion to meet Elena Petrovna last summer in Pyatigorsk. A fascinating woman. So... a seance! Did spirits actually materialize?"

"Yes."

"Right before your eyes?"

"Yes." He smiled at her. "I was as skeptical as you seem to be. It is something you must experience, I suppose."

"I would be terrified! I would be immobilized by fear. Imagine... spirits! It's rather horrifying. You weren't frightened at all?"

"No. Actually, I—"

"You thought it was a trick! Perhaps it was."

"I did at first. But it wasn't. Because the vision was of someone I knew."

"No! Impossible! Some departed soul? Oh, it gives me shivers just thinking about it! A member of your family?"

"A friend. A friend who is not dead. So far as I know."

"Not even dead? But how is that possible? How did she do it?"

"Some kind of mesmerism, I imagine."

"Well, I think you were very brave to submit yourself to such mesmerism. I have had a similar experience with her. Actually, it involved a friend of yours, Nikolai Barakov."

Hearing Barakov's name for the second time that evening, Azara felt a sudden and unexpected thrill of excitement, even of danger, the sort of frisson he always associated with the time he spent in the house across the river. He had taken Sofya Fyodorovna's conversation for idle chatter, hardly worth listening to. Now it occurred to him that she might be useful to him. But he would have to be careful with her. She might be more intelligent than she seemed.

"Do you know Nikolai Barakov?"

"I? No, I do not. All I know is that he's written a novel." She smiled at him and swirled the glass of champagne which an alert servant had recently placed in her hand. "Every editor in Petersburg is after it, including my sister. When I saw Elena Petrovna in Pyatigorsk that's what she said to me. She said, Tell your sister to find Nikolai Barakov's book. That's all. She appeared on a bench to give me that message. Then she—disappeared! I assure you, she did. Simply vanished. Like that. She is a strange woman, you must admit. But now everybody seems to be looking for this mysterious book. You don't happen to have it, do you?"

Azara made a show of vigorously patting himself down as though searching for something in his clothes, a comic routine he had picked up from Nikolai, who had a repertory of them. "No, not that I can find. No, no books. What book is it, exactly? He was writing a novel years ago."

"It's called *Monkey*," she said, smiling at his pantomime.

"The same one, then."

"Really? Have you read it?"

"A bit of it. Years ago."

"Well, how extraordinary," she said again. "You must tell me all about it later. Now shall we go and see if my sister has a few more bottles of champagne hidden away?"

He stood and offered his arm, and she took it, smiling at him charmingly. She was quite a delightful and attractive woman, and he felt quite pleased to have her on his arm. It had never occurred to him that Barakov's name would be bandied about in the drawing rooms of the literary elite, and he imagined that Nick himself would find it greatly amusing. But now, finally, he had discovered a clue. He felt quite pleased with himself indeed.

So, the evening passed pleasantly enough. Sofya introduced him to other guests, and he was asked many questions about crocodiles, the fate of Juan Manuel de Rosas, and even some of the finer points of the new Argentine Constitution, of which he was mostly ignorant. The mere idea of a constitution seemed to be of great interest to this group of people, as were the long years of civil war which preceded the approval of it. Though no one mentioned the situation in Russia, Azara knew from experience that everyone was thinking about it, seeing parallels, making comparisons, always thinking, never speaking. Bitterly, he remembered errors he had made in the past by speaking openly in the wrong places with the wrong people. He had learned his lesson. Had it not been for Nikolai, he might still be learning it, in a penal colony in Siberia. It was at such times, when he was reminded of how close he had come to disaster, that gratitude almost overwhelmed him, and fear as well. Russia was a dangerous country, and he had few allies here willing to protect him. It was really far safer to talk about exotic birds, mosquitoes, and cannibals.

By the end of the evening, he had made many friends, drunk a good deal of vodka, and even recited a poem, or a few lines of one, in Russian, which pleased his listeners and so led his drinking even more. *Gleams white a solitary sail, In the haze of the light blue sea. What seeks it, in countries far away? What in its native land did it leave?* It was a poem every Russian child knew by heart. Nikolai had taught it to him.

"I wish to speak with you privately before you leave," Marina Fyodorovna had whispered to him at one point in the evening, and so Azara lingered in the drawing room with Sofya Fyodorovna while the other guests said their goodbyes. Sofya was a painter, and Azara was quite interested in her ideas about Renaissance art.

After all the guests had finally left, Marina Fyodorovna came back into the drawing room. Like her sister, she was an attractive woman, despite her age, which he took to be well above thirty. The young judge everyone older than themselves as being ready to be swept into the dustbin of history, as Herr Marx might put it. Even Fyodorov seemed like an old man to him. The sisters, however, were both charming women, no doubt about it, women of the world. Marina Fyodorovna was a countess, he had heard, and a very important woman in the literary scene in Russia, one of the new "intelligentsia," as they were called, political intellectuals, men (or mostly men) who held liberal views about society. To be a liberal in Russia was to be radical. He might have found it funny, if he were thinking about it somewhere else.

"I imagine you know why I want to speak to you," Marina Fyodorovna said, sitting down beside him.

"Not at all, Madame. I am quite in the dark."

"Alexander... Do forgive me. I don't know your father's name."

"Felix."

"So then, Alexander Felixovich, I will enlighten you. The dark is never a good place to be." She smiled at him again and he began to feel a certain discomfort, as though he was soon to be led somewhere he did not wish to go. "Prince Kirill, who is an intimate friend, has told me of your quest to find Barakov. I am filled with admiration for you, and wish to help you."

"I see," he said. "I am grateful, Madame. Believe me."

She laughed. "You are not grateful. You are suspicious. Gravely suspicious. That's quite all right. In fact, it is good. Let me tell you then that I am Anastasia Barakova's editor, and so I, too, am interested, very, very interested, in finding your friend Nikolai Vasilevich, since until he is found his mother, my poetess, refuses to give me her manuscript. Perhaps this means very little to you, but it means a great deal to me. Therefore I am willing to help you as much as possible."

"That is very kind of you, Madame. So Prince Kirill told you I am looking for my friend?"

"He did. Don't be alarmed. It's true the prince loves to gossip, but in matters of this kind, he can not only be extremely helpful, but he is also utterly discreet. Shall we lay our cards on the table, Alexander Felixovich? You are a stranger here, and you are not sure whom to trust. Your patroness put you in the care of Prince Kirill. Trust him! I will tell you what he has already done for us, that is, those of us looking for Barakov, One of us was falsely arrested and imprisoned. He discovered where this person was being held, and thanks to that information, we were able to free our friend from captivity. This is the sort of man he is. Quite brave in his own way, and generous to a fault. So now, dear Alexander Felixovich, I hope your fears have been assuaged. Do let us help you. Tell us what you need."

"Yes, do let us help," Sofya added. "Not that there's much I can do, of course. But Marina is a genius at finding things. Let her help you, dear Azara."

"It is not a thing I am looking for, but a man."

"Of course," Sofya said. "Forgive me. I misspoke."

"I doubt that you ever misspeak, Sofya Fyodorovna. But it seems to me that your interest in finding Barakov's book, and my interest in finding Barakov himself give us a common cause, and a reason to combine our resources."

"What an excellent idea!" Marina Fyodorovna said with enthusiasm. "And let us prove ourselves to you. For we have been thinking... Tell me, have you tried to find any of Nikolai's friends? Surely there must have been a woman he was close to."

"The household was dispersed. I don't know where any of them went."

"I have a friend who travels in those student circles. He says they all read the same newspapers. Why not place a small notice in one of them, designed to attract the attention of his friends, asking them to contact you? We shall offer a reward for information."

"An intriguing idea. It may well prove successful."

"Well, then," Marina Fyodorovna said, smiling at him, "if it is agreeable to you, Alexander Felixovich, let us plan to meet again..."

Their discussion continued for some time. It was quite late before Azara finally bid the sisters a cordial goodnight, feeling far more hopeful than he had all day.

♣

Hope, however, was not what Fyodor Fyodorovich Fyodorov was feeling, poor man. It was the opposite of hope, it was despair, that was filling his soul. He had never in his life felt such grief. And how absurd it was, to feel grief over the loss of nothing, for surely she had no feelings for him, none at all. To leave with a few empty words of farewell... not even spoken but merely scrawled on a page. They had been talking to each other that very afternoon, she had said nothing to him about leaving, but when he returned to see her, after his dinner with Azara, she was gone, leaving him only a few words scrawled on a page of Nikolai's play.

He took himself to his laboratory and locked the door. He wanted nothing to do with anyone. He especially wanted nothing to do with actors or with that foul thing, *Wide and Crooked*, for what gives us joy when we are in love becomes hateful to us when love abandons us. There is no grief quite like that grief, which turns brightness dark and sweetness bitter and sears the soul with fiery brands of unfulfilled desire. So Fyodorov disappeared into his laboratory, Aleksey, the director, secured a role in a production at the Aleksandrinsky, the other actors went their separate ways, and Nikolai Barakov's play was not produced, at least not there, and not then.

CHAPTER EIGHTEEN

Rampage

Alejandro Azara was not a patient man, and he cursed himself up and down, hour by hour, that he had made such foolish arrangements, that he had set himself up to sit and wait night after night, for someone who would never come. Yet every time he decided he'd had enough and began settling his account, every time without fail, the same young man wearing a woolen cap and a workman's jerkin, would come into Osip's café and look directly at him, as though sizing him up, give him a nod, turn, leave... Or was it just his imagination playing tricks, this idea that he was being watched, sized up, tormented? Trial by waiting. Trial by boredom.

He had read entire books while he waited, he had finished *Lettres d'un Voyageur*, he had read a thick dissertation on the geological distribution of various quartz formations, he had drunk countless cups of tea. Every so often, Osip would stop by his table to see how he was doing. Osip remembered him vaguely, remembered Nikolai much better, had not seen the adorable Katya in months. "If she comes by, I will recognize her, and give her your message," Osip offered night after night. Perhaps he wanted the table for other customers. But Alejandro Azara had not come all this way, braved storms and sleet and wind, refused innumerable invitations from the delightful Vilinskaya sisters, even an invitation to the opera, only to be defeated by boredom and bad tea. He would stick to his post. He would stand fast.

When, therefore, on the fifth night of his ordeal, the girl finally appeared, and without saying a word took a seat at his table, he could barely believe his eyes.

"Don't stand!" she commanded, as he started to. "Don't draw attention to us."

"Thank you for coming, Katerina Ivanovna," he said, sinking again into his chair.

She looked at him searchingly. "The man from Quito," she said and smiled.

He was not from Quito. He had never set foot in Quito. It was just a bit of fun, one of Nikolai's jokes. He liked the sound of it. The Man from Quito. But it stuck, and turned out to be a good thing. Nobody in the Chancellery was looking for a man from Quito.

"You remember. I am flattered, Katerina Ivanovna."

"It is your name I have forgotten," she said, smiling at him. "Sasha is all I remember."

"Sasha will do," he said, smiling back.

"Then you must call me Katya. Now, quickly, we must go. You have been sitting here too long."

He certainly agreed with that. But Osip's at least was warm; outside it was freezing and snow was falling.

"Surely we can talk here. Unless you have another place in mind."

"I do," she said.

They had not gone far, walking arm in arm down the frozen street, when someone whistled sharply just behind him, Katya released his arm and moved away, a great weight hit him from behind, a coarse bag was pulled over his head, several pairs of hands lifted him up and flung him into what had to be the back of a cart. No one on the street paid any notice, nor did Katya scream or cry out in protest. A large sack of grain was thrown on top of him, and the cart rumbled forward. Struggling was useless. A voice told him to quit it or he'd be sorry. It was the sort of voice he tended to believe.

He was freezing before the cart stopped and he was lifted up and dropped onto the ground, pulled to his feet, pushed up some steps, and finally flung like a parcel into a chair. Bag removed from his head. Lamplight somewhat blinding. He squinted at the room, at the six faces looking at him. Looked around for Katya but she was not there. The only face he recognized was her brother's. Gutiev. A roughneck, as he recalled. A head-breaker. It was a relief, though, to be in the hands of bandits he knew rather than bandits he didn't. And it meant the girl was safe.

"The man from Quito," Gutiev said. "I remember you now."

"Likewise."

Gutiev sighed heavily, passed him a bottle. "Better warm up."

He took a long swig, as one should, hoping it would not kill him. Nearly spat it out, but resisted. Swallowed, and felt the burn, all the way down.

"So, man from Quito, you wanted to see us. What can we do for you?"

"It's Barakov I want to see. Trying to find him. Thought one of you might know."

"And tell you, you son of a—"

"Godforsaken piece of—"

"Who the hell do you—"

"Why do you want him?"

That was Gutiev. The loudest. The boss.

"I have a debt to pay."

"Do you? Fine. Good. Pay us the debt, we'll see he gets it."

Clever. Something he hadn't bargained for. Hadn't thought this through so well.

"I'd also like to see him, of course. It's been a long time."

"He's not available."

"You mean, he's not in the city?"

"I mean what I say. Not available."

"Well, then." He looked around at them, six big men, tough guys, scarred, bruised, bearded, unwashed, short-tempered, probably armed. What chance did he have of getting out in one piece, or at all? "I'm sorry to have troubled you. I'll be on my way."

Gutiev laughed. "Not so fast, Quito. You spent a lot of time at Osip's waiting for us. You dragged us out in the cold. Now you're gonna leave us so soon?"

"It's Barakov I want to see. No offense to you, of course."

"No offense taken. But let's look at what you did. You paid for a notice to get our attention. You even offered a reward. You sat in lousy Osip's for a week drinking lousy tea. Now that took perseverance. Worst of all, you disrupted our evening. We have things to do. Now you think you're gonna just walk away? I don't think so, man."

Gutiev passed him the bottle, and he took another long swig, shook all over, coughed, wiped his nose on his sleeve. He felt unmoored, and slightly afraid. He felt unfairly and unreasonably suspected, he wanted to insist on his innocence, his good faith, but their faces were so hard, their voices were so cold. There was no friendship here. And why not? What about their friendship? He had to appeal to it. He was their friend, not their enemy.

"Look, you know me. I'm Alejandro Azara. You remember me, don't you?"

"Sure we remember. So what?"

"What d'you want with Nick anyway? Who the hell sent you?" another one yelled in his face, a skinny, tough, very angry man whose name totally escaped him. He was getting scared now. They were sure to rough him up, it was something they enjoyed, but would they kill him, too? If they thought he was a spy...

"I'm not a spy!" he yelled back. "I'm a friend!"

The skinny one got in his face again. "You say! Who are you to say shit?" Other voices started yelling too until Gutiev shouted at them to shut up and they quieted down.

"You answer a few questions, and give the correct answers—then we'll see," Gutiev said. "One: where's the money?"

"I don't have it on me."

"Why not?"

"Didn't want to carry it around—"

"Too many crooks out on the street," someone said and started laughing, and others joined in.

"Pickpockets!"

"Bad boys!"

"Thieves!"

"Take it easy, you lot," Gutiev shouted and they quieted down again. "So you don't have it. We'll go get it for you. Where is it?"

"I will have to go to the bank."

"Fine. Tomorrow morning we'll all go to the bank. Meanwhile here's question two. You used the emergency code in that newspaper notice. Clever of you. Now tell me what the letters of the emergency code stand for."

He knew this. They stood for words one didn't use in polite society, and ones he didn't even know existed in Russian until Nick told him.

"You want me to say the words?"

"Yeah, genius. I want you to say the words."

He did. He said the words. They were no sooner out of his mouth than Gutiev growled and leapt on him and started to throttle him, shouting, "Don't you call me that, you piece of shit!"

Azara felt death grip him... panic overcame him... struggle was useless… and then, in an instant, it was all over. Gutiev released him and laughed so hard tears came into his eyes.

"Man, look at you! Scared the shit out of you, didn't I? Well, you're wide of the mark, brother. So Nick told you that's what it meant, did he? Hah! That's a good one!" And still laughing, he passed Azara the bottle.

Finding the bottle in his hand, Azara took a drink from it, and thought about her, for whom he was doing everything, for whom, it seemed, he was risking life and limb. Not for her mother, not to repay a debt… but for her, only for her. The thought of her cheered him. If he survived this, he would see her again. And, of course, he would survive. Yet, looking around, he had such a terrible feeling. The men were renegades, the room was shabby, even squalid. It looked like they used it for eating, drinking and sleeping, and now, for holding him hostage. There was no point asking them to let him go home and sleep in his own bed. No point at all. They wanted his money. He'd have to pay them off. Revolting as it was, he might have no choice. If he had no choice, he would have to use the resources entrusted to him. Use them, waste them; they'd get him no closer to Barakov. What a failure this was turning out to be! This whole endeavor, an utter failure.

"Now look here, Quito," Gutiev said, having controlled his laughter at last. "We have plans for tonight and they don't involve watching you. We have some business to attend to. You have a choice. Stay here, locked up, or come along with us."

"I'll come," he said, too eagerly.

"Sure you will. But I swear to God if you take one step out of line, you'll get a knife in the back. Understood? Now let's go."

They split into two groups, three and three, with himself making the fourth in Gutiev's group, along with the wiry, skinny kid—Mikha, he now remembered—and an older tough, a man with some girth, the heavy. When they'd go out, not exactly looking for trouble but always bound to find it, there was always one of these big men along, not too bright but powerfully built. Muscle, Nick called them. And it all came back to him, then, the old days, rampaging on the streets with Nick and the rest of them, it came back vividly, keenly, the joy of it, the thrill.

They passed out of the building and along the alley and down toward the river, padding along in the snow, and he had no idea where they were headed or what they were going to do, only that it would be wild and new and would become a good story to tell his staid Viennese friends.

It was a still night, cold, with no moon and few men on the streets. They were on one of the islands, he did not know which one; now they were coming to the river; now they were crossing a bridge. He did not know his way around this city, and even what he used to know, he'd forgotten. They marched along, a ragged phalanx, and anyone on the street, seeing them coming, moved quickly out of their way. The night belonged to them, at least in this run-down district. They came around a sharp corner, to a derelict street, stopped in front of a ramshackle house, and a flight of wooden steps rising up into solid blackness. Snow was falling again and now the wind was up. After a long while, or so it seemed, they heard an owl's call, repeated twice. Gutiev returned the call. The others were in place. It was time to move.

He was third in line to go up the rickety steps, holding on tight to the splintery banister, such as it was. Once up, they crawled through a hole, a disgusting hole it was, too, right through the wall and into a storeroom filled with junk, tools, garbage. Slowly and stealthily they made their way across the room, and into a half-lit hallway. By the sound of it, a raucous party was in progress in a room at the end of the hall.

Gutiev took hold of his arm. "Take this," he said, and handed him a short truncheon. He only then noticed that the other two men were carrying cudgels.

"What's it all about?" he asked in a whisper.

"Rats," Gutiev whispered back. "Extermination of rats. Let's get 'em!"

With a shout, he started running down the hallway. Then they were all running and yelling at the top of their lungs, even Azara, caught up now in the exultation of battle. In seconds they had reached the doorway and burst into the room swinging their clubs, shouting. Then there was more shouting and the sound of bodies being struck hard with batons and clubs, and there was blood in the air, and objects flying past him, and bodies falling. He was already feeling the exhilaration of pitting his body's strength against another man's, the thrill of victory in every striking blow. Oh, how he had missed it! For weapons, besides muscles and fists, they had broken bottles, legs of chairs, knives. They had shouts, cheers, grunts, curses. Once, when he was struck from behind, he pivoted, swung his truncheon, and swearing, slammed it down on the nearest body, and he heard the crack of breaking bones and such pure glee rushed through him, he looked around hopefully to see what other bones he could crush. Then there was a rushing of feet on the stairs and reinforcements arrived. But hard on their heels came half a dozen defenders, pushing, shoving, punching their way through the door to join the melee and add a new ferocity to the fight.

Amidst that rush of men, a giant emerged. The giant had his eye on him, was coming right at him, coming at a run. He tried to dodge away from the charge, but there was no room for dodging, the giant so clearly had set his heart on him, had chosen him as the apple of his eye. He lifted his club but it was like lifting a feather in front of a charging bull. He was grabbed by the collar, he was lifted into the air, he was thrown. He hit something hard that, breaking into a million pieces, a million shards, didn't stop him but let him through, out into the cold, sharp, glistening, cutting air, and he fell through that air until he hit something else hard that knocked the wind out of him, but not so hard that it knocked him out, for by God's grace, he thought, he had fallen into an embankment of snow.

The fight was still going on above him, but he was out of it now. If he could only get up and walk away. He wasn't sure he could. The snow was so soft, he was feeling so tired. But that was wrong. He had to move, he had to get up. The snow around him was sprinkled with red; looking down as he stumbled away from the house, he saw he was leaving a trickle of blood behind him, easy trail to follow, if they set out their dogs.

Not only the snow, but the air itself was red, blood in his eyes.

He knew he was lurching, and tried to walk upright, seeing a pack of rowdy boys coming at him. But he was a marked man. They surrounded him, knocked him down with ease, went through his pockets, took his watch and wallet, kicked him for good measure. Once down, down for good.

Now someone else was running up, bending over him. No more left to take, brother. But there was more. He had a wool coat, an excellent pair of boots, which hands were now trying to pull off him. To leave him naked on the street. And he would freeze to death. This thought roused him enough to kick, to shout, to protest, to fight back, he would fight them with his last breath... But still another group came running—was there no end to the brigands?—and it was all noise and chaos and fighting. They were fighting over him, over his coat, his boots, over his skin, his hair, his organs, over himself as the spoils of war...

Pull yourself together, Alejandro Azara! You are a man! Crawl if you must, but get away from the brutes. Get on your knees, push through the snow, use your arms, use your legs, this is how you save your life... inch by inch, foot by foot, yard by yard. So he crawled, crawled through the snow, crawled bleeding, crawled to the edge of a building, used the edge to pull himself up, got to his feet (feet still in his boots), and, holding on tight, using the building as a crutch, made his way to the corner, and around the corner, and there he saw, unbelievable as it was, a familiar sight, the single street lamp in front of the first bawdy house that marked the entrance to Stolyarny Alley. Sanctuary.

Yes, but to get there meant passing through a crowd of devils, and he could barely see anymore, and he could not stand, he was sliding down, his back to the wall, sliding down into soft soft sweet smooth snow, and it would bury him, and it would be sad, so sad, that he would never see her again, and she would forget him. The sadness of it was so great, so immense, so sorrowful... that they would find him frozen on this very street with her name on his lips.

Her name, like a prayer. He put his lips together to say it. He tried to. His lips would not move. His face would not move. Only his heart still beat... still yearned... still whispered... *Adieu sweet life... So soon it seems he sinks so softly sinking still so still and sweet her name so sleepy sleep in snow so deep...* As though in answer a voice, a man's voice, familiar and somehow dear to him, came to his ears singing... *bells are ringing and gongs sound heavy as though in a temple or a monastery... and all the trees are bowing down* ... and he did bow down, crouching down, coming through the snow blind he did bow... giant Nick, bowing to him... *Nick mi hermano he tried to say but could not move his lips and Nick said fucking shut up man you are freezing to death out here* and like a great bear grabbed him up out of the death waiting for him its crocodile jaws opening wide lifted him up above the jaws... *Nick amigo la muerte me está mirando desde las torres de Córdoba... What bullshit, Azara, no fucking way is death looking for you, man, not today* and lifted him up out of the snow.

CHAPTER NINETEEN

THE FOUR HYPOTHESES OF FYODOR FYODOROVICH

Washed, sewn, bandaged, wrapped in blankets, put to bed, now asleep, Alejandro Azara and his bludgeoned, stabbed, sliced, kicked, half-frozen body presented something of a puzzle to Fyodorov. Clearly he'd been attacked and robbed on the street and left, more or less, for dead. Somehow he'd ended up in the Stardust where Serafima took one look at him and sent for the nearest doctor, Fyodor Fyodorovich Fyodorov, who fortunately happened to be in the house. All that seemed clear. But who had attacked him? Where had he been? Somewhere nearby. He wouldn't have gotten far in the state he was in.

Nick Barakov, he kept saying. He'd seen Nick Barakov with his own eyes, and it was Nick Barakov who had brought him in from the frigid freezing deadly cold.

Fyodorov wanted to believe him, wanted with all his heart to believe him, but he knew it wasn't true. Little Abrasha had told him what really happened, how a peasant heading toward the Haymarket, a Good Samaritan, had found Azara on the street and called out for help, and how he, Little Abrasha himself, hearing a ruckus, had left his post, "... and come to find the young gentlemen all bloodied and half-froze, terrible thing, and so together we got him over here to Your Excellency."

Not Nick Barakov, Fyodorov told Azara.

"Then it was his astral body, dammit. Or his ghost."

In any case, Alejandro Azara was a very lucky man.

But it was irritating that he was now laid up in the Stardust, that he would need tending, that Fyodorov would have to see him, who did not want to see anyone, who had important work to do, who did not want to be bothered by having to care for Argentine spies. Or Austrian ones.

He gave one of the girls a few instructions for changing his bandages. "And if he runs a fever, if he seems disoriented, if when you change the bandages, you see pus, call me. On the other hand, if he gets fussy or tries to go anywhere—just give him a good slap and tie him down."

With that, he returned, grumbling, to his lab.

January was a dark month. His work was not going well. He could not concentrate his mind. He could not imagine solutions. He felt at a loss; he felt lost; he felt he had lost. And the more empty he felt, the less he had to offer, and the less he could do. Was it possible, then, that creation was the result of fullness, of hope, that to be drained and emptied was a sign of dissolution, of impending death? Was sorrow, then, not an emotion after all, but rather a kind of fabric, a form of matter? Did feelings affect the magnetic field?... And he would scratch out some ideas, and replace them with others, lackluster ones, pathetic ones... and so sink deeper and deeper into the morass.

One day the girl sent up a note. The patient insisted he was much better, completely healed, in fact, and was demanding to leave. What should they do?

"Let him go! Why should I care?" Fyodorov shouted at the poor messenger, whose face flushed a deep red. "Oh, never mind. I'll come," he said more calmly, and took up his medical bag and put on his coat.

"I know you, don't I? What is your name?" he asked the boy.

"Artemey Efrimovich."

"Ah, yes. You are the one who searched Marko Volchek's room, aren't you? Tell the truth, now, or I'll turn you into a toad!"

The boy stared at him in terror, for it was well-known in the Stardust that Fyodorov was an alchemist and a sorcerer, and that he did strange, dreadful things up here in these uncanny rooms. He had been frightened enough just climbing the stairs; now he was truly terrified.

"Yes!" he cried. "I did. On her orders, though! I would not do it otherwise."

"Whose orders? Serafima?"

"No, no. The magician. The spirit-caller. Madame Blavatskaya."

"Did you indeed? And what did you find for Madame Blavatskaya?"

"Some handwriting, she wanted. Just a page of handwriting and a strand of hair."

"A strand of hair! Dear God!"

"I took it from her brush. Forgive me!"

"Don't ask me for forgiveness, you miserable boy. I'm not the one whose room you searched. Though it's she who is to blame. That woman! She's studied sorcery, it's true. With the Kundyani of the Caucasus. You were probably wise to do what she said. I cannot turn boys into toads, but I am sure she can."

Could Elena Petrovna have put a spell on Marko, to drive her away? A spell, indeed! Truly, Fyodorov, you are going soft in the head, you are becoming as demented as your grandfather, the mad priest.

Azara was sitting up in bed, and truth be told, he was looking rather well, quite a good deal better, alive, at least. Fyodorov checked his stab wound, to see how the stitches were keeping; checked his bruises, his cuts, felt his forehead, looked into his eyes.

"It appears you have survived," he said. "And now you want to leave. Very well. I will want to take out those stitches, though, before you go."

"I can't thank you enough, Fyodorov."

He shrugged it off. "Let's have a drink," he said, catching sight of a bottle on the table.

"A toast to your recovery."

"How long have I been here?"

"Oh, a week, perhaps."

"It seems much longer."

"Perhaps it was. I am not one to ask about time."

"I thought you were exactly the one to ask about time."

Fyodorov poured them each a glass of vodka. "*Salud*," he said, raised his glass and drank it right down.

"You want to know what happened, I suppose."

"Not necessarily."

"I was with Barakov's old crew. Ilya Gutiev. Remember him?"

"How in the name of God …? Or, rather, why?"

"I want to find him. I told you that."

"But he moved out of that house. *I* told *you* that. Didn't you believe me?"

"I thought if I could just talk to Katya. I put a notice in a newspaper—"

"How very foolish, Azara."

"Why? I want to see him again."

"Is that all it is?"

"What else could it be?"

"Then why not put a notice in the newspaper for *him*? But you wouldn't do that, would you, because you know that not only is he not in the old house, he's not in Petersburg, either. What the hell are you up to, Azara?"

"I'm telling you, I thought Katya might know—"

"Bah!" Fyodorov said, and poured himself another few fingers of vodka. "You are lying to me. I don't care. I will drink this and go. You can take out your own stitches."

Azara laughed. It was, Fyodorov thought, a good, honest laugh, and, in a way, an endearing laugh. But good spies learn to laugh like that. Good spies have to know how to laugh and lie.

"All right, Fyodorov, if you must know." Azara held out his glass and Fyodorov refilled it. "I will tell you everything. It is a story—well, without a conclusion as yet.

"There is a woman named Princess Tatyana Volkonskaya. She is a close friend of Nick's mother, Anastasia Alexandrovna. When I was in trouble four years ago, Nick rescued me, remember? And to save me from prison, he bribed everyone. He didn't have that much money himself. He borrowed it from Princess Volkonskaya. Or, rather, from her daughter, Margarita Mikhailevna. Do you follow?"

"Yes. Go on."

Fyodorov was more than following; he was now paying very strict attention.

"Princess Volkonskaya remembered the incident, and remembered the debt I owe. For I still owe it. It is a debt of honor. I have never paid Nick back, so probably he has never paid Margarita back, or she, her mother. So when the Princess contacted me several months ago, and asked me to come here and look for Nick, as a favor to her, she did not need to remind me of the debt I owe her. I came immediately from Vienna and began to search."

"You might have told me all this before," Fyodorov said severely. "I had you working for some intelligence service. I had you pegged as an Austrian spy."

Azara laughed again. "Was I as inept as all that? Why, I thought I was passing quite successfully as an insouciant young traveler out on a *Wanderung*."

"Indeed. Well, then, explain this to me, if you will. How did the Princess Volkonskaya know how to contact you after all these years?"

"Still suspicious, Fyodor Fyodorovich, my friend? I will explain, gladly. I have been in correspondence with her daughter, Margarita Mikhailevna. I met her when I was here four years ago. We visited the Princess's estate, Nick and I. They, Margarita and Nick, are childhood friends. I fell in love with her, you see. It was all very romantic for me—the estate, the beautiful house, the art on the walls, everything so perfect, and this lovely young woman… I have proposed to her, and she has accepted. This journey, this search, I hope and trust, will end successfully. Then, our engagement will be announced, and soon after, God willing, we will marry."

"This is stunning news," Fyodorov said, and took out his handkerchief and wiped his brow with it. "I cannot take it in."

"Why, friend? Is it so impossible an American Spaniard should win the heart of a Russian princess?"

"Not at all. Don't assume you know what is in my mind."

"What is in your mind, then?"

Azara was peeved; Fyodorov was confounded and confused.

"It is a memory of a dream," he said. "Pay it no mind, I beg you. It is nothing to do with you… But let us drink to your happiness, and to your success."

They did so, being now reconciled, and soon after, having extracted Azara's stitches, Fyodorov excused himself and fled to the serenity of his laboratory, where he could think in peace.

Once he was there, he emptied his cupboard, pulling out in no particular order: collars, stockings, a pair of jodhpurs, ties, scarfs, unidentified woolen objects, brushes, a box of buttons, pins, clasps, and odds and ends, a bed pillow, a blanket; then, finally, hidden behind that barricade, in the very back by the wall, a stack of notebooks.

His dream journals, so-called. Notes from the Dream Time. The record of his episode of madness, his nervous collapse. He should have burnt them; he had not. And perhaps now he would be glad he had simply smothered them with a bed pillow and buried them behind a blanket.

He placed the notebooks on his desk, leather-covered journals, scraped and nibbled at, as though something had been gnawing on them. Mice in the cupboard? No, more likely it had been himself, gnawing on the pages, for he had written them while still in the cloud of unknowing, in the darkness, the dark night of the soul, so-called, when he had thought… No, when he had no thought, only the story which he was trying to capture before it fled like a dream.

Now, with some reluctance, some strong feeling of aversion, he opened one of the books, the page covered with his own writing, a scrawl no one but himself could ever read. Let us think of this as research, he told himself, as an investigation of some other scientist's archive, as a record of an experiment. Let us be objective. Let us not be afraid.

He did have a plan, a goal. He was searching for one particular incident, quite near the end… a conversation with a woman who bore the same name as Azara's fiancée, Margarita Mikhailevna. The name had triggered the memory, but he was so unsure of it, of what he remembered, and even of what it was he had remembered. The memory of a dream? Perhaps. But if a dream, a long and fantastical one. A dream that lasted days and weeks. A dream of a journey with a woman he did not know, to places he could never have imagined, for a purpose he did not understand, not until the end. Then—if he could only find it, the end… what he had written about the end.

He rifled through the notebooks, one by one, until he found what he was looking for. *We hurried after her, but some force stopped us on the threshold. We could only watch from there while, standing alone in the moonlight, something remarkable happened to Margarita Mikhailevna. It was as though all the light from the cold stars, all the light from the moon, was passing through her, making her first luminous, then diaphanous, and finally, right before our eyes, invisible, as though light itself had carried her away.*

This remarkable passage was followed by notes about something he had called a *time portal*; by some Blavatskian nonsense about a goddess and a Muse; by some final questions—about the nature of dreams. *It was like a dream in which things are happening that seem to have been happening for a long time, though you have only just become conscious of them and having a role in them…* Which, he thought, was very much like being born into the world, slowly becoming conscious of yourself in it, and of growing used to it, of forgetting its inherent strangeness. But he had not forgotten the strangeness.

And about this episode, this madness he had suffered... now, at this moment, quite sure of his sanity, he was able to look upon it with the detached curiosity of a scientist, and inquire about it, asking some of the same questions he had asked originally, just after he finished writing up his notes, but had not pursued, i.e.: If this was not a bout of madness, then what was it? Possibilities: mesmeric suggestion; use of morphia or other drugs; illness, accompanied by high fever, leading to hallucination. The latter suggestion had to be rejected for lack of any evidence that he had been ill. As for being either drugged or mesmerized... the next logical questions were: for what reason and by whom? At the time, these were questions he had not attempted to answer.

Now Fyodorov, pen in hand, could ask different questions. For clarity, he wrote them down: Were these options—mesmerism or drugs—the only rational explanations? Was it at all possible that he had in fact been transported to the places he remembered and had met the people he recalled having met? Let us, then, he said to himself, develop some hypotheses.

Hypothesis One: He really had journeyed with Elena Blavatskaya in search of Nikolai Barakov, and all his experiences had been real.

(Proof for this would lie in a rather simple experiment, i.e. if any of the people he recalled having met on his journey in turn recalled having met him. Had not Elena Petrovna herself provided such proof? She had appeared at the Stardust to hold a seance, and she did remember him, and treated him as an old friend. Moreover, he knew things about her psychic abilities, and when he spoke about her, to Marko Volchek, for example, his knowledge of such things as astral projection and telekinesis amazed even himself. He always meant to ask her about the journey they had taken together, but something held him back. What? Blavatskaya was a sorceress, a magician, a student of Voodoo, a priestess of uncanny gods. If she had manipulated his mind once and made him think he had taken such a journey, she might well do it again. Her reply to a direct question on this subject would be unreliable at best.)

Hypothesis Two: The extraordinary occurrences he had witnessed during this journey—inexplicably rapid changes of location and time, spiritual apparitions, even human beings changing form and becoming invisible—provided evidence for the existence of another reality beyond ordinary human observation and experience, whose laws differed from those scientific laws of nature based on predictability, causality, and rationality.

(It was a preposterous idea; yet, deep in his heart, he accepted it. The universe was mysterious, unknowable. Who were we to decide its limits, its laws? The universe is God, and everything God does is in accord with Reason because Reason is merely the name we give to what God does.)

Hypothesis Three: One such phenomenon was the mysterious woman, Margarita Mikhailevna, who (in the alternative reality of the journey) was both a woman—the daughter of Tatyana Volkonskaya, the wife of Nikolai Barakov, and the prisoner of Pavel Beriosov—and also, according to Blavatskaya, a sort of goddess, a Muse. If there were now yet another Margarita Mikhailevna, who was alive in the present, in this reality, and who was also the daughter of Tatyana Volkonskaya and engaged to marry Alexander Azara, there would then be three Margaritas, living simultaneously in three different worlds. Or one Margarita, able to move from world to world, by some means unknown.

That there was a Margarita Mikhailevna alive in this time, in this world, presented him with a God-sent opportunity to test his hypotheses, for if she resembled the woman he had met on his journey, if she remembered having met him somewhere before, if she had had similar experiences—why that would surely provide the proof he needed, it might well prove all his hypotheses at once, perhaps even Nikolai's favorite, the existence of parallel worlds.

Now something else occurred to him, as he sat calmly at his desk in the safety of his laboratory and the comfort of his chair, reading through his notes. There was yet another hypothesis.

Hypothesis Four: Time is not measurement, the ticking away of minutes and hours, nor is it fixed and immutable. The unchangeability of the past and the obscurity of the future are mental concepts, whereas time itself is mysterious and might better be understood as a fabric or a fluid. And that fluidity can be entered and exited at various points by means of gates or portals, which can be either discovered or created. The ray of light into which it appeared that Margarita Mikhailevna had vanished was not a ray of light at all, but just such a portal.

Suddenly—he could not believe his own stupidity!—he jumped to his feet and paced quickly up and down. How in God's name had he forgotten? He grabbed up his old notebook, his eyes fell again on the last sentences he had written, he read them over with a sense of mounting excitement. *Before that, where had I been? Had I not been in my laboratory? Had I not been reading a book? Then something had happened and it had thrown the universe out of whack.*

What book, you fool?

He stared all around as though the mysterious book would be lying about somewhere, shining at him. Was it *Monkey* he had been reading? He had been reading a manuscript, he had stumbled over a map of some sort, a design made of glyphs, it reminded him of something he had once seen displayed in a library in Vienna, the *Codex Mexicanus*. Had he actually seen it on the page or only remembered it? And then... he had begun thinking about extension and being, the infinite extension of space, necessary since God is an unlimited Being... the infinite extension of time... another continuum... And then... and then something had happened, and he had found himself sitting on a bench at the Patriarch's Ponds in an autumn evening next to a woman he had never met before, Elena Blavatskaya.

Finally the truth came rushing at him in a massive wave, understanding mixed with an equal force of incredulity—it could not be, yet it was. He himself had gone through a time portal!

He paced up and down the room, breathing hard, as though he had been running, feeling his heart beating rapidly in his chest...

He had brought a book with him on that journey, a manuscript, but it was not *Monkey,* it was the play, *Wide and Crooked*. Or was it? He had left something in a coach. Oh, what if it had been the book! No, no, the book was here, in his laboratory, it had to be. The secret to the time portal was in that book!

And he would find it. He would rip down the walls if need be, but it would be found.

BOOK FIVE

an Episode in Odessa

CHAPTER TWENTY

High Meadows

I put my pen down and gazed out the window. Snow was falling over the garden, spangling the boughs of the great elms with crystals, burying the newly forged pathways, silencing every sound. The quiet was like a blanket one had pulled over one's head, thick and protective. Yes, the snow lay thick on the land. We had reached a safe haven just in time, and now we were marooned on it, this tiny island of warmth and safety in a sea of fear and danger, ice and storm.

Chance had brought us here, though once we arrived it seemed almost inevitable that we should have come. After all, it was a logical way station. We were not planning on staying; we were still en route to our destination, though what that destination was we did not know, and so arriving at it would itself be a matter of chance, or fortune, or luck.

We had been lucky this once, at least. The storm had come down on us without warning, with blizzard winds, blinding snow, and cold so piercing not even the horses could bear it, and we were far weaker than they. Yet, by luck, it fell upon us as we were passing through the town closest to High Meadows, a place I happened to know, having visited it many times with Anastasia. In retrospect, it was really madness to have attempted those final miles from the district town, driving the sleigh across the fields to the estate, leaving what passed as a road and traveling as the crow flies toward the house with no landmarks to guide us since nothing was visible in the onslaught of snow, the air itself being thick and textured like a grey curtain flung in front of us, shrouding our way. We arrived in a dark twilight, in the midst of a tempest, half frozen, desperately tired, without even the strength to speak. We were barely human, Pavel Damianich and I; even our heroic driver, burly and bear-like as he was, could have gone no farther.

So, like mariners, lost at sea, carelessly cast back onto the same shore from which they had sailed, we found ourselves in a familiar house whose occupants were the very same Three Graces at whose urging we had originally set forth on our quest. And how they welcomed us! How amazed and delighted they were to see us! And how equally amazed we were to find them all there, gathered together in Tatyana Andreyevna's house, when by custom, I knew, Mariya Sergeyevna and Yevgenia Dmitrievna spent winters in their own houses in Moscow. Why were they here?

"Fate, my dear," Yevgenia Dmitrievna said. "We intended to go, we made plans to go, and then somehow the winter caught us dozing by the fire and it was suddenly too late to budge."

"And if you believe that..." Mariya Sergeyevna laughed.

"So the truth is?"

"The truth is... complicated," Tatyana Andreyevna said.

But truth-telling had to wait until we were bathed, and rested, and well fed; until the storm stopped and everyone, man and beast, was accounted for; until other guests who had been caught unaware by the storm and taken refuge at the house were sent on their way; until, in short, life returned to normal. I had time in that interval to take stock myself, and so I had decided to write a letter to Anastasia. It was a painful letter to write and took many long hours to compose. I was not happy with it, but I was not happy with much in my life, and my inability to do this one thing for her—difficult though it was turning out to be—made me feel so useless and incompetent and feeble that, for all the good I was capable of doing in the world, I might as well have stayed in that tower.

I was still sitting at the window, staring mindlessly out at the snow, my letter unfinished, when there was a knock on the door, and Tatyana's adopted daughter, Margarita Mikhailevna, came in.

"Am I disturbing you?"

"Not at all," I said. "What can I do for you?"

She smiled at me. "Offer me a chair?"

"Of course. Sit. It's your house, after all."

"It's your room."

"Then, please, be my guest."

She sat down with a rustle of skirts. If I was going to have to talk with this child, I wanted a cigarette and a brandy. This was how coarse I had become. Blame it on prison or on the Stardust or on Pavel Damianich's nefarious influence, but I could no longer bear polite intercourse, those empty courtesies we trade with one another, those empty sentences, no, I could not bear them.

"Marko," she said abruptly, startling me somewhat, "I must talk to you."

I waited, but she said nothing more. What drama the children indulge in! Did I need to encourage this confession, whatever it was?

"Go on," I said.

"Oh, Marko!" she cried, and burst into tears.

I was not much of a comfort to her, but I did manage to give her a handkerchief and a glass of water, and then a glass of something stronger.

"Can I trust you?" she managed to say at last in a whisper.

This is a terrible question for one Russian to ask another.

"To some extent," I said. "I can keep secrets. But, of course, it depends on—"

"I have to tell someone," she said. "And there's no one else."

I was the confessor of last resort.

"Very well," I said, and offered her my cigarette case. To my surprise she accepted one.

"I have been having such dreams," she said, inhaling the smoke. "I wake up and I don't know where I am. Is that common? Does that happen to you?"

This was not the way I expected our conversation to begin.

"Sometimes," I said.

"And the feeling lasts for a long time. I feel like I am... being pulled back. I wake up, but something keeps pulling me back."

"Back into the dream?"

"Yes."

"And is it always the same dream?"

"Yes. No. Not exactly. How to explain it? It is like each dream is a continuation of the last one. As though the story continues from where it left off, the way your life continues when you wake up from sleep. You're in the same bed, the same room, the same house. All that's different is that it's the next day. Though—is it the next day? It might be the same day all over again."

I ignored this last remark, the contemplation of which would surely lead us into the realm of philosophical speculation of the sort only a mind like Fyodor Fyodorovich's might welcome, and instead, merely to clarify, I asked, "So it seems to you that your dreams are always set in the same place?"

"Yes, and with the same people. It's like having another life."

"Does it frighten you?"

"Not when I'm dreaming, no. I am perfectly at home there and content. But... where is it? Where do I go? And why is it so real? That's what frightens me. Yes, that is what frightens me. That it's so real."

I considered carefully what she was telling me, or perhaps the question behind what she was saying. It was a deep question, if I had it right.

"Let me understand this. You are afraid that the dream may be your real life and that this life may be the dream?"

"Yes! That's it exactly! I knew you would understand. That is my fear... But I must be going mad, to think like that! I must be crazy. Oh, Marko, help me, please. I don't know what to do!"

I looked at her in her lovely blue gown, sitting just across from me, as real as anything else in the world... though I admit there were moments when it seemed she... flickered... but surely that was a trick of the light reflecting off the bright snow. The flickering, slight though it was, barely noticeable, reminded me of something... and I stretched my mind back, I sought in my memory... that flickering... what was it? Then I remembered: the hallway, the terrible, rolling hallway, the light flickering, the door at the end... Fyodorov...

"Marko?" The sound of her voice pulled me back, or woke me up. How rude to doze off like that. I apologized.

"Tell me, Margarita, in these dreams... do you recognize the people? Are they familiar? Are they people you know?"

"Yes. Some are. And some are new."

"And the ones who are familiar—who are they?"

She hesitated, and I wondered at her reluctance. She had become less emotional as we talked, and now she seemed entirely in control of herself. Perhaps she had conquered her fear without any help from me.

"It's complicated," she said, sounding exactly like her mother.

"How so?"

Again I could sense her trying to avoid the question, and I almost relented and brushed it aside, but something was bothering me now, something was wrong... The room itself seemed unsettled, the colors were far too bright and seemed to be pulsing. Suddenly my head was swimming… I heard her voice, coming from a distance…

My faint, such as it was, was only momentary, thank God. She quickly provided me with a glass of water and called for a plate of *zakuski,* for we both explained my moment of dizziness as the result of hunger and thirst.

Then, slowly, it all came out. She was dreaming about Nikolai Barakov. But why was she dreaming about him? Why, in these dreams, was she living with him in a small house, a mere cottage, somewhere in Moscow? Why, in these dreams, was the city of Moscow so different from the actual city, and yet why did it feel so real in the dream, with everything where it should be though somewhat transformed? And why, in these dreams, were some people so familiar to her, though when she woke she realized that she did not know them at all?

"Other than in your dreams," I asked her, "do you know where Nikolai is?"

"If I did, I would have told someone by now," she said in an injured voice. "Everyone is looking for him. Why wouldn't I tell them?"

"Perhaps he needs to remain hidden, and you're helping him."

"I'm not. I don't know where he is. And, to tell you the truth… "

Ah, the truth! Once the truth is announced it's certain what follows will be a tapestry of lies.

"… I don't care. What was between us ended long ago. It's absurd! Why should I be dreaming about him now?"

"What was between you?" I asked, brutishly. But I was tired of polite obfuscation, tired of tip-toeing around the truth. This was the story I wanted to hear.

Margarita—not the daughter of a revolutionary for nothing—poured us each a hefty glass of brandy.

"Yes, we were in love once," she began. "We adored each other. But we were very young. And Nikolai already had some very bad friends and he would go off with them. And I couldn't stand it, you see. I didn't know what he was doing with these friends but the fact that he would never tell me made me afraid he would end up like my father—arrested, imprisoned, sent east. I told him how I felt but he only laughed at me and told me not to worry, that nothing could hurt him, that he was invincible. So I stopped writing to him and refused to see him, and that was the end of it, I thought.

"Then one summer my mother brought us all to Oak Hills for a visit and Kolya was there. I was shocked to see him, really shocked. He had put on weight, he got drunk at dinner, he was argumentative and coarse... he wasn't my Kolya at all. But one afternoon, we took a walk and we talked, just the two of us, and, of course, he was the same, the same sensitive, funny, smart Kolya. It was like he was hiding himself, his true soul, the one I knew and loved, under a carapace of crudeness and vulgarity, an oafish caricature of himself. But why was he doing it? Maybe because he was living with *rasnochintsy*, and the worst elements of that class, many of them criminals. And he was writing about them, and about how they lived. Not to criticize them, or patronize them, but because he enjoyed them. I know, it's hard to understand. Or I found it hard.

"He let me read his play. *Wide and Crooked*, he called it. He was embarrassed to show me, he said, because he had put me into the play. Not me, as I am, of course, but he had created this woman who loved him and he thought of her as me. When he told me this—Marko, I just wept, I sobbed on his shoulder like a fool, but it broke my heart. In the play they escape together from all the dreadful things and all the horrible people... in a flying machine. It makes you smile, I know, but it is also so very sad, because it's so impossible. That they should escape, and be happy together, and not die at the end. Like my father did. Like my mother did." She paused and emptied her glass. "He always used to say that he was unstoppable. Nothing could hurt him. Who thinks that way, Marko? Only children."

"Was that the last time you saw him?" I asked, since I had to know.

"No. I went to his house once. In St Petersburg."

"Really? That was brave."

Foolish, I might have said. But women in love do very foolish things.

"We didn't stay in the house. He took me out of the city to an inn. It was very nice, the inn, and he seemed to know everyone there. We had a lot to talk about."

"I'm sure you did. Did he happen to tell you about his novel?"

She gave me a curious look. "You know about it, too? How do you know?"

"Many people are talking about it. But I have never seen it."

"I've seen it," she said. "I read part of it. That monstrous book! I hate it."

This was news indeed, and thrilling news at that. She had read the book! I wanted to savor the moment, but I couldn't. I had so many questions to ask.

"You hate it? Why?"

"It will destroy him, don't you see? I didn't have to read much of it to see that. I begged him to burn it."

"What is the book about? Why is it so dangerous?"

"Why? Oh, Marko, if only I could describe what it was like to read it!"

She shifted her gaze from my face to the window where the falling snow was still obscuring the view so that there appeared to be nothing beyond the room but a white void.

"How can I explain it to you? I only read a few chapters of it, mind you, that night in the inn. I couldn't read more, it was breaking my heart to read it."

"Tell me a little bit about it, Margarita. Please."

"I'll try. First I should tell you that the main character is called Nick, and he loves a girl who is only known by the initial M."

"M," I said. "Like Monika, the name of the girl in his play."

"Yes. I suppose," she said, almost dismissing this coincidence. It surprised me that Margarita did not make the obvious connection between the girl whose initial was M and herself, but sometimes the most obvious things escape our notice."But the world they live in is so different from ours. That's what's so frightening about the book, how different the world is."

"When you say a different world, do you mean the place where they live is in another country?" I was still hoping the book would somehow tell me where Nikolai was. I was still hoping for some small miracle.

This question seemed to puzzle her.

"No. It isn't that it's another country. It's Russia, but at the same time it's a totally different place. And a terrible one. Oh, Marko, what a terrible world he depicted. Can it really be the world we're living in?"

"Tell me about it."

"For one thing, all the people are violent and desperate, or cruel and angry, or so poor they have nothing, not even a roof over their heads. There is a mad woman who sits in the dirt outside her little hut all day, holding a book and yelling insults at everyone who passes by. There is a drunken man who falls down and suddenly a crowd rushes on him, empties his pockets, steals everything from him, even kicks him as he is lying there, helpless. Soldiers shoot unarmed peasants. A man beats his poor old horse to death in the street."

She paused for a moment and in that pause I was tempted to ask her questions, but, since at last I was learning something about Nikolai's book, I kept silent and waited for her to continue.

"In the chapter I read, the character named Nick drinks a tea made of special mushrooms and after he drinks it he begins having visions of a totally different world. In this world, everyone is happy and kind and free, everyone is treated as a friend. There is no suffering or poverty or repression, there are no serfs or black slaves, no, not even servants. All work is considered honorable, and everyone works. And everyone is loved. Even animals, Marko—even animals are loved and treated with care. He describes this place in such detail, how people feel there, and act there. The contrast between the two worlds—between the world the characters live in, which is the worst of our real world, though I suppose it is the world so many poor people live in, all our poor serfs and our destitute and desperate people, poor miserable souls... the difference between that world and the rich, full, joyous world he describes, well, it just tears at your heart. And yet, you know, he isn't happy when he is in the beautiful world because he keeps remembering the world he came from. He's like a traveler, just passing through, so everything is bittersweet for him. He longs to stay, you see, but he knows he can't. Then the vision ends, and he's back in the grim, sordid house where he lives. He wants to share what he's seen and learned with M, he tries to tell her, and he makes love to her... and he describes that too in such detail... I had to stop reading it. Oh, I begged him to burn it before it was too late."

"Burn it? Why?"

"It is more than a novel, Marko. It's a condemnation and a revelation. It's a call for revolution. Don't you see? My father was punished for discussing books that called for revolution, but Nikolai has actually written such a book. How much more will they punish him?"

"But he did not burn it. Did he?"

She sighed and got up and walked back and forth across the room, her hands clutched together in front of her... and how she resembled

MIKHAIL BULGAKOV

"Bulgakov? No, I have never heard of such a person."

in these movements Nikolai's other lover, Katerina Ivanovna! It was so remarkable I very nearly forgot the question I had asked. But Margarita had not.

"Yes, he did. Or he tried to. He built up the fire in the stove, he added wood until it blazed quite furiously, and he took his notebooks and began ripping out the pages and feeding them to the flames. 'Bulgakov will do the same one day,' he said. Who is that, do you know?"

"Bulgakov? No. I have never heard of such a person."

"Another writer, he told me. That's all he would say. Oh, he did it for me, you know, Marko. Not for himself. He was not afraid for himself, not at all. But the pages burnt so slowly! Then the room began filling up with smoke, and it wasn't long before the landlord came banging on the door, the smell of smoke was permeating the hall. So we snatched the half- burnt pages out of the fire, and I gathered them together for him because I could see it pained him to destroy them, though he said it didn't, he said it didn't matter to him at all. But that was always the problem with Kolya, always, that he refused to admit that anything mattered to him.

"He told me he would drown the monkey... that was the title of the book, *Monkey*. He said he had this monkey on his back, he would drown it in the river, he would wrap it in chains and weigh it down and send it into the sea... Did he do it? I don't know. He may have just left it on a bench in the rain. He may have thrown himself in the river for all I know... I don't know what happened because I never heard from him again.

"And how could he have done that to me? How? He loved me so much once. He always used to say it takes two... two to make things come out right. And we were the two. It was always that way. Then suddenly—nothing. As though I didn't matter to him either. As though nothing had happened between us. All I have left is silence, Marko. That's all. Just silence." She pulled a small lace handkerchief out of her sleeve and wiped her eyes. "So, you see, I hate him now, and I don't understand why I am having these dreams. Am I going mad? That's what I think sometimes. I think I am going mad."

"If it's any consolation to you," I said as gently as I could, "not even his mother has heard from him, not for over a year."

"How is that a consolation?" she cried, and tears began streaming down her cheeks. "It can only mean that he's dead!"

"Things have never been so bleak," Tatyana Andreyevna announced later that afternoon while we were all sitting in her drawing room drinking tea, all of us being the three Aunts and myself. "The world has never been in such a terrible state. Our country, our dear country, has never been at the edge of such ruin. And it can only get worse. Do you know how I know this? The level of sheer stupidity has risen, common courtesy has given way to the most abhorrent rudeness, no one treats anyone else with any respect, and worst of all, it is impossible to find anyone who has any hope that things will improve. No, on the other hand, every single person I know expects things to deteriorate—everything, roads, schools, farms, the arts, trust in institutions, in rational thought, trust in science, even the most basic social courtesies. What will rise will be the number of people living in poverty, and the level of violence and ignorance, and the number of arrests, of course, and the rate of incarceration and penal servitude. No, it's never been worse, not in my lifetime, and I have lived a very long time."

The Aunts often talked this way when they were together. They often lamented the state of the world. It was not surprising to hear it again.

"To what do you attribute this disintegration of our culture and social life—and our roads and farms and homes?" Mariya Sergeyevna asked. "Whom do you blame for it?"

"What a terribly indiscreet question, my dear!" Yevgenia Dmitrievna murmured.

"Well—has our courage also failed us in these awful times? Are we to be silenced in our own homes? Please do tell me who or what is to blame, or else let's stop talking about how bad everything is, since we can do nothing to change it, not even talk sensibly about it."

"The reverse of Progress," Tatyana said, "and I say this with the authority vested in me as an old woman of the so-called ruling class. The philosophers promised us Progress. They are fools. What we have instead is the unwinding of progress. Anti-progress. Civilization is a frail construction and is easily demolished. All it takes is a few demagogues and a few bombs. Oh, yes, and a cowardly leadership and a frightened paranoiac at the top of it."

"So we are to blame historical regression?" Mariya Sergeyevna said. "We are helpless? We are pawns of some spirit of Anti-progress? I don't believe it. You present evidence for something, true, because I do agree with the diagnosis. But the cause? About that, I disagree with you entirely. People make civilization, and people destroy it. You mentioned some of the culprits, so blame them and not History. Demagogues, bombers, aristocrats and our aristocrat-in-chief, our Imperial Autocrat. Why not say it? It's the truth."

"If we are casting blame," Yevgenia Dmitrievna said mildly, "why not start with ourselves? We complain but we do nothing."

"Don't be absurd! You do so much, Zhenya," Mariya said. "You do more than I do, certainly."

"Giving money to keep a little journal open—"

"Yes, it is vital! It keeps the journal open, the journal keeps our minds open—"

I lit a little cigar—Pasha had given them to me, where he came by them I have no idea—and stretched out and listened to their lovely voices arguing about which of them was the nobler soul. This, too, was something the Aunts did when they got together, and it was quite enjoyable to hear. And they deserved to be praised. I agreed with everything they said about each other.

When there was a pause in the laudations, I asked them if it was now possible for them to tell me how it happened that they were all here, in Tatyana's house, in the middle of December. How complicated could the answer be? Were they getting ready for Christmas?

"By knitting stockings and baking fruitcakes! What an excellent idea!" Yevgenia said, laughing. "And practicing our Christmas carols. We used to go caroling when I was a girl, in Vienna."

"We did, too, in Baden," Mariya said."The only good things about exile—caroling and fruitcakes."

"But in answer to your question," Tatyana said, "we are here together for another reason, and I imagine you can guess what it is. The remarkable thing is not that we are here but that you are."

"I think I can guess," I said. "You three can only be here at this time of year for one reason, and it has to do with Anastasia and her son."

They smiled at me, indulgently, as though I were a child who had just discovered that if a sound comes out when you put your lips together and blow, you've just learned how to whistle.

"Have you heard anything?" I asked. "Please tell me you have!"

"We have gathered here," Tatyana said, "so we can receive information together. We are expecting to hear some news very soon. If you feel strong enough to tell us."

Three old faces were turned toward me, expectantly, ironically, and, I feared, sadly. They knew very well I had nothing to say.

"It's a long and sorry tale, a dismal story of failure," I said. "I learned a lot, none of it of any use whatsoever."

"Tell us anyway," Tatyana ordered.

And so I did.

It was late afternoon by the time I finished. Much earlier we had moved from pots of tea to bottles of wine, and I could not tell if the report of my months of travail had entertained the Aunts or, with the help of a very fine Chateau Margaux, put them to sleep.

Mariya was the first to speak or, rather, growl "That Pavel Beriosov is a pig!"

"And a renegade pig at that. Well, we can stop him in his tracks, I think. Prince Kirill will see to that. Beriosov will pay for what he did to you, don't worry."

"Prince Kirill Pavlovich?" I said, marveling at Tatyana's words. "Do you know him?"

"Know him? My dear, once upon a time I almost married him. Marina Vilinskaya, Anastasia's editor—you know her, I'm sure—is also a friend of the Prince, and when you went missing she asked his assistance in finding you, and then informed Pavel Damianich—"

"He said he received an anonymous message."

"Well, it would have to be, wouldn't it? Good thing for you he paid heed to it."

"But none of this gets us any closer to finding Nikolai. Nothing I've done has helped in the least."

"We know where he isn't," Yevgenia sighed. "But the world is large."

This was a truth we pondered over another glass of Margaux.

"How is Anastasia?" I asked. It was a question I had put off asking since I arrived.

"The same," Mariya said. "Waiting."

"She is still in seclusion, as before?"

"She is still not seeing anyone, if that's what you mean."

"And the rest of the family? How is Vasily Yakovlevich?"

"Ah, dear Vasya!" Tatyana said with a smile. "You will find this hard to believe, but Vasily Yakovlevich has surprised all of us by rediscovering the brave young hero in himself, after all these years. He's gone off in search of his son. He's taken a different path, well, not so very different from yours, Marko. He's gone off in disguise, he and Aleksey Konstantinovich, if you can believe it."

"Uncle Alyosha? What do you mean, off in disguise?"

"They are making inquiries among the gypsies. And that is all I will say, because that is all that I know."

I laughed. I could not help myself, and the Aunts laughed with me, but I think their laughter came from a different and deeper source than mine, for when I thought of Vasily Yakovlevich and Aleksey Konstantinovich among the gypsies I saw figures of comedy, whereas they saw men they admired and loved.

"Well," I said, "what more can we do?"

"More to the point, what have we already done?" Tatyana said. "We have inquired through the Ministries. You, Marko, have inquired among the bohemians. Marina Vilinskaya has inquired among the literati and the intelligentsia. Vasily and Uncle Alyosha are inquiring among the gypsies, God help them, and there is another I've sent out who has yet to report back to us. Actually, he is Margarita's fiancé."

"Margarita is engaged?" I could hardly believe my ears. "To whom?" I had to bite my tongue to prevent myself from adding, *That's impossible! She's in love with Nikolai!*

"I doubt you know him," Tatyana Andreyevna said. "He is not Russian. He lives abroad."

Before I could add another word, a servant entered and announced it was time for supper.

♣

"So Nikolai Vasilevich has taken after his mother and written a book," Mariya said once we were settled at the supper table. "This is something I did not know. It will please her, I'm sure."

"Not if it causes him trouble," Yevgenia said. "Which it seems that it will. Or already has."

Unless he has destroyed it, I thought, remembering Margarita Mikhailevna's tale of the burning, but I said nothing. The book was of little importance to us. It was Nikolai himself we were in search of, not his strange and mysterious book.

"It once seemed like such a simple task, didn't it, finding Kolya?" Mariya sighed, seemingly reading my mind. "Poor Anastasia! I sometimes get so infuriated with him. Really, how can he do this to her?"

None of us said what we undoubtedly thought, or, at least, what I thought, which was that he might not have any choice.

Apparently Margarita wasn't having supper with us, and I was glad of it since otherwise, knowing what I did, I would not have been eager to have this conversation about Nikolai. It was clear that she still loved him, no matter what she said or to whom she was engaged, and watching her break into tears at the supper table would have ruined my appetite.

"I never thought it would be simple," Tatyana said, loading her plate with caviar, "but I didn't think it was to prove so difficult. I just heard from London. He is not with Herzen."

"He is not in Peter-Paul, thank God," Mariya said. "I have made inquiries."

"And you've established, Marko dear, and quite courageously too, I might add, that he isn't living in Petersburg any longer," Yevgenia said.

"We are still at a loss, however," Tatyana said. "I have no idea where to look next."

"Well," I said, "there's no lack of space in the world, is there? Maybe he's living in the forest with brigands or in the Caucasus with a band of Chechens or along the Volga with the Raskolniki or maybe he's on his way to America or Tibet or on a voyage to the South Seas... My God," I said, bringing my fork down onto the table with more force than I had intended, "don't you see? He could be anywhere on earth."

It was the moment when in a novel the door to the dining room would suddenly burst open, a man would step into the room, a man who had clearly just arrived from a long journey, perhaps still wearing a fur coat covered with snow, and in a strong but quiet voice, would say, "I could be anywhere, but I am here!"

I actually looked at the door to see if it would open.

Not surprisingly, it did not.

Later that night I had yet another light supper, this time with Pavel Damianich. He had spent much of the day talking about the weather with various servants, old men, and stableboys. The consensus was that the bad weather would not hold for long, there would be a window through which, if we were ready, we might escape.

"Defenestration," Pasha laughed. "We just need someone to give us a push."

We were drinking vodka with our supper and between the fire in the stove and the fire in the glass, we were feeling quite warm and disinclined to be defenestrated. At least I was.

"I want to go south," I said. "I want palm trees and bright umbrellas over little café tables and women in big hats and silk dresses."

"I want the same," Pasha said. "And a few gambling tables."

So we imagined ourselves in paradise, which reminded me of Margarita's dream.

"What do you know," I asked the man who knew everything, "about a drug that comes from mushrooms?"

"Well, there's the chaga mushroom, of course. The black ones you find on dead birch trees."

"Yes. But I don't mean medicinal drugs. Does anything like opium come from mushrooms? Are there mushrooms that give people visions?"

"There are such mushrooms, yes. I have read about them. They grow in the tropical forests of Spanish America. In Mexico and farther south. The Aztecs used them in religious rituals."

"Was it in Humboldt that you read about them?"

"Or some other traveler in those jungles. I don't recall."

He had a good deal of information on these mushrooms for someone who had merely read about them in a book whose author's name he could not recall. That they were banned by the Spanish. That the Aztecs called them God's flesh. That they gave revelatory visions.

After he talked for a very long time, he finally asked me why I wanted to know.

But by then I couldn't remember.

❧

We stayed at High Meadows until we were both quite rested and until the weather entered a short period of calm. Then we decided to go south. Once we announced our decision, Tatyana Andreyevna kindly offered us her house in Odessa. I needed a bit of peace and quiet to do some writing for it was by writing that I made my living, and I was rapidly running out of cash. Odessa might also prove an excellent spot for us to make some headway in our inquiries. Not only was it a year-round resort for the aristocracy, but an active port filled with many different people from all over Europe. Pavel Damianich, charming polyglot that he was, might be able to uncover some useful information about Nikolai Barakov while attending the opera or ballet, or promenading along the waterfront or under the trees of Primorsky Boulevard, or drinking with sailors or chatting up some French maids while sunning himself on the city's sandy beaches. Elena Blavatskaya had spent her childhood in Odessa. Perhaps she would show up there again and hold another seance. Anything was possible.

So early one morning, with the sun shining brightly, a few winter-loving chickadees chirping in the trees, and our sledge over-stuffed with gifts of warm clothes and rich food, we said goodbye to the Aunts and Margarita, and set off south, to the sea.

CHAPTER TWENTY-ONE

Sosa

Odessa is pleasant in winter, but it is paradise in spring which comes early and lusciously to the south, fragrant, warm, delicious, and decorated with sweet flowers like an exquisite French pastry. Petersburg might still be frozen solid under drifts of snow, but we sat outside at the cafés under umbrellas meant to shield us not from sleet but from sunlight. Oh, the sunlight on the sea! Sparkling, ever-changing, mercurial. The ancient Greeks did not call the sea either green or blue or grey, but rather described it in terms of light, how light struck it, its absence darkening it like wine, its presence making it sparkle and glimmer. Pavel Damianich informed me of this fact, having learned it from a classical scholar or a Greek sailor, and it seemed not only reasonable but right, the result of clear sight, for I spent many hours watching light play on the sea from the height of Primorsky Boulevard, that long, tree-shaded avenue that ran along the cliff-top overlooking the port. Twice a day, or more, I would stroll along that esplanade under those great plane trees, neo-classical mansions and palaces on one side, the wide and mysterious Black Sea on the other, and I, too, could not name the color of the sea, though at times that wonderful phrase of Homer's, *epi oinopi ponto*, would come to me and I would think, yes, the great poet had the keenest of sight, blind though he might have been: the sea is not black at all, but wine-dark.

Tatyana Andreyevna's house was not right on Primorsky Boulevard, but it was not far from it either, and close to the house in which Pushkin had spent a spring writing the first sections of *Yevgeny Onegin*. Incredibly, Odessa had once been a city where dissident poets were sent into internal exile, a place of punishment. Pushkin had certainly suffered in Odessa, being so bored he had taken the governor's wife as a mistress. After the governor quite reasonably expelled him from the city, other rebellious poets, Polish ones, were sent to take his place as resident writers-in-exile. I do not know what poems they wrote in Odessa, or whom they loved, though the city is such that love and poetry cannot fail to burst into flower here, even in the most rebellious hearts. I myself wrote a good deal in Tatyana Andreyevna's house, and the editor of the thick journal to whom I submitted the stories, my beloved Marina Fyodorovna herself, was pleased to receive them, though not as pleased as I was to receive Kataev's payment. Now I could pay my debts and still have enough remaining to continue on with my search. But I had become lethargic and complacent here, or perhaps I had simply allowed Odessa to work its spell on me, this beautiful city that felt not at all like a Russian city but far more like an Italian one, a city filled with people from many lands, speaking many languages, a city that felt free... Yes, that was it, of course. It was as though Odessa was its own city-state in which different rules applied, or a city that belonged to another country, in which people could speak their minds without fear. It was the absence of fear, that was the city's greatest gift to her citizens. How long could it last?

So I wondered as I walked under the plane trees and found myself at last by the statue of Richelieu at the top of the steep *Escalier Monstre*, the Great Stairs, gazing down into the crowded port. Every time I came here, I thought of Nikolai, I thought of maps, I thought of ships and voyages by sea, and I knew in my heart that he had stood here once, thinking those same thoughts. He had spent time in Odessa, according to Tatyana Andreyevna. In fact, he had lived in Odessa for several years. She told me this just after I had announced my intention of going south for the winter. I was shocked that neither she nor Anastasia had bothered to mention this vital fact to me before.

"When was this, exactly? Odessa seems like the sort of place he might return to. Has anyone looked there? Do you happen to know where he lived? Perhaps he still has friends in the city who may know where he is."

Tatyana had no idea where he had lived, but Margarita Mikhailevna did: he had rooms above a tavern called Sosa.

"He was really attached to that place," Margarita Mikhailevna told me. "In fact, I think he worked there."

So, of course, one of the first things Pavel Damianich and I did when we came to Odessa was to look for a pot-house called Sosa. We had not been able to find it. Like so much else in Nikolai's life, including Nikolai himself, it had just disappeared. Yet I looked for him on every street and in every café and tea house, and every time I stood at the top of the Steps I could almost see him running up them toward me, and sometimes I swore I did, though it never was Nikolai I saw, always some other young man.

Now that I had finished my three stories, each of which had consumed many more weeks than I had planned, and felt finally liberated from financial burdens and obligations, I had time to think about my promise to Anastasia again, about Nikolai and his mysterious novel, and about the ideal world he had described in it where, according to Margarita, everyone was happy and free. Where had he come up with such a crazy idea? Maybe right here in Odessa.

I lingered for some time, watching the ships in the port, so many of them, of such different kinds, both sailing vessels and steamships, and sailing under so many different flags. From here a person could travel anywhere in the world. Fyodorov was right about that. From any seaport it was possible to set sail to the ends of the earth.

With such thoughts in mind, I turned my back to the sea and continued my walk. I was meeting Pasha in a glass-enclosed café on De Ribos Street, not the sort of place I imagined Nikolai ever setting foot in. No, if Sosa still existed, it wouldn't be found in such fashionable districts or near the opera house or the mansions of the rich. It would be down in the port, or on the outskirts of the city where there were vodka shops and wine cellars and where nomadic Tatars had settled and now worked the land and prayed in their stone mosques. There were many places we had not yet searched. I had to shake myself out of this lethargy, and then shake my friend Pasha Damianich. We had both gone to sleep here, we had both relaxed and forgotten our mission, lulled by a sense of safety and the soft lapping of the sea.

"Sosa," I said to him, even before the waiter had finished pulling out my chair. "Remember?"

"Ah, you want to search again?" He sighed and since the waiter was waiting, he ordered two glasses of champagne.

"We have become soft," I said.

"I agree. Let us harden ourselves. It is always a preferable state, being hard."

I was about to punch him with a hardened fist when a person I did not recognize, wearing an ancient frock coat, even more out of date than mine, approached our table, bowed stiffly, pulled out a third chair, and sat down.

"Hello, Madame, how are you today?" he said. His accent was thick. So was his hair, so were his eyebrows, so was the journal he held in his hand and placed on the table in front of him. "I will drink with you," he added and smiled, showing a set of very white teeth in the midst of a very dark beard. Pasha gestured to the waiter—*three* glasses of champagne. "It is an honor for me," he said.

One hardly knows how to respond to such an introduction, or, rather, such a non-introduction, so I simply nodded my head, and waited for more.

"I have longed to approach, all these weeks, watching at a distance as you passed back and forth on the streets. Finally—abracadabra!—you appear before me! Brilliant and heroic, Madame! Our own George Sand! The George Sand of Russia!"

He stood, abruptly; he bowed, deeply; he sat down again, flashed his white teeth, reached into his breast pocket for a silver case, offered me a small cigar. All this was quite amusing, but I still did not know his name. Of course, Pasha did.

"Marko, permit me to introduce Odysseus Dimitrakos, poet."

"And other things," Odysseus Dimitrakos said, smiling, rising again...

"Do please stay in your chair, Kyrios Dimitrakos," I said. "This bobbing up and down... Oh, and here is our champagne!"

"Ah, the local brand. It is very good."

"Local champagne?" I said. "How do you mean?"

"Taste first," he said, and held up his glass for inspection. "Firm bubbles. Good color. Now, to taste!" He took a sip, and pronounced it *parfait*.

It was quite good, I had to agree.

"Our Tatars, you see. They grow champagne grapes. God knows how they do it."

"Here?"

"Yes, here! Right here! Here in Odessa! Pinot blanc! Excellent!"

"Of the other things you are, Kyrios Dimitrakos, is one of them an oenophile?"

"Ah! It is true. I am a wine-lover. A perfect Greek word, oenophile. You amaze me, Madame."

He continued praising Odessa's vineyards, while I smoked my cigar and wished him gone. I had had quite enough of Odysseus Dimitrakos, and was wondering how we might extricate ourselves from his company without causing offense. Perhaps he would leave us of his own accord, and I sincerely hoped he would. But, oh, how cruelly we misjudge our fellow men! Though it was Pavel Damianich I had misjudged, for I had come to the café today thinking it necessary to rouse his ardor for our mission, hardly suspecting that while I had been frittering away my time writing stories (though they did pay the bills), he had not been frittering away his time at all, but had made an astonishing discovery.

"Dimitrakos is also a ship owner and captain," Pasha said, once the Greek had finally ceased praising our faux-champagne. "What is she called, Odysseus? The *Argos*?"

"*Argos*! No, nor is she *Medea*. She is *Sosa,* sailing from Odessa to Constantinopoli, stopping at various ports of call..."

I almost choked on a mouthful of bubbles.

"*Sosa*? A *boat*?"

"Hardly a boat," Odysseus Dimitrakos said, in a wounded tone. "She is a magnificent and splendidly-appointed steamship, formerly owned and operated by the Black Sea Society of Steamships, now sadly defunct, currently owned and operated by Dimitrakos Brothers, of Odessa and Ermopoli."

As he spoke, I glanced at Pasha who was grinning across the table at me, that devil! How long had he known about this and kept it secret? How long had he planned this surprise?

"Is your ship currently in port?" I asked.

"It is, Madame. Perhaps you would like to come down sometime and see it."

"We would, sometime," Pasha answered, glancing around. "Now... perhaps we might move to a less conspicuous place."

"An excellent thought," said Kyrios Dimitrakos. "I also own a small taverna..."

"Also called Sosa?" I asked.

"No, no. My taverna is the Acropolis."

♣

We took a carriage away from the city center with its courtyards and cafes and soon found ourselves on a narrow, bumpy road, heading down toward the beach. We had not gone far along the beach road when the carriage stopped. There, surrounded by tamarisk and mulberry trees, painted sea blue, draped with vines, and situated not two meters from the sand, was the pot-house which a signboard proclaimed to be the Acropolis Taverna. Outside, seamen, fishermen, and stevedores, by the look of them, were sitting at long wooden tables under a canvas awning, eating, drinking, and talking, each group separate but seemingly ready to converse peaceably with one another, while sitting alone and to one side a man in a plain smock was playing a balalaika, more for his own amusement than to entertain an audience. Inside, with shutters open and a sea breeze blowing in, the rooms were comfortably cool. Dimitrakos brought us mugs of cold beer which was exactly what we wanted, and we sat by a window looking out at the sea, listening to strains of music wafting in along with the sound of many voices speaking in many tongues. There was something glorious about that polyglot sound; to me, it meant freedom.

After we settled ourselves and praised the location and ambiance of the taverna, Pavel Damianich surprised me again.

"Odysseus," he said, "perhaps now would be a good time for you to tell Marko what you know about Nikolai Barakov."

"You have said nothing?"

"You asked me not to, so I did not."

"What!" I cried. "Pavel Damianich! Don't tell me you've been keeping something from me!"

I was teasing him, yes, but that did not mean I was not annoyed.

"Spare him your wrath, dear lady," that obnoxious Greek said. "It was a condition."

"A condition of what?"

"I shared some information with him, but withheld more, to be delivered only in person to you, Madame, whom I longed to meet, whom I adore." And again he stood and bowed. I had to laugh, and so did he, and so did Pasha, that monster.

"Don't think you're forgiven," I said to Pasha. Then turning to our host, I said, "Very well, Odysseus. You have me here in your lair. Now speak!"

The story he told was long, intriguing, punctuated by paeans, interrupted by Greeks bearing gifts—trays of fish, olives, grapes, cheeses, sweet slices of watermelon, that most ubiquitous of fruit, and bite-size pieces of roasted meats, and mugs of beer, and glasses of wine—and it was altogether so entertaining, delivered with such skill, with so many digressions, such an indulgence of language, such delicacy of feeling… mere recall could do it no justice. What a storyteller he was, that Odysseus Dimitrakos! I wondered at myself that I believed a single word. Yet, I did.

♣

"Nikos had been in some kind of trouble up in Petersburg," Dimitrakos began. This was not an unfamiliar beginning when it came to talking about Nikolai. "There were people after him. Bad people. He had made some dangerous enemies."

We asked what sort of enemies. Political? "No, not political. More piratical."

"Piratical? What does that mean?"

What it meant was that, either by accident or intention, he and his crew had stepped on some toes, had robbed the robbers, plundered the plunderers, brigandized the brigands, bandited the bandits. (Dimitrakos, as a true poet, had no qualms about making up words when he needed them, or perhaps, since he used them, they did in fact exist, in some language, if not the one we were speaking.) As a result he was advised to leave Petersburg until things sorted themselves out, and he did. He went south for the winter, as far south as he could get, and landed on the beach.

"Right there!" Dimitrakos said, pointing toward the sand. "Right in front of the taverna. I found him sleeping on the beach. I roused him. I said, 'What are you doing here?' He said, 'Passing the time.' I said, 'This taverna is my place, and I don't allow no vagabonds, gypsies, layabouts, tramps or hobos to camp on my beach.' He said, 'You amaze me. I did not know a man could own a beach.' I would have slugged him, I tell you, but already I liked him. I liked the look of him. Then he starts reciting poetry to me! Who is this gypsy, this wanderer, reciting poetry to me, me, a poet? And how does he know I am Odysseus? Is he a magician? But, no, see, it's the poem he's reciting. *Only yesterday did I escape the wine-dark sea. Till then the waves and rushing gales had swept me on. Now some power has tossed me here, doubtless to suffer still more torments on your shores.* Yes, he knows the *Odyssey*. I must have looked stunned, because he laughs, he says, '*Acropolis Taverna*? And you're not a Greek? Give me some credit, and then give me some work,' he says, 'because like it or not I'm staying right here.' So I gave him a job. Like that. Why not? He could do anything. Cook. Clean. Pour drinks. All men are free here, and free men do all kinds of work, and all work is honorable, so I had him doing every sort of work there is, and we got along, we liked each other. Then, about six months later, I took him aboard the *Sosa*, and the real fun began."

The tale unwound at a snail's pace. *Odysseus, the great teller of tales, launched out on his story.* Yes, and, as I recalled, it took him the next four books of that enormous poem to tell it. Our Odysseus was no less long-winded, and it was late in the afternoon before he finished. But what a story it was!

For in those days, before the war, Odessa was a free port, proud, prosperous, pulsing with life and excitement, overflowing with travelers, traders, and tourists. *Sosa* was a pleasure craft, a passenger vessel for those who could afford to voyage in style, appreciating the best of everything—food, wine, entertainment. "Paying customers," Odysseus laughed. "The rich and titled, and thus *entitled*... to the best service, naturally." She carried travelers to all the Black Sea ports, terminating in Constantinopoli, though often enough she herself would pass through the straits and into the Aegean, carrying special passengers all the way to Greece. But with such passengers, the seas were not safe, for pirates were a constant danger, those criminals who plied the seas in search of plunder, attacking unarmed vessels. They had armaments of their own, of course, and under sail *Sosa* was fast and maneuverable. Still there were times when they failed to evade their pursuers and were boarded, and then they had no choice but to fight. Nikolai had been a successful street-fighter; he soon mastered the art of ship-fighting. It wasn't often they were attacked, but when it happened the crew of *Sosa* was more than ready to defend her and her passengers. "If needs be, if we couldn't outrun 'em, we would just have to lock the passengers up for the duration. Pirates have to be dealt with. Nothing to be done but fight. *I tan i epi tas!* Behind your shield or on it!

"Was Nikos wounded in these battles, you ask? Was he wounded! He almost gave his life. Oh, he bled for *Sosa*, I tell you, many times. Had his head bashed more than once. Knocked unconscious. Great gouges taken out of his scalp. Knife wounds, yes, and he even took a bullet in the shoulder. That laid him up for a bit. He had almost as many battle scars as our first mate who'd seen action at Navarino."

When he wasn't engaged in hand-to-hand combat with pirates, Nikolai worked in the galley, or served the guests, dressed in a sharp white uniform and no doubt looking very handsome. He was popular with the passengers, especially the young ladies.

All along the coasts they sailed, stopping at various ports, dropping off and picking up cargo of one sort or another, tobacco, wine, opium, silks, spices... and passengers. Often, in sundry ports, they would take on passengers whose papers were somewhat dubious, fugitives of one sort or another. Many were trying to get away from the Sultan; almost as many trying to get away from the Tsar; some running away from outraged husbands; others, the outraged husbands themselves, after they had avenged themselves, running away from the law; and the occasional wife, just running away. Blavatskaya had done that, I remembered, had run away from her husband the day after her wedding, had run to Odessa, and caught a ship to Istanbul.

"Nikos stayed—how long? Let me think. Three years? Four? Every year, before we embarked, he would say, No, this time I will stay on shore. He hated heights, you know, and in a ship... well, there's climbing to do, up the masts, and there's hanging off the sides for repair work... Not a great swimmer, Nikos, but then sailors rarely are. No, he didn't much like being at sea. But coming into port! Now that was something. Sailing up the Golden Horn, by God, nothing like it. And we'd plan how to take the City back. Oh, yes, we had invasion plans. She's a Christian city, you know, Constantinopoli. She belongs to us.

"Then we'd sail back to Odessa, we'd finish our business, we'd return here to the Acropolis again, and Nikos would be standing there, right over there, pouring drinks behind the bar."

I glanced over to the bar, trying to imagine him. How old would he have been? Twenty-two? Twenty-three?

"So many good years we had. I will never forget once in Sinope..."

We were his guests and we could not rudely interrupt, bang our fists on the table, make demands, ask the questions we longed to ask. Finally, as the day approached its end, he approached the end of his tale, and the circumstances that led to Nikolai leaving the *Sosa*. It was an unpleasant memory, and he dealt with it quickly.

"I loved that man with my heart. He was a *palikari*, a fighter. But... also I am sad to say a deserter. He jumped ship in Trebizond. Disappeared. Time to sail comes, he's not on board. We send up a flag. Still he doesn't come. I go down to his berth—everything gone. Cleaned out. Not that he had much, but, you know, the few things he had.... So we sail without him, and I curse him. I have to say, I did. To leave like that without a word."

Trebizond was a great port on the south-eastern shore. "The end of the Silk Road, the overland route from India. From there the riches of the east flow to the City and from there to Europe. Oh, it is a great city, Trebizond, a rich city. There are magnificent churches in Trebizond, great churches built by the Comneni Emperors. Their wine is incomparable, their fish market—you would not believe! Anything you want, anything in the world, you can find in Trebizond, once the capital of the Empire, you know, after the fall of the City. And that was where he left us. He had some pressing business there, undoubtedly."

"And you've heard nothing from him since?"

"Nothing. Not a word, until Pavel Damianich came to see me, and told me you were looking for him, that he had been living in Petersburg all these years. It has been a long time now. He was young then, and so I excuse him. But as to where he is now? Missing again, off on some adventure, but what it is I do not know."

"Do you have any idea why he stayed in Trebizond? Had he met a woman, maybe?"

"A woman?" Dimitrakos raised his chin and his eyes in that expressive Hellenic gesture for no. I suppose he felt no woman but Helen of Troy would be able to compete with the charms of Lady *Sosa*.

"Something he was interested in, perhaps? A business deal?"

"A trip to Persia? A trip to India?" Pasha suggested. "A journey he could begin from Trebizond?"

"It is true, many countries have consulates in Trebizond," Dimitrakos said. “There are Greek banks. If he wanted to travel to Persia, that would be the place to start. He could obtain everything he needed.”

“But he didn’t travel to Persia, did he?” I said. All this useless speculation was irritating me. “He went back to Russia. Back to Petersburg. So why not stay on the *Sosa*, which would get him back to Russia quite easily. There had to be something in Trebizond that he wanted.”

“Or,” Pasha said, smiling, “he just got drunk, passed out, and missed the boat. From what I know of him, that seems more than likely.”

Suddenly I wanted to jump up and shake the rafters, break glasses, or smash the furniture. Life was bitter, nothing worked out, everything was useless. We were just as far away from finding Nikolai as we had been before. We were on a wild goose chase, we’d never find him, we were just wasting our time.

“There is one thing I have just remembered,” Dimitrakos said slowly, with an expression on his face that betrayed a state of deep, and perhaps painful recollection. “There was a couple…”

Pasha and I leaned in closer to hear.

“…who disembarked in Trebizond. It is a city, you know, that is built upward from the port to the Byzantine citadel on the heights. There are two great ravines that cleave the hillside and the palace of the emperors rises up above them…”

I glanced over at Pasha, who raised his eyebrows, suggesting he had the same thought as I, which was that our Greek friend had drunk too much beer and Tatar champagne.

“About this couple…” I said, as a gentle reminder.

“Scientists, they said. Nikos had befriended them. I wonder now…”

“Do you remember their names?”

“Names?” He opened his hands in another universal gesture of futility. “All I remember is that the woman had most peculiar eyes, dull and protruding, like frogs’ eyes, and she smoked… Turkish cigarettes… The man, older, foreign…”

“The woman was Russian?”

“Oh, yes. Definitely Russian. The man… Egyptian. Yes, that is it! He was Egyptian. It is coming back to me now. He, especially—a most peculiar man. Metamon! That was his name. Doctor Paulus Metamon!”

It appeared Dimitrakos’s memory of this couple was now coming back to him in a flood. He remembered they boarded at Poti, a port in the Caucasus. He remembered the woman always wore black; the man ate only vegetables and fruit. They conversed with each other in French, though Doctor Metamon also spoke Greek. Dimitrakos remembered the doctor asking him the same questions every day: how soon they would arrive, how bad the weather would be, whether the vegetables were fresh.

"Did you learn why they had such interest in staying in Trebizond?"

"They wished to study some ancient books kept in the library of the Phrontisterion. A great center of Greek learning. The Phrontisterion of Trebizond. Opened its door in, I believe, 1683."

"Ah," I said, with a certain satisfaction.

"What?" Pasha asked. "Surely you don't think…?"

"I do," I said. "The scientists I know go out looking for plants or new species of butterflies, or they study bones or stars, or they make things with chemicals in their laboratories. They don't, in my experience, take long sea voyages to study ancient Byzantine books in ancient Greek libraries."

"Who does that? Tell me."

"Occultists." My two companions stared at me, one delighted with this idea, the other horrified. "Yes, friends," I said jauntily, for I was feeling quite confident now. "Occultists. Magicians. Alchemists. Those are the weird people who go searching in old books. I would guess—no, I would say, with some confidence—that Doctor Paulus Metamon, the Egyptian, was a practitioner of what was once called the Black Arts, and that his companion was none other than our old friend, Elena Blavatskaya."

I felt it was a dramatic moment, and worth at least a small gasp of surprise. But Pasha did not wait a beat before saying, rather brutally, "It's an interesting coincidence, certainly, but what does it have to do with Nikolai? You said he befriended these odd people, Odysseus. Do you think he left with them?"

But I had a thought of my own to follow.

"Wait! Do you know what this means? It means Blavatskaya knows Nikolai after all. So there was no need to use anyone else's memories at that seance. Unless… Ah!"

"Ah?" Pasha echoed. "What is this 'ah?'"

"Ah is—that she didn't know who he was then, and she doesn't know even now. She probably hardly noticed him at the time. Even if he was friendly to her, he was only a crewman, a hand, a waiter, an errand boy. Why would she remember him? But he was interested in her and her Egyptian so he jumped ship to follow them and see what they were up to. Something about them intrigued him enough... or worried him enough. I wonder what it was."

"Something else to ask him about when we find him," said Pavel Damianich, the eternal optimist. "I hope you're keeping a list."

"Black magicians, you say? Alchemists? On my ship!" Clearly Odysseus had been pondering this notion, and had worked himself up into a Greek fury. "To think, they might have harmed her!"

"Elena Petrovna claims to have gone to India, you know," Pasha said. "Maybe she left from there. It is the terminus of the Silk Route, isn't it?"

"Perhaps. But surely Nikolai did not follow her."

"We don't know, do we? Are there any missing years in his life?"

Missing years? He was joking, of course. Let's start counting them all, beginning when he was seventeen and went to university for a few months. The next two or three years he bunked down somewhere in the student ghetto. After that, evidently, he sailed around the Black Sea for three years or more. Then back in Petersburg to the house on the Vyborg side—four years or five. All these estimates were just that—estimates. He was now thirty-two, or maybe he had just turned thirty-three. Were there missing years? The last two were missing, for starters. And, adding up the others, I came up short by another two or three or four.

"Would it be worth a trip to Trebizond?" Pasha asked.

"You would be welcome on the *Sosa*. Her name means safety, you know. Her name means alive and well."

I thanked Odysseus Dimitrakos for his generosity. I thanked him for his help. I said we would consider it. Might Nikolai for some reason have gone back to Trebizond? I could not imagine it. I was too tired. All this listening and thinking had exhausted me. All this talk. But I didn't want to go back to Tatyana's house. I left the men still talking and drinking at the table, and went down to the beach to sit in the sand, for in addition to the joy of deep pockets, one of the great pleasures of wearing trousers is the ease of sitting anywhere you like, on the ground or in a tree or on the back of a horse or in the middle of a sandy beach. So I sat and watched the evening light play on the sea while the sky become streaked with brilliant plumes of pink and rose and luminous gold. I watched until the last of the western light faded, the sea turned dark, and night crept up, a long shadow moving ineluctably toward us from the east. Then a wind came blowing across the water, damp and chill, carrying the scents of wildness and brine. And what is that scent of wildness? It smells of great ocean swells; it smells of fear mixed with awe; it smells of wide horizons, and emptiness, abysmal depths, darkness, solitude, terror, and silence. It smells of death.

CHAPTER TWENTY-TWO

Two Corpses in One Day

Every ten days or so I wrote to Anastasia and to Tatyana and to my indomitable editor, Marina Vilinskaya. To Tatyana I reported on the condition of her house and garden, the health and happiness of her domestic staff, and the highlights (in detail) of the opera season, both those productions I attended in person and those I read about in the press. To Marina, I sent drafts, editorial changes, complaints, petitions, laments, the occasional love note, and requests for more money. The hardest letters to write were those to Anastasia, particularly because she never replied to them. It was not a correspondence so much as an ongoing report from the frontier, written as the barbarians stormed the gates. I tried to sound endlessly and eternally optimistic. The effort was beginning to tell on me. My dreams were often darker than I was used to. I was often angrier than I liked to be. More and more I found myself thinking the unthinkable: that Nikolai Barakov was lost beyond finding, either because he wanted to be or because he had been made to be. Then I would be forced to consider the many ways a man can be made to be lost, the many evils that can deprive him of his will and his freedom, and finally the last and greatest of deprivations that can rip away everything, and then my heart would consider, with terrible grief, the real possibility that Nikolai was no longer alive in the world. But these were not thoughts I could share with Anastasia Alexandrovna. Instead, I wrote to her describing guests at dinner parties, and passing on snippets of gossip Pasha brought back with him from his nightly sojourns, presenting them to her like little candied treats, not the way Pasha presented them to me, which was more in the spirit of a cat bringing home a mouse. I was careful to write nothing to anyone that could in any way be taken as critical of the government, its policies or its policy-makers. I was sure all my letters were intercepted and read.

One evening, a few days after our visit to the Acropolis, I was in the midst of writing one of these anodyne letters to Anastasia, so reminiscent of the newsless letters her son had written to her over the years, and wondering whether I should relay to her some part at least of what we had learned from Odysseus Dimitrakos, all the time knowing I could not, for who knew who would read my words before they reached her, though I dearly wanted to, and it was infuriating me that I could not. In my fury I had just picked up something near at hand—as it happened, a copy of *The Contemporary*—and thrown it across the room, when there was a loud disturbance at the door, someone insisting on seeing me while the doorman, poor old Vilya Illych, yapping like a hound on the scent, tried to bar his way. I threw on my old frock coat and, ready for a fight myself, went to see what was causing all the trouble.

I could see immediately why Vilya Illych had tried to keep this visitor out. He was a young ragamuffin, his coat stained, his trousers ripped, his hair long and wild. There was dirt and blood on his cheek and a greater blood stain on his shirt. Indeed, the blood was fresh and still seeping from his wound. I recognized him, despite the condition he was in. He was the man who had been playing the balalaika outside the Acropolis.

"Bring him in, Vilya Illych! Let him lie down, for the love of God! Run for the doctor!" Then Darya came rushing in and I sent her to fetch warm water and bandages, not that it looked like bandages could do much good. I saw how deep the wound was; the man was close to death.

Yet he had made his way to this house for a reason. Surely he had come with a message. I knelt by the divan where Vilya had settled him down and put my head close to his so I could hear what he had to say. It wasn't words he had for me though, or if there were words he was beyond saying them; but there was something clutched in his fist. He died there on the divan before water and bandages could come, but before he died he opened his hand for me and allowed that which he had been meant to protect, and indeed had protected with his life, to fall onto the floor.

It was a little golden charm in the shape of a monkey.

♣

The doctor came, reluctantly and too late, of course, but he did come, and told us what we already knew, that the man was dead. That fact confirmed, our next problem was what to do with the corpse. It would have to be removed, secretly and stealthily, without anyone outside the household learning about it. The servants would assist us; they were as loathe as we were to have any official agent involved. God forbid! To come within the purview of the police for any reason whatsoever—even as an innocent bystander to an accident—is a disaster to be avoided at all costs. Once you become known to them, your life is not worth a kopek, you are suspected of every possible crime, you are questioned, harassed, refused permission to leave the district, watched, followed, investigated, you spend days waiting in offices, hours and hours answering ridiculous questions, your friends are suspected as well, and your family and servants. Life becomes unbearable, and the only recourse is to ransom yourself by paying them to leave you alone. And how much it would cost us in bribes to the police with a dead man involved, I could not begin to imagine. But Pavel Damianich was already making arrangements to move the poor man's body out of the house, and no sooner had the doctor left, than he and the servants swept in and took it away.

"Where will take him?" I asked as they left with the corpse wrapped up in a carpet.

"To the Acropolis Taverna, of course," Pasha replied. "Where else?"

It was quite late by the time Pavel Damianich returned, but I was so eager to hear how he had managed that I suggested taking a walk along the esplanade so we could breathe in cool, fresh sea air, and try to understand what had happened and why, and what should be done about it.

"Did you speak to Odysseus Dimitrakos? What did he say? Did you discover who the poor man was? Did he give you any idea who might have murdered him?"

"Alas, I did not. The disposition of a corpse in the nighttime is a delicate operation, and so, once we had set our burden down on the sand, we did not dally for conversation. But I see why you would have wished me to interrogate Kyrios Dimitrakos, so I will return to the taverna straightaway, and make those inquiries," said my brave Pasha.

"Nonsense! We'll both go. Luckily, we'll be able to do so under cover of darkness."

At which remark, he burst into laughter.

It is difficult to retain one's *gravitas* around a man like Pavel Damianich.

The night air was luscious and cool, marvelously scented and refreshing. I had many questions and ideas but I waited until we were under the trees of the esplanade to ask the first: why had the balalaika player chosen to die on my divan?

"The monkey charm is somewhat suggestive, don't you think?" I said.

"I suppose you think he was bringing you some sort of message and that it had to do with Nikolai Barakov."

"That must be obvious."

He sighed. "Must it? Too many people know about that book. Too many people know you are looking for it."

"I'm not looking for a book. I'm looking for Nikolai."

"Yes, but the two go together. And who do you suspect sent him?"

"Odysseus, of course."

"Not 'of course,' dear Marko. We made no mention of Nikolai's book to Odysseus, there is no reason to suppose he knows about it. The musician might have come on his own, or been sent by someone else."

"But how would he know how to find me?"

Pavel laughed again.

"Have I said something amusing?"

"Marko, you are the most amusing person I know. Really, you walk around Odessa in your trousers and collars and waistcoats and ties and frock coats and top hats—love of God, Marko, do you think you go unnoticed? I expect everyone in this town knows exactly who you are. And where you live."

"All right," I said, taking this unsolicited information in stride, "say you are right. The balalaika player then, on his own or on the instructions of someone else, sets out last night to Tatyana's house. But he is waylaid, beaten, stabbed—a man dressed in rags. Does this make sense? Would a robber rob a man who clearly has nothing worth stealing?"

We had walked to the end of the boulevard, and sat down on a bench overlooking the sea. I took the little monkey out of my waistcoat pocket and examined it. It was skillfully made and heavy enough to be of solid gold.

"If I had this object," I said, "and I was a poor man, I would have sold it long ago."

"I agree. Then let's assume it didn't belong to him. But he was an honest man, and someone trusted him to bring it to you."

I tightened my fist around the little gold monkey, and thought of the poor balalaika player, clutching on to this object until his last breath. Why would he do such a thing? Why come to me with it? It was all infuriating—a man dying so uselessly.

"May I see it?" he asked. I handed it to him and he studied it carefully. "It might be worth having a goldsmith examine it."

"There are letters engraved on the bottom of the monkey's foot. I noticed them earlier. KK. It may be the goldsmith's mark."

"That is something, at least. We might find out who made it and to whom it was sold. If it was made in Odessa, and if there is a goldsmith here whose initials are KK."

"At least those are questions we can answer."

"Here are some we cannot. Not yet. If the charm did not belong to the balalaika player but was given to him by someone else, who was that person and why was it to be given to you?"

Suddenly it all seemed quite obvious, and in my excitement, I jumped to my feet. "But of course!" I cried. "Nikolai is here and he sent the man to me himself!"

"That is very unlikely," Pavel Damianich replied, sternly. "In fact, quite impossible. Come now, Marko, be reasonable, and sit down. You know very well I have been searching for Nikolai for months. Down in the port, on the docks, in the warehouses, in every tavern, beer shop, and bawdy house, and around gaming tables, and in cafes and tea houses, and out in the country, in the breweries and the wine cellars. Some people remember him, some even call themselves his friends. But nobody I talked to had seen him in a very long time."

"But what if he has just returned to Odessa?" I insisted. I was not ready to abandon my wonderful idea. "No one has seen him yet, of course not, because he has just arrived and he is in hiding because of that novel. Oh, Pasha! What if that's it! Nikolai is here, in hiding, and he gave his friend the balalaika player this monkey charm to show us so that we'd believe him, and go with him to wherever Nikolai is! That was the plan. But en route to us, the poor man was assaulted… Oh, I am sure that's it!"

"Now I see how you come to write your novels," said Pasha the Cruel. "You start with a dead man, and from there you make things up."

"Why can't it be true?"

"From everything you have told me about Nikolai Barakov, I would guess that if he wants to contact you, he's not going to send you a balalaika player with a little gold monkey charm as a token of proof. This is the sort of thing a woman does."

"A woman!"

"As Monsieur Dumas would say, *Cherchez la femme!*"

"A woman in Odessa. Well, of course, it only makes sense that he would have a mistress here. Remember when I asked Dimitrakos about whether Nikolai might have stayed in Trebizond because of a woman? Remember how he immediately said no? Without even thinking? He dismissed the idea far too quickly. Why would he do that unless he knew that Nikolai had a mistress to whom he was devoted? And I am sure he has been back since then, or at least is in communication with this woman. How do we find her?"

Of course, he had an answer to that. "If it is true that she sent the balalaika player to you, then clearly she knows how to find you. We'll just have to wait until she tries again."

"In the meantime, we must speak with Dimitrakos. Let us go now, and see what he has to say."

"Return to the beach? Very well, Marko. We might both benefit from a glass of vodka, don't you think? And I am glad to see you came armed."

I had brought my cane.

"And you?" I said. "Where's your yataghan?"

He opened his coat and showed me, not a curved yataghan blade but a good, solid hunting knife in a leather sheath at his belt.

"I am happy to see we go into battle well prepared," I said, and kissed his cheek in a most brotherly fashion so as not to scandalize the fashionable ladies taking the air under the plane trees. We hired a cab to take us down to the beach and along the shore road, such as it was, but we had the carriage stop about a quarter mile from the taverna and walked the rest of the way. This stretch of sandy beach south of the city would soon become the city's summer playground with its restaurants built on bamboo piles extending out over the water, its warm water baths, and its amusement parks with names like Little Fountain and Arcadia. Now, off season, everything was shuttered tight except for the few year-round fish stands and taverns like the Acropolis. North of the city, on the estuaries, were the more exclusive forms of amusement, expensive salt spring sanitariums and mineral water spas, with their mud baths and steam baths and the rest, meant for noble invalids, the wives of Polish merchants, and rich society women. I myself preferred this southern coast where now in spring the cliffs above the sea were blanketed with yellow broom, and yellow and purple Crimean iris, wild roses, juniper, and hawthorn. It was with such images in mind and memories of times I had visited Odessa in my youth, that I walked along the beach with Pavel Damianich, stars hanging like diamonds in the sky, the sea, murmuring secrets to itself, lapping gently against the shore. So when the two shots rang out they so startled me from my reverie that I clutched onto Pavel Damianich out of sheer surprise.

"What is it?"

"Pistol shots."

"Yes. Why?"

"A duel."

"A duel? Here?"

By then we had taken cover, if cover it could be called, under the skimpy boughs of a tamarisk tree.

"I don't—" he began, but his words were drowned out by another blast from a pistol, so close we could smell the gunpowder. There was shouting and movement ahead of us, men running down toward the water where a small skiff was pulled up on the sand. In the blink of an eye they had pushed her into the surf, climbed in, and rowed away just as another group of men rushed down to intercept them, but to no good end as the rowers were quite strong and expert with their oars and were out in deep water before their pursuers could catch them.

"What were you saying?" I whispered.

"That I don't think we should try to speak with Odysseus tonight. It appears he is keeping himself quite busy."

We turned around and went swiftly back the way we had come. It was a long walk since we had no carriage, but Pasha was quite insistent that we go the long way around and not through the port and up the

Steps. The port of Odessa, he claimed, was no place for a woman, even one as armed and dangerous as myself. I objected but he held firm. So we walked up the road in the dark, puffing and complaining, stumbling over ruts, falling into holes, getting mud on our boots, and it was a long time before we sighted a cab for hire. By then we were practically home.

"I wonder what it was all about," I was saying, if not in those exact words, in words much like them, and I was sure that Pavel Damianich was quite prepared to elucidate the occurrence for me now that we had been relieved of our muddy boots and were sipping Tatyana's exquisite French brandy and filling our pipes with good Turkish tobacco. But he did not get a chance, for at that moment there was once again confusion in the hall, our poor doorman apparently being unused to opening the door for people, inquiring about their business, discovering their names, and announcing them properly. The man who strode into the drawing room had to announce himself, and did.

"Your pardon, Madame Markova," he said, bowing slightly, reluctantly, the way officials do. "Chekovich, assistant to the chief of police."

Merde! My heart sank like a stone. We had been discovered! The musician's body had been found and traced back to us—how, I could not begin to imagine. We were in terrible trouble. I wondered if I had anywhere near enough money to extricate us from it.

"What can I do for you, Assistant Chief of Police Chekovich?" I asked, forcing myself to smile at him with his stiff uniform and his stiffer expression. Clearly he did not expect to see Madame Markova in her waistcoat and trousers, smoking a pipe. But then, what can you expect when you barge in on a woman in the middle of the night?

Pavel Damianich by then was standing beside my chair in his bulldog stance, practically growling at our visitor, and even Vilya Illych, poor man, was puffing himself up like an adder about to strike. Chekovich had come alone, which was a good sign, unless, of course, he had reinforcements waiting outside.

"What is it you could possibly want from us that couldn't wait until the morning?"

He glanced around at the room, the silk-covered walls and damask-covered furniture, the high ceilings and curtained windows, the graceful chandeliers, the amber decanter, taking in at a calculating glance the wealth represented by the room, not my wealth, but Princess Tatyana Volkonskaya's. Then he shifted his gaze to me.

"I have come," he said, "at the behest of my superiors. I am sorry to be the one to tell you this, Madame, but there has been a tragic event, here in Odessa, which has led to the death of your husband, Yevgeni Markov."

A hush fell on the room.

But my heart had recovered its strength and was filled now with indignation rather than dismay. Once more master of myself, I stood to face this impertinent and dangerous man. "I would thank you for your kindness, Assistant Chief of Police Chekovich, but I have no husband, no husband named Yevgeni, no husband whatsoever. There has been some mistake. How did this poor man meet his end?"

"He was shot to death in a duel not three hours ago," Chekovich said. "We were informed he was your husband."

"I am afraid you have been misinformed."

"For your sake, Madame, I am gratified to hear it."

"Had he no identification on his person?"

"No. Duelists rarely carry their passports."

"So someone present gave you his name and sent you to me?"

"Someone present, yes, gave the police your name as next of kin. Madame Valentina Markova. And this address."

"Remarkable," I said, knowing it was a remarkable lie. Who would give the police my name? "There is, however, a rather famous Yevgeni Markov. I have just read his article in *Notes of the Fatherland*. It is about his voyage around the Black Sea. He mentions following in the footsteps of his distinguished cousin, also a writer." The reference had struck me when I read the article, which was why, in the midst of everything, I could recall it so clearly. "The cousin's name is Elena Blavatskaya."

"I thank you for your assistance, Madame, and beg your forgiveness for coming to your home at such an hour." As he spoke, his eyes alighted on the bottle of brandy on the table—and remained there. I might not have to bribe him, but it was clear I was not going to get him out of the house without first offering him a drink.

He accepted, of course, and settled down in a comfortable chair to drink and chat. He proved to be quite forthcoming. The poor dead man, he told us, who may or may not have been the travel writer, Yevgeni Markov, had met his death on the beach near the Acropolis Taverna.

"A den of pirates and smugglers," Chekovich mentioned after his second glass. "You know, there are Greeks in this city, men like Rallis, Mavros, Mavrokordato, Iannopulo, rich merchants, people of the highest quality. Then there are the other Greeks, of the lowest quality, rich men, too, mind you. They rule the underworld, they control the port, they run contraband in and out, and all the criminal activity that goes on down there—they run it all. And Odysseus Dimitrakos, owner of the Acropolis, he is one of them, a big man among them."

This news was so unexpected I could not think of any response. Odysseus Dimitrakos, an underworld villain? It seemed preposterous. Yet, it would explain Nikolai's attraction, for why would he spend years of his life serving drinks to wealthy passengers on a Greek steamship unless there was something else—something dark, dangerous, and interesting—on offer?

While I was contemplating this extraordinary turn of events, Pavel Damianich was asking if the police were convinced the man had died in a duel.

"Not at all. I said that to you, Madame Markova, when I thought it was your husband who had died. Better to think your husband died in a duel of honor than that he was shot to death by pirates."

"You think he was shot by pirates?"

"I think there is a war going on in the underworld, and Markov was caught in one of its skirmishes. Maybe we'll be lucky, and they will all kill each other. If this Markov is who you think he is, then perhaps he was writing about them or they were afraid he would."

"Or he just stepped out from behind a tree at the wrong time," Pavel Damianich said, and I was sure he was thinking, though he did not say, "As we almost did."

Chekovich became loquacious as he helped us polish off the bottle. Before he left us, he had imparted a good deal of information about the darker side of the City of White Acacias, the Little Paris of the Black Sea. He talked about the white slave trade, through which hundreds of girls every year were sold for shipment to Constantinople, the opium trade, even the trade in subversive magazines, for evidently Herzen's *Kolokol*, published in London, was smuggled into Russia through the port of Odessa. There were even secret revolutionary societies, and socialists and agitators at work in the city. Odessa had given shelter and support to partisans of the Greek independence movement in the '20s, and she was disposed to shelter Polish and Ukrainian revolutionaries now. Besides that, the city was aswarm with swindlers of every kind; frauds, thefts, murders, and other disorders were ordinary occurrences. Sailors were mostly to blame but also the carters who brought in the grain, the warehousemen who stored it, and especially the stevedores who loaded it—Russian tramps and drunkards, Turks in dirty turbans, Persians who colored their hair and nails—a disgrace! And then there were foreign thieves and receivers of stolen goods who came in easily across the border and over the sea, all of them indulging in the most lascivious vices and excesses, which the city seemed eager enough to provide.

"It is an interesting phenomenon, the proximity of the two worlds. Noble ladies walk on the high esplanade under the plane trees, while two hundred feet below them... *Lasciate ogne speranza, voi ch'intrate.*"

"I am glad I did not know all this earlier, when we were walking home in the dark," I said to dear Pasha after Chekovich had departed, and we had resumed our original positions, he on one chair, I on the other. "And I see now why you were so reluctant to allow me down into the port. You were afraid I might get sold to a sultan. But, tell me, can it be true that Odysseus is a smuggler and pirate and chief villain of the Odessa underground? Did you have any idea of this? I assume not or you would not have introduced him to me."

Pasha sucked in his cheek, a sign of his displeasure. "Of course I had no idea! And I must say this whole affair is becoming more and more mysterious. Who gave your name to the police?"

"It had to be Odysseus himself. I know you think I am an inveterate fictionalizer and therefore a person of poor judgement and little practical use when it comes to fathoming the workings of actual, living human beings—"

"Marko, I never—"

I dismissed his objections with a regal wave of my hand. "Nonetheless, I did notice the other afternoon when we met Dimitrakos in the café, that he was carrying this very same edition of *Notes of the Fatherland*, the latest edition, as it happens. If I read Markov's article, it's just as likely he did as well. It concerned Dimitrakos's own business, after all, since it described Markov's journey by steamship from Odessa to Constantinople."

"So?"

"So—the article gave him a name for his corpse. Assuming the corpse isn't really that of Yevgeni Markov. Who knows? Maybe it is."

Pasha snarled, another sign of displeasure. "And in the process implicated you. I assume you have an explanation for why he would give your name to his corpse—if it is his corpse and not ours—"

"Ours? But ours was stabbed, not shot."

"Indeed, but it was deposited on the same beach. Still, assuming a second body, why attach your name to it?"

"It was a message."

"Ah. A message. *Don't push your luck, Markova, or the next body might be yours?*"

"No. But you will think my idea is nonsense."

"Probably, but tell me anyway."

"He wanted to inform us that he had avenged the death of his musician."

"A nice story. Very romantic. But, you must admit, absurd."

"I don't see why. The balalaika player worked for him. The balalaika player was murdered. Dimitrakos is evidently an underworld hegemon of some kind, and can't allow his people to be murdered on the street. He discovers who among his enemies is responsible, he lures them to his taverna, and shoots one of them. Then he decides to let us know about it. After all, I have a right to know. The balalaika player died on my divan."

"And so he sends the assistant chief of police to your door? Unlikely. How much easier simply to send you a note! Besides, I thought we had decided a woman sent the balalaika player to you."

"Perhaps the woman is somehow connected to Dimitrakos."

"It's quite a tangled web you're weaving, Marko Volchek."

"I did not weave it. I am trying to untangle it."

He sighed. "Then add this to the tangle: doesn't it strike you as odd that Madame Blavatskaya's name keeps coming up?"

"That she seems to be *haunting* this investigation?" I smiled at him. "Coincidence, undoubtedly."

"Coincidence that she was a passenger on the *Sosa*? Coincidence that she disembarked at the same port as Nikolai did? Coincidence that her cousin, the travel writer, took that same voyage eight years later? Coincidence that he may or may not have been shot tonight on the beach? And my guess, for what it's worth, is that the dead man is indeed Yevgeni Markov. It is a crime to purposefully misidentify a corpse, and I doubt Dimitrakos would do it just to send you a message. A letter would serve the same purpose."

"If it is—but, Pasha, if the body is Markov's, how will his family ever know? Who will identify his body? And if no one does…"

"Come now, Marko. They'll find someone."

"Will they? Will they bother? How many men die on the street with no papers? How many men die at sea, or are washed up on the shore? How many die in squalid rooms, all alone, and no one ever knows? Oh, Pasha, it's terrible!"

I found I was shaking, for I had had a terrible vision. I had seen Nikolai dying in such a way, friendless and alone, his body like some abandoned overcoat left lying anywhere, nowhere, and none of us ever knowing, seeking him always and never finding him.

"I must go myself and see the body," I said. "I might recognize him after all. Even his clothes might tell us something. And someone must see to his burial."

Pasha took my hand and smiled at me, lovingly. "All right. We'll see to it."

"What a very long day it's been!" I sighed, feeling suddenly that I could not stay awake another moment. "Two corpses in one day. It seems—excessive. It is the same day, isn't it?"

Just then the clock on the mantle began to chime.

"Not any more," Pasha said.

CHAPTER TWENTY-THREE

THE GIRL WITH THE GOLDEN MONKEY

By the next morning I had changed my mind. I did not want to get entangled with the authorities. I did not want to look at a dead man, I did not care if it was the corpse of Yevgeni Markov.

It is simply a fact that minds change from day to day. They make their decisions while the rest of the body sleeps. Or perhaps it is the soul that changes, that travels during the night to places unreachable by day, that sees and learns, grows or lessens, becomes bolder or more timid, braver or more afraid. Or perhaps in sleep we are visited by dreams that speak to the deepest part of ourselves, that give it wise counsel, then vanish like smoke in the morning light.

However it happened, I woke in the morning with a new mind.

"This entire Markov affair has diverted us. We must retrace our steps. We must find the goldsmith with the initials KK, discover who purchased the monkey charm, and talk to that person. If it turns out the charm was lost or stolen, all right, at least we'll know. But I am hopeful that it will lead us to Nikolai. Whoever sent it to us might very well know where he is."

Pasha poured me another cup of coffee and handed me another piece of buttered bread. He was unusually quiet. Perhaps he, too, had been visited during the night by a mind-changing dream.

I asked him if that was the case.

"No," he said.

"What then?"

"Marko, I think we should leave Odessa. It will begin to get hot soon, the dust will rise, the cholera will break out, and you have done what you intended to do here. I am sorry I brought Dimitrakos to you. I regret it now, but I don't want to have to regret it for the rest of my life."

"Leave Odessa? What an idea!" Pasha was sometimes subject to these sorts of erratic notions. The best way to handle him at such times was to divert his attention by changing the subject. "As for Dimitrakos, how did you ever meet him in the first place? You never told me."

"You did not ask." He shifted in his chair. I knew next he would begin complaining about uncomfortable furniture.

"Please tell me," I said, offering him a cigarette.

"I was introduced to him by Prince Mrozinski."

"Really? Where?"

"At a dinner."

He was being uncharacteristically coy. It could mean only one thing.

"All right. At the home of what lovely Polish lady were you eating this dinner?"

"Countess Zuza Glowacka. And her husband, the Count."

"It did not strike you as odd?"

"That I should be invited to dinner?"

"That you should meet a Greek smuggler at the home of a Polish count."

"He was introduced to me as a poet."

"Ah."

"An admirer of Adam Mickeiwicz. Listen, Marko, there is more here than meets the eye."

"Please don't tell me we have landed in the midst of a Polish conspiracy!" I found this idea laughable and told him so. Of course, the Poles still wanted their freedom, and Polish students were always being arrested for subversive activities like writing anti-Russian poetry or singing Polish songs on the street, but the Polish nobility in Odessa were grain merchants. They came to negotiate the sale of wheat. They bought country houses and built grain warehouses the size of palaces. Their wives came for the spas and the shops that sold Parisian fashions.

"You are too cynical, Marko," Pasha said, somewhat sternly. "Even rich men and merchants can love their country. But I am not suggesting that Prince Mrozinski or Count Glowacki are plotting to liberate Poland. Theirs is an interesting circle, however. It draws men with many different interests, and what better place to hide a spy?"

"A spy for whom?"

"A spy for the Third Section. A spy for the Polish-Ukrainian Revolutionary Committee. A spy for French intelligence. A spy for the Sublime

Porte. A spy for the governor of Kherson. A spy for Wladyslaw Czartoryski. Give me a few minutes, and I'll think of more."

"Fine," I said, my head spinning. "But what does such a spy discover at dinner with Count Glowacki?"

"Perhaps only the price of next year's wheat. On the other hand, one might wish to know where our Polish merchants stand on certain issues. Where their sympathies lie. Are they sending money to Paris? Are they preparing another Polish legion like Czaykowski's Ottoman Cossacks? Are there plans—real plans, not Russian fairytales, but real Polish plans—to assassinate the Tsar? People talk, Marko."

"And so you were at such a dinner, listening to people talk, when Prince Mrozinski introduced you to Odysseus Dimitrakos. Whose ship carries passengers and freight back and forth from Odessa to Istanbul."

"Whose ship smuggles people and contraband back and forth from Odessa to Istanbul. Where Czaykowski is still living. Under his new name, General Sadyk Pasha."

"And no doubt still plotting."

"Yes. There will be another Polish uprising soon. I can feel it coming. In the way people talk. The way they say nothing, and yet the air all around them seems to crackle with intrigue and excitement."

"You amaze me. Why didn't you mention these dinner-table faux-conspiracies to me before?"

"I didn't think such dinner-table faux-conspiracies interested you."

"No, but you could have told me about the food."

Pasha laughed and I could feel something in him relax back into his usual Gallic insouciance. "All I remember is that the watermelon was exceedingly juicy. I wonder they can keep them fresh through the whole winter."

I raised an eyebrow at him. "And I wonder you can find time to consort with the Polish aristocracy through the whole winter. I am not keeping you busy enough."

"My job is to protect you. I am doing my job now by recommending we leave Odessa."

"Why? Do you think I am in danger?"

"Two dead men, and you have witnessed both their deaths."

"There is no reason to think both dead men are linked to me. The musician, yes, maybe. But the man on the beach..."

"Listen to me, Marko. Last night you had the idea that Dimitrakos gave Chekovich your name because he wanted to send you a message, do you remember? And last night I disagreed with you. This morning I agree absolutely. It was a message. Everything he said. It was a warning."

"Why have you changed your mind?"

"Because this morning while you were sleeping I went to the police station. I wanted to inquire about viewing the body of Yevgeny Markov."

"A bold move. And did you inquire?"

"Yes."

"And you were told..."

He looked at me. I looked back at him. *Dear God!* I thought. *I know what he's going to say!* And a chill crept through me, a cold shiver creeping up my spine, raising bumps on my skin as it went. He must have sensed it, because he poured me a finger of cognac, which happened to be in a handy decanter on the table.

"I've already put some in my coffee," he said. "For courage."

"So at the police station they told you ... there was no body?"

"There was no body. And when I asked for Chekovich..."

"There was no Chekovich."

"There was a Chekovich. A minor clerk. I demanded to see him. He is a little, pink-faced mouse of a man, certainly not the man who came here last night."

I sat for a while, stunned.

"What can it mean?"

"This is what I think. I think Dimitrakos knows who comes and goes on his road. He knew very well that someone had come last night and left the balalaika player's body on his beach. He knew that later you and I arrived by carriage. Of course he needed to discover why we had come, what we knew, and what, if anything, we were going to do about it. How can he find out? He sends a policeman right to your door in the middle of the night. If you intend to make an official report, there is your Assistant Chief of Police himself to take your information."

"But this fake policeman has to have a reason to come to my house in the middle of the night. So Dimitrakos makes up the story about my husband being killed in a duel, though he knows very well I have no husband. We say nothing about the dead balalaika player or about what we've seen on the beach, which may mean we know nothing and we've seen nothing, but just to be sure we remain silent our policeman will scare us nearly to death with stories of what a dangerous man Odysseus is. And so he did."

"Yes. Fine. He's done his job. Dimitrakos has nothing to fear from us. Then this morning, what did I do? Walked right into the police station and asked about Yevgeny Markov. Do you see now why we have to leave Odessa?"

"No. I see now why we have to stay. Now it's getting interesting."

"Holy Mother of God!" he cried, a sign he was deeply upset, for it was only then that he reverted to prayer.

"All right, Pasha, *mon cher.* I will leave Odessa, I promise, as soon as we find the goldsmith, find the owner of the golden monkey, and find out who sent it to me. Maybe we'll even find Nikolai, though, please note, I do not set that as a condition. Only after we solve the mystery of the golden monkey will I leave Odessa and not a moment before. They won't scare me away... You know I found it rather marvelous last night that a policeman could quote Dante. But now I marvel even more that a pirate can."

"By all the saints and angels, Marko Volchek, you defeat me!"

"I don't mean to," I said. "But surely you know me well enough to know I can't let a band of brigands frighten me."

"A band of brigands! I think you must be mad. But you're also the boss. So, very well, Madame, if it's your will that we stay, we stay. What is your plan for the day?"

"We go jewelry shopping. Though I am afraid that little monkey has traveled. He may even have come from Istanbul, from the gold market in the Covered Bazaar."

"Then we are wasting our time looking here."

"Except for that KK."

"They could be the initials of the woman to whom it was given."

"Then we'll search for her. Listen, Pasha, my dear, we can discuss this all day. But, look, the sun is shining. Let us arm ourselves and go forth to hunt for gold."

♣

Hunting for gold in Odessa was not difficult. There were shops filled with gold in all its many forms: gold brooches, gold rings, gold bangles, gold earrings, gold necklaces, gold cuff links, gold pill boxes, gold cigarette cases, gold coins, gold brocade, gold crowns, gold plate, gold frames, icons covered with gold leaf, gilt-edged pages of books, gilded glassware and porcelain. But we were looking for gold in the shape of little figurines with the maker's signatory initials engraved on them, and these had proved impossible to find.

The weather was lovely, though, and we spent a few pleasant hours strolling up and down Catherine and DeRibos, looking in shop windows, examining golden items, asking shop owners for the names of jewelers and goldsmiths, stopping in tea shops along the way, and admiring the views, for one of the joys of living in Odessa was being able to look up and down its straight, broad boulevards and see unbounded space in both directions, the rippling sea at one end of the street, the rippling steppes at the other; in one direction, a vastness of blue or grey, in the other, depending on the season, a vastness of yellow or green, white or dun.

Finally, some clever shop owner suggested that we look for a goldsmith where goldsmiths did their work, in their own districts, where their workshops had stronger locks and better guards.

"He's sending us on another wild goose chase," Pasha muttered as we left the shop and looked around for a carriage to hire. "Maybe we should stop and have dinner now, like normal human beings."

I was ready to agree with him, and would have with just a little more persuasion, when the entire question of dining became quite moot. A carriage rolled to a stop in front of us, a beefy footman in livery jumped down, opened the door, and invited us to make ourselves comfortable inside. He was a giant of a man, and the driver, peering down at us, was no less gigantic.

"Why should we?" I asked. "Who sent you?"

Then I noticed the gold monogram painted on the carriage door, and decided it would be wise to accept the invitation without any argument.

The carriage headed west, away from the city center. Soon we were crossing the boulevard that marked the boundary of the old free port, passing the military barracks, whose building so resembled a Greek temple, and driving into the countryside. How pleasant it was to be in the country! Amidst the walnut trees and mulberry trees were the elegant country houses of the rich, built of limestone with tiled roofs and terraces, painted light blue or pale pink or yellow, surrounded by gardens, vineyards, and orchards. Some of these villas were quite large, of a type one might be more likely to find in the Tuscan countryside rather than at the edge of the Central Asian steppes; most were summer dachas but others were used year-round. We passed little villages; we passed coffee houses and vodka shops; we passed carts and cows and fields.

"I wonder where we're going," I said. "We must be miles from the city."

"You have asked that question several times, and I have answered it. You've been dreaming, Marko."

"Forgive me. What answer did you give?"

"You know, Odessa was settled mostly by runaway serfs. Half the population had no passports in the early days, and Catherine didn't mind. She wanted settlers. She didn't have them captured and brought back. Very kind of her. That was sixty years ago. Today most of the tradesmen in the city are sons of serfs."

"If this was your answer, no wonder I fell asleep."

"When these run-away serfs were asked questions, they had one answer. Where do you come from? I don't know. Where is your passport? I don't know. What is your father's name? I don't know. So they were called *neznaiyooshchie*."

I grinned at him. Pasha's stories always have a point, eventually.

"Know-nothings. So that was your answer? You know nothing?"

"Correct. I don't know where we're going but I am enjoying the ride."

"A nice philosophy of life."

"The golden Ks on the carriage door are suggestive."

"Yes, I agree."

"Traditionally, you know, goldsmiths were bankers."

"Were they?"

"And sometimes bankers were goldsmiths."

"So our goldsmith is a rich banker."

"And he's invited us to his country house for dinner."

"You are an optimist, aren't you?"

"Or perhaps he has a vast estate upon which he keeps sheep. It must be shearing time, don't you think?"

"And he wants us to help shear his sheep? As long as we're not being conscripted to work in a tallow factory."

"It is one of the unpleasant facts of life, that if you want unnatural light you must obtain it by unnatural means. We must kill to live. It is our fate as human beings."

"Now you've really cheered me up. Thank you."

Meanwhile our carriage was slowing almost to a crawl.

"I could walk faster than this," I said. "And I think I will."

"Don't be rash, Marko. We're turning off now. Look, we'll be arriving soon."

He was right. The carriage was turning into a drive lined with trees.

"I could still walk faster."

"You would sink into the mud and be stuck fast. We would have to get a team of oxen to pull you out."

"How bovid our conversation has become! Cows boiled for tallow, oxen hitched up to drag pedestrians out of bogs, and sheep shorn of their wool! See what happens when you venture into the country!"

Just about then the carriage lurched, the horses made a racket, and there was great commotion as footman and driver struggled to keep both beasts and carriage upright. I opened the door and jumped out. The villa was close, and most of the space between house and carriage was paved with brick. Thank God, I could walk the rest of the way, and I did.

"We have been waylaid, we have been snatched off the street, we have been driven out into the country to God knows where, we have been rattled, bumped, and bruised along the way, and now we are here, miles from civilization. Do you have a good explanation for all this?"

"The only way to deal with kidnappers, in my limited experience," Pasha had whispered to me, as we waited in the reception hall, "is to seize the upper hand right away." That's what I was attempting to do. The borzoi I was addressing, however, seemed unimpressed. He came up to us, sleek and beautiful, with his long tail wrapped around his back legs, and sat and waited for us to admire him, which we did.

"Hard to imagine such a beauty chasing a wolf," I said, patting his head.

"Not at all," another voice replied. "Divo runs like the wind, don't you, marvelous? But I must apologize. It was not my intention to inconvenience you. But surely you received my message. Please tell me you did."

She was a beautiful young woman, twenty-three or twenty-four, no older, tall, dark-eyed, and raven-haired, standing with her hand on the magnificent wolfhound's head, and she sounded so disappointed that I could not stay angry at her. I wondered what message she was referring to. Could she mean the golden monkey, or some message the poor balalaika player was meant to deliver? It was difficult to imagine how this rich young woman could have anything to do with the Acropolis Taverna or its musician.

"No matter. We are here."

"Yes, thank God. Though I truly regret your discomfort on the road."

"That, too, is of no consequence. Yet you have us at a disadvantage."

"Forgive me, Madame Markova. My name is Alexandra Kirillovna Kantrovskaya. But, please, before we talk further, let me make you comfortable. Let us sit on the terrace. Some wine after your journey? A light meal? Anything to restore your good humor and convince you of my friendship."

I introduced Pavel Damianich, and agreed a glass of wine would go a long way to restoring our good humor, but secretly I was delighted. Now I was sure she was in some way connected to the monkey, his foot branded with a double K, and that she held some key to the mystery of Nikolai Barakov. But these things take time and subtlety. I knew she had sent us the golden monkey. I had to be patient until she was ready to tell us why.

Accompanied by Divo, she led us outside to the terrace. The air was filled with the sweet fragrances of springtime. The fruit trees of the orchard were in flower, birds were chirping and fluttering in the branches, and in the garden below, covering the ground like a brilliant Turkish carpet, hundreds of red tulips were in bloom. Beyond the cultivated garden was a flowering meadow, and beyond that, reaching out toward the horizon, flat and endless, were the steppes.

"We are at the edge of the civilized world, you see," she said, smiling at us. "Beyond, for the time being, only sheep and wheat. But you saw how the city is creeping up on us. Soon this will be all built up. Soon this will be the city, and there will be factories here, and congested streets, and poor people sleeping in hovels, ten to a room. My father can foresee this."

"Well, then, we should appreciate its beauty while we still can," I said.

I was willing to let her take her time. Pasha was never so patient. He did not wait long before saying, "When will you tell us, Alexandra Kirillovna, why we are here, enjoying this lovely view of your poppy field."

Was it a poppy field? "I'm sure those are tulips, Pasha," I said.

While Alexandra and Pasha discussed poppies and tulips, I sat back, listening and enjoying the sunshine. I was content for the moment. The wine was a deliciously light and slightly sparkling muscat. It went a long way to restoring my good humor, as did the slices of sweet watermelon and the creamy cheese that accompanied it.

"Of course, poppies are useful flowers, for a number of reasons. We use their seeds in the making of bread."

"Indeed, Alexandra Kirillovna. But surely their better use is for the extraction of opium, from which we obtain morphia, of the greatest benefit to mankind, and laudanum, of the same importance for our health and well-being."

"Have you read *The Confessions of an Opium Eater*?"

This question startled us both. "I have not," Pasha admitted. "Have you, Alexandra Kirillovna?"

"Please call me Sasha, as you are now my friends. And, yes, Pavel Damianich, I have. It was lent to me by a dear friend. Rather, it was *left* to me. I am sure he did not intend me to read it. But I found it most enlightening."

"And who was this friend," asked Pasha, clearly with great interest, "who kindly left you *The Confessions of an Opium Eater*?"

"Ah," she said. "But first I must ask you a question. Another friend was to visit you yesterday with a message from me. He did not come?"

"Someone did come yesterday," I said, cautiously.

"Thank God!"

"A musician."

"Yes, he is a musician. And he delivered the message?"

"He was unable to speak to us."

"Unable to speak?" Just at that moment, Divo, evidently a most sensitive animal, sat up from where he was lying at Alexandra's feet, and lay his head in her lap.

"Was he a good friend?"

"Yes, Why? Why didn't he speak to you?"

"The poor man had been brutally attacked on his way to us, and I regret to say that before he could speak—"

"Oh, no!" she cried. The borzoi lifted his head from her lap to look at her, and she clutched his head in her hands and put her own dark head against his, creating a tableau of grief that was saccharinely romantic and yet somehow deeply moving. They were both handsome animals; perhaps that was what redeemed it. I said nothing, but again Pavel Damianich stepped into the breach, offering, in quick succession, words of comfort, his handkerchief, and a glass of sparkling wine. Soon she was capable of speaking to us again, and she asked us to tell her everything in detail. Pasha did this with his usual dispatch, stopping at the moment when the musician opened his hand and the little gold monkey fell to the floor.

"So you have it!" she cried. "Oh, I am so glad!"

I fished it out of my waistcoat pocket, the little golden monkey charm, and showed it to her. I have rarely seen such a rapid change in a person's emotions, from deep grief to delight in a matter of moments.

"I would have been grieved to lose it," she said, reaching for it. "It belongs to Niko. To Nikolai Vasilevich."

Eureka! I put the little charm in her outstretched hand. "So you asked your friend to bring this to me. Why?"

"My dear friend, Perikles Stepanovich," she said, and wiped the tears from her eyes with Pasha's handkerchief. "I cannot believe he has died. He was a wonderful musician."

I realized she needed a few minutes to grieve before answering the many questions I was dying to ask. I am useless at comforting people, but Pasha is skilled at it. He took her hand and spoke to her soothingly, in that gentle tone he reserves for unhappy horses and distraught women, and soon extracted the entire story.

Perikles Mavros, Black Perikles, was a balalaika player, but also a pirate, an Allen a Dale to Dimitrakos's Robin Hood, as Alexandra put it, whose familiarity with English literature was the happy result of her having an English grandmother. He had been a friend of Nikolai's, whom she called Niko, and it was through Nikolai that she had met him and come to trust him. So when she wanted to get a message to us, she made use of him as a messenger. She arranged to meet him, and she entrusted him with the little golden monkey. I poked Pasha to let him know that he could gloat if he wanted, for he had accurately predicted that we would find a woman behind this monkey business, but he only frowned and gave me a very slight nod of acknowledgment. He was becoming quite entranced by Sasha and didn't want to be disturbed.

"He was to tell you who I was and that I would send a carriage for you and when and where it would be waiting. The charm was a sign so you would know it came from a friend of Niko's."

"And why would I know that?"

"It is quite valuable," she said. "And clever. Did you discover its secret? See how it works?" She held the monkey in one hand and with the other she twisted and pulled the monkey's tail, and its back swung open, revealing a tiny hiding place inside. "My Uncle Khayim is a goldsmith. He made this for me when I was a child. I loved the secret door. I used to hide all sorts of things in it. Little things, of course."

"So the monkey is yours. I thought you said it belongs to Nikolai."

"I gave it to him, but after a short time he gave it back to me. He said he always loses things or they get stolen. He really hates owning anything. And in answer to your previous question, Pavel Damianich, it was Niko who left me the de Quincey book. He gave me many books. And one book, especially, which he showed me, a book that is a great secret, and which I swore to him I would never mention to anyone."

"*Monkey*," I said.

She gave me a beatific smile. "Yes! I knew he would have told you, I knew you would recognize the monkey charm. Forgive me for not saying so at once. But I did promise him never to mention its name."

"Do you have this book? Did he leave it with you?"

"No. But it is because of his book that I asked you here, as Perikles Stepanovich would have told you."

She blew her nose, kissed the borzoi's head, and sat back in her chair. Her face was flushed and lovely, her dark eyes smoldered. She was finally taking in the full consequences of what had occurred, and now anger was replacing self-reproach. I was glad of it. She had a passionate nature, one could easily see, and righteous anger is a far more productive emotion than guilt. She knew Nikolai, she probably knew a great deal about his life, and if we were to be successful in our search here, it was clear that we needed her help. I was convinced that beneath that meek feminine exterior, she was strong and she was brave, much like her animal companion, Divo the Magnificent.

"We have a house in town," she began, "and I'm there more often than here. One day, over a month ago, I met Perikles on the street. It was not an accidental meeting. He had been waiting for me by the house and had followed me. He was quite agitated and it took some time to get the entire story from him. He worked for Dimitrakos, and he knew everything about his business. He told me that Dimitrakos was becoming alarmed because there was a man going around the port asking questions about Nikolai Barakov, a Frenchman—"

"Tut-tut," I muttered.

"—and that he was going to have to do something about it."

"Why would our asking about Nikolai alarm him?" My heart leapt up. "Is he here?"

"That is the question, of course."

"Do you know the answer?"

"No. But the fact that Dimitrakos became so concerned makes me think he may be."

"You mean, Nikolai may be here, working for Dimitrakos?"

"It is possible. Which might be why, if someone comes along, asking questions, especially a Frenchman—"

"Wait!" I said. "Odessa is filled with Frenchmen. And Italians, and Armenians, and Jews, and Slavs, and Greeks, even Tatars. Why should Pavel Damianich cause such concern? Plus, he speaks excellent Russian. I'm surprised anyone would even know he was French. What does Dimitrakos have to hide?"

They both humphed at this absurd remark.

"Everything," Alexandra said.

"Why a Frenchman in particular?"

"Opium, perhaps," Pasha suggested. "France consumes more opium than any other country in Europe. It comes overland to Trebizond, gets on-loaded into ships there, and passes into the Mediterranean through the Straits. A ship sailing under a Russian flag would pass through Istanbul and into the Straits unhindered. But if the cargo never arrives in Marseilles, or arrives much lighter than it should, some powerful French merchants would be unhappy indeed."

"Or it might have to do with Dimitrakos's other work," Alexandra Kirillovna said. "His very secret work."

"What? He is an informer? Not for the Third Section, surely."

"Heavens, no! He works for foreign intelligence agencies only. Niko used to tell me stories about what they did. There was much involvement with French agents. And, of course, the Polish government in exile has its headquarters in Paris."

"So Dimitrakos passes information back and forth between Odessa and Paris?"

"Information and people. Through Czaykowski's organization in Constantinople. At least, he was doing that before the war. Perhaps things have changed. Who knows what Dimitrakos is involved in now. But this is not what Perikles was concerned about. What he wanted me to know was that Dimitrakos had made inquiries, and had learned your names and true identities."

"That wouldn't be too hard," I said.

"No," Alexandra said, smiling at me like I was another marvelous borzoi. "Marko Volchek. You are undisguisable and unique."

"He must have been quite relieved to learn that we were not disgruntled French opium addicts or enraged Polish spies."

"Correct. Instead he discovered you were a famous writer. And being written about is something he fears more than anything else."

"Does he indeed?"

"He has a terror of it. So as soon as Perikles learned that Dimitrakos intended to meet with you, he came to me so I could warn you. Of course, Niko had talked to us both about you, his dear friend, the writer Marko Volchek, and so I was as concerned as Pericles. I especially wanted to implore you not to mention anything to Dimitrakos about Niko's book. Dimitrakos cannot ever learn about it, he must never know it exists, especially if Niko is here."

"Tell me why."

"Because it is a book full of secrets. It is a masterpiece but it is dangerous."

"You have read it?"

"Parts of it. He showed me parts of it. And he made me swear I would never talk about it to anyone. And I have not."

And I knew from the sound of her voice that she would keep her promise and so, rather than ask her about *Monkey*, I asked the question whose answer I most desired to know. "Oh, Sasha, for the love of God, tell me the truth! Have you seen him? Is he here?"

"No. No, I haven't seen him. Not for two years. Two years! And he used to write to me, such beautiful letters. But I haven't received a letter from him in a long time."

This was an interesting piece of new information, that Nikolai had been in Odessa two years ago. I glanced over at Pasha who had reacted to the news with the dismay of a hound who had somehow missed picking up the scent.

"He came here to visit you?" I asked.

"He did visit me. But why he came, what reason he had to come—that I don't know."

"How did the two of you first meet?"

She gave me that sweet smile again. "Oh, we met at my cousin's birthday party, ten years ago. My English grandmother gives us English birthday parties, you see, and Niko just appeared at one. He was so charming, and of course we all assumed he had come with one of our friends, but we could never discover which friend it was, and later he confessed that he didn't know any of us but had been walking by and just decided to came in and join the fun."

"So tell me this, Sasha dear," I said. "If Nikolai were here in Odessa, working for Dimitrakos as you suggested, why wouldn't he contact you? Why wouldn't he do that?"

"I don't know."

"And where would he be living? He seems to be nowhere in the city, and no one has seen him."

"They have caves," Sasha said. "They have great caves filled with contraband in the old limestone quarries. There are labyrinths down there, catacombs. Before they smuggle people out, they hide them down there. Men in trouble pay great sums to be hidden in the catacombs. They have fitted some of them out quite nicely. Niko took me down there once to show me. It was forbidden, of course, but he did it. If he is in Odessa and working for Dimitrakos in some clandestine business, God knows what, he would probably be living in some cave down there. No one would ever know, and he would be quite safe."

"Excellent! Will you take us there?" Pasha began to object, but I waved his objections away. "Is it possible to enter without being seen?"

"I don't know how guarded it is. Everyone knows the quarries are there, of course, and boys play in them, but they don't go far in because everyone also knows they are dangerous, used as depots for contraband, and are dens of smugglers and thieves."

"Do the police know this as well?"

"Of course. But the police are paid to forget what they know."

"We have to try, don't we?" I said to Pasha. "After all this time, don't we owe it to Anastasia to look?"

Pavel Damianich rubbed his face, tightened all his muscles, narrowed his eyes. "We would have to be very prepared."

"And we shall be! We shall be extremely prepared! When would it be convenient for you to take us, Alexandra Kirillovna?"

"Anytime. I am at your service," she said. "But it will very dangerous. You must go armed."

And so we made our plans.

It was late by the time we began our return journey, and the sun was low in the western sky. As we drove eastward toward the city, the light of the setting sun made it glow, burnishing the great stone buildings set high on the ridge. How they resembled palaces and columned temples! How easy it was to imagine one was looking back through time at an ancient Greek city, perhaps Odessos, from which Catherine had taken the city's name. Then the sun sank, and the city shone with different lights as the street lamps were lit and in the houses lights sprang out into the evening gloom like lighthouse fires guiding sailors home. I lifted my eyes from the city to the lights in the sky, and then out at the lights flickering in the village houses we passed, flickering in the villas, and in the hamlets farther away, and I could see how Kirill Kantrovsky might fear for his pristine countryside, for all around the city immigrants had built villages and settlements, and even those villages were being overwhelmed by more people moving out of the city, being pushed farther and farther out for lack of room. So among the farms, gardens, vineyards and orchards, mud huts were being built, and taverns were opening, and streets and roads, not one of them paved, but merely dirt tracks, were being cut across fields and meadows by the wheels of carts, the hooves of oxen and horses, and the feet of working men. In Petersburg and Moscow, they still referred to the south as a frontier, and to Odessa as another San Francisco, a city of desperate and hungry adventurers, searching for their pot of gold.

I remembered studying the map of the world with Fyodor Fyodorovich, up in his strange laboratory above the Stardust; I remembered how he traced the sea journey Nikolai might have taken to reach the west coast of America and the city of San Francisco, a journey that would have begun here, in Odessa. I remembered thinking then how very far away it was, how very long it would take. It did not seem so far away anymore.

So I was thinking as darkness fell, and our carriage lamps lit narrow patches of the road ahead, if it could be called a road, so rutted and pitted and bumpy and slow, but there were lights in the distance, little diamonds shining out in the blackness, like a ship's lights seen shining far out at sea.

CHAPTER TWENTY-FOUR

In the Pirate Caves

"I don't understand why all those Italian ships in the harbor are flying the Russian flag."

"I see we need to educate you in economics."

"I am not so naive as to think this has nothing to do with greed."

"Economics is merely an explanation for greed."

"I see. Just as theology is merely an explanation for irrational superstition?"

"Yes. And philosophy an excuse for complacency. Progress is inevitable, say the philosophers, so we need do nothing to help it along."

"Herzen says that the idea of progress should join the other lost illusions of mankind for it is merely a secular version of religious teleology. Progress, he says, is a need, not a law."

"That is well put."

"He also notes that while Malthus says poverty and suffering have their origins in natural law and so cannot be changed by human institutions, the truth is that poverty and suffering result from human relations, and so can be changed. They are not the result of natural law, but are economic facts."

"I gather you have been reading the latest edition of *The Bell*."

"I wonder if we'll find stacks of them piled up in the smugglers' caves."

"Along with silks, opium, gunpowder, and tobacco."

It was difficult to imagine those caves from the comfort of Tatyana Andreyevna's morning room from whose windows we had a perfect view of her newly blossoming garden. We had slept well, we were drinking strong coffee, we were comfortable and safe, and we could do anything we wanted. We could leave Odessa, as Pavel Damianich had more than once suggested, and return to Petersburg. We could take ship to Constantinople. We could make the circuit of Caucasian spas. We could follow in Blavatskaya's footsteps, and trek eastward, to India. Instead, we were planning to spend the afternoon climbing around limestone quarries and into smugglers' caves. It was going to be dangerous, and we were trying hard, both of us, to contain our excitement and anticipation by talking about serious, though, at the moment, inconsequential things. But I kept my eye on the clock, I was so eager to set out on the adventure. Yet we still had hours to wait before we could leave. We were to meet Alexandra Kirillovna at a designated spot just beyond the old free port boundary line. She would direct us from there.

But time went by, as it does, and soon enough we were on our way. We had dressed warmly, we had brought two dark lanterns with us and a length of rope; we had stuffed our pockets with useful items like chalk to mark our way and matches and extra candles, cigarettes and apples, bottles of spring water and flasks of brandy; we had for arms, one cane, one hunting knife, and Pavel Damianich's old short sword, which he called his *coupe-chou*, his cabbage cutter. We hired a carriage to take us to Moldavanka, and there, under a tree some fifty meters from the gates to a rather magnificent building housing an institute for the education of noble young ladies, we waited for the arrival of Alexandra Kirillovna.

To pass the time, I asked Pasha to tell me about the family of the young woman into whose delicate, gloved hands we were about to place our lives. I knew Pasha had spent the past few afternoons and evenings since our meeting with Alexandra doing his usual investigations. He had undoubtedly spoken to a vast array of citizens, to coach drivers and denizens of various cafés, to tea house *habitués* and ladies taking their ease on park benches, to his Armenian barber and our water carrier and gardener and probably to his banker as well, and so by now knew everything there was to know about the Kantrovsky family going back several generations.

"They are Galician Jews, as you probably suspected," he said, "and originally from the city of Brody, again as one might expect. The family made large contributions to the building of the synagogue twenty years ago and they give financial support to the Jewish hospital. Kirill was born Khiram, but Russified his name when he began taking an active role in his family's banking business. His brother, Khayim, is a well-known and highly regarded goldsmith, even in a city so filled with exceptional craftsmen. Khayim has a daughter who married a Pole. Other than that, no scandal is attached to the family."

"Is it scandalous to marry a Pole?"

"Only if you are a Jew and he is not."

"What about Alexandra? Does she have a suitor?"

"Many, but she has so far delayed making a choice."

"She seems to have delayed making this journey as well."

"Perhaps it is for the best if she does not come at all. You know, dear Marko, it is extremely unlikely that we will discover Nikolai living in a smuggler's cave beneath the city of Odessa. What is more likely is that we will wander in that underworld like lost souls in Hades, and come to no good end."

Before I could respond to this dismal picture, a carriage drove up and Alexandra Kirillovna, dressed in a smart riding outfit, leaned out the window, apologized for her tardiness, and asked us to join her inside. "Only a little farther," she said. "We are nearly there."

"I had not expected to be in the country," I said as we settled ourselves in the carriage. "I expected we would be closer to the sea."

"We are close to the sea," she said. She did not elaborate but merely asked if we had brought extra candles, which I assured her we had. She seemed nervous, unsettled, and her jitteriness made me jittery too. But it was not long before the carriage stopped by an open field. There was nothing to distinguish it from any other field. Surely the driver had mistaken the place.

"Here we are," she said, opening the carriage door and getting out before Pavel Damianich could assist her. We followed, bemused. I could see nothing like a cave anywhere. We might as well be out on the steppes, the field was so flat and overgrown with grass and wild flowers. I could not imagine by what sign she had recognized it as our destination. She gave the driver instructions to go some distance ahead and wait for her there. "I will take you as far as the entrance," she said to us. "We will have to cross the field."

She walked back along the dirt road a few paces and then turned into the field on a barely noticeable path. Following that track was like wading into a sea of grass, as so many writers before me have noted who have traveled across the steppes. We followed her. Just when it seemed the track had disappeared entirely, she would find it again, though it was narrow and barely visible. However, I could see it was somewhat cryptically blazed, for every time the path forked, I noticed a stone marking the way. Still, as I looked around, I could see no possible entrance to a cave. When she finally stopped, I was horrified to find that the entrance to the catacombs was nothing but a bump and a hole in the ground.

"The contraband caves are by the port," she reminded us, "but you could not enter there because the entrances are so well-guarded. From here you can slip in behind the watchmen. This is the way Niko brought me in. I don't know where we came out. He told me he could never find his way out the same way he came in.

"It will be steep at first, and narrow. Then you will reach the mining tunnels. But as you go in farther, it will become more labyrinthine. You will descend to a deeper level near the sea, where the natural caves are. Some of the chambers are vaulted and very beautiful, but be careful there because they are also more likely to be occupied. If Niko is living in the caves, that is most likely where he will be. Don't worry about finding your way back. There are many portals out of the catacombs, all over Odessa and in the countryside. The straight, wide corridors will eventually take you to an exit. They have been made by miners who cut the blocks of stone and use oxen and mules to drag them out. If you see lights, they could be miners. Or they could be smugglers. Remember, if you can see their lights, they can see yours."

She had told us all this before. Clearly, she was well-versed in the intricacies of catacomb exploration. I had the feeling she had accompanied Nikolai underground more than once.

"You had better light your lanterns here," she said. We did as she advised. Then she kissed us both and wished us good luck, and since she was watching, she of the raven hair and the smoldering eyes, we had to look brave and competent and boldly descend.

It was like entering a tomb. The dwarf-size entrance was overhung with a tangle of grass roots. Its ceiling was so low we had to bend our necks and stumble along in a crouch, first down about a dozen stone steps, then along a steeply sloping passage. Pavel Damianich was in the lead, holding his lantern in front of him to light the way ahead; but as we walked, darkness crept up behind us and settled around us, a darkness so black no night could rival it, a darkness so black it was as though no light had ever been.

In the tightness of the low and narrow shaft, with the only smell that of damp earth, I had the strongest feeling of terror: I felt I was in my grave; I could not breathe; I had to escape, yet I could not. The roof was so low and the passage so narrow it was impossible to turn around and go back. I was about to cry out like a coward when suddenly I found no roof crushing down on me, but rather enough space overhead that I could at last stand straight, and there was a blissful sense of space and openness even in the darkness. Our lanterns, held aloft, showed we were in a large chamber.

"Thank God," I said. "I could not have borne that much longer."

"Yes. We are through the birth canal now," Pasha said with a laugh. "And here we are, out in the world."

"It is a rather dark, cold, and stony world."

"Shall we turn back?"

"Absolutely not," I said, shivering at the thought. "We must go on."

We crossed the chamber and found ourselves in a wide and straight tunnel. Soon, however, I realized that though it felt like we were walking in a straight line, the tunnel was actually veering, first one way, then another, and we were always passing openings into other tunnels. In the dark, with only the lanterns to show us the way, I could not tell if we were still in the same tunnel we had started off in or if unknowingly we had turned into a new one. Not that it mattered; we were not intending to return the way we had come. Still, I had a terror of going around in circles, and I meant to mark in chalk the places where we deliberately chose a direction in which to go. But we had not yet chosen any direction; it was too dark to see what choices we had. Instead, we meandered down one tunnel after another, with no idea where we were going, knowing only that we were underground and, were our lanterns to fail, we would be wandering these catacombs forever in the dark. So stumbling along, I searched for some source of inner strength or comfort or courage. What came to me were lines from Anastasia's little poem "To Comfort Me, They Talk of Journeys."

To comfort me, they always say
that life's a journey on which we choose
the safest paths through the darkening woods.
If so, then even I misunderstood
the perils of the way.

For there are no paths to take or leave,
we are always making our lives as we go,
wandering on, like a stream in its flow.
Who of us ever chooses a road,
knowing exactly where it will lead?

I don't know how long we wandered along those stone corridors deep beneath the earth. With no daylight to mark its passage, time played tricks on us: we might have been walking in that underworld for hours or days. Our ears played tricks on us, too, for the tunnels were so silent that every stone we crunched underfoot, every whispered word, every squeak of the lantern or tap of the cane resounded in those cavernous passages with a volume more characteristic of the sound of a marching army than of two stumbling human beings.

"A bit monotonous, isn't it?" I whispered to Pavel Damianich after we passed through yet another vaulted chamber that led to yet another narrow tunnel. "Room after room, tunnel after tunnel. I wish we'd get somewhere."

"Where, for example?"

"Oh, a café. Or a garden."

We stopped and lifted our lanterns up to see the way ahead. No café. No garden.

Soon after that the tunnel began twisting, so that it seemed we were walking inside a giant corkscrew. We took another, and it zig-zagged in a meander pattern only to dead-end in a room the size of a little box. Tunnel after tunnel led us to the same grim end. Turning back from one of these culs-de-sac, we noticed that even the roof had slowly lowered as we walked, and I began to feel that same terror again of being confined in smaller and smaller spaces. Had it only been brighter, had we only been outside in the sunshine, I might have felt more like a child playing in a fantastic boxwood maze, but there was nothing in the least charming about these damp, narrow passages that brought us into little black boxes with walls closing in on us on all sides.

We could not escape. With every step, we were lured deeper and deeper into the labyrinth. A tunnel would turn us one way, then the other, then it would simply stop. We would come to a wall; there would be no other way to go but back. But once we turned back, we were confronted with a multitude of openings and passages. Which one had we come through?

"I am defeated!" I cried at last. "We must get out! But how?"

"We must recall our goal, Marko. The smugglers' caves are near the sea. We must follow the downward slope."

I lifted my lantern and caught sight of some sign, a symbol carved on the wall. Stooping under the archway, we entered another vaulted chamber. But this one was different from the others. As we looked around, we noticed that squared stones had been placed along the sides of the chamber as though to be used as tables or chairs.

"Your café," Pavel Damianich said with a smile. "Shall we rest here? Have a drink of water? Something to eat?"

"Rather cold and damp for a café," I said. "But a bit of brandy might take the chill off."

We sat on the stone benches and drank a little water and brandy and shared an apple.

"I wonder," Pasha said, "if that mark you discovered is a sign telling miners or smugglers that there is a place to rest here, or if once it had been supplied with provisions or blankets, if it had been a kind of underground hostelry. Perhaps we are getting close to the smugglers' caves."

After resting a bit, we went on, stooping under a low archway, and found ourselves in a tunnel that was narrowing and, thank goodness, sloping downwards. Perhaps we were getting closer to the port, but we were also getting farther away from the surface and its many exits. Soon the tunnel split in two; we took the right-hand way. It ran steadily downward, and came to an abrupt end in a pile of rubble.

"They've closed that exit," Pasha said. "I wonder why."

"Maybe the roof fell in," I said, looking up. The thought of so much stone over my head was terrifying.

Up we struggled. I was tired and, worse, I was also beginning to feel afraid. I wanted to be out in the air again under the sky, which would not fall on me and crush me under tons of stone. My mouth was dry, and I was feeling the cold, or perhaps what I was feeling was a cold fear that we were trapped now in this blackness, and would never get out.

When we finally stopped to catch our breath, Pasha shone his lantern on the wall and there we saw another low archway, but I could not take comfort from it. There was no end to these archways and chambers, these culs-de-sac, these damp tunnels leading nowhere. I marked this wall with my chalk, and we went under the arch. It did not take us into a chamber, however, but only to another tunnel. This one did not run downward, but seemed to flow like a stream, lolling sometimes in one direction, sometimes in the other. The ground under our feet was uneven, rising and falling in little bumps and mounds. Clearly, it had not been smoothed by the passage of draft animals dragging blocks of stone, nor had the walls and roofs here been mined. The stone was still rough and in places it took the form of long decorated columns as though chiseled by a sculptor's hand. We could hear sounds now as well, muffled and hard to distinguish, but it certainly seemed we were getting near to some human activity, which could only mean that we had finally reached the area of the old caves.

"This is good," I whispered to Pasha. "We are nearing the sea."

The passage now took a turn, opening up into a cavern. I saw something just ahead, and only barely caught myself from crying out in delight, for at first I took it to be daylight. It was not. It was torchlight, and it was coming toward us.

At once we stepped back, darkening our lanterns as we did, taking refuge in the blackness of the cave. The men coming were speaking, we could hear their voices now, but they had not seen us yet, and so we tried to make ourselves small and still as stone. It would do little good, however, since they were carrying torches that threw a good deal of light. I was trying to imagine the words I would use to excuse our presence, when the entire troop—disappeared! They had made some turn, taken some fork we could not see… but they were gone.

Close beside me, I heard the sound of Pavel Damianich unsheathing his blade.

"What are you doing?" I whispered. "Put that away! We are here to look for Nikolai, not start a war. Do you want to get us killed?"

"On the contrary," he whispered back. "Besides, you have your sword-cane ready to hand. Are you the only one permitted to go armed?"

I could not argue. His logic was impeccable.

"Do we dare go forward?"

"We cannot go back," he said, and, daring man that he was, he slid the darkening shield away and let his lantern's light shine forth. After only those few minutes in utter darkness, even that small light seemed to illuminate the entire cavern, and to announce our presence in it. Fortunately no one was there to see us, huddling like frightened children against the wall.

"Let's see where they went," I said, and struck out boldly into the cavern, lantern in one hand, sword-cane in the other. I could not help thinking what a good story this escapade would make, should we survive to tell it. Or what a wonderful letter I could write to Anastasia about it, should we succeed. I was imagining it as we crossed the cavern, going as silently as we could. I was thinking of a happy ending, Nikolai's smile, his warm embrace, and so was not as fearful as I had been, or as I should have been.

There were many men in the next cavern. That was clear from the sound of loud voices and of all the other sounds, the usual thumping and bumping that men in groups tend to make. Perhaps they were loading things or unloading them. There was no way to slither by such a group unnoticed. But there is always another way out, Alexandra Kirillovna had told us, and in any case I was sure there were other rocky chambers all around us, all opening onto this large cavern. Where did they store their contraband? Where were the silks and spices, the stacks of tobacco leaves, the bundles of hashish and copies of *The Bell*? Where were those comfortable apartments where men who paid small fortunes to be smuggled in or out of Odessa spent their time waiting out their pseudo-quarantine here in the pirate caves? And, if Nikolai were indeed here, where would he be?

Hugging the wall, we slid behind another of those stone columns, and watched and listened. Our lanterns were no longer necessary; these caves were lit with large lanterns suspended from the ceilings and torches attached to the walls. The utter darkness of the winding tunnels had been terrifying, but the light was far more dangerous. Still there were shadows we could slip into and alcoves in the rock we could use for concealment. I had to discover the secrets of these catacombs, the storerooms, the quarters for guests, the well appointed chambers. I wondered if the men in the large cave were bringing in a shipment of contraband; I wondered what time of day it was, or whether by now it was night. It might well have been, I was so tired. I felt I had been walking for years down the empty streets of this underground city. How many miles of streets, how many little box houses, how many secret entrances and exits, all through the city, all over the surrounding countryside, how many access points to the sea?

Then, as though the cave's light had finally penetrated my dulled and benighted brain, I began to see... It came to me with the force of a revelation. I felt like someone who had been staring for hours at a rectangle of blue color and had only just recognized it as the sea. Or like a starving man who had been sitting for hours staring at a plate and only just realized there was food on it he could eat. No, no comparison did justice to the feeling I had. I wanted to shout it out. *Eureka!* This labyrinth of tunnels and caverns which small-minded men were using as a warehouse and bolt-hole was in fact a great underground city, a potential city, a city-in-waiting. Unlike the great underground cities of Cappadocia, it had no past; it was newly formed and awaiting a future. If Nikolai had walked these tunnels, he would have seen it, too—not what it was, but what it could become. And if he had seen it and grasped its full significance, he would surely have set it down in his very dangerous book. But surely he would not have been the first to see its many uses, for it was made for times of strife and war, it was waiting for such times, for invasion, for civil war, for insurrection. And if others were already thinking those same thoughts, perhaps going further, perhaps incorporating the catacombs into their plans, and Nikolai had written about it, how dangerous his book would be!

These thoughts flew through my mind as we slipped under a stone archway. Then Pavel Damianich thrust me hard against the wall, into the shadows. We were standing at the mouth of a cave, the very sort of Ali-Baba cave I had imagined thieves and smugglers would have, the floor covered with rich carpets, the walls with tapestries, the tables with boxes of gold, the furnishings with sparkling, jewel-encrusted brocades, a veritable treasure trove, the sort of chamber one might find in a Pharaoh's tomb. The richness of the room took my breath away. But as I looked, taking a measure of the incomparable wealth set out before us, something else caught my eye. Sitting on a throne-like chair at a grand table in the center of the cave, light from golden candelabra shedding a warm glow all around her and giving her black hair a gleaming iridescence, was a woman who bore an uncanny resemblance to Alexandra Kirillovna Kantrovskaya.

CHAPTER TWENTY-FIVE

La Donna é Mobile

Pasha had seen the woman, too, and pressed me gently backwards, deeper into the embrasure of the archway. We were caught now between cavern and cave. From the large cavern behind us, we could hear the hum of men's voices, and from the cave in front of us, magnified by the acoustics of the rock, the sweet tinkling of Indian bells, and the sputtering of coals in the brazier at the woman's feet. The brazier reminded me of how cold I was, while the perfumed scent of oriental incense that so thickly pervaded the air made me fear I would soon begin to sneeze.

Then the woman, who had been gazing down at something on the table in front of her, lifted her face and looked right at us, or rather toward us, for I was sure we were quite invisible to her, hidden as we were deep in the embrasure of the archway. Not for the first time that day, I caught my breath in surprise. She was beautiful, this woman who was not Alexandra Kirillovna, but enough like her to be an older sister and, given that she was sitting like a dragon amidst the treasures of a pirate cave, undoubtedly more dangerous.

"Yurochka?" she called out, but since neither of us was named Yurochka, we did not reply.

Pasha gestured to me that we had to go back. Going back meant easing our way into the large cavern, and from there, through the chain of caves and caverns, into the labyrinth. This escape route held no appeal for me. I wanted to leave by the front door. And now I was intensely curious. Who was this woman who so resembled Alexandra Kirillovna? What was she doing here? Still I hesitated to step into the cave and reveal our presence. One man involved with us had already died; these smugglers had killed another man on the beach. They had no scruples, they did not mind spilling blood. What would keep them from killing us if they chose to, and dropping our bodies into the sea, which is what they must have done with the dead man on the beach?

I had not yet moved, but was still standing in the embrasure, pressed up against the stone wall, when, darting with the speed of a small animal, a man rushed by us and into the treasure cave. His movement so startled me I very nearly cried out in surprise, and even Pasha, always so steady, jumped a bit as the figure passed. It was a miracle he did not notice us, but it appeared he had eyes for no one but the woman at the table. Pasha gripped my arm and pulled me backwards into the adjoining cave.

Here there were many of those stone columns that appeared to be suspended from the cave's roof, and so there was an ample supply of places for us to conceal ourselves while we crept along in the deep shadows close to the walls. Unfortunately, a group of men had decided to squat down amidst the crates and bundles strewn around them, and drink something from a bottle. They were outlandishly dressed for such a group of scoundrels, and, evil as they undoubtedly were, one could not help but imagine that they had acquired their wardrobes by looting the costume wagon of a traveling opera company. One wore bright pink pantaloons, a richly brocaded waistcoat, and a red fez; another, an old Hussar's uniform decorated with lace-and-frogging, complete with fur-trimmed pelisse, a red silk scarf tied over his head, and gold rings in his ears; a third was wearing a sheepskin coat over bright blue breeches. Seeing them drink reminded me how thirsty I was, how hungry, how tired, and how cold. We squatted down, too, behind a fat, bulging sort of stone, watched with envy as they emptied their bottle, and listened with curiosity to what they had to say. Sadly, I could not understand a word of it. In a city where thirty or more different languages could be heard on the streets, it wasn't an unusual experience to be unable to follow other people's conversations. Odessa was not a good city for eavesdropping. I could not even determine what language it was, and I wanted to ask Pavel Damianich if he understood it, but of course I could say nothing to him. We were too close to them; indeed, we were close enough to smell them, and what they exuded was not a pleasant perfume.

After a while—long enough for my bones to fully absorb the cold and damp and for my legs to cry out to be stretched—Yuri, if that was his name, emerged from the treasure cave and barked at his entourage, and like faithful dogs they all struggled to their feet and followed him out of the cavern. I wanted to struggle to my feet as well, but Pavel

Damianich ordered me to wait, and he was right. Within minutes the woman appeared. She wore a pearl-encrusted dolman over a dress with heavily jeweled sleeves, an ancient sartorial style reminiscent of the Byzantines. Regally bejewelled and barbarically perfumed, she swept across the cavern and disappeared through one of its several archways.

Without a moment's delay, we pulled each other up, and padded after her in the hope that she might lead us to the apartments we were seeking. These caves were clearly in use. They were well-lit and also well-guarded. I had just begun to wonder whether we had chosen the best course of action, when she disappeared through a very narrow crevice in the rock wall. If I had not seen her slip through it with my own eyes I would never have detected its existence, it was so camouflaged by the surrounding stone wall. Pavel Damianich tried to hold me back, but I was determined to follow her, so putting down my lantern and gripping hold of my cane, I squeezed through the opening in the wall, and emerged on the other side.

What greeted me was a gaping hole in the rock, the mouth of the cave, and before it, in a great open space, a scene that might have come directly from the stage of an Italian opera: a group of cut-throat ruffians, pushing and shoving, gathered around the figure of Little Yuri, fair-haired, red-faced, and very angry, who was barking at them, in some form of Russian. Would he begin to sing his aria? Unlikely. Instead he gripped hold of one scoundrel's arm, pulled a pistol from his belt, and began waving it in the air while the others scrambled about, yelling vociferously. Since escape in that direction seemed impossible, I slithered back into the crevice, and hidden from their view, watched them carefully. Pasha had his sword in his hand, and by the gleam in his eyes, I knew he was ready to use it. I tightened my grip on my cane. Meanwhile, Yuri seemed to be finishing his invective, his roaring was becoming less full-throated, and for a moment he even paused. In that moment, and in a tone of authority, a woman's deep, sonorous voice said, "Yuri Mikhailovich!" Instantly, every other voice ceased, and all eyes, including our own, turned to the glittering faux-Alexandra, whose Byzantine headdress alone was probably worth a tsarina's ransom, and who had just stepped forth from the shadows. "I wish to leave. These men are standing in my way."

Immediately, Yuri directed a roar toward the scoundrels, and they

COUNTESS MORA SABANSKA

Instantly, all eyes turned toward the glittering faux-Alexandra who had just stepped forth from the shadows.

dispersed to the sides of the cave as swiftly and nervously as sheep, leaving a broad avenue for her majesty. I was surprised that no red carpet was flung down at her feet.

"Timur!" she called. Instantly a huge turban-wearing, pink-pantalooned scoundrel stepped forward and bowed. Yuri bowed low as well, and kissed her gloved hand. Then, with Timur walking several paces behind her, she strode across the cavern and out through the mouth of the cave. It was a most dramatic exit.

And having seen it, and appreciated it, we squeezed ourselves back through the crevice and conceal ourselves in the cavern as quickly as possible.

"Shall we continue our search?" Pasha asked in a whisper. "Or would you prefer some fresh air? We might attempt to leave by the front door."

"But how can we?"

"Look!" he ordered. And I did. To my surprise and delight, the cave was emptying before our eyes, the pirates dispersing in different directions. Their exodus was swift; they lifted crates and bundles and disappeared rapidly through various passages.

"I believe some air might do us both good," I said, and so, clutching our weapons, we ran with all speed across the open space and out of the mouth of the cave into the sweet air of the night. The sun had set, and the moon was shedding her silver light on the smooth stones. I could hear the sea lapping against the beach and smell the briny sea air and hear the last calls of the sea birds, and, by God, I was glad to be above ground and alive!

We found ourselves on a stony plateau from which roughly carved steps led steeply downward toward the sea. We did not want to take that route, and evidently neither did the lady and Timur. We could see their lantern light heading in the opposite direction, away from the sea. They were going toward what appeared to be a sheer stone massif, a great wall of stone. We followed behind them.

Even with the moonlight, it was hard going without lanterns of our own; we had left ours behind in the caves. Scattered all around were blocks of cut stone and piles of rocky debris left from the days when this had been an active quarry where men had hollowed out the very bluff upon which the city stood. We had to do a good deal of climbing and scrambling around them, all the time keeping Timur's lantern in view as it bobbed about, weaving its way across the stone-strewn plateau.

Then, at some distance in front of us, the twinkling light began to rise. It was something wondrous to see, and magical, like watching a star ascend. We soon discovered why it was happening. At the foot of the massif, a well-trod path led up from the quarry to a set of rickety wooden steps. Faux-Alexandra and Timur were climbing these steps, and we followed faithfully behind them and so at last reached the top of the cliff. Thank God, we were back in the city now, perched hundreds of feet above the world below like birds of prey gazing down with keen sight and cool indifference at the old quarry, and the port, and out to sea. A few more meters along a dusty trail brought us to a road.

There a carriage was waiting, the horses already hitched in readiness, the driver smoking, as drivers in this city are wont to do. I myself would have enjoyed to sit high in a driver's seat, and smoke a cigarette, and drink from my flask, and so I looked on him with envy, and wondered if I would have been happy with a life like his, and wondered if he could imagine living a life like mine. I suppose none of us knows in the least what other people's lives are like, even those closest to us, for each of us has his secret universe, populated by his own memories, embellished and burnished over time, and his very own loves and hatreds, desires, compulsions, obsessions, terrors, beliefs, longings, fantasies, miseries, and sources of joy. How could one imagine living in another man's skin, thinking another man's thoughts, having another man's friends and lovers and children? We were each of us a world in ourselves, a world deep and full and rich and entirely inaccessible to others. I was meditating on such thoughts when Pavel Damianich completely undermined them by reading my mind and offering me his cigarette case. Meanwhile, Timur had fastened his lantern to the carriage, helped the lady of the caves climb into it, and taken his place beside the driver. The horses whinnied, the carriage rocked ever so slightly, and pulled way, leaving behind it only darkness and dust.

"Now what?" Pavel Damianich asked.

"Now we walk," I said.

"Why didn't you ask her to give us a ride? You are losing your touch, Marko."

"Not at all, I just thought we needed a little more exercise. We have been far too sedentary today."

We lit our cigarettes and began walking down the road.

"I still feel like an outlaw or a rebel, smoking on the street here," Pavel Damianich said wistfully, blowing a stream of smoke into the air. "It is so frowned upon in the capital."

"Everything pleasant is frowned upon in the capital, and smiled upon here. Now, tell me, Pasha, confess! Didn't you think for a moment that that woman was Alexandra Kirillovna? Our own Sasha, with a slightly different face, and probably a very different soul?"

"There is a striking similarity, I grant you, yes. A family resemblance."

"Perhaps a cousin. Perhaps the scandalous cousin who married a Pole."

We trudged on. We were coming close to populated streets where if we were lucky we might find a cab willing to take us home. Soon we found ourselves on busy, café-lined Deribasovskaya, where in the warm spring evening people were strolling arm-in-arm, or sitting over a coffee, chatting and laughing. A young man passed us, whistling "*La donna è mobile,*" and the tune was taken up by another man passing in the opposite direction. Suddenly I felt light hearted, but I was light-headed, too, having gone so long without food.

We stopped at a small restaurant for supper before making our way back to Tatyana's house. It had been a long and tiring day, a rather frightful day, a day that had raised many questions and provided few answers. I did not think I would be able to sleep for thinking of them all, but I was wrong.

"It is too bad that we left so much undone yesterday," Pavel Damianich said the next morning over breakfast. "I'm sure you'll want to go back to the catacombs today and finish exploring."

I always appreciated his sardonic wit first thing in the morning, but in fact I had been thinking seriously about the same thing. We had much more to learn. I wanted to find out who the woman in the cave really was, yes, most avidly I wanted that. But I had an idea I wanted to pursue, an idea that might require investigating the Polish-Ukrainian Revolutionary Committee, and for that I would need Pasha's help. He did not seem to be in a very helpful mood. But Pasha liked to talk, and I knew if I asked him some questions, he would enjoy answering them, and so be better disposed to do whatever unpleasant or impossible thing I later asked of him.

"Have you ever been to Cappadocia, Pasha? Do you know about the underground cities there?"

"I have not been there, but I have read about them. They were built under the Byzantines during the time of the Muslim wars. Some are even older. They have multiple levels, three, sometimes five, and on these various levels there are vaulted chambers connected by a web of tunnels. They have built chapels, stables, storage areas, work rooms and living spaces for five or ten thousand people, maybe more. In times of trouble, people take all their worldly goods and disappear underground until the trouble is over. I recall reading that they are ventilated by air shafts and their water supply comes from deeply dug wells. They are also cleverly defended. Great boulders can be rolled to seal off entry ways, and there are hidden pits and traps throughout the mazes, and stashes of arms."

He knew many other facts about these cities—where exactly they were located, how they were built and expanded, how the Greeks in Cappadocia managed to maintain their religion and language despite living under Ottoman rule—and I listened to him with interest as I always did and drank my coffee without interrupting. When he had finished, we sat in silence, contemplating the resourcefulness of mankind.

"Let me guess what you are thinking, Marko," he said after awhile. "You are thinking Odessa's caves are a great resource, and wasted on smugglers and thieves."

"I am thinking that under certain circumstances they could be put to better use than they are."

"What sort of circumstances? I can't see the population of Odessa seeking shelter in the catacombs in the event of a Turkish invasion. Or a British-French invasion, for that matter."

"Not if they had any warning, no, of course not. They would simply evacuate the city and retreat onto the steppes. But in case of such an invasion, you might hide an army of defenders down there. Or, alternatively, in case of insurrection, an army of insurgents."

He did not reply to this.

"Pasha, I know you sometimes think I get fantastic ideas, like a writer of romances, although I do not write romances, as you well know—"

"Forgive me. I did not mean my silence to be interpreted as a criticism. On the contrary."

He got up and walked across the morning room to the window. I took the opportunity to help myself to one of his cigarettes.

"But, no!" he said, coming back to the table and throwing himself into his chair. "What you are thinking is a completely mad idea."

"Tell me, please, what you think my mad idea is since I haven't yet told you what it is."

"If I know you, you are thinking thus: Odysseus Dimitrakos and others of his ilk use the caves for illicit business purposes, but they could as easily lease them, so to speak, to other interests. One interested group might be the Polish nationalists. The Poles are planning an uprising; there are Poles in Odessa willing to support such an endeavor; they need to get men and arms into Warsaw. We are very close to the Moldavian border here. The Dniester is an easily navigated waterway into Galicia, and from there into Poland."

"True. But I am not thinking simply about Dimitrakos expanding his smuggling operation. I am thinking something else." Even thinking these thoughts made me nervous. I got up and looked into the hall to be sure we could not be overheard. I did not mistrust Tatyana Andreyevna's servants, but when one is raised in a police state one always takes precautions, no matter how absurd and unnecessary they may seem.

Pasha was smiling at me when I returned to the table. "You have that look,' he said. "I fear I am about to be exposed to some subversive ideas."

"Indeed you are!" I said and laughed at him for suddenly I was feeling quite gay "This is my thought and it is so simple I can hardly believe I am the first to consider it. Listen, Pavel Damianich, and you will hear: Poles are not the only men who want their freedom. We Russians want our freedom, too. As for Ukrainians, I have spent a good deal of time in the Ukraine, and I can assure you that Ukrainians are also desirous of freedom. And you yourself informed me some time ago that the Poles and the Ukrainians have joined together and formed a Polish-Ukrainian Revolutionary Committee, right here, in Odessa."

"So you imagine... what exactly?"

"Only that if there is ever another Polish uprising, how useful it would be if there were a Ukrainian uprising at the same time, and if it began here in Odessa."

"Another fascinating idea. How would it be? While the Poles attack Warsaw, Ukrainian partisans, having concealed themselves and their caches of arms in the caves, stream out and seize the port. They take the heights, they raise the flag—do they even have a flag?—they recite the patriotic poetry of Taras Shevchenko. Their Russian comrades join them and together they overthrow the autocracy and bring freedom to us all. Alas, Marko, I know very little about Ukrainian history, but I do know that Poles and Ukrainian Cossacks have been slaughtering each other time out of mind. What could possibly unite them now?"

"That one, eternal truth, that the enemy of my enemy is my friend. And despite the conflicts of the past, at the moment the common enemy is Russia. Russia partitioned Poland, and Russia absorbed the Ukraine without abiding by any of her promises to give Ukrainians their independence."

"Oh, what a story it would make!" Pasha said with admiration. "Imagine it... Well, evidently you have."

"Yes, I have. I wonder if Nikolai imagined it, too. I wonder if he also thought it would make a good story."

"Ah," Pasha sighed. "I see now why this interests you."

"I am trying to piece things together, that is all. If anything like this were happening, Nikolai would not have been able to resist putting it into his book. No wonder he made Alexandra Kirillovna swear not to speak about it."

"But it isn't happening, Marko. It's only a story."

"Of course, at the moment it is only a story. But it is not unknown for a story to start a war, or inspire one. And you must admit there are some suggestive elements. For example, how did Nikolai—working in a taverna for a Greek smuggler—ever come in contact with a banker's daughter, Alexandra Kantrovskaya? Isn't it likely he met her through her cousin's husband, the Pole? How else? The Pole had dealings with Dimitrakos, and through Dimitrakos the Pole met Nikolai."

"Alexandra Kirillovna said he came uninvited to her cousin's birthday party, and, from what I know of Nikolai, it seems just the sort of thing he would do."

"Come now! Do you seriously think they would allow someone like Nikolai to walk in on such a very exclusive, very special party, just off the street like that? No, the cousin's Polish husband invited him. They already knew each other. They met in Dimitrakos's caves."

"Where the Polish husband was busy plotting a Polish uprising. Well, it is excellent story-telling, my dear, but it is story-telling nonetheless. You are writing fiction again, dear Marko. It might become a brilliant novel—it has romance, adventure, intrigue—but it is a fantasy. I think there is something about caves that tends to inspire such poetical fantasies."

"All right. Say it is a fantasy. Say Nikolai was inspired to create a similar fantasy. Say he imagined a use for the catacombs, say he imagined a secret conspiracy, an uprising, a revolutionary base hidden deep underground—"

"But according to what Margarita Mikhailevna told you about Nikolai's book, it is all about drug addicts and hallucinations."

"She read only a small part of it. She doesn't know what the entire book is about. How could she? And you do see, don't you, how dangerous it could be for him to write about something like this."

"Yes, I do see," Pasha said with a sigh, "So now I suppose we shall have to visit Alexandra Kirillovna again and ask about her cousin."

He did not like taking carriage rides onto the steppes. He would rather be pickpocketed on Greek Street or lose heavily at cards. Our steppes bored him. He had read Baudelaire and it had ruined him for such mundane pleasures as watching grain grow or contemplating grazing sheep.

"I expect she will send us a note today," I said, soothingly. "Perhaps she'll be in town."

"And after we see Alexandra, you will want to visit her cousin. And then we shall have to arrange that... And that will lead to something else, and that to something more. Marko, I must advise you again and urge you most strongly to leave Odessa as soon as possible. And by as soon as possible I mean today or at the latest tomorrow. I implore you."

"Well, then. If we must leave no later than tomorrow, we had better get going, because we have a great deal to do today. We must find the woman, yes? *La Donna é mobile, qual pluma al vento.* I would rather find Nikolai, of course. Oh, Pasha, what if he's here?"

It was a question to which there was no answer, an exclamation needing no response. If I knew he was in Odessa, or even had a good reason to suspect he was, I would not budge until I found him. But I did not know, and it was the not-knowing that was so hard to bear. So I would compromise with Pavel Damianich. I would leave as he demanded, but not today and not tomorrow. I would give myself two full days. If I did not find a trace of Nikolai in two days, then we would leave. As to where we would go next, that I would leave in the hands of the Fates.

Before we finished our coffee, a note from Alexandra Kirillovna arrived just as I had predicted, inviting us for dinner that afternoon, not at the villa, but at the family's house in town. Sasha had written that she was eager to hear about our adventures of the day before, but I noted with satisfaction that she had been careful not to mention where those adventures had taken place.

Alexandra herself welcomed us at the door, delighted to see us, but anxious to warn us that we would not be having the intimate dinner she had hoped. There were several other guests whom her mother had invited, and a few members of the family had also dropped in unexpectedly. We would not be able to speak freely at dinner, but, she assured us, these guests would not stay long.

"Perhaps we should return later, then," I said. "I would not mind in the least, and it might be safer to do so."

"Not at all, dear Marko! I could not have you leave!"

"But how will you explain our presence to your mother? How will we have made your acquaintance?"

These were the very questions I had been asking myself about Nikolai and his introduction to the Kantrovsky family, and I was interested to hear how she would reply. Her response was instant and admirably well-rehearsed.

"Why, you are Marko Volchek! We have all read your stories and novels; we are all great admirers. So when I recently learned that you were a guest at Princess Volkonskaya's, I felt emboldened enough to write to you and invite you to dinner, and you graciously accepted my invitation, you and your companion, Pavel Damianich."

"Well done," I said. "Have you really read my stories and novels?"

She smiled sweetly at me. "Of course. I have read them all."

With that, she led us into an opulently furnished drawing room where the guests had gathered waiting for dinner to be announced. We were first introduced to Sasha's parents. Her father was a stern man who gave me such a reproving look that I felt inclined to make my excuses and depart at once; her mother, however, smiled most graciously and immediately offered me a sweet. Of the other guests, there was an archeologist named Osip Kobyakov, a sugar merchant named Abraham Brodsky, and Sasha's uncle, Khayim. We had barely time to make their acquaintance when another guest arrived, at which point I lost any interest I might have had either in sugar beets or Scythian burial mounds.

She swept into the room the way she had swept out of the smugglers' cave, with that same proud, swift stride.

"My cousin," Alexandra Kirillovna said, presenting her.

And so we met Countess Mora Khayimyevna Sabanska.

Her black hair was as lustrous in daylight as it had been in the torch-lit caves, her clothes were as lovely, though today they were encrusted with far fewer jewels. She looked me up and down with interest, but with no sign that she had ever seen me before, though when she gave Pavel Damianich her hand, she smiled at him in a much friendlier and more familiar way.

Almost immediately dinner was announced and we passed through a lavishly decorated hallway into a large dining room and took our places at the table. I was seated between Uncle Khayim and Cousin Mora. Alexandra sat across from Mora and beside Osip Kobyakov, the archeologist. Farther down the table, talk was all about interest rates and sugar production, but at our end, it was about gold dug up from underneath the earth. On this subject, Kobyakov had many interesting and amusing stories to tell.

"The ancient past is so fascinating, isn't it?" Mora Khayimyevna said, turning to me while the soup bowls were cleared, plates of watermelon were set out before us, and there was an appreciative pause in the archeological conversation. "I wonder, have you ever thought to write about it?"

"The ancient past holds no interest for me as a writer. The more recent past, yes, perhaps I will write about it someday."

"Yes, you must wait until the present changes so that the more recent past can be written about truthfully." She smiled at me somewhat wistfully as though I were a beloved child who had disappointed her hopes. "Yet I have recently read a novel about Petro Konashevych Sahaidachny, the seventeenth century hero of the Ukrainian Cossacks, that was both truthful and inspiring. Though perhaps you would not think of the seventeenth century as the recent past."

Now it was my turn to consider her with interest. Sahaidachny had led a Cossack army to the walls of Moscow in support of the King of the Polish-Lithuanian Commonwealth. He and his Cossacks had slaughtered their way to Moscow and slaughtered their way back.

"Who is the author of this novel?"

"A Polish writer. Michal Czaykowski. Do you know of him?"

"Under the name Sadyk Pasha, yes. I was unaware that he wrote novels."

"He did, when he lived in Paris. They are all very popular."

"Not in Russia."

"No, not in Russia."

"Mora, dear," Alexandra called from across the table. "What is the name of that place where you saw the Scythian tombs?"

"The *kurgans*?"

"Yes."

"Well, they lie about us everywhere around here, don't they? They are always underfoot."

The archeologist laughed at this remark.

"But the ones you told me about," Alexandra insisted. "The special ones. Oh, I remember now. It was a place called Kelermes, in the Kuban. You had a feeling about them, remember?"

"Whatever feeling I had is long forgotten," Mora Khayimyevna said, piercing a piece of pink watermelon with her fork. As she was impaling the melon, her father leaned over me to address her, and said, sharply in Ukrainian, "Say no more about this."

I am by no means a linguist, but Ukrainian is a language I understand.

"I know Kelermes," I said, insouciantly. In fact, I had never heard of it. "One does get a very special feeling there. Do tell us about your experience, Mora Khayimyevna."

Beside me I could feel her father bristle. I wondered why he didn't want this subject discussed. Kobyakov, sitting across the table, was also looking a bit uncomfortable.

The third course was served.

"Myself," said the archeologist, "I prefer the *kurgans* of the Ukraine. The excavation in Alexandropol is most interesting. Luchenko from the

Kerch Museum of Antiquities and Bukhteev from the Odessa Society of History and Antiquity did the work."

"Ah, that's where they found fourteen horse burials, didn't they?" Mora said with a laugh. "That's the sort of thing that sticks in the mind. Buried with one's horses. Now I would prefer being buried with my hats!"

"You have such lovely ones," said Uncle Khayim. "My daughter spends all her money on hats. What do you think of that, Madame Markova?"

How brilliantly Mora had managed to change the subject!

So while we ate our spring lamb and refreshed our palates with mouthfuls of sweet, succulent watermelon, we talked of millinery subjects: Parisian styles, the mysterious disappearance of the straw bonnet, and the resurgence of the hat in its many variations: hats with crowns, hats with brims, hats with ribbons and feathers, hats with felt and lace. Parisian hats might have brought us back quite naturally to French novels, or Polish novels popular in France, but instead it led to different topics altogether: the joys and discomforts of travel, travel by rail versus travel by sea, the horrible ordeal of the quarantine.

"The quarantine is unbearable," Alexandra Kirillovna asserted. "I would rather be smuggled into the city inside a crate."

"Is it possible to be smuggled into the city in a crate?" I asked, sounding, I hoped, both ignorant and innocent. "I would think it might be quite dangerous."

"It certainly would be, considering who would be doing the smuggling," Khayim said sternly. "From what I understand, it is operated by criminals, for criminals."

"So such a thing does exist, Papa?" Mora Khayimyevna asked. "I had no idea."

"Don't be absurd, Mora!" Alexandra said with a laugh. "Of course you know about this! Why, they use the old quarry—"

"I confess, I have heard about the quarry and the caves, but I have never in my life been near them. Certainly, Sasha, you never have either."

In a moment, Sasha would have admitted having visited the catacombs, and heaven only knows where that might have led. Fortunately, Pavel Damianich, who had been unusually silent during the meal, launched into a story about a journey he had once taken to some caves in France, and from there the conversation drifted to other topics, thankfully unrelated to caves, caverns, smugglers, or the discomforts of quarantine, until the appearance of dessert.

Dessert was our undoing.

At the other end of the table, Abraham Brodsky and Kirill Kantrovsky had been talking about grains and sugars, selling and buying, borrowing and lending, or whatever bankers and sugar merchants talk about at dinner, but at the arrival of dessert, the inevitable Turkish sweets, the conversation turned to more familial topics.

"How is that husband of yours, Morishka?" Kirill Kantrovsky asked. "Where is he this afternoon?"

"The husband of mine is quite well, Uncle. As to where he is this afternoon, he is on the estate, working."

"I am surprised he stays. I am surprised he does not return to Poland," Kirill Kantrovsky said. "All things considered."

"What things are those?" Mora asked. "I can't imagine why you would think he should leave, especially at this time of year. "

"Mora, please—" Khayim began, but the Countess was irritated and, ignoring her father, continued to address her uncle. "I have told you many times, Uncle, that my husband does not share the views of *his* uncle, who paid a heavy price for his devotion to the cause of Polish freedom. My husband is a more cautious man, a man who believes in profits not patriotism. Whether you agree with that position or not—"

"We agree entirely," her father said

"Not all of us!" cried a voice from the end of the table.

"Myself," Kirill said, somewhat grandly—it was, after all, his house—"I approve of the Pole who said Jews can fight as bravely as Christians, and put them in his legion to fight, and they did fight, very well. They were just fighting in the wrong war. Jews should not fight with Poles for the liberation of Poland. Jews should fight with Jews for the liberation of Palestine."

"Hear, hear!" said Abraham Brodsky. "Some day, God willing."

"The Greeks succeeded in freeing their country," Kirill continued. "Why not the Jews?"

"The Ottomans are weak. Unlike our Russians, who are strong," Kobyakov said. "Like the Greeks, the Jews might win, who knows, but Poles never will. They would be fools to try again."

"They would," Kirill said. "Let's hope your husband is not one of the fools."

"Mora's husband's uncle supported the Rising," Alexandra informed me in an undertone. "His property was seized and he was exiled from Odessa."

Meanwhile tempers were rising all around the table.

"My husband is less a fool than you, Uncle," the Countess said, angrily, "with all your talk of a Jewish homeland. It is far more likely that the Commonwealth will be restored than that the Temple will ever be rebuilt."

"The Commonwealth will be restored, though," said that voice from the far end of the table. The speaker was a small man who had come late and to whom I had not been introduced.

"Don't talk nonsense, Troinitsky," Khayim shouted down the table. "You only upset everyone with your talk."

"It isn't talk!" Troinitsky shouted back, quite loudly for such a little man. "Hotel Lambert still exits. Prince Czartoryski still heads the national government in exile. The struggle still goes on." Suddenly, he jumped to his feet and shouted:. "For our freedom, and yours!"

"Nonsense!" someone said quite loudly, and Brodsky took Troinitsky by the arm and lowered him back into his chair. Many people were talking at once. In the midst of it, Mora leaned over the table to Kobyakov and said, again in Ukrainian, "Are they ready?"

"Yes. I have them," he answered. "Let us meet after."

Hearing this, I had to struggle within myself to suppress a visceral desire to flee—flee the table, the room, the house, the city itself. Conspiracy was all around me, on every side, and who could tell, among such people, who was an honest fool and who a government spy?

Madame Kantrovskaya rose from her chair. Dinner had finally come to an end.

We had left the table and were walking back down the hallway to the drawing room, when Alexandra, who had taken my arm, said in a low voice, "Now that dinner is over, we shall finally be able to have our tête-à-tête. I am eager to hear all about your adventure yesterday."

"Where can we have this conversation?" I whispered back. "There are so many people."

"What adventure are you two whispering about?" Mora Khayimyevna, coming up behind us, asked with a laugh. "Some secret rendezvous? Some *affaire de coeur*?"

Alexandra denied any such romantic assignation. "On the contrary," she began, and, as my heart sank, she blurted out, "Madame Markova went into the catacombs yesterday. I am eager to hear all about it."

"Did you indeed?" Mora Khayimyevna asked, smiling her treacherous smile. "How intrepid of you! I must hear all about it, too."

"She is terribly brave," Alexandra said, squeezing my arm. She was proud of me. She was happy to present my achievement to her more sophisticated but far less intrepid cousin who by her own admission had never in her life been in the caves or even near them.

"Where are we going, Sasha, dear? To your room? I'll ask for tea to be brought in, shall I? I am terribly thirsty."

So instead of returning to the drawing room with the others, we went along another corridor to the family's private rooms.

In Petersburg, every building is a microcosm of a country estate, divided by income and class into the spacious apartments of the rich and the squalid little rooms of the poor, and always in the same manner, with the well-to-do living on the first and second floors, and the poor in the cellars and the attics. Odessa was no different, though the buildings being lower, the rich had to make do with one floor rather than two. Such was the case in this apartment, which expanded horizontally rather than vertically. Sasha's room was far in the back of the building, equally away from the noise of the guests and the noise of the street, with a view of a small garden below. We entered the room, we sat at a small table by the window, made ourselves comfortable and waited for the tea. Meanwhile, Sasha was saying far too much, about me, about the quarries. Of course, she had no reason to suspect her cousin of being—whatever she was.

While Sasha spoke, I watched Mora carefully. She was very good at lying, I had to admit. I had seen her in the cave with my own eyes, I had seen her with Yuri and the pirates; yet, she almost convinced me that my eyes had deceived me and that she had never entered the quarries in her entire life. As an actress, she was skilled and talented. But what role was she playing? Was she a respectable married woman playing at being a bandit queen, or was she a bandit queen playing at being a respectable married woman? What did she have to do with the archeologist, Kobyakov? What was her husband, Count Sabanski, really like? Was he only a Polish grain merchant, as she portrayed him to be, or was he the patriot she insisted he was not? If only he had accompanied her to dinner, I might have been able to make a guess. Now with Sasha, she was acting the role of older cousin, teasing her and indulging her whims, flattering her. Before we could speak confidentially, we had to wait for the tea, and in the meantime, Mora had to approve of and admire Sasha's new hat—"All that talk about hats at dinner, I just have to show you this new one, Mora!"—and she had to agree to accompany her cousin to a new shop on Catherine Street, and she had to give Sasha her opinion about a new perfume… I listened to them chatter, and I could not tell who was the better actress, for this Sasha was quite a different young woman than the one I had met a few days before.

Finally a servant arrived not with tea, but with a pot of coffee and a decanter of a liqueur.

"Now," Mora said when we three were alone again, "about this adventure…"

"Yes, tell us!" Sasha urged, smiling at me. Then turning to Mora, she added, "Madame Markova has been looking for an old friend of hers, who also happens to be an old friend of ours. Nikolai Barakov."

"And looking for him in the old quarries?" Mora asked lightly. "How very odd. Did you find him?"

Her voice was light, yes, but her look was dark, and there was something slightly threatening about it, though I might have been imagining it. I did feel a slight chill, and I even looked to see if a window was open and a breeze from the sea coming in.

"Sadly, no," I said. "But we hardly spent any time in the caves at all. They terrified me."

Sasha's expression changed from expectation to disappointment. "What a pity!" she said. "You remember Nikolai, don't you, Mora?"

"Nikolai Barakov? Let me think. Oh, yes. Your friend, the sailor."

Now the chill in the room was even stronger. I looked from Mora to Sasha to see if she had felt it, too. It appeared she had not.

"Yes, I remember him, vaguely," Mora continued. "Anyway… it was years ago. Yet here you are today, Madame Markova, looking for him! But why search for him in the caves? They are such dangerous places. One even hears of bodies being found in them." She paused for a moment, rather dramatically I thought, lifted the lid of the coffee pot, and peered in. "I wonder that it would even occur to you to look for him there, or how you would know how to enter them. Though I suppose the entrances to the quarries are well known in some circles."

As she spoke, she busied herself moving cups, sugar bowl and creamer from the tray to the table. She had beautiful hands, with long fingers adorned with gleaming gold rings and precious stones. She was altogether a magnificent woman. I wondered what it was she so ardently wished to know. And then she simply asked:

"I would think no one would be down in those grim tunnels. Did you happen to see anyone at all?"

"No," I said. "We saw no one."

"Good. For one hears such terrible things about the caves. Had you met the smugglers—good heavens!—you might not have gotten out alive."

She smiled at me, disarmingly, and began pouring coffee into our cups As she was doing so, her elbow bumped against the sugar bowl, knocking it to the floor.

"Goodness! What an oaf I am!"

Sasha bent down to retrieve the bowl and gather up the sugar cubes. Most of them had fallen nearer to me, so I felt obliged to help her.

"We'll have to sweeten our coffee with liqueur," Mora said. "I'll pour a little into our cups, shall I?"

While she did, I asked her how well she knew Nikolai Barakov.

"I hardly knew him at all. He was Sasha's friend, wasn't he, dear? What do you think of the coffee? Is it too bitter? I think it is. We really need more sugar, Sasha. Would you be a darling and ask Galya to bring us some?"

The Countess had choreographed this scene perfectly, and I was extremely curious to see what she would do once Sasha was out of the room. Still, the transformation she underwent the moment we were alone surprised me greatly. She turned to me with an expression of intense sincerity, and, speaking rapidly, as though she could not contain herself any longer, she said, "You are in grave danger here. You must say you are feeling ill and I will offer to take you home. Please believe me."

I was not inclined to believe her.

"What danger—?"

"Does the name Pavel Beriosov mean anything to you?"

It was a shock to hear his name after all these months.

"He is here in Odessa. He knows you are here, too."

"But why—?"

"Why am I telling you this? Listen to me, Madame Markova, you who love Nikolai Vasilevich. I love him, too. I love him, I broke his heart—yes—but I love him still. For his sake, don't endanger yourself, but come with me now. I will say I am taking you home."

At that moment, Sasha came back into the room.

"Madame Markova is feeling unwell. I am leaving now anyway, so I will take her back to Princess Volkonskaya's in my carriage. Do let Pavel Damianovich know, darling. Now, come with me, Madame Markova. You'll feel much better once we get outside."

In fact, I was feeling unwell. Something strange was happening to me. I found I could barely stand. Both Sasha and Mora Khayimyevna had to help me to my feet, and once I was standing, the room began to spin. Looking down at Mora's hand on my arm, I understood why. Perhaps it was insurance in case she was not able to persuade me to go with her, but she had surely used that little diversion with the sugar cubes to drug my coffee, and I even knew how, for I could see that one of her rings opened on tiny hinges just like the golden monkey her father had made for Sasha. The poison ring was still slightly open, though seeing this was of no good to me, since I had lost my ability to speak. I could say nothing to Sasha, I could not protest, it was as though all my muscles were melting away.

How the rest happened I cannot say with certainty. A servant came and, directed by Mora Khayimyevna, carried me down the back stairs and through the garden to a coach which was waiting in the alley behind the house. My legs were utterly unable to hold me up, and I could not cry out for help. As I was lifted into the carriage beside Mora Khayimyevna, someone passed in the alley whistling that catchy little tune from *Rigoletto,* so popular these days, *La Donna é mobile*. It was the last thing I heard.

Chapter Twenty-Six

The Many Lives of Countess Sabanska

That same afternoon, while the Kantrovsky family and their guests were gathered around the table, dining, Major Semyon Semyonovich Semyonovsky was at home in his study, working at his desk. As the afternoon wore on, he dealt with his correspondence, wrote several letters, reviewed a report to the Minister, and finally glanced through all three local newspapers, the *Journal d'Odessa*, the *Odesskii vestnik*, and the *Odesskii almanakh*, reading thoroughly and carefully certain articles that he felt warranted his full attention. What he was really doing, however, was waiting.

Major Semyonovsky was a handsome man, a sociable man, and a shrewd one, a good host, an entertaining raconteur, an excellent judge of horses and of men, but his most valuable asset was his ability to wait, as he was waiting now, calmly, without anxiety, without impatience, with the full confidence of a man who had faith in the effectiveness of his own skills. So when his mistress finally entered, late as she often was, he was not perturbed in the least. He was happy to see her, as happy as she was to see him. These separations were unpleasant, but there was no reason to extend their unpleasantness by giving even a moment over to moodiness or chagrin. In this, as in most things, they were of the same mind.

"How was dinner, my dear Countess?" he asked, helping her off with her cloak, kissing her cheeks. "Your family is well, I trust?"

"I ate too much and drank too much. Is there tea?"

"I doubt it," he said, and laughed at her. The samovar had been ready for some time, but he did not tell her that. He only wanted to kiss her, and he did.

"Oh, Senya, I have so much to tell you!"

"Surely it can wait."

"Of course," she said. "But I have met Marko Volchek."

"Have you indeed! You are a wonder."

He held her in his arms, his beautiful Jewess, most beloved... and most dangerous. One could take an agent to one's bed, but one must never take her to one's heart. Still, she was lovely. He was an excellent judge of women, too, was Major Semyon Semyonovich Semyonovsky.

"Was your husband there?"

"No. The Count remained on the estate to oversee the harvest."

He kissed her hair, her neck, her throat. He felt a shudder pass through her body, that first response to his lovemaking that despite himself nearly always drove him mad with desire for her. It was a piercing and erotic thrill he found impossible to resist. Marko Volchek would have to wait.

"What is she like, this George Sand of Russia?" Semyonovsky asked some time later. Mora Khayimyevna, sitting up in bed, her dark hair lying in rich waves over her shoulders, was finally having her tea. "One hears such things."

"About Marko? What sorts of things?"

"Oh, that she is ugly and masculine, sharp-tongued, a virago."

"An Amazon?" Mora laughed lightly. "She is none of those things, although she is an intelligent woman and so frightening to someone like my uncle, who doesn't care for women in trousers and waistcoats who know a thing or two about stocks and can put a sensible sentence together. He was not pleased with her at all."

"Well, my stock will rise at the Ministry once Beriosov learns she's in Odessa. He's had a bee in his bonnet about that woman for some time."

She laughed lightly at that remark. "What does he want her for? She surely is no threat to the state."

"She has information he wants."

"Which she is unwilling to give, I take it."

"Evidently. He tried once... but she escaped."

"Escaped? From Beriosov?" Now she laughed harder. "Oh, my dear, you must admit..."

"Yes. Well, the *affaire de Volchek* is a dark operation. It is unofficial... until it succeeds. So his humiliation, though widely known, is not officially known."

"You mean he is not being officially laughed at. Still he is in a vengeful state of mind, I imagine. Well, she is here, staying at Princess Volkonskaya's. She has only a male companion with her. The household servants are old and won't put up a fight."

"I doubt he intends to arrest her here. He can't arrest her anywhere, really. He has no official orders."

"I see. Well, what can I do to help?"

"Nothing right now. Let's see what he says when I inform him that she's here. See what he wants me to do, if anything."

"I can't imagine what it could possibly be about, Senya. She is a writer of romances and adventure stories. She dresses strangely, yes, but that is a mere affectation. She seems so perfectly harmless."

"What did you discuss at dinner?"

"With Marko? Let me see. It was all quite unremarkable. We talked about hats. Parisian fashions. Oh, a book I read recently. A book she read recently."

"What book had she read recently?"

"Herodotus."

"Herodotus! In Greek, I suppose."

Mora smiled at him. "You will want me to maintain this relationship with her, I imagine. I could invite her for tea."

"Yes, do that."

"Shall I invite you as well?"

He shook his head. "As pleasant as it sounds, talking over tea about Herodotus and hats."

"Oh, there is one more thing I took note of at dinner that I thought might interest you. Apparently there is some illegal digging going on around those burial mounds that were excavated recently in Alexandropol."

"Hardly my area of concern."

"I just thought I'd mention it."

"Well, yes, it's good you did. I'll pass it on. Nothing said about Poland, I take it?"

"Not a word at dinner, no."

"Not a word at dinner. But… there was a word?"

She sighed and sipped her tea. "It is all so vague, Senya."

"My darling, everything we hear is vague at first. Now, tell me what you heard. No matter how inconsequential it seems."

"Apparently Stanislaw Rzewuski has written to Paris."

Despite his amazement, even shock, at hearing this news—Rzewuski, a traitor?—Semyonovsky remained utterly calm.

"To Czartoryski? You are sure?"

"I haven't seen his letter. But I have it on good authority."

"Your husband?"

"No. I don't believe he knows, and if he does, he did not tell me. He would be terribly upset by this news, and undoubtedly deny that it's true. It is such a shock. Rzewuski has always been loyal to His Majesty. His entire family has been. I found it hard to believe myself, but the source is impeccable."

"Who is the source? Tell me."

"I received a letter from my husband's sister who mentioned it to me. Stanislaw's own sister had told her. They are all very close-knit, those Poles."

"Close-knit in their conspiracies. Close-knit in their treacheries. Well, my dear, this is information worth exploring. It could be nothing. Rzewuski may be writing to Hotel Lambert merely to curse them for the fools they are. Or perhaps Prince Czartoryski contacted him for some rapprochement of his own. He must be nearly in his grave by now. Perhaps he's decided to make his peace with His Majesty. Such a gesture would be well-received."

"Shall I tell Adam what I heard from his sister? I hesitated to do anything until I spoke to you, my dear."

"How do you suppose he will react?"

"He will be enraged. He will confront Rzewuski and break off relations with him. He wants no more trouble for the family. He never forgets what his uncle suffered in '31."

"Then best say nothing. If Rzewuski is indeed writing to make contact with Hotel Lambert and that conclave of Polish rebels, then we will want to watch him carefully. I am afraid a confrontation with your husband might flush him out too soon. But write back to your husband's sister, show some slight interest, see if you can gently prod a bit more out of her."

"Ah, so much work!" Mora sighed, smiling at him, teasing him. "It makes me weary just thinking about it. Anyway I must leave now, *mon cher*. I'm sure I have some sort of engagement tonight. Perhaps it's the opera."

"What a life you lead!"

"Yes? And you, Senya? What terrible and weighty tasks await you tonight?"

"Oh, a bit of drinking. A bit of gambling."

"With Beriosov?"

"Beriosov! No, Morisha, sweetness, Beriosov is far away in Petersburg. Not likely he'll come here either. He'll send orders."

She got up then and stretched and began to dress, slowly, almost lazily, the way a cat upon waking will slowly stretch and lazily begin to lick its fur. He sat at the edge of the bed, fully dressed himself, and watched her until she asked for his help and he was able to touch her again, re-fastening what he had loosened, lacing up what he had pulled apart. He wanted to loosen everything again and feel her soft body in his arms once more. With effort he restrained himself, and with as much self-discipline as he could muster, led her to his door and watched her go.

♣

Adam Sabanski, a lean, middle-aged, bespectacled man, had also been working at his desk that afternoon. He, too, had dealt with correspondence, all involving business, and also with grain orders, bills and receipts, and complaints from his bailiff, giving the charade he was forced to live his full attention, for many lives besides his own depended on his maintaining it.

When he heard his wife's voice in the hall, he was filled with relief and happiness, but he, too, managed to disguise his feelings, for, as usual, there were guests in the house whom he did not entirely trust. So instead of running down the stairs and greeting her, as he would like to have done, he remained in his study and waited for her to come to him. All he did by way of welcome was to set out two glasses, a soda syphon, and a bottle of brandy.

The moment she strode into the room, her face flushed with excitement, he knew what had happened, and knowing, he jumped to his feet, threw his spectacles onto the desk, and rushed to her. Throwing his arms around her, he lifted her off her feet and swung her around with the energy and strength of a much younger man.

"Adam! Put me down!"

She was laughing gleefully, like a child.

"You have succeeded! I know you have! Ah, Morashka, darling, tell me everything!"

"All right, I will if you stop squeezing me. And give me a drink!"

While he made their drinks, she unpinned her hair and loosened her clothes and stretched out on the divan.

"It has been a very full day."

"You have managed everything perfectly, I'm sure. Now, tell me. What's still to be done?"

"Very little. I've already delivered the gold to my father, the pieces I acquired from Yuri."

"Which he obtained from the Kelermes *kurgans*?"

"Yes. It pays to cultivate the friendship of thieves. Then today, Kobyakov gave me his drawings. All the details are beautifully rendered. And since my father now has some of the original Scythian work as models, he will have no problem reproducing the tiara. Are you still set on bringing it to Paris?"

"I wouldn't trust anyone else with it."

"Once the tiara is sold, we will have all the money we need. Oh, Adam, it will be a fortune!"

"It will be a considerable sum and we'll put it to good use. You have accomplished this brilliantly, my dear. And your father is not opposed to doing this work?"

"He doesn't know for whom he is doing it, of course. He thinks Kobyakov intends the tiara as a gift to the archeologist Alexey Luchenko, a token of his esteem, and a means of propelling his career forward. The sort of thing my father understands." She sipped her brandy and soda, a new kind of drink just imported from France along with the cognac. It was very good. "Then I stopped to see Semyonovsky and delivered the message for you. It amazed him that Stanislaw Rzewuski could be in contact with Hotel Lambert."

"Of course it did. But did he believe you?"

"Oh, yes. He wanted to, and so he did. I also told him that if you ever found out that Rzewuski was a traitor to His Majesty you would be so enraged—your loyalty to His Majesty being so great, your hatred of rebels likewise—that you might do something rash."

"And perhaps I will. Hah! How I would enjoy going after him with my cane!"

For a moment, he allowed himself to imagine this encounter. If only they could snare Stanislaw Rzewuski in such a trap—what a perfect act of just revenge it would be against a man who had betrayed the cause of Polish independence for his own advantage. Even the mere suggestion that Rzewuski was in contact with Hotel Lambert, seat of the Polish government in exile, would be enough to set the tsarist hounds on him, for Russians never trusted Poles no matter how loyal to the Tsar they might appear. And what joy that would give Polish patriots everywhere! What joy he would feel himself, what sweet revenge that would be!

While he considered this, Mora studied him. He was looking older, yes, and there was a touch of grey in his black hair, but it didn't matter, she would never tire of looking at him or admiring him. He had been her savior, just as he would one day be the savior of his country. Saving the lost... that was his life's work. But it was dangerous work, and he had not wanted to share it with her. How she had managed to convince him, how she had overcome his objections—that it was no work for a woman, that Poland was not her country—still amused her whenever she remembered it, for it was a brilliant strategy that had come to her quite out of the blue. They had been sitting in this very study, years ago now, and again he was being chivalrous and refusing her help, when she had laughed at him and told him to go and read the Bible. "Think of Judith, and Esther, and Ruth. I may not be an Eve to you, dearest Adam, but I will be a true helpmate, and always stand beside you, and fight for your people as though they were my own."

Remembering that, she smiled at him.

"Anything else?" he asked.

"There are a few more items of interest."

"Yes?"

"That writer Semyon has been trying to find—Marko Volchek, who is really a woman named Valentina Markova—happened to be at dinner today."

"*Happened* to be?"

"Sasha invited her. Sasha collects writers. You know how she is."

"So you have found her for him. Was our major delighted to hear this?"

"Extremely delighted."

"What will he do with her?"

"He's awaiting orders from Petersburg. But he will have waited too long. I intend to send her on a little journey. She will disappear from Odessa."

"Good. Anything else?"

"Yes," she said. "I'm afraid so. Adam, you must do something about poor Mateusz Troinitsky. He spoke up again at dinner. Yes, we were at home, and he probably felt it was safe, but he frightens me. He has no self-control."

"All right. I'll deal with it."

She smiled at him. "I think that's my report for the day, my dear Count. May I have my supper now?"

"If supper is what you want, you shall have it."

"In an hour?"

"In precisely an hour."

They kissed at the door, and parted.

Zuzana, a Polish woman in her mid-thirties, was not only Mora Khayimyevna's maid but her spy in other households, those they happened to visit and those in which Zuzana's friends worked, for Zuzana was a trusted servant whose family had served the Sabanskis for generations. Now, after helping Mora Khayimyevna undress, bathe, and dress again, this time in a simple gown, she obeyed her mistress and took a seat on the divan to await further orders.

"I have a particularly dangerous task for you, Zuzana," the Countess began. "You may refuse it if you wish. It will require you to travel."

Mora Khayimyevna described the particularities of the task, and Zuzana agreed to accept it without hesitation. It did not seem too dangerous to her. She had lived through the bombing of Odessa. Nothing could hold much terror for her after that.

Once Zuzana left to prepare herself for her journey, Mora sat down at her dressing table and unlocked a shallow drawer. From the drawer, she took a rectangular object wrapped in deep blue silk and laid it on her lap. Gently, almost reverently, she caressed the silk; its blue was the exact color of his eyes. Then with great care she unwrapped the bundle, revealing the manuscript's title page. *Wide and Crooked.* His play. Carefully she turned the pages, smiling at some of the more imaginative marginalia, until she found the scenes he had written and inserted the last time they had been together, the scenes featuring his new villain, the golden-tongued and traitorous Semyon Semyonovich.

Oh, Nikos, Nikos, why did we ever part?

She knew the answer: fear.

Yet how she had loved him, how madly she had loved him long ago when they were young, before the war! They had been so in love, they were like children at first, utterly without fear, heedless of consequences. She had even gone into the catacombs with him, and he had told her amazing stories there, tales of pirates, corsairs and buccaneers hiding in the tunnels, of Ukrainian freedom fighters living secret lives below ground, of holy saints hiding in the crevices, and magicians and alchemists working wonders in their caves. He had thrilled her with stories, he had won her heart, just as, she knew, she had already won his. Of course, her family would never consent to their marriage, so they made plans to elope.

He was working as a crewman for Odysseus Dimitrakos then. He would sail on the *Sosa* as far as Trebizond, a city busy enough with its own concerns to take little notice of them, and wait for her there; she would follow on the next passenger steamer to Constantinople. It was such a romantic idea, to rendezvous in Trebizond, to marry there and set off on great adventures together, to travel the world.

So he sailed away from Odessa, trusting that she would follow him. But when the time came to book her passage, she lost her nerve. It was impossible to leave her family and go off with a madman—for Nikos was quite mad, always full of wild plans, always telling crazy stories, and he had no money and no prospects, his father had given away all his land to his serfs, or was planning to, and Nikos himself had no desire to make his way in the world, for he had nothing but disdain for careerists and sycophants and men who only cared about wealth and power. It was the very thing she loved about him, that madness, that wild abandon. She loved it, and she feared it, and so, suspended between fear and desire, she stayed where she was, in her parents' house, listening to them make their own plans for her, ones she hated but was not strong enough to resist.

Yes, it was her fault, hers entirely, she alone was to blame, she had been weak and afraid... and so she had not boarded the steamship to Trebizond, she had not kept the rendezvous, she had sent him a letter instead and broken his heart. He told her that years later when they met again, confessed it to her without recrimination or resentment, as though it were a case of some near-fatal war injury which he had survived, though with the loss of a limb, a disability he had learned to live with over the years and which now did not bear mentioning.

It was then, during his last visit to Odessa, when he found her married to a rich man, a conservative Polish count, that she had to make a confession of her own and break the code of silence and tell him everything, the whole truth: her parents' plans for her marriage to a rich banker whom she despised; her inept attempt to end her life; her introduction to Count Adam Sabanski; his gallant offer of a fictitious marriage; his secret work for the Polish government in exile; their plans for another rising; her own clandestine work as a spy; the necessity of her involvement with the abhorrent Major Semyon Semyonovich Semyonovsky. Hearing about that, his outrage at the count was so intense she had to work hard to calm him, to physically restrain him from rushing off at once to challenge him or whip him like a serf, he deserved no less. His intentions toward the major were equally murderous. His ferocious anger, when it blazed up like that, fierce and frightening and righteous and raw, reminded her of why she had adored him when she was young.

It should not have surprised her—yet it did—that she found herself falling in love with him all over again, for he had not changed, not in the least. Unlike so many other men, he had not been crushed or made bitter and cold-hearted by living in such terrible times; he had not lost the nobility of spirit and passionate nature of his youth. And so, as though no time had passed, they were lovers once again. He told her about his life, he told her about his novel, he even showed her the part of it set in the catacombs, a part he had written at such a distance from her, knowing nothing about her life with Adam or their plans, that reading it almost frightened her, it was all so uncanny, the way he had predicted everything: using the caves to hide partisans, and the tunnels as escape routes; employing smugglers as guards, guides, and foils.

"How do you know all this?" she had asked, seized with dread and the terrible fear that all their plans had been betrayed.

"Come now, Mora!" he said, smiling at her. "It's all pretty obvious. You do realize that, don't you?"

But when she read about the partisans robbing the Scythian tombs of their gold and creating a faux-tiara to sell to effete French aristocrats to obtain money for guns, she laughed, the idea was so fantastical and amusing, so whimsical.

"Where did this idea come from, to make a tiara out of Scythian gold?"

"What are you talking about? Don't you remember? We thought it up together."

Then she did remember.

Nikos had such a talent for devising illicit schemes for making money; it was he who had dreamt it up. It involved raiding the *kurgans* in Kelermes for some bits of ancient gold—"No security anywhere, not a guard in sight!"—and then finding a goldsmith who could create a barbaric tiara in the Scythian style. "And we won't have to look far for someone like that! If you can't persuade your father to do it, you can certainly persuade his apprentice." The next step would be the easy part: taking the tiara with them to Paris, and selling it to the Louvre. "They'll never know the difference, and we'll make a fortune, Mora, my love! We'll be rich as Croesus and we'll live in style in one of those grand French hotels!"

"I do remember now," she said, laughing. "I thought it was such a splendid idea."

"I still think it's a splendid idea," he said, smiling at her. "Just don't use it to help that damn Pole."

And now, she thought, smiling to herself, remembering those blissful few weeks with him, here it was, two years later, and she *was* using his idea to help the damn Pole. He would be furious if he knew.

And now, too, Marko Volchek was in town, looking for him, sending the Frenchman around, upsetting everyone—Dimitrakos, Yuri, even Kobyakov had heard and become alarmed. Steps had to be taken, and would be taken. But if Nikos's friends were that concerned, he must have gone missing some time ago. Two years ago he had left without a word. Could something terrible have happened to him then? This was the question whose answer she needed to know.

Right now, though, Adam was waiting for her. She would eat supper with him; she would go to bed and sleep. Marko Volchek was safe enough for now.

"Marko Volchek will trouble us no more, I assure you," Countess Sabanska said, shifting her parasol a bit, and making herself more comfortable on the bench. Before her, the sea was rippling and sparkling in the morning sun, overhead the new leaves of the great plane trees were rustling in the breeze, and sitting near her—fortunately, not too near—dressed in his old fashioned frock coat and pretending to be reading the *Journal d'Odessa*, was Odysseus Dimitrakos. Having spent the night before thinking so much about Nikos, she could not help but hear his voice in her head now, and his laugh: *We have to stop meeting like this*. But she certainly did have to stop meeting Dimitrakos on Primorsky Avenue. This had to be the last time.

"I had hoped to frighten her away," he said.

"Evidently she does not frighten easily."

"I lost a good man."

"That had nothing to do with us."

"It had to do with your cousin."

"I am not my cousin's keeper... But, you are right. Fair is fair. How can we compensate you for your loss?"

"My dear Countess, you misjudge me. I am not here to ask for compensation. In sending Black Perikles to Marko Volchek, your cousin intervened, innocently, no doubt, in a surveillance operation of ours."

"You were watching Marko? Why?"

"Not Marko. We were watching that Frenchman, the one asking all the questions. For reasons of her own, no doubt, having nothing to do with us, your cousin sent Perikles to that house, an innocent man, having no intention of betraying us to French Intelligence—for that Monsieur Paul de Bourguignon is a French spy, or so we have reason to believe. Yet there Black Perikles was, and there our men were, with strict instructions to let no one from the catacombs pass... and there it was, an unfortunate result, as you know. It is no one's fault. These things happen."

"Really, Odysseus, you amaze me! Can you seriously believe that Madame Markova's little pet is a French spy? Your absurd suspicions will be the death of you one day, as they were the death of poor Perikles. And what of that other incident? By your taverna?"

"That? That was of no importance. Merely business.."

"Your drug trade is your own concern, Odysseus. We appreciate all you do for us. We are thankful."

"Your thanks, dear Countess, is more than enough."

"Nevertheless, pray accept this small gift from us. Perhaps for his family." She laid the book of poetry she was holding down onto the bench beside him. "The cover gives little indication of the riches within."

"My deepest thanks, Madame," he said, slipping the book into his coat pocket. "If there is anything I can do for you—"

"There is one thing. You might tell me what you know about the disappearance of Nikos Barakov."

"Barakov? I know nothing. It is what I told de Bourguignon, and Madame Markova."

"It may be what you told them, Odysseus. But what do you tell me? The truth, if you don't mind."

"Ah, Countess... It's true, I did make inquiries of my own."

"Go on."

"It bothered me, you see, that the French should send an agent here asking about him. *If* they did send him, *if* he is a spy. But if he is, then I have to ask why. Why do they want to talk to Nikos? What does he know? Well, yes, Nikos knew a lot about my business once, but that was years ago. Has he returned to Odessa? Is he here now? So I began asking around, and what did I discover? History. Only history. Two years ago, he was seen in the city, but not since. He told his friends he'd been living in Petersburg, but he was not planning to return there. Said he was planning to get himself a berth on a Stambouli steamer and ship out. One day he did, and no one has heard from him since. But I learned one thing more: that right now, all kinds of people are talking about him because of some book he's written, a dangerous book full of secrets, or so they tell me. And that is all I know, Countess, and that is God's truth."

"You spoke to friends of his?"

"I did, yes."

"Was one of them Black Perikles?"

"Yes. In fact, yes."

"The man who is now dead."

"Yes, Countess. Purely a coincidence, I assure you."

"To whom else did you speak?"

"Let me think... Petrov, the poet. He's the one who told me about the book. He's a great keeper of secrets himself, but this secret he could not keep under his hat. And Plitov, of course, the barkeep at the Five Friends."

"And these men have not heard from him since he was here two years ago?

"Not a word. And I believe them. Nikos is not one for staying in touch. What is your interest, Countess, if I may ask?"

"I have no interest. Only curiosity. Thank you for satisfying it."

"My pleasure, Countess. If there is anything else you need..."

"Yes. I will contact you."

Without looking at him or saying another word, her interest in Nikos Barakov, like all her other interests, perfectly concealed behind an imperturbable facade, she rose from the bench and strode off down Primorsky Avenue, a lovely woman, holding her parasol aloft against the harsh rays of the morning sun.

Some time later, a steamship bound for Istanbul left the harbor. By then the wind had come up, the sea was choppy, and most of the passengers stayed in their cabins. One woman in particular, who had been ill even before she boarded—nothing contagious, merely a migraine, but one so severe it required her to seek the darkness of her cabin immediately upon boarding—was not seen on deck at all that day, nor, in fact, at any point during the entire voyage, for, according to her Polish maid, who cared for her most devotedly, she suffered terribly from *le mal de mer*.

BOOK
SIX

THE Final Dispensations OF Fyodor Fyodorov

CHAPTER TWENTY-SEVEN

Of Monkeys and Mushrooms

"Oh, it's a monkey! Natasha! Come and see! Look at the monkey!" Misha was jumping up and down, and pulling on her hand. He had excited everyone—Madame Marie, his brother Sasha, the stall-keeper, the people standing about, even the monkey himself, who was jumping up and down as well, pulling on his little chain, and, instead of chattering sweetly as monkeys should, was making horrible screeching sounds. "Oh, do look!"

Natasha looked and felt very sorry for the monkey who, it was quite clear, desperately wanted to be free and run around and knock things down and swing from awnings. The big parrot was upset now, too, and was screaming at everyone in Italian—the vender had bragged that he was the only Italian-speaking parrot in Petersburg ("Only one hundred rubles, Madame. Only one hundred rubles!")—and all the other birds were fluttering in their cages and those who could squawk were squawking and those who could not were chirping loudly in distress. Only the finches seemed unperturbed and were singing lustily, poor little things. Oh, how she wanted to open their cages and free them, for it was spring at last and every living thing in the world wanted to be free, to fly, if they could, and sing in the treetops. Yet how much better it was to see these living creatures, caged or chained though they were, than the poor dead and frozen animals that were sold at the markets in the winter. She had written a poem about them, but it had not turned out well.

Madame Marie had finally calmed Misha down, and the vender had calmed the monkey by giving him a piece of fruit, and now Natasha could look at him more closely. He was small and furry with a clever face and bright eyes. He looked, indeed, like he understood everything that was said to him, and made quick and accurate judgements about everyone around him. She felt he could be friendly, but also deceitful and even malicious. She took his measure and decided she did not like him. He, meanwhile, was eating and chattering, almost laughing, and any minute he would begin doing tricks. He was a performer, and no doubt wanted to be purchased and freed from the constraints of market life. Surely it was no fun for him to be on display all day, chained to a stall in Stock Exchange Square.

"Ah, Obezyana," a man's voice said behind her. "He's quite the entertainer, isn't he? He will ride around on your shoulder, if you let him. But better not. Once he gets comfortable on your back, he'll never want to get off."

She recognized the voice, and turned to him with a smile.

"Fyodor Fyodorovich! Good day to you."

"Good day to you, too, Miss Natalia. Madame Marie. Sasha, my boy. Misha!" They had all gathered around him, the boys shouting out happily, recounting their adventures with the monkey, and earlier with a dancing bear, while Madame Marie, apologizing for their behavior, tried herding them as best she could. Natasha just smiled at Fyodorov and waited for her brothers to move on. One stall over was a giant tortoise she felt sure would attract their attention, and very shortly, it did. She took Fyodorov's hand and stood with him behind the others.

"We have not seen you for so long," she said.

"Not so long. It was only a few weeks ago. But time is relative, and goes at different rates of speed for different people."

"Does it? So two weeks seems long to me, but short to you?"

"It depends entirely on which two weeks. If I am waiting for a letter from a friend, two weeks can seem very long indeed."

She considered this idea with some care.

"My grandmother is waiting for a letter from my uncle, so time must go very slowly for her."

It was odd, he thought, that Nikolai was now in both their minds, though in his case it had been because of the monkey.

"How is your dear grandmother?" he asked.

"I don't know. I haven't seen her in a very long time. But we are going to Oak Hills soon. In a few weeks." She smiled up at him. "They will go very slowly."

"I'm sure they will seem to, my dear. I, too, am traveling to the country soon. Alexander Felixovich and I are going to visit your grandmother's friend, Princess Volkonskaya."

"You're going to High Meadows! That's wonderful, dear Fyodor Fyodorovich! Then we shall surely see you in the country because Aunt Tatyana always comes to visit us, and you shall come with her! That will be lovely!"

They had reached the tortoise stall and Natasha let go of his hand to get closer to the huge creature. Fyodorov waited a few minutes, watching the three children and feeling the bemusement a man like himself feels when he finds himself suddenly and unexpectedly taken up by a family and included in their lives. It had happened so easily, almost naturally. He found it inexplicable; yet, he took great pleasure in it. A child taking hold of his hand—it was an extraordinary feeling, and filled him with an utterly unanticipated joy.

It was Azara who had thought of visiting the Chernovs, for he was sure that if anyone knew where to look for Nikolai it would be a member of his family. He had met Sofia Vasilevna only once, and briefly, when he was living with Nikolai, but as Nikolai's friend, recently arrived in Petersburg, it would be rude of him not to send his card to Sofia Vasilevna and it would be natural to expect at the very least an invitation to tea. As it happened, he was invited to dinner, and, with Sofia's permission, he brought his friend, Fyodor Fyodorov, along with him. In so far as they had hoped to get news from Sofia Vasilevna about Nikolai's whereabouts, they were deeply disappointed, for she knew less than they did, but they enjoyed their dinner and were quite taken by Sofia Vasilevna and Ivan Ivanovich and the children, especially Natasha. Sofia was equally glad to hear their reminiscences of her brother. A week later, they received a second dinner invitation, and after that, they were frequent guests, and were even encouraged to stop by whenever the spirit moved them. In this respect, Azara said, Sofia Vasilevna was following in the tradition of her parents, whose home was always open to friends and acquaintances, and who never kept to the strict and burdensome formalities of social life.

After watching the children for some minutes, Fyodorov called out to their governess, "Madame, I must go. Please give my regards to your mistress. Children, enjoy your afternoon. I will see you soon." And waving goodbye to them, he continued on his way across the square. He had an appointment with another of Nikolai's relatives, his other sister's husband, Arkady Ulanov.

It was this other sister, Irina Vasilevna, who intrigued Fyodorov, and in particular, it was her husband, Arkady Andreyevich Ulanov. Ulanov worked for the Ministry of Justice. He had contacts in the Third Division and even claimed to be an acquaintance of Pavel Beriosov. Irina, a charming woman, though somewhat dreamy and naive, seemed quite unaware of her husband's work and associates. Not so Sofia Vasilevna, however. She knew very well what Ulanov's politics were, though it appeared clear to Fyodorov that even she assumed that, as he was a member of the family, Ulanov would use his position to protect Ivan, if need be—and Nikolai, if need be—and that, despite any official offers or inducements, family ties would always act as a restraint on his ambitions. Fyodorov had no such expectations. He did not like the man or trust him, but he believed he could make some use of him since he loved to show off his connections and was easily flattered into revealing whatever secrets had been entrusted to him. News of the inner workings of the Third Division was hard to come by, so Fyodorov, that very afternoon, was meeting Ulanov at his club.

Natasha turned away from the tortoise and waved goodbye to Fyodor Fyodorovich. What she wanted to do was skip along beside him and talk to him the way they had talked when he last visited her house. It did seem like a long time ago, but she would never forget it as long as she lived. She had written a poem about it and memorized the poem; that's how she would never forget the visit, or what he had said to her, and how happy it had made her. Because Fyodor Fyodorovich knew Uncle Kolya, knew him very well, and could tell stories about him, and agreed with her entirely that Uncle Kolya could easily be on a quest to rescue Princess Zinaida—or someone equally beautiful and worthy and in need of rescue. In fact, Fyodor Fyodorovich knew of a real princess who loved Nikolai so much she had traveled a huge distance in a magic carriage just to find him. Her name was Margarita.

"So is he really lost?" she had asked. "Is everyone looking for him?"

"Many people are, yes."

"People who love him? Or people who want to hurt him?"

"What makes you say that, my dear? Why do you think anyone

would want to hurt him?"

"I hear things, Fyodor Fyodorovich. They speak and I hear. I can't help it."

"Ah. So you have heard them talking about someone who might hurt him. They did not say who it was, did they?"

"No. Just that he might be hiding from them, whoever they are. He might have left the country. Are you looking for him, too?"

"I am, yes. He's my friend, you see, and I have something that belongs to him."

"What is it?"

"A play."

"A play! What sort of play?"

"A play he wrote."

"A play he wrote! Oh, how wonderful! I want to see it! Does it have firebirds and angels and flying carpets and queens in velvet gowns and lots of singing?"

"No, it's a different kind of play. Not quite so much fun, I'm afraid."

Then he laughed his funny, half-stifled laugh, which frightened her a little when she first met him because of the unfamiliar sound—more like a groan or a grunt—but which she now knew was just his way, though it was not anything like the loud and jolly laughter she was used to.

There were other odd things about Fyodor Fyodorovich which had frightened her a bit at first, but which she now found quite endearing, his habit of muttering under his breath, for example, a mumble which sometimes burst into discernable words—"Bombast!" he had muttered far too loudly once—and then his loquacious apologies, which were often more confounding than the original interruption. One thing she had loved about him from the start, however, was his little notebook which he carried in his waistcoat pocket and which he pulled out and wrote in at any time the fancy took him, even at the dinner table, something she herself was never permitted to do even when a poem came to her while she was eating a strawberry ice.

"When I am an adult, I will write at the dinner table, too," she had told him, in confidence. "I will only eat the foods I like, I will only go to sleep after midnight, and I will travel everywhere and see everything there is to see in the world."

But that was a different conversation on a different day. The day she wrote her poem they had talked about Nikolai and the magical Princess Margarita who had traveled so far to find him, and who was still looking for him. That was what the poem was about. It was really a sad poem, though it was a happy poem, too. Sadness and happiness were never too far apart, she thought. It was the oddest thing of all.

"You don't know my grandmother?" she had asked him once in amazement after he said something that suggested he did not. "But you must! You are so much alike!"

When he asked her to explain what she meant, she could not do it.

"Only that I talk to you the way I talk to her," she said after thinking about it for awhile.

He said, quite seriously, that he had never received such a compliment. "Your grandmother, Anastasia Alexandrovna, is one of the great poets of our time. Her work is incandescent, luminous, incomparable. What a joy it must be for you to be loved by her, and to be able to talk with her. I am deeply honored and touched, dear Natalia, that you think me to be like her in any way. I thank you for such a compliment. I will treasure it."

He was a very odd man indeed.

"But you must meet her," Natasha had insisted. "Perhaps she will want to meet you, too, since you know Uncle Kolya. Perhaps you will come to see us in the country and she will receive you. That would make all of us happy."

Now that would come true! Fyodor Fyodorovich was coming to Oak Hills. He must come! He would be visiting Aunt Tatyana, and Aunt Tatyana would bring him with her to Oak Hills. Anastasia would see him, and he would tell her about Nikolai and that would make her happy.

But still the questions remained. Where was Uncle Kolya? Why could no one find him, not even Princess Margarita in the poem Natasha had written:

Her sledge flew high, and quick as flame,
for finding Nikolai was her aim.
His deeds had won him great acclaim,
in every town, she heard his name.
To rob the rich was his favorite game,
but he gave the gold to the poor and lame,

to hungry children to end their pain,
and he fought the bandits who kill and maim,
and the evil landlords we all disdain.
For this he earned the greatest fame,
and never was the least to blame.

"Where are you, Prince? Have you lost your way,
in the dark forest where the light is grey,
or in the hills where the shepherds stray?"
So she called him, as all men say,
flying high in her magic dray,
like an osprey circling, or a bird of prey,
crying, "Come with me, Prince, let us fly today
to Istanbul or Mandalay!"
But though she searches over field and bay,
and loves him dearly, and for him prays,
she cannot find him in the night or day.

The poem continued in this vein for several pages. Natasha loved rhymes, but still she felt the rhyming made the poem suffer, constrained it somehow, as though it was caged like the birds or chained like the monkey, and she was eager to talk with Anastasia about it, for only another poet would understand the vexing relationship between sound and meaning, form and content, which she, Natalia Ivanovna, at nine years of age, was struggling with for the first time. For words and rhymes could take you to places you didn't want to go, as they had done, unexpectedly, in a stanza at the end of the poem, quite independently of her intention, which began its rhyming with innocent words like bread, led, and wed, but ended quite terribly with shed, bled, and dead.

❧

Vexation was nothing new to Arkady Andreyevich Ulanov. He was plagued with more problems than any man alive, and foremost among them was his wife, Irina Vasilevna, and her family, his family now, more difficult people it would be impossible to imagine—Vasily Yakovlevich, the mad *pater familias,* who spent all his time in the woods with a band of crazed *Dukhobors;* Anastasia Alexandrovna, the little empress of the family, who could not write a line anymore and never came out of her attic; Ivan Ivanovich, his brother-in-law, the professor, whose own views and whose students' antics might well ruin him and bring his whole family down with him; and most difficult of all, Nikolai Vasilevich, Irina's ruffian brother, her scandalous, subversive, criminal brother, whose whereabouts he was under oath to discover—whose whereabouts, if he discovered it, would make him, Arkady Andreyevich, a titled nobleman overnight, and put a medal on his chest, and a big reward in his pocket... Oh, the frustration of it! How his bile rose every time the fool's name came up! Because he knew, absolutely, that they knew where Nikolai Vasilevich was, of course they did, but they refused to tell him, his own wife refused to tell him, and of course he could not ask outright, he could not let them see how important it was to his future, for then they would never tell him in a million years, they being such brutes, such monsters, such impediments to his happiness.

But Fyodorov! That was a different matter altogether. Fyodorov and that Argentine spy, they knew something, and he would get what information they had from them, it would not escape him, not this time. So he had arranged this little supper with Fyodorov, in masculine comfort, in his own club, no women to pester him, no eavesdropping wife, no constraints, and he would get what he needed, man-to-man, directly, without any bother. Fyodorov was abstemious, it was true, but he was also absent-minded, overly philosophical, and unworldly, and so, in Arkady's estimation, a man who could be easily confusticated and thus tricked into idle confabulating, from which Arkady would indubitably glean the verities he sought. (Arkady Andreyevich was often subject to such fits of verbal obfuscation.) So it was with mounting anticipation and high expectations that he awaited the arrival of Fyodorov. While he waited, he polished off the *zakuski* his club provided as hors d'oeuvres, washing down the pickled herring, caviar, and dumplings with enough vodka to strengthen his resolve, his firm resolution. He would not be bamboozled, he told himself, as he threw back another glass, smiling to himself reptiliously. He would not allow Fyodorov to leave the table until he had satisfactorily wrung every bit of information he could from that bumbling cosmist. Was he not Arkady Andreyevich Ulanov, Titular Counselor, soon to be promoted to the rank of Collegiate Assessor, whereupon his future rise in the Ministry would be assured? Unless Fyodorov this very day handed him Nikolai Barakov's head on a platter, a golden platter! Then he would be elevated at once to the hereditary nobility! And he deserved no less, though others far less worthy were promoted before him, for the civil service was corrupt at its core, as everyone knew, and the dross were often honored ahead of the true and pure, the scum rising to the top, while men like himself, noble-hearted, dedicated men, labored beneath them like slaves… So Fyodorov found him, cheeks already flushed, eyes already dulled, puffed up with wounded vanity and resentment, fractious, bilious, and ready to take offense.

They greeted each other cautiously, Ulanov barely rising from his chair, Fyodorov, barely recognizing him in his half-drunken state, bowing uncertainly.

"Sit! Sit, Fyodorov! No formalities here! A men's club, you know. English-style. How d'ya do, old man? Ha ha ha."

Fyodorov, taken aback by this jollity, sat down as directed and accepted the glass of vodka thrust into his hand. To settle himself, he glanced around at the room, taking in the heavy drapes, the paintings of hunting scenes, the great antlers over the fireplace, the tables around which groups of men were sitting, talking and eating, the waiters in their liveried jackets, and he thought he could be in another country entirely, how well Russians mimicked the style of others, though not the substance—as the short lull in sound was broken by some raucous Russian laughter from one of the tables—and how truly unpleasant such places were, with their false fronts, like Potemkin's villages, behind whose facades were the usual squalors, sicknesses, and sorrows.

"I am afraid I am late, Arkady Andreyevich. My apologies."

"Not at all late. No, not at all. I arrived early. And ate up all the *zakuski*. Ha ha ha."

Since Fyodorov could think of no satisfactory reply, he said nothing, but looked with regret at the remains on the plate. He was quite hungry.

"Supper's coming, though, supper's almost here. My dear Fyodorov, what have you been doing with yourself? Keeping occupied, have you? Not like us lazy bums in the ministries, eh? No, science first, science forever, and let the paper-pusher push away, isn't it true? Oh, it's true enough. Indeed, yes."

"I would disagree, Arkady Andreyevich. The government has duties it must fulfill, and your ministry especially has a noble task, to see that the people are treated justly and by the rule of law."

"Well, that's handsomely said, it is indeed, though I wonder how many believe it, eh? That we are the guardians of justice. How many believe it? Can't say I do, but then the closer you are to the pig sty the less likely you are to eat pork, isn't it true? But what about you, old man? Eh? What about you yourself? Tell me now, how are your experiments coming along? Have you perfected your rocket ship? Ha ha ha. You are a man of such value to us. Oh, yes. His Highness, were he to know of your work, would be most appreciative. His Highness should know! Indeed, he should be told. Perhaps you would receive a pension, a position, a professorship. Not this peripatetic life you live now! No, something solid and substantial. Shall I make inquiries? Shall I become your advocate? I think it is what you need, for the successful completion of your work, don't you think? After all, we are in competition with the West, we must prove our mettle, the glory of our Autocracy, the strength of our Faith. They have science, we have religion. Isn't it true? And we are in a race, don't you see, a race to achievement, to greatness... Yes, a relay race, and you, Fyodor Fyodorovich, you are part of the relay, you have been passed the baton. You must exert yourself, yes, but we can help, the government can help. Why not? You are working for the greater good, are you not? Colonizing space! What could be better? We send the criminals to Siberia now, but soon even Siberia will not be big enough. We'll need another planet to put them on. Ha ha ha!"

Fyodorov, squirming in his chair and once again hard-pressed to find a suitable response, gazed around him in futile search of a subject to remark upon, anything to turn the conversation away from himself. But Arkady Andreyevich was not to be deterred by his guest's obvious embarrassment, and plunged ahead.

"Yes, position, prestige, monetary assistance—why, they'll be calling you Your Excellency soon! I can be of such service to you. Really my own position is secure, of course, but even I might benefit from your success. This is how the world works, does it not, Fyodor Fyodorovich? One hand shakes the other. But, look, here is our supper now! What have they come up with, those scullions, nothing shabby I hope."

Plates and cutlery were set in front of them, bowls of beet soup and platters of meat, fish, pickled vegetables, pancakes, cheeses and fruit. Another bottle appeared, from which Ulanov poured generously into both their glasses.

"Now, let's see if your appetite can rise to this occasion, eh, Fyodorov? Let's see what we can uncover here, like spies, eh? By the way, how is your Argentine friend, Azara? *He* must have some uncovering to do, but for whom is he doing it? Well, a man must make his way however he can, and we all know the situation is dire in Spanish America, always has been. But that is not the point, is it? Not at all the point. Point is..." He stopped speaking long enough to chew and swallow. "The point is..." (stopped again to wash it down) "... we are all trying to achieve the same goal, my friend. Happiness! Yes, that is the goal of life! Happiness!"

Fyodorov, his own mouth full, merely raised his eyebrows, nodded his head, and chewed more deliberately, as slowly as he could, hoping Ulanov would continue to speak and relieve him of the need to do so.

"Now my dear wife, Irina Vasilevna, tells me that your friend Azara is a friend of her brother's. And you are a friend of her brother's. You know, Fyodorov, my wife's happiness is of great importance to me. You know that, don't you? A wife's happiness—why it makes the household run smoothly and happily. An unhappy wife—well, only misery comes from an unhappy wife. You're married, are you? No? Well, believe me when I say, an unhappy wife is worse than no wife at all."

"I do believe you," Fyodorov said.

"So here you are, a friend of her brother's," he repeated, smiling at Fyodorov as though he had just won him as a prize. Taking up his napkin with a flourish, he wiped away the dribbles of beet soup running down his chin. "Two of you. Indeed, two at one time. A gathering of old chums, is it? All of you such close pals. You and Azara and Nikolai Vasilevich. I would lay odds that you are all meeting somewhere to talk about old times and lay one on, eh? Have a good time, that's the spirit! I envy you, I do. Springtime, in the country? Or are you getting together right here in Petersburg? I would, if I were you. Mud season. Flies. Difficulties crossing rivers. Dear God, the country in spring! No, the city's the place for you lot, isn't it?"

He smiled across the table at Fyodorov, a crocodile smile.

It had occurred to Fyodorov that if Ulanov didn't choke on a mouthful of meat first, he might eventually get around to the subject of Nikolai Vasilevich on his own, without any prompting at all, but he had not expected the subject to come up so quickly and in such an overt manner.

He was not a subtle man, Arkady Andreyevich, or a clever one. He had given the game away before he'd even finished his soup.

"Forgive me, Arkady Andreyevich," he said, also scrupulously wiping his lips. The napkin was white linen, overly starched and rough to the touch. "But I fear you are mistaken if you think Azara and I—"

"Listen, Fyodorov. Let's stop pussy-footing around here. My wife wants to see her brother. Simple as that. Now where the hell is he?"

"But, my dear Ulanov, I have no idea. I was hoping you could tell me."

"Tell you! How the devil can I tell you?" Ulanov's face had turned as red as the beet soup stain on his napkin, the exact color, Fyodorov noted with some interest, and his voice had risen dramatically so that diners at neighboring tables took notice. His chest heaved, his hands gripped his cutlery, his eyes bulged, in short, he appeared to be a likely candidate for a fit of apoplexy. Yet what reason could he possibly have for such rage?

"My dear Arkady Andreyevich, please calm yourself. No one I have spoken to knows where Nikolai Vasilevich is. No one at all has any idea. And if you and your family are all as much in the dark as we are, perhaps... well, perhaps he has left the country entirely."

But Ulanov, incapable of heeding anything sensible, was breathing deeply, heavily—rather like a bull, Fyodorov thought—and looked like he was about to turn over the table and break it in his bare hands into bits of kindling. A waiter came rushing over in anticipation of such an event... but no, not at all, only to bring yet another bottle of vodka... dear God, how they drank, these civil servants!... and only a single glass was broken in the exchange of bottles. The glass, however, cut Ulanov's hand and suddenly there was quite a gush of blood spilling over the tabletop.

In the ensuing confusion—calls for a doctor, further upsets on the table, a gathering of onlookers from nearby—Fyodorov, having wrapped a napkin around Ulanov's hand and assured him the wound was not life-threatening, shouted out his farewells amidst the turmoil, and not forgetting to grab his hat and cane, made his escape.

Back home in his laboratory once again, if home it could be called, Fyodorov felt the burden of despondency fall on him as it so often did these days, as it had all winter long, during those dark days when slowly but surely, inch by inch, he had stripped his garret and searched in vain for Nikolai Barakov's book. He had dismantled his shelves, emptied his drawers, closets and cabinets, taken up his floorboards—all to no avail. The book, like its author, was nowhere to be found. Then, finding himself living in shambles, he returned everything to the way it had been, and now at winter's end he was back where he had started at winter's beginning, desperate and utterly at a loss. His work had suffered. Indeed, he had lost interest in it entirely. All he wanted, all he cared about, the only thing of any importance in his life, was Nikolai Barakov's book.

How such desire—desire for what is unattainable, for what is beyond one's reach, for what may not, in fact, even exist—how such desire took over one's life would be a fascinating subject for study, and indeed he believed it had been studied, for surely there were books examining the lives of those seekers of God who fled into the desert or up onto mountaintops and lived solitary lives of prayer and sacrifice, of mortification, those on Athos, those in the Sinai, those, of whom he had heard, living on bare rocks in the northern ocean, their passionate desire for God having driven them mad. As the days and weeks and months of the winter passed, he began to recognize in himself a similar desire, and he even contemplated turning to God Himself, and using prayer as a means to obtain *Monkey*. Better prayer than mesmerism, better prayer than seeking the help of gypsies or fortune tellers or Elena Blavatskaya with her elemental spirits and astral bodies.

The fact that he had lived in the same house with Nikolai Barakov, had eaten with him, drunk with him, talked to him, considered him a friend—and all the time, not really known him, or known what he was doing; that at any time during those years, he might have asked about the book Nikolai was working on, might, in fact, have read it; that he had been so close to the secret, to the man who knew the secret, and that he had entirely missed it, it had blown right by him like a puff of smoke or like a cloud or like a butterfly—these were truths that kept him awake at night, that haunted him in the darkest hours, and that often seemed about to drive him mad.

And yet, when he was in his right mind, when he was calm and thinking clearly, not overcome by desire, frustration, or hopelessness, he understood very well that Nikolai's book existed somewhere in the world, in some time and in some place, and that with determination, strategy, patience and cleverness, it could be and would be found. He simply had to wait until winter's end and then he had to act.

He had just settled himself in his chair and closed his eyes—after so much vodka, and so much disappointment, a short nap was in order—when he heard a familiar rattling at his door. Young, red-cheeked Artemey Efimovich with a message for him. Alexander Azara was in the drawing room of the Stardust. Would Fyodor Fyodorovich care to join him for a drink, or might he come up to the laboratory? Fyodorov had completely forgotten that they had arranged this meeting in order to discuss his interview with Arkady Andreyevich. Of course, he told the boy, tell Alexander Felixovich that I will come right down.

"But my dear Fyodorov, this is good news!" Azara exclaimed with his usual light-hearted optimism. The man could see the bright side of any catastrophe; it was an attitude that always struck Fyodorov as distressingly callow, and especially so in the face of tragedy and grievous loss, or, in this case, grievous disappointment.

"I can't see how it can be."

"It can be by process of elimination, my dear fellow. For if Ulanov expected information about Nick from you it means he does not have the information himself. Well, we wouldn't want him to have it, would we? He works for the Third Section, doesn't he? Or he's close to men who do. It means, don't you see, that they don't have him in custody, he's not imprisoned or in the mines or on the front, if there is a front... Oh, be glad of it, man! It's good news."

"Oh, yes, I see how you're looking at it. Yes, I see. I, on the other hand, was hoping that since he does work for the Third Section or know men who do, he'd have discovered Nikolai's whereabouts if only for the family's sake. For, by all the saints, Azara, someone on this earth must know where Nikolai Vasilevich is, someone must have some idea! It's an outrage that we can't find him, an outrage!"

"You surely wouldn't have expected him to give that information to you, though, even if he had it."

"No. Of course not. But he doesn't have it, that's the point. If he had, he wouldn't have brought it up in the first place. I was expecting to try to worm something out of him, if only a hint, if only a supposition. Instead he jumped onto the subject on his own, began interrogating me, looked like he wanted to beat the answers out of me. I tell you, he was frightening."

"Well, then, have a drink. Calm yourself. You did well. And so we have eliminated the family. Or that part of it."

"His sisters know nothing. I'm quite sure. Their mother is utterly desolate due to Nikolai's disappearance. If they knew anything they would surely have told her."

"Yes, of course. So Arkady was our one possible source, and you are quite convinced he knows nothing. All right. We go on." He poured another finger of vodka into Fyodorov's glass. "You're not drinking, my friend. Come now! Be of good cheer! I have a surprise for you."

"What sort of surprise?"

Azara smiled at him. "Feast your eyes!" he said, and, reaching into his coat pocket, he pulled out a folded handkerchief, which he unfolded carefully on the tabletop. There, lying on the white handkerchief, was what appeared to be a small pile of plant detritus. Upon closer inspection, Fyodorov was able to discern that the detritus was in fact the dried stems, gills, and caps of mushrooms. "They arrived only today. I had them sent from Vienna."

"Vienna? They grow there?"

"Certainly not. I brought them with me from home. They were stored in a cabinet in my rooms, inside a kind of reliquary, like bones of a saint. I had a friend ship it to me along with some lighter clothes so it would go unnoticed. And here they are."

"But they are all dried out and useless!"

"Not at all, my friend. They only sleep; they come back to life. What you have here is the divine mushroom, the Aztec's *teonanacatl.* Indeed, when dried it will retain its power for many years, perhaps for centuries."

"This is the mushroom you gave to Nikolai?"

"This is the mushroom we ate together, yes. This is the mushroom you asked me to obtain for you. What is the matter, Fyodorov? You are looking unwell."

For Fyodorov, looking at the fungus before him, was taken with a sudden and inexplicable distaste. The dried mushrooms, grey, twisted, ugly, struck him as sinister, and the thought of ingesting them filled him with loathing. But perhaps this aversion was not the fault of the mushrooms but a result of the humidity, the vodka, the futility of his afternoon.

"It is nothing," he said. "When can I try this drug, Azara?"

"In some few days," he said. "We must prepare ourselves."

"How do you mean, prepare ourselves?"

"Like taking a sacrament, my friend. One must fast and pray. But do not worry. We shall purify our bodies and minds, and I will be your guide on the journey to encounter the god, and all will be well."

"I hope you are speaking metaphorically, Alexander Felixovich. I have no desire to encounter a god."

"What do you expect then?"

The map! The key! The portal!

Yes, that was the truth. He had been longing for this mushroom ever since Azara had told him about it. There was some mystery about its use, yes, some deep secret. It was eaten by the descendants of the people who had made the *Codex Mexicanus* which he had once seen in a library in Vienna. He had seen the same kind of writing, if writing it was, in his own memory the day in his laboratory when he recalled—so clearly!—the page of *Monkey* he had been looking at just before he had—perhaps—traveled through a time portal and into the arms of Elena Blavatskaya. Perhaps there was no connection between these four things: mushroom, codex, *Monkey,* portal. But Nikolai had eaten these sacred mushrooms, and after that, he had written his book, and into that book he had written a great secret. There was no doubt about the sequence; the only doubt was about the causality. So he would eat the mushrooms, too, and he would see. Perhaps a door would open for him; perhaps a secret would be revealed.

"I don't know what to expect, my friend. I am putting myself entirely into your hands."

Azara smiled at him mysteriously. "Good. Then leave it all to me."

Natasha's life in the city was not at all unpleasant, and yet now that spring was coming—and on some days, particularly sunny days, seemed to be quite near—she began yearning for Oak Hills, her real home. She lay in bed at night and imagined walking through the garden along the narrow paths she had always loved to the wild and overgrown back garden, to the great bushes she could easily crawl beneath, to the maze, and the dry fountain with the pretty stone nymph, and on into the woods, to the woodland paths, the dear bent old trees, the rippling streams, all the way to the campground where Pyotr Panov and his troupe of actors had set up their wagons and their stage. And there, too, in the country, in those cool rooms overlooking the garden, she would see her grandmother again, and how she longed now to see her! It seemed a lifetime since she had snuggled into the bed with her and kissed her cheek and heard her voice. Sometimes she would try to remember her grandmother's voice, and what she had said, how she would call her *mon petit chou* and give her treats to eat and help her with her poems, though she did not write any poems any more herself, or so she said. No one seemed to believe that, though. Her mother didn't believe it and neither did Aunt Irina. She herself didn't believe it, either. Poets didn't stop making poems, even if they only kept them in their minds and their hearts and never wrote them down. Meeting Fyodor Fyodorovich in Stock Exchange Square and talking with him about her grandmother had made her yearn even more for the estate, and all the rest of that day and all the next day and the day after that, she found many things to complain about, she refused to concentrate on her lessons, she sat in corners and worked on her poem about Nikolai and the Princess... and found herself rhyming head with bled and fled with dead... and was, most uncharacteristically, quiet and cast down.

On the fourth day, a dreary, rainy Sunday, she was surprised to discover Fyodor Fyodorovich himself being greeted at the front door by her father. Being a curious child, she followed them down the hall to the study, and since her father did not close the door behind them, which she took as an invitation to join them, she slipped into the room as quiet as a mouse, and settled herself in her favorite big chair in a corner by the door.

At first the conversation was far too scholarly for her to pay it much attention. It was in the area of the natural sciences, her father's special subject, but one filled with long words in languages she did not understand. But after awhile it appeared they were speaking about something quite common after all, only mushrooms, though they had confused her at first by using such very incomprehensible names for them. By the time she realized this, however, the subject had shifted again, to something of intense importance, and she sat very, very still and pricked up her ears so as not to miss a single word.

"Would Nikolai Vasilevich have taken such a risk?"

"Risk? My dear Fyodorov, I thought you knew him. Nikolai lives for risk. His entire life is one risk after another, and the riskier something is, the better he likes it."

"You are quite right about Nikolai and his love of risks. Yet physical risks are quite different from risks to one's—inner life. One's soul."

"I cannot say. On the subject of souls I would have to defer to the judgement of theologians. For myself, as a scientist, I have grave doubts that such phenomena exist."

"I expect Nikolai shares those doubts. When we lived under the same roof and saw a good deal of each other, whenever he returned from a visit with you, he would always mention how enjoyable it was to have conversations with you."

Ivan Ivanovich laughed at this.

"Conversations? Arguments, more like it. Oh, how Nikolai loves to argue. He will argue with you about the color of the sky! Still, I also enjoyed those discussions, and I miss them. I haven't seen Nikolai—goodness, it must be five years!

"I confess, Fyodorov, I have many criticisms of Nikolai Vasilevich, for like everyone else, I recognize his talents while at the same time I see how flagrantly he wastes them. He is a man who is easily bored and exceedingly disposed to the fantastic and the chaotic. He will do anything for the thrill of it; yet, as I often argued with him, it is possible to find adventure even in occupations that are legitimate. One does not have to be a criminal to find life thrilling. I would say this and he would laugh at me. He told me once that he actually didn't know how to live lawfully, that he didn't know how to relate to law-abiding men, that everything he did was on the sly, under the table, or through the black market. The fact is, Kolya always needs to feel the exaltation of danger. Join the army, I told him once. Battle will give you that sense of danger. And he laughed at me and said he could battle any day of the week in any inn or tavern in the city, he didn't need to wear a uniform to get into a fight."

"This is true. He does love fighting. Any brawl at all."

"He is smart enough, you know, to see the situation clearly. To see it too clearly, in my estimation. Vasily Yakovlevich respects him for it, admires him, I would even say. Yet I cannot admire him. He lives with the down-and-out and rejects his own family. How is that admirable?"

Fyodorov began to speak but stopped himself. Poor Fyodorov, Natasha thought. He lived with Uncle Kolya once. Was *he* down-and-out?

"Vasily Yakovlevich admires his rejection of inherited wealth. How is that admirable? If he ever wants a family he'll see how important inherited wealth is, mark my words. I will not say Nikolai lives off other people. Yes, I have given him money in the past. Sofia used to give him money, too. Or lend it to him. He always promised to pay it back. But the truth is, he has never had a reliable source of income. Why not? He could have managed his father's estate. God knows, it needs managing. He refused. He could have worked in one of the ministries, or in an office of the municipal government. He refused to consider it. He could have started a small business, some enterprise of his own, even a literary journal, if he was so inclined. Vasily Yakovlevich would have given him the capital. Again, he wouldn't hear of it. Instead he would borrow, he would steal. Yes, he would rather steal.

"After awhile, you know, a man gets tired of drinking all night, he gets tired of having ideas that never amount to anything, telling stories of what could be but isn't. A man—how can I say this?—takes on a certain role, becomes serious, decides on a career, works to attain a place in the world. The world is not perfect. We know this. We struggle to do the best we can in an imperfect universe. This is what it means to be a man, in my opinion. But Nikolai refuses to accept this. Or he hasn't yet accepted it, or hasn't to our knowledge. God knows what he's up to now. I certainly don't."

"When you say he sees the situation clearly, do you mean the political situation?"

"Yes. Of course. What other situation of any importance is there?"

"It seems that in that case he would be involved in societies... in organizations. That he would be known. By young people. By your students, for example."

"He'd only be known if he was active. He isn't. He isn't a joiner. He's an anarchist, Fyodorov. He's against organizations. He's against movements, against working with people, against finishing a task. That's all boring, don't you see? It's tedious work. Deep in his soul, Kolya is a man who cannot work with other people, and has no desire to."

"He's an artist, I think," Fyodorov said mildly.

"An artist! You must be joking."

"A writer is an artist, is he not?"

"I would like to see one thing that Kolya actually wrote. He talks well. He can be very entertaining. But to actually sit down and write something? I would very much doubt it."

"But it is true. I have one of his works in my possession, and I am well aware that there is another."

"Are you talking about that monkey-business with the novel? *Monkey*, he called it? Come, come, Fyodorov, you don't give that any credence, do you? Why that's one of Kolya's jokes. There's no such novel. It doesn't exist."

"Some people have read it."

"Some people? Who? People who are pulling your leg, my dear fellow. No, I love the man, I do, but he's not on the straight and narrow, and he never will be."

"I suppose you're right," Fyodorov said.

"Well, I hope I've set your mind at ease at least in respect to *Agaricus semilanceatus*. I would be happy to examine the specimen you have and see if I can make an identification. Without seeing it, it's impossible."

"I thank you with all my heart, Ivan Ivanovich."

Natasha heard the shuffling and movement which meant the men were rising from their chairs and shaking hands, as scientists did.

"You will stay for tea, of course. Sofia Vasilevna will never forgive me if you leave without seeing her."

At this juncture, Natasha slipped out of her chair and out of the room, and scampered away down the hall as quickly as she could so as to be in another part of the house should she be invited into the drawing room for tea.

She was not invited; Fyodorov did not stay.

But she had learned a very important thing. She wondered if Anastasia knew about *Monkey*. She wondered if she should tell her. Yes, she would tell her! It would make her so happy.

CHAPTER TWENTY-EIGHT

Teonanacatl

He had fasted. He had dressed himself in loose-fitting clothing; nakedness was preferable, nakedness might ultimately occur, but for the time being he felt comfortable enough. Azara had chosen the place, a small house on the grounds of one of Prince Kirill's estates, not far from the city. Here they would be quite safe, they would not be disturbed, they would have shelter and food and access to the gardens—to trees, plants, fresh air, water, peace. They had arrived a few days before, so as to familiarize themselves with the place and become acquainted with the domestic staff of the main house, those servants who lived in the house and maintained it over the winter. Azara went about preparing everything, obtaining the supplies they needed, and removing from sight anything that might distract or alarm. While he did, he instructed Fyodorov on various useful techniques for preparing himself for the ceremony: how to meditate, how to clear his mind, how to relax his muscles, above all, how to remain calm. Now at last the time had come to sit at the table they had set out in the garden, and eat the god, as Azara put it, god in the shape of dried, twisted bits of ancient mushroom stems and caps, chewy, horribly dry in the mouth and bitter-tasting, needing to be washed down with tea.

Soon he felt the nausea Azara had warned him about. Do not think of it as sickness but as an awareness of your own physical being. True enough. In fact, he was feeling his entire body in an altogether strange way, being aware for the first time of its own existence apart from himself. He felt like a soul inside a body. For surely there was himself, and then there was this object of weight and oddness—of blood pulsing and stomach acids excreting and nerves feeling, tongue moving, saliva dripping into his mouth—the very body in all its dutiful activities—lungs breathing, hair growing, skin shedding—God, he could see the pores of his skin!—and within it, somewhere within it, himself, a small voice or thought, a sense of being. He himself. His soul.

"Now while we wait, we can walk under the trees," Azara said, interrupting his thinking, smiling at him.

Indeed, the trees were well-worth walking under and admiring. They were just coming into leaf, the tiny furled leaves just opening, the color of them so extravagantly brilliant against the bright blue sky: golden-green, yellow-green, chartreuse, with the contrasting, eye-popping, bright red of the red maples. And then the flowering trees, the fruit trees, delicate pink, pure, snowy white, deep purple. Had he never noticed these trees before? Even their barks were extraordinary, and their gnarled trunks, the texture of them, so rough in contrast to the smoothness of their flowers, their petals, their delicacy.

Their living presence.

Yes, their presence was—daunting. How huge they were! How alive!

One great tree-creature—its scientific name he now discarded as useless, having no importance compared with the rich reality of the living being—this great tree-creature allowed him to touch its bark and stroke it... listen to it... feel it moving in the soft breeze under the gentle light of the sun. The breeze gusted now and then and when it did the new leaves and newly awakened branches rustled and whispered. Sometimes the rustling became loud and the sound filled him so that nothing else mattered to him but the rushing of sound.

He could hear everything now, every sound came to him brilliant and clear—and over great distances, for he could hear hammering coming from the stables, geese honking from the pond, a dog barking, a rhythmic, deep-throated bark, and voices of men who could not be closer than the road, and that a good half mile away, and hear it all with the same clarity that he heard the chirping and tweeting in the trees around him and the scurrying of chipmunks amidst the undergrowth and residue of dried leaves.

While part of his being delighted in these new sensations, another part was considering his inability to put what he was feeling into words. Where once he might have taken out his notebook and recorded what he was experiencing for further investigation—the experience of enhanced hearing, the experience of enhanced sight—now such a response seemed laughable to him. It was enough to attend to the fact that he was thinking, an incredible activity he had previously taken for granted but which he now found quite astonishing. Thinking, he realized, was done in words, and words were inadequate for describing the world. Worse than inadequate, words distorted reality. The word *tree* distorted tree-reality, attempted to capture in a single sound the image of an enormous and magnificent being. In fact, he thought—and what a revelation it was!—language was created to mask truth, it was created to deceive, to keep the reality of actual sensation and experience far away and hidden from view.

This idea took such hold of him that he could barely think about it, because thinking—his thinking, at least—was done entirely in words.

Yet, how foolish to think words had any power at all. All the words he knew meant so little. They were only sounds meant to itemize and label, manipulate and mask. Words were like little picket fences, like little toy fences, men tried to put around giant living beings.

He saw the little fences; he saw the giant creatures. It was funny, really, how foolish men could be.

Amusement at the follies of men occupied his mind while, sitting in the prickly, sweet-smelling grass—he found himself sitting in the grass; how he came to be there exactly he did not know—he watched the movement of small insects, very busy insects—ants, beetles, bees, a butterfly—who were not in the least foolish but were concentrating on their considerable tasks, performing them with industry or grace, each to its own work in its own way, in its own time.

The grass sighed, the wind blew in little gusts. Delicate flowers fell from the sky. An ant ran rapidly up his arm. A bee buzzed around his ear. A shadow fell over him. A man squatted down.

Nothing had disturbed him until then, until the man squatted down across from him and began to talk. So many signals were being sent to him from this man—he named them signals having no other name to give them—that he felt utterly overcome and could make no sense of anything, that is, he could not put into any order the multiple signs he was receiving or interpret them in a satisfactory way.

To realize the reality of a man—it was an overwhelming prospect.

First the body, the clothing hiding the body, the gestures of the body, the expression on the face, the movement of eyes and mouth, the sounds coming from the mouth, how false they sounded, how untrue. Yet what was true? The expression? The eyes, very black, very large, all pupil; or the mouth, moving; or the smooth skin, the black hair? The teeth?

What white teeth he had! And the strength of the body. He felt it, the muscles, a tautness. Very well. The other signs. The words. How they ran out of the mouth, joined together, galloped about, this and that, drinkeat, sitwalkbreathe. The smile on his face. Those teeth again. Then a solemnity. The change was quick. Too quick. It startled him. From smile to frown. The expressions changed, one to the other, they flowed, they never stopped. *Stop!* he cried, or tried to.

Yes, he had said it. *Stop!*

The man—startled. Gazed at him with deep seriousness. Eyes so black and deep. How deep is a man! What worlds live within him!

And in himself. He felt—he feared to feel—the depth in himself, as though he might dive into it as into a deep pool or into the bottomless sea.

The man, smiling again.

A bird, singing in the tree.

What is that?

A sparrow.

The word amazed him for it brought to his mind an exact image of the little brown bird whose song he was hearing but whose body he could not see.

So that is the purpose of words.

He did not want to sit with the man any longer and tried to get up. That is, he willed his body to move. It seemed unwilling. Indeed, it seemed he could not get up from the ground at all. Must someone help him? The man sitting across from him rose up quite easily, gracefully, but he could not imagine standing in that way, in one movement, and when the man offered his hand, he refused. No, he must do it himself. He shifted his limbs, pivoted onto his thigh, struggled to his knees, then lumbered up, off balance, one leg at a time. It was hard work, awkward and difficult. This body of his was cumbersome indeed. But standing felt good. To stand on two feet, to breathe, to fill the lungs with air. To stand tall. He and his body were somewhat estranged, it seemed, but as they were joined, they had to learn to get along. His body appeared to like walking rather than sitting on the ground, so they would walk. Perhaps a chair would appeal to it more. Perhaps a divan.

The idea of furniture came to him, and architecture. The building of houses. Shelter. The things men made. He turned to the man accompanying him, but that man was no longer there. He had said: something to drink.

Something to drink. Yes, he was experiencing thirst. His mouth was dry. Very dry. How had he not noticed how dry his mouth was? And was he also hungry? Was that the feeling in his stomach, a great void, an emptiness, and a sound like groaning? Was that hunger? And was he tired? Was he sleepy? Was he feeling heavy? Or light? Or drunk? It was like being drunk, but then he couldn't really remember the feeling of being drunk. He could only see what was in front of him. A path. Trees on either side. Stones underfoot. A long path, rather straight, like a corridor. And things floating in the air. Petals. Seeds. Stardust. Then the air trembled, the sun was so bright. The light wavered. It was so hot, so bright, so sweet, the air, so heavy with stardust and earthseed, so thick with beings, spirits, so heavy and thick and hot and bright, he could barely move through it. They danced ahead of him on the bright stones, under the trees. What were they, those dark dancing shapes? Surely they had a name.

Shadows.

Once again he sat down, this time on a wooden bench, to watch the shadows playing under the trees and smell the air and swallow the wetness in his mouth that was not wet enough. His body felt less strange but still an incumbrance. It did not always do what he wished it to. Right now he wished it could rise into the trees so that he might examine the birds more closely, or it might also suit if his eyes had better sight. Suppose they had and he could see... The thought stopped there for he was seeing, perfectly, a tiny creature making its way along the arm of the bench, a tiny creature with tiny legs... three pairs of legs, one pair of antennae... moving its three-part body in a three-part motion... a creature with delicate diaphanous wings... What name had they given to this perfect little creature, this tiny creature with wings? Gazing up at a sound—suddenly there was enormous sound everywhere—a flight of sparrows passing by, the swishing sound of wings in flight—and was that the sound of water? Was there perhaps a fountain or spring nearby? How thirsty he was!

Or was he? Perhaps not. For he did not want to disturb anything, the shadows at his feet, the sounds in the air, the insect beside him, the birds above him, the moment in time in which he sat still, that stretched out around him and lived within him

just as time past lived within him, through memory

and time future lived within him, through imagination

and time present, the living moment, in which he breathed… the breath coming and going, the heart beating, everything in motion, moving, changing, no stillness ever anywhere in life. The present was fugitive, in eternal and infinite movement. The present was in eternal flight. The present was winged.

He looked down and the insect had gone, flown away, no doubt, on some insect mission unknowable to men.

But now something was coming. He could feel something large moving toward him in the bright air, something that came bearing a combination of sounds, birds in alarmed flight, a kind of grunting and coughing… and there appeared at last a man, a foreigner, with dark skin, and straight black hair wearing rough peasant clothes, wearing a straw hat as well, and sandals on his feet, a sort of shaman, perhaps, or Amazonian Indian, or character out of a book… which idea or image came thundering toward him… ***Book***… at the same time as the man, shaman, foreigner, head-hunter, cannibal, stepped out of the shadows, stepped up to the bench upon which he was sitting as though paralyzed, and handed him a cup of what appeared to be amber liquid.

"Your tea," the foreign cannibal shaman said. "Fyodor, my friend, how are you feeling?"

It is tea. The tea is warm. How can it still be warm?

"If you had your watch," said the smiling shaman, "you would notice that very little time has gone by since you left this cup on the table and walked down the path to this bench. We measure time differently now."

He heard and didn't hear. The warm tea quenched his thirst beautifully and he was filled with gratitude for it. But he was also interested in the man whose name he knew to be Alejandro Azara but whom, he realized, he did not know at all.

Tell me who you are.

"A long story," said the man.

We have time.

That word again.

The man began to speak. He had a soft voice, a kind voice. Appealing. He was telling a story, but one did not need to listen to the words. The essence of it all was clear. The man was talking about someone he cared for. Ah, it was his father.

My father... an interesting life... adventure... making maps, Amazon, animals, naturalist, botanist, Mayan astronomer... Mayan something... something... Humboldt...maps for him...

They were walking now under the trees, and now under the sky, across a meadow. He noted the movement of the grasses, and felt the heat of the sun, and wondered about spring and summer. A different story came to him—about Demeter and Persephone—and for the first time it struck him as a deep and profound truth. The daughter of the Mother of All Life is stolen by Death and taken to the underworld. In her grief, her terrible grief, the Great Mother stops creating life on earth, nothing is conceived, nothing grows. The situation is dire, Death is forced to give the girl back—for half the year—and during that half, life is renewed on the earth, though in the other half, it dies again.

What a joy it was to be alive on the earth!

The earth is God. The universe is God. Life is God. And we who live are also God. God is all around us and in us. We breathe in God. We breathe out God.

A joy to be alive. A pleasure. A gift.

"Yes," said the man Alejandro Azara, son of the map maker. "I agree. A joy. A feast."

Then words came to him, a sort of rhyming, rhythmic song. He felt he should think about it, but instead the words started dancing around his mind and made him smile, something so silly about them, about all the words.

I must sit... Maps, you say?

Just to keep the man talking so he himself could sit in the grass and listen to the little song. Where did it come from? Someone had written it, someone he knew. A little ditty, a short-hand version, a way to remember.

"What is that you're humming?"

A poem. A little song. No, it has no music. I can't remember—

"If you just begin, it will come flowing out of your memory like water flowing from a spring. Try!"

He enjoyed the image of his memory as a spring of water flowing...

There is the First, the One,
infinite, without limits.
The One cannot be named.
The One engenders Intellect,
its essence an infinity of parts,
and Intellect generates Soul,
which, entering time,
produces Nature,
a visible God.
But cast down without wings
and entombed in a body,
Soul is filled with desire
for union with God.
This desire is Love…

It lilted, it sang. But he had forgotten how it ended, it had gotten all confused in his mind, and it was all nonsense anyway. It was impossible to explain—he opened his arms wide—all this! Impossible to put it into words.

Azara was speaking.

"I remember that song. I remember when the two of you wrote it."

The two of us?

"Yes. Your happy Plotinus poem. You wrote it together. You and Nick."

There in the meadow, sitting in the grasses, the smell of the earth, the sounds of the earth, the sun beating down but the breeze cooling, the name revealed a memory and now the memory was coming to him over the meadow—he could almost see it coming. But so much else was happening, his body breathing, the clouds passing, the beetles and ants and bees and flowers, being… his mind thinking, his heart beating, and memory coming over the grasses, a figure… a figure, a voice, and there he was, Nikolai, the memory having arrived, and then he was back in the communal house, and Nikolai was making up the song of Plotinus because *philosophers hardly know what they're saying themselves, I have to make it simple or I'll forget it, the mind can only remember so much nonsense, pardon me, Fyodorov, I know you love this man, but if you want me to remember his ideas you'll have to help me make them into a little doggerel, forgive me, because I'm not as smart as you and I need things to be easy, now let's see how it goes, and be sure to stop me if I get it wrong. There is the First, the One...*

A happy poem? Yes, yes, it was a happy poem. He felt like he was a child again. Everything was fresh and new. Magical.

But it was the man who called it happy. Had the man read his mind?

Did I say it?

"What?"

There is the First, the One, infinite without limits? Did I speak the words?

"Yes. Just now. You did."

Did I laugh?

The man laughed. "Yes, you did. It is funny, isn't it? No, not funny. Happy. That men think like this."

Like what? How do men think?

"About everything, in every way. Mind keeps thinking, all the time. *Its essence, an infinity of parts.* Ha ha ha. Even dreaming. Always making. Always producing. Like you say—like God, always busy. Produce, make, sing, dance, eat, sleep...make up language, religion, cosmologies, world views... ha ha ha. Think of the hubris! *World views.*"

Philosophy.

Then all the philosophies of the world turned their eyes on him to gaze at him as though each had its view of him and where he was sitting in the golden-green grass, the garden-of-Eden grass, the first-day-of-the-world grass... and they were all—wrong. But it didn't matter. He dismissed them. And they departed.

Nikolai remained, sitting on the grass right at the edge of the little dirt path. He was clean-shaven and his head was also shaved like a new recruit or a prisoner—had he been in custody? had he escaped?—and he was wearing his usual peasant shirt and baggy trousers, his old blue jacket. Now he was lying on his back in the grass.

Are you real?

The man was now talking to him about something else. Ancient writing. Carved in stone. Glyphs.

What are you talking about, Faya? Of course I'm real. As real as anything else.

"My father could read them, the glyphs. I am not sure how much he told Humboldt about these things, if Humboldt even cared about them."

He glanced down to where the shaman was drawing images in the dry dirt with a stick. Squares with lines inside. The lines seemed to make pictures. The pictures seemed to be of faces. Of animals, perhaps. He bent down closer to the dirt to see. He had left his spectacles somewhere. Close now, he could make out pictures from the lines, bumps, squiggles, and circles inside the squares. There were heads. Faces in profile. Patterns. Designs.

Maps.

In his mind, he saw a picture of a page. The page in the book. He remembered the book.

Monkey.

"Yes, there is a Monkey," said the man drawing in the dirt. "Here. This is Lord Monkey."

He drew a square with a circle at the top and lines coming up from the bottom like plants growing from the earth toward the sun.

Did you know about this, Kolya, when you wrote your book?

Just one of those weird coincidences.

Coincidence? Is there such a thing?

I know, right?

"Monkey is the name of a day. *Ozomatli* in Nahuatl. The days are gods for them. They are pagans, and worship strange deities."

He kept drawing the squares in a long line along the path. He spoke in a strange language. Pagan words and pagan gods. The air bristled around him. Little flames sprang out of the dirt where he moved his stick, and the stick itself left a trail behind it, of color or movement, as though he could see the movement, the displacement of spirits in the air as it moved, or of light, which was perhaps the same thing.

A wave of light, disturbed in its flow, interrupted, would part and allow the object of disruption to cast its passage through the wave... and now he was seeing it... with his own eyes... his now perfect vision... He moved his hand, and it too left a trail of light behind it.

Are you made of light, Nikolai Vasilevich, or are you here, in flesh and blood? And where did you come from, dear friend? Do you know we've been searching for you?

"They say Lord Monkey is the great craftsman. The god of art and knowledge. A good day."

By now the shaman had filled all the dirt with symbols.

Nikolai sat up suddenly.

Look what he's doing! He's making a map of the mind.

Those pictures?

They take you from day to day. They take you through time. They're pictures of thoughts. Of how the mind moves. The mind is the space-ship, Faya. You do realize that, don't you? Or should I say, the time-ship.

These sentences cut through the air, which had thickened. The words sliced through the thickness. He saw the map in front of him, floating in front of him. It was a chart, a nautical chart, with lines and arrows and figures. Impossible to read it. Or was it a musical score? Or a set of equations? Then pages and pages of writing in many different languages, written in many different scripts, with many different writing instruments—thick black Gothic letters and graceful Arabic script, the delicate brushwork of Chinese ideographs, the deep wedge-shaped carving of cuneiform, the pictorial carving of Egyptian hieroglyphs, a spidery Byzantine Greek—all flew past him as though a library of books had been released from their bindings and had taken to the air.

Maps of the mind.

His mind—it seemed he could think about different things at the same time. It seemed he was having several different conversations at the same time. Almost it seemed he was living several different lives at the same time.

But now he could not think at all because the world was racing ahead of him, and before him—before his own eyes—the spirit world was unfolding like a fan unfolding or a Japanese screen. He could almost see it, each panel opening in turn, each telling its own story but linked in some way with the panels that came before and the ones that would come after. And the air was thick with seeds and stardust, the spirits ranged about, spirits filling the air like gossamer, moving on silken pathways, in astral time, subtle bodies, Elena Petrovna called them, made of light.

And there was another world still, superimposed on that spirit one, the third world, in a dimension beyond them, and in that world was the dwelling place of Ideas, the perfect and pure Ideas of which all human ideas were a pale and meager copy. Oh, how intense the joy! He had dismissed philosophy, and rightly so, for this was not philosophy but truth. Not words on a page, not the stuttering of children, not dry theory, empty promises, false logic, cynicism, lies. All that was a mere shadow of THIS... and we are in the cave, encaved, entombed, like in Plato's story, the so-called myth of the cave, but the cave was no myth. Oh, Plato had seen this! He had known! Spirits, Daimons, Ideas—all real, just as he had said. He knew! Plotinus knew! It was not fabrication, myth, metaphor, lies. No, it was true!

His heart banged in his chest. His blood pounded.

He would die because his heart would burst from joy.

And then he would be released from his cumbersome body—his soul now encased in matter—and he would become part of that beautiful *anima mundi*, which he could see now in all its colors and its music, he could hear the colors, the sound of the colors, and see the music, the notes of sound. Yes, it was magnificent!—Even the choir of angels, that was true, too, for there they were, winged, glorious... and he knew in this blessed world in which all is soul even the tiniest creature was blessed and beatific and not lost.

Nothing was lost, ever, for it is all one, it is all existent, it is all present, everything at once.

Everything at once for there is no time.

Time is the lie.

Then amidst the colors, all the colors, a single star, the brightest star, came closer. He reached out to it, without fear. His soul reaching out for reunion with God. Everything was coming true.

And there standing before him was Nikolai, his friend.

What is it, Kolya? Tell me! Is it God?

Not God, my friend. Only the passage, the portal, the gate.

Are you going through? I will come with you!

But the light was so bright.

He turned to the shaman, but he was not there. What was there: an empty meadow, and a kind of mist in the air, and in the mist, the tunnel, just as he imagined it to be, a bright tunnel, a time portal. All around him, light was fading, and colors were dimming. Clouds above and below, and the tunnel, flickering, all alight.

Oh, he should follow Nikolai now! He should go through the tunnel. Margarita had done it. He had seen it with his own eyes.

But he was not alone after all. Fear was standing beside him. It closed his throat against voice, it closed his mind against love, it closed his heart.

What will I find inside it, beyond it?

Fear answered him. *Disembodiment. Disintegration. Emptiness. The void. Darkness. Death.*

He was so cold suddenly. He was trembling with cold.

Now he heard sounds. A rumbling, getting louder and louder. So much sound. Bellowing sound. A voice, shouting, speaking, saying words. He could not make them out. Then someone was there beside him. A human being. A blanket of some kind thrown over his shoulders.

"We have brought hot tea and some things to eat. Come now, have a little tea."

Who are you?

"I'm Sasha. I'm your friend Sasha. Now, drink this, Faya. It will do you good."

And who is that man, standing next to you?

"Mitya. He's Mitya. He's just bringing tea. He's leaving now. See? He's gone."

Every movement left its wave behind, left a streak of light in its wake. Every movement disturbed the field. Energy sparked and sparkled everywhere. The meadow was bright again, the cloud had passed. The mist had dispersed. Had taken Nikolai away with it. His friend.

The tea tasted bitter, so bitter. It was not tea at all.

He did not trust any words.

He looked around, but by then the door, the portal, the gate had closed, and, like Nikolai, it had disappeared.

⁂

He awoke with a start. It was night.

He was lying in the grass under a soft woolen blanket. The ground was cold and covered with dew.

He smelt smoke and heard the crackling of a fire. Yes, nearby a fire was burning, a little fire burning in the dark, from which came amazing sparks and flames of red and gold, and delightful warmth.

Sasha, his friend, was squatting there beside the great god of fire, holding a stick in the flames, playing with it like a child.

And overhead the dazzling stars, those blazing beings, those fires of the cosmos, were sparkling and twinkling and glistening in the velvet black sky.

He had traveled and now he was back on the good, solid earth, inside the comfort of time.

He had seen it, though. The portal had opened but he had not gone through, and now he never would.

And Nikolai?

I saw him with my own eyes. I saw him here and I saw him leave.

Where was he now? Where had he gone?

Tears were running down his cheeks, but for what? For what he had lost, or for what he had gained? He had seen things, he had seen miracles. The world had changed. Everything was different now, and different it would always remain.

CHAPTER TWENTY-NINE

The Doom of Margarita Mikhailevna

Like a physical journey—long, tiring, and uncomfortable as they always were—Fyodorov's spiritual journey took some time to recover from. For some days afterwards he could barely speak in anything but the simplest sentences. Objects—all objects, animate and inanimate—still had a glowing radiance about them. Light still moved slowly across his field of vision, leaving trails of color behind it. He found this fascinating and could watch it for hours on end. He felt satisfied with everything; everything pleased him and many things struck him as so funny that they made him laugh out loud. These were quite ordinary, everyday things: forks, buttons, Mitya's donkey, a rain shower.

By the end of the week, when he was again capable of formulating thoughts, he understood that the divine mushroom had lasting effects, that it had permeated the very cells of his body, enhanced the power of his senses, and fundamentally altered the character of his thoughts. He saw the world now with new eyes and understood it with a more expansive mind; and he knew for certain now—knew it in the very fabric of his soul—that everything in the world was holy, everything was sentient, living, and he was a living part of it, of this Oneness, this glorious Whole. *The World is God. God is the World.* It was a truth he felt sure he had once known very well but had somehow forgotten, to his great loss. Love for the world and all beings in it filled his heart. Joy filled his heart. He lived in a state of pure exaltation; everything around him wore a halo of light. At the same time, the practical concerns of life and the philosophical ideas that once consumed his attention lost all their power over him. It wasn't even that they no longer mattered; they simply ceased to exist. He was satisfied with where he was, in the little cottage on Prince Kirill's estate. He enjoyed listening to Alejandro tell his fantastic stories, and he chatted about the weather twice a day with

Mitya, who brought their meals, and he watched the progression of the spring with deep pleasure, in a state of bliss.

After awhile, however, he felt a need growing in him to record the experience he had had, to put it into words. He recognized this need as the beginning of his disenchantment. He realized what it was: he was returning to his former self. The god, the strange god, was leaving him.

His first impulse, once he recognized what was happening to him, was to eat the divine mushroom again, immediately. But Azara, keeper of the god, said no. It was too soon. In any case, it was impossible to reproduce the first encounter, and dangerous to try. Especially since there was no shaman guiding them, they had to take great care. The truth was that Azara himself had been quite frightened during their journey, frightened for Fyodorov, whom he thought might have been journeying too far. Some people did, and it was difficult to get them back. Some lost their minds entirely. In short, unless one was guided by a shaman, one should not approach the mysteries at all, and certainly not as cavalierly as they had done.

His initial response was annoyance, then suspicion… Azara wanted to keep the mushrooms for himself!… then anger. Once these feelings ebbed, a period of sorrow took him into its grip. It felt like a grip; he could not loosen himself from it. The sunlight lost its glimmer; the spring lost its magic. He felt empty and bereaved. When the grief finally passed, he was faced with summer heat and lethargy and boredom. There was nothing for him in the country. It was time to leave. But where would he go? The thought of returning to his laboratory filled him with dismay.

Before he made any decision, however, Fyodorov decided he should indeed write as full an account as he could of his drug-induced experience, for now that the wonder had worn away, he acknowledged that the mushroom's power was no more miraculous than that of the opium poppy; Nature provided men with such potent substances, to use or misuse as they chose.

But then, to his amazement, as he wrote and brought the experience back to mind, as he meditated on what he had felt and thought and seen, something wonderful happened: joy returned to him. He could feel it slowly unfurling within him again like a new leaf opening or a small flower. He remembered how time had vanished, he remembered how the world had appeared to him, beautiful, and whole, and good. He had experienced that reality vividly, he had experienced it as true, and it was true, even though from now on he would have to take its truth on faith, being unable to feel it again as he had felt it when the mushroom had revealed it to him.

Just as clearly, he now remembered his friend Sasha, his guide, caring for him, bringing him tea; he remembered Sasha writing in the dirt with a stick, and how the glyphs he had drawn had reminded him of the page in Nikolai's book, and how Sasha had called them maps of the mind. If he had only been able to find the book! But the book was lost, irretrievably lost, and he would never know its secrets. No, that was untrue. He had been offered its secrets, the portal had opened up before him, but he had turned away.

Oh, now it all came back to him in a flood of images and memories—how he had recited the Plotinus poem and how Nikolai had appeared, wearing his usual old jacket, and had sat down by him in the grass. He remembered the coming of the great light and his thinking it was the Beatific Vision, and Nikolai's words: *It is the portal, the gate.*

Now as he wrote, tears filled his eyes and ran in streams down his cheeks. He had been overcome with fear and not gone through the time tunnel, if time tunnel it was. But worse than that, he now understood what it meant that Nikolai had left him and vanished into the mist. It was what he had known for some time but had refused to admit. Nikolai, his friend, so dear to him, he had never known before how dear, was no longer living in this world.

"Back to Petersburg?" Azara exclaimed in some horror. "Surely not, Fyodor. Surely the city in summer… it's unbearable! And up in your garret? Oh, in the name of all that is holy… my dear friend, don't be a fool!"

He laughed, and clapped Fyodorov on the back, a friendly familiarity which was one of his charms. He was a charming man, no doubt about it, but Fyodorov did not think he could charm him into staying in the country, and he said so.

"Stay in the country? But a visit to a country estate is hardly 'staying in the country,' as you put it with such disparagement. Don't you remember we have an invitation to visit Princess Volkonskaya? Surely you haven't forgotten! You said you would come to High Meadows with me. You planned to come. Fyodor, my dear friend, it may be a special occasion, it may be the occasion of the announcement of my engagement to the lovely Margarita Mikhailevna. I need you to come and be by my side. An engagement is an ordeal. One must have friends about one at such an agonistic time."

"You are so eager to see the Princess, yet you have no news to report."

"I have no news, it is true. But I cannot wait any longer. I must make a decision, to stay or return to Vienna. I have spent the winter here and the spring. I regret having been unable to fulfill my promise to the Princess, but I am running out of time."

"And you have written and received an invitation?"

"I have. And the invitation extends to my dear friend, Fyodor Fyodorovich Fyodorov. You see, you, too, have been invited. You, too, are included. Come now, Faya, don't be stubborn and difficult. Come with me and meet the princesses. Anyway, you have already met Margarita, haven't you? You told me so."

"I have not met her. Never in my life."

Azara shrugged. "It will be a pleasant surprise then. What do you say?"

"Let me consider it," Fyodorov said.

An agonistic time indeed. For it would be a sure test of his hypotheses, to meet the enigmatic Margarita Mikhailevna, to discover whether she had any memory of him, or he of her. And what if he remembered her but she denied any memory of him? What would he do? Alternatively, what if she did remember? What then?

For the rest of the day he pretended he had some choice to make, but in fact there was no choice at all.

"I will accompany you to High Meadows," he said over supper that evening. "But there are some questions I must ask you, Sasha, and I trust you will tell me the truth. It is very important that I know the truth."

Azara sat back in his chair, black eyes flashing in the candlelight, and said that of course he would answer and of course he would tell the truth. "We are friends, and compañeros. We have taken the divine mushroom together. This is a deep bond."

"When we were taking the mushrooms together..." He did not know how else to put it. "...why did you show me the Mayan glyphs?"

"Why?"

"Yes. Why."

"I don't know why. I had a stick in my hand. I started drawing them. I enjoy drawing them. They remind me of—being a child, being with my father, being home. I was happy to tell you the story of them. To share them with you. They upset you though, didn't they? They were too—strange? Forgive me."

"No, no. Not at all, Sasha. Listen, you took the divine mushroom with Nikolai Vasilevich, too. Can you remember taking it with him?"

"Of course I remember."

"Did he talk to you about it afterwards? Did he tell you what happened to him?"

First Azara smiled, but seeing how serious Fyodorov was, he immediately changed his own expression to one of thoughtfulness. But Fyodorov was still close enough to the god of the mushroom to recognize the falseness of this change. Azara felt the question he had asked was funny and he could not disguise that feeling.

"Why do you laugh?"

"I am not laughing. But you must admit that it is difficult enough to understand what happens to oneself, and to speak about it. How much more difficult to understand and then remember what someone else said about his own experience. And it was years ago. Really, Faya, you ask too much. Let me think a moment."

While Azara thought, Fyodorov refilled their glasses and took out his pipe and tobacco. While he was doing these things, he also thought. He thought about *maps of the mind* and he tried to remember if he had thought those words or if Azara had. For surely his very clear memory of Nikolai's presence in the meadow had to have been a hallucination, and hallucinations, naturally, do not come up with ideas of their own. Surely not, he insisted to himself. Some things are patently and absolutely impossible. The entire notion of time travel, of time portals, of mind maps, of Mayan glyphs, of a day called Lord Monkey—all nonsense.

"Yes, I do recall it," Azara said. "Yes, and I wonder now how I could have forgotten. The mind has dark old storerooms one hardly ever enters. But now the candle's been lit, and who appears in the circle of light but Nikolai Vasilevich."

Fyodorov waited, listening. It would be a long story. Long-winded. Round-about. Circling around and around. Never quite getting there.

Nothing direct. Nothing to the point. It would begin at the beginning of time and meander through the ages. There would be magical incantations and bizarre, esoteric references. Truth was always hidden, draped, concealed, missing or misplaced.

"Yes, I remember. I taught him some of the glyphs. He was interested, you see. In the stories. In traveling. We had always talked about traveling there together, into the jungles, to see the great temples. But Nick hates trees. He was lost in a forest once, and he came to hate trees. He claims that trees terrify him. What a funny man he is!"

"Being lost in a forest is frightening."

"Yes. That is true."

"Is that all you remember? That you showed him some glyphs? Nothing else?"

"No, no. There is more."

But what more there was was so woven into Azara's own tale that it was impossible for Fyodorov to untangle it. There appeared to have been a fire, and forms of gods had emerged from the flames. The gods had come alive, they had spoken—in what language? Azara could not recall, but he understood them and so did Nikolai—and they had traveled with them. Yes, they had traveled with the gods, they had flown, out of body; they had been taken on a voyage.

"Are you sure that Nikolai was on this voyage with you? It seemed to me, when I was under the influence of the mushroom, that I was quite alone, that my experience was not one that could be shared."

"True, it was like a dream, but we were dreaming it together. We were taken up, as though our spirits were gripped tight in the talons of great birds. We flew with them. Flying, Faya! That is the truth. Flying. We were taken into a different world. Perhaps it was heaven. The colors! The sensations! Unbelievable. And the spirits there, and the love one feels for them... the communion with them, the unity with them. That is why I laugh at Madame Blavatskaya and her astral bodies. I have seen astral bodies, my friend, in all their glory. I have seen angels."

"And Nikolai had this same experience?"

"Yes. Yes, he did. We took the journey together."

"And you talked about it?"

"Yes. We talked as it happened to us. We talked afterwards, too, for days afterwards. We were both so happy. We both remembered everything. And didn't you feel it as well, Faya? Didn't you feel you were entering another world, a world filled with love? Perhaps you did enter it? Perhaps you saw it, too? But, of course, you and I took a much smaller amount. I had so many mushrooms with me the last time, I think Nick and I must have eaten four or five grams each."

"The mushrooms have some chemical power."

"The mushrooms have spiritual power. Listen, I am a scientist, too. I know the world is made up of atoms and energy, chemicals and compounds. Matter and spirit. A theologian will say the same. Plotinus says the same, doesn't he? The mushroom is also matter and spirit. The more you consume of the god, the closer to the god you come."

"I see," Fyodorov said. "Yes, I understand."

Two days later, they left the little cottage on Prince Kirill's estate and set out for High Meadows, Azara, optimistic and in the best of moods, despite the mud-clogged roads, Fyodorov somewhat pensive and somber. He had spent the day before trying to imagine a meeting with Margarita Mikhailevna and what might result from it. The more he tried to imagine it, the more complicated each possible scenario seemed, and the less confident he became of having the wherewithal to go through with it. Finally he decided that the lady would not recognize him, that it was impossible that she should, and that therefore he had nothing to worry about. His hypotheses would not be proven, but that was all to the good. His hypotheses were no longer of any interest to him. His goal all along had been to find Nikolai and his book, and now that he was sure neither was possible—both man and book lost forever and never to be recovered in this life—the thrill had gone out of the chase. It even seemed to him as he rode along that the thrill had gone out of life as well, and that he had nothing to look forward to but disappointment, solitude, and defeat.

Despite the beautiful spring day, the blossoming groves, the sweetness in the air, that was his state of mind as they drove through the gates of High Meadows, and arrived at the front door of the house. Palace, he corrected himself. The windows gleamed in the sunlight, the yellow stone glowed. The building seemed to stretch out on both sides like a beautiful woman, just awakening, stretching her arms—oh, what foolishness, Fyodor Fyodorovich! now you fancy yourself a poet!—and Alexander Felixovich bounded up the steps as though he already owned it, he was already master of the house.

But it was clear from the first that something was very wrong. Outside, the palace was all grace and charm, gardens and meadows, flowers and fountains, but within, there was a darkness, a gloom. Fyodorov was not an intuitive man, but he was still imbued with the spirit of the divine mushroom which gave him a certain insight, a certain sensitivity to emotion, and the emotion of the house was grim.

They were met by an elderly, black-clad lady who introduced herself as Yevgenia Dmitrievna, a dear friend of Princess Volkonskaya, offered them refreshments, inquired politely about their journey, informed them of the various times meals were served, invited them to make themselves comfortable in the house or explore the grounds, and made apologies on behalf of the princess, who regretted she could not be there to greet them, but would most certainly see them at supper. They were then led away to their rooms by a kindly old servant who, when gently questioned by Fyodorov, admitted that things in the house were not as they should be, but would say no more.

"If there was sickness in the house, they would surely have told us," Azara said. "It can't be that."

"No. It isn't illness. Something else."

Yet, as they moved around the house, there was that palatable hush in the rooms that signified a suspension of normal life, that signified illness or even death.

Fyodorov spent only a short time in his room before going out into the gardens to escape the oppressive silence of the palace. The gardens were extensive and alive with the chattering and piping of birds, the buzzing of bees drawn to the sweet scent of flowers, and the reassuring sounds of human voices and human labor, the gardeners at work among the flower beds.

He sensed rather than saw the figure of a woman, sitting quite still and almost completely concealed beneath a vine-covered pergola. For a moment his heart leapt, his pulse began racing, he felt almost dizzy, weak... What if this was Margarita! What if she turned to him now and recognized him! His clothes weighed on him, his collar oppressed him, he felt too weak to stand, and looked around for some seat, a garden chair, a bench... How absurd if he were to faint away... Then a workman appeared at his elbow, saying, "Now, then, sir, now then, take a breath..." and he realized he was lying on the path. He had collapsed. And there was the woman, tall, dressed in blue, standing over him, saying, "Poor man, it's the heat, bring him inside....Carefully now!" Then strong arms were lifting him off the ground, brushing him off, yes, he could stand, he was quite all right... "Nonsense," said the woman, "bring him onto the terrace. Get him a whiskey and soda..."

Installed quite quickly on the terrace, in the shade, with a cold drink in his hand, Fyodorov, highly embarrassed and apologetic, was exhorted to drink up, to loosen his collar, to think nothing of it, but to be so kind as to introduce himself, which he did. The kind, voluble lady in blue was yet another dear friend of Princess Volkonskaya, Mariya Sergeyevna, and it took her very little time to find out everything of importance about Fyodor Fyodorovich: his rank, occupation, place of residence, marital status, relationship with the princess—"None whatsoever"—mode of travel, traveling companion, relationship with same, until they arrived at last to the purpose of their visit, upon which question, like a ship crashing against a reef, he finally foundered.

"Never mind," said the lady. "Now I am prying. Forgive me."

"Not at all," he said.

"Tatyana invited you and you came."

"Yes. Well, to be sure, she invited Alexander Felixovich, and, with her permission, he invited me."

"And you are a doctor of medicine?"

"I have studied medicine, yes, but I am not—"

"And a cosmist, you say. What is that, exactly?"

He began to explain his scientific work as succinctly as he could, but got no further than the first few sentences when once again Mariya Sergeyevna interrupted him.

"We are getting rather desperate, you see."

He did not see, but said nothing.

"Tatyana won't have anything to do with priests, of course, and I don't blame her in the least, but I am beginning to think the situation calls for something of the kind. I believe we need a scientist of the soul."

What an extraordinary statement, he thought, in some confusion, until, almost immediately, it occurred to him that, of course, he understood: she was explaining the situation in the house, alluding to a particular desperation.

"And you believe I may be of some assistance?" he said.

She smiled at him. "I do sincerely hope you may be. I am not entirely unacquainted with you, you know. We have a dear friend in common, who spoke so kindly and admiringly of you when I saw her last that I almost feel that I know you very well myself. Marko Volchek."

For the second time that day, he felt as though his heart might stop.

"Marko," he whispered. It was all he could manage.

"She is a scrupulous judge of character. We trust her entirely."

He should have answered politely, but he found he could not speak at all.

Marko! His heart throbbing, his mouth dry, he felt a great fool, the greatest of fools, and yet some foolish part of him could not help jumping for joy, just at the sound of her name, and another foolish part of him could not resist asking Mariya Sergeyevna, once he could speak again, a single, simple question, "Where is she?"

"In Odessa. Or she was, for the winter."

"Odessa!"

"The green roofs of Odessa!" Mariya Sergeyevna sighed. "Yes, and the mud and the dust. Well, it's bearable in winter, at least. Evidently she is writing there. Well, as for our problem here... But I should let Tatyana explain it to you. And she will, in her own good time."

♣

The time for explanations did not come that afternoon, nor did Princess Tatyana join them for supper, a very fulsome meal, served not in the great dining hall, but a smaller supper room. At the table, besides Fyodorov and Azara, were Yevgenia Dmitrievna and Mariya Sergeyevna, several other house guests and several resident relatives, distinguished-looking men and well-dressed women, whose names Fyodorov tried valiantly but vainly to remember. Who was not present, he noted, besides Princess Tatyana, was her daughter, Margarita Mikhailevna. Poor Azara, having so anxiously awaited his meeting with her, was so crushed by her absence that he sat silently at the table, barely raising his eyes, hardly touching his food. The relatives and house guests chatted among themselves, making the occasional attempt to draw the newcomers into their conversation, but Azara, petulantly (Fyodorov thought) refused to say a word, and Fyodorov himself, never an overly talkative dinner guest at the best of times, relied entirely on the prolixity of Mariya Sergeyevna, sitting on his right, to navigate him safely through the meal with as little embarrassment at his own shyness as possible.

After supper, she took his arm, and whispering, "She will see you now," steered him across the gallery and up the stairs. They walked down a corridor and entered a large, pleasant room done in ivory and pale rose. A tall, elegant woman was standing at a large window whose drapes had been pulled back to reveal the deeper rosy glow of the sunset and a golden ray of light that so gilded her figure that his first impression of Princess Tatyana as she turned to greet them was of a golden-framed icon, a stern angel or a saint.

They sat on velvet-covered chairs. She offered him brandy, which he refused. Mariya Sergeyevna left them, and when she did, that same strange hush fell over the room which her lively presence had for a time dispelled. By then, the sun had set, the sky had darkened. A servant came in quietly and closed the drapes.

"It is as though some sorcery is at work, though I am enough of an old-fashioned rationalist and liberal to despise myself for saying so. And, yet, Fyodor Fyodorovich, I swear to you, I have no other explanation for what has happened to Margarita Mikhailevna."

"What *has* happened, Princess? You see, I am quite in the dark."

Princess Tatyana stroked her lips with her fingertips, as though trying to silence herself or erase her words, either those she had already spoken or the ones she seemed now to be unwilling to utter. In the pause, the silence was heavy, thick, unbroken. He felt he had suddenly gone deaf.

"Well," she said, though it was more a sigh than a word, "it appears she has lost her mind. Yes, for all intents and purposes, she is mad."

"Brain fever?" he said. "There are treatments."

She gave him a small, condescending smile. "Those treatments have been tried. Let us call her illness by its proper name."

"How does this illness manifest itself?"

"How? She will not leave that miserable hut she has taken to live in. She will not speak to us when we attempt to talk to her. She sits and stares out the window, at nothing, or else she sits just outside the threshold, in the dirt. Poor child! She barely eats, she does not wash. She wraps herself in rags and sits outside the hut in the dirt. And she weeps."

Fyodorov picked up the decanter of brandy and poured himself a glass. He drank it. He set it down.

"How long ago did this begin?"

"How long? Let me see… I suppose it began in January. I blame myself. We should have gone to Moscow for the winter. I don't know what possessed me to stay here. Yes, proximity to Anastasia, of course, but I might have sent Margarita to my sister's. There was nothing for her to do here. Then Alexander Felixovich wrote to us, and I suppose she was looking forward to seeing him… But time dragged on and on, you know. The winter was particularly severe…"

"Did it begin slowly, or was it as though something changed for her overnight?"

"I can't say. I didn't see her every day. We didn't always have our meals together. Perhaps I was … inattentive. But, yes, it appeared that it happened without warning. Suddenly she decided to sleep in the hut. She calls it a cottage. It's hardly that. Then she began spending all her time there. I would send messages. She never sent back a reply."

"This hut is at a distance?"

"Yes. At the far end of the estate. When I go there to see her, she does not acknowledge me. It is like she is sleeping, but with her eyes open. As though she were in a trance. Hypnotized. Of course, I had doctors come. They diagnosed brain fever, They advised rest cures. Rest cures! I dismissed them all. What good were they? Rest cures!"

"I would like to visit her, if I may."

"Do you think you can help her, Fyodor Fyodorovich? Please, I want you to tell me the truth."

"I don't know if I can help her, Princess. But I would like to try."

"Tomorrow morning, then, we shall visit her together after breakfast. I am most grateful to you."

The interview was over. He rose then, bowed, and left the room, so filled with emotion he felt he might burst.

The house was still. He went down the stairs to the hall, through the drawing room, onto the terrace. No one was about, everyone having retired to their rooms. It was palpable, the sense of doom that hung over the house, and no one wished to be caught in it, that much was clear to him. Better to disappear into a corner than arouse the fury of whatever devils were ranging about, leaving chaos in their wake. Not only the guests and resident relatives, but the house serfs and servants, the maids and cooks, the cleaners and porters, the panoply of domestics who would normally inhabit the lower floors, even they had vanished, leaving a ghostly silence. The light was ghostly, too, for clouds had moved in, covering the moon and stars, bringing the sky closer to the earth, as though a curtain of gauze had dropped over the heavens. The air itself had thickened so that it was hard to breathe.

To return to a sense of normality, he sat in a chair and prepared his pipe and deliberately lit it and smoked it although he had no real desire to do so. The night was still, the smoke, rather than dispersing in the air, hovered around him, he felt how falsely he was behaving, but then he felt how false the world was behaving, becoming every day stranger and stranger. Still, he soon knocked the burning tobacco out of his pipe and walked down the terrace steps into the garden where he could breathe in the freshness of plant life and the purity of the soil. Everything was hanging in the balance now, disaster or exaltation, madness or salvation. Either she would recognize him or she would not. He felt in the secret darkness of his heart that she would; he felt in the bright clarity of his mind that she would not and that even to imagine that she might was itself a kind of madness, his own madness.

Remember, Faya, fortune favors the bold!

He stopped in his tracks, and held his breath. Impossible, yet he had heard it, as clearly and distinctly as any voice speaking to him, as someone speaking to him who was standing just beside him. But no one was there. He waited, pricking up his ears, listening, listening.

Kolya?

Was it possible that he was here? Of course it was. Why not?

Kolya!

Yes, of course! This was exactly the place where he would be. Why hadn't they thought of looking for him here? High Meadows—the perfect bolt hole! Safe, secure, protected, with luxurious accommodations, and the best food and drink—a palace!

And, of course, Margarita.

Love leaped out in front of us like a murderer in an alley and instant-

ly struck us both at once. Though she insisted that we'd loved each other for a long, long time without even knowing one another.

Sensing a movement behind him, Fyodorov spun on his heel—*Kolya, is that you?*—but it was only an animal, a cat, slinking away under a bush. But now the garden was filling up with sound, croaking and piping, buzzing and cooing, rustling and bubbling, and with shapes, and with movement, for a breeze had come up and the young plants were swaying... *and all the trees are bowing down, bending back and forth, back and forth, in the gale...* Lines from a poem Margarita had not remembered, Anastasia's poem, one of Nikolai's favorites. It all came back to him now, that day in the inn: how Margarita had told them, Blavatskaya and himself, that she was Kolya's wife, told them that Kolya had burnt his novel, told them that she had saved a few pages from the flames. Then she changed shape in front of their eyes and disappeared into a ray of light. *I must go back now,* she had said, *or I will never find him again.*

Who was that creature? Blavatskaya had thought she was a goddess, a Muse. A Muse would have the power to transform herself into a lovely young woman or a ferocious bear. A goddess would be able to disappear into a ray of light. But was it rational to believe in Muses or goddesses? And should such a divine being exist, was it possible that she might also be this girl, Margarita Mikhailevna, daughter of Princess Tatyana Volkonskaya? No, it was utterly impossible unless the world was a very different place than what one was taught to believe.

But it is, Faya. It is a very different place than we were taught to believe. Our ignorance of the world is only rivaled by our arrogance in refusing to acknowledge it.

What then? Tomorrow, when I go to her, what will I find?

You'll only know by going. You worry too much, Faya. You do realize that, don't you?

Surely, it was his voice. He strained his eyes in the dark, but he could see nothing.

Where are you, Kolya?

No answer.

The next morning after breakfast, they set out for the cottage, he on horseback, the princess in a well-appointed pony cart accompanied by a driver and a groom. A bridle path took them through a small wood and along the edge of a meadow. Fyodorov was not a particularly good horseman, and would have preferred riding in the pony cart, too; thankfully the cottage was not as far from the house as he had imagined.

They had barely come in sight of it when they realized they were not the only visitors that morning. A horse was calmly grazing some distance from the little house while some terrible argument seemed to be in progress on the doorstep. Fyodorov, insisting the princess remain with the cart—she did not, of course, but followed right behind him—went rushing into the midst of the fray. He recognized that one of the contending parties was his friend Alexander Felixovich, holding his arms over his head to protect himself, and that the other, wielding a thick walking cane with which she was pounding him, was the lovely Margarita Mikhailevna.

"Murderer!" she was shouting. "Devil!"

Fyodorov rushed up and, pushing Azara back, placed himself in front of Margarita, in the process taking a glancing blow from her cane.

"Get away! Let me at him!" she cried, and then shouting at Azara over Fyodorov's shoulder, "I know who you are! I know what you did!"

"My dear Margarita Mikhailevna—" Azara cried, pleading earnestly, but she was still shouting at him.

"Demon! Monster! And call me by my proper name. You know it! And I know yours, Azazello, you poisoner! Have you come to poison us again?"

Azara stood helplessly before her. It was obvious that her rage was quite beyond him, and Fyodorov felt a wave of compassion for him as well as for the graceful, beautiful, aristocratic woman she must once have been, now transformed into a virago, attacking him in a mad frenzy.

"You spy! You liar! Informer! Monster!"

Princess Volkonskaya, rushing up to her daughter, pleaded with her to stop yelling, to calm herself, to put down the cane. "Margarita, my darling!" the Princess kept saying. "Margarita, my love," while trying to embrace her, but Margarita kept pushing her away.

"Monster! I remember every word you said! *Fire!* you said. *Fire, with which all began and with which we end it all!* And you drew out a flaming brand from the stove and you set the room on fire, you burnt his books, his manuscript. *The novel, the novel!* I cried. *I remember it by heart,* he said. *I remember every word. I'll never forget anything now!* Then we escaped from you, we mounted on black steeds, they rose into the air, they broke through the linden branches, they soared into the sky and raced over the rooftops."

"She is mad," Azara said, backing away from her. "Mad! What a pity!"

"Pity?" she cried. "You dare say the word? You, Azazello? You can deceive *them*, you can wear that Spanish disguise, but I know you for what you are. Informer! Spy!"

"Sasha," Fyodorov said, "you must go now. Immediately! Princess, please, take him with you. Take him away."

"Yes. Of course. Come along, Azara. You've done enough harm for one day."

"Harm? What harm?"

"Do your best," she said to Fyodorov in a low voice. Then she called for the groom, who stepped right up, gripped Azara by the arm, and led him somewhat forcibly away to his horse.

"Margarita!" he called back to her over his shoulder.

"Devil!" she said, and spat on the ground like a peasant.

They stood a little apart, beside a flowering lilac bush, staring at each other.

Yes, she was the same young woman he and Blavatskaya had rescued from the house of the dreadful Pavel Beriosov, the same raven-haired beauty who had spoken about Nikolai Vasilevich with such ardor, the same ravishing creature who had vanished into a ray of light, but how changed she was now, how sunken her cheeks, how dull, disordered and knotted her hair, how roughened her hands and ragged her nails, how coarse and hoydenish her voice. She was like some strong, young tree suddenly devastated by blight, or some wild animal, a panther or lioness, trapped and caged, surrendering itself to bitterness and grief, but with just enough spirit left to claw and bite and roar.

"I know you," she said. "What is your name?"

He bowed, and told her.

She turned her head, first to the right, then to the left.

MARGARITA MIKHAILEVNA

She was the same young woman they had rescued from the dreadful Pavel Beriosov—but how changed she was!

"They have gone."

"Yes, they have."

"But you remain. Why?"

"I am pleased that you recognize me," he said, gently. "You do recognize me?"

"I have seen you before. Haven't I? In one... place or another."

"I believe so, yes. Might we go inside?"

She hesitated for a moment, then opened the door and nodded him in.

Inside, what Tatyana referred to as a hut was more like a cottage, clean and neat, though small, with a low ceiling. In the front room was a table covered with a red velvet tablecloth, upon which was a small vase filled with lilies of the valley. There was also a low cabinet, a china stove, a worn red sofa with several embroidered pillows. The adjoining room contained a bureau and a narrow bed. But what he noticed first and foremost was the small uncovered table against the window upon which was a tall stack of paper. A manuscript!

"I have nothing to offer you," she said. "But sit on the sofa, Fyodor Fyodorovich. It is old but comfortable."

He sat on the sofa; she sat facing him on a rough-hewn wooden chair. And so, here we are, he thought.

"How do you wish me to address you?' he asked.

"Margarita."

"And your patronymic?"

"It is unnecessary." She sighed deeply. "Nothing is necessary."

He had a vision of all the necessary things, one by one vanishing into thin air, showing themselves to be of no account at all. Vanishing into nothing...

"In that case, please call me Fyodor."

"So then, Fyodor... why have you come here? What is it you want?"

He had imagined this meeting for so long, but now he could not frame an answer to that simple question.

"I am so full of words right now, dear Margarita, I don't know how to begin."

"They oppress me, words."

"I find them quite inadequate to the task we have assigned to them."

"You say you are full of words. How does it feel, this fullness?"

His chest felt tight, his heart beat fast and loud, his throat was closing, his sight darkening, he couldn't breathe…

"See? They are choking you, poor Fyodor. Speak! Say whatever you want. It doesn't matter to me."

"You *are* a Muse, then," he whispered, just getting his breath back, just feeling his chest expand again, allowing him to breathe.

"A Muse? Better to say it is my doom to drive men into spewing out an endless stream of empty words, to choke us and strangle us with words, as though the world were not full enough."

She got up and went to the cabinet, returning with a bottle and two glasses.

"Only mineral water, I am afraid," she said, pouring them each a glass.

The water was delicious, cool and sweet. It relieved his thirst wonderfully.

"Now, please, Fyodor, say what you came here to say."

What had he come to say? *Who are you?*

"You say you remember me, and I remember you; yet, we have not met before. How is that possible?"

"Perhaps we have dreamt about each other. Perhaps we have met in a dream."

"A dream about the house of Pavel Beriosov? For that's where I first saw you, Margarita. You were a prisoner in his house."

"Yes. Betrayed and brought there by Azazello, that monster!"

"But not the man who was here. His name is Alejandro Azara. Surely you are mistaking him for someone else."

At the mention of Azara's name, her eyes narrowed, her mouth contorted in anger, she almost bared her teeth.

"Mistake him? I would never mistake that devil, devil, murderer, betrayer. He is a snake, he slithers, simpers and sneaks. He's a drug addict, and, worse, he's a rat."

"I have heard those words before."

"Of course you have. I say them to Venka in *Wide and Crooked*."

"So—you are Monika?"

"Of course."

"And Azara—is Arif?"

"The devil. Yes. There are many devils in the world. One recognizes them on sight. What difference what names one gives them?" She poured more of the sparkling clear, honey-sweet water into his empty glass. He had not realized how thirsty he was. "Nikolai has a nose for these devils, he gets to know them personally so he can use them in his work. Sometimes he gets too close, he takes risks, he plays with fire, sometimes he even seems to become a devil himself, to sink into that life, to lose himself in that world—yes, to fight, to steal, to lie drunk on the streets. But any real artist must do the same, for to forge from such gross materials as we have at hand a work of art that tells the truth is a dangerous task, it takes heroism, and, indeed, very few survive its battles. Misha Bulgakov also fills his novel with devils in order to make it true to his time, which will be even more devilish than our own. Azazello is the name of one of his devils. A minor one. It is a name that suits Azara, who is a minor one as well. Our major devils have good Russian names, normal Russian names. Great Russian names..."

He tried to think logically, and logic told him that in her madness Margarita Mikhailevna had begun to confuse fictional characters with real people, Azara with Arif and with this mysterious Azazello. Very well. But what about himself? He had experienced something, too, that might well have come from the pages of a book.

"It was real, though, wasn't it?" he muttered to himself. "Yes, it happened."

"Our meeting at the house of Beriosov? Yes, it happened. But dreams also happen. Dreams also feel vivid and real while you are dreaming them, but when you awaken, you barely remember them and they fade away... We are dreaming even now, don't you see? ... Oh!" she cried, jumping to her feet. "And it is a terrible, terrible dream! Please, please, let me awaken!"

Rapidly she walked back and forth across the room, and back and forth again; she flung open the door and stared out. More and more she was resembling that wild creature, the Margarita he remembered from the inn near Finland, the Margarita who had paced the room there, the goddess-shape-shifter who had changed herself into a bear, who had disappeared into a ray of light. There was something magnificent about her now, like a great, wild creature caged, and also something quite terrifying.

"If you would only come with me, Margarita. Leave this place. Your mother—"

"I can't leave this place. Are you blind? Don't you see? I have a rendezvous here. I am waiting." She stopped pacing and flung herself into the wooden chair, looked into his face, laughed. "Dear Fyodor, I am frightening you. Forgive me. Oh, but it is terrible, terrible, to be caught in the web of time! But I see that all this emotional talk is making you sleepy."

"Do excuse me," he said, shocked at himself, for he had just yawned, and done so unconsciously, without any attempt at concealing it.

"Never mind. Only I wonder—have you said what you came here to say? Have you asked the questions you came to ask? Are you satisfied with the answers? Here, I will recite a poem for you. Not a good one, but then of all the poems in the world there are so few one would care to remember at the last moment of one's life, so few indeed. But this is almost a lullaby. Oh, how one might sing it to a child… to console him… for all he must lose…

Farewell, dear world, that I must leave.
Farewell, swift flying birds, abounding trees.
Farewell autumnal gold and wintry gales,
And summers spent on greenwood trails.
Farewell song and music, games and art,
And you, I bid adieu to you, my Love, my Heart,
Of all lights in this world, the last to fail.

How full life seems until, with joy's retreat,
We sense the emptiness beneath our feet,
Like petrels, dancing on the ocean's foam,
When nothing lies below us but the deep.

As he listened, great waves of fatigue washed over him, and by the last line, he felt such a great swell of sleepiness, he could barely continue sitting upright.

"Lie down," she said softly. "Lie down, lie down, rest your head. The sofa is old but comfortable…"

♣

Perhaps the sofa was comfortable, but the coach had very poor springs and it rumbled and bumped along in the dark, the roadway being, as usual, rutted and unpaved.

"The rotten roads of Russia!" his traveling companion said with a laugh. He had the shaved head of a convict or a new recruit, but his cheeks were round like a child's or a cherub's. "Another of life's bitter disappointments."

The lady in the black veil sitting across from them shook her head. She was so thoroughly draped in lace he could not see the expression on her face, whether she was smiling in agreement with the sentiment or frowning at such unpatriotic criticism. Surely she could not be disagreeing with the assessment itself, as a huge bump sent them all a few inches into the air.

He gazed out the window and saw that even though it was night he could see quite well in the dark. He could see they were passing a village, and he could even see some of the sad faces of the poor children sitting in the dirt in front of the old wooden houses, and he could see also, to his great amazement, inside the houses and inside the bare rooms where people were eating their frugal suppers, the men's beards bobbing up and down as they chewed their crusts of bread, the women's torn and ragged skirts, the crying children, in every passing house the same scenes of poverty and sorrow.

He turned from the window and trained his gimlet gaze on the woman in black but he still could not penetrate the veil and see her face.

"I expect we'll get to the river by dawn," his companion said. "Nothing like being on a river early in the morning."

"It's just a crossing, isn't it?" he said, nervously. He was not fond of riverboats, or really boats of any kind.

"Yes. Just a ferry crossing. Still, the great thing is that anything can happen on the water. The river is deep, the currents are strong, the ferrymen are usually drunk, there's a lot of water under your feet, you're way out of your depth."

"You say it as though you enjoy that feeling."

His companion laughed. "Of being scared to death? Absolutely. Don't you?"

"The fear of death gives life its thrill," said a low voice from behind the black veil. "Ironic, isn't it?"

"But quite true," his companion said. "Life has few pleasures that rival the thrill of coming within spitting distance of death and escaping with your life."

"Few pleasures that rival it, you say?" the lady in the black veil replied. "What might they be, I wonder? Perhaps no pleasure comes close to it, not the pleasures of love, or the pleasures of creation, or the pleasures of the contemplation of beauty. What if in fact there is no rival at all to the pleasure of coming face to face with death?"

A feeling of horror was creeping in on him.

The woman across from him took hold of her veil with her black-gloved hands and began to lift it up. The face beneath the veil was—

"Ah!" he cried. "No!" and sat up, his heart banging in his chest.

"Well, I see you're finally awake. How was your nap?" his companion asked.

"I had a terrible dream," he said, staring all around as though he could not believe where he was.

"What was it?"

"I was in a coach, going to the river, to a ferry crossing. To cross over—"

The carriage lurched, and his companion laughed. "Well, you are in a coach, there's no doubt about that."

"There was a woman with us. A woman in a black veil. She was Death."

"I have never had a dream like that. How did it feel, coming into such close proximity to Death?"

"I did not like it at all."

His companion laughed again, and beautiful Margarita Mikhailevna, stylishly dressed in a light blue traveling coat and sitting directly across from him, just where, in his dream, the lady in the black veil had been sitting, said, "Of course you didn't." Then, addressing his companion, "The tone was all wrong. It was far too Gothic for him. The other one was far better."

"The Surreal one, you mean? I totally agree," his companion said.

"Well, of course you agree. It was so completely Bulgakovian."

"I know, right?" his companion said with a laugh.

"I don't follow," he said. "What 'other one'? And what is the meaning of Bulgakovian?"

"He doesn't remember," Margarita said sadly.

"Oh, yes, he does. He's just pretending he doesn't. He's always pretending he doesn't know what he knows." Then addressing him directly, his companion said, "Listen, you were in another coach, much like this one, with another woman, quite different from Margarita. She was ugly, bossy, opinionated, she smoked the stinkiest cheroots—"

"Blavatskaya!"

"See?" his companion said. "He remembers. And, as Margarita just said, it was entirely in the style of Bulgakov, or, anyway, the style he will develop for the novel he will write."

"Yes, it had all his tricks," she said, somewhat wistfully. "His spirits and his magic."

"His mesmerism and his humor."

"His belief in true love."

"His need for redemption. Even his politics. Dressed up as satire, of course. Or is it irony?"

"Excuse me," Fyodor said, interrupting this literary litany. "But who is Bulgakov?"

His companion put his arm around his shoulders in a brotherly embrace. "Never mind. It's not important. Listen to me. Forget Bulgakov. Forget Blavatskaya. Don't get mired in detail. Either God is in the detail or the Devil is, and one is never quite sure which of them one is dealing with." Then turning to Margarita, he said, "It's all about testing his four hypotheses, you see. He's a scientist and requires proof."

"Proof," Margarita sighed. "And what sort of proof does science require?"

But before he could answer her, there was a terrible noise, in fact, many terrible noises, all at once. A gun was fired, or several guns, the coach creaked and some vital part of it cracked, making the entire carriage lean precariously to the side, men's voices were raised, there was shouting, more shooting, and smoke and the smell of gunpowder wafted into the carriage which had begun to pitch and heave. Suddenly the entire vehicle lurched onto its side and water began pouring in.

"Quick!" his companion cried, shoving hard against the upper door which now resembled a hatch. A few hard shoves and the hatch opened, he pulled himself through, and reached down to help the others climb out after him. "Hurry! We're sinking fast! Into the life-boats!"

Fyodor found himself on the steeply slanted deck of a large ship on the high seas and in the midst of chaos. A mast had cracked and fallen, canvas and rope and enormous splinters of wood, not to mention huge pieces of ordnance, were rolling to the starboard side; men were rushing about amidst the rubble; water in huge waves was coming in over the gunwales, while not far away another ship, heavily armed, was firing cannons at them.

"Follow me!" his companion yelled, and taking Margarita by the hand, began forging his way forward. He had spied a lifeboat; clearly his plan was to get to it and put it over the side before the ship sank. But the seas were heavy, very heavy indeed, and the thought of being in that small boat in the midst of those massive waves so terrified Fyodor that he could not follow his companion and Margarita, but looked around for some other means of salvation. And so, standing there on the heaving deck, frozen in place, gripped by terror, looking about him for some miraculous rescue, he saw her.

She was almost indistinguishable from the sailors, being dressed much as they were, even to the cutlass in her hand and the scarf tied rakishly around her head, and like them, she was standing at the rail, armed, waiting for the enemy ship to try to fasten on, unless their own ship were to founder first and send them all into the sea. Indeed, it seemed to him the ship was bound to go down, and go down soon, as greater and greater waves were now flowing over the deck. He had no sooner thought this than, with a terrible lurch and shudder, the ship began to roll onto her side. "Marko!" he shouted, catching one last sight of her just as another great wave struck the deck and flooded it. He shouted again and moved toward her, slipping, sliding, falling... but she had disappeared over the side, which was no longer even a side, which had vanished completely leaving only flotsam in its wake, and men desperately clinging to whatever objects they could find. For a moment he saw her in the swirling water. Without another thought, he stripped off his coat and jumped in after her.

Down, down, the bitterly cold water closed in over him. Cold blackness, taking his breath away, and he sank down, down, never to rise again. How heavy, so hard to struggle up, and too much debris around him, something catching at him as he rose, dragging him down again... kicking it away, but impossible to free himself or see or breathe or struggle in this darkness, in this black night... when, suddenly, to his joy, he broke the surface, a simple, singular light buoying his heart, and he saw her, rising and falling on the swell. Marko! He cried out her name, but in the terrible noise of the sea, she could not hear; yet, he knew she saw him and was making her way to him, and he struck out toward her, flailing in the water, yes, but coming ever closer to her, closer with every stroke.

"Marko!" he cried as loudly as he could...

... and opened his eyes and found himself gasping for air, crumpled on the floor of the coach, clutching onto Margarita's knees.

"It's all right, dear Fyodor Fyodorovich," she said, stroking the top of his head. "She is quite well, our Marko Volchek. She is not drowning in the sea. But you did well. You would have saved her."

"So it's to be a romance after all," his companion said. "Shipwrecked and washed up on a desert island... perfect! Or maybe not a desert island, come to think of it. You'd want a good meal and some decent wine after something like that. But is it more convincing as a romance? That's the question."

"Love is the only true proof," Margarita said with a sigh. "Always the last light to fail."

"Is it convincing enough, though? What do you say, Fyodorov? Have we convinced you?"

"Of what am I being convinced?" he asked. He had managed to pick himself up off the floor and straighten his clothing, but he was still quite abashed at his behavior, and was trying to compose himself by retrieving his hat and his cane.

"Many worlds, existing simultaneously, the possibility of. Or, alternatively, one world, different times, access to. Time itself, the fluidity of. Time portals, the existence of."

"My four hypotheses!"

"Yes, your hypotheses. We are testing them for you. Scientifically. As you wanted."

"Look," Margarita murmured, glancing out the window. "It's getting light."

"Well, I'm ready for breakfast," his companion said. "Hungry, Fyodor?"

He was. In fact, his stomach was grumbling and growling.

"Where shall we eat? Or rather, *what* shall we eat? What do you feel like, Margarita?"

"Blinis and knishes, pickled herring, gefilte fish with beet sauce and horseradish, a plate of bialies, and a pot of coffee."

"Just the sort of breakfast I used to eat with my friend Sasha Kantrovskaya. Back in the day."

Margarita laughed. "Back in the tunnels. Look, here we are!"

The carriage had stopped in the middle of a field. The sun was rising, the air was full of wings and song, colors popping out of the gloom and shadows springing to life again, long and lean, otherworldly creatures. He breathed in the fresh, cool air, rejoicing at being on unmoving, solid ground.

"Come along or all the food will be gone," his companion said cheerfully. "I know these pirates!"

Then he noticed an opening in the ground, a shaft of some kind, and crude steps leading down. He started to object but he was already bending over, holding a lantern in his right hand, taking the narrow steps down into the darkness of the underworld. The roof became ever lower, the tunnel ever narrower, until he was crawling on his hands and knees and barely able to breathe. Just as he felt he could go no farther the tunnel opened up into a cavern flooded with torchlight, and he could stand again and breathe and see... a long table, tin plates and bowls laid out, and many bearded men wearing old, worn uniforms sitting down for a meal.

"We got here just in time," his companion said. "The bombardment is starting up above."

And he could hear it now, a deep rumbling, like thunder.

"Where are we?" he asked.

"In the catacombs underneath Odessa. A place to avoid if you have any fear of confined spaces. Many of these galleries have no exits, many of the tunnels lead to dead-ends. You can wander around down here in the dark for a lifetime, and, trust me, many do. A lifetime of dark passageways and dead ends. A life that ends in a cul-de-sac. I know it well."

"My dear!" Margarita said, throwing her arms around their companion and kissing him on the lips. "A life lived unflinchingly and with magnificent contempt!"

"These partisans, for example, are always found down here," his companion continued as though she had neither embraced him nor said a word. "From some kinds of heroism there is no escape."

"What can you mean?" he asked in some confusion. The rumbling overhead continued.

"He is speaking of heroic despair," Margarita sighed. "It is another form of romance."

"Yes. Perhaps you are right," their companion said. "Still one must admit the catacombs are the safest place to be while the war is going on."

"War?" he cried. "What war?"

"You name it. Any war you want."

"But I don't want a war."

"No? That's right, we didn't want a war, did we? We only wanted breakfast."

In the blink of an eye, cavern, torchlight, soldiers vanished, and they were sitting at a small but well-laid table on a flower-filled terrace overlooking a lake dramatically framed by a range of snow-topped mountains. The air was crisp and sweet. A waiter in a white uniform was pouring coffee for them into delicate china cups. The rolls on their plates were still warm.

"Ah, the Caucasus!" his companion sighed. "This is far better! Fresh air, nice scenery, and I hear the water's pretty good."

"A place where poets come to die," Margarita sighed back.

"Come to get themselves shot, you mean, the fools."

"*The poet's dead, a slave to honor. He fell, by rumor slandered, Lead in his breast, and searching for revenge, Hanging his proud head! Slain! What use is weeping now, The futile chorus of empty praise—*"

"Stop!" his companion cried. "You're ruining my breakfast."

"You haven't got your breakfast yet."

"What are you talking about? I've got a hot roll right here."

Margarita smiled across the table at Fyodor. "What's wrong, dear Fyodor? You're so quiet."

"I am merely—perplexed."

"Merely perplexed?" his companion said with a laugh. "Well, I would be more than perplexed with all this talk of poetry and romance, all these *musings* on the work of our Muse. But we've made our point, haven't we? And you've taken the point, I'm sure. That is... not to put too fine a point on it..."

"What he means to say is that we hope that your hypotheses have been thoroughly tested and that you can now draw proper conclusions. That's how one puts it, isn't it?" She addressed this last remark not to Fyodor but to his companion, who nodded in agreement. "And let me add that we hope your dreams come true. Only the good ones, of course."

He stared from one to the other. The clear morning light, the radiantly bright morning light of the high Caucasus, was shining on Margarita's pale skin and gleaming blue-black hair, burnishing the reddish gold of the man's short, well-trimmed beard, thick brows, and long lashes, illuminating the dark blue of his eyes.

"Nikolai!" he exclaimed, only now recognizing him. "My God, Kolya! It's you!"

The light was so bright it quivered in the air, as though all around him invisible doors were opening and closing, and through one of those doors where mirages floated magically in the air... glimpses of palaces, palm trees, pyramids... through one of those blindingly bright openings Kolya and Margarita now slipped and the golden door closed behind them.

"No!" he cried.

♣

And sat up, distraught and confused, on the sofa in Margarita's little cottage. Margarita herself, disheveled as before, was sitting on the wooden chair across from him, holding several sheets of paper in her hand. She gazed at him, with some curiosity.

"Did you sleep well, Fyodor?"

"Was I sleeping? I... I had many dreams."

"Dreams, yes. I, too, have many dreams."

"But they were so real."

"They are real. They are real dreams."

"And so detailed. And so... revelatory."

"I am glad. And now that you have had your revelations, perhaps you should go." She lifted the pages in her hand. "For as you see, I am busy."

"Can those be pages from *Monkey*?" The thought that they might be wiped away all remnants of sleep.

She glanced down at them. "Can they be? No. He burnt *Monkey*. I didn't like it. I told him I didn't, and so he destroyed it."

"But that's impossible!" he cried, feeling, horribly, that it was not impossible at all.

"Ah, now you will tell me manuscripts don't burn. Which is utter nonsense even though Bulgakov will say it and insist on it. But I assure you, *Monkey* is no more. It is utterly destroyed. It no longer exists in this world. And then he left me here, marooned in this place. He died and broke my heart."

Her words seared into him, like venom entering his blood.

"*Farewell, dear world, that I must leave. Farewell, swift flying birds, abounding trees. Farewell autumnal gold and wintry gales...* Not that he ever cared a fig for birds or trees. He was only mimicking a style. It was all in fun, you see, until the last lines. The last lines were sincere. Oh, God! What am I going to do?"

"Is there anything at all I can do to help you?"

"Nothing. We must each bear our own grief."

"But is he really dead?"

She fixed her eyes on the page in her hand; she did not answer. After a few long moments, he rose, bowed deeply to her, feeling that his heart was on the verge of breaking, and with tears filling his eyes, left the cottage.

It took the freshness of the breeze, lifting the flowering branches and the leaves, and his mare's soft whinny, the chattering of sparrows in the trees, the scents and colors of the earth to bring him to his senses. *Fool!* he cried to himself. *Coward! You cannot leave her in that state. You must bring her out.* A memory came to him, clear and vivid, a memory of standing on the sloping deck of a sinking ship, of stripping off his coat and jumping into the sea. *You must go back!*

The door had slammed shut behind him. He tried the handle. When it didn't move, he used force and burst it open.

"Come!" he cried, striding up to her, taking her by the hand. "We must leave. You must come with me now!"

"Leave? No, I can't leave! This is the rendezvous. I must stay here, here, or I will never find him again."

He paid no attention. He had her by the arm now, and was pulling her toward the door.

"Margarita! I must insist!"

"I cannot leave, I tell you!" she cried angrily, twisting out of his grip, pushing him away, backing up toward the red-covered table with its vase of tiny, white lilies-of-the-valley. The breeze that came through the open door ruffled the pages she had set down beside the vase, and light coming in with the breeze illuminated the motes of dust in the air, shifted the palette of the room, saturating the colors, revealing the most mundane objects in their ideal state, enhancing them the way grace enhances the soul, and the fairies of the air, the spirits of the air, nestled around her, settling on the tabletop, on the lily buds, in her hair. Everything in the room was transfigured, became more real, more vivid, more deeply to be loved. But more transfigured than any of the objects was Margarita herself. A radiant calmness flooded her face, her eyes shone, her dark hair gleamed, and sparkling light danced all around her, and all around the place where she stood. He rushed toward her, but too late. She had already passed through the portal into a shaft of light.

CHAPTER THIRTY

Heaven on Earth

Fyodorov opened his eyes and discovered he was lying on the floor. He pulled himself to his feet, and staggered to the table where, to quench his terrible thirst, he drank the rest of the mineral water left in the bottle. It was warm, but it refreshed him somewhat, enough to allow him to begin to collect his thoughts, which were scattered and strange. His brain felt bruised, as though it had been badly shaken, as though some mental disaster had occurred so that all the familiar pathways of his mind had been blocked or washed away. Still he remembered to look for the pages of manuscript Margarita had been reading, but they were not on the table, nor were they anywhere around. As he looked for them, he realized nothing was as it had been: the cottage which before had been so tidy and homey now had a most weird and eerie feel to it, the way places do that have been long abandoned, and as he glanced around he noticed great cobwebs hanging from the corners, a table leg broken, the old sofa ripped and torn, and dust accumulating even as he watched, all the motes of dust settling and thickening, and the lilies-of-the-valley, dead and dried in their empty vase.

Panic seized him then, and he ran out the door and to the very edge of the wood. It was no longer morning, the day had become quite hot, and the horse he had ridden that morning was no longer tethered there in the shade. This did not surprise him. What sentient animal would remain in such a place? Turning back for a moment from the safety of the great trees, he saw that what had been Margarita's cottage had further decayed into a broken-down hut, its roof caved in, its walls crumbling. The mere sight of its decomposition sent a shiver of horror through him, for now it appeared that the phenomenal world itself, the world perceptible through the senses, had become weird and uncanny, untrustworthy. Either that or he was still in the grip of the mushroom, and nothing he perceived with his senses could be trusted, nothing that seemed to happen to him was real, and, by the standards of normal men, he was indeed utterly mad.

He turned away from the hut and began walking back toward the meadows, his thoughts so disjointed, his feelings so contradictory, he might be suffering from brain fever himself. He even had the physical symptoms: his head ached, his eyes seemed overly sensitive to light so that even under the shade of the trees he could barely see for the blinding brightness, his thirst was great, and he was so hot he had to remove his coat.... his waistcoat... his tie. Oh, God, so many layers of clothing in this terrible heat!

Water was what he needed, and it could not be too hard to find. The land was crisscrossed by little streams, dotted with ponds, a river wrapped itself around the estate, forming one of its boundaries. Surely there would be water somewhere, he would stumble on water, he would soon be cool and refreshed. Thinking of coolness brought the great house to mind. The palace itself would be cool, bathed in afternoon light, its yellow stone in bright contrast to the dark green of its gardens and grounds—yes, it would be blissfully cool inside. But no sooner did he imagine it than he knew he could never return to it; he could not bear the thought of facing Azara, who would undoubtedly demand an explanation, or of meeting with the Princess, who would be owed one. No, he would have to take a different path, there were many in the woods. He would wander through the countryside until he came upon the river; he would continue along it; it would lead him somewhere. There was no hurry. He had no place to go, no home to return to, no friend waiting for him, no task to fulfill.

So he walked on, his mind beset by fearful doubt. If he were to believe his eyes—and he was not completely sure he did—he had witnessed something extraordinary. If his eyes were to be believed, his hypotheses were correct. Yet to know this brought him no joy, for if Margarita, whoever or whatever she was, had in fact escaped this world for another, he himself had not. Once again he had been left behind. The portal had opened before him, but he had not gone through.

Our summer days are long. Even so, the light eventually dims, something like night eventually comes, and when it does it is best not to be caught out of doors, alone. Poor Fyodor Fyodorovich was caught out of doors, alone. He had found the river, at least, and with it a miserable horde of biting insects, a grave dampness rising from the earth, and the threatening sounds of men, a group of whom were encamped nearby. He would have liked to join them for they had a fire, but he was afraid of them and so stayed where he was, serenaded by a chorus of crickets and croaking frogs, the incessant buzzing of mosquitoes, and the splashing of nocturnal animals along the riverbank. He did not sleep a wink, until he did.

He awoke chilly, stiff, and hungry. The air carried the good scent of smoke and food, and, starving as he was, he thought it might be safe now, in the morning light, to approach the men, but when he made his way to their campsite, there was nothing there but the drenched remains of a fire, and traces in the grass and dirt that at least one wagon had recently passed. Gypsies, he thought. Travelers.

His hunger was becoming troublesome to him, but at least there was fresh, clean water, for just here, where the gypsies had encamped, a spring-fed stream flowed into the river. He drank, and felt remarkably better, remarkably well. He could do worse than follow behind the gypsy wagon, for they would stop where there was fresh water and places to forage for food.

All day he trudged along, following the tracks of wagon and horse. He knew they stopped at mid-day, and to his delight they left some crusts of bread behind, and some apple cores which he was able to retrieve before other scavengers swooped in and swept them away. Fortified by crumbs and cores, he continued his journey, but at a slower pace as the afternoon wore on and heat descended on him. Finally, baking inside his clothes, he stopped in a patch of shade to rest.

He had been walking through woods; now he was at the edge of a field. Half the field was ploughed, the other half still unfurrowed, the work seemingly abandoned mid-way through. He did not know much about agriculture, not being a landowner himself. Not that many landowners knew much about agriculture, either. No, only peasants knew about the land, how to cultivate it and make it produce wealth, not for themselves, of course, but for their owners, for those who owned the land also owned the men who worked it.

To put it in such words, so simply, was to reveal the true horror of it. Yet who spoke about it? Who cried out against it? Some few did, yes, like poor Radishchev, who ended up in Siberia, or Yosif Rozental, condemned to imprisonment for life. For life! And for what? For speaking the truth. But if speaking the truth was a crime, keeping silent was a sin, a violation of Christ's command that we love one another. How could living in constant violation of that command not lead to damnation? *So we are all damned,* he thought. *There is no honorable way out, except Siberia or the gallows. We are dancing on the edge of the abyss, and only hell awaits us.*

Sitting on the ground in the ever-dwindling shade, staring out at a half-ploughed field baking under a blazing sun, he felt he was already in hell, the heat was so great, as great as his hunger and his thirst, and his mind was in such disarray, and his sense of direction so confused. He was somewhere but he did not know where. Did he even know what day it was? His watch had stopped; he did not even know the time. *I do not even know the time,* he repeated to himself. The irony of it made him laugh.

"Yes, they do make us laugh, our dear, darting redwings, our swooping swallows, our thrushes," a man's voice said, and without more ado, the man himself squatted down beside him, startling him greatly. "It is their nature," he continued, pointing upwards into the air, "to be free as they are, to live with such joy. Birds, bless them, are not oppressed by time. Of course, being a man of science, you must know them all far better than I."

He was a man of indeterminate age, with a great flowing beard, his skin creased and browned by the sun, wearing the usual peasant garb of belted tunic over baggy trousers, his feet and legs wrapped in rags secured by twine, a pack on his back and a staff in his hand. Yet he did not have the voice or bearing of a peasant, his eyes held a sparkle unknown to slaves, and his laugh and the natural friendliness with which he had squatted down beside Fyodorov was a sign, true and final, that this stranger was not now a serf, nor had ever been one.

"How do you know I am a man of science?" he asked.

"Before we talk seriously," the man said with a smile, "let us have a bite of apple and a bit of bread to restore our strength."

He opened his pack and took out a loaf of bread, a hunk of cheese, a sausage, an apple, placing each in turn onto the grass.

"Eat!" he said. "Do not hesitate! Look! Already the birds of the air have taken notice of our feast. Already they are planning how to distribute the crumbs!"

His laughter rang out; it was music to the ears just as food was music to the stomach. Oh, how hungry he was, and how this simple meal satisfied him! He ate it with such joy, he could not believe how happy it made him, how it filled him with energy and hope.

"Forgive my gluttony," he said in distress, appalled at himself, for he had eaten everything, not even a crumb of bread remained, and his companion had taken nothing. "I do beg your pardon."

"No need," said the man. "I had already eaten my dinner, and you had not. So, now, shall we talk about birds? Look there! Isn't that a kestrel hovering there, just overhead?"

"I fear you have mistaken me, my friend, for I am not an ornithologist and know very little about birds, far less than you. But I must thank you from the bottom of my heart for this delicious dinner you have provided for me. I am in your debt."

"Bah!" said the man dismissing it all with a wave of his hand. "There are no debts among friends. Now let me propose something to you, and consider it an offer you can refuse with no hard feelings in the least. I am an actor, by name Pyotr Illych Panov, traveling with my troupe in the caravan just ahead. We have noticed you walking behind us, and I've come to invite you to join us. If you are traveling for a time in our direction, you might find it more comfortable riding in our wagon... Ah! Look at her make her dive! Has she succeeded? I think not, bless her soul. I think this time the vole has escaped her!"

"That is most kind of you," he said. "I do thank you, and accept gladly. May I introduce myself?" And he did. "I, too," he added, "have had some experience in the theatre."

"Have you now? An actor, are you?"

"No, indeed. But I have worked with actors. I tried at one time to produce a play written by a dear friend of mine. We had a venue. We rehearsed. We even had an opening date...We had no money, of course."

"And actors need to eat," Pyotr Illych said with a smile. "Would I know this play, or your friend's name?"

"Neither, I am sure. Ours would have been the first performance of his play, and he has written no other so far as I know. His name is not known in the theatre world, I am sure. His mother, on the other hand, is well-known. She is a poetess. Anastasia Barakova. Perhaps you have heard of her? In any case, her son's play is extraordinary, I think, but hardly likely to ever be performed at the Aleksandrinsky."

Pyotr Illych gazed at him in wonder.

"'Let sorrow vanish into dust! Let malice perish! And into our hearts, grown young again, let unending joy descend!'... A poem, my friend, by our great poet Nikolai Nekrasov, and one fitting indeed for my feelings at this moment. For if I take your meaning, if I understand you properly, then joy has indeed descended on me. But we shall speak more about this later. Now let us leave our crumbs for the birds and walk on. The wagons are waiting for us in that copse over yonder, there on the far side of the field."

They helped each other to their feet, and Pyotr gathered up his pack and staff.

"We must go carefully these days, dear friend," Pyotr said as they walked along. "There is trouble at hand. Great trouble brewing and coming closer. I fear we must pass through it to get to our destination, for I see no way around it."

"What kind of trouble?"

"You have noticed the unploughed fields? After three hundred years of slavery, the serfs in this district have chosen this moment to rebel. They sense freedom in the air, they know one day they will be free, but their landlords say no, that even if freedom comes one day, they will still have to work for them because freedom will come without land. But how then is freedom different from slavery? Our dear peasants don't believe the landlords when they tell them this. They don't believe the Tsar could be so unjust and cruel. No, they fervently believe the Tsar has already given them not only their freedom but also the land they have worked all their lives, but the landlords and their officials have concealed the Tsar's decree. So they will no longer work for the landlords, and so the landlords have called for troops to come and put down this uprising, this up-rising of hope and liberty. We shall see what comes of it."

"All that can come of it is massacre."

"Yes," Pyotr said sadly. "Massacre. Floggings, hangings, bullets, death."

"And yet you can feel joyful, Pyotr Illych?"

"Joy and sorrow often come hand-in-hand. Grief is never far from the soul, for she is so full of love and innocence and joy that grief is drawn to her for consolation. You see, she retains in herself an echo of the music of our childhood which is the music of heaven. For the true world that God created for us, my friend, is the world we knew as children, when our lives were rooted in belief and trust, and we were intoxicated with the joy of life and every day was filled with bliss. Alas, we have fallen out of that world and into this one, this dark world of delusion and suffering and terror, but it is not the real world but a false world. The true world is the one in which children dwell, God bless them, the world from which we have been expelled and whose joys we cannot recapture without becoming like children again, as our dear Lord said. 'Unless you become like one of these little children, you shall not enter the Kingdom of Heaven.' And Lord Jesus never lies to us, never, though oftentimes we don't understand what he means."

"I thought he meant we should become humble as children are."

Pyotr laughed merrily. "Do you know any children, dear Fyodor Fyodorovich? I know many and none of them are humble! No, indeed, children are not humble, not unless humility is beaten into them, and their spirits will resist it even then and for a very long time. Now, see, here we come and we shall have a bit of kvass and then off we go. Perhaps, God willing, we shall put on cloaks of invisibility and slip by."

The wagons rumbled along slowly but steadily, bouncing them over bumps in the road, if road it could be called, this dirt track that wound its way alongside the river, that jostled them across shallow streams and careened them down hillsides. When the day declined into evening, they stopped the wagons beside the river in a grove of chestnut trees, and set about making themselves comfortable for the night. He had been sitting beside Pyotr Illych in a driver's box all day; now he met the other members of the troupe. There were more of them than he had imagined: men, women, girls, boys, children.

The children were permitted to play for a time after they ate their supper while the adults sat at their ease around the camp fire, talking and singing. The songs they sang were of the nature of hymns, yet the

PYOTR PANOV

"We believe the living spirit of God dwells in each human being."

words were different from those of the psalms and other religious songs with which he was familiar. Nothing about this troupe of actors was familiar to him, or rather nothing was the way he had expected it to be.

"Yes, we are a family," Pyotr said in answer to his question. "Not blood-relatives, but sisters and brothers in the faith and in our art."

"What faith is that? Are you Dissenters?"

"No. We are Dukhobory. Spirit Wrestlers."

"I know the name, indeed I have heard it often, but of all else about the Dukhobory I am ignorant. I yearn to know the nature of your faith."

"We believe the living spirit of God dwells in each human being."

"The Orthodox Church teaches the same."

"Does it? One would not guess it, living here, in a country ruled by the Orthodox faith."

"Yes. I do take your point. Tell me, then, how do you live your faith, in good conscience?"

"We try to live as much as possible in the manner Lord Jesus would wish us to, given the situation in which we find ourselves. We share all we have. We do not work for personal gain but for the well-being of all. We serve in no army and fight in no wars. We need no church, no priests, no icons. We live in our own communities and we live in peace with our brothers. That is how we live our faith day by day, though for this we are persecuted and punished, since we do not adhere to the practices of the Orthodox church. But our true work is in the realm of the spirit. There we wrestle—yes, the word is accurate enough—we wrestle with our spirit, each of us, in prayer, in meditation, in joyful song, in order to bring the spark of the divine that dwells within each of us out into this world, and to grow stronger in the spirit of love. Love is the essence of our work and of our lives, our joy and our need, to manifest the spirit of love within, which is the spirit of God. There, then," he added with a twinkle in his eye and a smile, "I have overstepped and preached to you, brother. Forgive me."

"No need. I am grateful for your explanation Yet, if I may say so, it surprises me greatly that a religious man like yourself should be traveling about the countryside putting on plays."

Pyotr Illych laughed quite merrily at this comment, nodded his head, stretched out his legs, tickled the little girl who had jumped onto his lap, and let her go to run off with her friends, just as one of the women, announcing it was bedtime, began herding the children in from their play with the help of a little brown dog.

"Oh, how right you are, dear Fyodor! How right you are! It is surprising indeed. It surprises everyone. It surprises me every day. But it is my calling. There is nothing I can do about it. To make sad people laugh. To do little magic shows for the dear children. To bring joy to joyless places. It is what makes me happy, you see. The Spirit works in mysterious ways. And, you know, not everyone is meant for a settled life. Some of us are born to wander. All these..." he spread his arms to embrace the campground, the caravans, the children. "... are holy wanderers. We carry our village with us wherever we go."

They spoke a little longer, but Fyodorov was so tired he could barely follow the conversation. Soon Pyotr took him by the hand and led him to the wagon where they had made up a place for him and where he fell asleep instantly the moment he stretched out on the mat.

The next day passed much the same as the day before. Fyodorov again rode beside Pyotr Illych in the driver's box. Again he watched the road, the fields, the sky, and listened to Pyotr Illych hum to himself or talk about the trees they passed beneath or the birds they saw flying over the meadows. He himself said little. His mind had no content; he thought about nothing. Sometimes he even fell asleep, dozing beside Pyotr, the rocking of the wagon soothing him into slumber. A jolt would startle him awake, but soon enough he would begin to doze again. Once in a while he would remember that he did not know where they were going and that perhaps he should inquire, but the thought did not linger. He did not worry about it. He felt light, unburdened, unconcerned. It was a new feeling; yet, when he wondered how it was different, when he tried to remember how he used to feel, he could not do it. It was as though something had come sweeping by and erased his past.

They stopped to eat a midday meal and to rest the horses. Everyone had specific tasks to perform. Fyodorov wanted to be of help, but did not know what to do and was standing around feeling useless when one of the children came up to him and asked him if he would please play with them. Before he knew it, he was sitting in the dirt with a group of children playing a game of jackstraws with them.

"And who won at jackstraws?" one of the men, Misha, asked.

"Fyodor Fyodorovich!" two of the children said in unison. "He is the winner!"

"No, indeed," Fyodorov said. "I could not pick up a single stick."

"That makes you the winner!" a child said, laughing.

"Is it true?" he asked. "No, surely not!"

"It is how they play," Misha said. "So the little ones don't feel bad if they can't pick any up."

"In that case I am the winner for certain," he said, smiling at the children. "And I will win every game we play."

They were all in such good spirits and were packing up to return to the wagons and the journey when one of their number came running into the campground and, going up to Pyotr, whispered something in his ear.

"Dear Ones," Pyotr said in a loud voice so everyone could hear. "Alyosha has just scouted ahead and returned with news. As we feared, the village is filled with armed men and the landlords have sent for troops to put their rebellion down. We are caught between the two, village ahead and troops behind. Can we ford the river here or not? Misha, what do you think?"

"I fear it is too deep for the wagons, Pyotr dear," Misha said.

"Then we must decide what to do."

Everyone gathered together and sat in a circle, even the children, who sat on their parents' laps. Fyodorov sat with them as well, though he had no opinion of which choice to make. There were three to consider: first, to stay where they were, in the hope that the troops coming up the road would either not see them or not bother them; second, to continue on as before, in the hope that they might pass through the area of disturbances before the troops arrived; third, to go into the village and take shelter there, in the hope that a peaceful solution might arise before the troops burnt the village to the ground. It took very little time for them to decide. They would go on, in the hope of passing through. They sang a hymn together, finished packing, hitched the horses to the wagons, and set off down the narrow, overgrown track. Beside them, the river flowed placidly on, over their heads leaves rustled and birds chirped and sang, but ahead of them? Who could say what was awaiting them on the road, or into what furnace they were bound?

Yet they were not somber, and as the wagons rattled along, he could hear the sound of children singing and laughing, the voices of adults speaking in light and friendly tones. He had not once heard a voice raised in anger the entire time he had been with the actors, which seemed to him to have been a very long time, or rather that, having lost count of time, it seemed that he had been with them forever and would remain with them forever, time itself having stopped, or perhaps—this thought now and again crossed his mind—he was asleep and dreaming this, dreaming everything. But then how could he ever tell what was real and what was fantasy, illusion, hallucination? How could one ever tell? And as he began to think of this, images returned to him of his meeting with Margarita Mikhailevna. He remembered her rage at Azara, her accusations; he remembered the dreams he dreamt while asleep on her little sofa; he remembered his last sight of her, disappearing into a great ray of light. With that memory, his entire body began trembling, trembling fiercely, as though he were having a kind of fit, and he thought, *This is how it will end!*

Pyotr Illych threw down the reins he was holding so lightly (the horses kept going, the horses knew their way), and gripped Fyodor Fyodorovich in a tight embrace.

"Fyodor, brother," he said, shaking him gently. "You are dreaming! Wake up!"

"I am awake!" he cried, and there were tears on his cheeks now which he wiped away with the back of his hand. "Oh, how inexplicable! How contrary to reason! Oh, how is it possible? For I swear I saw it all with my own eyes and yet it cannot be! So I must be mad, I must be a madman, or near death, or else I have seen such strange wonders that now the whole world is turned upside down, Pyotr Illych! The whole world, upside down!"

"Now take a deep breath, my brother, a very deep breath. Breathe once more. Breathe! Let your heart become calm, like a ship at sea after the storm, setting herself once again upon her true course. You did dream and now you are awake. See how the world restores itself to its harmony, see how all is well again."

He wanted to say: *It was not a dream. I saw it all. I saw a woman disappear before my eyes. I saw her vanish. I saw her fall out of time.*

"I felt I was falling," he said.

"Yes, we are riding so high up here, there is always that fear. We become drowsy, we wake with a start, feeling we are about to fall."

The idea of falling brought to his mind what Pyotr Illych had said earlier about men falling out of the true and joyful world of childhood into the false world of suffering and terror. How did it happen, that falling from one world into another? For surely it was true that childhood was another world from the one in which he found himself, that little Natasha and her brothers inhabited a different world entirely, and he wanted to ask Pyotr how it happens that we fall out of that world and into this one, although he knew the answer very well. Already he felt a growing terror of what lay before them, which might be a false world but was certainly a real one, in the same way that pain is real and undeniable and overwhelming. He feared for them, for they were like children, Pyotr Illych no less than the littlest girl who had asked him to play jackstraws with her in the dirt.

So he thought, and time passed.

"You are pensive, dear Fyodor," Pyotr Illych said gently over the rumbling and creaking of the wagon. "Perhaps you are wondering where we are taking you in our magic caravan. You wonder why we are on this particular road, where we are going, or even if we have any destination in mind at all."

"No, I was not wondering that. I have no destination in mind myself, and so I am happy to be traveling with you wherever you are bound. What I was considering was the existence of evil, how it arises, and from whence it comes."

"It is an ancient question, dear Fyodor, and has never been answered. It has no answer, no more than its opposite: where comes the good, the gift of life, the joy of creation, the upsurge of love. We live in ignorance of our beginning and our end, like a little child who can recognize his mother but has no notion of where he is living or who rules over him. And we must accept that or we ruin the gift we are given, this miraculous gift of life which appears to have no cause or reason or meaning. It is like a magic show or a play which can only be enjoyed by those who allow themselves to believe in its illusions. The same holds true of life. One must believe in it or it all collapses into nothing, and one sinks into the depths of confusion and despair. But you, Fyodor, you ponder ideas without allowing them to poison your heart, and so you do not lose your belief in life. I know this is true about you, and I salute you for it."

"What we meet ahead might well poison my heart," he said.

"Grief wounds the heart, yes, but does not necessarily destroy it. Grief is common to all of us, no one escapes it. It can turn us against our brothers, but it can also fill us with greater love for them if we are able to see that suffering is something we all share. Even our Father in Heaven shares that sorrow with us."

"Yet I feel that it is easier to believe in evil than in good. Doing evil seems to be more in line with our nature, more natural to us, while doing good takes determination and effort."

"We all live our lives the best we can, dear friend. No one thinks he is doing otherwise."

Fyodorov considered this statement while the wagon rattled and jolted along the road. It was one of those statements of faith, utterly unscientific, based on no evidence; indeed, it flew in the face of all evidence, for surely one had only to look around to see how badly most men lived their lives. How seductive it was, though, this idea that men really wanted to be good, how satisfying, how simple-minded, like believing in Heaven. And yet he himself believed in Heaven. He himself believed, as did these poor serfs, that the Tsar was God on earth. *How come you by such beliefs?* Blavatskaya had asked him once, in a dream. Was he then as much a fool as this holy fool sitting beside him?

"And do you also believe in Heaven?" he asked, knowing what the answer would be.

"Are we not in Heaven now? Is this not Heaven?"

"Heaven on earth? No. It certainly is not."

Pyotr turned to him with a look of profound care. "You fear for the future? Do not. We are like the birds of the air to Him, the flowers of the field."

"I want you to tell me, to assure me. If my friend is dead," and in an instant an image of Nikolai Vasilevich appeared in his mind's eye, "I want to know, not that *if* there is a Heaven, he is in it, but that there *is* a Heaven and he *is* in it."

Pyotr smiled at him and hummed a fragment of song. The little tune lifted Fyodorov's heart, it was so cheerful.

"You know," Pyotr said, still smiling, "how a horse finds pleasure when he is let loose over a green heath where the ground is smooth and level and he can gallop as fast as ever he can over the grass? It is his nature to gallop over the grass and in it he finds pleasure. In the same way, it is God's nature to love us and to pour himself into us, and he finds pleasure in doing so, and because he does pour his own nature into us, heaven is here with us, always, wherever we may be."

Pyotr took up his sprightly little tune again, and sang, "'Let sorrow vanish into dust! Let malice perish! And into our hearts, grown young again, let unending joy descend!'"

"Nekrasov," Fyodorov said. "I met him once."

"Did you? Oh, do tell me about him, dear Fyodor. What a saint he must be! What a hero of the soul!"

"I was on a strange journey. I was traveling... Ah, but Nekrasov, yes, a kind man. He took me into his home. I was unwell. He cared for me. As you are doing, Pyotr Illych. It seems to be my fate to be a burden to others."

"Nonsense, Fyodor! You are no burden to us. We enjoy company on the road. And I'm sure you were no burden to Nikolai Alexeyevich. Poets take delight in such encounters for we poor souls who are not poets ourselves feed their imaginations, isn't it true? Without us, and the birds, and the clouds, and the night sky and the moon, what would poets have to write about? Now may I tell you something about a poet I know? For the verse of Nekrasov's reminded me of a joy you brought me which I have yet to share with you. You mentioned the son of Anastasia Barakova. It happens young Nikolai is a dear friend of mine, and so is his mother, and it is to her home, to an encampment on her estate, that we are this very moment bound. You see? Can anything be more God-sent than our meeting? Is it not a sign of His grace that we should meet on the road? It filled my heart with such joy, Fyodor, when I heard you say her sweet name!"

"I am amazed by your words," he said. "I am astonished."

"It's good, isn't it, to be amazed sometimes. Wonder is the source of all philosophy, they say, and also all gratitude and praise. But, look, here is Alyosha. We must be getting close to the village."

The young man, who again had been sent ahead for news, came running back to the wagons.

"The village is just yonder, over that little hill, the leader is speaking and rousing his men, the army is coming from the north and is not half a mile away."

"And we are going east. Surely we have time to pass through."

Slowly, slowly, the wagons inched up the little hill, and over its crest, and slowly they descended into the village. There a sight met their eyes that none of them had seen before. A crowd of peasants, three or four hundred strong, armed with sticks, pitchforks and scythes, was gathered in the center of the village; a skinny young man with a powerful voice, standing on some structure—it was impossible to see what—was addressing them; around them clustered women and boys, shouting agreement along with their men. The essence of the speech was clear from the few fragments Fyodorov was able to hear: the land is ours; the Tsar has given us land and freedom but the landlords have withheld the decree; they want to keep us slaves, but we don't have to work for them anymore; and we shall not work for them anymore. "We are free!" Those words came clearly to them. "We are free!"

Then someone in the crowd noticed the three wagons rumbling slowly down the street toward the east road.

"Look! Wagons! Soldiers! Stop them!"

The cry went up, the crowd turned, and like one being surged toward them. In a moment they were surrounded by wild, armed men, shouting at them, cursing them. Pyotr stood up and tried to calm them, but they did not heed him. It took a child, a terrified child, screaming and clutching onto her mother in the back of the second wagon, to make them stop and look at what was in front of them.

"Tinkers!"

"Gypsies!"

"A traveling show!"

"Puppeteers!"

Now the focus of the crowd turned from the peasant speaker to the caravan. Anger was dissipating like wind going out of a sail, jollity was taking its place, laughter and good humor. The wonder aroused by a magic show, the excitement of the village children, the promise of a bit of fun had distracted them for the moment. But not for long. A group of young men came running into the village from the north, shouting that troops were approaching along the northern road, were less than a mile away, were led by a general in uniform, were armed. At once, attention turned away from the caravan to the peasant leader again, and when he shouted, "Seize the wagons! Use them for barricades!" his followers obeyed.

There was no point in arguing or struggling against them. The flood tide was rushing in, sweeping everything aside. Roughly pulled out of their wagons, they could only watch as all their precious sets and costumes were tossed into the dirt and crushed underfoot.

"Set them at the north entrance!" men shouted and other men climbed up, took the reins, whipped the horses, and drove the wagons away, followed by the peasant army, shouting for freedom and land.

"Poor souls," Pyotr said, watching them go, they and the whole village behind them, even the children following behind. Then he turned to his troupe. "Well, friends, they have left us some things. Let us take what we can and go on our way."

"What about our horses?" Misha asked. "Are we leaving them behind?"

"Unless you want to go now and get them," Pyotr said. "But the army is very close."

"I will," Misha said. "I'll find them, wherever they are."

"Two of us can get them, Pyotr," Alyosha said. "They are docile creatures."

"Three," said Fyodorov. "I will come, too."

So while the troupe set out on foot along the eastern road, Misha, Alyosha and Fyodorov followed the peasant army toward the north end of the village. They were quicker than the women and children; they wove their way through the crowd until they came close enough to the place where the north road entered the village to see their wagons being overturned and joining some old carts and hay wagons to form a barricade across the road. The troops, led by an officer on horseback, were now visible on the road. Their own horses were nowhere to be seen. They turned back and began looking down all the lanes. Soon Misha spied one of the horses and called out to them to follow him. Fyodorov was about to do so when something else, something far more compelling, caught his eye.

It was the back of a man, a man wearing an old blue jacket, a tall man, broad-shouldered, a man with a familiar gait. Immediately he left his new friends who were following after their horses, and followed after his old friend, perplexed, yes, and yet filled with a growing excitement and delight, for surely he could not be mistaken, a man's gait was as unique as his face.

Walking at a brisk pace in order to keep the man in the blue jacket in sight, Fyodorov soon reached the edge of the crowd at the north end of the village. Just as he approached, a great cheer went up and the cheering continued, growing in volume as he drew nearer. "Freedom! Freedom!" they were shouting, but Fyodorov kept his eyes fixed on the back of the man in the blue jacket. When he disappeared into the crowd, Fyodorov rushed in behind him as another cheer went up. "Freedom and Land!"

But where had the man gone? Everywhere he looked he saw rough faces, old and young; he saw flashing eyes and open mouths; he heard shouts and curses and calls and exhortations. The crowd was pushing from behind even as he pushed his way forward, one minute catching sight of Nikolai, the next losing him in the mob, the press of men.

Up ahead, some of the peasants had mounted the barricade and were standing with their weapons in hand, pathetic weapons though they were. Still the barricade would be enough to protect those who sheltered behind it, and to give those who wished to flee enough time to do so before the troops broke through.

Now up ahead a cloud of dust appeared along with the sound of five hundred marching feet. A voice barked orders. More voices echoed it. There was the foreboding clang of musket and sword.

At once a great hush fell on the crowd. Men's faces became serious, attentive, alarmed. Fyodorov was now quite near the barricade. There, in the front ranks, were the young men, strong, powerfully built, most determined. He turned around and around, in a circle, searching for Nikolai, or the man who so resembled him, but he could not see him in the crowd. *I cannot give up now. I know he is here!* With this conviction in his mind, he pushed forward to the barricade, the upended wagons, and pulled himself up onto one of them. From there he could see the general on his horse, sword in hand, the soldiers, lined up in formation, their terrible guns.

"Disperse!" the general shouted in a powerful voice. "Disperse, I say, in the name of the Tsar, or you will be fired at!"

"You are not the Tsar!" the leader called back. "The Tsar has freed us! Fire on us and you will be firing on him!"

"I am sorry for you, my lads," the general replied, "but I must fire and I will fire. Those who feel themselves innocent, move off!"

No one standing on the barricade moved. Instead, the men shouted back in anger, “No envoy will we believe. Only the Tsar!”

“One salvo!” the general shouted.

At that moment, Fyodorov saw the man in the blue jacket jump down from an overturned wagon and spring out in front of the line of soldiers. Filled with joy at the sight of him, a joy he had not expected and could not fully understand, and calling his name, Fyodorov jumped down from where he was standing into the open space between the barricade and the troops, and ran toward him. As he did, the first rank of soldiers raised their guns. There was a sudden blaze of light.

BOOK SEVEN

Death and the Poet

CHAPTER THIRTY-ONE

Marko Considers What Is to Be Done

"From what I understand, the ship foundered off the coast in rough seas and high winds. Those steam engines are worse than useless in a storm. Under the circumstances, to have been captured by corsairs in a more seaworthy ship was a stroke of luck."

"I have no memory of it."

"A pity. It was most exciting."

"Why don't I recall it?"

"You were drugged, my dear. You were heavily sedated and quite immobilized."

"A pity, indeed. Please continue."

"As I was saying, our vessel was boarded and all the women taken off. Well, it's what they do, isn't it? Women have husbands and fathers. Husbands and fathers pay ransom. If not, there's always the slave market in Constantinople. Where Pushkin's great-grandfather was bought by Tsar Peter, if I'm not mistaken. In any case, their plan was foiled. The storm that destroyed the steamship drove the corsair's vessel into port here, where it was seized and we were rescued."

My host, a rather heavyset, moist-eyed woman in black, relit her cheroot which had gone out and poured a bit more vodka into my glass.

"All quite as romantic as one of your novels, my dear," she said.

"I am most grateful to you, Elena Petrovna, for caring for me as you have. I don't know how to begin to thank you." I glanced from her face to the window behind her through whose elaborate latticework I could just make out a bit of Poti's harbor spread out at our feet. The sea was quite blue now and calm. "But what an astonishing coincidence that we should both be on the same ship."

"These things happen," Elena Petrovna said.

"I understood that you had gone to Tibet."

"I do intend to travel to that blessed land. But I have some work to finish before I go. It is keeping me here longer than I expected."

I knew what that work was: finding Nikolai Barakov and his book. Another coincidence, that it was the same task upon which I myself was engaged. Of course, Blavatskaya knew I knew Nikolai; Fyodorov had told me that. But did she know I was also searching for him? And did she know I knew she was searching for him, too? I had to assume she knew both these things since she was a clairvoyant and mind-reader, a sorceress and magician, a psychic and occultist, and rich enough to buy any information she wanted. She probably had an entire platoon of spies working for her. Most successful fortune-tellers did.

"By the way, your maid, Zuzana..."

"I have no maid named Zuzana."

"Odd. She seemed most attentive to you on the ship. She disappeared once we arrived in port, however, and I haven't seen her since. But you say she was not your maid?"

"No. I have no memory of her," I said, which was perfectly true.

"How strange," said Elena Petrovna, strangest of women. "What is the last thing you are able to recall before you awoke from your coma and found yourself in this house?"

"The last thing I remember..."

Oddly, I had not given much thought to what I had been doing last or where I had been. I remembered eating dinner with the Kantrovsky family; I remembered walking down a corridor with Sasha and her cousin; I remembered drinking a cup of coffee...

Suddenly I was very angry. I was sick and tired of being manipulated, lied to, threatened, drugged, imprisoned, abducted, and, most of all, I absolutely hated being interrogated by black magicians even if they were providing me with shelter, food and Turkish tobacco.

I got up and walked across the room to the lattice-covered window. Walking was not easy. I was wearing clothes that were not my own, a silk kimono and a pair of Turkish slippers. The kimono was too long, the slippers, too tight. I could not leave the house dressed like this even if I knew where to go, or had the money to get there.

"What happened to my valet? Was he also taken by the corsairs? Or did he remain on the ship that sank?"

"I do not believe your valet was on board the ship to begin with."

"Well, that's good news, at least."

From what I could see of the harbor through the carved latticework, there were many ships at anchor or tied up along the quay, and a passenger steamship was even now pulling away from the dock. With different clothes and some pocket money, escape was possible.

"But… the last thing you remember… you were saying?"

"Was I?"

"Yes. And what was it, my dear? Your last memory…"

I was being urged to turn away from the window. I struggled against that urge. I kept my eyes fixed on a little two-masted xebec making its way into port. Such a graceful little boat with its lateen sails. I had seen them often sailing into Odessa harbor, a Mediterranean ship, Pasha had told me, who knew so much about so many things, who knew how to guard his mind. Fill your head, he'd laugh, like an overstuffed attic, so that anyone searching it for something in particular might find the searching difficult. So I began counting off the types of boats whose names I knew, and such names they were! Brigantine, caique, corvette, felucca, frigate, galley, galleon, gondola, launch, sloop, schooner, skiff, tserniki, trehantiri…

"Let me help," she said.

"To remember? I don't need your help. I remember quite well. I was visiting a friend. I was taken ill."

I turned around and walked back to the sofa. The late afternoon sun was shining into the room, a room decorated in Turkish style, with divans and pillows, low tables, and brightly colored rugs, and its rays, coming in through the latticework, were leaving diamond-shaped spots of light on the floor.

"A Polish friend, perhaps?" Blavatskaya said in a low, deceptively soothing voice.

"I wonder why this is of such interest to you."

"I would think it would be of greater interest to you. Why would you not wish to discover who drugged you and sent you off to some deadly fate, to slavery perhaps, to some sultan's harem?"

"Oh, for goodness sake," I said. "You're becoming highly dramatic."

"Not at all. It is perfectly possible. I have found this quest we are both on to be highly dramatic in all its aspects."

Having so dramatically confessed her interest, as well as what she supposed was her knowledge of my own intentions, she leaned back in her chair and took a long pull on her cigar, exhaling a tremendous cloud of thick, evil-smelling smoke. Just as suddenly as I had earlier become angry, I now had to restrain myself from bursting into laughter. The whole thing struck me as funny: Blavatskaya, dressed in her black sack, smoking her cheroot, the room with its elaborate *mashrabiya*, the joke of my being a guest here. I was not at all a guest; I was a prisoner again. And all this for the sake of a book!

"I wish you would tell me, Elena Petrovna, what it is about *Monkey* that so fascinates everyone? I myself don't give a fig about the novel. It's Nikolai I'm looking for. You can have the damn book as far as I'm concerned, if it even exists, if it hasn't been ripped to shreds and burned to ash or thrown into the Neva or left on a bench in the rain. But what is it that makes everyone want it? That's what I'd like to know."

At that very juncture, just when I thought that for once I might get an honest answer to a question, the door to the room opened and a tall, thin, bespectacled man, a man who in his figure and his movements quite resembled a praying mantis, walked in.

"Valentina Grigorevna, may I present Dr Paulus Metamon."

The Coptic magician, of whom Odysseus Dimitrakos had spoken, who had traveled with Blavatskaya to Trebizond in the *Sosa*, and whom Nikolai may have jumped ship in order to follow, bowed and said how pleased he was to make my acquaintance. He made my skin crawl.

"If you'll forgive me, Elena Petrovna," I said, "I am feeling quite fatigued and shall retire now."

I began getting up, but Blavatskaya raised her hand, a gesture which seemed to physically restrain me from moving.

"Ah, but you asked me a question, and I would be pleased to answer it for you. You asked about *Monkey*, did you not?"

The dappled light on the carpet seemed momentarily to quiver.

"What is it about *Monkey*, you asked, that fascinates... And fascinates is indeed a well-chosen word. But, of course, you, too, are a writer. You understand the power of words."

Dr Metamon, meanwhile, had taken a seat on one of the divans lining the walls, and was watching us from under half-closed lids.

"As for others, I cannot speak. For myself, I search for it because it is required by my Master, my Guide. Why does he require it? Because it contains occult knowledge which must not be divulged to the uninitiated. It is that simple, my dear."

"Whatever can you mean? Are you suggesting that Nikolai Barakov is in possession of this occult knowledge and has put it into his novel?"

"Possesses it. Acquired it. Stole it. Yes. However he obtained it, he did so without permission."

"Permission of whom? Is there an owner of such knowledge?"

"Of course. Knowledge is the property of those who can wield it."

"You make it sound as though knowledge were a weapon."

"In many hands that is exactly what it is. And Nikolai Barakov, for reasons known only to himself, having acquired this secret knowledge, passed only from master to pupil over many centuries and under the most guarded circumstances, put it into a novel. A novel! Can you begin to comprehend—first, the sacrilege, then, the danger such a thing poses, that these teachings be cast like seeds, cast to the wind, to land wherever they might, to infect whatever poor wretch comes in contact with them? These secrets are immensely powerful and without the proper control, and in the wrong hands, God only knows what they might unleash on the world. Indeed I fear that this book has the power to distort time, reverse temporal linearity, and destroy the very integrity of narrative."

"The integrity of narrative, indeed!" I said with a laugh. "What an interesting story. Forgive me if I don't believe it."

"It is of no consequence to me whether you believe it or not. But I must know everything you know about Nikolai Barakov, and the names of everyone you have contacted in your search for him—and I must know these things without delay!"

At these words, as though they had been a signal, Dr Paulus Metamon, a grotesquely tall and thin creature, rose from his divan and came toward me. At the same time, Blavatskaya reached out her hands as though to grip hold of my arms. I jumped to my feet, relieved that I was no longer restrained, and tottered to the door in my tight slippers, yelling as I did, "Fire! Fire! Help! Fire!" I had barely crossed the room when the door burst open and several servants piled in, carrying nothing with which to extinguish a fire had there been one, and while they pushed their way in, I pushed my way out and ran down the stairs and out the front door into the street.

Fortune favors the bold, Nikolai always said, and fortune was with me. There on the street, not two meters away, a horse was being led to a stable by a young boy, a mere child. What luck! I grabbed the reins from the child, put my slippered foot into the stirrup, swung myself into the saddle, and at once the dear creature and I were clattering away down the street, going as fast as ever we could, down toward the harbor and its precious ships, my salvation, my escape by sea.

A kimono-wearing woman in Turkish slippers galloping down a cobblestone street on a swift steed—what could be less ostentatious, less noticeable? What could cause less disturbance? Only a kimono-wearing woman in Turkish slippers jumping off such a creature and leaping from the quayside onto an outgoing caique, one of those trusty, single-masted fishing boats that plied the coast, one that had just cast off and was moving out on the ebb. The fishermen would have been well within their rights to shove me right overboard, and I half expected them to do so, but I threw myself on their mercy, told them I had been kidnapped, begged them to save me, and offered them a handsome reward—all in a language I was quite sure they did not understand. By then we were almost out of the little harbor, the wind being strong and from the east, and to throw me overboard that far from shore would have been nothing short of murder.

Looking back toward the harbor, we could see that the incident had drawn the attention of a number of on-lookers; the horse was causing a bit of trouble, a large, excited animal being left unattended on the quay; officials were coming out of their holes and starting to ask questions; and I was sure I could see some of Blavatskaya's servants running down toward the beach. From the safe and ever-increasing distance between ship and shore, the entire drama was taking on the aspect of a comedy, and so it appeared it would remain. No one took hold of me to toss me into the sea. Instead the crew of three young men went back to the task of sailing their little boat while their more grizzled captain gestured me to go below. There he sat me down and began asking questions. This being the Circassian coast, he was a polyglot: besides his native language, he spoke Russian and Turkish, and even, it would later turn out, a little Greek. Who was I, he asked, and who was I running away from, and how much did I intend to pay him for risking his boat and therefore his livelihood by taking on board a possible criminal or runaway wife?

"And tell it to me quickly in case they should be sending another boat after you even now."

I told him my name. It did not impress him in the least, and I did not expect it to. I then related the entire story to him as Blavatskaya had related it to me—the steamer, the pirates, the storm, the corsair ship driven into harbor, the captives freed. Surely he had heard of these events. But, no, he had not. He was a poor fisherman. He did not know everything that happened in the world, and he did not want to know.

"But why jump onto my boat in such a manner when you can easily take another ship back to Odessa?"

"After we were freed from the pirates, a woman took me into her home. I thought she was being kind, but she kept me a prisoner. She took my things, as you see. I left her house with nothing. She is dangerous and powerful."

What sort of tale was I telling now? It was true, all of it, more or less, but even to my ears it sounded like the plot of a romance novel or a story concocted by a woman who was utterly mad.

He sat back to consider the matter.

"What am I to do with you? If I set you down anywhere along this coast, you will be alone, helpless and destitute. Where do you have friends?"

It was a troubling question. I could not answer it.

"You want to get back to Odessa. There are many ships in the sea, many going to Odessa. Better I get you onto one of those. But you will have to pay passage. Or work." He laughed; he found the idea most amusing.

"I can work," I said.

He ignored this and continued thinking out loud. "But why should I help you? Your people slaughter us. Why shouldn't I throw you into the sea?"

Another troubling question I could not answer.

He rummaged around in an old chest and pulled out a pair of trousers, a shirt, and a jacket, and handed these items to me. Proper fisherman's clothes, worn, far too big for me, but quite adequate. Just then one of the boys shouted something down to the captain and he quickly went up on deck.

I threw off the kimono and dressed myself in the captain's old clothes. Then I looked around for a weapon in case one was needed. Instead I found a bottle of something that smelt like raki and took a gulp, for fortitude. Meanwhile the ship had heeled to starboard. Voices were raised on deck; our speed increased. Were we being pursued? It seemed absurd that Blavatskaya would have taken such a step.

The captain called down to me, "A Greek merchant ship. Maybe en route to Odessa. I will see."

Time passed. It was now evening; bow and stern lanterns were being lit. There was more shouting, ship to ship. Vessels hailing each other over the sound of blowing wind and rushing water must yell very loudly. A lady, I heard my captain say. *Kyria.* It was one of the few Greek words I knew. A few minutes later he came down to tell me the ship was indeed en route to Odessa, that he had told the Greek captain I was a survivor of a shipwreck and desperate to get home, that they were sending a boat over for me. They would take me on faith; I would pay them on arrival. "No need for you to haul sails or scrub decks," he said and laughed again.

I insisted on knowing his name and promised I would send his payment, that I wished to do so. He shook his head, a skeptic for sure, and suddenly I was filled with love for him, who had saved me and clothed me and asked nothing in return. All I had of any value was a little ring I had bought in the gold market in Istanbul many years before and always wore. This I placed in my captain's hand, closing his fingers over it and pressing his hand tight, in friendship.

From the deck I watched bobbing lights approaching, the skiff being rowed toward us.

"*Kalo taxidi,*" my captain said, handing me over the side, and with that wish for a good journey, he turned his little caique back toward his fishing grounds while I was rowed toward the large, graceful, three-masted merchant ship, which had kindly heaved to for me, and was floating gently on the water like a swan. I wondered how rich a lady my captain had portrayed me to be, how many titles he had given me, to persuade the Greek to stop his ship and take me aboard. I wondered how much it was going to cost me. Then I climbed the rope ladder and was helped onto the deck, she made sail again, and I stopped wondering.

It was wise to do so. I had so many problems, I could never have solved them all by musing, or by any other means. How I had come to be in Blavatskaya's house puzzled me terribly, but I could not unravel the puzzle, and what I learned from the Greek captain only increased the mystery: there had been no report of pirate activity along the coast, there had been no storm, no ship from Odessa had gone down in rough seas, and no corsair or pirate vessel of any kind had been taken into port in Poti. All this was intriguing, but a more pressing problem at the moment was how I was to be smuggled back into Odessa since I had no papers, no passport, no respectable clothes, and no money. Fortunately, the captain was a clever Greek and not a fearful Russian. He didn't think of rules as laws to be obeyed but as annoyances to be overcome and so rather than see me detained for a month or more in quarantine, being examined, fumigated and kept from normal society (and my bank), he immediately thought of a solution that would be beneficial to us both.

So it happened that one morning at first light, after a relatively smooth sea journey of many days, I was discreetly rowed ashore near the summer resort town of the Fountains some short distance from Odessa, where, still in my fisherman's disguise, I easily made my way into the city, arriving at Princess Volkonskaya's house in time for a late breakfast, to the great surprise, and I might say, even delight of the servants and of poor, distraught Pavel Damianich, who had almost despaired of ever finding me again. How joyfully we embraced each other, both of us skinnier and a bit more battered than before, and over a breakfast of pancakes, cigarettes and pots of coffee, each a delight in itself, we told each other our tales.

Mine, as I told it, beginning with the Countess's clever use of her poison ring, was as full of near calamity, last minute rescue, and miraculous escape as any adventure novel, lacking only an element of romance. Still, Pasha appreciated it. He loved such tales, much as he poo-pooed them as mere juvenilia, though it is just such juvenilia that paid our bills.

His story was equally dramatic, filled with danger and heroic determination. He, too, had been drugged at the Kantrovsky house. He had awakened the next morning in an empty room in an abandoned stone house on a deserted country road miles from the city. Since the only way back to Odessa was on foot, he set out, already hungry and thirsty, with no clear idea where he was. He walked all day and into the evening before, exhausted, footsore and dying of thirst, he stumbled up the steps of Princess Volkonskaya's house where, to his great distress, he learned that I had failed to return from dinner the previous night.

Early the next morning, he began searching for me. First he returned to the family's townhouse, but there he learned from the few remaining servants that the family had moved to their country house for the summer. He spent days driving around the countryside, searching for the house Alexandra Kirillovna's carriage had brought us to, but he could not find it. With some difficulty, he was able to discover the location of Khayim Kantrovsky's goldsmith shop, but the man himself was away and no one could say when he would return. He wrote to Countess Sabanska with inquiries, but received no reply. Nor, though he made frequent stops at the Acropolis Taverna, was he able to find the once ubiquitous Odysseus Dimitrakos. He had run out of ideas, he was desperate, frantic; he seriously considered taking the extreme step of reporting my disappearance to port officials and the Odessa police, a drastic measure which would surely have resulted in nothing but masses of paperwork; he was about to write to the princess and inform her of the catastrophe when—*voila!*—I dramatically and miraculously appeared at the door.

"It appears we have two mysteries here," Pasha said when he had finished his tale. "Are they related or are they not?"

"I am not sure I am capable of contemplating even one mystery so early in the day."

"Come now, Marko, you must be intrigued. Two mysteries—one, why were you drugged by the Countess and sent away on a steamship—in the care of that Polish maid, Zuzana, I suppose; and two, how did you end up in Blavatskaya's house in Poti."

"You think the Countess and Blavatskaya are in league? To what end?"

"It certainly appears that Blavatskaya thinks you know something of importance to her, and she is determined to find out what it is."

"She told me that *Monkey* is full of secret occult knowledge. That's why she wants it. It's absurd, of course. Kolya hates all that spiritualist nonsense. He always makes fun of it."

"Maybe he put it in the novel in order to make fun of it. Maybe Madame Blavatskaya has no sense of humor."

"She must think I know where the book is."

"Or you know something that would help her find it."

We sat in silence for awhile, digesting this idea along with our breakfast.

"Well, damn," I cried out finally. "What the hell is it that I know?"

"Whatever it is, it won't do us any good," he said. "It's a piece of a puzzle, but we don't have the puzzle it goes to."

"But it's not a puzzle I give a damn about," I said. "It's Kolya I want to find, Kolya! Not his blasted book!"

Pasha laughed and said I'd clearly been spending too much time around seamen and from there launched into a long discourse about the various linguistic means used to establish class identity and the idea of salty language being a particular and essential class identifier for sailors. It was oddly calming, as Pasha's intellectual discourses usually were.

"But just think of it, Pasha," I said, calmly, once he had finished. "Elena Petrovna must have had her minions spying on us all these months. Somehow she learned that I was a passenger on that steamship, and somehow she managed to get me off the ship—and concocted that absurd story to explain how I came to be in her house. She imprisoned me and tried to read my mind, she and that black magician, Paulus Metamon. They frighten me, these people."

"Yes, that could be how it happened," he said, thoughtfully. "She learned you were a passenger, and she took advantage of the situation to kidnap you from the steamship. Yes, it is possible that that is how it occurred, and there was no conspiracy involving herself and the Poles. Then we would have to turn our attention back to the Countess. What reason would she have to drug you and send you off on a ship to Constantinople? Did she say anything to you, Marko, that might explain it?

"Not that I remember. What a mysterious woman she is! I imagine there is quite a story to be told about Countess Sabanska."

"And I imagine you are already writing it."

"Not at all. But if I were..." I stopped to allow him time to light my cigarette. For the first time I was thinking fondly of Mora Khayimyevna, the way one does when first considering an actual person as a potential fictional character. "Yes, if I were I would make her the ravishingly beautiful daughter of an Odessan banker, a man with liberal sympathies and aspirations, who would often host Poles visiting Odessa for secret meetings. She would listen carefully to all these conversations, and at times she would even express her own thoughts and declare herself a passionate supporter of freedom for the Poles."

"A beautiful, passionate heroine. Excellent. And is she also a secret partisan?"

"No, indeed. She is actually an imperial spy."

"What! A spy for the Tsar?"

"Yes. She is secretly engaged to a member of the intelligence services, who has persuaded her to assist him by reporting on the comings and goings of the Polish nationalists."

"Dear God! Then what happens?"

"Then she meets a young man, a Pole, handsome, dashing, brave, a true partisan. They fall in love, of course, and she confesses what she has been doing, she begs his forgiveness, she declares herself willing to do anything to make up for the harm she has done the noble cause. He suggests that she continue making her reports, but that she falsify all the information in order to mislead and deceive the Imperial Intelligence Service. This is dangerous, he warns her, but she agrees."

"A romance and an intrigue! Marko, you must write this! It is brilliant!"

"Of course, our heroic Pole must always wonder if his beloved has truly changed sides, if she is truly devoted to him and the cause, or if she is still, God forbid, in the pay of the Tsar."

"Naturally. There must be that tension. He must always suspect her, though unfairly."

"Indeed. But what if his suspicions are justified? How would he know? If men disappear, if couriers are murdered on the street—well, Odessa is a dangerous city. As for those smugglers, pay them what you will, they are outlaws, thieves and murderers. You can never rely on them not to turn on their friends. In this way, the revolutionary cadre can be decimated while all the blame for it can be laid at the doorstep of ordinary criminals."

"But what possible motive could she have for betraying him and the cause? Surely she can't so love the Tsar!"

"Not at all. But she does love her fiancé, the Russian spy. Oh, one could excuse it in operatic fashion by saying her father is a gambler, and she must pay his debts or the family faces ruin. The Imperial Treasury has a good deal more money in its coffers than the Polish-Ukrainian Revolutionary Committee. But that would make the story pathetic and overly sentimental. No, she is simply enamored of her Russian, her handsome and dashing officer of the Third Division. And she enjoys the thrill of it, the risk and the danger, the excitement of living on the edge."

"But it is so reactionary, Marko! A romance in which the heroine is an imperial spy? A double-agent? No, it's impossible that you should write such a thing!"

I had to laugh at him. Poor Pasha. Sometimes he took things far too seriously.

"I am only joking," I said. "I would never write such a story, as you should know by now." Still, I thought, it was a good story, and it could easily be true, for no matter how much people talked about idealistic reasons for taking one position or another, or espousing this cause or that one, in the end it was only love that moved us to act, only love that motivated us to do anything, desire in some form or other, desire for something we lacked. I could easily imagine Mora Khayimyevna, a passionate woman, a woman of spirit, acting bravely, risking everything, for the sake of love. But love for what, or for whom?

Suddenly something flashed through my mind, a sentence, a few words... but so quickly I could not grasp it. There was something—I barely remembered—something she had said to me in those last moments before I lost all memory... something in her voice... something about love...

"I will admit it is an intriguing tale, Marko. Look how it has diverted us! But now we must return to the question. Why did the Poles kidnap you and send you out of the country? What reason could they possibly have to want you out of Odessa?"

"Wait!" I cried. "I am trying to remember... Oh, dear God!" Now the memory was coming back to me, and I could barely restrain myself from jumping to my feet. "Beriosov! We have been in such danger! Oh, is it even possible? And is it even possible that the tale I just made up for your amusement is actually true, and Mora Sabanska is a spy?"

"I can't imagine what you—"

"No! Wait! Oh, I have it now! I have just remembered! It is not conspiracy, dear Pasha. It is love! Love! *Amor, ch'al cor gentil ratto s'apprende... amor, ch'a nulla amato amor perdona...* She told me! I remember now. She is in love with Nikolai!"

"Who?"

"The Countess, of course! She confessed it to me! Dear God, what a romance!"

"When did she make this confession?"

"As she was drugging me. Yes, just then she spoke from her heart. She told me Beriosov was looking for me, was intent on finding me, that I was in terrible danger. And then she said she was warning me because I was Nikolai's friend and she was in love with him, although she had broken his heart. Oh, it is a romance, you see! How could I have forgotten?"

"That changes things considerably. If Beriosov is here in Odessa searching for you, then she had the best of intentions, hustling you out of the country as she did."

"Yes. But why do it so brutally? Did she think I would not listen to reason?"

"Do you ever listen to reason, dear Marko? But now you must. It is imperative now that we leave Odessa at once."

"I must pay my Greek captain first," I said. "Maybe you could do that for me. I would be happy if I never saw the sea again as long as I live."

"What? No more adventures at sea?"

"Never again!"

"Very well. I'll see your captain. But then, Marko—"

"Then... yes, yes. I agree. It is time to return to Oak Hills."

He nodded, but said nothing. It was defeat and we both knew it.

So, without more being said, we prepared for our departure. Pasha went down to the port to deliver my compliments and my money to my Greek captain and to bid adieu to his favorite drinking haunts. I gathered my books and papers and packed my trunks. I also had a number of letters to read, which I intended to save until evening, though by evening I was too tired to do more than glance at them and put them in my pocket to read in the coach.

Early the next morning, our coachman drove us to the station where we boarded a post-chaise for the first leg of our long journey north, first to Moscow, and then, as quickly as possible, spending no time at all in the city, on to Oak Hills.

CHAPTER THIRTY-TWO

Return to Oak Hills

"Poor Fyodor Fyodorovich! I feel so sorry for him!"

Sofia Vasilevna smiled at her daughter. "You are very dear, Natasha. But why do you feel sorry for Fyodor Fyodorovich?"

"He's not coming to the country with us. I feel sorry for everyone who isn't coming to the country with us. But especially Fyodor Fyodorovich because he is so unhappy. And I want him to meet Grandmama!"

Sofia Vasilevna studied her daughter's face for a moment. She was changing so much, changing every day, growing so tall, straight and slender, her clothes hardly fit her anymore. But it was her face that so surprised Sofia every morning that she found herself examining it with intense curiosity at the breakfast table, wondering what feature might have been newly sculpted overnight. One morning, it was her nose that had become more delicately formed, another morning, her eyes seemed darker and more almond-shaped. Now, where just yesterday her cheeks were still childishly chubby, suddenly today she had cheekbones, giving her face the contours of the steppes, as though whatever exotic blood had made its way into her veins was expressing itself at last. It was abundantly evident that little Natasha was no longer a child, but was rapidly becoming a young girl.

"... but I think he will come with Aunt Tatyana."

"Fyodor Fyodorovich? With Aunt Tatyana? It's quite unlikely. I hardly think she knows the man, Natasha."

"But he told me he was going to High Meadows with Alexander Felixovich. And won't Aunt Tatyana come to see us? Maybe he will come with her. I hope he will."

Sofia gazed out the window of the carriage at the rather monotonous landscape, green at least now rather than snow-covered or dull brown. This was the last day of their long journey, which had brought them steadily deeper and deeper into the countryside. First the train from Petersburg to Moscow, where they visited Ivan Ivanovich's parents; then, with all their bags, trunks, boxes, servants and children packed into wagons and carriages, the slow advance into the country on roads that became ever narrower and narrower, muddier and muddier. Midway, as always, they stopped for the night at the house of an ancient cousin of Vasily's. There the children ran wild in the meadows surrounding the old house, and slept soundly in the low, rambling bedrooms, so old-fashioned and unchanging in their furnishings that Sofia always felt she was stepping back in time whenever she set foot in them.

Now at last the journey was almost over. It was always like this, she thought, this last stage, always agonizingly slow, jarring, the boys riding in the open wagon, yelling as usual. Poor Natasha had so wanted to ride with them, but she was too old now to tumble around in an open cart, shrieking and jumping about with the boys. She had hoped they might read but it was too difficult, the road was all ditches and pot holes when it wasn't thick with mud or washed out entirely... Vanya was quite right to say that the country would never prosper without decent roads, not that anything would be done to improve them, not under this regime... And all this trouble, packing and traveling, moving the whole household into the country... every summer... when instead they might have a lovely, relaxing holiday at the sea. If Mother would only agree to go, she thought bitterly, but she won't even leave the house.

Thinking of Anastasia reminded her of Fyodorov and Natasha's strange desire to have him come to Oak Hills. What an odd child she was!

"You must tell me, Natasha. Why do you want Fyodor Fyodorovich to meet Grandmama?"

"Because he's a friend of Uncle Nikolai's, and so I know she will love to talk to him."

"Uncle Nikolai has been gone a long time. Perhaps it will make her sad to talk about him now."

"No. Why would it?"

"Because sometimes it hurts to remember people who—"

She stopped herself, frowning at the words that, without her volition, were about to come out of her mouth.

"Who—what, Mama?"

For absolutely no reason, she felt her eyes fill with tears. She shook her head to drive them away and sat up straighter as the coach bounced over yet another rough spot in the road.

"Who have been away a long time. And whom we miss very much. Now read your book, Natasha. I am going to close my eyes and try to sleep."

To sleep. To dream. She had dreamt about her brother quite recently, a dream that had stayed with her all the next day. They were children again, traveling in a cart together, just like her boys were now. There were other children in the cart with them, and animals of all kinds, and somehow she had confused a small animal, perhaps it was a kitten, with her brother. The kitten, if it was a kitten, had fallen out of the cart and she had jumped out of the cart to try to find him. She was running down a dirt road, searching for him, when she woke up. This dream had so disturbed her that upon awakening she took his last letter out of the locked casket in which she kept it and read it again. When she first received it, it had made her angry; now, it aroused a terrible fear.

"Well, at least he doesn't come around borrowing money from us anymore," Vanya had said, cruelly when she expressed her fear to him, and then had immediately apologized and told her it worried him, too, it was worrying him very much, and, really, he loved Kolya, thought he was one of the smartest people he knew, missed their discussions, their long talks, missed drinking with him, missed hearing his point of view, etcetera, etcetera.

"You say that but you never do anything about it."

"What am I supposed to do? Tell me! I'll do it. Just tell me what it is."

"Don't you know anyone you can ask?"

"Who? Who am I supposed to ask? And ask what? What am I supposed to ask?"

"You are the professor, Ivan Ivanovich, not me. You are the intellectual."

"I swear to you, Sonya, if I knew—"

It was useless. Irina got the same sort of answers from Arkady Andreyevich: who can I ask? what do you want me to do? As though they were children, as though they were not, respectively, a university professor and a well-placed civil servant. She did not believe it was cowardice on Ivan Ivanovich's part, for he was brave enough when it came to protecting his students; nor did she think it was a secret dislike of her brother, for they had always gotten on well together. There was no logical explanation for Vanya's refusal to help her except that in his own way he was trying to protect her from a truth that would hurt her deeply and bring suffering to everyone. But if that were the case, would it not be better to have the truth come out, to suffer and mourn rather than hold onto false hopes and expectations? Whenever she thought about her brother, she felt such overwhelming emotions, and one of them was rage at Nikolai for dying, if dying was what he had done, or for his endless silence, if he were still alive; in either case, for the pain he was causing them all, this pain she felt in her heart.

On and on they drove, passing flat, endless fields of corn. Then the road went into the cool forest, and that meant they were getting closer. The land rose around them into hills. Closer and closer, and Natasha became more and more excited. Finally the big hill, and up and up they went, and then, at the crest, they could see it all: the village of lovely little painted wooden houses, the little white, blue-domed church, the double line of lime trees leading to the big house, with its barns, its garden, its pond, the oak-covered hill behind it, and the woods stretching out beyond, while looking all around in a circle one could see for miles and miles a great ocean of corn, dotted with bright villages and the dark green of woods, the great forests, so many different greens.

"Oh, it's so beautiful!" Natasha cried. "Please, let me get out and run down the hill!"

"I will let you do no such thing, you little monkey!" Sofia said, laughing, because she, too, in her heart, wanted to get out of the carriage and run down the hill. Instead she started tickling Natasha, who shrieked with pleasure, and so they were both laughing hard when the carriage finally reached the road shaded with lime trees and drew up to a stop in front of the old house.

"Now you may," Sofia said, and Natasha pushed open the carriage door and flew out like a caged bird, freed.

Her brothers were already running around in circles, in delight; the house servants were opening their arms, everyone was hugging, and Grandpapa was standing on the steps, laughing at them all. Natasha ran to him and hugged him tight.

"Where is she?"

"Upstairs. In her room. Waiting for you."

"I'm going."

"Kisses first."

He bent down and she kissed him on both cheeks. Then up the steps she ran as fast as she could.

The return was always so wonderful, the windows, the shutters, the steps, the hall, the chairs, the rugs, the little table. Everything was where it should be, where it always was, where it would always be. When she dreamt about Oak Hills, everything was just the same, too. Nothing could ever change. And then she was running up the stairs, one flight, two flights, running through the doorway, running into the room and into her grandmother's arms.

♣

Anastasia sat on the divan, Natasha sat on the little Turkish stool in front of her. Between them was the low table that looked like a big bronze platter and on the table was a plate of little pastries and sugar-covered dumplings, a pitcher of cold lemonade, and pretty glasses with gold rims. All around the room were Anastasia's little stone gardens and little altars, all the pictures of Uncle Nikolai, some with little vases of pretty flowers in front of them. The room which Natasha loved so much was the same as it had always been. Anastasia's lovely silk shawl with the gold fringe was lying over the back of her chair. The beautiful books were on the shelves. The window was open and she could hear the gentle rustling of oak leaves and the piping voice of a thrush. Beyond those sounds were others, so dear and familiar, sounds of the barnyard, a donkey braying, a cock crowing, someone hammering. Natasha was so happy she could barely contain her joy.

If Anastasia was thinner, if the lines on her face were deeper, if her eyes were duller, her voice weaker, her smile sadder, if she seemed frail and old, Natasha did not notice. What she saw was her dear grandmother, and she had so much to tell her, it seemed she would never be able to remember it all. But of everything she wanted to say, there were three important things she needed to tell her grandmother right away so when Anastasia asked, "What are the best things that happened since we saw each other last?" she knew exactly what to answer.

"I have been investigating."

"Really? What have you been investigating?"

"Grandmama, I have met someone who knows Uncle Nikolai. His name is Fyodor Fyodorovich. Do you know him?"

"I do not."

"He came to visit us. With another friend of Uncle Kolya's, a man from Argentina named Alexander Felixovich."

"Ah. Alexander Felixovich," Anastasia repeated after a moment's thought. "Yes, I do remember him. From years ago."

"They are going to High Meadows to see Aunt Tatyana."

"How interesting."

"Perhaps they could come here. I think you would like to talk to them. And I found out something else, Grandmama. Which I think will make you happy. Nikolai is a writer! He has written a play and a novel!"

It surprised Natasha that Anastasia said nothing in response to this wonderful news. She sipped her lemonade. She smiled at Natasha. Finally she said, "These men told you this?"

"Fyodor Fyodorovich told me about the play and he told Papa about the novel. I overheard them. It's called *Monkey.*"

Anastasia took another sip of her lemonade.

"Thank you for telling me this, Natasha, dear. Thank you very much. Have you learned anything else?"

"I learn things every day," Natasha said.

"And you are writing, too, I hope."

"I have filled several notebooks."

"I am proud of you. Say one of your poems for me."

She did, and Anastasia listened, but her heart was elsewhere and when Natasha finished reciting her poem, Anastasia said she was getting very tired and needed to take a rest.

"May I come up after supper?"

"Of course you may. By then I shall have had my nap."

Anastasia kissed her and Natasha went dancing out of the room, leaving distress and upset in her wake.

For a long time Anastasia sat very still with her eyes closed, waiting for the sea to become calm. Perhaps it never would become calm, perhaps this was the end of calmness, quietness, and retreat. Of waiting. Of hoping. Waiting could make you mad. Hoping could make you mad. Stillness. It was what they prescribed for madness, for neurasthenia, for depression, malaise, acedia... lying still in a darkened room. But the cure was the same as the disease.

She thought she had made her peace with it. With the terrible truth. She thought she had made her peace. It had been forced out of her, wrung out, the way you wring water from a piece of clothing, with strong hands, with force, with determination, painfully; she had wrung it out of herself with her own hands, her own mind. She had forced it out and she had looked it in the eye. This is the truth, she had said. Then it had destroyed her, as she knew it would.

What these men, these men, strangers, what they had said was nothing. It was what they had not said. What they could not say. He is living there, he can be found here, in this place, he's gone overseas, he is living in New Russia, New Spain, New Orleans, in Jamaica, Sumatra, Algeria, Alexandria. The vast world, anywhere in the vast world, would satisfy. But nowhere in the vast world, this was the answer she received, always the same answer. He is not here.

She would not see these men.

She would not hear their stories.

That he had written a book, a play, poems... all useless things. Who cared about words, about stories, ideas? Who cared about feelings stored on pages of old and useless books? Life was what mattered, only life, and there was no life in words. All that would satisfy was his presence in this room. His footsteps on the stairs. His figure at the door. His arms around her. His voice. His smile. Nothing else would answer.

Finally she stood and stumbled across the room to her desk. There, deep in a drawer, deep as a grave, was a stack of papers. She sat down in her chair, she opened the drawer, she took out the poems which had been wrung out from her, which had been written in tears, in fury, in blood. Fifty-six poems. Each one, a horror. Pathetic hopes expressed and dashed, each one a testament to bitter truth, that honor alone forced her to face, torn out of her, each one, torn out with fiery tongs.

Only a flock of angels coming on a wind,
and tearing through this bitter screen
between the worlds, might then
so upset the way of things,
that the done deed might be undone,
and I might hear your footstep on the stair,

and when I glance up you might be standing there
where you will never stand again.

They had done the deed, which could not be undone. They had convinced her, they had made their case. No one else would tell her the truth, only the poems did. The only value of words, to say what had to be said, to break the will and then to break the heart, to shatter it or turn it into stone.

The only hope left to her, and the only joy, came to her in her dreams, as the one she had dreamt that very morning, so early in the morning that when she awoke the stars were still shining in the sky, a dream so wonderful, a dream in which she came down the stairs and found him home again, sitting at the table with Vasily, eating pancakes.

And with what joy she had awakened! The joy of seeing him had been so keen it had caught in her throat, and opened her eyes wide inside the dream, so wide, she could feel her eyes opening with joy, but as she opened her eyes inside the dream, she opened them outside the dream, too, and woke up and found herself in her bed, in her room, the dream already fleeing, her son gone.

♣

Sofia Vasilevna linked arms with her father, squeezed tight, and kissed his cheek.

"How are you, Papa?"

"I am well, my dear. I am very well. And you?"

"I am well as well," she said, smiling at him.

The ritual greetings, call and response. They had already hugged and kissed in the hall, Sofia had already settled the boys, washed her face and hands, changed her clothes, and had a cup of tea. Now, before supper, they were finally alone, strolling in the garden, admiring the first flowering bushes and the newly planted herbs. They had not seen each other all winter, and now it was late spring. She thought he looked older, his face seemed thinner, and his hair was now entirely white.

"You are looking fit as a fiddle," she said.

"You are as lovely as ever."

They laughed.

"Now," she said, "tell me the truth. How are things here?"

"Do you mean how is your mother?"

"Yes."

"She is the same. Reclusive. Unhappy."

They walked along the path between the flower beds in silence until they came to one of the garden benches and sat down. From the bench, which faced the back of the house, they could see Anastasia's two windows, shuttered, like blind eyes.

"I spent some time in the fall traveling around with Pyotr Panov. You remember him, I'm sure."

"The puppeteer?"

"Yes. The same. He and his troupe were passing through on their way south for the winter."

"You traveled with the actors, Papa? I can't believe it. Whatever for?"

"I was looking for your brother."

"For Kolya? With tinkers and gypsies and traveling actors?"

"Those were the kind of people he liked."

"Well, I take it you didn't find him."

"No."

"Did Mother know about this?"

"Of course I told her. Perhaps I should not have. I may have raised false hopes."

Sofia thought her mother was not so naive as to have her hopes raised so easily, but she did not say it. Instead she asked what traveling in wagons with a troupe of actors was like, and listened to her father talk with some enthusiasm about the adventure, the excitement, even the discomfort of their journey. Uncle Alyosha had come with him. They had done a bit of fishing along the way.

"There is something to be said for the gypsy life. There's physical rigor to it, outside all day, always moving, you see a lot, believe me. The country has its beauty, you know, but it has its bitterness too. Poverty in the villages. Homeless men, wandering on the roads, children too, it's terrible. And of course we ourselves were considered vagrants in various places, harried, threatened. By officious officials. Who do they think they are? Bah! Still, we took byways, avoided certain estates, and Pyotr has done that journey so many times, he knows where it's safe and where it's not—unless things had changed meantime, and every so often, they had."

He and Uncle Alyosha had gone with the actors as far as the Volga where Pyotr intended to take barge and steamboat all the way down to Astrakhan.

"Such a journey! How we wanted to accompany them! But then, the thought of returning… and the weather changing… going upriver a bit slower than going down… and then, of course, your mother…"

Sofia glanced up at her mother's windows. She would go up to see her soon, have a good talk with her. No more nonsense! To think of it! Anything could have happened to him on the road. He could have been killed.

I must tell them about the letter, she thought suddenly. *This has gone on long enough.*

"But in terms of its purpose, it was not a wasted trip, Sonya, dear, not at all. I found out some things about your brother I did not know, and learning these things, I feel quite comforted. I feel quite… reconciled."

"Reconciled? To what?"

Muttering something under his breath, Vasily leaned over and plucked a rogue weed out of the flower bed on his right.

"So much to do," he said. "Work never ends."

"Reconciled to what, Papa?"

"What?"

"You were talking about Kolya. You said you felt reconciled. To what?"

"Ah! Well, I suppose, simply put, to his way of life. After all this time, yes, to his way of life. You know, while he was still living here, and even afterwards, whenever I saw him, whenever we talked, I would always recommend he do this or that. I would say, You can still change things for yourself. Why don't you take my advice? And he would say, Why are you always trying to get me to change my life? My life is good. I love my life. And I would say, How can you love living the way you do? He couldn't answer. He wouldn't try to answer. That was always between us, Sonya. I think between you and him also. Isn't that right? We did not approve. We wanted him to change. We wanted him to be different than he was. We didn't appreciate what he was doing, how he was living. Of course we didn't! How could we? But spending time with Pyotr and the actors, living with them for weeks at a time, I learned something. Nikolai's life is good. To live like that is good. It's not safe, it's not easy, it's dangerous. There's a rawness to it. It's primitive. But it is exciting, too. It's new every day. That's not to say that Nikolai lives that way all the time. Or that he's living like that now. But for those years that he wandered around, that he consorted—as we put it—with the worst sorts of men... they are not the worst sorts of men, in fact. Seeing from the other side, it is the officials, the police, the magistrates, the landowners, with their minions and their punishments, their arrogance, their lawless power over other men—it's they who are the worst of men, not the poor souls who travel the roads and live hand-to-mouth, and try to enjoy what small pleasures they have."

Sofia smiled at him. "Papa, dear, this is what you have always said. You taught us all this, you yourself. Don't you remember?"

"Did I? Then I taught you what I didn't even know."

"No. You always have known it in your heart. Your very good heart. And you have lived that way yourself. Admit it! In your own way you have always defied convention. You have always lived a free life. You and Mother, both of you."

"Irina will be arriving soon," he said, changing the subject somewhat abruptly, shying away from his daughter's praise. "Oh, how good it is to have all the children here again!"

The conversation turned then to summer guests and visitors, and plans for the children's amusements, but Sofia could not shake the dismal feeling that had taken hold of her, the conviction that grew stronger and stronger every day, that something terrible had happened to Nikolai, and that it had happened while she had been busily concerned with mundane and unimportant things. They had lived in the same city, after all, not hundreds of miles away from each other; yet they never saw each other. He never responded to her invitations to dinner or to the children's name day parties, and he never sent presents, and when she invited him for holiday celebrations or for family picnics, he never came. And so she had stopped inviting him. She had not gone to see him, she had not inquired about his health, she had not attempted to discover if he was in trouble. No, she had simply assumed he didn't care about her or her family, and she had become angry and annoyed, and yet it was possible, it was even likely, that something terrible had happened to him and she had not cared enough to investigate and find out what it was. Then his letter had come and she had ignored it. No, worse, it had angered her, it had turned her against him. Now she saw that it was all her fault, this endless wondering, this worry, this ignorance they were suffering from, for if she had done her duty, if she had only taken the time to look in on him, to go to across to the Vyborg side of the river, to visit that house, horrible place that it was... but such a simple thing, really... if she had persisted and kept him close, insisted on keeping him close, in the embrace of her family, might that not have saved him?

"Oh, come, my dear!" Vasily Yakovlevich exclaimed, and put his arms around his daughter. "Come, come, don't cry! What is the matter, Sonya darling? Why are you crying?"

"I'm a bad sister, Papa," she sobbed. "I'm a dreadful, awful woman."

Shocked and confused, he held her tight in his arms, and tried to soothe her, but just then they heard children's voices and the boys came running down the path, calling "Mama! Mama! Grandpa! Come see the lambs!" Quickly she sat up, dried her eyes, and smiled at them.

"Right away, my darlings. I'm coming right away."

"Come with us, Grandpa!" they shouted, but he shook his head.

Vasily watched her take the boys' hands and walk with them—they were tugging at her arms to make her walk faster—down the path through the rose garden and across the barnyard toward the sheep's meadow. The lambs! How they danced around and played, how they danced in the grass, sweet, dear creatures. May they not learn, the boys, what became of the lambs. How vividly he remembered now how Kolya had reacted when he first discovered what became of the lambs.

The world is full of grief, he thought.

Getting to his feet, he glanced up at Anastasia's shuttered windows. She's right, he thought, close the shutters! Keep the world out!

Then slowly, like an old man, he took his cane and walked back to the house.

CHAPTER THIRTY-THREE

"ONLY A FLOCK OF ANGELS COMING ON A WIND..."

It took us nearly two weeks to get to Moscow. Thirteen nights in mostly miserable inns. Terrible food, terrible roads. At least I was traveling in trousers, boots, and cloak. I had nothing but pity for women who put themselves through such misery with the additional torment of corsets, crinolines, and hoops.

I was suffering from a different sort of torment, and it would have been unrelieved by better coaches, better inns, faster horses, smoother roads. Over and over again I read the letters I had received from High Meadows and Oak Hills, compelled by some need to make them say something other than what they said, as though by reading them again and again I could erase the words on the page or change their meaning. But words are often as powerful as deeds; they are acts, as powerful in their own way as a blow or a kiss. These words were blows, and I could not defend myself against them.

Pavel Damianich sat across from me day after day, reading *Les Trois Mousquetaires*. He understood me very well, and asked me no questions, though he was quite aware that I was distressed if not entirely disconsolate. Finally, when we were within forty-eight hours of our arrival in Moscow, and were resting in our room, having just finished another one of those grueling twelve hour traveling days, nine hours sitting in the coach, three hours waiting around for horses to be changed, I handed him the letters and let him read them for himself.

The first one was from Tatyana Andreyevna. In it she described a series of extraordinary events that had occurred at High Meadows. First, she wrote of the terrible neurasthenia which had struck her daughter, Margarita, a mysterious illness which caused her to separate herself from her family and take up residence in a small, abandoned hut in the forest. Some time later, two unexpected visitors arrived on the estate.

One was Alejandro Azara, whom I had met at the Stardust and who, according to Fyodorov, was an old friend of Nikolai's and possibly a spy. I now learned from Tatyana that he was also, surprisingly, Margarita's fiancé. The other visitor, just as surprisingly, was Fyodor Fyodorovich himself. Finally, she described the subsequent disappearance of Fyodorov Fyodorovich and Margarita Mikhailevna, followed by the abrupt departure of an insulted and furious Azara, set on overtaking the fugitive lovers and demanding satisfaction from Fyodorov for the outrage to his honor.

A farce worthy of Alexandre Dumas himself, Pavel Damianich declared when he had finished reading. And yet...

"Yes," I said. "And yet."

"The discrepancies," he said. "The details."

"Yes. The discrepancies. The details."

"So," he said, after thinking it all over for some time, "you suspect the veracity of this account?"

"Not of the account, not at all. I am sure the princess is reporting what she believes to be true."

"Yes. But you doubt that Fyodorov is the sort of man to elope with a seriously ill woman engaged to be married to someone else."

"Indeed, such an act would be uncharacteristic. The idea of it is absurd. Then there is Tatyana's description of Margarita's cottage which overnight turned into an abandoned ruin. It looked, she said, as though everything had *aged*. She called it uncanny."

"Uncanny is a remarkable word to use under the circumstances."

"Yes, it is. But it was uncanny, wasn't it? Overnight, a little cottage in the woods *aged*. And I would shrug it off as an old woman's fantasy but uncanny things have happened to me too, once at High Meadows when we were there last, and another time in Petersburg when I was going into Fyodorov's laboratory. Though it's impossible to describe what exactly made these moments *uncanny*, I'm afraid."

"Impossible? Don't be daft, Marko. You're a writer, aren't you? Try, for God's love."

Pavel Damianich had been rolling a cigarette and now handed it to me and lit a match. "Maybe this will help."

I smoked and tried very hard to focus my mind.

"First something happens to the light. It quivers. It becomes unstable."

"The light?"

"Or what is seen in the light, I suppose. Objects appear unstable. They seem to fade. One can see through them as though everything in this world, which appears so substantial and real, is only a scrim or a screen, concealing another world behind it."

I stopped speaking and smoked the cigarette Pasha had given me, and remembered smoking a cigarette with Margarita in my room at High Meadows, and remembered what she had told me then. The memory sent a shiver down my spine.

"Margarita was having dreams that frightened her because they were as real as waking life. She had the same dream night after night, and in this dream she was living with Nikolai in a little cottage in Moscow, a *cottage*, mind you. Well, what if that cottage of her dreams had somehow materialized over an ancient, ruined cottage in the woods? What if she was dreaming it? And when she stopped dreaming it, it returned to its ruined state again? Is such a thing even possible?"

"Like any rational man, I would have to say no. Yet, to presume that the world is entirely rational may be an act of unwarranted rationalism."

"Margarita and Fyodorov disappeared, Pasha. That appears to be a fact."

"Disappeared? That may be too fanciful a word. No doubt they left by carriage."

"Perhaps. Yet when you consider all the *uncanny* circumstances that have accompanied our search for Nikolai... the odd coincidences... Elena Petrovna's fascination with *Monkey*, the lengths she will go to in order to obtain information about it... And consider further that Margarita Mikhailevna is one of the few people in the world who has actually read portions of the book..."

"Are you suggesting that Blavatskaya had something to do with Margarita's disappearance?"

"I am merely pointing out a coincidence."

"Coincidence be damned! You are thinking that there is some magic contained in this book."

"Well, what if there is? Of the three of them involved in this mysterious disappearance—Margarita, Fyodorov and Azara—two have definitely read parts of the book, Margarita and Fyodorov, though in Fyodorov's case, Nikolai read a section to him when he was drunk and so he doesn't remember any of it. It was when they lived together in the communal house. And who else lived there for some time? Azara! So all three of them—"

"Yes, I take your point. But Sasha Kantrovskaya also read parts of the book."

"And she said it was a book full of secrets, remember? Listen to me, please, Pavel Damianich. I have been thinking about this for days now, and I am becoming convinced that *Monkey* does contain some occult knowledge. As difficult as it is for a materialist like myself to entertain such an idea—"

I was interrupted by a knock on the door and a servant entered with our supper on a tray. Just as well, since I really didn't know what idea I was about to entertain, everything was so confusing and difficult.

We were both hungry and thirsty and we ate for a few minutes in silence, I, for one, trying to collect my thoughts while at the same time thoroughly enjoying the meal before me. Not for the first time it struck me how utterly joined together were the intellectual realm and the physical one, how easily one could pivot from mind to body and vice versa, and how odd and yet wonderful it would be if we could move from one world to another as easily, and I wondered, while I quenched my thirst with a long swallow of cold kvass, what that other world, were it to exist, might be like. These were unusual thoughts for me; of course, I blamed them on the influence of Nikolai's book.

But it wasn't his book that I cared about, it was Nikolai himself. And, oh, what sorrow, what grief lay just there! What anguish for myself and for her whom I loved! How could we bear it? And so I turned away from it and thought only about the book he had written, the book that had to be found, as though his life depended on our finding it, or as though without that testimony of his life, there would be no trace of him left in the world.

"Let us put Tatyana's letter to one side for the moment," Pavel Damianich said. "There are the others to consider."

Pasha picked the letters up, and glanced through them again. I knew them very well, having read them over many, many times, having wept over them at night, having let their meaning sear itself into my soul.

"The very sad ones," I said. "Must we consider them over supper?"

"You are sometimes a terrible person, Valentina Grigorevna," he said sternly.

"I am always a terrible person, Pavel Damianich. But since I am a creator of fictions and thus a master of lies, I am usually able to conceal it. But, all right, I've eaten enough. Let's consider the letters from Oak Hills. Not that there's much to consider about them. They need no interpretation."

"There is a coldness to this one, don't you think?" he said, laying the pages down on the table. "There is something almost brutal about it."

"There is anger, surely. Sofia Vasilevna sees her mother suffering. Of course there's some anger—"

"No. This is more than that. If I read it to you—"

"Please don't."

He did anyway.

"My dear friend," he began in a stern, cold voice, quite unlike Sofia Vasilevna's, holding her letter aloft in his right hand, "there is something I must tell you, something you must know. Therefore I will break a silence I have kept for far too long and tell you the truth. My brother, Nikolai Vasilevich, was an unhappy man. Some time ago, he sent me a letter in which he revealed to me the depths of his unhappiness. He longed for a family and children, but his mistress, his so-called wife, had miscarried his child and then left him. He was far away from us, utterly alone, abandoned, and unloved. He had failed at everything he tried to do, and he felt there was no reason to keep living. This is what he wrote to me. I dismissed it as childish nonsense. He drank excessively, as you know, and men who drink excessively often descend into morbid self-pity. So I told no one about the letter. I assumed he had written similar letters to all of us. Evidently he had not. Only to me. But since none of us has heard a word from him since then, I am now quite certain this letter was a declaration of his intention to end his life. I am convinced my poor brother is dead. Recently I learned that you have taken it upon yourself to look for him on our behalf, and so I feel it my duty to inform you of the contents of this letter so that you do not spend your time in a futile search for someone who cannot be found. Please say nothing about this to my poor parents since I have not yet told them about it myself, though I will, I must, for they suffer so with anxiety for him. I remain, your very dear friend, etcetera etcetera"

He stopped reading and looked up at me.

"A cold-hearted letter if ever I read one, Marko."

"I did not read it that way. Do you not see the tiny blots on the page? Do you not see how in places the ink has smeared? Those are marks made by tears, Pasha. She wept as she wrote it. No, this is a letter from someone who is in mourning, announcing a death of someone she loves."

"Do you believe her?"

"I don't doubt her."

"I mean, do you believe her interpretation? The idea that he wrote to her to declare his intention of putting an end to himself? Does that sound like the Nikolai Vasilevich that you know?"

"I would say no, on the face of it, except that—well, we haven't found a trace of him, have we? No one we've asked about him has seen him in a very long time."

"Before I accept that Nikolai Vasilevich is dead on the basis of a letter he wrote to his sister, I would have to read the actual letter itself and not rely on her gloss of it. Did he really mean to suggest he was about to take his life? After all, it is not at all uncommon for young men, when they are unhappy, to write letters full of self-pity and despair to their older sisters. One might argue that is precisely what older sisters are for. And, as both God and you yourself know, Marko, any piece of writing can be misinterpreted very easily. Satire, for example, is very often misunderstood. Even Voltaire—"

"Let us please not discuss the writings of Voltaire," I exclaimed in some distress. "Not when there is so much pain in the world!"

"Very well. But I am not convinced by Sofya Vasilevna's letter, not in the least, and I hope you are not, either. I would want to see the original, and I would also want to know where he was when he wrote it. And, of course, who this so-called wife is, whose child was stillborn."

"Such an event must have a terrible impact on a sensitive soul."

"Indeed. The next two letters, on the other hand, are unambiguous and need no analysis."

"But so terribly sad! Poor Vasily Yakovlevich. She broke his heart, telling him about that letter. I can't understand how she could have brought herself to do it. Though I know why she did it. She wanted to spare them the endless suffering parents must feel when their son has disappeared, who every day expect to hear word of him, who every day expect him to appear at the door—and every horseman who rides up the drive might be him, and every carriage that passes might be the carriage that is bringing him home. To wake up every day with that hope. But isn't it better than to wake up every day with no hope at all?"

"Still, he wrote you a very gracious letter, Marko. A nobleman's letter, clear, dignified, restrained, yet filled with kindness and gratitude. I do not know Vasily Yakovlevich, but from this single letter I feel deep admiration for him."

I smiled at my dear Pasha, who sometimes amazed me by the depth of his feeling. I had to remind myself that he was half Russian as well as half French.

The third letter was from Anastasia. It was brief. She thanked me for writing to her so faithfully and asked me to come to see her when I was in our district again. She had enclosed a poem.

"Please read it to me," I said. "If I try to read it aloud, I will only cry."

So he did.

I woke this morning from a dream,
so full of joy, so free and safe—
for in the dream I'd seen your face—
that resting in a blissful state
I lay at peace, it pleased me so,
until, forced to let it go
and wake...

I found the sky above still grey,
my joyful dream a bitter ruse,
and what was done still done,
for unlike words an act can't be erased
but locked so tight in time's embrace
not even light can penetrate that space
nor an earthquake shake it loose.

Only a flock of angels coming on a wind
and tearing through this bitter screen
between the worlds
might so upset the way of things,
that the done deed might be undone

and I might hear your footfall on the stair,
and glancing up I'd see you standing there
where you will never stand again.

He finished reading the poem and neither of us spoke for some time.

"This is a terribly callous thing to say," I said, "but the existence of this poem means Anastasia is writing again."

"It is a terribly callous thing to say, but it is true." He smiled at me encouragingly. "Now, Marko, once we arrive in Oak Hills, you must speak with to Sofya Vasilevna. We must hope she has saved Nikolai's letter and is willing to let you read it. You must see if you can glean some information about the woman in question. Once again it is a question of *cherchez la femme!*"

I had almost given up hope. But Pavel Damianich was only half-Russian and so not entirely given to fatalistic despondency; in most situations his French half buoyed him up handsomely.

"And you don't think this is simply another exercise in futility?"

"It may well be. But isn't that what everything in life is? Isn't life itself such an exercise? And do you have anything more pressing to do?"

Another question to which I had no answer.

It took five more days of travel before we arrived at my house, weary, dusty, hot, and sore from nearly three weeks of constant jostling and jolting. I delayed going to Oak Hills; I had to put my own house in order first and recover from the journey. After a week, however, knowing I could no longer postpone a visit, for word of my return home had by now certainly reached them, I sent a note to Anastasia asking if I might pay a visit. The return note from Vasily Yakovlevich urged me to come to the house for supper that very evening, if possible. It would give them so much pleasure to see me.

"Pleasure must be in short supply at Oak Hills these days," I muttered to Pavel Damianich upon reading Vasily's message. Already the thought of seeing Anastasia in her grief was making me weary.

"You expect the house to be in mourning," he said, glancing up at me from his newspaper. "But I find it hard to believe that a single letter of the sort Sofya Vasilevna described could bring despair to so gallant and intrepid a heart."

"But even last summer some part of her was already in mourning."

"For that matter," my dear Pasha said grumpily, "we should all be in mourning all the time since each one of us is doomed to die, eventually."

"I blame the poets," I said. "The damn romantic poets. They are the guilty ones." Pasha raised a cynical eyebrow so I elaborated for him. "Lermontov and his ilk. What did they do but make the desperate seem heroic, the despicable, noble, and the criminal, romantic? And boys like Kolya saw them parade around in their cloaks and spurs with their pistols and swords, and fancied that that sort of flamboyant nonsense constituted the best life had to offer. Perhaps it's true that our grandfathers spent their time dressing up and pretending to be French, but at least they never tried to convince anyone that standing ten feet in front of a lunatic with a gun pointing at your heart was the perfect way to either start your morning or end your life, and the one was as good as the other."

"I thought it was our grandfathers who began that lurid custom in the first place. Or great-grandfathers. I believe dueling was quite popular in the latter part of the last century. And I seem to recall that despite the best efforts of the government to outlaw it, ten thousand duels were fought in France during the reign of Louis XIV."

"Really? Well, you would know about such antics in France. But here in Russia it was Pushkin and Lermontov who turned dueling into a death cult. Though that is not my point, Pasha. My point is ..."

But by then my point had quite slipped my mind.

"You were blaming romantic poets for Nikolai's way of life."

"So I was."

"I am also willing to condemn them—for false representation of reality. But Kolya's generation has other, worthier villains to blame for their despair. Your autocracy must be held accountable since it is ultimately responsible for the state of the country. Culture is informed by social and political forces, it responds to these forces, it reflects them."

"Yes, of course," I said, becoming wearier by the minute. "Tell me, is it worth reading the newspaper? Is there any news in it?"

"None whatsoever. You would think nothing was happening anywhere in this fair country. And yet I heard from the stableboy—the stableboy, mind you—that troops had fired on an angry mob of peasants not one hundred versts from here."

"Really? Fired on them? How dreadful! Why?"

"They refused to work for their landlord, I suppose. That's usually why troops are called out. And they resisted returning to the fields, no doubt. And so a few shots were fired at them to put them in their place. The stableboy said fifty men were shot. I assume that's an exaggeration."

"My God! Maybe it's starting!"

"Don't get overly excited, Marko. I imagine this was just another little incident in a long chain of incidents."

"One will eventually tip the balance."

"Indeed," he said, without much enthusiasm.

He went back to his reading, and I to my journal. The afternoon wore on. Before long it was time to dress and ride over to Oak Hills for supper.

On the surface it was the same house I'd always known and loved, the same bright, welcoming doorway and windows, the same carved wooden shingles, the same sloping roof, the same flower garden, the same broad, generous terrace. On the surface, it was cheerful, with children running around screeching with pleasure in the garden, playing a game of hide-and-seek, and the garden itself seemed as colorful and lively as it ever had. But something was different, something was not quite right. The house had a feeling of impending abandonment about it, everything was a bit out of kilter, a bit unsteady, the way houses seem whose people are about to move out of them, a sense that everything was provisional, hastily set up so as to be the more easily knocked down, the china about to be packed in excelsior, the furniture hauled away, the windows boarded up, the garden allowed to grow wild. It was not merely that the poor old house was in desperate need of repair, of fresh paint, of sprucing up; its troubles went deeper than that, went to its core, its heart. Its upper rooms were enshrouded in deep shade, windows locked and shuttered tight against the slightest hint of summer, or ray of light.

Vasily was expecting me, and took me directly into his study. It was pleasantly cool inside the house, and especially so in the study with its dark furnishings and heavy drapes.

"How the children can run around in this heat!" he sighed. "Well, I suppose we all did it once."

He seemed like a man who had surrendered and was now unable to imagine how he had ever fought at all. So I was right: something had changed.

"May I see her?"

"I must tell you, my dear Marko... she is unwell."

"What do you mean, unwell?"

"She has developed a bad cough. She is very weak. The doctor—"

"She is seeing a doctor?" This was dire news. Anastasia never called in a doctor. I had never known her to do so in her entire life.

"Yes. I insisted. The doctor is hopeful she will recover, but no visitors, he says. He is quite adamant."

"I see."

"I told her you were coming. She gave me a letter for you." He took an envelope out of his breast pocket. The dear man had been carrying it next to his heart. "You may want to read it now. I can leave you alone in here, or if you would prefer to walk in the garden..."

"The garden," I said.

He smiled at that. "Yes, it is lovely now. Purple is in its ascendency. Let me send someone out to you with a cold drink..."

It took a few minutes to arrange the drink, the location of the chair in the garden, a small table to be brought out into the shade. Then with some reluctance but with superb gallantry, Vasily Yakovlevich left me alone with Anastasia's letter.

With some reluctance of my own, I opened it. Tiny slips of paper fell out onto my lap, slips of paper covered with tiny words, sometimes two together, sometimes three, forming a single line. I caught them, for they were at risk of being blown away by the breeze, and gathered them together, and thrust them back into their envelope, and felt that my world was being torn into pieces as these poems most certainly had been, that my world, like Anastasia's, was shattered forever.

♣

It was Sofia who came out to fetch me in for supper, Sofia of the cold heart, as Pavel Damianich would have me believe. But one look at her told me that she was suffering terribly. Surely her decision to share the contents of Nikolai's letter with her parents had been made with the best of intentions; yet, like much we do with the best of intentions (may they be eternally damned!) it had resulted in the exact opposite of what she had wished.

"I beg you, Sofia Vasilevna," I said as we walked back toward the house, "tell me about your mother. Have you seen her? What is her condition?"

"She is weak. She will not eat. She will not speak to any of us, only to Papa. She is breaking Natasha's heart."

So, I thought bitterly, there is some justice there, since you have broken hers.

"I take it that you showed her Nikolai's letter."

"No. I only told her about it. I did not bring the letter with me. Why would I do that?"

"Well, that's a pity, I must say." I was losing my temper and had to struggle to keep it from showing. I knew if I lost patience with her I'd never get the information I wanted. So I took a deep breath and continued in a calmer voice. "One can gather quite a lot of information from a letter besides what's written on the page. If you had the actual letter—"

"But I don't have it. I told you."

"You were angry—"

"Of course I was angry! Such self-pity! Such—" She had stopped beside an immense rhododendron bush, and now looked around in some confusion. Somehow we had taken a path going away from the house not toward it and were now in the jungle of rhododendrons and other wild and unpruned bushes, privet and honeysuckle and mock orange.

"Such what?" I asked. "What was it that so infuriated you?"

"Such emotion," she said.

"Ah."

"So exposed."

"He must have trusted you," I said as mildly as I could, trying to keep any trace of blame out of my voice.

"A woman had broken his heart."

"It happens."

"She had lost a child."

"His child."

"Yes. He wanted to be a father. He had even married her. Married her! Can you imagine? That I could not forgive!"

"You didn't say that before."

"No. How could I? And I did not tell them either. And you mustn't tell them, Marko. Please."

"Of course. So she became pregnant, he married her, she lost the child. Then what?"

"She left him. Because he got drunk. Because he was crushed, losing the baby, and he got drunk, and she punished him by leaving him."

"What was her name?"

"He never mentioned her name. He called her 'my wife.' My God, how that word cut into me! Like a sword thrust, Marko."

"But why, dear Sonya? Why should he not marry?"

"Yes, he should marry, of course he should! But a woman of our own class, a respectable woman he could bring home to us, to his mother and father, and marry properly. Properly, in church, with the family assembled and a wedding feast after. Not on a ship en route to America!"

"Wait a moment! He was going to America?"

"So he said. To Spanish America. A place called Panama. But I didn't believe him, Marko. Why should I? He lied about everything."

There was a bench by one of the rhododendrons and Sofia sat down heavily on it. I sat beside her. The great purple flowers were beautiful, the bush enormous, this part of the garden being so untended. Sparrows were chirping madly all around us. It was as though we had entered a world apart, a tropical rainforest, perhaps a place called Panama. I almost expected to see monkeys swinging from the branches of the trees.

"So in his letter he said he was en route to Panama, but you didn't believe him, and so you never said anything—"

"I was so angry at him, you understand."

"I understand," I said. I didn't understand at all but I wanted to keep agreeing with her. I wanted her to keep talking. "Please continue. They were married—en route to Panama?"

"See? See how unbelievable it is? To a girl he met in Pera, a girl without a name! And Kolya always lied so well, lied constantly, lied to all of us, I simply couldn't give it any credence."

"So they met in Istanbul, and took ship from there. Where was he when he wrote to you?"

"On the high seas, he said. Alone. She had left him in some port of call. Abandoned him. Broken his heart. Yes, she left him and broke his heart. His only hope, he said, was getting to San Francisco. As though there was something there, waiting for him. Such nonsense! All he wanted was distance. To be as far away from us as he could get."

"But, Sonya, this is amazing news!"

"News? It's no news at all! I received that letter two years ago. Can't you see what happened? He never arrived in Panama. He was despondent, despairing, and he threw himself into the sea."

I had recently been on the sea. The idea of throwing oneself into it was more horrifying than any thought I had had in a very long time.

"It's a pity you don't have the letter with you. A pity we can't read it. Even to discover the name of the ship he was traveling on. You have no memory of that?"

"No. Only that it was an English ship. That's all. But, Marko, what possible difference can it make now? No word from him for so long!" She took a handkerchief from her sleeve and wiped her eyes. "And now poor Mama!"

By now the light was beginning to fade, and the evening chorus of insect, amphibian, and bird was beginning to rise up and fill the garden with sound.

"Let's go back to the house, Sonya. They will wonder where we are."

But as we walked back to the house my heart was racing and I could barely contain my excitement. At last we had information, and a direction to go in, and we had a final destination: San Francisco! And now I was certain that we would find Nikolai there. After all, he had told us so himself, he had written it at the end of *Wide and Crooked*, though poor Fyodorov had suppressed it, thinking the reference too fanciful or obscure for the Stardust. *San Francisco, a place far, far away where it's always summer and we can be free.* How I wanted to rush home and tell Pavel Damianich about it and congratulate him for his insights and his faith, his optimism, his perseverance! Of course Pasha was right, of course Nikolai had not taken his own life. It was only that, being in a place so far, far away, our letters never reached him, nor did his reach us.

We would leave as soon as I could work out the finances, we would set out on a great voyage, we would track him across oceans and continents, we would go to San Francisco, the city of his dreams, and we would find him at last. We would not fail.

There were just the three of us at the table, myself, Sofia, and Vasily Yakovlevich. I missed Natasha's bright presence, but she and her brothers had been fed their suppers earlier and were being readied for bed. How hard it is to be a child in the summertime, being made to go to bed when the day is not yet ended! I always thought of it as a cruel punishment to which I had to submit though innocent of any crime. Perhaps this is how we learn to submit to autocracy and repression; perhaps our long summer days, our white nights, are to blame for our passivity in the face of injustice and outrage. Be that as it may, there were the three of us at supper, and a dismal group we were, each of us struggling to find topics of conversation that might bring a bit of cheerfulness to the table, none of us succeeding in doing so. Anastasia's illness hung over us, a sorrow we could not thrust away even for the duration of a meal. Since we were already so despondent I thought I'd inquire about the peasant trouble that Pavel Damianich had mentioned, just to see if the stableboy was in any way a reliable source of news.

"A terrible, terrible thing!" Vasily Yakovlevich exclaimed with more passion in his voice than I had heard all evening. "Yes, what you heard is true, or partially. Thank God there were not so many deaths, only one, though many were wounded. And very near Tatyana's estate, too, though not on her land, of course."

"What happened exactly?" I asked, thinking that this subject at least, though tragic, would bring some life to the conversation.

"Fortunately I am in a position to tell you what happened exactly. Fortunately I have more than the official report upon which to base what I say."

"Papa!" Sofia cried. "Don't upset yourself! You mustn't!"

"Bah!" Vasily Yakovlevich replied, waving her objections away with a gesture of his hand. "I will tell you, Marko, this event will spark some controversy! There will have to be an investigation. Why? Because the man they killed was not a peasant but a professor, a scientist, and not an agitator, either. He had been visiting Princess Tatyana, and he was on his way here—to us! Yes, he was traveling to our house! A friend of Nikolai's, on his way to pay us a visit!"

"My God!" I said. "What happened?"

"The official story states that some *raskolnik* or some old soldier who had fought against Napoleon and been to Paris in '14—notice how they always blame Old Believers or veterans of the Patriotic War for these things—in any case, a man who could read or who pretended he could had come through the district preaching about a writ of emancipation which abolished the corvees by order of the Tsar. The peasants believed this, had been expecting it, rejoiced in it, and stopped working on their landlords' land. When the landlords told them there was no imperial decree, they still stubbornly—*stubbornly,* mind you—refused to return to work. The landlords being unable to prevail upon their serfs to pay their corvee, requested help from the local troops, and General Alexander Apraksin led a squadron to the village. The peasants would not disperse, and he was forced to shoot a single volley into the mob. Some injuries were reported, but only one death, that of a man who rushed the troops with the intention, says the official report, of interfering with their orders."

"What a brave man," I said. "Or what a fool."

"A fool perhaps, but in his death he has become quite a hero in our district. You see, it was not General Apraksin's intention to shoot professors, only peasants, so when he saw his men had shot and killed a gentleman, well, he was so shocked he stopped the action immediately. The peasants were equally shocked, since they were not expecting to be fired upon at all, they thought the threat was a ruse. They truly believed the Tsar had freed them and that the Tsar's soldiers would never shoot at them, poor deluded souls. In any case, it's clear that there would have been a massacre had Fyodorov not sacrificed himself."

"Fyodorov!" I cried. "Not Fyodor Fyodorovich, the philosopher?"

"The same." Vasily said, sorrowfully. "And now we will never know what he was coming here to say."

It was in this way that I learned about the death of my dear friend, Fyodor Fyodorovich, whom I had treated in so cruel and cavalier a manner, and left in Petersburg without even saying a proper goodbye.

"Was he traveling alone?" I asked, thinking of Margarita Mikhailevna.

"No. He was with a friend of mine, Pyotr Panov, and his troupe of actors."

"Ah," I said. "I am glad to hear that, at least. Traveling with actors would have made him happy. He loved the stage. But what does Tatyana Andreyevna say? She must be terribly upset."

"To be honest with you, Marko, she is far more upset about the disappearance of her daughter, Margarita. She's had the entire district out looking for her, but she's nowhere to be found. We fear the worst."

"And what is that, exactly?"

"That she may have drowned herself in the river. Evidently she had become quite mad, poor thing."

I thought drowning oneself in a river was just as unpleasant as drowning oneself in the sea, and I wondered why everyone seemed intent on imagining these watery deaths. Myself, I thought it far more likely that Margarita had run off with Alejandro Azara, since clearly she had not run off with Fyodor Fyodorovich, and I was about to ask what had become of him when Vasily Yakovlevich answered the question without my even having to ask it.

"There was another young man staying with Tatyana, a friend of Fyodorov's and of Nikolai's. A fellow from Argentina. Alexander Azara. He has been helping her organize the search. He and Margarita were about to announce their engagement, and he is quite devastated by this terrible turn of events."

"We seem to be surrounded by misery," Sofia Vasilevna sighed.

Universal grief is the supreme characteristic of our times, as Herzen says, but there is a difference between universal grief and the very intimate grief that strikes one's own soul, breaks one's own heart. It is the latter, in its millions of forms, its millions of distinct and individual iterations, that forms the great ocean of grief on which we sail our little barks or our great sloops or drift on our fragile rafts, but whatever our craft, or craftiness, the ocean of grief will wash over us in time. Hence, perhaps, these ever arising images of watery deaths, for we are all condemned to the same dark end, and from that final drowning there is no escape whatever. *Only a flock of angels coming on the wind and tearing through this bitter screen...* But there were no angels, as Anastasia well knew, and there would be no tearing through the screen between the worlds, for there was no screen, there was no other world, there was only this one, drear and miserable as it was.

"Listen!" Vasily said, breaking through my bitter thoughts. "The yellow warbler is singing!"

⁂

It was quite late by the time I left the house, and so I was surprised indeed to catch sight of little Natasha hiding in the bushes beside the entrance to the flower garden. I couldn't imagine what she was doing outside by herself. I strode over to her with every intention of hauling her back inside, but when I saw her little sorrowful face, her trembling lips, her big brown eyes filling with tears, I didn't have the heart to scold her but instead knelt down beside her. She threw her arms around my neck and began to sob.

"Natasha, darling, what's happened? What are you doing out at this hour?"

"Oh, Marko!" she whispered. "Everything is horrible!"

I could not argue with that.

"Is it your grandmother?"

"Yes. Dear Grandmama. And Uncle Nikolai. And poor dear Fyodorov. And, oh, Marko, I will be in such terrible trouble. And—"

"Enough," I said. "Come inside now. Cook will make us tea."

I took her by the hand and we went around the house to the kitchen door.

"Dear Cook, give us tea and bread and butter, if you please," I said. "Send it up to the nursery."

Then up the stairs we went. The other children were already in bed. We went into the little alcove room off the nursery where Natasha slept and we cleared a space on her little table for the tea and settled down on her bed.

"Now," I said. "Speak to me. Tell me everything."

She dried her tears with her handkerchief and blew her nose.

"I am very sorry, dear Marko, and I apologize, but I couldn't help it, you see. It's my place to read and be alone and write poems, under the rhododendron bush. I didn't mean to overhear."

It took me a moment to understand what she was telling me. What rhododendron bush, I wanted to ask her. Then I remembered.

"Ah. So you heard us talking about Nikolai."

"I heard he got married to someone Mama does not like. I heard he set sail to America on an English boat. I heard that he jumped off the boat into the sea. But he couldn't have, Marko! Not Nikolai! He would never do that!"

She sobbed a great heaving sob, and tears began running down her cheeks again. The poor child was devastated. I had no idea what to do to keep her from becoming hysterical and ill.

"I am sure you are right. Now listen to me, Natalia Ivanovna. What your mama thinks is not necessarily true. Perhaps Nikolai did go to America on an English boat, but we don't know at all that he jumped into the sea. We don't know that. Your mama was just—expressing a fear."

"Expressing a fear," Natasha repeated very seriously, as though I had said something she wanted to remember.

"Yes. Our fears sometimes get the better of us. It does not make them true."

"You don't believe he jumped into the sea either. Do you, Marko?"

"I do not."

"Oh, I'm so glad!" she said, and hugged me very tight. What a strong child she was! "But what about dear Fyodor Fyodorovich? What they say about him, being shot—is that true or not true?"

"I think that is true, Natasha. But you didn't know him so—"

"But I did! I did know him. I knew him very well! And I loved talking to him. And I so wanted him to meet Grandmama. He knew Uncle Nikolai. Oh, it's so awful that they killed him. How could they?"

I thought she was going to start crying again, but, no, her anger was getting the better of her sorrow. A good thing, I thought. Be angry! Tears do no good, as Achilles tells Hector's father. Tears make no difference in this world at all.

"Pyotr Illych was with him. I know Pyotr Illych very well, too. I have been to his caravan. And he told me that Fyodor Fyodorov is a saint now, in heaven. He says he's like Jesus. He laid down his life for his friends just like Jesus did. But I don't want him to be in heaven, Marko. I want him to be here."

It was the moment for me to offer her such platitudes as *But he is here with us, dear, and always will be* or *He's gone to a better place* or *He has found peace* or *He is now with the angels or one with the universe.* I would not insult her intelligence with such claptrap so I said nothing at all.

Masha came in with a tray for us: cups of cocoa and a plate with little pieces of bread and butter and a tiny bowl of jam. I was pleased to see that Natasha was not a child to let sorrow get in the way of her appetite. After politely inquiring if I was hungry—I was not—she quickly devoured every morsel.

"Well," I said, "now that you feel better, you're no longer famished, and you understand that when we express our fears—which is normal and good for us, in a way—we don't expect other people to take what we say as the truth... now that you've accomplished all that, it's really time for you to go to sleep."

"Are you going to San Francisco? Are you going to look for Nikolai?"

What questions the child asked!

"Yes," I said. "Yes, I am."

She took my hand and squeezed it tight.

"Before you go," she whispered dramatically, as though I were a secret agent about to set out on a secret mission that very night, "there is something I must show you."

"Well do it quickly before we both get in trouble. You are up very, very late."

She was wearing a little red jacket which she now took off. Sewn into the inside of the jacket was a deep pocket, big enough to hold a book or journal, and out of that pocket she drew a bundle of papers, the sheets folded in half as one would fold a letter, all tied together with a blue ribbon. She looked up at me with such a solemn expression, her entire face was transformed by its solemnity. For a moment she resembled one of our dark-eyed icons; I caught a momentary glimpse of the strikingly handsome woman she would one day become.

She held the bundle in both her hands, like an offering.

"What do you have there?" I said, although my body already knew: my heart was beating harder and more rapidly, my mouth was dry, my hands were trembling.

"First I have to tell you the story," she said.

I took a deep breath. "Very well. Tell me."

A child, and yet what she had done had taken the gumption and intrepidity that not many adults in the same situation would have shown. And, as she told me the story, I thought: this child has Nikolai's spirit; had he a daughter, she would be like this, bold and fearless, yes, but this child is not only clever but also sensible, thank God... Then I stopped thinking and listened to what she had to say.

It had begun some weeks ago, before Anastasia became too ill to leave her bed. Natasha went up to her rooms every day to visit her, and she began noticing some odd things, bits of paper on the carpet making

NATASHA

She laid the bundle of poems
on my lap. "They are very, very sad," she said.
"I am afraid they will make you cry."

little paper trails from Anastasia's study across the room and down the stairs. She began collecting the bits of paper and she soon recognized what they were. Anastasia was ripping up her poems and sending them downstairs with Masha every afternoon with her tea cups and plates of untouched bread and cheese and fruit. And what was Masha doing with these bits of paper? Burning them in the stove!

Natasha, though horrified, realized at once that she could not persuade Anastasia to stop ripping up her poems and burning them, and so she did the only thing she could think of to do which was to steal as many as she could and so preserve them from the fire. She knew where the poems were kept—in the deep drawer in Anastasia's desk—and so every day she would find some opportunity to be alone in the study. Then she would quickly run to the desk, open the drawer, take out a few pages, and stuff them into her pocket. But every day the pile of poems in the drawer grew smaller and smaller, and then one day there were none left at all.

"And just at the same time, she became so ill, she wouldn't get out of bed, she took every portrait of Nikolai and set them up all around her in the bedclothes, and then Mama told me I couldn't visit her anymore until she got better, but I don't think she will get better. I don't think she wants to. That's why you must go and find Nikolai, Marko. Please!"

"I will do my best, Natasha," I said. "I promise I will."

She laid the bundle of poems in my lap and kissed my cheek.

"They are very, very sad," she said. "I am afraid they will make you cry."

As though she were the grown-up and I were the child.

"I will take them and give them to your grandfather."

"No, Marko. You mustn't do that. No, please don't do that, or give them to my mother either. I will get in terrible trouble if you do. And then they will burn them, too. They don't care about poems."

I wanted to object but I feared that in this as in so much more she was quite right.

"But you aren't giving these to me, are you?" I asked incredulously.

"Yes. To keep them safe. Please, Marko. Just keep them and don't tell anyone. I know I can trust you."

"How do you know that?" I asked. "Adults are quite untrustworthy as a general rule."

"I know because my grandmother loves you and she doesn't love many people. She is careful in her loves."

I stared at the child in amazement. Perhaps I knew nothing about children at all, and so perhaps I knew nothing about human beings; perhaps people were much wiser than they led others to believe.

"All right," I said, smiling at the child. "I will keep them safe. And perhaps when Anastasia gets well again and Nikolai returns, she will be glad to have them."

"I think when Nikolai returns she will not want them at all, they will be all untrue, and maybe that's why she was burning them. Because she knows he's returning, she has great faith that he's returning. I didn't know what they were when I took them or I wouldn't have taken them, you see. But I can't burn them and I can't give them back and I can't tell Mama..."

I told her not to worry, not to concern herself at all, that I would keep both the poems and her secret safe.

"I knew I could trust you," she said.

And I saw Anastasia in her eyes and in the tilt of her head, and I heard Anastasia in her voice, and in the assurance that she would be obeyed.

I kissed the child goodnight, stuffed the bundle of poems into my coat pocket, and left the nursery. A nanny was pacing in the corridor outside, waiting for me to go. I bid her goodnight, but I wasn't yet ready to leave the house. I had to see Anastasia. I didn't care what the fools of doctors said. I had a terrible feeling that if I didn't see her now, I might not have another chance.

All at once there was sudden rushing movement throughout the house. A servant I did not recognize came running down the stairs from Anastasia's rooms, another came running up the stairs from the kitchen, subdued voices floated up and down the staircases with them.

In a state of mortal fear, I took the stairs two at a time and burst into Anastasia's rooms. Lamps were lit and people were standing around. Vasily was there, sitting beside Anastasia's bed, sobbing, with Sofia, pale and trembling, kneeling beside him, together making a portrait of grief. But she, my darling, my sweet lady, my Anastasia, was no longer there in the room. It was not she but merely a shell, an empty form, lying cold and still in the bed, images of Nikolai scattered in the bedclothes all around her. A terrible keening began, Masha, her oldest servant, kneeling behind me, wailing. Then Natasha came running and crying into the room, the nanny coming up behind, helpless to catch her, and flung herself on her grandmother's bed.

I could not bear it. I turned and went down the stairs and out of the house into the cool night.

CHAPTER THIRTY-FOUR

NIGHT

For days after Anastasia's death Oak Hills was in that state of disarray a house falls into when its mistress departs this world, the family in distress, the servants in mourning, even the animals disgruntled and unhappy, and the children undisciplined and running wild. At Vasily's request, I stayed and made myself as useful as I could, writing letters, greeting guests, offering what comfort I could, though I had little comfort to give, and dealing with the hundreds of little tasks that needed performing and that no one else in the household had either the patience or the time to attend to. With my hours filled with such duties, the days were somewhat bearable. Not so the nights. Either I did not sleep at all, or else, exhausted by work and grief, I would fall into a deep sleep, only to wake suddenly in the dead of night, and find myself in such misery that I might have sunk into a stark black void, blacker even than the blackness of the Odessa caves. There is no solace in the night, and since in that grim and silent dark, time itself ceases to exist, the suffering is endless, suffering without words or, worse yet, only words, streams of words, oceans of words, empty and futile and worthless words.

Night after night I awoke into that dimension of timeless misery. Usually I would toss and turn for awhile, then light a lamp and read or write... anything to keep my mind from the abyss lying in wait for it. For although I had many joyous memories of Anastasia, many sweet memories, what came to me in the dark were not the joys, not the sweetness, but the tortures of regret, and bitter memories of all I had neglected to do for her over the years, and the greatest regret of all, my failure to fulfill the one task she had given me, my failure to bring her back her son, my failure even to see her at the last, to speak with her, to offer her some final hope. That failure tortured me more than words can say.

One night, I found I was so weighed down with remorse I could not even toss and turn, or move my arm to light the lamp. The mere act of breathing seemed futile, the very fact of being alive seemed absurd. To be alive. What did it mean? To be a conscious animal, a thinking animal, to be tortured endlessly by useless thoughts, to suffer endlessly beneath these cascades of useless words. I wished it all to stop. I wished most fervently for my life to end.

Then it seemed that everything was emptying out of me. It was the most remarkable feeling of loss, everything I had once loved or valued, cared for or esteemed, turning into liquid and pouring out, as though I were a glass, being emptied. One by one they came to me, in images or words; one by one they vanished into nothing. What was there really? No lover was steadfast, no friend was faithful—had I not proven that myself, unfaithful, unsteadfast as I was? Those ideals of eternal love and loyalty were mere mirages, fantasies, the imaginings of poets. No ideas were true, or rather, no ideas were real. They, too, were creatures of the pen, of some mind weaving fantasies. There was no object precious enough... no land dear enough... no work important enough... nothing to hold onto, nothing greater than the desire for death. I saw before me my own work, my books and stories, which were like children to me, and they appeared in their true light, not as monuments to thought or imagination but as rather shabby little tales a child could tell, that little Natasha could put into verse with more ingenuity... stories that concealed rather than revealed, that had nothing true in them at all. And then the final revelation came, winging wordlessly into my mind, and caught hold of me, and stunned me into silence.

Nothing mattered. That was the revelation. Nothing mattered, nothing I did, nothing anyone did, nothing mattered at all. Books, poems, inventions... empires—what difference if men colonized Mars or if the Poles won their independence or if Anastasia's last poems were printed? In what universe did such things matter in the least? Not in one in which we died, each and every one of us, and disappeared into nothing. To think otherwise was to live in delusion, to live a lie. We are that very smoke that vanishes into the air, and all our riches and powers and ambitions, all our loves and hates, all our desires—everything we consider important—watch a moment and see how they all melt away, like dreams.

Yes, like the dreams of that poor soul, Margarita Mikhailevna, before she went utterly mad and drowned herself in the river.

Lying there, cold and still like a corpse myself, I recalled the conversation I had with her that snowy afternoon at High Meadows, I remembered the story she told about reading Nikolai's book, about how she hated and feared it, and a picture came to me of Nikolai himself, standing by a stove, burning it for her, tearing up the pages, feeding them to the fire. I saw him in that light, in the light of those flames, in the squalid room, with a woman he loved but who did not love him, or did not love him enough, who wanted him to be something other than he was... burning the pages of his marvelous book... How could it not pain him to do it? To destroy his work utterly, to watch it burn? Or did it truly not matter to him at all, as he told her? Perhaps it did not matter, perhaps Nikolai had reached that point, that realization, the one I myself was experiencing at that very moment, that nothing whatsoever mattered in this life, that his book was nothing, just words on bits of torn paper, like Anastasia's last poems, to be fed to the fire, fed to the winds. Even the gesture of burning the book was overly dramatic, overly significant. Nothing signified. Better to leave it on a bench in the rain.

Suddenly stricken by that image, I sat up in bed, hot tears running down my face. Tears I had not yet shed for his mother I was now shedding for Nikolai, the picture of him in my mind, walking away from a bench upon which lay, for a moment at least, before the wind took them, the half-burnt pages of his marvelous book.

The tears brought me back from the brink.

The tears saved me.

♣

That was all I recalled of the night when I awoke in the morning. The new day presented me with her tasks, all the cares and concerns that come with being alive in the world, and they, in conjunction with the sun's warmth, the birds' song, the bright colors of Vasily's flowers, even the overarching reality of our grief, dispelled all other memories of the night, all except one which stayed with me: the image of Nikolai Vasilevich ripping *Monkey* into shreds and feeding it to the flames. That image was so convincing that I had to take it as truth. But the conviction that *Monkey* had been destroyed by an act of the author's own hand left me in such confusion that I put it to one side, the way one puts to the side the knowledge of one's own mortality, for I did not know whether such an action was a sign of despair or of freedom, or whether, ultimately, there was any difference between the two. What I did see, quite clearly in the light of day, was that I was not yet ready to welcome the great emptying out, the great flowing of self into the void, though I had no doubt that it would come to me at last, in its own good time.

Chapter Thirty-Five

Natasha Finds Her Way

In the midst of all the uproar, confusion, grief, preparations, all the frantic activities, somber though they are, that attend a death, the children were ignored. The younger ones were instructed to behave and handed over to their nursemaids or nannies; having few memories of their grandmother to begin with, they soon forgot all about her.

Not so Natasha.

Natasha, poor child, had never in her life felt so devastated. It was as though she had lost everyone she loved all at once, all in one stroke. And no one paid any attention to her, no one talked to her or tried to comfort her, they were all busy doing things, they would not even let her go into her grandmother's rooms, they shooed her away when she told them she needed to water the stones. For the first time ever, her grandmother's rooms were locked, and as much as she insisted that she had to go into them, she had duties to perform, no one listened to her at all.

Since they did not care for her, and the one person who had cared for her and loved her was no longer on the earth, she decided it was time to leave them all and set off bravely on her own, to live her own life in her own way. She made up a bundle of necessary things, she took some food from the kitchen, she dressed in her sturdiest clothes. She did not even wait until dark, but left one morning just after breakfast. No one even noticed she had gone.

The woods were cool and damp and surprisingly quiet. After all the hubbub in the house, the silence of the forest was surprising, even a bit uncanny. There was not even a rustling in the trees, or the song of a bird. She, too, walked under the great boughs of the ancient trees without making a sound, as though she were walking on a featherbed or a cloud.

In the little meadow where the summer before she had first set eyes on Pyotr Illych, she sat down on the little stone where her grandmother had been sitting that night. Perhaps it was a holy stone or a magical one. She remembered the pale moonlight falling on the meadow, and how she had imagined that the figure in the long cloak was Princess Zinaida and the peasant prince was Nikolai. How foolish she had been! Nikolai would never return now. She would never see him or talk to him. He had gone away forever, and he would never return.

Sitting there on a hard stone, all alone and more miserable than she had ever been, she was overcome by a profound sorrow, and although she was ashamed for doing it, she could not stop herself from crying like a baby. Tears rolled down her cheeks, salty tears went into her mouth, sobs choked her. Oh, the world was a cruel place, an empty, worthless, desolate, miserable place, and people were heartless, and life was unjust, and death made everything useless and stupid.

"Oh," she said, taking a huge breath, wiping her tears away, looking around at the meadow in surprise. It was the same place, of course, but she was seeing it differently.

"What a strange thing," she said aloud to herself, since there was no one else to hear her. "It's like a stage, isn't it? It's real but not real. No, that's not it at all. Oh, how I wish dear Fyodor Fyodorovich were here! He would understand what I mean."

"I'm sure he would," Pyotr Illych said. He seemed to have just popped up out of the ground beside her.

"Pyotr Illych! Wherever did you come from?"

"Why, from just yonder, from the wood. You didn't see me coming?"

"No. I was thinking."

"Ah, mustn't do too much of that, my child. Very bad for the health."

"Thinking? How is it bad for the health?"

"How? Why it takes you away from where you are to a place where you are not."

"Ah. And that makes you ill?"

"Easily. You worry about the future, which does not exist. You fret about the past, which also does not exist. While all the time what does exist right in front of you is fleeting by you and you are missing every bit of it. How can that not make you ill?"

"But even when I am quite truly here, I miss the people who are not here, and so I wish I were somewhere else, wherever they are. And where are they, dear Pyotr Illych? Where do they go?"

"People go here and there. The world is large, my dear."

"What about my darling Anastasia? What about poor, dear Fyodor Fyodorovich? Where are they?"

He smiled at her, his dark, creased face lighting up, his eyes twinkling. "There's no great mystery to that, my dear. They are in Heaven. They are in the Blessed Land. Your grandmother is there right now, and Fyodor Fyodorovich, too, and they are having a good talk, the two of them, a very good talk."

She considered that answer for a long moment. It was what everyone said, of course, and everyone claimed to believe it, but no one really acted as though they did. No one seemed in the least consoled by the idea of Heaven, it stopped no tears, it cured no grief.

"What are they talking about, Grandmama and Fyodor Fyodorovich?"

"Why, not being there, I don't know. Poetry, perhaps, or flying machines."

"Or Uncle Nikolai."

"Indeed. I am sure they both have a great deal to tell each other about Nikolai Vasilevich."

"So, is it true then, dear Pyotr Illych, that you don't believe that this world is the only world there is? I mean, that it's the only real world?"

He laughed, a deep, merry laugh. "Goodness, no! How miserable we should all be if that were true. No. This is not at all the only world, and what we see, though it's all real enough, is not the only real thing there is. No, child, it is an empty shell we must fill up with love. It's the love that's real, my darling. Only the love. Now, sweetheart, are you hungry at all? I have been thinking about cooking you some delicious pancakes."

He offered her his hand, and she got up happily.

"Is your caravan in the same place as last year, Pyotr Illych?"

"It is."

"I have left home, you know. I want to travel with you. I want to travel all around and put on plays, like you do. It's my heart's desire."

"Well, we'll go to the wagons now and have some little bite to eat, and then we'll see how the day goes."

"I am quite determined," she said, though in her heart she knew that determination would not be enough.

"Anastasia Alexandrovna told me once how proud she was of you, you being a poet just like herself. I wonder if you could recite one or two of your poems for me as we walk along now."

She said she could, indeed she could, she would be happy to, and so she did. She began reciting her long poem about Prince Nikolai and the witch.

Prince Nikolai Vasilevich
Did not know he was so rich
Until one day he met a witch.
The witch said, Prince, give me your gold,
As many sacks as I can hold,
A sack for every year you're old....

And so she continued for all twelve stanzas. She did not stop until she had finished.

An evil wizard, as you can tell,
Had put her under an evil spell.
The prince broke it by acting well,
And bowing to her as a prince should do.
This tale now ends that I wrote for you,
And may you be happy and blessed, too.

"Well, well, that's very fine, that is, very fine indeed!" Pyotr said, with one of his chuckling laughs. "And we might make a bit of a play out of it, for the children. Why, I can see the prince, I can see the witch."

"And the princess!" Natasha said. Suddenly she felt like dancing around. She felt like wings were sprouting on her feet. She could see the little stage, she could see the prince and the witch and the princess. "Oh, a play!" she cried out. "We'll make it into a play! Uncle Nikolai wrote a play once, you know."

"Did he? Did he, indeed? Well, then, we shall write one, too, you and I, dear child. After breakfast. Ah, poems, plays, pancakes," he cried, leaping into the air as he did and twirling like a top. "What a world, dear child, that has poems, plays, and pancakes in it! What lucky ones we are, praise God, to live in such a world!"

BOOK EIGHT

Passage to Panama

CHAPTER THIRTY-SIX

Pavel Damianich Makes a Confession

"But such a journey—it's impossible!"

Pavel Damianich glanced up at me darkly. He was in a foul mood and my doubts were only exacerbating it, I knew. But I was unsure of what to do and I needed him to convince me. He wasn't cooperating, however. He had his own concerns. He was trying to decipher some obscure code.

"It is," he said gruffly. "You're quite right." He flung down his pen. "Good. I will not bother trying to make sense of these timetables then, these many routes, this absurd cartography, this gobbledygook. *Tiens!* Let us instead play a game of whist, shall we, or perhaps go to the theatre."

I got up and paced up and down the drawing room, which was what I had been doing all day, all week, ever since Anastasia's funeral. I had cried enough, I had drunk enough, and now I had to make up my mind. It wasn't easy. My charge had been to find Nikolai for Anastasia, but Anastasia was no more. Very well. My general was dead; my orders were rescinded.

On the other hand, I myself wanted to find him, I myself, for myself. I wanted to follow his trail across the ocean to America, to San Francisco. Oh, what a journey! What an adventure! But could it be done? For one thing, it would cost a fortune. But I might get dear Marina Fyodorovna to pay me to write about it, I might get her to advance me some money for the trip. I might, quite easily, in fact, since I had something she wanted very, very much. I had Anastasia's last poems.

Still, finances aside, it would be a difficult journey. I would have to get official documents in order to leave the country. All right. We had contacts; it could be done. Then I had to arrange the passage. Did we even know how to get to San Francisco? This was what Pavel Damianich was in the process of determining. Of course, it was a sea voyage, which meant being on the sea, and I had sworn I would avoid sea adventures for the rest of my life. I would have to retract that oath.

"Oh, it's nonsense to think we won't go," I cried. "We must go! For one thing, I promised Natasha I'd find him, so I will."

"Well, a decision at last!" Pavel Damianich said.

"We will need to go to Petersburg first, however, though it is in the wrong direction, but I must see Marina Vilinskaya and give her Anastasia's manuscript and try to squeeze some ready cash out of her. If we're to go off adventuring, we need some money."

"And I must go there as well... Marko, do you think you might sit down for a moment? I have something to say to you, but I can't say it if you keep pacing around the room."

I threw myself into a chair and said, "Ah, you are about to make a confession! You've already bought the tickets, the ship sails in a week, we must leave without delay, there isn't a moment to lose. Is that what you want to say to me?"

"Not exactly," he said. "Not entirely."

"You are getting married in Paris, and you must be there within the month."

"No. Stop guessing and listen, please."

"My ears are yours!" I said. "Speak!"

He pulled his chair over closer to mine and gave me a very stern look. "Promise me you will not interrupt. What I am about to tell you, you must let me finish."

"Of course," I said in an injured voice, taking his proffered cigarette. "I never interrupt."

He gave me one of his Gallic grunts, and lit my cigarette.

"Very well. I do have a confession to make, in fact. I confess that I have not been entirely candid with you all this time."

"What do you mean, *all this time?* How much time?"

"That is an interruption, right there!" He jumped to his feet and stormed over to the window. "You are impossible! I try to tell you—"

"All right. All right. Do come back and sit down, for heaven's sakes. I swear not to say another word until you are quite finished."

He shrugged, skeptically, and returned to his chair, lit his own cigarette, and began to speak.

With enormous difficulty, I kept my word, I held my tongue throughout his discourse and did not interrupt him, despite the fact that his story was not only quite incredible but took an exceedingly long time to tell. Without the scholarly tangents, the myriad parentheses, the internal monologues, and the excessive number of French quotations, it went something like this:

As much as he admired me and felt great affection for me, Pavel Damianich was often most astonished by how naive I could be and, despite my cynical exterior, how trusting of others. For example, I took him into my service without even a cursory investigation into his background, which was all for the best since his personal references were completely fabricated as were all the other pieces of information he had provided, regarding, for instance, his parentage, his education, and his place of birth. His passport and other forms of identification were equally fraudulent. Why all this deception? For what purpose was it devised, and by whom? These were obvious questions and he would answer them as best he could. As to the other most obvious question—why he was confessing all this to me now—he assured me that the answer would become clear very soon.

In contrast to the rather romantic and completely fictitious story of his life which I had accepted as true—his father, a dashing French sailor; his mother, a beautiful Russian opera singer; their dramatic meeting on board the *Halcyon* during a storm off the Balearics; his subsequent birth; his somewhat erratic upbringing in various ports of call and opera houses—he was, in fact, entirely French, and came from a family of some distinction: both his grandfather and his father had distinguished careers in the French diplomatic service. During his youth, before what the French referred to as the *Guerre de Crimée*, his father had been attached to the embassy in St Petersburg. Pasha had gone to university in France, but spent part of every year in Petersburg with his parents, which explained his perfect command of the Russian language. It was during one of those sojourns, while attending a lecture on Humboldt's theory of terrestrial magnetism, that he had made the acquaintance of Nikolai Barakov.

(*Aha!* I thought, loudly, but did not let so much as a murmur escape my lips.)

They were both quite young at the time, and rebellious, and ardent. Pavel Damianich introduced Nicolas (as Pasha called him) to radical ideas then current in Paris while Nicolas educated Pasha about the true nature of Russian autocracy, the horrors of serfdom, and the extent of state repression. They became the best of friends.

One year, however, Pasha returned to Petersburg to discover that his friend had left the city in some haste and was living in Odessa. It was impossible for Pasha to go to Odessa to visit him, but he obtained Nicolas's address and they continued their correspondence. Long before Russia began the war with Turkey, Pasha's father knew that if war broke out between the two, France would join in on the side of the Porte, and Odessa and the Black Sea coast would become a theatre of war. Pasha warned Nicolas about this—by then, knowing full-well the tactics of the Russian secret police, they were writing to each other in a secret code—and Nicolas replied by sending Pasha stories, fantastical stories. It was only when he read them carefully that he realized that Nicolas, his friend, had buried within them the most precise and detailed information about the Black Sea ports and about Odessa in particular. They had always said, the two of them, that all tyranny had to be opposed, the tyranny of the Tsar most particularly, that free men were not slaves to kings but bound only to their fellow men by ties of affection and friendship, and that they did not consider themselves citizens of any nation state but citizens of the world. In remaining loyal to these ideas Nicolas was taking a tremendous risk; however, the stories he sent were so fantastic and romantic that they passed through the postal inspectors' hands without being censored at all. Pasha was able to share some of this information with his father, never revealing its true source, though whether any of it made its way through bureaucratic channels to the French admiralty he did not know. Months before the declaration of war, Pasha alerted Nicolas and told him to leave Odessa and take his girlfriend with him, a girl Nicolas only ever referred to as "M."

(*Aha!* I thought again. And who could this girlfriend be but Mora Khayimyevna? I yearned to mention this obvious fact, but once again, and with renewed effort, I restrained myself from saying a word.)

Nicolas, Pasha was explaining, had long been estranged from his family. He regarded his father as one of those liberals who wanted to undermine the old order and yet clung to it, who, as Herzen put it, "lit the fuse and then tried to stop the explosion." He was convinced his father regarded him as an unmitigated failure. They had little to say to each other. His older sister had married an academic who treated him with the condescension with which the over-educated regard the autodidact. Furthermore, in such repressive times, the professorial class had to be extremely vigilant about the political views of the men with whom they kept company. Nicolas, as cognizant of that as he was of his brother-in-law's mild disdain for him, kept away. His younger sister had married into the class he most despised, the civil servants, those bureaucrats who colluded with the system for their own benefit. A nihilist brother-in-law who consorted with *raznochintsy* and gypsies, revolutionary students and Poles could hardly be a welcomed guest in his home. So, for different reasons, Nicolas saw little of his sisters or their families.

The only member of his family to whom he remained devoted and who was aware of his friendship with Pavel Damianich was his mother, Anastasia Alexandrovna. Pasha met her only once, but they took to each other right away, and even had a short correspondence, mostly on the subject of French poetry. At that one and only meeting, Pasha was struck by the resemblance between Anastasia and his friend. It was not so much a physical resemblance but an intellectual and spiritual one. They laughed at the same things. They understood each other. Sometimes they even sounded like each other. Pasha recognized the deep love between them, the admiration and regard they had for each other, and so when Nicolas stopped replying to his letters, Pasha did not hesitate to contact Anastasia, express his desire to maintain his friendship with her son, and ask her for Nicolas's new address. She replied to his note: Nicolas's address had not changed, it was the same one he had been writing to all along, in Petersburg. Knowing what he knew about the Third Section, Pasha became greatly concerned. And when, about a year later, Anastasia wrote to him asking if he had heard from Nicolas within the past year, because she herself had not, his concern turned to genuine alarm. By then he himself had joined the French diplomatic corps, held a small post from which he could without too much difficulty obtain a leave of absence, and at the same time provide himself with the necessary papers and introductions, and he was soon able to travel to Russia incognito. (*Well, well, so you are a French spy, after all!*) He made his way to Oak Hills, to Anastasia Alexandrovna, and offered to help her in her search for her son.

But how was it to be done? Anastasia decided the best plan was to take him on as her secretary. Under such a guise, he could easily travel back and forth to Moscow and Petersburg, and make inquiries for her. It was just around that time, however, that I returned home from Kiev, and Anastasia, now desperate for news, asked me to help search for Nikolai and I agreed. Once she gave it some thought, she realized she could not let me go off alone. I needed a bodyguard, and Pavel Damianich was the perfect choice. She arranged it all: she herself composed his dossier specifically to appeal to my romantic nature; she had Vasily Yakovlevich recommend him to me as a man of ability and experience; and she instructed Pasha himself how to conduct himself with me, most specifically not to attempt to win me over by flattery or flirtation, as I was not susceptible to either. Finally, she made him swear that he would wait until our investigation was complete (she could hardly have expected it would take so long) before revealing his true identity to me, this as a way of protecting both of us should any questions arise in official circles, in other words, should I be questioned by the likes of Pavel Beriosov. Her strategy was successful, I innocently offered him a position as my valet, and *voila!* here we were. Now, of course, I might ask (*indeed I might!*) why, since he had kept this secret from me for an entire year, he was willing to break his promise now, or why he had not done so sooner. His answer to the latter question was simple: he enjoyed his role as my valet and companion, he was quite happy to leave things as they were, and, naturally, the longer he kept the secret, the harder it became to confess to it.

"Being so truthful and candid yourself, Marko, and esteeming friendship so highly as you do, I feared you might feel devastated by the deception I had perpetrated on you and turn against me. In fact, I fear that now. I can only hope you will be able to forgive me… But, I beg you!" he said, seeing that I had taken a deep breath in order to respond. "One more moment and I will be quite finished."

The conclusion was rapid and sincere. Rather than endanger our friendship by telling me the truth, he might have kept the secret forever, but information of critical importance to our journey had just come to him from a colleague, and in order to convince me of its veracity, he felt it necessary to reveal its source: French Intelligence. France had a long-standing interest in the activities of certain Russians, one of whom happened to be Elena Blavatskaya. From his source, he had learned that Blavatskaya had traveled from Poti to Odessa, and from Odessa to Moscow, where she was busy making inquiries about me. She would not give up the pursuit, she was a determined woman, a dangerous woman, and he did not doubt for a moment that she would do everything in her power to discover my plans and follow me all the way to America.

"I beg you to consider this and weigh it carefully before you make your decision."

Silence descended on us. It appeared he had finished speaking at last and it was now my turn to say something. However, I found I was quite speechless. I poured a little cognac into two glasses and handed one to him.

"A toast, then, dear Pasha, to our next destination. To Panama!"

His dark, handsome face broke into a wide smile. "You are the most gallant woman! Then it is *bon voyage*," he said, raising his own glass to me. "And we must leave tonight."

"I knew it! I knew it would be something like that. The whole long tale of spies and intrigue all comes down to the same old song: we must leave tonight! And how are we leaving? By what magic carpet or flying machine or spaceship? How are we to escape her?"

"By means of extreme secrecy and celerity. First, I must visit my embassy. I will need better papers, a passport, and a new identity. Not insurmountable problems: I am acquainted with the ambassador. Then we do the least expected thing. We take our cue from Nicolas Barakov. One minute we are in Petersburg, the next minute—poof! We disappear."

"And where do we disappear to?"

"Riga. We smuggle ourselves out of Petersburg and take ship from Riga through the Baltic and across the North Sea to England. From there, across the Atlantic to Panama. It is thankfully the right time of year. We follow Nicolas's trail. We go west."

"You amaze me," I said, smiling at him.

"I am glad to hear it," he said.

"All this time, searching for Nikolai, and you never once let slip a single hint that you know him, that, in fact, he is a friend. How were you able to keep that from me?"

"I have put my memories of him in a locked chest and stored it so deep in my mind that even now, speaking to you about him, I find I am struggling against the lock. And it is just as well, Marko, for so much emotion would escape if the box were open, so many memories. There, then, we shall keep it all under lock and key until we find him again. All right?"

"Yes. All right. Though I long to hear about him, and about your friendship with him. But I must honor your discretion."

"It is not discretion, but a desire to keep my memories of him pure and untarnished. To remember his gestures, his way of speaking, to retain the sense of him, smartest, most brooding, most profoundly nihilistic of men, yet one so willing to give you his friendship and his love. The only authentic anarchist I have ever known, living without rules or direction or ambition, and, I swear, the only authentic artist, letting himself be swept away by life, seeing it all as research for his book. To remember him, Marko! The way he has of acknowledging you from across a room, with an ever so slight lift of his head, a kind of upward nod... that gesture, so characteristic, so familiar... and the sense of complete freedom you feel around him, as though his only wish for you is that you be as free as he is. It is such intimate memories that I keep in mind, so that in the midst of all the lies and deceits surrounding him, I will not forget him. For I cannot tell you, dear Marko, how difficult it has been for me all these months, listening to what other people say about him. When I was asking about him in those bawdy houses and drinking dens in the old port of Odessa, it nearly destroyed me to hear their stories about him. How true they were, of course, is another matter."

"In what way—"

"Just this, and this is all I will say. Russians drink. We know this. They drink to excess. Yes, we know. But there is a kind of drinking, not celebratory and joyous, but cold and determined and self-destructive, whose only goal is the obliteration of the mind and the senses. It was a dipsomania of this type that they described to me, the compulsive drinking of a man whose heart has been broken too often, and now wishes nothing more than annihilation. And I know this, at least, to be true of Nicolas, that he has never been happy in this world—how can I say this?—that the world does not suit him, that he was not made for it as it is, and he has always suffered greatly because of it. So he drinks as a man will who wishes to put an end to his suffering. Still I am loathe to believe much of what they told me, how many times he came close to drinking himself to death, how he was felled by terrible seizures, how often they took him to hospital and only medical intervention saved his life. If this is true, he must have known it was killing him, but he either would not or could not stop. He had a monkey on his back, he told them, and couldn't shake it off. I blame women, of course, though I might as well blame the Tsar, the Church, your revolting social system, the entire nineteenth century. We live in a world in which everything innocent and good and honorable and idealistic is crushed to powder under the heels of capitalists, warmongers, lechers, gluttons and buffoons. How can we not drink ourselves to death or throw ourselves into the sea?"

"Indeed," I said, suddenly angry, thrusting aside the image of Nikolai that Pasha's words had conjured up for me, shocking, yes, and yet, I had to admit, not entirely unbelievable. "Given the state of things, it is certainly a wonder, perhaps even a scandal, that both as individuals and as a species we so doggedly persist and persevere."

He gazed at me in all seriousness for a moment before the sarcasm of my remark hit home. Then a smile broke through the somberness of his face like the sun breaking through a nacreous sky.

"You are such a tonic, Marko," he said. "Forgive my ranting. It shall not happen again."

"Very well. But you must pay a penalty. I demand an answer to one more question."

"Only one more?"

"Yes, for the moment. Tell me, my friend, is Paul de Bourguignon your real name?"

"No more than Marko Volchek is yours."

"I see. Well, I suppose it hardly matters what your real name is if you're about to get a new one very soon. I would certainly get confused, having to learn two new names in such a short time."

He leaned over to me and whispered his family name in my ear. It did not surprise me that it was a well-known and distinguished one.

"Now," he said, "let me return to my role as your valet and pack your trunk."

A few hours later, we left my house under cover of darkness, (an expression Pasha finds most amusing), and reached the nearest station by mid-morning, in time to catch the Petersburg express. I had taken this train many times. It was a strange feeling to think I might never take it again.

My life was about to undergo a great change, and yet the core of it, the heart of it, remained as familiar as ever. I was a writer and I would write, and what stories I would write now! What adventures we would have, traveling across an ocean and a continent in search of our elusive friend, Nikolai Barakov, and his even more elusive book, for although part of me was convinced he had destroyed *Monkey*, another part of me still believed in it, the way one imagines knights once believed in the Holy Grail, as something that must be sought although it can never be found.

And, too, the idea of being pursued by the mad Madame Elena Blavatskaya, a flotilla of subtle bodies and deranged spirits trailing in her wake, was itself an exciting prospect, and one that I could turn into the sort of ghostly Gothic tale dear Marina Vilinskaya would most certainly delight in and pay a great deal for. Our adventure would be costly; I would have to work hard during our transatlantic voyage and send her a manuscript from Panama. I could only imagine how astonished she would be to receive such a package, and how pleased.

These were the thoughts that were in my mind when the train pulled into the station closest to High Meadows, the estate of Tatyana Andreyevna. Several new passengers entered the car, and I recognized one of them immediately. He was Alejandro Azara, whom I had first met at the Stardust, at Madame Blavatskaya's seance, but had only come to know over the past few weeks due to his presence at Oak Hills. He had accompanied Tatyana to Anastasia's funeral, being her almost-son-in-law, the almost-fiancé of her daughter, Margarita, though poor Margarita herself had not yet been found and by now everyone accepted that she never would be. He was immensely surprised to see us, though not as surprised as we were to see him.

It had been such a sad time for all of us, Anastasia dead, Fyodorov dead, Margarita presumed dead, Nikolai missing... and Azara, having known each one of these people, to one extent or another, and being a Spaniard, and therefore a passionate and highly emotional man, had taken his state of mourning very seriously, had worn the deepest black, had hardly spoken a word to anyone, had wept openly from time to time, and in general had looked, for the all the world, like the most bereaved of men. Now, however, he seemed rather chipper, and when he caught sight of us, he brightened even more and asked if he might join us, a request that was impossible to refuse. It was not that I disliked the man, but I remembered what Fyodor Fyodorovich had told me about him, and I did not trust him. Pavel Damianich, on the other hand, not only did not trust him but did not like him in the least, and I could feel that beneath his placid exterior, he was bristling at this rude invasion of our privacy.

Azara put on a sad face and talked for a bit about how sorrowful he was, how sorrowful I must be, how terrible it was to lose friends, how short life was, how vital it was to enjoy it, though how seldom one remembered to do so it in the course of a day or a week or a lifetime, how he himself—now that his dream of happiness was dashed, his life destroyed, his future dark and black—had to remember every day to feel grateful to be alive.

Pavel Damianich could not allow such cant to go unchallenged, and so launched into a diatribe worthy of the great cynic Diogenes.

They argued their respective positions like philosophers.

So time passed.

At a certain point, when their interest in the argument began to fade, I asked Azara what his plans were, and learned that he was not returning to his post in Vienna, as one might have imagined he would do, but instead was abandoning Europe and going home.

"There is much to accomplish in my own country, so much to be done there. I owe this decision to Fyodor Fyodorovich's influence, may his soul rest in peace. He reminded me of the richness of my own culture, the resilience of my own land, the wisdom of my own people. I mean, native people. I am half-Indian myself. I have deep roots among them."

"Fyodorov did all that? How remarkable."

"Yes. In that way he was much like Nick Barakov. A man who could step outside himself."

I thought about this remark for some moments, and felt that it was quite insightful and in fact quite true.

"So you are embarking on a long voyage," I said. I almost added the word "too," but thankfully caught myself just in time.

"Yes," he said. "I will not return to Vienna. I will leave from Petersburg. There are steamships that traverse the entire Baltic. Step by step I shall make my way to London and from there I shall take a ship to Buenos Aires. I cannot tell you how I long for home."

I could almost hear Pasha groan at the thought of a long sea voyage in company with Alejandro Azara, but at that moment Azara looked quite young and lonely and I felt sorry for him.

"You will be happy there," I said. "I am sure you will find happiness."

"Perhaps," he said. "Though I shall have neither wife nor friend."

Tears came into his eyes, and to hide them, he turned his head to face the window. I followed his gaze. We were coming into the city. The air was grey with smoke and fog. Somewhere something was burning, perhaps the entire city was in flames.

Perhaps the great conflagration had finally begun.

If not now, soon.

CHAPTER THIRTY-SEVEN

Marina Vilinskaya Gets Her Heart's Desire

Marina Vilinskaya kissed her beloved friend, Marko Volchek, on the lips and wished her *bon voyage*. It had been a quick visit, and Marina was still a bit breathless from it.

"Here is your long-awaited manuscript from Anastasia, her final poems," Marko had announced with her usual *élan*. "Dedicate it as I have written on the title page."

The shock of it all had been nearly overwhelming. Anastasia's poems! At last! Marko had no time to spare so Marina had had to show her gratitude with unusual and rather unseemly haste, heartfelt though it certainly was. Now they stood together at her front door, Marko looking as dashing as ever, and it was already time to say goodbye.

"Now kiss me, Marina," Marko had said with a laugh. "I am off to find *Monkey* for you, and I must be gone this very instant."

And so, having been kissed goodbye, Marko took her top hat and her cane and strode out the door, the very figure of a debonaire young man, but with the soul and heart of a magnificent and generous woman. For having in her possession the last poems of Anastasia Barakova, she could have struck a much better deal than she had. Marina Fyodorovna was well aware of that, and knew that the advance she had offered Marko for her proposed book of travel tales did not in the least correspond to the value of the poems Marko had given her. Still business was business. She had offered what she could; the offer had been accepted. And the poems, the priceless poems, thank God, were now finally in her possession. Anastasia's death had been a terrible shock and a great tragedy, yes, but the poems had been saved and the poems were all that mattered in the end.

She carried the package of poems with her into her study. The room was dim, the shutters having been closed against the afternoon heat, and was delightfully comfortable and cool, with the coolness of smooth surfaces, wooden furniture, and thick drapes. Marina Vilinskaya sank into a deep voltaire and gently caressed the manuscript in her hand. Her heart was filled with a primitive joy. She had won the contest, she had succeeded. After all the machinations and supplications, the devious plotting, the debasing flattering of old men and young ones alike—none of which in the end had done any good—she had finally obtained everything she wanted. These pages, these poems, these words, they were treasure to her, and riches, and gold.

So she rejoiced deep in her heart, in the darkness of her room, while outside the bright summer day was shining forth in all its glory on Marko Volchek, on Pavel Damianich, on Alejandro Azara, and on all the other living men and women who walked the streets of the city, just as we hope deep in our own hearts the bright light of an eternal sun shines down its glorious and eternal light upon the dead.

CHAPTER THIRTY-EIGHT

"IT CANNOT END LIKE THIS."

It did not take long to finalize our plans and secure passage on the *Katarina*, sailing from Riga through the Baltic and across the North Sea to London, from which great port we would depart on our transatlantic voyage to the Isthmus of Panama. The *Katarina* carried both passengers and freight, and a crew which might have stepped off the pages of a pirate novel by Eugène Sue, Alexandre Dumas, or Edouard Corbière. Pavel Damianich, of course, had been in complete charge of all our arrangements, which meant that our paperwork was perfectly correct while our berths left much to be desired. Not that it mattered that we were cramped into a hole below deck, since, as he pointed out, all I did was lie in my bunk all day and scribble in my journal, and in any case the journey to London would be mercifully short, no more than ten or twelve days, if all went as it should.

And if all did not go as it should? What a wretched end to the adventure it would be, drowning in the terrible North Sea. The thought of it was always with me. By day I wrote, but by night I clung to Pavel Damianich, who, for all his faults and foibles, was warm, strong, and alive. In the dark of night, in the terrible black emptiness of the open sea, the rolling, rocking, frigid blackness of nights at sea, I clung to him, coward that I was, for in my soul there was no fear more primitive, less accessible to reason, than the fear of death by water, the terror of death at sea. In this way, days and nights passed. I did not count them, I merely endured them, and hoped for them to come to a speedy end.

One afternoon, with the wind blowing hard and the ship rolling more dramatically than usual, making writing not merely difficult but impossible, I turned my thoughts to what might be in store for us when we arrived in California.

"The Gold Rush is long over, isn't it?" I asked Pavel Damianich who was likely to know.

"If not long over by now, it surely will be by the time we get there. I believe it began in '48, the same year as the revolutions in Europe. However, the miners were known as '49-ers. No doubt because the two words—miners and forty-niners—rhyme in English. There is that famous song—"

I sat back and listened to his curious theory about history bending to the whim of song-writers until I completely lost the thread of the argument.

"But," he said in conclusion, "artists always distort what we call history. And why not? What we call history is fiction anyway. Look at Herodotus!"

I did not want to look at Herodotus and told him so.

"A storyteller like yourself," he said. "He travelled, he listened, he wrote down what he heard. Indeed, he is a model for fiction writers everywhere."

"Perhaps you're right," I said half to myself and half to him. "I find I am somewhat at a loss."

"What is the problem?"

"I cannot seem to bring my story to an end. Too many characters. Too much must be left unresolved."

"Like life, in that sense, Marko. We know too many people but too little about them, and we leave them abruptly with everything left hanging—meals uneaten, letters unanswered, books unwritten, lovers unwarned, and children unconceived. Yes, one thing is certain, if your story is at all realistic, it can't end well."

"I know, right?" I spoke in imitation of Nikolai Vasilevich, and Pasha smiled at me in appreciation.

"Yes," he said, with conviction, "if it is to be true to life, it must end badly, as life always does."

"I suppose, in that case, it would be best not to end it at all."

"That does appear to be the only solution," Pavel Damianich replied wisely. "I recall hearing a story about a certain writer, an Austrian, I believe..."

I settled myself more comfortably in my chair.

"...who began a book, a very ambitious one, and completed an entire volume, and most of a second. At that point he found to his dismay that he had written over seventeen hundred pages and still did not know either what the story was really about or how to conclude it. Suddenly he came to the realization that all he had to do was stop writing and the book would end completely by itself. He could then turn his attention to something more productive. He was Austrian, after all."

"A Russian would never do that."

"Turn to something productive?"

"No," I laughed. "Never that! Nor would he ever abandon his book without a proper conclusion. No, no, a Russian would make up some sort of ending even if he had to kill off all his characters or have them taken up on a magic carpet and flown into the land of the Firebird. To a Russian reader, either would be equally acceptable. But to have the story simply stop, in the middle, with no conclusion? Impossible!"

"Poor author," Pavel Damianich said, smiling at me lovingly, or perhaps ironically, it was hard to tell. "Either you must kill all your characters or else have them magically fly away, leaving you behind to record their flight. What if the author wishes to fly off, too?"

"This might present something of a problem, I suppose."

"Yes, like the captain of a sinking ship, the author must always remain behind, pen in hand, wrestling with insoluble problems, like the pathetic fallacy."

"But is it a fallacy? I must say, I find it inconceivable that storm clouds *don't* harbor evil intentions."

"Indeed," he said, smiling at me. "Shall I see about some tea?"

"That would be kind. I'll join you on deck in a few minutes."

"Of course," he added as he was leaving the cabin, "if you must kill everyone off, a shipwreck is an excellent device."

Barely had the door closed behind Pavel Damianich than I found myself trembling with anguish and desperation, seized by a great foreboding that the very disaster I had been fearing was about to descend upon the poor *Katarina*. I knew I had to leave the cabin immediately and make my way to the upper deck. Indeed, the floor was bucking and rolling beneath my feet, bringing to mind that uncanny corridor leading to Fyodorov's laboratory high above the city of St Petersburg. Just as then, lights began flickering around me like fireflies, there was a sound like buzzing, the air tingled and seemed to be teeming with forces and energies and forms being made and unmade. I pushed my way forward against these energies, following a narrow corridor of light, while all around me a grey and misty darkness gathered.

Then, to my horror, the ship lurched violently, staggered, and recoiled, as though it had struck something huge, an iceberg, perhaps, or a much larger ship; there were terrible cracking and roaring sounds, a great pounding of feet overhead, and from the companionway many voices could be heard shouting.

The lower deck was tilted sideways, dark, and filled with panicking passengers, all afraid and aflurry, shouting to each other and trying to feel their way blindly along. Pavel Damianich was among them, though struggling against the tide, as he was intent on returning to our cabin to assist me. Together we soldiered on and had just reached the foot of the companionway when a great rushing wave of icy cold water poured down on us through the hatch, flooding the corridor, knocking down everything and everyone in its path.

"Hold your breath, grip hold, and climb!" Pasha yelled in my ear, and so I did, pulling myself up the ladder into the chaos on the upper deck.

There, despite the tempest and turmoil, we saw salvation sailing toward us in the shape of a much larger ship, not topsy-turvy but looking quite majestic and weatherly and not in the least about to sink as we surely were. And indeed soon a flotilla of little skiffs appeared, gallantly rising on the gigantic waves, plunging into immensely deep troughs, and rising up again onto mountainous swells. We watched their rolling progress with great interest, some of us stoically, others in desperation, clinging to whatever we could find still attached to the deck in order to keep ourselves from being swept into the sea. Wind blasted us, salty spray blinded us, an incredible howling deafened us, and some of the less sea-worthy of us added violent vomiting to the mix of miseries. Slowly but surely, the sturdy little boats drew up alongside our tipping, foundering vessel, and one by one we crept, crawled or stumbled to the railing and flung ourselves overboard into the waiting arms of our saviors, strong seamen who by some miracle could keep their heads and their balance while all around them the sea, turgid and angry, swirled and lunged and flung itself at them. Once in the boats, we were so severely rocked and thrown about that I barely realized that the men were rowing us through the roiling water to the safety of their ship. Meanwhile, poor *Katarina*, the ship we had just abandoned, tilted even farther, lay down on her side, and slowly slipped sadly into the deep.

Drenched and terrified, we dozen or so survivors were hoisted, shoved, and pulled on board, escorted into a large saloon, and offered blankets and tea. We had been rescued by an English ship, so much larger and stronger than our former vessel that it hardly seemed we were being battered by a terrible storm at all. That being the case, our fellow rescuees began doing what people do who have just been saved from certain death: they began whining, complaining, and stomping about in a rage. All their property lost, their possessions sunk beneath the sea, only left with the clothes on their backs, incompetent captain, drunken crew, worthless hunk of garbage, shouldn't have been allowed to sail, bring the bastards before a court of law, etcetera etcetera.

Pasha and I found a corner table and gratefully sipped our good English tea.

"I thought the North Sea was relatively calm this time of year," I said.

"To say the North Sea is relatively calm is like saying a lion is relatively tame."

"Travel is never easy, is it? I suppose it's meant to be difficult to encourage people to stay where they are and so avoid the spread of revolutionary ideas and infectious diseases. But at least this near disaster has solved the problem of bringing my story to an end."

"Has it? How so?"

"Or if it has not solved the problem, it has most certainly postponed it. For it appears another problem, of far vaster dimensions, is about to engage our attention. Or didn't you notice the two passengers on this vessel who are so curious about us, and are even now peering in at us as we speak?"

"Who?" he asked, turning around to face the saloon door. Then "*Merde!*" he muttered under his breath, for he had caught sight of Alejandro Azara, grinning in at us. Then Azara was pushed aside and Elena Blavatskaya, looking as sinister as ever, her short, squat figure draped theatrically in a black cape, strode into the saloon, Azara trailing in behind her like an acolyte.

"I knew it!" Pasha whispered to me. "They are conspirators together, and here we are, flies in a web, stuck in the middle of an ocean with them, trapped!"

"It does appear that we are now all in the same boat," I whispered back, feeling philosophical. "Perhaps it's fate."

I detested the woman and all her hocus-pocus, but I was beginning to admire her determination. Indeed, it was dawning on me that if anyone could help us find Nikolai Barakov, it might well be none other than Elena Blavatskaya. Meanwhile, the lady herself, having fixed her protruding frog eyes on me, and taken Azara's arm to steady herself against the ship's increasingly severe roll, was even now careening toward me across the room.

"Marko Volchek!" she exclaimed as she drew closer. "What a happy surprise!"

Beside me, Pasha invoked the name of God.

I, too, invoked a dear name, not God's but another's, and to her I offered a prayer. *Oh, divine Anastasia! If there is any true justice in this world, you are now enthroned as a goddess in that heaven philosophers dream of. Protect us as we journey forth in your service, guide us safely westward over oceans and continents so we may fulfill your command to find your son, Nikolai Vasilevich—and perhaps even Monkey, his book.*

This invocation, fanciful as it was, so sweetened my temper and buoyed my spirit that, as the ship rocked and Elena Petrovna, still hanging onto Alejandro Azara's arm, continued swaying back and forth on the now precariously tilting floor of the saloon, I was taken by the idea that Lady Fortune had played a large role in this meeting on the high seas, and that by joining our forces we might actually succeed, the four of us, unlikely companions that we were, for surely we comprised exactly the sort of odd fellowship that would be needed to track down so slippery a trickster as Nikolai Barakov. I would have shared this thought with Pavel Damianich had not the sound in the saloon suddenly increased to a deafening level, whether caused by the ship's machinery or the force of the gale, it was impossible to tell. Perhaps I had been too sanguine about our rescue and ultimate survival; perhaps this strong English ship was going to sink just as our poor Latvian barque had, leaving us floating in tiny lifeboats in the great, chilly expanse of the North Sea.

I was looking around at my fellow travelers, wondering how they would act in such an eventuality and what sort of lifeboat companions they would turn out to be, when, glancing past the stumbling, swaying figures of Blavatskaya and Azara, my gaze was drawn to the doorway of the saloon where a familiar figure, a tall young man in seaman's clothes, was leaning insouciantly against the door jamb. He caught my eye and acknowledged me with a slight upward nod, a slight lift of his chin. The gesture so startled me that I reached out to Pasha and gripped his arm.

"Look!" I cried. "There! In the doorway!"

In the terrible din, he barely heard me. I shook his arm and pointed.

"Look! Look! Don't you see him?"

But it was becoming impossible to see anything. The vessel was pitching quite sickeningly now, rising and falling on great swells, and creaking portentously, and one by one the lights in the saloon were going out. People were clutching onto each other, or onto anything that was nailed down. Even Blavatskaya had yielded to necessity and taken a seat farther away from me than she might have wished.

It did not matter. I had to cross the room to that stranger, who might be no stranger at all but our own Nikolai, our own dear friend. Pressing down hard on the armrests, I raised myself up to a standing position and set out. Again it seemed I was following a narrow corridor of light through a gathering darkness. I did not look into that darkness, however, but kept my eyes fixed on Nikolai Vasilevich who, impervious to the storm, was slouching comfortably against the doorframe. And although my mind kept insisting that it was not rational to think that Nikolai could be standing right before me in the doorway of the saloon of an English ship, and that what I was seeing was some sort of hallucination, perhaps one of Blavatskaya's materializations or astral bodies summoned by her occult powers, I pushed those thoughts aside and continued on, accepting for the moment that what was happening to me was neither dream nor vision, but something else, quite extraordinary and mysterious, for which I had no name.

Then, suddenly, out of nowhere, a terrific wind sprang up and blew against me, drenching me in icy water. Only the fact that I was gripping onto the ship's railing—and how had I come to be on the deck, gripping the railing?—saved me from being knocked off my feet. The wind sighed, inhaled; there was a pause in the rushing force and howling sound, and in the pause the tall man standing beside me took a handful of paper out of his pocket and tossed it into the sea. He emptied another pocket, and this time the scraps of paper rather than sinking were caught by the wind and flew up over our heads.

"Kolya!" I cried joyfully, for indeed it was he. I would have embraced him but I feared letting go of the taffrail. "Can it really be you? I've been searching for you everywhere—But what are you doing here?"

As he pulled a handful of narrow notebooks from his inner pocket, what he was doing became perfectly clear: he was destroying *Monkey*, obliterating each and every page.

"Stop!" I cried again, and indeed I was crying, my face was wet not only with the spray lifting up from the sea, but also with tears, frozen tears stripped away by the wind, carried off like scraps of paper, like scribbles of words."Oh, why are you doing this? Why?"

He didn't answer but only continued emptying his pockets of thin notebooks and scraps of torn and half-burnt paper, and tossing them into the air. The notebooks sank into the sea, the scraps were taken by the wind, though some blew back onto the deck which was awash with seawater. On the deck, a clean-shaven young man with a long ascetic face, wearing a strangely cut suit, and an odd collar and tie, was walking slowly, bent over, painstakingly picking up the scraps of paper with both hands and thrusting them into his pockets.

"Misha Bulgakov, the writer," Nikolai said, nodding over his shoulder. "Some of these words are his, and he'll hold onto them as long as he can. Everything else goes into the cloud, the great memory, where it will be saved and lost forever. Like some great—"

A roar of wind and an icy slap of saltwater drowned out his words and pushed me backwards so that I almost fell over Bulgakov, crouching behind me, picking up sodden bits of paper, muttering words to himself, poor man.

"Forgive me," I said loudly, so he could hear.

"No need, no need... Everything has ended, and everything ends... Burn, burn, former life! Burn, suffering!" He straightened up, somewhat painfully, and lifting his arms over his head, began grasping some of the bits of paper out of the air as they flew away in the wind. "Under the arch of the gateway, the restless flame of torches!" he cried out. "Why has he changed so, Margarita asked. He says that even the moon gives him no peace..."

Another great wave of seawater flooded the deck, thoroughly drenching poor Bulgakov and nearly knocking him over. Yet soaked and staggering as he was, he continued chasing down what scraps he could from the torn pages Nikolai was flinging into the air.

"Oh, do stop, Nikolai!" I shouted, gripping his arm.

He paused then, and glanced at me with that glowering look he could summon—how I had forgotten it!—knitting his brow in feigned anger, slitting his eyes in feigned fierceness, a look that had always made me laugh. Now I could only manage a smile. "Nikolai," I said. "My dear."

"Listen, Marko, you know it is better to live one year as a tiger than a hundred as a sheep. So I've had my tiger years. And they've been good." With that, he tore apart his last notebook and threw its pages into the sea. "And now this monkey's finally off my back."

"The end of *Monkey*," I whispered. Still clutching his arm, I tried not to look down at the sea, its horrible depths. Was he intending to throw himself into those terrible roiling waves? If so, how could I stop him? "Please, Kolya! It's madness."

"Madness? Of course it's madness! Mad men in a mad world, racing toward oblivion, drunk with destruction, intoxicated by annihilation, wanting nothing more than to burn it all to the ground? What else is it but madness? One death more or less—what does it matter? Everything has ended, and everything ends."

"I can't lose you," I whispered, knowing he would not hear. The wind was pounding like fists against a door, great gusts pounding and shaking the place where we stood.

"Even the moon gives me no peace. But I'm finally done with all this nonsense. Now I can leave."

"Leave? Where are you going?"

He smiled at me. "Wherever the winds choose to take me."

His smile was so innocent and so full of warmth that it relieved my mind of fear.

"I will come with you!" I cried, and my heart lifted at the thought. What we had planned once, what we had promised each other long ago when we were both young—to travel the world! A memory came to me then, a memory so real I felt I could reach out and touch it, the sky so blue, the meadow flowers yellow as the sun, and Pyotr Illych's wagon rumbling along the track, bells on the horse's bridle tinkling in the breeze, and Pyotr himself, dancing along beside it, his magician's jacket all covered with buttons made of mother of pearl. Nikolai, walking beside me, shouted out to him, asking him where it was he was bound, and Pyotr, laughing, replied, "The Enchanted Isles! I am on my way to the Enchanted Isles!"

"Take us with you!"

Twirling around so the sunlight caught the pearl buttons on his jacket and made him shine like a star, Pyotr sang, "It is a long, long journey, my dears. It will take a lifetime to get there."

"And we have a lifetime!" Kolya replied. "That's exactly how much time we have!"

The memory faded away, but Kolya was still beside me, standing so close beside me at the taffrail and I was still clutching his arm. Over the din of wind and sea, I shouted again, "I want to come with you!"

"We'll have to go by flying machine," he shouted back. "You do realize that don't you?"

"Fyodorov's flying machine?"

"The professor's magic ship. Ready and waiting for us."

"Where will it take us?"

"To San Francisco, a city far, far away, a place where it's always summer, a place where we can be free."

Hearing those lines from the last scene of *Wide and Crooked* made me smile. Next a crowd of people would rush onto the stage led by Semyon, a pistol in his hand. But instead of Semyon and his pistol, what rushed in was a dark, thick cloud, we were wrapped in a grey, watery mist, and great gusts of wind struck us, drenching us in sea water. Wind and sea roaring in my ears, I felt I was about to be sucked into a maelstrom. Something powerful was close to us, something immensely strong, looming nearby. Was it Fyodorov's flying machine? Or was it—"Kolya! Wait!" I cried, but—

"Oh! Here you are, Marko!" Pavel Damianich said, coming up beside me where I stood at the taffrail, gazing out at the ship's wake. "I have ordered our tea. Shall we drink it inside or out here on the deck? I find that the sea air is rather refreshing."

Shocked into momentary speechlessness, I gazed about, and was utterly perplexed by what I saw: passengers strolling calmly on a sunlit deck. My clothes were perfectly dry and the ship was sailing smoothly on a tranquil, sapphire sea.

"Oh, dear God!" I cried. "Where is he? Tell me where he is, Pasha! Tell me where we are!"

"We are sailing to London on the *Katarina,* and as for whoever this *he* may be—"

"The *Katarina!* She did not sink in a storm?"

"Of course not."

"Of course not," I repeated stupidly, staring around me. "And this is not a British ship?"

"No," he laughed.

"And Blavatskaya isn't on board, is she? And neither is Azara."

"No, thank God." He laughed again. "Have you decided to take my advice and end your story with a shipwreck? Have you been standing out here, imagining it?"

"No! Not at all! He was here, Pasha. Nikolai was here. I spoke to him. I swear I did. And there was a great storm, and—"

"Come, come, Marko," he said kindly, taking my arm. "Let's go in and get out of the sun."

The sun was quite bright, the glare from the water almost blinding. I stared down at my gloved hands, clutching the wooden railing, and I willed my fingers to release their grip. I exerted my will further and turned my body away from the sea. I had to speak calmly to my friend, to share my thought with him, to say what needed to be said.

"Do listen to me, Pasha, please. Dear Fyodor Fyodorovich, may his soul rest, explained this to me once, but I did not understand, I did not believe. How could I? Imagine, he said, that there are many worlds, not just this one we live in. Imagine that it is possible to find a gate or door from one world to another, to travel between different worlds or even to a different time in our own world. Time, he said, is not what we think it is. He even told me Nikolai was traveling in the future, and I thought he was talking nonsense. There are more things in heaven and earth than our philosophy can dream of, he said to me, and he smiled—remember that shy smile of his? Of course, he did not expect me to believe him. But now I am convinced that what he said was true and that it is possible to step into a kind of parenthesis in time where everything is different, everything is changed. Oh, I know it's absurd, Pasha, but I believe that it happened to me just now. I was not on the *Katarina*. I was somewhere else. I was with Nikolai."

Pavel Damianich was silent for a few moments. Then he took my hand and looked at me with great seriousness. "Marko, my dear, please consider that what you have described is not so very mysterious, but is precisely the state of mind you enter when you write your stories. You imagine another world, a parallel world, and you enter it. You step out of time when you create. How many meals have you missed when you're writing, Marko? How many hours and days fly by and you have no idea where they've gone? Now you think something uncanny has happened. Very well. Let's say it has. We still need to have our tea. And while we are having it you can tell me how you intend to end your story."

Dear Pasha. He was so rational, so French. Of course he would be unable to believe me, just as I had been unable to believe Fyodorov. And what proof did I have to offer? If only I had caught hold of even a single torn page of Nikolai's book!

"How will the story end? Badly, of course, as you said, the way life always does."

"I am sorry I spoke those words to you. For art exists to soften the blows life delivers, to point to what is beautiful and good and lovable in this world, and so make bearable the pain we suffer living in it."

Art! All at once I wanted to laugh at him with his pompous ideas about art. To speak the truth is hard enough, to let it spill out from the heart, not in cries and tears, but in words, weak though they are. Standing there at the rail of the *Katarina,* standing on a frail wooden deck with the horrible depths of the sea just below my feet, I felt profoundly how weak words are, these meager sounds, what frail vessels they are to hold so much feeling, how perhaps Anastasia was right to burn her words, to tear up her poems, how perhaps Nikolai was right to rip his notebooks and toss his pages into the sea.

"Oh, this terrible world!" I cried, quite beside myself with emotion. "This frightful, cruel, terrible world! No wonder Kolya could not bear to live in it! He was never at home in this world, never, even as a child. He would not accept it, and I believe—with all my soul, I believe—he finally found a way to escape it. As for art—it has no power to save us from the cruelty of the world. The beautiful and the good and the lovable are ephemeral and fleeting, like our very lives. We are creatures of the moment, all of us, and in the end we are forgotten as though we had never been. Even my Kolya—Oh, but it was so real, Pasha! I was standing beside him, I was holding his arm, we spoke, we laughed together, it happened only moments ago—but now he is gone. And I think—oh, I think that's what killed Anastasia, finally, that she could not hold onto him. For see how it is: a boy leaves his home and is gone for years and years, and one waits and waits, and one hears nothing, and time goes by, and the silence and the loss and the grief devastate the heart and leave nothing behind but ashes, like burned pages, leave nothing behind, not even a memory. Then, at last, it isn't that he has left you, but that you have left him. You see? You have left him behind, you have gone on to live while he has vanished, and so he fades and soon you have forgotten everything about him, which is the greatest grief of all."

For some moments Pavel Damianich stood in silence, staring out into the distance with great intensity, as though forcing his eyes to see into the past.

"No, it cannot end like this," he said in so soft a voice I barely heard him, for the wind had come up and was blowing from the north. "He has not faded for me, he has not vanished, I have not forgotten him. I will not abandon the search. I will go on. And you will come with me."

"Will I? Why?"

"Why? Because we are doomed by our nature to persist and persevere, as you yourself said to me once. And, more compellingly, because you have given your word to a child."

"That is true," I said, for it was.

"Then, my dear Marko, rather than stand here getting cold in the wind, let us go in and drink our tea and have no more of this despair. It does not suit us."

I had to smile at him, he was so stern and sincere. Seeing my smile, he returned it and took my arm and we began to amble across the deck to the door of the saloon. We were nearly there when I had the feeling that something—a small bird, perhaps—was fluttering just above me. I looked up, and saw what it was—not a bird, but a bird-like form, a flying machine made of a thousand tiny shreds of paper, hovering in the air right over my head. I reached up to it, but just then a gust of wind swept the deck and scattered the shreds, lifting them far above my reach, far away into the air.

epilogue

THE TWELVE LAMENTATIONS

The Twelve Lamentations

by Anastasia Barakova

For Nikolai,
my son, my springtime,
my sweet child.

I.

Every morning by the window
overlooking the garden
where you used to play,

every morning in this attic room
I sit and place words
on a page,

one word after another
as though it were a way to pray,

a way through,
a making way.

No more can I do.
A writer writes,
though on water.

2.

Morning after the first great storm,
full moon setting in the western sky,
the east just tinged with pink,
I took a shovel and went outside
to break the white crust of the snow.

No one yet was on the road,
and all was mercifully still,
like a winter morning when you were a child,
with its stillness, snowdrifts, and a sliding hill,
and the whole world, for a moment,
infinite and white.

Then I would dress you in your little coat,
your mittens and scarf, a fur hat on your head,
and we'd go out together into a shimmering world.

There are days I remember, and days I forget.

Taking you out into the snow,
the world as strange to me
as it was to you,
both of us seeing whiteness
with new eyes.

3.

Strong winds lift up the snow
lying lightly on frozen ground
and blow it, sparkling, all around,

And blow dry leaves
left over from the fall
while spring leaves still huddle in their tender balls,

Still budding on snow-decked branches
like tiny shoots of plants
halted in their dances,

Halted by this killing air,
unexpected, fierce and bold,
this arctic vortex of heart-stopping cold.

And so with sorrow, memory and remorse,
fade they may, but leave an open door
into the heart's most tender core

Where, in a sudden rush,
a squall of grief
can overcome all defenses, all relief.

Not that I want a single memory lost,
for every source
of memory helps recall
that you were here, were present in this world.

But it is not your presence
but your absence that I feel,
that shakes my heart, as fierce, as real,
as the frigid winds that shake the house,
this cold that grips me in my deepest soul.

4.

I woke this morning from a dream,
so full of joy, so free and safe—
for in the dream I'd seen your face—
that resting in a blissful state
I lay at peace, it pleased me so,
until, forced to let it go
and wake...

I found the sky above still grey,
my joyful dream a bitter ruse,
and what was done still done,
for unlike words an act can't be erased
but locked so tight in time's embrace
not even light can penetrate that space
nor an earthquake shake it loose.

Only a flock of angels coming on a wind
and tearing through this bitter screen
between the worlds
might so upset the way of things,
that the done deed might be undone
and I might hear your footfall on the stair,
and glancing up I'd see you standing there
where you will never stand again.

5.

There was no sleep for me last night,
only memories that rose and fell like breath.
So few, so weightless, and so light,
when I tried to grasp them, they only fled.

I thought you were mine forever,
in the whole vastness of life,
you would always be my son,
I would always be your mother.

A sad joke and cruel,
like so much we believe,
so much we think is true,
lost as we are, following a trail of crumbs,
or shipwrecked, clinging to a fragile raft,
passengers on a ship of fools,
awaiting a rescue that never comes.

6.

Today the air is thick,
and heavy with unfallen rain,
and still my heart is filled with pain,
like a body, sick
and barricaded behind a door.

At Sofya's party, though, amidst the children's play,
their fun and laughter,
and name-day flowers,
I was able to forget for hours
what happened after
you left the house that day.

How long ago it was!
Now I can't remember
that last embrace,
and how I must have kissed your face,
and yet the fear I didn't
burns me like an ember.
Oh try!

Try to find
hidden deep in memory
some residue,
some proof of kissing you—
though I know there is no remedy
in holding a mere image in the mind.

For moments gone
are lost
as finally as fallen leaves or dried up flowers
or words or empty hours
spent carelessly, at no cost
but time, like water, running on and on,

Until without a warning sign
and in quite ordinary places,
time stops—there, in the midst of life—
and all that's left is memory, rife
with mindless bits and empty spaces
where I search in vain for things I cannot find.

7.

Out on the peninsula
where streets are encrusted with ice
and mist hovers over housetops,
where in the tangles of bush and brush
huddle the early-migrating birds
and from their high windows
gaze down the idle and impervious rich,

There, across the high road,
on the other side of the park,
the other side of the ridge,
were places you used to know
in the town that used to be yours,
long ago when you were a boy.

Sometimes when I walk there,
on the narrow, winding streets
where you used to walk,
I will catch a glimpse of you
in the stride of another boy,
in his hooded jacket, his baggy pants,
or in the way he nods
across infinity
toward me
before he passes by.

8.

You were always growing away from me
though slowly.
Each new step,
a burst of energy,
to carry you far enough away.

Just now the sun has broken through
a cloud bank in the east,
to shine full-face in my window
where icicles hang, glistening,
and frost makes lacy patterns on the glass.

How beautiful each moment of the morning,
each different stage of light,
turning the sapphire sky to palest grey,
before that great star, our sun,
sends shadows skittering across the snow.

Each step you took, a new meridian,
moving ever westward, like the sun,
until you reached a place
beyond meridians, beyond stars,
beyond this morning light,

This finitude of morning light.

9.

Between the sparrow's chatter and the blue jay's call
I dreamt you were an infant I was taking for a walk.
I held your head carefully so it wouldn't fall,
Then you sat up in my arms and started to talk.
What you said was so clever, even ironic,
I was sure it was you, alive after all.

We walked, (I was holding you),
down a busy street,
to a supper party, quite complete
with writers I knew
who asked questions intensive
about putting prepositions at the end of a sentence.

Then we took a cab with a family of tourists
who mistakenly thought they were somewhere in Europe.
The cabman tried to collect the fare,
but I didn't have money to pay our share.
You said it was improbably expensive,
so we crossed the street where, surrounded by fences,
a block of brick buildings was standing in ruins,
and a white dog appeared to see what we were doing.

But how happy I was,
so filled with joy,
holding you in my arms,
my little boy.

A joy I will never feel again,
in this bitter place
where the pleas we send
are never answered,
nor lighted candles,
nor prayers nor hymns,
and hopes are false as promises or whims
and all our joys are lost without a trace.

10.

This is the winter that will never end,
the entire world in mourning,
thickness in the air, and clouds are weeping.
They used to say it was angels crying,
when they believed in angels.

Here in this hamlet clinging to the steppes,
we expect harsh storms and blizzard warnings.
It is the perfect place for grieving,
with its fogs and dour seasons,
offering no easy answers or diversions.

Now waves of hailstones pound upon the roof
and outside my window darker clouds are forming.
I think of how you left your home here, seeking
brighter days and clearer skies,
hot sun and balmy breezes.

How could I know that you would not return,
that you wanted freedom not belonging,
always packed and ready to be leaving,
the open road was always calling
and you never wondered where the road was leading.

Crows fly by but still the rain is falling
like tears, lost hope, and endless longing.
I miss your laughter and ironic observations,
even your lies and fabrications
would be sunshine in this desolation.

11.

That I will never see you again
or hear your voice,
or share a meal with you,
or walk with you through the park
in the city you loved,

Is unimaginable.
I cannot think it,
like looking into nothingness
or being nothing.

Unimaginable
your everlasting absence,
and so I feel my way
like someone newly blinded
in this dark, empty place,
feel my way,
not in the hope of finding
or holding
or catching hold,
but like an animal
that has no choice
except to stumble on.

12.

And what if I forget you?
What if some morning—innocent, innocuous,
a full moon setting in a pale sky—
I wake without thinking of you?

Or if an entire day goes by
without a single thought of you
striking my heart hard, like a gong
or like a bell in some steeple
sounding out over a desolate plain?

Acknowledgements

Some of the characters in *Monkey* are based on real people who lived in Russia in the mid-nineteenth century. I doubt they would be entirely pleased with the way I re-imagined them, and I want to take this opportunity to acknowledge them and apologize to them. Please forgive me, Maria Vilinskaya/Marko Vovchok, Elena Blavatsky, Nikolai Nekrasov, Avdotia Panaeva, and Nikolai Fyodorov. I have also relied on the work of other writers for inspiration and information. My particular thanks to Mikhail Bulgakov, author of that great novel, *The Master and Margarita*, and to Alexander Herzen, Franco Venturi, Neal Ascherson, and Anna Akhmatova.

My son, Nick Bushell, was working on a novel called *Monkey* when he died in 2016. After his death, not a single trace of his novel could be found. That missing novel became one of the main characters in my version of *Monkey,* as did Nick himself. I also tried to fill my novel with incidents and characters he might have appreciated, but, except for the Russianized excerpts from his screenplay *Wide and Crooked,* my novel is unlike anything he would have written. I only hope it became a book he might have enjoyed.

I was able to write *Monkey* only because of the enormous and sustaining love of my family—Jim, Jessie, John, Silas and Sean. I also depended—as I continue to do—on the companionship and affection of my friends, especially the always inspiring Greek Ladies—Judy Allen, Marcia Brown, Jennifer Clarke, and Kathi Fields. I am grateful to Bonnie Blythe and Kate Kennedy who were the first brave readers of this very long book, and whose enjoyment of it was so encouraging. Very special thanks to Bob Coe and Merrily McCabe, perceptive readers and excellent critics, who have been mainstays for me as a writer ever since they published *Days of the Dead* thirty years ago. The publication of *Monkey* would not have been possible without their enthusiasm and generosity.

Portland, Maine
January 2022